KATIE FLYNN

The Girl From Penny Lane

A Liverpool Lass

arrow books

This edition published by Arrow Books in 2004

Arrow Books
The Random House Group Limited
20 Vauxhall Bridge Road, London SW1V 2SA

Random House Australia (Pty) Limited
20 Alfred Street, Milsons Point, Sydney
New South Wales 2061, Australia

Random House New Zealand Limited
18 Poland Road, Glenfield
Auckland 10, New Zealand

Random House (Pty) Limited
Endulini, 5a Jubilee Road, Parktown 2193, South Africa

The Random House Group Limited Reg. No. 954009

www.randomhouse.co.uk

A CIP catalogue record for this book
is available from the British Library

Papers used by Random House are natural, recyclable
products made from wood grown in sustainable forests.
The manufacturing processes conform to the environmental
regulations of the country of origin

ISBN 0 09 190290 8

Printed and bound in Great Britain by
Cox & Wyman Ltd, Reading, Berkshire

KATIE FLYNN

The Girl From Penny Lane

arrow books

For Tim and Sylvia Turner,
who introduced me to the Rock.

Acknowledgements

My thanks go once again to the late Richard Brown, whose wonderful stories have helped me to build up a picture of Liverpool some seventy years ago, and whose experiences 'on the tramp' as a youngster have been freely adapted to enrich my tale. Thanks also to the staff of the Local History section of the Central Libraries on William Brown Street, and to the café on the top floor, for feeding me when reading got me down!

In addition, thanks to Rosie Hague and her mother, Lily Evans, who introduced me to *Her Benny*, by Silas Hocking (essential reading for all Liverpudlians), and last but not least a big thank you to Terry Billing of Norwich, who was kind enough to lend me, gratis, a keyboard for my word processor when I found myself in his area, with a book to write and no keyboard to type it on.

Chapter One

1924

'Kitty Drinkwater, ain't you the idlest kid ever to come out o' Paradise Court? Didn't I tell ye an hour since to take them trimmin's over to the milliner for me? Might just as well save me breath. Now will you put that handful o' rubbish down and git over there right this minute, afore I catch you one across the side o' your lug!'

Kitty guiltily lay down on the doorstep the three fragments of broken pottery she had been holding and got to her feet. Trust Ma, she thought crossly, to interrupt the only winning streak she'd had for days and days ... she'd lost her five hoarded cherry stones the previous day to Humpy Alley, who had amazing luck, and she could scarcely remember the last time she'd actually owned an olly; for weeks now she'd been forced to borrow other people's for the odd game, which meant anything you won was theirs, and made playing pointless, almost.

'All right, Mam, if the stuff's ready I'll git a-going,' she said as soothingly as she could. Sary Drinkwater's temper was legendary, not only amongst her large brood of neglected children but amongst the neighbours, too. Little Etty O'Mara, who had been playing with Kitty and Ellen Fosdyke, stumbled to her feet as Kitty did and prepared for flight. Etty knew full well that Sary, with drink inside her, could fetch you a thump which would knock you halfway into next week whether you were her kid or not, and Etty was too little and weak to risk that sort of violence.

'Well? If you're just a-going, why ain't you here, takin' the stuff off of me?'

'You put it down on the step, an' I'll fetch it,' Kitty said diplomatically. 'I wasn't born yesterday, Mam, I's not comin' too near, not I!'

'Nasty, sly little slut,' her ungrateful parent mumbled, eyeing her first-born broodingly through slitted lids and clenching her fists in a horribly workmanlike way. 'You'll come 'ere when I sez or . . .'

She swayed and clutched the doorpost. Inside herself, Kitty chuckled. Sunshine was the enemy of the morning after, she reminded herself gleefully. Mam had been down at the Black Dog on the corner of Vauxhall Road until the early hours, she wouldn't come into the bright afternoon willingly. 'Where's the box to go, Mam?' Kitty asked. She could tell her mother's head must be paining her something shocking, what with the drink and the close work which making the trimmings entailed. 'Which milliner do you mean? Is it Miss Hughes on Upper Freddy?'

Sary made another threatening gesture with her fist but it was weaker than the first. She's yaller as a wax candle, Kitty thought gratefully. She ain't going to belt me one, not now she ain't. If only I can get her to bring the box out onto the step . . .

'You know bloody well I only works for Miss Hughes, now,' Sary Drinkwater said thickly. She put a wavering hand to her brow and half-closed her eyes, but Kitty could see she was still watching with spiteful intensity through her swollen lids. 'Oh Gawd, me 'ead's splittin'. Come 'ere, Kit, or . . .'

'Put the box on the step, Mam,' Kitty coaxed softly. 'I aren't going to let you tek a swipe at me, you don't know your own strength an' that's the truth! If you give me a broken arm I ain't likely to get that box delivered this side o' Christmas, am I? Put the box on the step and I'll be over to Upper Frederick Street and back again afore you've had a chance to miss me.'

'Me own child ... ungrateful ... never a word but she's wicked as the devil ... what've I done to deserve ...'

Sary's muttering retreated as she began to go back into the house behind her. Kitty waited. If she got within a couple of feet of the door and her mother was hiding behind it she'd not escape, but if she stood well back and bided her time ...

A small figure appeared in the doorway. Kitty's sister Betty stood there, both arms wrapped round a large cardboard box. Like all Sary Drinkwater's children she was barefoot and dirty, but she wore a proper dress and not a man's shirt with a piece of orange rope round the waist, as Kitty did, and her fair curls were tied back from her face with a piece of once-white ribbon. She was an appealing child, round-faced, healthy-looking, but now her blue eyes were saucered with apprehension and her small mouth drooped pathetically. She kept glancing behind her as she came out onto the step, a clear warning to Kitty that her mother was still lurking. 'Ere you are, our Kit,' she said. 'For Miss Hughes.'

'Righto, Bet, fetch it over here,' Kitty said briskly. 'Did Mam give you a penny for me tram fare?'

A muffled roar from behind the door was answer enough – not that Kitty had the slightest expectation of having to do anything other than lug the box, on foot, half across the city. And for nothing, too, she knew. If Mam had made one of the other kids go it would have been a farthing for a gob-stopper or a couple of liquorice sticks, but if she sent Kitty ...

3

'You're the eldest,' she would say briefly, if Kitty ever questioned her treatment. 'You owes it to us.'

Once, Kitty had felt forced to point out that though she was indeed the eldest, Arny and Bob, the twins, were a mere eleven months younger than she, and both bigger and stronger. Her ears had rung for days from the resultant pounce and pounding, so that was one point she had not laboured. It was useless expecting fairness from Mam, and Pa, when he was home, was worse. The other kids got ha'pennies, sweets, even hugs. All Kitty got was abuse. Pa even grudged her food, wouldn't have her sitting near them when he brought in a paper of chips or a hot pie. She was forced to lurk in the back kitchen, a noisesome hole with no fireplace and a damp earth floor, waiting for a brother or sister to have pity on her and sneak her a mouthful or two.

Sometimes Kitty indulged in a beautiful fantasy – that she was not Mam's eldest daughter at all but a changeling of some sort, which was why Mam treated her not like her own flesh and blood but more like a slave, or an enemy, even. She would look at her reflection in a window pane, seeing not the tangled mop of red-brown hair tied back with a bootlace nor the man's shirt which reached to her knees and was all the dress her mother bothered to provide. Instead, her mind's eye saw white skin, coppery curls, a pretty dress ... and shoes on her bare and dirty feet. After all, Mrs O'Rourke, who had lived only two doors away from the Drinkwater's, though her home was as different from theirs as it could be, had once hinted that there was something special about Kitty, but she wouldn't go the whole hog and say what that something was. Mrs O'Rourke had been a nurse in her young days and had gone abroad with Florence

4

Nightingale to nurse wounded soldiers, so she should know.

Kitty and Mrs O'Rourke had first become friends when the older woman had found Kitty in the Court, weeping bitterly over a cabbage. Kitty had been small and the cabbage was large, so lugging it home from the Great Nelson Street market, where she had stolen it from a busy stallholder, had been a task which had taken her most of the short winter afternoon. So when her mother had snatched the cabbage from her arms, snarled at her for being out late and slammed the rickety door in her face, it had seemed like the end of the world to the young Kitty.

She had cast herself down on the dirty flagstones and not only sobbed but railed against fate, too – and railing against fate, when you are seven years old and don't have much experience of life to call upon, consisted, in Kitty's case at least, of using the worst words at your disposal at the top of your tear-choked voice.

'Bloody, bloody, bloody-bloody-bloody cabbages,' she shrieked. 'Lazy, sluttish, greedy, idle cabbages! Stinkin', rotten, bastard cabbages!'

In her heart, she half-hoped her mother would come out again, even if she only battered her for swearing and then took her inside, but Sary did not reappear; the stained and crooked wooden door with a hole where the handle should have been remained closed.

After she had cried all her tears away and was at the sad, hiccuping, snuffling stage, a quiet voice spoke to her from out of the increasing dusk. 'Now what do we have here? Well, if it isn't little Kitty Drinkwater, a-lyin' on the flags an' bitin' great chunks out of 'em, very like! Sit up, lovie, an' tell me what's caused you grief.'

Kitty sat up, knuckled her eyes and looked around her. Mrs O'Rourke was standing on her neatly whitened doorstep looking down at Kitty. She was wearing a blue serge coat with shiny buttons over what looked like a navy wool skirt and she had sensible lace-up shoes on her feet. Her thick grey hair was neatly parted in the middle and drawn back behind her ears and she wore a tiny pair of spectacles perched on her fat little nose. Behind the spectacles twinkled a pair of shrewd grey eyes.

'Well, darlin'?' she said now in her soft, Irish voice. 'What's caused you grief? Is it hurt you are? Knocked your knee?'

'Mam shut me out; she snatched me cabbage an' then banged the door in me face,' Kitty said, the words bringing her tears to the surface again. 'It was 'eavy, that c-cabbage, it m-med me late, it waren't my fault!'

'Shut out, are ye? Did you give de door a bit of a knock, then? Or a bit of a shove?'

Kitty shook her head. She found herself reluctant to describe the conflicting emotions which made her accept her dismissal, since it would also entail admitting that if she did go indoors she would probably be in more trouble, though for what she could not be certain. She knew, without understanding why, that the mere sight of her could put Sary in a rage and though, by and large, she accepted this unwelcome fact and did her best to keep out of her mother's way when she was in a mood, she was still baffled by the violence which could descend on her head simply because Sary had forgotten to buy the bread, or even because a younger brother or sister had been difficult.

'No, ye wouldn't, of course,' Mrs O'Rourke said, having given the suggestion of Kitty knocking the

6

door some thought. 'Well, how would ye like to 'ave tea with me, chuck? There's soda bread, sardines an' a fruit cake for afters. 'Ow about it?'

Kitty scrambled to her feet, all thoughts of unfairness and grief forgotten. The food sounded weird and wonderful, but what she valued most was the invitation. To get beyond that whited doorstep and to see the wonders within! It was rumoured that not only did Mrs O'Rourke's house have all its floorboards still intact, it had carpets as well, and linoleum in the kitchen to cover the bricks. And there were embroidered squares on the chair-backs so your greasy head didn't mark her covers and pictures on the walls, to say nothing of refinements such as wallpaper and a sideboard with polish on.

And now Mrs O'Rourke had opened her front door – a wonder in itself, painted a lovely deep green with the panels picked out in cream and the doorhandle and door knocker not only present, but made of well-polished brass – and was ushering Kitty inside.

Kitty stopped on the doormat to stare. All the rumours were true, in fact they weren't the half of it! A broad mantelpiece supported a ticking clock, some beautiful ornaments, and two vases each containing three pink roses. There was marvellous carpet on the floor, a very pale creamy brown colour with wreaths of pink and red roses scattered over it. Because it was summer there was no fire in the grate, but where in winter flames would blossom now Mrs O'Rourke had a big blue vase filled with bulrushes.

Kitty's eyes travelled slowly over the wonders. White net curtains across the lower half of the window panes, and a red baize curtain by the front door though this was pulled back in deference to the warmth of the July day. And the chairs! They had pictures on the seats and backs and the couch had half-a-dozen cushions thrown casually down upon it, whilst against one wall was a little bookcase crammed with books, and against another a dresser with gleaming china – all roses and arbors – laid out carefully to best advantage. Against the third stood a small upright piano made of some reddish coloured wood, with a picture above it of a wistful lady leaning on a sun-dial with a sheet of music in one hand and her mouth open, so you guessed she was singing.

'Sit down, chuck, while I put the kettle on,' Mrs O'Rourke said hospitably. 'It's on the hob in the back kitchen, so I shan't be two minutes. Can you read?'

Kitty had attended school sporadically for two years and could read better than most children of her age but she nodded rather doubtfully. 'I can read from readin' books,' she said. 'Them Rainbow Readers ... stuff like that.'

'If you can read them you can read anything,' Mrs O'Rourke assured her. 'Take a look at the book on the little table by the fire – it's what they calls a magazine – it's got pictures of the King and Queen in there it has.'

Kitty sat down, suddenly conscious of the state of her clothes and the smell of them. All she wore was a shirt, but it had never been washed – never been off her back since her mother had slung it at her a couple of months earlier. She had seen Mrs O'Rourke going to and from the hospital where she worked and was sure her hostess changed her clothes, probably as frequently as once a month! But she would be very careful with the magazine ... she put out a grubby hand to pick it up, then pulled it back. She would look with her eyes, there was no need for hands to be involved; that way the magazine would stay clean.

And fortunately Mrs O'Rourke was as quick as she had promised, so she had only looked at the shiny cover of the magazine, wondering which of the people illustrated thereon were the King and Queen since everyone was dressed, so far as she could see, in perfectly ordinary clothes with not a crown nor a coronet in sight, when Mrs O'Rourke wheeled a trolley into the room. It held a teapot under a knitted cosy, two white china cups, two plates and the promised food. Kitty wouldn't have known that the object was a trolley – she thought it looked a bit like a miniature tram in fact – except that Mrs O'Rourke referred to it as such. Sitting herself heavily down on the sofa she leaned forward and took the cosy off the teapot.

'A trolley's a deal lighter than a tray, to be sure,' she observed, tapping the side of the round white teapot approvingly. 'And it'll hold more . . . do you like tea, chuck, or would you rather have a cup of milk?'

Kitty had never tasted milk, so the choice was agonising. She screwed up her face, praying for guidance – this chance might never come again – which would she prefer?

'You'd like the milk,' Mrs O'Rourke said, deciding for her. 'Better for you . . . put some flesh on those bones.' She poured herself a cup of tea, then poured milk for Kitty. The jug was small and white with a frill round the rim, and the cups proved to have a full-blown rose on either side. She handed a cup of milk to Kitty and Kitty tasted it. It was lovely, though somehow unexpected – she had thought it would be thicker, had not imagined it would slide down so easily, quenching thirst.

'Now . . . here's some buttered soda bread and a

9

sardine . . . you squash the sardine flat on the bread, see, like this, with a speck or two of salt. I'm rare fond of sardines so I am.'

Kitty decided after a mouthful that she, too, was rare fond of sardines. She wished she could have a little sardine squashed up on a piece of soda bread every day of the week – and then Mrs O'Rourke cut the cake.

That cake was the nicest thing Kitty had ever tasted or ever hoped to taste, for that matter. Mrs O'Rourke, handing her a crumbling slice, explained that the fruit was in fact sultanas, currants and mixed peel and not fades from the market, as she had at first supposed. It was made with eggs and flour and milk, butter and dried fruit, and it was moistened, as Mrs O'Rourke put it, with brown sugar . . . it was a prince, nay a king, amongst cakes.

And while she ate, filling her starved and empty belly, Mrs O'Rourke filled her achingly lonely mind.

'Your Mam give you a clat round th'ear, is that right?'

Nod, nod, went Kitty's head as her mouth dealt with mashed sardine and soda bread.

'For bein' home late, is that it?'

'I brung 'er a big cabbage,' Kitty said thickly. 'She bawled at me an' slammed the door in me face.'

'And you don't know why, eh, queen? Because she ain't so rough with the other kids – that about the size of it?'

Nod, nod, *nod*, went Kitty's head again, emphasising that it was very much the size of it.

'Ah. Well, you's different, queen. Always has been, always will be. There's nowt wrong wi' being different mind, but your Mam had a rare bad time givin' birth to you. It's often that way wi' a first child. And . . . I don't know if you knew, you was born th' wrong side o' the blanket, which sometimes meks a woman more fond an' sometimes meks her uncommon grudging.'

Kitty swallowed her mouthful, cleared her throat, and said what was in her heart.

'Was it my fault, that I was born the wrong way round, like? Was it suffin' I did?'

Mrs O'Rourke took a sup of her tea and wagged her head at Kitty. Her grey eyes looked kindly, as though she really did sympathise.

'No, chuck, it were more . . . but ne'er mind that. You've got an 'ard cross to bear, that's for sure, but it's nothin' you done, it's more what you are . . . can you understand that?'

Kitty nodded again, not because she understood – she had not the faintest idea what Mrs O'Rourke was talking about – but because she wanted to please this wonderful warm, motherly woman who had taken her in and been kind to her.

'You do?' Mrs O'Rourke looked doubtful, then smiled. 'Oh well, tell you what, chuck, you come an' see me when things get too much for you, and we'll 'ave a nice cuppa an' a nice chin-wag. 'Ow about that, eh?'

And Kitty, full of delicious food and with a white milk-moustache round her upper lip, agreed with starry eyes that she would come and see Mrs O'Rourke often. And by the time she left, her small belly as hard and full as a new-laid egg and her mind warmed from the attention and kindness she had received, she was almost reconciled to her lot. It no longer seemed so important that her mother hated her and her father despised her. Indeed, over the days that followed she somehow managed to convince herself that what Mrs O'Rourke had actually said to her, what she had really meant, was that Kitty was not a Drinkwater at all, but someone different. Someone finer, more intelligent and sensitive than any Drinkwater could possibly be.

However, right now, with the round hat-box clasped in her arms, it was hard to remember that first meeting and the ones that had followed without also remembering where Mrs O'Rourke was now.

Dead. And it had been Kitty who had found her.

Walking as fast as she could, which was not particularly fast as the box was both heavy and awkward, Kitty cast her mind back to that December more than two years ago, when she and Mrs O'Rourke had had their last tea together. It had been a cold, miserable day: with Christmas only days away and Hector Drinkwater home from sea and nasty-drunk most of the time Kitty had been outside her house more than she had been in, so the sight of Mrs O'Rourke gesturing to her in her doorway had been more than usually welcome.

'I bought's a pair of bloaters,' Mrs O'Rourke said, when she had closed the door safely behind Kitty. Sary Drinkwater had early shown belligerent fury that her daughter should be asked in to a neighbour's house, so by unspoken consent the visits had become a secret between the two of them, with Mrs O'Rourke beckoning from her window and Kitty, like as not, sneaking in under cover of darkness. 'And I made one of those treacle tarts you like.'

Ecstatically, after their tea, the two of them talked: about books, because Mrs O'Rourke had joined Kitty and herself up at the big library over on William Brown Street; about sewing and knitting, because Mrs O'Rourke was teaching Kitty to do both; and about Father Riordan, because Kitty went to Mass with Mrs O'Rourke if she could get away, a couple of times a month.

Kitty had been reading *Her Benny* and wanted to discuss it with her friend, whilst Mrs O'Rourke was rather anxious to discuss the recent disappearance, from the shop shelves, of tins of red salmon. Between the two of them their tongues had never stopped until, at close to midnight, Kitty decided it would be safe to go home.

She kissed Mrs O'Rourke goodnight, said she'd come round again before Christmas and sneaked into her own home. By moonlight, she joined her small sisters and the twins in the fusty little back bedroom, diving into the big pile of rags which constituted their bed. She had slept soundly with a full stomach and a happy mind, for Christmas meant a present from Mrs O'Rourke and Kitty had saved some pennies to buy her friend a gift in return. She intended to shop for it in the morning.

But next day the knife-grinder, meeting Kitty as she hurried off on an errand for her mother, told her he'd not been able to get an answer from Mrs O'Rourke's place and he had a pair of scissors for her, well-sharpened, and would Kitty like to take them and hand them over when her friend was in?

'Well, she's in today,' Kitty said. 'She don't go out much, mornings, an' she said last night she'd be workin' on her knittin', today.'

You couldn't peer through Mrs O'Rourke's windows because of the net curtains, but the door wasn't locked. Kitty went in, worried that her friend might be ill, and found her, dead and cold, sitting in her fireside chair with the jumper she had been knitting still in her lap.

Relatives who had never bothered with her in life

came to the hooley after the funeral. Father Riordan preached a lovely sermon and everyone cried, even if only Kitty meant it. The lovely, clean house which Mrs O'Rourke had worked so hard to keep decent was let to a young married couple, and within a couple of years the man lost his job, the girl had two babies, and the floorboards came up to light a fire during a hard winter. The house, Kitty knew without ever setting foot in it, would be very similar to the Drinkwater establishment soon. And she averted her eyes from it as she passed and planned how, one day, she would run away and find her real parents, the Duke and Duchess, or Prince and Princess, and live happily ever after.

But Mrs O'Rourke had died more than two years ago, and Kitty had grown resigned to the loss of her friend. She still went to the library and borrowed books, but she had to hide them well or her mother would have sold them. She had never told Sary, or any other member of the family, about her ability with a needle, for if her mother knew she would force Kitty to help with the trimmings. Life was hard enough, Kitty concluded, without taking on more unpaid and unappreciated work. When Sary could catch her she made Kitty light fires, chop wood, cook whatever food was available and keep an eye on the kids. Kitty had no desire to add sewing to the long list.

So now, peering over the top of the box as she crossed the Scotland Road to make sure there was no traffic about to mow her down, Kitty considered her lot. Twelve years old, thin as a lath and generally dirty and unattractive, she had almost no chance of a job, yet work would be her only escape from Paradise Court. She was happy enough in school, mixing with other kids and finding the work well within her capabilities, but there were always those embarrassing occasions when a parent was summoned to come to the school, or an outing was planned, or a group photograph taken. It went without saying that Mr and Mrs Drinkwater would not turn up and would not cough up, either. Whilst Mrs O'Rourke was alive she had slipped Kitty oddments of money for errands run or small tasks performed, but now she was dead it was steal or go without, and though Kitty was by no means averse to a spot of thievery, she knew that her friend had disapproved and did her best to stay on the straight and narrow. Besides, though her brothers stole and her father brought things home from sea which Kitty doubted he had acquired honestly, she knew without any doubt that if she was *caught* pinching, her parents would kill her. Not half kill, but finish her off once and for all.

Any excuse, in fact. Kitty's left eardrum had been perforated when her father had punched her in the side of the head, she had had ribs fractured and a broken wrist after an encounter with her mother when drunk, and her skinny arms were always black and blue from the automatic, almost casual, blows which were the result, it seemed, of a parental eye lighting upon her.

One day I'll go, she told herself now, clutching the increasingly heavy box of trimmings. One day I'll just up and off, and they won't even pretend to be sorry!

But right now she was on her way to Upper Frederick Street, where the small milliner's shop run by Miss Hughes and Miss Morton was situated. The two spinster ladies ran a very successful small business and they would give Kitty the money for the trimmings in a small brown envelope, a new bundle of

15

ribbon and lace for embroidering and finishing, and, if she was lucky, a piece of cake, an apple or even, as had happened on one momentous occasion, a meat and potato pie.

Kitty never thought about the money in the envelope because it had no significance for her. Her father's allotment was paid to her mother monthly, she believed, and so far as Kitty could make out the extra earned from the needlework enabled Sary Drinkwater to lift her elbow more frequently than she would otherwise have done. That was its only significance for Kitty, though her mother frequently told friends and neighbours that without her earnings the kids would have starved. Kitty, getting by on the scraps her mother allowed her and the odds and ends she picked up, usually made herself scarce when the family were having their evening dinner, the only significant meal of the day. What was the point in getting too near her mother's strong right arm just in the hope of a chunk of bread and a cup of weak tea? She could go in late and get anything left over, then go to bed.

Not that she would be able to do that today, because she would have the money and a new bundle of trimmings to take back for Sary to work on. So she would have to go straight home today . . . but she would be safe enough, this time. She had noticed that she was always safe when she had been performing an errand for her mother, so perhaps she should regard that as payment enough.

On a tram the journey between Paradise Court and Upper Frederick Street would have been long and slightly tedious but perfectly possible. On foot it was as long as a route march. Kitty went right the way along the Scotland Road, never noticing or caring as it became first Byrom Street and then the Old Haymarket. Trams passed her, ringing their bells, but since she had no pennies for her fare they, too, meant nothing but an added hazard should she want to cross the road. Pedestrians dodged the small girl with the big box – some smiled, others frowned – but no one offered to give her a hand and indeed, had they done so Kitty would have been highly suspicious. The box might look like nothing much but the trimmings were worth a lot of money, she wouldn't hand them to anyone, not she.

On Old Haymarket the trams were lined up, nose to tail, waiting for departure time. Kitty glanced at them, but continued doggedly to walk, dodging the people hurrying for their homegoing trams. She had set off at a good pace, but it was late afternoon by now and women, shopping in the centre of the city, were turning their steps homeward in order to cook a hot meal for husbands and children. At least, so Kitty enviously surmised, for thanks to Mrs O'Rourke she knew what mothers were supposed to do, even though her own parent seemed to remain largely ignorant of her duties. Along Whitechapel she went, past the sailors' home, into Paradise Street, and finally, when she had traversed Cleveland Square with its big houses and leafy trees, she dived left into Upper Frederick Street at last and knew she was almost halfway through her journey – for once she had handed over the box she would be given another and would begin the weary trek back.

Unfortunately, Upper Frederick Street was a very boring thoroughfare for someone of Kitty's age. Warehouses, public houses and tradesmen's properties jostled down either side of the road, with never a shop window to please the eye. Until you got to the milliner's shop, of course.

Miss Hughes and Miss Morton had a lovely window, Kitty considered. Two or three wax heads with disdainful expressions displayed the most expensive hats, and the rest were laid out tastefully on swatches of material or beside a vase of artificial flowers. In spring, Miss Morton, who was the artistic one, always put a china hen and a clutch of china chicks amongst the hats. In summer, it was a bucket and spade and a cleverly constructed sandcastle made of cardboard, and in winter a Christmas tree dominated the window, all decorated with tinsel and toys. Kitty, who knew about the seaside only from books, stopped to look in the window and envy those children lucky enough to possess buckets, spades and sandcastles. She rather liked the hats, too – the big straw one with artificial poppies round the crown, the fluffy, feathery one, the one which had a brim so wide that Kitty doubted whether the wearer would know if it rained or shone – and anyway, looking in the window gave her a breather, which she needed before going inside.

She did take a look through the half-glazed door, though, because she knew that the Misses Hughes and Morton much preferred her to enter the shop to transact her business when they were not busy with customers. A severe-looking lady was at the counter, paying for a purchase, but as soon as she had left, with a rustle of unfashionably long skirts and a fearful glance at the blue sky overhead, as though she spent her life expecting a downpour, Kitty nipped inside and heaved her box up onto the counter.

'Trimmings from Miz Drinkwater,' she said breathlessly: the counter was high and the box heavy. 'An' can I tek the nex' lot, please?'

Miss Hughes, who had been serving the severe-looking lady, had gone into the back of the shop as soon as her customer left, but a plain and spotty girl, not a lot older than Kitty herself, moved forward to take the box from her. 'Drinkwater,' she said heavily. 'Wait on, I'll git the new lot.'

She was about to disappear in her turn when the shop door rattled. Kitty turned automatically as it opened, intending to give just a quick glance behind her – and instead of glancing, stared. The newcomer was the most beautiful young lady she had ever imagined. Thick, softly shining red-gold hair was coiled into a bun at the nape of her neck, her skin was white and clear and her eyes large and violet blue. She wore a beautiful navy blue dress which fitted her slender figure to perfection and a little jacket made of the same material. She went towards the counter and the girl who had been talking to Kitty turned automatically towards her.

'Yes, miss?'

'Miss Hughes is making a hat for my sister to wear at a wedding. It's white, with a wide blue ribbon – I wondered . . .'

The spotty one nodded violently, turned without a word and went to the door behind her, opening it to reveal the beginnings of a flight of stairs.

'Miss 'Ughes!' she shouted up the stairs. 'It's the gairl from Penny Lane, she's called for th' weddin' 'at!'

A voice shouted a muffled reply which evidently made sense to the spotty one. She turned back to her customer.

'She says it's ready, Miss. I'll jest go up an' fetch it down for you.'

She disappeared and the beautiful young lady said, apparently to herself, 'The girl from Penny Lane, indeed! What sauce!'

Kitty nodded earnestly and the movement caught the young lady's eye. She swung round, looking properly at Kitty for the first time.

'Oh! I'm sorry, I didn't see you there – are you being served or did I push in ahead of you?'

'S'orlright,' Kitty said. 'I ain't a customer, I's brung work in.'

The young lady nodded.

'I see. Well, if the hat's ready I shan't be long, since Nellie – that's my sister – paid the first instalment, and there's only one shilling and sixpence owing, which I've got in my purse.'

'I'm fetchin' trimmings,' Kitty confided, delighted that this pretty, beautifully dressed young lady was disposed to chat. 'Me Mam makes 'em for Miss 'Ughes an' Miss Morton. They sends plain ribbons an' she 'broiders 'em, an' stitches lace an' makes button-'oles an' all sorts.'

'She must be very clever with her needle,' the young lady said. 'My sister can sew, but I'm not very good. Can you embroider?'

'Well, I can, me friend taught me, but I wouldn't tell me Mam,' Kitty confessed. 'She'd make me do it all, else. 'Sides, don't suppose I could do all them fancy stitches an' that.'

'You should practise,' Kitty's new friend said kindly. 'Then, one day, you'll be able to help your mother, perhaps in the evenings, when you are home from your job of work. Fine needlework is always useful.'

At this point someone began descending the stairs heavily. Miss Hughes, who was carrying a huge, wide-brimmed hat with great reverence, began to speak almost as soon as she appeared in view.

'Miss Larkin! I thought it must be you when my niece said . . . dear Sophia remembered you had been staying with Mrs Gallagher in Penny Lane, but that is really no excuse, as I told her, for rudeness! But there, she's my elder sister's only child and is new to our work, though determined to do well, quite determined, and as I said to Miss Morton, better to keep it in the family, with so many valuable materials, to say nothing of all the new lines we're beginning to stock . . .' She held the hat out to her customer. 'Now what do you think? Will it not make madam quite the best-dressed lady at the wedding?'

'It's beautiful,' the girl said, eyeing the hat admiringly. 'I have the rest of the money here, and thank you very much, Miss Hughes, I'm sure my sister will be delighted with your work.'

'I hope so, I hope so indeed. And should your employer ever desire something a little special, a little out of the ordinary, and should you feel able to recommend us, I should be most grateful . . . you would not regret such a recommendation, you may be sure.'

'My employer has been ill and rarely leaves the house,' the girl said sadly. 'If you could put the hat in a box, Miss Hughes, and let me have a receipt . . .'

'Of course, of course,' Miss Hughes said. She frowned slightly at Kitty, who was leaning against the counter and drinking in every word. 'Yes? What do you want, my dear?'

'Me Mam's money,' Kitty said promptly. 'An' the new trimmin's.'

'Ah, yes, you're the Drinkwater child,' Miss Hughes said. 'When I finish with this lady I'll call Sophia; she's fetching the box and your Mama's wages.' She turned back to the girl, gave her a practised smile and then dived under the counter, reappearing with her hands full of white tissue paper. 'Now, I'll just wrap the hat up for you.'

Kitty watched, fascinated, as the hat was swathed expertly in the tissue paper and plunged into the depths of a handsome hat-box only just big enough to contain it. Then the box was tied up with string and pink sealing wax and the string formed into a neat carrying handle.

'There you are!' Miss Hughes said triumphantly, handing the beautiful, light parcel over to her customer. 'Good afternoon, Miss. Convey my respects to Mrs Gallagher.'

'Good afternoon,' echoed the girl. She then turned to Kitty and gave her the most brilliant and beautiful smile. 'Good afternoon, Miss Drinkwater, and thank you for your company.'

Politeness costs nothing, Mrs O'Rourke used to say, and *Good manners are a sign of good breeding.* So Kitty smiled and gave a little bob and said, 'Same to you, Miss, I'm sure,' and then watched as the beautiful young lady, the hatbox swinging from one hand, left the shop, closing the door gently behind her.

'Well, well,' Miss Hughes said vaguely, as Kitty turned reluctantly back to the counter. 'Where were we . . . ah Sophia!'

There was a faint hail from up above, then a thundering of heavy feet descending the stairs which made Miss Hughes's earlier progress sound positively fairylike.

'Ere we are, Aunt,' Sophia said, thumping down the last stairs. She had a box in her arms which looked, to Kitty's despairing eyes, even bigger and heavier than the one she had just delivered. 'Trimmin's for Mrs Drinkwater an' the money for the last lot.' She waved a small brown envelope, then put it down on top of the box. 'Miss Morton's just mekin' a cuppa. She says if you go up now, I can go up later.'

22

'Ah, tea,' Miss Hughes said, half-closing her eyes and smiling fondly at her niece. She turned to Kitty. 'Here you are, child. Carry them carefully, there are a lot of expensive materials in there. How far have you to go?'

'Paradise Court, off Burlington Street,' Kitty said. She usually put the envelope containing the money inside the box, but decided that it might be safer slipped down inside the neck of her shirt-dress, where it would lodge against the rope which spanned her middle. 'It's a helluva walk.'

Miss Hughes's eyebrows rose almost into her thinning grey hair but the fat Sophia giggled. Kitty gave her a cold glance. You could see that Sophia hadn't done much walking, not with a belly on her like a woman six months gone! She would have liked to tell Sophia so, but prudence demanded that her good manners remain with her for a little longer. Miss Hughes usually came up with something.

And today was no exception.

'Burlington Street! That must be several miles ... but of course it's on a direct tram route.'

'I walked,' Kitty said bluntly. 'Me Mam don't 'ave no gelt to spare for leccy-rides.'

'You *walked*?' Miss Hughes stared at Kitty for a moment as though doubting her own ears, then she gave a quick little nod and reached under the counter. 'Well, here's a penny, catch a tram home. And – wait a moment.'

Whilst she was gone, labouring up the stairs, Sophia came and leaned over the counter the better to see Kitty, apparently, for presently she remarked, 'Where's your boots?'

'Ain't got none,' Kitty said at once. 'Me feet's 'ard, I don't need no boots in summer.'

'And in winter?'

Kitty shrugged.

'None in winter, either? Nor clogs? And that ain't a dress, it's a man's old shirt. You aren't 'alf dirty, an' all.'

'I might 'ave boots, next winter,' Kitty said, ignoring the slur on her apparel and her cleanliness. There was little she could say, since her dress was indeed a shirt and she knew herself to be very dirty. Curiosity getting the better of her, however, she added, 'What's it like up there, above the shop? What does you do? Are you learnin' to mek 'ats? Ow d'you get a job like that, eh?'

But Sophia, whilst apparently thinking her own nosiness justified, drew back in offended astonishment at Kitty's questions.

'That's none of your business,' she said sharply. 'You need brains and a good 'pearance to work in a nice shop like this. And boots.'

Kitty had filled her lungs for a quick – and insulting – retort when Miss Hughes came thumping down the stairs again. She had a thick slice of bread and jam in one hand and a tin mug of milk in the other. She put them down on the counter, breathing hard.

'Lord, but it's hot,' she remarked. 'Drink that, child, then eat the butty as you go. You want to get home before dusk.'

Kitty was thirsty and drank the milk at a draught, with murmured thanks, but had only just sunk her teeth into the bread when the shop door opened once more and Miss Hughes made violent shooing motions and began to brush the crumbs Kitty was making off the counter. She drew herself up and smiled brightly across the top of Kitty's head whilst hissing, 'Off with you!' under her breath.

Kitty glanced at the handsome old lady with crimped grey hair, and at her companion, a stringy girl in her twenties, and then made for the door, with the bread and jam resting on top of the enormous box. She would get herself to the tram stop with all possible speed and eat her food in comfort once she was there.

She might not have caught a tram from here before, but she had often wished she could, watching enviously as the huge Oceanics whisked by full of rich people. That girl, the one from Penny Lane, would undoubtedly have caught a tram, lucky thing, and would be home by now. But Kitty was lucky too, with a penny in her hand for a ride and food to eat.

Kitty reached the tram stop just after a vehicle had picked up the waiting passengers, so she put her box down on the pavement, sat on top of it, and began to eat the bread and jam. Presently one or two other people came up, and Kitty thought gleefully that the tram would soon be here and then she could get rid of the heavy box. She felt no curiosity over the contents; trimmings were trimmings, after all, but for the first time in her life she wondered just how much money her mother was paid for all that close work. After all, if the girl from Penny Lane was right, when she left home she would have a vested interest in how much one could earn for sewing work.

The envelope, however, was comfortably wedged against her ribs; to get it out and start trying to open it, or even to feel for the size of the coins in front of the people gathered at the stop would be a silly sort of thing to do. Instead, she finished off her bread and jam with deep contentment, wiped her sticky hands on the dusty pavement and got to her feet just as the tram came whooshing down upon them.

'Move along there,' the conductor shouted jovially.

'Want an 'and wi' that thumpin' great box, chuck?'

'Sounds as if 'e's 'ad a skinful, dinnertime,' someone behind Kitty muttered as the conductor heaved the box aboard, but Kitty was just grateful for the man's strong hand, and watched him stow the trimmings under the seat, wishing everyone was as kind. This was turning out to be a really good day, despite the long and tiring walk.

The tram was full and at every stop there seemed to be people jostling to get aboard, so it took longer than Kitty had anticipated to reach the Black Dog on the corner of Vauxhall Road and Burlington Street, but they got there at last and Kitty climbed down, hoping that someone who knew her was watching. It was not every day that she caught a tram. The conductor handed her down her box, Kitty shifted its weight onto her hip, and the Oceanic trundled off with its load whilst Kitty began the short walk home.

Halfway down the street, however, she remembered her curiosity over the contents of the little brown envelope. She slid her hand across her front. There were coins, she could feel them pressing into her ribs, but she thought she could feel a sort of rustling, too. Did that mean paper money? Good lor', there might be a ten shilling note inside the scruffy little envelope! Mam never opened it in front of her, just snatched it and shoved it into her own capacious bosom, but . . . oh, she would simply have to get it out and see whether she could discover the contents without actually unsealing the flap.

Kitty looked around her. She was fast approaching a shop she hated because of the smell. A fishmongers, with white trays holding crabs and lobsters whilst the fish nestled in beds of ice. Down the side was an entry, where fishboxes, buzzing with bluebottles, awaited collection. It wasn't a very pleasant place, what with the smell and the flies, but it struck Kitty that if she went down the strong smelling little back alley, at least she wasn't likely to be disturbed. So, still lugging her heavy burden, Kitty stole past the fishboxes, past the big black delivery bicycle propped against the wall with the fishmonger's name in white letters across the wrought iron basket on the front, and down to where the back of someone's privy formed a conveniently private place to examine the envelope. She put the box down and delved into the front of her shirt, but she had scarcely got her fingers round the fascinating envelope when someone's shadow fell across her. Startled, she looked up.

Two boys stood there, grinning at her. One of them wore the filthy, stained apron of a fishmonger's apprentice, the other had a very large checked cap pulled down over one eye and pieces of string tied round his trouser-bottoms. Oh 'eck, Kitty thought, dismayed, I didn't oughter be down here and them's the lad what guts the fish and the lad what delivers. Now I'm in trouble!

She took her hand out of her shirt front and went to pick up the box of trimmings but one of the boys, the one with the string round his trouser-bottoms, put a foot down on the top, only just missing her fingers.

'No you don't, gal! Wharra you got in there, eh?'

'Nothing! Well, only ribbons an' that, for ladies' 'ats,' Kitty said nervously. They were large, well-nurtured boys of fourteen or fifteen, a clack from either of them would hurt! 'Me box is that 'eavy, I stopped for a bit of a rest.'

'Ribbins? What's de user dat?' The delivery boy went to turn away but the other stood his ground. It struck Kitty for the first time that they might rob her – thank heaven she hadn't pulled the envelope out of her shirt, for money could always be spent but what use would a couple of lads have for a box of unworked trimmings?

'Got any gelt? Dey pay you for what you brung 'em?'

Kitty cursed the perspicacity of fishmongers' apprentices; the other turned back immediately, his narrow face menacing. He brushed impatiently at a bluebottle which seemed to have followed his rich smell down the entry.

'That's ri', dey pay for t'ings like dat! Where's de cash?'

'They pay me Mam, not me,' Kitty quavered. 'I's jest to fetch an' carry. Come on, let me go 'ome.'

The delivery boy would have let her go, she was sure of it, but the other was altogether a nastier proposition. He stared at her hard for a moment, then bent and picked up the box.

'Tell you what, you go 'ome an' tell your Ma that she can 'ave 'er ribbins back for a coupla bob. 'Ow about dat?'

'She'll kill me,' Kitty said fearfully. 'She will, she'll kill me. She ain't overfond, me Mam. Come on, fellers, gi's me box back.'

'Where's your money, then?'

'I ain't got none,' Kitty squeaked desperately. 'I 'ad a penny what the shop lady give me, but I caught a tram, the box is that 'eavy. C'mon, gi's me box.'

'No money, no box,' the apprentice said. 'And jest in case you've gorrit in mind to tattle . . .'

He put a hand into the long pocket in front of his filthy apron and pulled out a knife, a huge thing, sharp, wicked. He stepped forward, and whilst his companion tucked the box under his arm in a very final sort of way, pressed the knife against Kitty's throat, so hard that she dared not even swallow, convinced that any movement would send the razor-edge deep into her flesh.

'Understand, chuck?' his whisper was more frightening than a shout or a cuff would have been. 'One word from you, jest one word, an' your Mam'll find you up dis entry tomorrer wi' your t'rottle cut from ear to ear. An' don't t'ink you can escape from me, 'cos I'll git you, I swear on the face o' God.'

Kitty, rigid with terror, said nothing. She could feel perspiration running down the sides of her face but she was deathly cold. He would kill her and get pleasure from it, she was sure. She could do nothing to save the trimmings, but if she said she'd come back later with the money perhaps . . .

'Off wit' you!'

A hand grabbed her shoulder and twisted her out of the corner into which she had shrunk as a pin twists a winkle from its shell. A violent push sent her staggering up the entry, and as she regained her equilibrium she simply flew, her feet scarcely touching the slippery, smelly cobbles.

Out on Burlington Street, with people about her, she dared not glance back. That knife – and the threat that went with it – had been all too real. She kept her head down, dodging passers-by, heading hopelessly for Paradise Court. She reached it and then shrank back, suddenly realising what a fix she was in.

If she went in without the trimmings her mother would kill her, even if she handed over the money. And would she be allowed to explain what had happened, how she could get the box back if she took a couple of bob to pay the boys' blackmail demand? Her hand stole down across her shirt-front once more. She still had the money, but because she had lost the trimmings the money would mean nothing to Mam, who would have to pay it all back, and more, probably, to Miss Hughes to make up for the missing work.

Caught on the horns of a horrible dilemma, Kitty stood there, gazing into the tiny, cobbled court. If only Mrs O'Rourke had still been alive, she might have helped Kitty to explain her predicament to her mother before the blows began to fall. But she was not. This problem was Kitty's and Kitty's alone.

Tears began to form, to fill Kitty's eyes, to trickle down her cheeks. Oh, God, what was she to do? She realised, suddenly, that if she took two shillings back to those boys they would think that she had a source of income and would probably give her back a few ribbons and demand more money. What was more, they had made no arrangements for the handing over of the cash, she could scarcely walk into the fishmonger's shop, hand over money and expect to receive her box of trimmings in return! She could hang around the entry, she supposed doubtfully, then knew she would never dare. The boy with the knife was mad, he would probably take her money and then slit her throat, she never wanted to go down that entry again as long as she lived.

But what was her alternative, really? If she ran away then they would have the scuffers after her because she'd stolen money. If she went indoors without the trimmings then she was as good as dead. She wondered about going back to Miss Hughes's shop and explaining, offering to run errands for a hundred years, if only Miss Hughes would replace the trimmings and say nowt to Mam. But the shop would be closed, it would be dusk soon, there was no hope there.

Kitty sat down, with her back to the side of the wine merchant's shop, and began to sob.

Chapter Two

Lilac Larkin, with the new hat for her sister Nellie nestling in its tissue wrappings, had to catch two trams to get back to Penny Lane, so she decided, since the afternoon was sunny, to walk the first part of the way. She would enjoy the exercise and besides, she needed time to think.

The truth was, despite appearances, Lilac was not comfortably settled in a nice job with an employer to look after her. Not any more. She had said nothing to Miss Hughes, but her entire life had just been thrown into turmoil and she was still none too sure what course to take. Because for the first time in her working life Lilac was about to become unemployed. It was a bad time to job-hunt, too. Although the first Labour government was in power, and the British Empire Exhibition had been opened at some place called Wembley, up London, and everyone said that could mean more jobs, as yet there was little to show for either event.

And though Lilac had been a valued member of the household as personal maid to Mrs Matteson, a doctor's wife, she was otherwise untrained. Indeed, she had been there ever since she had started work and had fancied herself settled there until such time as she might meet Mr Right and marry him. In fact several Mr Rights had come into her life, only to be spurned at the last minute. And then a couple of months earlier Mrs Matteson had had a stroke, and after nursing her back to a semblance of health her husband had decided that his best course would be to take her out of the city and into the countryside, to the small village of Scarisbrick, just outside South-port. There, she might be near her sister, Lady Blanche Elcott, yet far from the noise, grime and strain of living in a large city like Liverpool. But the house to which the Mattesons would move was small, too small to allow them to employ a lady's maid, and besides, Mrs Matteson would be living quietly and in a very different style to that which she had enjoyed in the city.

'A little gardening, a little sea-bathing when we're in Southport, perhaps – for her health, you know – and gentle visits to her sister will be all the excitement she either needs or wants,' Dr Matteson told Lilac gently. 'We will give you an excellent reference, I'm sure you know that my dear, but it would be quite impossible for my wife to employ a personal maid in such cir-cumstances. For though I hope to help the local man out when he's overstretched, I shall no longer have a practice of my own.'

Lilac quite understood, of course she did, and had hurried round to Nellie's comfortable little house in Penny Lane to ask her adopted sister's advice. For though Nellie was a mere thirteen years older, she had considered Lilac as her own particular responsibility ever since Lilac had been found on the doorstep of the Culler Orphan Asylum, where Nellie had been living since her parents' death when she was not much more than five.

When told that Lilac was about to lose her job Nellie was a brick as usual, and had suggested that Lilac should move in with them. She knew, however, that having had financial independence for so long,

Lilac would not be happy without a job of some sort. 'Think about it, and decide what you'd most like to do,' she had urged. 'Something tells me you won't want to stay in domestic service, not with anyone other than your dear Mrs Matteson. There's plenty of other jobs – you could nurse, like I did – but you must make up your own mind, Li, love. And there's no hurry, you're lucky there. So give it some thought and then we'll talk again.'

So Lilac, sauntering along and swinging the hat-box idly in the bright afternoon sunshine, had plenty to think about. What did she really want to do? Nellie was right, domestic service, or skivvying as the unkind called it, had only been bearable because the Mattesons had treated her more like a daughter than an employee. But nursing did not appeal to her; now that the war was no more than a memory nurses did not have interesting soldier-patients, so you were likelier to end up slaving for a crabby hospital sister on a women's ward than meeting a handsome man who would offer you his hand, heart and fortune. And shop assistants were notoriously underpaid and over-worked. You were on your feet all day, she had heard, and could be sacked immediately if a customer complained. And customers were always complaining, it was their natures. During the war, Lilac remembered, it had been perfectly possible for women to do all sorts of things – they had driven trams, dug ditches, managed offices, delivered the post, even – but now the choice was limited once more.

What about working in an office, then? Lilac asked herself. She could not type, but she had neat writing and a good grasp of arithmetic. She could probably do bookkeeping work of some sort, though with such a large number of unemployed men in Liverpool, it was not easy for a girl to get a job which a man, who had probably fought for his country, could do as well or better.

As she walked, Lilac glanced in at the windows of the offices she was passing. Solicitors, accountants, surveyors, insurance companies, they all employed some women. She could see them poring over ledgers, carrying cups of tea between the desks, sitting beside bad-tempered old men taking dictation. The offices, from out in the sunshine at least, looked fusty, dusty and traplike. No, she did not think she would want to become an office worker.

What about making something, then? Hats sprang to mind, having just visited Miss Hughes's establishment. That might be quite fun, except that she had never enjoyed sewing, and even inventing a confection with a wide brim, on which she would balance a positive greengrocery of artificial cherries, plums and hazelnuts, would mean stitching the fruit into place. The materials were lovely, though – would she not enjoy working with tulle and straw, felt and feathers?

But then she remembered that most milliners employed at most one girl, and decided against that, too. Lilac enjoyed the company of girls her own age and, truth to tell, had begun to fret a little even at the Mattesons once they cut their staff down as the doctor began to see fewer and fewer patients. Polly, who was Lilac's particular friend, had gone, and the fat cook and bright Liza. The woman who came and scrubbed twice a week was a taciturn creature with a large family and very little conversation and Mrs O'Malley, who described herself as a good plain cook, might have been good and was certainly plain but did not excel in the kitchen. Lilac, who enjoyed her food, had begun to quite look forward to the moment when the doctor would come roaring down to the basement, a broken tooth in one hand and one of Mrs O'Malley's scones in the other. But it hadn't happened and now Mrs O'Malley was looking for another situation and had probably been promised a good reference, which meant someone else would soon be tackling her hard pastry, overcooked meats and soggy vegetables.

A sweet-faced girl in a grey coat and matching hat, pushing a heavy pram and holding the hand of a small and sticky boy, approached along the pavement. Should I be a nursery-maid? Or perhaps a governess? wondered Lilac idly, rather admiring the uniform. Except that governesses had quite gone out, the rich were sending their children to school just as the poor did, although to far superior establishments, of course. And although everyone knows babies are lovely, I think I'll admire them from a distance rather than get really involved with them, Lilac decided. Being an honorary aunt was one thing but changing napkins, mopping up puddles, soothing the fractious, smacking the naughty ones and buying chocolates for the good – Lilac's ideas of bringing up rich children were hazy to say the least – appealed to her no more than domestic service, now that she considered it seriously. After all, in the nature of things she would marry one day and have kids of her own; there was no sense in having all the work and none of the pleasure, which was how being a nanny struck her. And marriage, so far as Lilac was concerned, was something for the future, not entirely out of sight but quite far off. A number of ardent young men dancing attendance on her was fine, but actually settling down with one of them seemed like the end of the story. Lilac felt she wanted a good deal more fun before she settled for a tiny house, a husband and a number of noses to wipe.

But marriage was beginning to seem more attractive, ever since her path had crossed that of Alan Blake. She had met him whilst waiting on a party in a smart house in Huskisson Street. He had been one of the guests, a tall, handsome young man in naval uniform, who told her that he was First Officer aboard a liner, the *Lady Mortimer*, plying between Liverpool and New York.

'May I have the next dance?' he enquired presently, smiling down at her. 'I'm sure you dance divinely.'

'Dance? Me? I'm *waitressing*,' Lilac had told him. 'You'd get me dismissed without a character, and I enjoy these evening jobs. They pay quite well, too.'

'Come out into the corridor,' the young officer had said, his light blue eyes dancing. 'Come on, if we just nip through the baize doors . . .'

She went, not because she took him seriously but because she had a trayful of empty glasses to return to the kitchen. But he took the tray from her, stood it on the floor and swept her into a modern waltz, though she was sure the music was playing something quite different.

In his arms, leaning back to look up at him, laughing, protesting, she had seen the light eyes darken as his mouth drew nearer her own – and had broken free, recaptured her tray and made for the kitchen once more. But back in the ballroom he had lain in wait.

'Meet me afterwards?' he had begged. 'I'm on leave for a couple of days and this is my aunt's house so you'll know where to find me. I'm Alan Blake, First Officer on my ship and a pillar of respectability, I assure you. Ask anyone, I never seduce beautiful girls – not unless they ask me to! But if we meet when you finish work we'll talk about a proper evening out. We could have supper at that big hotel down by the waterfront – they have marvellous oysters – or I'll hire a car and drive you to New Brighton, just ask, beautiful lady . . . what's your name, by the way?'

'Umm, I'm Lilac Larkin,' Lilac murmured. 'And by the time I'm finished here you'll be tucked up in your bed. We have to wash and clear, you know.'

He nodded, the merry eyes still holding her own.

'Right. Ask, Lilac Larkin, and whatever you want shall be yours! What about tomorrow night? After you finish work? Only I sail on the tide the day after that.'

'I've got to go and see my sister tomorrow night,' Lilac said, trying to sound casual. She would have loved to agree, but something told her that if she didn't want to be thought of as a pushover, an easy conquest, she had best play a little hard to get. 'Still, if you're in the Pool regularly . . .'

'Oh, Lilac, those are beautiful words, words of hope! Where d'you live?'

She laughed, shrugging.

'You'll forget, but for the next couple of weeks I'm at the Mattesons' house, on Rodney Street. After that I'm not certain where I'll be, though 39 Penny Lane will always find me. It's my sister's address.'

He nodded, scribbling in a tiny pocket-book.

'Right. I'll drop you a line and we'll paint the town red when next I'm here.' He squeezed her hand. 'Don't forget,' he commanded. 'Alan Blake of the *Lady Mortimer*. I shan't forget you, Lilac!'

But as she hadn't seen the young officer since that night, Lilac, reaching the tram terminus on the Old Haymarket, dismissed Alan Blake from her mind. He would probably forget all about her, never get in touch, but at least she'd enjoyed their brief acquaintance and it had made her see that there could be a future for her which did not include either skivvying or marrying a bank clerk.

She scanned the line of trams and there was the one she wanted, waiting. The driver was leaning against the door chatting to another driver and smoking a cigarette. Lilac jumped aboard, settled herself on the slatted wooden seat and decided to tell Nellie she simply couldn't make up her mind. No need to mention Alan, definitely a ship that passed in the night. Nellie always knew what was best for her, anyway. Why, by now she might well have a dozen schemes to put forward. So Lilac pushed the hatbox under the seat, drew her money out of her pocket, and sorted out her fare. Then, with the tram under way, she simply gave herself up to the pleasure of a free and sunny afternoon and let her future take care of itself.

'I'm anxious that you get the right sort of job this time,' Nellie said later, when the two of them were settled in the kitchen preparing a meal together. 'Stuart has always said you were wasted in domestic service, and I do think he's right. You know you're welcome to move in with us, but even then you'd want a job of some sort, Li, my love, because you're used to a bit of independence . . . unless you've decided to make marriage your career and take on Art, or one of your other admirers?'

'I'm not going to marry anyone, yet,' Lilac said firmly. 'I like Art all right but I reckon we've known each other for too long, we're more like brother and sister than anything else. And banking's awfully boring when you come to think and anyway, he couldn't afford to marry me for years and years, and I want some fun before I die!'

'Well, you aren't yet nineteen, I suppose, and I didn't settle down until I was a good deal older than that,' Nellie admitted. The two women were in the kitchen, Lilac shelling peas into a large zinc saucepan whilst Nellie, enveloped in a huge white apron and with a smudge of flour on her nose, made the pastry for a steak and kidney pudding. 'It's just that you're so pretty, Lilac love, and I do worry about you.'

'You're very pretty yourself,' Lilac said gently. Nellie had a fine-boned and delicate face, she looked a real lady, Lilac always thought, with her grey eyes, light brown hair and very white skin. Lilac knew her own red-gold hair and deep blue eyes were instantly striking, instantly memorable, but she thought, with rare humility, that perhaps it was Nellie's face which stayed in the mind the longer, whilst Nellie's loving, giving character could be read in the sweet line of her mouth, her straight and honest glance.

'That's very sweet of you, Lilac dear,' Nellie said, twinkling. 'But no one could accuse me of prettiness right now, especially carrying all before me as I do.' She stroked a hand down her stomach, distended by the child within. 'Still, I do feel fit and well, so perhaps I don't mind being hideously fat. And Stu's as excited as a kid at the thought of being a father.'

'And I can't wait to be an honorary aunt,' Lilac said. She ran a finger down the last pod, popping the peas into the pan with a rattle like gunfire. 'So what do you advise, dear Nell? Another job in service, or a complete change? Only I don't know whether I could stand starting at the bottom again, as a kitchen maid.'

'You wouldn't have to, chuck,' Nellie said at once.

'You've had a first-class training, any fine lady would be glad to employ you. Go down to the employment agency in Clarence Street and see what they've got to offer. But personally, I don't think you're going to find another Mrs Matteson, and perhaps it might be better to get right away from that type of job from the start.'

'I suppose I could give the agency a try,' Lilac said reluctantly. 'The only thing is, being a lady's maid and companion is all I know, and I've often thought it would be fun to work for a younger lady, with more interest in fashion. It's a pity Stuart's salary doesn't run to a lady's maid, dearest Nell, or you could employ me and we could all be happy.'

'I'd hate to have a maid, it would make me feel useless, although Stuart's doing awfully well,' Nellie said. She was lining a large earthenware pudding basin with pastry, working quickly and methodically, as was her wont. Having completed the task she took the steak and kidney which she had already cooked and tipped it into the basin, then topped it with a circle of pastry, nipped it together, tied a clean piece of cloth over the top and went over to the stove. She lowered the basin into the pan of water already boiling over the gas, then went back to the sink and rinsed her floury hands. She picked up a striped towel and began to dry them, moving slowly across the kitchen as she did so, her glance abstracted. Lilac, who knew the older girl better than most, was instantly alert.

'Nell? What is it?'

'What do you mean?'

'Something's happened,' Lilac said positively. 'Something you aren't too sure I'll be pleased about. I can read you like a book, our Nellie!'

'Oh, Li, you're right, I've been meaning to talk

to you for weeks, only . . . then Mrs Matteson was taken ill, and Stu said it wasn't likely to happen for a bit anyway . . .'

'Nell, you aren't frightened of telling me your news, surely? Don't say that something bad's happened? Tell me at once, before I invent some awful sorrow for us and make us both needlessly miserable.'

Nellie smiled but shook her head.

'No indeed, not an awful sorrow at all, just an upset. Li, love, Stuart's been offered an excellent job with very good prospects.'

'An upset? But Nell, that's marvellous news! I always knew he was undervalued, now . . .'

'Now he's been offered the chief crime reporter's job with the *London Evening Telegraph*,' Nellie said. 'But it will mean moving down to London, you see, and we hadn't meant to do that until you were settled.'

Lilac shook her head sadly at her sister's worried frown. 'You mean you didn't intend to go *ever*?' she said with mock incredulity. 'Because I may never settle, not in the sense you mean. Nellie, I'm going on nineteen years of age; when you were that old you were taking care of me, earning your living in miserable circumstances at the Culler, working in your spare time . . . you weren't much older than that when you went off to France to nurse the soldiers, risking your life every day, working your fingers to the bone, and happy to be doing both. Why, compared to you I've had no life at all, yet! I've got all sorts to do before I "settle down" as you call it, so you and Stuart mustn't think twice, he's got to take this new job – think of the baby, chuck.'

'We do think of the baby, of course, and of Stu's future,' Nellie admitted. 'This is a lovely house, so new and modern, and we've been awfully happy here, but we'd both like a garden and Stu says we won't live right in London but in the suburbs, so we can have a bit of space around us. Why, Stu wants me to learn to drive a motor car, Li, so that the baby and I will have some independence whilst he's at work!'

'Cor!' Lilac said inelegantly. 'Nell, you're a lucky lass, you are indeed. And why shouldn't I get a job in London, eh? I'm told there's plenty of jobs down there.'

'And leave . . . all your friends?' Nellie said tactfully. 'You wouldn't want to do that, chuck! You've a good many admirers, not just Art O'Brien, and when I saw Polly last she said she had helped out waiting on some party or other where you were much admired by ever such a handsome young man. I know you're sensible, but handsome young men at posh parties don't always mean well by young girls. Of course I don't know who he was, he might have been someone you knew from school, but it wasn't Art, Polly said; she knows Art.'

'Oh, Nell, that young officer was only being polite, and he was fun, not dangerous or anything. Anyway, I've more sense than to be taken in. I wouldn't meet him, after. He says he'll write, though I daresay he won't. But you're still hoping I'll settle for Art O'Brien, aren't you? Well, you can forget it, same as Art can! We was pals as kids, I don't deny it, and we had some fun together, but now he's a ploddin' young bank clerk an' I can do better'n *that*.'

'How you drop your fancy accent when Art's name is mentioned,' Nellie said teasingly. 'You go broad scouse, chuck! But Art's a good lad and a good friend to us all, so I can't help hoping. This officer of yours is probably a good lad as well, but as Stu said when we were discussing Art . . .'

43

'I don't want to hear Stu's opinion of Art, not one bit I don't,' Lilac said crossly. 'I've told Art a hundred times I'm not gettin' tied up yet and I'm prepared to tell him the same a hundred more. And now I'd better go or Mrs Matteson will wonder what's happened to me.'

'Oh Lilac, love, don't go off in a huff just because I mentioned Art – and anyway you can scarcely call it mentioning him to say it *wasn't* Art you were with at the posh party! There's no need to be horrid about him either, queen, because he's been a good friend to all of us, not just you. But I understand how you feel – you want to make up your own mind who you'll marry, you don't want us deciding for you, and you want to have a choice, even if you decide – sorry, sorry, I nearly put me foot in it again! So sit down and I'll make our tea and we'll have it early, before Stu gets home, so's you won't be leaving Mrs Matteson alone for too long.'

'She won't be alone, exactly,' Lilac admitted. She had taken her jacket off the hook behind the back door but now she hung it up again, then walked over to the pantry and got out a loaf of bread and some butter. 'All right, I'm silly to be huffy with you, dearest. I'll stay to tea, I won't be missed for a bit. Shall I slice this loaf and butter it?'

'Please. And I'll tell you what, why don't you get a job for now and then come and stay with us in London once we're settled? Then, if you like it, you can try for work down there.'

'I might,' Lilac said, slicing bread. 'Nell, this move . . .'

'I know what you're going to say. Is it for ever, that's what you're thinking, isn't it? No, love, of course it isn't, but Stu knows it's important for him

44

to work on a London paper as well as a provincial. He's been a foreign correspondent, but never on the staff of a big daily. As for staying away, I don't think either of us could settle far from the Pool for long. Our life is here, all my relatives, you ... but Stuart needs the experience, needs to get away for a bit. Then he can put in for Mr Mullins' job when the old feller retires, and get to be editor, which is what he's aiming for, eventually. So his plan is to get the necessary experience in London in order to be able to apply to the *Post* or the *Echo* when a first-rate job comes up here.'

'I can see that,' Lilac said, buttering bread. 'So there really wouldn't be much point in me moving to London, would there?'

Nellie pressed a fist into the small of her back and then sat down in one of the fireside chairs.

'That's better – I've been on me feet all day, just about! You're a shrewd one, our Lilac, that's just what Stu said. No point in her settling down there and us moving back, he said. Better let her get on with her own life. Because I won't deny that when he first told me I said I wanted to take you with us or I didn't want to go.'

'Oh Nell, you are kind,' Lilac said. 'But I've got to stand on me own two feet, Stuart's right about that, at least, and as you say, all my friends are here. I'll visit you, though ... come to think of it, if I get a job in a shop or a factory I'll get set holidays, won't I? Domestics get half a day here and a day there, and though the Mattesons were very good they still expected me to take a holiday when they did, even if it wasn't very convenient. So I'll start looking in the next few days. All right?'

'I suppose so. When will the Mattesons be moving out to Southport, then?'

'Within a month,' Lilac said rather guardedly. 'When are you going to London, Nell – the truth, now!'

'We-ell, Stuart's going in a fortnight,' Nellie admitted, pink-cheeked. 'I said I wouldn't go until you were settled, love, but it does go against the grain to stay here when he leaves, so if you really can manage, I'll go when Stu does.'

'Of course I can manage,' Lilac said stoutly, though her heart sank a little. 'But that means you won't have the baby before you go!'

'No. My little lad or lass will be born in London, though he or she will be Lancashire through and through, 'cos Stu and me are both Liverpool born and bred.'

'I shan't see it until I can get down to London to stay with you, then,' Lilac observed rather sadly. 'Still, these things happen and must be faced. I'll get on a train and come down as soon as I possibly can, just to take a peep. After all, he's me only nephew.'

'Or niece,' Nellie observed, heaving herself out of the chair. 'You're as bad as Stu, he always talks as if I'm bound to have a boy. But for my part, I think a girl is likelier. Boys lie high, this one . . .'

'Oh? Who says?'

'Everyone says,' Nellie insisted. She walked over to the pantry and began to lay the table for the main meal of the day, always taken in the evening when Stuart was home. 'Girls lie low, like this one, and boys lie high. Wait and see if I'm not right, anyway.'

'I don't have much choice,' Lilac pointed out. 'Shall I put the kettle on now, our Nellie? That steak and kidney pudding isn't for tea tonight, is it? Because meat puds take hours to cook and I've got to get back before Mrs Matteson's bedtime.'

'No, it's for tomorrow. Tonight it's casseroled mutton – can't you smell it, cooking away with thyme and rosemary and nice little new potatoes – with apple pie and custard for afters. You feeling hungry already, then?'

'I am. But I do love steak and kidney pudding,' Lilac confessed. 'Can I come back to tea tomorrow, our Nell?'

Nellie pretended to consider, head tilted, whilst her eyes twinkled at the thought of Lilac actually asking for an invitation to tea instead of just announcing that she would be attending the meal.

'We-ell, the mayor will be poppin' in, and Stu said he'd asked Lord Liverpool, being as how steak and kidney's his favourite pudding too, but I daresay there'll be room at the table for a littl'un. Yes, our Li, you come along. When you pull the kettle over the flame, just stand the pot to warm, would you?'

Lilac complied and the two girls began the final preparations for the meal, bustling round Nellie's neat, modern kitchen. Lilac, even as she bustled, found herself looking wistfully round her. She had known some very happy moments in this room – indeed, in this house. It didn't belong to Stuart and Nellie, of course, only the rich owned their homes, everyone else rented, but they had rented it when they married two years earlier, and Lilac had helped to hang the dark red damask curtains in the sitting room, had gone with Nellie to choose the square of pink carpet, had picked the wallpaper for the little front bedroom where she slept when she stayed over, and had varnished the chest of drawers and the small wardrobe which Stuart had bought at Paddy's Market and carted home on a coal wagon, or so he claimed when the stuff arrived.

'What'll happen to the house, Nell?' Lilac asked at last, when the table was laid, the tea made and the bread and butter tastefully arranged on Nellie's best china cake plate. 'Who'll have it, d'you suppose?'

'Well, Stu and me were wondering whether you'd like to have a couple of friends in and share it,' Nellie said hesitantly, astonishing Lilac totally. 'Working girls sometimes share houses and flats in London, Stuart said, so if you and a friend or two want to take over the rent – it isn't expensive, not between three or four.'

'Oo-ooh!' Lilac squeaked. 'I never thought of doing that, but it's a really clever idea, our Nell! Surely we could afford it, if we got enough of us? Why, Polly left the Mattesons two months ago, she's working in a factory, and Liza's in Lewis's, selling wedding gowns, and then there's Blanche who was at school with me – 'member Blanche, she was the one with bright red hair? – and there must be heaps of girls who leave the Culler and don't stay in domestic service, even if they start out there.'

'We've got the three bedrooms, so if two of you shared the double and you had one each in the singles, that would be four of you sharing the rent,' Nellie said. Lilac could see how enthusiasm and excitement were lighting Nellie from within, taking the anxiety out of her expression and curving her mouth into a happy and hopeful smile. So Nellie was not really as easy in her mind at the thought of leaving me to my own devices as she pretends, Lilac thought. Their lives had been too closely interwoven for too long for either to contemplate losing the other without a good deal of pain. Lilac felt a warm glow at the realisation that even now, with her own husband and a baby on the way, Nellie still thought a lot of her adopted sister. She's been mother and father to me for too long to let me go my own way and not worry a bit, Lilac told herself, and was happy that it was so.

'Then there's the sitting room, and the little room Stu calls his study . . . you could have a couple more of you downstairs if you wanted,' Nellie went on, still planning how Lilac could best manage when she and Stuart had left the city. 'It 'ud take a weight off me mind, our Lilac, if I thought you were with pals.'

'I'll have a word, tomorrow,' Lilac promised. 'Oh, but would the landlord mind? I mean with you and Stu living here he knows everything'll be seen to and done right, but with a parcel of girls . . .'

'Stuart's already had a word with Mr Ellis,' Nellie said. She went a little pink. 'Truth is, Stuart said he'd still keep it in his name and see to things . . . we're bound to want to come back one day so you could say you were keeping the house warm for us. And it'll be nice for us to have somewhere to stay when we pop back for a day or so, just to see how you're getting on, like. So when we come back Stu says he'll tackle anything you can't manage.'

'Nellie, love, if you're thinking about climbing ladders and carting loads you don't want to worry about that sort of thing, not if we get Polly, Liza, Blanche and me all living here. I don't want to sound swelled-headed, but there'll be fellers queuein' up to give us a hand, four girls living alone, to say nothing of Polly's young man, who won't be far off. Not that we'd need help, not after having been in service, because we've all done our share of lifting and carrying.'

'Yes, I suppose you're right,' Nellie admitted, 'I got pretty strong nursing, I suppose I'm inclined to forget the cans of hot water and the buckets of coal you heave up and down stairs without a second thought when you work in a private house.'

'That's it. Water up, slops down, empty chamber pots, fill ewers, get a laden breakfast tray from the basement to the furthest bedroom on the first floor and don't spill a crumb or a drop,' Lilac said wryly. 'Then there's coal for the bedroom fires, carrying down the ash-cans . . . domestic service may not be everyone's cup of tea, but it keeps your muscles in trim.'

'Well then, I shan't need to worry about you at all,' Nellie said cheerfully. 'Is that Stuart's key I hear in the lock? Mash the tea, our Lilac!'

After weeping dolorously for ten minutes or so, Kitty scrubbed her eyes dry with the backs of her hands, blew her nose into her fingers, and scrambled to her feet. Kitty Drinkwater, you've bin a-tellin' yourself these past two years that you'd leave, one of these 'ere days, she told herself fiercely. Well, now's your chanst, girl! If you poke the gelt through the 'ole in the door when they're all asleep, with a note to say what 'appened and who took the trimmin's, then probably Mam won't set the scuffers on to you. What's more, since you'll be far away by then, she won't be able to mek you go back to get 'em yourself. Kitty had no illusions about her mother; if there was a choice between never seeing her trimmings again or having her daughter's throat slit from ear to ear but regaining her property, she was sure Sary would have plumped for her trimmings without a thought.

Unfortunately, however, she didn't have a stub of pencil or a chalk on her, which made the writing of a note difficult, to say the least. And she was too near to Paradise Court; at any moment her mother or a brother or sister might stumble out to see what was taking her so long – at the thought of the explanations, the blows, Kitty turned pale all over. Best clear off until the early hours, then return with the note written on the envelope. If she wandered down the Scottie, she was almost bound to see a friend who might lend her a writing implement of some description, particularly if she looked in on Paddy's Market. They stayed open late and someone there, a stallholder or a customer even, might have the necessary pencil or chalk.

Despite the lateness of the hour it was still not dark and the air, after the sunny day, was warm and pleasant. Kitty began walking rather gloomily along the pavement despite this, but very soon the good humour of the women shopping and the men lounging in front of the pubs lifted her spirits and she began to look about her and take more notice.

Scotland Road was a wide thoroughfare, and most of the shops didn't close until very late, so that goods and lights spilled in a prodigal fashion out across the pavement. Shopkeepers shouted their wares, house-wives shouted back, bargains were struck and baskets piled. Kitty was not usually out so late, since Sary tended to shout the kids to bed early in order that she could go off out, and the brightness and intensity of this side of the city's night-life intrigued her. Who'd 'a thought it, she marvelled, all these folk wanderin' the streets when us is abed! Oh, there's Wally Mick – wonder if 'e's got a pencil on 'im?

Wally Mick was in school with Kitty and lived a bit further along the court but since he was older than she they rarely exchanged more than the most casual of greetings. But Wally Mick's sister Dora was one of Kitty's cronies, which meant that they were on quite good terms, since Wally Mick was a fond brother and Kitty had long admired his kindness to his sister as well as his fair, cheeky face. Asked for the loan of a pencil, however, Wally Mick could not help. He had no pencil right now, he was helping the greengrocer. But later, when the shop closed, he would get given any fades that were going besides a bob for his pains.

'Waddyer want wi a pencil?' he asked rather plaintively, rubbing a filthy hand across his spiky fair hair. Kitty thought it was Wally's yellow head and round blue eyes which had got him his job – he looked so trustable, somehow. 'Most kids is after a plum or a handful o' cherries, which I can manage, now an' then.'

'I want to write a note; just a little one,' Kitty said persuasively. 'I only want to *borrer* it, it ain't for keeps.'

She had noticed that the greengrocer, a strapping fellow with bright ginger hair, had a well-sharpened pencil tucked behind one ear. Now she directed her gaze meaningfully at the older man.

'That's for addin' up wiv,' Wally Mick said doubtfully. ''E can't borrer you that one. 'Ere, wait on.'

He disappeared into the darkness of the small shop at the back of the mounds of fruit and vegetables and came back a moment later, breathing rather heavily, with a tiny, blunt stump of pencil.

'Bring it back,' he muttered, pushing it into her hand. 'Don't be long, either; we shuts in 'alf an hour.'

'I will, and thanks, Wally,' Kitty said fervently. 'You're a pal, you are. Dora's real lucky, wish our twins was like you.'

'Oh, Arny an' Bob's awright,' Wally Mick said awkwardly. 'They's only kids, an' your mam's a real frightener.'

'I knows it,' Kitty agreed fervently. 'I'll bring the pencil back awright, you see.'

She would have returned it under any circumstances, but the thought that Wally Mick might act as messenger and put the envelope through the door for her was an attractive one. On the other hand, there was money in the envelope and Wally might be less trustable than his round blue eyes and yellow hair seemed to suggest.

Considering the problem, Kitty found a quiet corner by a knife-grinder's cart and settled herself, back to the wall, knees up. She spread out the envelope, pondering deeply. There wasn't a great deal of room – what should she say for the best? Sitting there, it was suddenly not quite so easy to explain, but she must do her best or have to contend with the police on her trail as well as the other dangers of the streets.

After five minutes of fruitless wondering she began.

Mam. No point in trying for a pleasanter tone when your pencil was old and blunt and your paper just a small and dirty envelope. *Mam. Here is the muney from the Hat Lady. Them boys at Harraps Fish stowl the Trimmens off me. Kitty Drin*

At this point she ran out of envelope and pencil simultaneously, the one being filled with her uneven writing, the other now reduced to the scatching of bare wood.

Still. It was readable, even in the flickering light of the gas lamps, and it said what needed saying. As for the half signature, if anyone knew her name it should be her mother, so that was all right. She had said nothing about her future plans, but why should she? Sary Drinkwater would not care, she would say good riddance to bad rubbish, until she next needed an errand running or a head to clack. And by then,

Kitty thought gleefully, scrambling to her feet and shaking her head to clear it of the desire to sleep which kept creeping insidiously over her, by then I'll be far, far away!

Chapter Three

Deciding to run away was all very well, but when, in the early hours of the morning, Kitty crept cautiously back to Paradise Court, number eight looked almost inviting. Darkness and quiet brought their own beauty to a place singularly lacking in attraction, and the moon, high in the clear night sky, even managed to make the house look as though it might possibly be more comfortable than a cold doorstep.

Kitty knew well that this was an illusion, but just for a moment she toyed with the idea of stealing silently up the two filthy steps and pushing open the creaky wooden door with the missing panel, through which the naughtier of the neighbours' children watched the Punch and Judy fights, rows and beatings in which Sary and Hector Drinkwater specialised. Facing Kitty then as she stepped through the doorway would be the Drop, a gaping hole in the floorboards into which generations of tenants had tipped the ash from their fires. It was really dangerous now that Sary was in the habit of ripping up floorboards whenever her need for a fire became urgent, because an unwary step could mean death by choking as you sank over your head in ash five or six feet deep.

But Kitty, used to the Drop though rightly terrified of it, would walk carefully round the sinister, coffin-shaped hole and up the shallow wooden stairs. At the top she would turn right into the slit-like room where the children slept on old newspapers, rags and anything else they could scratch together. Although it was a balmy night, Kitty thought wistfully of that heaped-up bed. In sleep there were no animosities, no tale-bearing, no snatching. They would all cuddle up close, like puppies in a pet-shop window, and for a few hours the illusion of loving togetherness would envelop them all, even Kitty.

But then morning would come, and discovery. She would have to tell her story . . . her flesh crept at the thought . . . and take whatever punishment her mother meted out. And it was bound to be something dreadful, really bad, for a girl who had lost a whole box of trimmings.

Once, Sary in one of her real furies had threatened to hang Kitty with a length of orange-box rope from the top bannister, cutting her loose before she was quite strangled so that she might drop into the ash below and die of asphyxiation. Kitty had fled the house then – she had been only seven – and taken refuge under Houghton Bridge by the Leeds & Liverpool Canal. She had been driven back on the second night by a tramp who had coveted her bed and threatened to drown her if she didn't git, an' quick. Kitty had been as much frightened by his hissing, bubbling voice, the result, someone told her later, of being gassed in the trenches, as by his threats. She had stumbled off home, sobbing drearily, but when she went downstairs next morning her mother had been too preoccupied with the fact that she wanted some coal nicking from the railway depot to even comment on her absence, let alone ask where she had been.

Might that happen again, perhaps? Might it be safe to join her brothers and sisters in their warm and smelly nest? But she knew it was no good, not really. The small Kitty had annoyed Sary by some tiny misdeed; she had not lost a fortune in trimmings. And that first time Kitty had been away almost two days and nights ... perhaps if I'm away for a week this time, Kitty told herself hopefully, turning away. Or a fortnight, or a month ...

But it was silly to start regretting anything or planning to come back. Once I'm gone I'm gone, Kitty told herself grimly. She crossed the Court, climbed the steps and applied an eye to the hole in the door. Darkness. Nothing stirred, nobody creaked up or down the stairs. Nobody snored in the front room, which meant that Sary had got herself up the stairs and into bed. She must have decided that Kitty would be a while, having to walk such a distance so heavily burdened.

Kitty raised the envelope to push it through the hole, then hesitated. If she tore the envelope just a little, perhaps she might abstract a coin or two, just to see her on her way? After all, Sary owed her a good deal one way and another, even if you only judged what she would have had to pay a neighbour's child to trek right across the city for her trimmings. She don't even feed me, not like she feeds the others, Kitty reminded herself. She glanced across at Mrs O'Rourke's house. In her mind's eye she could see the elderly woman with her head tilted thoughtfully as she gave the matter her full attention. Then she smiled at Kitty and nodded slowly. *Aye, lass*, she seemed to be saying, *you're owed it a dozen times over; no harm to pay yourself a few pence for your trouble*.

Trembling a bit, Kitty turned her back on the door and sat down on the step. She put a finger under the flap and opened the envelope, just a tiddy bit. Then she opened it a bit further. Coins, big ones.

Two half-crowns, round and silver and heavy, then notes. Nothing smaller.

Oh 'eck, Kitty thought, dismayed. She turned, in her mind, to Mrs O'Rourke's benign shade. Wharrer we goin' to do me old pal? There ain't no kick, not even a bob, only the 'alf dollar. Can I tek so much? But I's scared to 'ave no gelt at all and that's gospel truth.

In her mind's eye, Mrs O'Rourke thought, then nodded, so Kitty put the half-crown into her lap and turned her attention to the envelope. She had torn so carefully that it had parted right along the fold. With a bit of luck, Mam would snatch it up from the floor, rip it open, and not even notice anyone had been before her. As for the sum within, it was a fortune, so surely she would not bother her head about a missing half-crown? Indeed, from what her mother had let drop from time to time, her payments did vary and she was often at a loss to understand why.

Kitty stood up and put her hand, with the envelope clasped between her fingers, through the hole. With the skill born of long practice she lobbed the envelope gently to the right, heard it clunk softly down on the odds and ends of materials which Sary thriftily saved to use on the trimmings, and then, with the half-crown rapidly growing warm in the palm of her hand, she gave one last, valedictory glance at her home and set off at a determined trot in the direction of Houghton Bridge.

The canal might not be very far from home, the bridge might not offer much shelter in case of rain or prowling policemen on their beats, but at least it was somewhere definite to stay until morning. Another night, when she had more strength in her legs, she might make her way up to Exchange Station and try to kip down in the subway which ran from Pall Mall to St Paul's Square, but for now the bridge would have to do.

Padding barefoot along the pavement she passed the Black Dog, where her mother liked to drink of an evening. It gaped blankly at her, doors and windows locked and barred, deserted for once by the revellers who usually crowded the benches and spilled out onto the pavement. She crossed Vauxhall Road, strangely quiet without the hum and clank of trams or the clatter of horse-drawn carts, the thunder of motorized vehicles. Only the moon looked down on the shiny tram lines and the open-air swimming baths and the looming bulk of the Tate & Lyle sugar refinery beyond the strong curve of the girders of Houghton Bridge. Only the moon looks down on me, Kitty thought, as she climbed nimbly around the side of the bridge and dropped down onto the canal path below. And let's hope the moon tells no tales, because I don't want no humping great scuffer disturbin' what's left of the night for me!

After enjoying the beautiful mutton and the lovely apple pie, Nellie and Stuart insisted on walking Lilac as far as her tram stop because exercise was good for Nellie in her condition and Stuart said he had been working in the office all day and would be glad to stretch his legs.

'I'm perfectly all right to walk up to Ullet Road on a sunny evening in July,' Lilac said, touched by their kindness but not wanting to put them out. 'Honest, our Nell, when you move I won't be fussed over like this.'

'When we move you'll be living on Penny Lane and probably working nearby, and even if you aren't you won't be visiting much after dark,' Nellie pointed out. 'And you'll have Polly and Liza and whoever else you get to share to keep you company. Besides, though this isn't a rough area, you get strange people in the parks sometimes. They're lonely for a girl to walk through as dusk is falling.'

'I could catch the tram up on Smithdown, instead of coming to the Ullet-Croxteth circus,' Lilac pointed out. 'Then I needn't go through the parks at all.'

They were walking three abreast, arms linked, with Lilac, feeling very loved, in the middle. Stuart un-linked himself for a moment in order to wag a re-proving finger at the younger girl, whilst the dark eyes in his thin, brown face sparkled with amusement. Lilac had once fancied herself in love with Stuart and even now, knowing how he and Nellie felt about each other, she was perhaps fonder of him than she should have been. But if he knew it he never made her feel uncomfortable or guilty, and he treated her just right, with a mixture of affection and teasing, so she pushed to the back of her mind the knowledge that Stuart still meant more to her – a bit more – than a brother-in-law should, and behaved naturally towards him.

'Will you be grateful, young woman!' Stuart said now with mock severity. 'We're not going to admit twice in one evening that we need the exercise, nor how much we like walking in the park, so let's just get on and enjoy our little excursion. And don't forget, we shall expect a letter every other day and a postcard in between, just to reassure our Nell that you haven't been sucked down the plughole whilst having a bath, or pecked to death by a parrot escaped from the Sefton Park aviary.'

'Or got dragged down by an octopus on the lake,' Nellie contributed. 'Really, young people these days – you just don't know what they'll do next.'

They were walking down Greenbank Lane, Lilac trying to peer through the screening trees and bushes at the big houses on the left-hand side of the road, whilst Nellie gazed dreamily out over the fields and trees to the right.

'I don't suppose we'll ever live anywhere nicer than this, not even if we do move into the country, and just think, if we'd still been here, living at 39 Penny Lane, our littl'un might have gone to that school,' Nellie remarked as they drew level with Greenbank School in its beautiful wooded grounds. 'Imagine a kid having all that wonderful space to wander in! Why, it's as big as Sefton Park, very near.'

'Might be bigger,' Lilac said, peering through the hedge. 'Well, when I marry my millionaire, Nell, I'll pay for your tiddler to come back here and get his education – isn't that a fair offer?'

'By the time you marry a millionaire I'll be one in my own right,' Stuart said. 'And by the time young Gallagher is thinking about school we'll be back here anyway, I'm sure.'

'Or cleaning out Buckingham Palace for yourselves,' Lilac said. 'Ouch, Nellie, don't pinch!'

'Stop gabbling you two and step out,' Stuart advised. 'Come on, Nellie love, you know what it said in the book about exercise, the more you take the easier the birth will be. Besides, we've got to prove to all those soft southerners that Liverpool lasses make the best little mothers in Britain. Left right, left right!'

He unlinked arms once more and began to walk with a ridiculous goose-step, lifting his knees to hip level with every step and swinging his arms so vigorously that Nellie and Lilac fell back to give him room.

'Come *on*, girls!' Stuart adjured them. 'Follow my example and use your whole body when you walk. March like little soldiers – come on, show me what you're made of!'

'If we walked like that we'd show you our bloomers,' Nellie grumbled. 'And if you had young Gallagher kicking and squirming inside you, you'd take things a bit easy too. So stop fooling about, Stuart, and take my arm. Lilac's coming to tea tomorrow, as well, so we'll be able to discuss our plans for this house-sharing business then.'

'Oh. Right. I'll consider myself cut down to size,' Stuart said. He put his arm round Nellie and gave her a squeeze. Nellie squeaked, then squeezed back and Lilac, watching, felt a curious little stab of something very like envy twisting in her breast.

But I don't want to marry and settle down, she reminded herself as they began to cross the park. I want some fun before I start letting some young man order me about. Time enough for all that, and certainly there's nothing I'd like less than to have my figure ruined by some wretched baby!

But later, when she was aboard her tram and turning to wave, she watched the two figures strolling slowly back the way they had come, Nellie's head very close to Stuart's strong shoulder, his arm comfortingly round her thickening waist, and the curious little stab of envy pricked her once more.

They were going far away, and they were going together. But she, Lilac, would stay here growing older, all by herself, with only her friends for company, with no lover to warm her.

The conductor shouted to someone to hurry up

please, the bell ting-tinged and the tram lurched into motion. Lilac noticed someone who had been standing some yards from the stop suddenly decide to jump aboard; she saw him leap, heard the conductor shout, and then a tall figure was pushing its way between the seats and slumping into the one beside her.

'Art! What on earth are you doing here?'

'Doin'? Catchin' the tram, our Lilac, same's you.'

Art grinned affectionately down at her. He was tall and husky, with bright brown hair which fell in a cowlick across his forehead, a broad, almost simple grin and a pair of shrewd brown eyes. He would probably have been the first to say that his face was undistinguished and his figure too chunky, but even if she didn't want to marry him Lilac still had a soft spot for her old playmate and smiled back at him whilst shaking her head sorrowfully.

'Catching the tram indeed! Well I know that, puddin'-head! But I've been to supper with the Gallaghers; what are you doing in Penny Lane?'

Art chuckled and put an arm along the back of the seat. Lilac edged forward a bit; she did not want to be cuddled in a public service vehicle!

'This isn't Penny Lane, Miss know-it-all, this is Ullet Road. Do you remember Tippy Huggett?'

'No. Should I?'

'Oh, queen, you must remember Tippy! He was the feller who got turned out of the Rotunda for making spit-balls. Don't you remember, we were all kicked out by the commissionaire – you said . . .'

'Oh *him*,' Lilac said hastily. The tram was crowded, she did not want the other passengers to hear all about her misspent youth. 'What about him?'

'He's lodging on Ullet Road; he's working for

William Griffiths & Son, the tailors in South John Street. Doing well for himself is Tippy.'

'I can just imagine him sitting cross-legged on the floor, but I can't imagine him using a needle and thread,' Lilac observed. 'He was a right devil was Tippy.'

'So was I,' Art said regretfully. 'So was you, queen! Fact is, we all have to change as we grow up or we'd starve. But Tippy doesn't sit cross-legged – whatever give you that idea? – he's in the showroom. He shows patterns and takes measurements; he was always kind o' neat, wouldn't you say?'

'Ye-es,' Lilac agreed. She remembered Tippy as a small, aggressive boy with sores round his mouth and hair which looked as though mice had nibbled it. 'Smartened himself up a bit, has he?'

'Haven't we all?' Art said reproachfully. 'I call to mind the day you fell on your face in Mersey-mud an' Stuart chucked you in the bath . . .'

'Don't keep getting so *personal*,' Lilac snapped, 'or you can move to another seat! Kids are always mucky. So anyway, Tippy lodges in Ullet Road and you were visiting him and just happened . . .'

'Don't get swelled-headed,' Art advised kindly. 'I just happened to walk down to the tram stop and saw you get aboard, I nearly didn't bother to come on as well, I meant to walk, only . . .'

'You thought you might as well ride,' Lilac said sarcastically. 'Oh well, if you're getting off at my stop you can walk me up to Rodney Street if you like.'

'And give you a kiss and a cuddle on the door-step?'

'No!' snapped Lilac, all too conscious of listening ears. She moved pointedly further along the slatted

64

wooden seat. 'I've got my good name to consider, Art O'Brien.'

'Aw, c'mon, Lilac love, don't get all starched up wi' me, you knew I were only joking!'

But Lilac settled primly back in her seat and gazed out at the summer dusk and the hissing gas lamps on a level with the top deck. I won't marry till I'm good and ready, she told herself crossly. And when I do it won't be a bank clerk with a worn suit and cracked black shoes. That smart young ship's officer, he's more my style! I could see he liked me, and he came of a rich family, that house was full of good stuff.

Then she thought about Nellie and her Stuart, who would be happy, she was sure, on a desert island sharing their last coconut between them. But she was different, she did so like her creature comforts, pretty dresses, money in her pocket, warm fires in winter and iced drinks in summer! She would find it very hard to settle for anything less than the sort of life she had grown to enjoy with the Mattesons. She doubted that she could be happy with anyone who didn't have money and some sort of position, and Art really wasn't cut out even for clerking in a bank. He's rough, she told herself virtuously, and I'm not. Not now. And I won't end up like Mrs O'Brien or the other women in Coronation Court – overworked, always hungry, fighting a losing battle against the filth, the vermin, their menfolk.

Yet Nellie, whose life had been considerably harder than Lilac's, would have followed Stuart to hell and back, barefoot. Lilac knew it as surely as she knew she drew breath.

I'm made of weaker stuff, she thought sadly as the tram rumbled on. Even if I thought I loved . . .

someone . . . which I don't, I couldn't marry just for love. I'm not strong, like Nellie.

It was a curiously humbling thought.

Kitty woke when the sun came up the next day. She had found a patch of long grass by the canal and since the night seemed fine and likely to remain so, she had curled up amongst the soft blades, not bothering with the dubious shelter of the bridge.

Now she sat up, knuckled her eyes, and looked about her. A horse the size of an elephant was coming along the path towards her, towing a canal boat. It was a brightly painted boat with elaborate pictures all over it, and it towed in its turn another boat, the second one heavily laden with timber. There was a scruffy lad of about Kitty's age balanced on the timber, steering with a long pole-like rudder, a little girl in a blue cotton dress was watering the big earthenware pots of tomatoes set out on the roof of the first boat, and a good smell of bacon cooking came wafting over the water to Kitty's suddenly interested nose.

The boy spotted her and raised a hand.

'Marnin,' lass, an' a gradely one at that,' he observed, in what Kitty considered a thick country accent. 'Sleepin' rough, art tha? I see thee in thy nest, earlier.'

'Oh, I only come 'ere till me mam cools off,' Kitty said hastily. 'I'll go 'ome to get me butties.' But she fell into step beside the first boat, her nose pointing towards the bacon as though given the chance it would have leaped the gap and helped itself, if only to the rich and delicious smell.

'We'm 'avin' bacon,' the little girl chimed in. She picked up a thick sandwich from the cabin roof and waved it in a friendly sort of way towards Kitty. She was a pretty child of six or seven, with curly fair hair

66

and blue eyes. 'Tis only t'best for us, eh, Cally?'

'That's right,' the boy agreed. 'On a Sat'day, any-road.'

'I'll likely get bacon too, when I goes 'ome,' Kitty lied manfully. She swallowed. 'Yours smells a treat,' she added.

The little girl looked back at the boat containing her brother. He obviously interpreted her glance for he said, 'Go on, 'en.' He turned to Kitty. 'Wanna bite?'

'I can't tek your grub,' Kitty began, but the little girl carefully put her watering can down on the roof of the

boat, picked up her sandwich and held it out.

'Oh, I can't . . .' Kitty began, then the smell reached her and she was lost. Her hand stretched out of its own volition, her grubby fingers sank deep into fresh-baked bread, and the sandwich was in her mouth, her teeth feeling first the softness of the loaf, then the delicious, greasy crispness of well-fried streaky bacon.

'S'orlright, innit?' said the little girl. 'I'll git another from me mother, don't fret yoursel'.'

'Thanks,' Kitty gasped. The bread and the bacon had already disappeared, were already nothing but a happy memory. 'Thanks a lot.'

She slowed her pace, wistfully watching as the small group moved further along the canal and entered the patch of shadow under Houghton Bridge. The horse's huge round hindquarters gleamed with grooming, its head was up, its step long and comfortable. The first boat was clean and homelike, the second sensible and properly packed so that the horse might not have to drag an uneven load. How enviable were the lives of those two children! Bacon sarnies, a horse to ride, a boat to steer – and a warm and comfortable Mam, who not only handed out bacon sarnies to small daughters, but would hand out a second, it appeared, and no awkward questions asked!

She stood and watched until the boats had disappeared behind the bulk of the Tate & Lyle warehouses, then walked along to Houghton Bridge, swung herself back on to the road, and considered the morning.

It was still very early. The sun, a red ball occasionally glimpsed between the buildings, seemed to promise another fine day. How lovely it would have been had she been asked aboard the canal boat, given a job, and more bacon sarnies, told she might stay with them! But things like that only happened in stories, in real life you were likelier to get thumps than kisses, so she'd better start moving. Sary never got up till noon, especially when she'd had a skinful the previous night, but the eleven-year-old twins Arnold and Robert – known as Arny and Bob to their friends – were often abroad far earlier and had been known to visit the canal for the purpose of either nicking off the boats or fishing in the turgid water with a bit of string and a bent pin.

'All they'll catch will be colds in the head,' Mrs O'Rourke used to say when Kitty explained why her brothers were somehow never expected to work as she did. 'They'll grow up bad, those two.'

Kitty thought they were pretty bad already, but you couldn't altogether blame them. Sary didn't much like any girls, but she did adore the twins, so they got their own way with everything, waxed fat on their own thieving and Sary's sporadic generosity, and never gave a thought to the sister who had pretty well brought them up, save to tell tales of her to their mother whenever the opportunity arose.

So where'll I go, then? Kitty asked herself, looking

round the early-morning street, already beginning to bustle as the night-shift got ready to leave the factories and the day-shift began to stream in. What'll I do today? By 'eck, that sarny were good – I wouldn't mind another one jest like that! And I've got the 'alf dollar an' all – I could get me some grub to set me up for the day.

It was strange to know that the day was her own, and whether it was the unexpected kindness of the boat-people or the comfortable fullness engendered by the bacon sarny, Kitty was beginning to feel that her life was on the up-and-up, that there was hope for her, a future, even. Other girls left home and prospered! Boys, too – did not her favourite book, *Her Benny*, tell the story of two Liverpool kids from the slums who made it to better things? The uncomfortable thought that little Nellie, the book's heroine, had died and gone to heaven before real good fortune came to Benny was easily dealt with; Benny was the eldest, as she was, so she was bound, like Benny, to be all right, to make her fortune, and to live happily ever after.

But not, of course, if the twins found her and told Sary, nor if either Sary or her father came across her. All they would consider would be how many bones they should break before tossing her remains into the River Mersey for the fishes to nibble. They'd brand her a thief no matter that she'd handed over the money and told them where the trimmings were to be found. Oh well.

She was walking along the pavement when a woman drew level with her. As she did so she glanced down at Kitty, sniffed suspiciously and produced from her handbag an embroidered hanky, which she pressed defensively to her nose. She also increased her speed, plainly eager to get past the younger girl as quickly as possible.

Reckon I niff a bit, Kitty thought unconcernedly, for was she not always dirty and unkempt? She glanced down at her stained and filthy shirt, then looked again. Oh dear Lor', she thought, look at them 'ands!

They were not only black, they were striped, where the bacon fat had run down. Kitty guessed that her chin was probably fatty too, and she remembered that at home, unless her mother was up betimes and chased her out, she usually did her best, without soap or a flannel, to wash her face and hands under the pump shared by all the houses in the Court. And if you wanted anything, you were more likely to get it if you were at least clean.

There's the deserving poor, someone had said to Mrs O'Rourke in Kitty's hearing, and there's the squalid, idle drunkards and wife-beaters. Charity isn't any use to the latter, they abuse it or drink it; the former hate being the recipients of it but at least use it to escape from the poverty trap. So if she wanted help from anyone, Kitty reasoned, she had better set about becoming deserving poor right away.

Kitty returned to the canal. She knelt on the bank and rubbed at her hands and arms until they were pink and only lightly smeared, then she doused her face and rubbed that too. And finally, because it was a lovely morning and the sun was shining on the water – and also because her nits were itching her something cruel as they wandered across her scalp – she ducked her whole head in the canal and held it there for two or three lung-bursting minutes, then sat back, gulping air and squeezing water, dirt and even one or two nits out of her tangled locks.

She sat on the canal bank until she was pretty well dry, though her hair would probably stay dampish for a while yet, then climbed over the bridge once more and looked cautiously about her. No one so much as glanced at her. A passing scuffer, with his helmet in one hand to let the sun warm his curly dark hair, did not even see her, though he trod on her little toe with his great clumping black boots. Kitty said a few things under her breath, but continued to walk – or rather, limp – along Vauxhall Road, heading away from home, leaving the richly stinking tannery, the coal wharves and the small, familiar streets behind. She could feel the half-crown, wrapped in a bit of rag, nestling near her roped-in waist, comfortingly solid against her bony ribs. It represented food, safety, hope. Public houses were still locked and barred but drowsy, blowsy women wrapped in big aprons were emerging from them to scrub steps and brush pavements, to shout curses at horses who left piles of steaming manure too near their doorsteps and to hail the milkman as his dozy steed dragged the milkcart up and down the small streets.

Kitty didn't know many eating places, but everyone knew Paddy's Market, and she did consider going there. They sold marvellous, mouth-watering food and it was cheap, too, and though she would not be able to afford even a second-hand dress she might beg or nick one, explaining – or not, of course – how she wanted to be the deserving poor and not the idle and feckless. But you could meet anyone in Paddy's, the twins nicked all sorts from the stalls, and kids of all shapes and sizes hung about it, including half Kitty's classmates, so it simply wasn't safe. No, she would have to get a lot further from home before she stopped to eat again.

But if there was one thing Kitty was used to, it was being hungry and not being fed. So it was with the bright optimism still burning within her that she began the trek to another part of the city, somewhere where the name Drinkwater wouldn't have people clutching their baskets and covering their pockets.

I'll make me fortune, she told herself, peering interestedly into shop windows as she passed. I'll run messages and carry shopping, I'll scrub doorsteps and hold horses, but I'll keep meself a deal better'n me mam ever did.

And with that thought to hold on to – and it wasn't so very much to attain, after all – Kitty plodded on through the bright morning.

Kitty had lived in the city all her short life. She knew the streets, the canal, the gas works, the factories and the tannery, the rice and flour mills, the various railway lines and stations, the smells and the sounds of it all. But her Liverpool consisted of a smelly, crowded mile to mile and a half at the most. When she ran errands for her mother, making her way to Paddy's Market to fetch rags or to the fruit market on Great Nelson Street, she was still more or less in her own territory. But when she went to and from the millinery shop on Upper Frederick Street, sneaked down to nick ends of timber from the yard opposite St Anne's on Rose Place, hung around outside the Free Library on William Brown Street, too scared to go in yet longing for the books which Mrs O'Rourke used to borrow for her, she was in Indian country, a stranger in a strange land.

So, padding along the dusty summer streets and wishing that the water-cart would come along and spray her hot, aching feet, it was not so very long before Kitty began to feel herself safe from the entire Drinkwater clan. Her father was a stoker on a merchant ship which plied across the Atlantic, taking goods to the United States of America. It was a long journey and so Hector Drinkwater was away more than he was home, for which fact Kitty was frequently devoutly thankful. She knew he was a seaman of course, that Liverpool was a great port, but since she was a far cry from being a favourite child she had never been taken down to the docks to view her father's ship from afar, nor lifted down onto the muddy sand at low tide to play with other kids in the rich, sticky mess.

Yet in a way the sea was in her blood, for the wind which blows nine days out of ten over the city was sweetened with salt, as well as with the oily, tarry, fishy smells from the docks. Kitty had breathed in the smell all her life and, indeed, knew no other.

So when she had passed, with a half-wistful glance, the end of Upper Parly, as the kids called it, she turned left along Park Lane, where those great, swaying land-ships, the trams, thundered along sounding their warning bells, and then she turned right into Beckwith Street, with the smell of the sea stronger than ever here and a strange excitement mounting in her. It was an ugly little road, too. She passed a huge building which announced that it was Heaps Flour Mills, then a shipyard, only by now the street had begun to call itself Carpenters' Row; no wonder, thought Kitty, appreciatively sniffing the smells of sawdust, tar and engine oil, a great many carpenters must be employed to make huge ships!

She emerged from Carpenters' Row on to Chaloner

Street – and saw the overhead railway for the first time. It scared her when the train came rattling and chugging along, but then she saw the docks, and her attention was caught and held.

Ships! Water, lots of it, and when she skirted Wapping Basin and began to cross the swing bridge which looked just exactly like another piece of road – if she hadn't been able to read she would never have known it was a bridge at all – she found the sea! Wide and blue today, with the buildings on the opposite bank shimmering in a heat-haze and looking very far away, but undoubtedly the great ocean she had read about, which divided Liverpool first from Ireland and then from the United States of America, though she was not quite certain how this division worked.

A girl of about her own age was playing hop-scotch with another girl on the wide dockside. Kitty approached them.

'Hey, is that the sea?' she asked, sure of a confirmatory nod. But instead, two shaggy heads shook.

'Nah, chuck, that's the Mairsey,' the smaller of the girls assured her. 'Ain't you never seen it afore? Biggest river in the 'ole wairld, me da says.'

'Oh!' Kitty said. She had lost face, but the girls didn't seem to care at all. The taller one threw her piece of slate into the crudely chalked squares and began to hop. Kitty watched for a minute, then ambled on. She had found a fish and chip shop on Chaloner Street, squeezed between the Great Western Railway goods station and a small tobacconist shop, and still had the paper which had held the chips, though she had eaten the contents hungrily within moments of handing over her half-crown and watching sadly as it was reduced to two shillings, a threepenny joe and two pennies.

She'd had a drink of water just before accosting the two girls, because there was a drinking fountain at the side of the road, so she was comfortable enough in herself. And now she began to wonder if she might find employment of some sort amongst the ships which thronged the docks, or perhaps someone needing an errand run. For in fact Kitty, a gregarious little soul, was beginning to find the loneliness of her wandering almost as trying as the fear of being picked up by the police or the dread of dying of starvation: fates which, she well knew, did befall unwanted children.

But the afternoon was wearing on and fascinating though the dockside was to one as new to it as Kitty, it was patently no place for a skinny, barefoot girl. Mostly she was ignored, but now and then someone spoke to her – not always in English, either – and a strong sense of self-preservation warned her that the men who called out to her and cajoled her with sweets to come and talk to them meant her no good and might well be as dangerous as an encounter wi:. Sary or Hector Drinkwater.

So she abandoned the docks and wandered back into the city proper once more, this time into a better area where the houses were big and very clean and the pavements wide and well-swept.

She glanced up at the road sign nearest her. *Rodney Street*, it read.

Kitty walked on. A great many of the houses had brass plates on the door; she stopped to read one. *Dr G.B. Matteson. Member of the Royal College of Surgeons.* Wondering vaguely what the wording meant, Kitty continued. But she was getting tired and Rodney Street did not seem like the kind of place where she might find a fried fish shop, nor one of the delightful cocoa rooms where a cooked dinner might be had for sixpence – not that she intended to waste her substance on cooked dinners, of course, when chips were available for so much less. Besides, it was evening and she really ought to be finding a nice warm nook for the night, not wandering gormlessly on with no thought for the future.

So she turned and began to retrace her steps.

Chapter Four

Lilac had settled Mrs Matteson tenderly in bed, put
a glass of iced water within easy reach, arranged a
light shawl comfortably round the older woman's
shoulders, and gone downstairs to the kitchen to
fetch up Mrs Matteson's tray, on which there should
already be a light and tempting supper. Since she
was going to the house in Penny Lane for a meal
she wanted to get her work over so that she could
change her print gown and flat shoes for something
a trifle more fashionable, but she would never have
dreamed of hurrying her mistress. Nevertheless, she
entered the kitchen hoping devoutly that the evening
meal was prepared.

The plain cook, stomping about her domain, gave
Lilac a nasty glare as she entered the room; Mrs
O'Malley had found another place and the dislike
Lilac felt for her was now seen to be mutual. She
had already prepared two plates of food, one for the
mistress and one for Dr Matteson, and when Lilac
looked at the unappetising helpings she felt a cold rage
envelop her. The woman had cut the cold mutton into
chunks and scarcely warmed the cabbage, whilst the
potatoes, small, new, toothsome, had been boiled to a
miserable mush. She had made a thick, solid-looking
gravy and the mint sauce, which should have been
sweet and green with the well-minced herb, was last
week's, so it was brown as a cup of milkless tea. She
had used one of the best plates, it was true, but there

was a smear of gravy across the gold-rimmed edge and she hadn't bothered to match up the knife and fork: the knife had a heavy pearl handle and the fork had embossed ivy leaves on its silver surface. Bullied by Lilac into at least a semblance of caring, she had put a rose in the silver vase on the tray, but the rose was half-dead and heavily infested with greenfly and the vase had smears of plate polish down one side.

'This is disgraceful,' Lilac said shortly, not bothering to hide her annoyance. 'Mrs Matteson is an invalid, cook; we are supposed to tempt her appetite. Do you remember what the doctor told you when he first employed you?'

'He never told me no jumped up orphing from a 'sylum 'ud be 'titled to order me about,' the cook muttered rudely. 'Tek it or leave it, Miss.'

'Mrs Matteson will leave it, because it's badly cooked and stale-looking,' Lilac said firmly. 'Get the bread and butter out, please. I'll make her a few sandwiches – if you haven't ruined the rest of the food in the pantry, that is.'

The cook snorted; her big, work-roughened hands went behind her to untie her apron.

'Do it yourself,' she snapped. 'I'm orf.'

'You aren't due to leave for another hour and a half,' Lilac said. 'What do you think Dr Matteson will say when he sees what you've prepared for him and his wife?'

The cook continued to shed her apron, then snatched her coat off the back of a chair where it had plainly been hung ready for her departure.

'Don't care what the 'ell 'e finks,' she said. 'I've got a new place waitin' for me, unlike some. I'm orf now and I won't be back. Put tharrin your pipe an' smoke it, you snotty bitch.'

78

Lilac, fairly trembling with rage, cleared the tray of the greasy, rapidly cooling food and threw the dying rose into the bin. Then she watched as the older woman struggled into her coat and jammed a felt hat down over her greasy hair.

'So you don't even intend to work out your week! Well, good riddance to bad rubbish is what the Mattesons will think,' she said to the cook's back as the woman headed for the kitchen door. 'Now that you've gone, and your nasty, lazy habits with you, perhaps I can get my poor mistress a meal that's halfway decent for once.'

Mrs O'Malley did not deign to reply but sniffed scornfully, then slammed the kitchen door resoundingly behind her, just as Lilac filled her lungs for another blast of truthful abuse. Seeing that she would be talking to herself, Lilac began to scrabble round, preparing a tray from scratch since there was nothing whatsoever left to hand once the original plateful had been consigned to the bin.

As she worked, she wished she could have got word to Nellie, to say she would be late. She guessed Nellie wouldn't start the meal without her and poor Stuart would be hungry as a lion by the time she had finished here. The Mattesons knew that she had to find a new place and had told her, with all their usual sympathy and understanding, that she might have as much time off as she wished provided Mrs Matteson was never left alone, but tonight she had the cook's job to do as well as her own and was bound to be very late indeed arriving at Penny Lane.

However, wishing was not much use and working hard was likelier to shorten Stuart's wait. So she ran into the back garden and found a beautiful white rosebud, just unfurling. She picked it, put it in the silver vase which she had already wiped clean and polished with a duster, then she went into the pantry. Looking round her, she realised that cook had been steadily using up all the available food and not bothering to spend the housekeeping money she was given to stock up again. A very small pat of butter, a tin of sardines in oil and another of ham in jelly, together with a heel of bread met Lilac's eye. The bread was stale, she could see that at a glance, and Mrs Matteson did not care for ham. She opened the meat safe, expecting to find the rest of the mutton reposing therein, but it was empty. What cook had done with the mangled remains of the joint she could not imagine, but it was nowhere to be seen.

Still, they say, necessity is the mother of invention. Lilac cut two thin slices of bread and toasted them, mashed the sardines with a little vinegar, salt and pepper, and spread the resultant savoury paste on the toast. Then she covered the fish with thin slices of tomato and ran into the garden again to pick some parsley, which she chopped and scattered over the food. She lit the gas-grill and slid the toast under it, then got a bottle of white wine out of the sideboard in the dining room and poured her mistress a modest half-glass. She deserves something to help that down, though it'll be tastier than the muck cook had prepared, she told herself grimly, putting the hot food onto a warmed and clean plate and setting it carefully on the tray, with matching cutlery beside it and the glass of wine beside that.

Upstairs, Mrs Matteson's eyes brightened at the sight of the tray.

'Looks – n-nice,' she said hesitantly. 'Pretty. Ooh, wine!'

'Her speech is improving,' Dr Matteson had said

to Lilac earlier in the day. 'With peace and quiet and no worries, and with me on hand all day, she'll make a complete recovery, I'm sure of it.'

Now, Lilac arranged Mrs Matteson's pillows so that she was sitting upright, cut the hot toast into small squares, and sat down beside the bed.

'The doctor won't be long, now,' she said cheerfully. 'You eat up, Mrs Matteson, and think how pleased he'll be to see a clean plate when he gets back!'

'Umm,' Mrs Matteson said. She picked up the wine glass, her hand shaking, and carried it to her lips. She drank, then replaced the glass. A smile curved her lips. 'Nice,' she said again.

'Yes, it's a good wine I believe,' Lilac said. She had never tasted wine, but she knew what Dr Matteson would have said. 'Can you manage the toast?'

'Umm. Oo-oh, sard . . . sa . . .'

'That's right, sardines. Do you like them?'

'Mmm!' A vigorous nod of the head accompanied the hum. 'N- nice.'

Lilac sat by the bed, watching for the first sign of tiredness, for the fork to drop from Mrs Matteson's thin, nervous hand, but all went well. Apparently sardines on toast were a treat to someone who habitually tackled a heavy cooked dinner at night – particularly heavy lately, since Mrs O'Malley believed in sending up large helpings as a method of disguising her inability to present palatable food. And presently Lilac hurried down the stairs with an empty tray, and carried up the only dessert she could find: a helping of raspberries, sugared and topped with thick cream.

Coffee followed that and Lilac tried very hard not to think how time was flying by, nor how late Dr Matteson was. Indeed, when his step sounded on the stair she did her best to stand up casually, as though she had all the time in the world.

'Evening, doctor. As you're late, should I bring your meal up on a tray? Then you can sit with Mrs Matteson whilst you eat. Your wife has only just finished!'

'Excellent,' Dr Matteson said heartily. 'Many thanks Lilac – what has cook prepared for us tonight, then?'

'Nothing. She's done a bunk,' Lilac said briefly. 'Good riddance, I say. The pantry's bare, but I can do you toasted ham sandwiches with mustard, and there are raspberries and cream to follow.'

'*Toasted* sandwiches? Why not plain old bread sandwiches?' Dr Matteson said, tiredly sitting down in the chair Lilac had just vacated. 'Anything will do, my dear . . . and I'll have a glass of wine, too.'

'The bread's stale,' Lilac said. 'It toasts fine, though. Shan't be a tick, sir.'

But she was, of course. The doctor didn't need a rose on his tray but Lilac knew he would like a clean tray-cloth and she had to make up fresh mustard. The tin of ham was easily opened and despite Lilac's suspicion of tinned meat, proved to be fresh enough. But by the time she had found another tomato and sliced that as a garnish on the side of the plate, poured the wine, changed her mind and put the bottle on the tray, sugared the raspberries . . . goodness, it's going to be dark before I get there, Lilac told herself, dismayed at the way time was flying.

As soon as the meal was served she hurried up to her room. She changed with great rapidity into a light green skirt and white blouse and donned a pair of neat black shoes with a medium heel. She brushed her hair, coiled it round her hand and wedged it on top of her head with a number of hairpins, snatched up her jacket and headed for the attic stairs.

On the first floor, she remembered the tray. Damn! She fetched it, the doctor having cleaned both his plates and emptied the bottle, and hurried down the two flights of stairs into the basement kitchen. And though it wasn't her job to wash up she had best do it rather than have the poor doctor go down later to make his wife's hot milk and find the kitchen in disarray. The washing up was done at speed, Lilac snatching crocks in and out of the water and slapping them on the dresser without pausing for breath. When it was done she looked round the kitchen, decided it would have to do, and headed for the front door, making a lightning decision as she went.

She would go to Nellie's by cab!

She descended the steps and stood on the pavement, looking about her. There was a cab rank outside the Philharmonic Hall and it wasn't far to the Philly, she would simply turn to her left and walk up Rodney Street until she reached the crossroads, then turn right along Hardman Street, past the School for the Blind and St Mary's Church and there you were, with the bulk of the Philly to your right and cabs lined up against the pavement waiting for fares.

But she was in luck. She had scarcely walked more than ten yards on her way when a cab came towards her with its flag up; cruising for fares, no doubt, possibly having just dropped someone off further up Rodney Street. As she stepped into the cab, having told him Nellie's address, she heard a shout. She looked round, the vehicle already on the move, and saw a skinny child waving at her from the pavement.

Puzzled, the glanced about, because the child

couldn't possibly be waving to her, she didn't know the girl. The street was empty though, so perhaps the kid just thought she recognised Lilac. Or was her skirt caught in the door? It had happened, Lilac knew, and could result in a nasty mark on a precious garment. She checked, but her skirt was all in the cab with her and very nice it looked, spread out on the cracked red leather seat. And presently, as the cab made its way towards Penny Lane, she forgot about the child and began to think about the steak and kidney pudding she would presently enjoy, and Nellie's wonderful lemon chiffon pie which would follow. How odd it is that this evening I'll be eating a much better meal than the Mattesons, who are very rich compared to Nellie and me, she thought. What a topsy-turvy world it is – money can't always buy you the best. And she decided to get Nellie some really good chocolates as a thank-you present, to eat on the journey down to the snooty south of England.

Kitty had walked up as far as Leece Street and bought herself an enormous bowl of pea and ham soup and a wedge of bread at the refreshment rooms opposite St Luke's Church. Considerably heartened by this repast, she bought two blackjacks for a farthing from Thomas Henry's, a very superior sort of provisions shop, and decided to save the sticky sweets for the long watches of her second night under the stars. Not knowing quite where to go, she then returned to Rodney Street. It was quiet, the lamplighter had not yet been along and the sky was a peaceful greenish blue, deepening to red-gold along the western horizon. No one was about, so she found a house with deep steps, under which was a dry, cave-like hidey-hole. She clambered into it and stared out down the street.

A door opened somewhere, then shut with a sharp snap. High-heeled shoes clack-clacketed down steps and along the pavement. A woman, quite young, Kitty decided drowsily. Wonder what she's doin' out at this hour, when everyone else seems to be settled indoors?

The woman came into view. Only it wasn't a woman, it was a girl and a very pretty one, too. With renewed interest, because the pretty girl looked somehow familiar, Kitty eased herself out of her hiding place and stood up, then her heart gave a great bound in her skinny chest.

It was her! The girl from Penny Lane! And she was walking swiftly and confidently along the pavement, any moment she would be on a level with Kitty!

She'll help me, Kitty thought unhesitatingly. She will, she's a real lady, Mrs O'Rourke said real ladies were always willing to help. I'll 'splain about me mam and the trimmin's and all that, she'll tell me what to do and where to go.

She moved hesitantly forward just as a car came past and the girl gestured to the driver, who pulled over and stopped by the kerb. Kitty waited; she would speak to the girl from Penny Lane just as soon as the cab had driven on. How lucky it was that she had chosen a Rodney Street doorstep for her bed! But it seemed her luck had run out, for the girl from Penny Lane said something to the cab driver, then opened the door of his vehicle and jumped inside. Kitty ran forward, waving, calling, desperate that her one hope of help should not disappear. In fact she pursued the cab all the way down Rodney Street, turned the corner onto Hardman Street at such speed that she burnt the side of her bare foot, and saw with real dismay that the driver was accelerating and would presently outstrip her.

Kitty ran on, but she knew it was useless, and presently, sobbing with effort and with a hand to the stitch in her side, she slowed to an amble and then a walk. She would never catch up, not if she ran and ran, and even if she'd had the money to get into a taxi herself and shout 'Follow that motor!' she would never have the nerve. Why, for all she knew, Penny Lane might be miles and miles away.

She had been shuffling along the pavement, intermittently sobbing and hiccuping, whilst tears spilled down her cheeks, but now she stopped short and stared sightlessly at the building ahead of her. Penny Lane! Her new friend was the girl from Penny Lane, they had said so in the milliner's shop. So all Kitty had to do to find her friend was to find Penny Lane!

'Lilac! Well, our kid, you had us well worried!' Stuart gave his young sister-in-law a friendly hug and drew her into the small, square hallway. 'My lady-wife was all for calling out the scuffers to search for your body, but I told her you were probably working late and would arrive in time for the meal if we hung on a bit.'

'Oh Stu, you didn't wait supper for me? I couldn't help it, honest . . . that wretched cook I told you about left without warning and I was landed with gettin' Mrs Matteson her tea and cookin' for the doctor . . . *how* I wished you were on the telephone, so I could have let you know I was going to be late.'

'We'll be on the telephone in London, since I'll need to be in contact with the newspaper,' Stuart said. 'So there'll be no excuse for not getting in touch, young lady. Come on, let's get sat down now you are here.'

'I'll just put me jacket on the stand,' Lilac said, wriggling out of her short coat. 'Ooh, I've been thinking of steak and kidney pudding all the way . . . I caught a cab, you know, like a proper lady!'

Stuart looked down at the vivid little face so near his own and remembered the first time he had met Lilac. A skinny, scruffy kid she'd been, covered with mud and stinking like . . . like the Mersey at low tide, which was where the mud had come from. He'd made her take a bath in the old tin tub before her aunt's fire and had been astonished, when she emerged from the water, to find she had a mass of red-gold curls and very white skin as well as a pair of dazzlingly blue eyes. She'd been a regular little brick then, for all Nellie mourned her selfishness and quick temper, and she was a regular little brick now, though she did still tend to see life strictly with a view to her own best interests. But Nellie was all she had in the world, apart from a few friends her own age and a good many ardent young men, and Lilac had stressed that she would cope happily with life alone to make it possible for Nellie to go down to London with a clear conscience. Stuart was well aware that, had Lilac bemoaned her fate, said she'd pine for Nellie, his wife would have felt guilty and unhappy about putting her husband before the girl she had treated more like a daughter than an adopted sister, and would have been unsettled and unhappy in their new home as a result.

'You are a lady, chuck,' Stuart said now, throwing open the kitchen door and smiling across at his wife, standing by the table enveloped in a huge white apron, whilst the steam made her hair curl in tiny tendrils around her face and turned her cheeks scarlet. 'Here she is, Nell darling, as safe as houses and as pretty as a picture.'

Lilac walked into the room and kissed Nellie's hot cheek, then turned back to Stuart, her blue eyes dancing with innocent flirtatiousness.

'Oh Stuart, I wish I were a lady, for if I were I'd do all sorts of exciting things, but there's no gainsaying that I'm just me.' She turned to her sister. 'Nellie, love, I'm sorry I worried you, but it wasn't my fault I was late, honest to God.'

'It never is, honest to God,' Nellie said drily, ladling the steaming pudding onto three plates. 'Tell us what happened; is Mrs Matteson all right?'

'Fine, now. Better for that wretch of a cook leaving without warning just at dinner time,' Lilac said. 'That was why I was late, I had to get some decent food and Mrs O'Malley, the awful cook, had left us with a bare pantry, so it took a while. Shall I put the spuds round whilst you do the greens, Nell?'

'You sit yourself down and be a guest for once,' Stuart ordered her. 'She hasn't told you how she got here, Nell. What a girl she is!'

'I came by cab,' Lilac said proudly, when Nellie looked an enquiry across the table. 'I was so desperate to reach your steak pudding, our Nell, that I didn't grudge the money one bit. And it were a good drive, too. I enjoyed it, though right at the start I thought I'd caught me skirt in the door of the taxi, which could easily have spoiled it.'

'There you are; eat up,' Nellie ordered, pulling her own chair up to the table and picking up her knife and fork. 'What made you think you'd caught your skirt in the door, chuck?'

'I can't remember . . . yes I can, it was a little girl,

a real street arab, standing by the kerb screeching something at me and waving. And then when the cab started to move she ran behind for a few steps, so I thought she must have wanted to warn me I'd trapped my skirt. Only I hadn't.'

'I see,' Nellie said placidly. Stuart, eating, grinned to himself. He did love feminine logic, and anyway he was feeling supremely happy. The two women he loved best in the world – he was very fond of Lilac even when she was acting like any other pretty, empty-headed youngster – were sitting at his table, his wife was expecting a baby, and they were about to move south to a well-paid job. Furthermore, he had always wanted to work in London because the city fascinated him.

But thinking about the baby made him think about something else, something he would rather have forgotten. When he had asked Nellie to marry him she had told him that long ago, when she had been little more than a child herself, she had borne an illegitimate son to another man. He had been shattered, astonished, hurt. Nellie had always seemed perfect to him, a delicately beautiful, sensitive girl whose main aim in life had been to guard the child Lilac against all ills and to strain every nerve to bring back health and happiness to the wounded soldiers in her charge – for Nellie had been nursing when they had first met as adults. He had been so sure of her innocence, too, and for a couple of days he had kept away from her, feeling betrayed and cheated.

But it had not lasted: Stuart was too fairminded not to see the double-standards he was applying to Nellie's unwelcome and unexpected revelation. He had had a good few experiences himself, and he had not got the excuse of youth and innocence, either.

A pretty Parisienne, a warmhearted brunette from Bootle, a blonde and bubbly girl-reporter covering the same story as he in France, had all shared his bed at one time or another and he had instigated the relationship in each instance. Yet even knowing that he had no right to expect Nellie to be different, he still felt, irrationally, that he had been cheated. If only she had talked more about the affair, explained . . .

Apologised, you mean, Stuart said crossly to himself. After what that girl suffered during the war, surely you aren't still of the opinion that women are in some way different to men? That your little flings are to be tolerated with a smile whilst her one fall from grace must be frowned upon as a deeply immoral act? You know Nellie, you know she's a sweet, giving person. She must have thought she was in love with the chap . . . she never said what happened about the baby . . . Oh but it's different, I can't bear it, she's mine, all mine, I've got her present and her future in my loving hands and the truth is I want her past, too!

'Stu? What a grim expression!' Lilac smiled at him, breaking into his train of thought, bringing him abruptly back to the present, to the cosy kitchen, the untouched food on his plate. 'If you don't want your dinner, I know someone who does!'

'Don't say you're still hungry, our Lilac!' Nellie exclaimed. 'Better start your meal, Stu love, or the poor, hungry orphan will be whipping it off your plate and on to her own!'

'I am, I am,' Stuart said, hastily beginning to eat. 'Nellie, you're the queen of cooks,' he added through a full mouth. 'This is prime! I can't blame the kid for wanting seconds.'

'There's a bit more pudding left, and some veggies, if you'd like them, Lilac,' Nellie said. 'Pass your plate, queen.'

Lilac laughed but shook her head.

'Couldn't, I'm stuffed fuller'n a Christmas turkey,' she declared. 'And did someone say it was lemon chiffon for afters?'

'Someone did. And now since Stu's come out of his brown study and started to eat I'll fetch it through. It's on the marble slab in the pantry, keeping cool.'

Nellie got up to fetch the dessert whilst Lilac cleared the table and Stuart, conscience-stricken, ate as fast as he could. He was just thankful that no one had offered him a penny for his thoughts though, because a guilty blush might have led Nellie to make a pretty shrewd guess as to why his face had seemed grim.

'All done, love?' Nellie said as he pushed back his plate. 'Lemon chiffon? Or would you rather have cheese and biscuits?'

She always asked, almost always provided a dessert, though she knew Stuart invariably chose cheese. His wishes, he knew, came first with her, she studied to please him in everything, never really considered herself at all. So why could not he, in his turn, be more generous over the only action of hers which he could not entirely understand and condone? This evening, to make up for his unkind thoughts, Stuart eyed the lemon chiffon appreciatively and said he would try some, thank you, dear.

'You can have cheese afterwards,' Nellie said, twinkling at him. 'A chiffon is ever so light.'

I wonder if he was dark or fair, her first fellow, Stuart's mind wondered perversely as he began to eat the delicious, lemony dessert. Or he might have been grey haired, or a red-head ... he could even have been bald, with a great white beard!

'Go on, Nell, you're eating for two, remember,' Lilac remarked. 'Take the last bit of chiffon, it'll make young Gallagher grow up big and strong!'

Stuart finished off his dessert and reached for the cheese. What on earth was the matter with him tonight? What did it matter if her lover – even thinking the word was like a knife twisting in his guts – was dark or fair, grey or bald? He was past, perhaps dead, certainly out of both sight and mind. Or out of Nellie's mind, anyway. So why should the bloke, whoever he was, persist in entering Stuart's thoughts on the least possible excuse, to plague and irritate?

'Biscuits, love?'

Nellie held out the small, round tin. Stuart selected two, cut himself a wedge of his favourite cheese and watched the two girls as they bustled round clearing the table, for they were later than usual and Lilac would have to be walked to the tram stop soon or she would miss the last one.

As he ate, it occurred to him that there might be a rather nasty secondary reason for his sudden preoccupation with Nellie's past. The obvious reason was her pregnancy, because every time he looked at her he could not help remembering that this was not the first time her stomach had slowly swelled and ripened with a child. He thought guiltily that the secondary reason might easily be that with Nellie's pregnancy pulling her out of shape and making her tired and pale, he was noticing Lilac's ripe young beauty more than ever before – and perhaps as a result was very conscious of the fact that Lilac still had an almost childish affection for him, which took the form, often, of friendly flirtatiousness.

If it wasn't for Nellie . . . he found himself thinking, and was appalled at his own shallowness. He loved his wife deeply, devotedly, and he loved Lilac as one loves one's wife's pretty little sister. He harboured no carnal desire for the younger girl either, despite her lovely looks; he was simply intrigued by the sneaking suspicion that, should he make advances, Lilac would fall into his hands like a ripe plum.

'Finished, dearest? Then pass your plate and go and read the paper whilst Li and I wash up and have a good gossip.'

Nellie gave him her sweetest smile and Stuart, muttering that he really ought to help, left the room, clutching the evening paper and feeling a complete cad.

Well, he had looked himself squarely in the face and he didn't much like what he had seen. A man who could not bring himself to forgive his wife for a long-dead, girlhood love-affair, yet admitted to a prurient interest in her pretty younger sister. What sort of a fellow was he, for goodness sake? He sat down in the basket chair by the window and opened the paper. He would never think about Nellie's past again, what did it matter, it was over, finished! Though one day, when they were both much older and wiser, he might just ask her . . .

Nellie set down her teacup and eased her aching back, then stood up. Stuart must be roused from his newspaper so that he and she might walk Lilac to the tram, and Lilac must be brought indoors and put into her coat, because at present she was gossiping over the back wall to Ena Evans, next door.

Nellie sighed and began to walk slowly across the kitchen. Having a baby was a tiring business, her legs hurt, her back ached and now even her mind was uncomfortable, because she knew her dear Stuart as well as she knew herself, and she had known as soon as she saw the expression on his face at supper-time, that he was thinking about Davy again.

Not that he knew about Davy, he just knew he wasn't her first lover, that this baby would be her second child. He had sworn it didn't matter, wouldn't affect their love, and it hadn't, not at first. Not until she told him she was expecting his child and she saw how his first joy had been tempered by the thought, *she's done it all before.*

It was a pity, really, that they had both agreed never to mention the matter again, because some things, Nellie believed, needed discussion before complete understanding could result. She had never told Stuart that Davy was married, and happily at that, to a girl called Bethan from the little village of Moelfre in Anglesey. Never told him that Bethan's eldest child, Richart, was the baby to whom she, Nellie, had given birth on that chilly March day in 1915. Not that anyone had known she was the child's mother. Bethan, believing Davy dead, had longed for a child and Nellie had known she could not give Richart a tenth of what would be his as Bethan's boy. So they had padded Bethan with cushions, and covered Nellie with voluminous aprons and a cloak, and Richart had stayed in Moelfre where he was totally accepted as Bethan's son. Even Davy, who had been posted as missing but who had in fact been picked up by a passing ship and was in rude health, thought the

boy was his and Bethan's. Conceived on his last
leave, born in his absence ... Davy was sure that
Richart was the best thing that had ever happened
to him.

So though Nellie could have told Stuart that her
child's father was a married man and to the best of
her knowledge alive and kicking, she could never tell
him who that father was nor that the child was living
with his father and that father's legal wife on the Isle
of Anglesey. It was not her secret to tell and she and
Bethan had vowed silence. To break that vow would
have been unforgivable.

So perhaps not mentioning it ever again was the best
idea, after all. If only Stuart could have put it right out
of his mind, pretended it had never happened. Nellie
did just that, most of the time. There was no point in
dwelling on it; what can't be cured must be endured,
her Aunt Ada used to say. Well, it was true and she
was doing her very best to endure, but when she saw
Stuart looking at her as though she was somehow evil
... well, it was hard.

I needn't have told him anything, she reminded
herself sometimes. I could have kept it to myself, same
as I have with everyone else. But everyone has their
own set of rules, and Nellie's rules said that you didn't
hold back, not with someone as important to you as
Stuart was to her. She could not be totally frank and
tell him everything, because it wasn't just her secret,
but she'd done her best. Besides, if he had wanted to
back out, not to marry her, he'd had his chance, and
he'd not taken it. So why should he keep dwelling on
it now, when she needed his love and support as never
before?

Nellie was Liverpool born and bred. In the poverty-
stricken court off the Scotland Road where she had

been born, the air she had breathed for the first twenty years of her existence had held the whiff of Mersey mud and the rolling fog which came in from the Irish Sea, and was dyed yellow and sulphurous by the fumes from the factories. She had travelled to France during the war and been kept going by the accents of her home city all around her, as Liverpool girls clung together and did their best to save lives. The city was her home and she loved it; when the war ended she had come home and vowed never to leave again. But that was before Stuart had been offered a job in London, of course. A wife must support her man; she had agreed unhesitatingly to go with him. Far from home she would go, far from friends, far from Lilac, too, who was more than a sister, dearer than any friend.

But she would do it all, for Stuart. She would even consent to her child being born in the soft south, picking up heaven knows what horrible habits and accents and affectations amongst those effete Londoners who had never eaten scouse or conny onny butties, wouldn't know a stirring cart if it ran over their feet, and probably thought a scuffer was a doormat.

And how did Stuart treat this selfless devotion to duty, this denial of her natural wish to be in her own place, to bear her child amongst friends? Why, with grim glances, a downturned mouth, a secret grudging of her one dreadful mistake – she had loved too well, and as it turned out, very unwisely. Was she to suffer for it for the rest of her days?

She had crossed the little hallway and now saw Stuart asleep in his chair. Her heart, hardened by what she imagined Stuart had been thinking, softened at the sight of him. Brown curly hair flopping over his forehead, the worry lines smoothed out, mouth open, dark eyes closed . . . he did work hard, poor Stu, and anyway she supposed that he was right; it was wicked to make a baby with a man before you married, she had done it and suffered the consequences. Perhaps she should take Stuart's disapproval on board, along with all the rest – her guilt over leaving Richart, lying to Davy's parents, deceiving her relatives and friends.

She moved softly across the room, her simple dress rustling over its petticoat. Stuart stirred and opened his eyes. For a moment he stared up at her, looking puzzled, then his eyes lit up with the most loving and tender glance.

'Nell! I was dreaming . . . such a nice dream . . .'

'Stu, we've got to walk our Lilac to the tram now, but when we get home, I want to talk.'

He frowned. Not crossly, but as though she had puzzled him.

'We talk all the time, sweetheart,' he said gently. 'What's different about talking later this evening?'

'I want to talk about – about what you were thinking, at supper tonight. Thinking so hard, love, that you forgot to eat.'

'Oh.' He looked stricken, then guilty. 'Nell, I try not to even let it cross my mind, I try to tell myself it never happened. But . . .'

'I know. I'm the same in a way. We'll talk about it though; right?'

He smiled, nodding a bit, and then rubbed his eyes like a child.

'Right,' he said.

Lilac climbed to the top deck of the tram and took the vacant front seat. Then she turned round to wave to Nellie and Stuart, already setting off for home.

Lucky them! So happy together, so ... so *complete*, somehow. Small, slender Nell – slender from the back, anyhow – walking with her arm round tall, dark Stuart's waist, whilst his arm encircled her and their heads drew close. They were made for each other, Lilac decided, fishing in her handbag for her fare. Absolutely made for each other. The two of them would face the move, the new job, the strangeness of London, and come out happily smiling, glad to be together. Perhaps it would even be a relief to them not to have Lilac forever on their doorstep, forever popping in for a meal or a chat.

But she didn't believe the last bit, not really. She knew herself to be loved and valued. So she smiled sunnily at the conductor when he came round, and presently, when Suzie, who had worked with her a year or so earlier, climbed up to the top deck, she hailed her to come and share her seat and they gossiped all the way back to Rodney Street.

Despite her resolve to find Penny Lane, Kitty speedily realised that it was not practicable to set off tonight. She had no idea where it was and though the commercial streets would still be buzzing with people for some time yet, the quieter, residential streets were not. It would be hard to find someone to give her directions once she got out of the main city, and she had a feeling that Penny Lane was a residential district which at this time of night would be deserted save for the odd householder returning from the pub or walking a dog. Accordingly, she made her way round the backs of the houses, searching for a gap in the hedge or a wall she could climb, and sure enough soon found one.

Long ago she had learned to climb walls, using

her bare toes with great cunning to find every tiny crack in the brickwork, and throwing any garment available over the broken glass set into wall-tops by provident householders. Lacking a jacket or even a pair of knickers to throw over the broken glass, she now resigned herself to scratches at best and a few deep cuts at worst, but luckily the householder she chose was either less canny or more trusting than his fellows, for the wall was merely topped by a single piece of barbed wire. Kitty got over without a mark on her and dropped down into the garden as quietly and lightly as a cat.

Once there, she looked consideringly round her. Rows of vegetables and some fruit bushes met her eyes, with a patch of lawn beyond and the house itself beyond that. Up against the back door there were dustbins – she could dig about in them – and a door in the wall which was swinging open. It's their privy, Kitty thought, pleased with her own perspicacity. She had heard that grand houses had their privies indoors and had only half-believed it, which was as well since she could now see with her own eyes that it had been a lie. She stole up the garden, a shadow amongst shadows, and sneaked into the privy. It was a proper flush one, a real lavvy, not a stinking enamelled bowl with a wooden seat on top shared by all thirty people in one of the courts off Upper Burlington Street. Kitty enthroned herself, used the lavvy as nature had intended, found a neat little box of toilet paper and used some for the proper purpose and stuck the rest down the front of her shirt in case she needed paper some time. She might want to send another note. Then she climbed down, not daring to pull the porcelain pear hanging from its chain in case she woke the whole house, and set off to explore.

There was a coal house, but it was summer so there wasn't much in it and anyway she had no need of coal: you could neither eat it nor sleep under it. There was a garden shed, however, and though she could not see much through the tiny, dusty window she thought it might be worth investigating. She was right. The door was locked but the key was still in it. Carelessness brought its own punishment, Kitty thought smugly, nipping inside and pinching two wonderfully warm sacks, which had once held seed potatoes and would very soon hold Kitty Drinkwater. She found a lovely big ball of string but took only a few yards, since it was a bulky thing and would be difficult, she imagined, to either use or sell. She was terribly tempted by a little fork, the sort of fork some people used in their window-boxes, but decided against it. I can always come back another night, she told herself, conveniently forgetting that she was bound for Penny Lane, and in any case she could scarcely make her fortune by prigging forks from garden sheds.

Having decided that the shed held nothing else of interest, Kitty abandoned it, not bothering to shut or lock the door again since if she tried it would probably squeak and bring someone down on her. But she did get herself a long, satisfying drink from the rainwater barrel – she thought the water tasted interestingly different and imagined that the householders probably preferred it to the dull stuff which came out of pumps – and also took a duster which someone must have forgotten to take in off the line earlier in the evening. I can wash me face wi' that, Kitty thought, stowing it down her shirt-front.

Next was the vegetable patch. In the dark it was difficult to differentiate between what was edible and what was not, but Kitty went back for the little fork, dug up a root of potatoes with it, and ate them raw, though after the first two she washed the rest in the water butt because the grit got in her teeth. Then she dug up another root for breakfast and found that the pea-pods were full, so she picked a score or so, flitting busily up and down the rows, thoroughly enjoying herself. Finally, she filled her shirt-front – already bulging, and most certainly not with Kitty – and set off for the wall once more.

She was tired now, but still managed the climb all right, avoided the barbed wire, and was about to drop down into the entry when something made her glance to her right. Someone was standing there, very still, against the wall. Someone big and dark, almost invisible save for the whiteness of face and hands.

A scuffer! A bobby, a busy, a bloomin' peeler, a policeman! Kitty had heard them called all sorts, but right now she didn't care what this one was called, she just wanted him to clear off. Heart thumping so loudly that she feared he might hear it, Kitty peered cautiously towards the man. She didn't think he had seen her because his face was in profile, but she dared not move and draw his attention . . . she could never get off the wall and run faster than he, not with her shirt full of her ill-gotten gains.

After a few seconds, though, she wondered why he was standing so still – and, what was more, facing the wall. Then she heard a gentle swishing sound and understood his choice of this dark and private entry. In the darkness, Kitty grinned. Even scuffers were human, he'd been taken short and was having a widdle, so it wouldn't be all that long before he took himself off and left her to make her escape.

And she was right. A few more moments passed whilst Kitty kept her head down and scarcely breathed and the policeman attended to his trouser buttons. Then, with majestic tread, the officer of the law walked slowly down the entry, turned left and disappeared. As relieved as the policeman, Kitty nipped down off the wall, slid along close to the bricks until she reached the pavement, then peered cautiously out. Nothing. Not even a broad back. The policeman had gone on his way and she, Kitty Drinkwater, could find her nice warm nook and settle down for the night.

Back on Rodney Street she identified her chosen doorstep easily, for the lamplighter had been and the soft glow of the gas made identification simple. She spread out her sacks, one to lie on, one to pull over her in lieu of a blanket, arranged her booty right at the back, where the cement wall divided her steps from next door's, and lay down. She ate a few peas, not deigning to take them out of the pods but crunching down the whole works with an eager appetite. They were sweet and young and sweetness was something that Kitty frequently craved. Then she pulled the second sack over her shoulders. Within five minutes her breathing had deepened; Kitty slept.

Chapter Five

Kitty had thought it would be easy to find Penny Lane, but she had reckoned without the city dweller's reluctance to stray far from his roots.

'If it ain't on a leccy route, queen, I won't know it,' a tram-driver said, when asked which way she should go.

'Penny Lane? Sure an' haven't I hord folk mention it over 'n over? But whether tes out Aigburth way, or over to Bootle, or a bit past Everton, that I couldn't tell ye, love,' said a knife-grinder, stopping his hissing, sparking machine to answer her query.

And what was more, because she was alone and more than a little afraid, she found she did not fancy moving far from her doorstep home in Rodney Street. During the day it was far too busy a spot for her, since the house above it was inhabited by a number of doctors, who appeared to have divided the whole house into consulting rooms. Caretakers, a very old man and his very old wife, lived in the basement in decrepit squalor, but they were both deaf and half-blind and never knew they had another tenant who slept each night under the front steps and always picked up her bed and walked by sunrise.

After a couple of weeks of searching the streets within half a day's tramp of Rodney Street, Kitty began to lose heart. Just what would she say when she caught up with the girl from Penny Lane anyway? Kitty looked down at herself, at her shirt, which no longer even looked like a shirt but more like a filthy scrap of rag, at her limbs, stained to a rich brown with outdoor living and dirt. She carried a sack over one shoulder with all her worldly possessions in and would have defended it, had anyone tried to snatch it, to the death. She had given up on her hair though she still attacked her little visitors by dipping her head into the water barrel from time to time. Givin' me nits a swimmin' lesson, she always thought as she ducked her hair and rubbed vigorously, though she was wryly aware that though she might lose a few in the water the rest would cling on and survive. The nit nurse had a painful steel comb, paraffin, and other smelly, efficient douches; water alone could never do the trick.

Thinking about the nit nurse made her think about school, and that made her wonder what she would do come September, when school started again and the dreaded attendance officers would be out, scouring the streets for kids sagging off school. She liked school all right, but the teachers would take one look at her and realise something had happened ... even Sary would have sniffed and found her some sort of dress for school had she seen the state of Kitty's present garment.

Although nothing would have persuaded Kitty to go home, she was in a quandary over what she should do. She was beginning to think she would never find Penny Lane and even if she did, she doubted that she would dare approach the girl, not in her present state. But how to get herself cleaned up and respectable she could not think; she dared not return to the canal, it was too near the Court. Yet despite the fact that she was dirty, nit-ridden and sometimes very lonely, and would soon be indecent, for her shirt was falling apart, she felt surprisingly well, and hunger, her constant companion in the old days, had been routed by the vegetables and odds and ends of food which she nicked each night from the gardens and dustbins of the rich.

So going home was out of the question – she still shuddered at the thought of the violence and abuse which would greet her if she tried – yet Penny Lane had come to seem an insubstantial dream, somewhere to think wistfully about, but not a place which a girl like her would ever actually visit. And time was passing. In a few days – she had lost track of time – the school holidays would be over and the authorities would undoubtedly find her and either put her into the workhouse or force her to return home.

If only I was clean, Kitty yearned. A clean, well-dressed child could do all sorts and no one would ask where they were going or what they were doing, but a filthy little street arab was everyone's enemy, from the school truant officer to the scuffer on the beat.

And then, when she was beginning to lose heart and to think about going back to Upper Burly and throwing herself on someone's mercy, she had a stroke of luck. Sack on shoulder, she was trying a new direction, a way she had not gone before. She decided to try going in a straight line instead of wandering randomly, and eventually she struck Lark Lane and, crossing it, Linnet Lane. Lark Lane was busy, with a great many shops and businesses, but Linnet Lane was quite different. The houses on her left as she walked were huge and set so far back from the road that she could only make them out by peering, and even the houses on her right were substantial, with nice big gardens and motor cars standing in their driveways.

Then she reached another intersection, Park Lane, and when she looked to her left now, she could see a public park, an absolutely huge one, and what she thought must be several miles of grass and gravel walks, hundreds of trees and, in the distance, what looked like water ... a canal? A river? A lake? She knew it could not be the sea, but it was worth investigating. So Kitty set off across the park and was soon in a daze of pleasure over its many attractions.

She found a half moon of cages, each one containing various species of rare and exotic birds. Children's nannies, in navy coats and heavy shoes, with their small charges in high perambulators or running alongside, sat and gossiped around the gravel sweep, and called to the children not to run on the gravel or they'd fall and skin their knees and then what would Mamma say? Kitty stayed close to the cages and eyed the children with interest but without envy. What a quantity of fussy clothing they wore, considering the warmth of the day! And although they were fat and well fed, with lovely clean pinafores and dresses, how the nannies nagged at them!

'Master Reginald, don't tease the pretty parrot!'

'Miss Dora, you'll feel the weight of my hand if you spit; little ladies do not spit!'

Kitty, who had just spent an absorbing ten minutes teasing the parrots, and who did not grudge the beakful of skin one of them had endeavoured to gouge out of the back of her hand, smiled with secret sympathy at the would-be parrot teaser, slouching back to his minder with hanging head, but then she began to notice that she was the object of attention from several of the nannies. They were looking at her oddly and she realised that she was very out of place in this beautiful park where the children of the rich came to feed the birds, row on the water and play ball on the soft, green grass. However, just as she was about to turn tail and continue her search, a stop-me-and-buy-one came trundling along one of the walks, and the attention of the nannies was immediately diverted. Almost with one voice, the children demanded ices and the nannies, equally with one voice, reminded their charges that tea would be spoilt – and pretty dresses and trousers ruined – should they be allowed such a treat at this hour.

The stop-me-and-buy-one winked at Kitty, then began to shout his wares. Kitty, like a moth to a flame, drew nearer. The stop-me-and-buy-one leaned over and lifted the lid off his chilled container. The most glorious smell wafted out. The lad – for he was little more – picked up a metal scoop and began to pile the rich yellow ice-cream into a large cone until it looked like the picture of a pyramid in Kitty's school primer.

'Want one, luv?' he said enticingly. 'Only 'alfpenny to you, queen.'

'I 'aven't . . .' Kitty began, but picked up at once on the tiny shake of the head he gave, and the warning glance in his rather watery eyes. 'Oh, thanks,' she said instead, holding out a filthy paw gripped into a fist, as though her closed fingers held the money owing.

'Master George, little gentlemen don't ever hit ladies. If you do that again . . .'

A nanny had been kicked in the shins for her refusal to part with pennies for an ice-cream, Kitty realised. She grinned, taking the cone from the lad and conveying it slowly and with maximum effect to her mouth. The afternoon was hot, however, and the ice-cream was already beginning to melt so she shot out her tongue and swiped an all-encompassing lick at the sweet, slithery mountain of frozen cream.

'*She's* got one and she's only a guttersnipe,' whined George. 'Georgie's hot, Nan, Georgie wanna nice-cweam!'

'If you call names you'll get nothing,' the nanny in question said quickly. 'Come along, Master George, time you wasn't here.'

'You said guttersnipe,' Master George said sulkily. 'You said it was a rum thing when little gutter-snipes. . .'

'That's enough,' the nanny said sharply, her spade-shaped face reddening. 'Speak when you're spoken to, Master George.'

'Mamma often lets Philly and me have ices when we've been good,' a tot in a pink cotton dress, with a butterfly bow in her curls, said persuasively to her nanny. 'Sometimes when it's hot she comes up to the nursery and gives us pennies so's we can run down when we hear the man's tinkle-bell.'

'Very well, Miss Rose, you may have a cone this once, but only because it's so very hot. Yes, Master Philip, you may have one too, and since you're the gentleman you may take the pennies, and go and buy two cones . . .'

It started a rout, of course.

'Ices, ices,' rose the babbling cry. '*She's* got one . . . everyone gets an ice but me!' Nannies fished in pockets, in handbags, down the side of perambulators and presently the stop-me-and-buy-one, with his leather bag full of pennies, prepared to ride on, giving his big black bicycle a shove off, accompanied by another wink at Kitty.

But Kitty, seeing what amounted to the first real friendliness she had known since she left home about to disappear, forsook the aviary, crammed the rest of the best food she had ever tasted into her mouth, and followed.

'Oy, mister,' she said, desperately trotting. 'D'you know where Penny Lane is? I come along Park Lane an' Linnet Lane . . . is it near, eh?'

'Oh, aye, everyone knows Penny Lane, chuck; it's only t'other side of the park,' the lad said. 'Know Greenbank, do you?'

'No, I don't know anything much round 'ere,' Kitty admitted, padding along on her hard, bare feet but rather regretting the gravel, nevertheless. 'I'm from Upper Burly, meself.'

'Oh aye? I'm from Coltart Road; Colly, we call it. Let's think . . . Upper Burly . . . eh, queen, you're a long way from 'ome! So far's I recall, that's the far side o' the Scottie, ain't it?'

'That's right. But I've got a friend lives in Penny Lane, I never been there though. Nice, is it?'

'Yeah, nice 'ouses,' the lad said. 'Foller me, I'll put you on the right road. 'Cep' I'll 'ave to stop off at the cricket ground if there's a game goin' on.'

So for the rest of that hot afternoon Kitty followed the stop-me-and-buy-one and they chatted of this and that and Kitty admitted she'd run away from home and told the lad why. But she gave him a false name – Kathleen Legatt – and told him her da was on the ferries. It wasn't that she didn't trust him, exactly. More that she trusted no one. And with Penny Lane no longer a dream but about to become reality she had no desire to feel a hand on her shoulder and hear a constable's voice saying, 'Hello-ello-ello!' in the time-honoured fashion.

The roundabout route taken by the stop-me-and-buy-one meant that day was fading gently into dusk by the time Penny Lane actually came into view.

Kitty's new friend, who had been pedalling slower and slower, came to a halt and pointed at the road opposite.

'There y'are, chuck! Want the last of me ice-cream?'

Kitty accepted the cone eagerly, then looked doubtfully down the road which the stop-me-and-buy-one had indicated. It was longer than she had imagined, and much smarter, though the houses seemed to be mostly terraced or semi-detached. But now she had arrived she began to wonder how she would ever get up the nerve to knock on one door, let alone dozens and dozens, always assuming she did not strike lucky at once. And if she did, what was she to say?

'It's gettin' late,' she said pensively. 'A bit late for callin', would you say?' The lad chuckled and began to push his heavy old bicycle away from the kerb. 'Don't purrit off, love,' he advised kindly. 'Tomorrer's a long way off an' you've walked your feet down to the ankles I shouldn't wonder, jes' to get 'ere. A friend's a friend, no marrer what time o'night you turns up, so she'll tek you in. Cheerio, Kat'leen, an' good luck!'

'Bye, and thanks,' Kitty said earnestly. 'Thanks for everyt'ing. You're a real pal, you are.' But he had gone, with one last wave, pedalling tiredly away, his whole body drooping with fatigue.

Kitty stood on the edge of the kerb, contemplating the length of Penny Lane. As she did so a figure came cycling slowly along Greenbank Road, stopping at each lamp post as he reached it. The lamplighter was doing his rounds. If I don't get up me courage an' start a-knockin', the Lord above knows what I'll do tonight, Kitty reminded herself stoutly. Git a move on then, kid!

Obedient to her own command, Kitty crossed the road and began to walk along the pavement.

Immediately it struck her that these neat little suburban houses had no great flights of steps under which she might hide herself for the night, nor could she even begin to think about a return to Rodney Street until she'd had a few hours rest.

So you've got no choice, Kitty Drinkwater, she told herself firmly. It's find the girl from Penny Lane or get took up for a vagrant and chucked into the work'ouse. So start, Kitty, or git back to that park afore the gates is locked an' barred.

Lilac heard the bad news about the house only a matter of days before Nellie and Stuart left for their new home in London. She had been given a day off because Mr Matteson had hired a car to drive himself and his wife up to their cottage in Scarisbrick to choose curtains and carpets, so she had come round to help Nellie with her packing.

In fact she was full of her own plans as that very morning Polly had confirmed that if the house in Penny Lane was really to be theirs, she had a fourth girl eager to join Lilac, herself and Liza.

'Marie's little sister 'ad twins two days ago; Marie's Mam thinks it'ud be better if Marie moved out, though she'll still want a bit of money from 'er, especially now,' Polly had said. 'But wi' four of us rent-sharin' . . . .'

Stuart had told the landlord of Number 39 that he had passed on the property to respectable relatives, who would pay the rent as promptly as he and Nellie had done, but unfortunately, whilst discussing the hand-over, the landlord suddenly realised that his new tenants were four young girls. As soon as he did so, his whole demeanour towards Stuart changed.

'I'm a God-fearin' Cat'olic, and dere's no bawdy 'ouse bein' run in any of *my* properties,' he exclaimed angrily. Although Stuart did his very best to reassure the man that the girls were decent, hardworking young women who would not dream of entertaining young men on his premises even during daylight hours, he simply tightened his self-righteous, rat-trap mouth and shook his head.

'Dey isn't comin' 'ere, Mr Gallagher,' he repeated with parrot-like obstinacy and a complete disregard for every word his tenant had uttered. 'What would de priest say to me, allowin' such a carry-on?'

'I'm that sorry, queen,' Stuart said, when he let Lilac in and took her through to the kitchen where Nellie was wrapping china in newspaper and placing it in tea-chests. 'I did my best to explain but there was no hope of his even listening properly once he found you were under fifty. He's an old fool, but it is his house.'

'Well, I suppose it was too good to be true; anyway, the house is a long way from my new job,' Lilac admitted. She was to start work at the bag and sack factory in Bridgewater Street the following Monday, and had consoled herself for having to put up with what would, she believed, turn out to be a boring and repetitive job with the thought that at least she was to have a little house to run and friends to share it with. She was bitterly disappointed over Stuart's news, but did not intend to let Stuart and Nellie believe they had let her down. 'Polly and Liza are both keen, though, so perhaps we'll find somewhere else, even if it's not as nice.'

'Try for a good neighbourhood, love,' Nellie urged. 'Oh dear, if I'd known . . . but there are decent little rooms to let round here, I suppose you could get one of them.'

'Look, we'll be all right,' Lilac assured her. 'Don't worry, our Nell, it's not good for the baby when you worry, and anyway Mrs Matteson will let me stay on in Rodney Street till the end of the month so there's no hurry. I'll let you know as soon as I find somewhere and it will be somewhere respectable, honest to God. I won't go back to the courts, even if I'm offered.'

'Most of the people in the courts are grand: clean and hardworking,' Nellie said quickly, guiltily. Lilac knew that Nell tried very hard not to be ashamed of her background. 'But there's the bugs . . . you'd not want to tackle them, chuck, having been away from it for a bit. Aunt Ada used to say it was one long battle . . . oh do try for a nice little place.'

Lilac nodded rather impatiently. She could remember summers in the Court when all the cleaning in the world could not entirely get rid of the fat grey bugs which came out of the walls and made themselves at home, fastening on to your flesh so nimbly that you scarcely noticed until they had sucked your blood and gone, leaving the swollen, itchy spots which were their trademark. And then there were the fleas, hopping ceiling-high on their long legs, driving you mad if they got a hold. And the nits which bred in your hair, and cockroaches and rats . . . She would have to be very desperate indeed to take that lot on again!

'Honest to God, our Nell, I wouldn't dream of living somewhere which wasn't clean and decent,' Lilac said, shaking her head sadly at her sister's lack of faith. She picked up Nellie's best teapot and began to swathe it in newspaper. 'There's respectable houses letting rooms, you know, as well as slum-dwellings. Polly and I will share one room between us and Liza will probably get Marie to share another, now that Marie's sister's had the twins.'

Overcrowding in the courts was always a problem. With rents high, even for property which should have been condemned and torn down years ago, people tended to double up when children were born or times were hard, and most houses in the city tenements contained three generations – grandparents, parents and children, often with a widowed cousin and her family thrown in.

'Aye, I know you're sensible. But what am I doing, letting you wrap up me teapot, which will be on the go until the removal men come and after?' Nellie took the pot from Lilac and unwrapped it, then looked round the room, already cleared of everything but the furniture. 'Honest to God, me mind's going, I swear it. Don't say I've been and gone and packed all me cups and saucers away?'

'I'll get the kettle out,' Lilac said tactfully. 'You root for the cups; don't bother with saucers for heaven's sake, our Nell.'

She could see that Nellie was disturbed at having to leave her without lodgings, but apart from promising to be careful in her choice, there was very little she could do about it. She guessed that Nellie would want to take a look at whatever she chose, but since she would be leaving the city in forty-eight hours, there was no chance of that.

'Bless you, chuck. Lor', I'm tired ... if I sit down for a moment, can you make a brew and take a cup through to Stuart? He's packing the books in his study, that'll take him most of the day I reckon.'

Two days later Lilac came over on the tram, walked through Sefton Park in a drizzling rain, and watched rather mournfully as Nellie and Stuart saw the removal van off with all their worldly possessions aboard.

'We've got a cab coming,' Nellie gulped. She had been crying for hours if you could judge by her red eyes and swollen nose. 'Can you come with us to Lime Street, our Lilac? Wave us off, like?'

'Of course I will,' Lilac said gently. 'Cheer up, Nellie love, you're not going to the ends of the earth, flower!'

'And I'm going with you,' Stuart said, putting his arm round Nellie's bulging waist. 'Poor old lady, she's been up half the night with backache and indigestion and now this!'

'Why indigestion?' Lilac said, hoping to lighten the mood. 'I always thought you'd a digestion like an ostrich!'

'I f-fancied p-pears and custard. We had 'em for supper, only I didn't f-fancy them then,' Nellie stammered tearfully. 'So when I c-couldn't sleep I came down and ate 'em cold, acourse. It must'a been around two o'clock in the morning and they sat on me chest and kept trying to get out ... oh, Stu, I don't want to go! Can't we change our minds?'

'If you're unhappy we'll come back,' Stuart said soothingly. Lilac saw his thin, brown fingers cross behind his back and smiled to herself. 'Don't worry, queen, just give it a go, eh? For me and the littl'un.'

Nellie's tear-garbled reply was lost as a taxi-cab screeched to a halt beside them.

'Gallagher? For Lime Street? 'Op in then, or you won't mek it afore your train leaves.'

This galvanised Nellie into action. She seized her lightest case and heaved it on the step beside the driver, watched whilst Stuart put the rest of their luggage on top, then climbed awkwardly into the cab.

'Come on, our Li,' she urged. She looked happier, to Lilac's relief. 'You heard what the driver said, we've no time to lose.'

It's odd the way Nellie blows hot and cold now, Lilac thought to herself. Once, she was so calm and sensible but now everything upsets her and she doesn't like anything for long. I suppose it's all part of having a baby, though . . . fancying pears and custard at two o'clock in the morning indeed!

'Move over, love,' Stuart said, getting in beside them. 'I'll drop you a line in a couple of days, Lilac, to tell you how we've settled in. Where's the string bag? It's got our carry-out in it, and the flask.'

'It's on my lap,' Nellie said. 'Have you got my knitting, Stu? I might as well knit – better than sitting on the train staring out of the window and feeling miserable.'

'I've got *everything*,' Stuart said forcefully. 'Every hand-hemmed handkerchief, every nappy, every safety pin, every . . . oh my God!'

'What?'

'We left the kitchen sink! I bet you never thought to pack that, our Nell!'

And Nellie laughed and slapped Stuart and Lilac laughed and hugged him, and the three of them tried not to look out through the window at the city speeding by, the city which two of them were to leave and one was to find a lonely place, without her Nellie.

Kitty knocked half-a-dozen doors that first evening without success and the woman in the last house she tried set the dog on her. To be sure it was a very small dog, but it had sharp white teeth and when they buried themselves in Kitty's ankle they hurt, and she kicked out so that the dog went sailing back up the garden path.

'I'll 'ave the law on you, kickin' me little Mitzi,' the old woman who had set her dog on Kitty shrieked as her pet, uttering an undoglike scream, sailed backwards towards the front door. 'Oh, you dirty little slut, knockin' doors in the dark an' kickin' me only friend!'

Kitty felt guilty; it was getting dark and she supposed the old woman had a right to be wary, but even so the bite hurt. Her ankle was throbbing something awful and she could feel tears only just behind her eyes. 'Sorry missus,' she called. 'But the dawg's gorra lump out of me ankle, honest to God.'

'Clear orf, clear orf,' the octogenarian shrieked, shaking a tiny fist as wrinkled and brown as an old walnut. 'There's a copper lives down the road a ways, get outa here or I'll set the law on you!'

'Well, I reckon the girl from Penny Lane don't live there, any road,' Kitty mumbled to herself as she set off along the pavement once more. 'She wouldn't ha' looked so purty an' 'appy if she'd lived wi' an old witch like that 'un. So what'll I try next?'

She eyed the nearby houses uneasily, for she had seen several curtains twitch during the fracas and though she suspected that the old woman was lying, policemen, she supposed, lived in ordinary houses when they weren't hounding homeless children. It had not occurred to her before but she'd be in real trouble if she knocked a door and a scuffer answered it! It was dark now, seeming even darker than it really was because of the streetlamps with their circles of hazy gold and it was time she settled for the night because although she'd had two ice-creams and there was half a cabbage in her sack, she really ought to have a drink and something solid inside her, or sleep would be courted in vain. She looked hopefully up and down the road but there were no dustbins standing out and she found, suddenly, that she was far too tired to think about climbing walls and prigging herself a meal.

What was more, she had remembered the palm house.

Earlier, in Sefton Park, she had noticed the palm house admiringly, not consciously considering it as a place to sleep. But now, *in extremis*, she was pretty sure that she could kip down on one of the benches, with her sacks around her and the cabbage to gnaw on until she fell asleep. If she chose a west facing seat, what was more, she would not be woken by the sun in her eyes.

The park was locked, of course, but railings, though not easy, were meant to be conquered. With the aid of her sacks and her rope-belt, Kitty was over the railings and back inside the park in seconds. She found she was very disorientated by the darkness, and by the fact that she had not entered the park the way she had left it, but after scouting around for a bit her eyes grew accustomed to the lack of light and she began to recognise landmarks. She remembered that the palm house was surrounded by trees and had a flagstaff nearby, and in a remarkably short space of time she was there, selecting her bench, spreading her sacks, and curling up. She thought about the cabbage, but since she was resting her head on it and had got comfortable she thought she would save it for breakfast. Besides, all the walking and the excitement had tired her out. Within five minutes of settling down on the bench Kitty was sleeping the sleep of the totally exhausted.

She woke when someone coughed nearby. It was a deep, rasping cough and whoever had coughed also rustled. Kitty pulled her sack up a bit higher and shivered. Who was it? Some old tramp, waiting to murder her in her bed for the half cabbage? Or a park attendant, patrolling the grounds, eager to throw out any kid who might have planted themselves on a bench by the palm house? Grown wise in the ways of sleeping rough though, Kitty did not sit up, she merely kept as still as she could, opened her eyes wide, and stared around her.

Nothing. No one. Only the trees, their branches moving slightly in the wind, and the palm house behind her, its glass still reflecting warmth from the day's sunshine. And the bench beneath her.

Someone cleared their throat, sighed and rustled again.

Whoever it is, they've settled down for a sleep so they probably don't know I'm 'ere, Kitty told herself thankfully. Now all I've gorra do is wake up first, in the morning. And with this comforting thought she closed her eyes again and immediately plunged into a lively dream in which she was playing cricket with a cone for a bat whilst the stop-me-and-buy-one bowled at her with a cabbage and Mitzi rushed around yapping and biting ankles.

She woke the second time to broad daylight. During the night she had managed to roll onto her stomach so the first thing she saw were the wooden slats of the seat on which she lay. The second thing she should have seen, of course, was the ground beneath the seat, but instead, between the seat and the ground, she saw a pale face topped by rough, hay-coloured hair.

Whoever had coughed during the night was now curled up asleep under her bench, with old newspapers below and above, which was why he had rustled as well as coughed. It was a lad, age uncertain, temper equally so, for Kitty knew lads were only men not yet grown and as likely to clout as pass the time of day with the likes of her.

Very gently, so as not to disturb the sleeper, Kitty moved a bit, so she could see how much lad there was under the seat and judge his dangerousness, for she saw lads, all lads, as the enemy. Mostly the lads who lived rough were bigger than her, stronger than her and very much nastier than her; they could make mincemeat of her if she crossed them so she tried very hard to steer clear. This one was quite tall, taller than she, and bony. But having looked long and hard at his sleeping face, Kitty decided he did not look dangerous. His eyes were closed of course so she did not know how the expression in them might change if he woke and caught her staring, but he had a mouth which looked as though it smiled a lot and an unlined, though exceedingly dirty, brow.

However, there was no sense in courting trouble. Kitty sat up and started to get off the seat, to go through the preparations for the day ahead – and then stopped short, staring.

The palm house was surrounded by gravel, then trees, and then miles and miles of glorious grass. But if she had not remembered this from the day before she would never have known, for now the grass was invisible beneath a smooth, soft blanket of white mist, which twisted and swayed between the tree-trunks and even sent a few tentative smoky tendrils curling across the gravel, whilst the sun, suddenly appearing between the trees, dyed the top layer of mist goldy-red, turned the trees' tall trunks to glowing flame, and gilded the edge of every leaf, every tiny twig.

Kitty knew very little about natural beauty, but she recognised this sunrise as beauty unparalleled and gave it the attention it deserved - an open-mouthed, wide-eyed attention which not even her desire to be gone before the lad woke could break. So she was still sitting there, with unexplained and unwanted tears suddenly filling her eyes and blurring her vision, when a voice behind her exclaimed: 'Christ A'mighty, ain't that suffin? Wharrer sight, eh?'

Kitty turned. The boy had crawled out from under the seat and was kneeling on the gravel, staring as she was at the mist, the sunrise, the edges of the grass gradually coming into view, every blade topped by a diamond drop.

'Yeah, it's pretty,' she said inadequately, having glanced round and made sure it was she that the lad was addressing. 'I never seen the sun come up in the country, afore, though I've read about it in books.'

'I 'ave, but not so . . . oh, I dunno.' The lad heaved a deep sigh and then looked properly at Kitty for the first time. 'So you read books, does you? What've you read?'

'Lot's an' lots,' Kitty said promptly. 'Well, one a week since I was seven, an' I'm twelve now.'

'Get on! I'm fourteen, but I reckon I ain't read many more'n you. What's your name, kiddo?'

'What's it to you?' Kitty said immediately, poised for flight. Talking about reading was one thing, discussing names another. But then she remembered she hadn't yet put her belongings into the sack and looked uneasily at her companion. Suppose he decided to nick her stuff? He was older, taller, stronger, but somehow, she decided, as he grinned down at her, she didn't think he had theft in mind. And the cabbage on which her head had rested all night didn't look all that appetising, either.

'Fierce, ain't you? What've you done, eh? If you've nicked that scrawny cabbage, chuck, I can't think anyone's gonna fight you for it, an' sacks are mostly give away. So why not be civil, eh? No 'arm in it, surely?'

He had a pleasant voice with a smile at the back of it. Kitty didn't know why she thought that, she just knew she did. She looked at him properly, harder. He was tall and bony, as she had surmised even through the newspapers, but he was a lot cleaner than she was and his shirt and trousers, though by no means new, were respectable. She found that she liked his face, from the broad brow to the deep blue eyes with laughter creases already forming, to the straight nose and the curled, amused mouth. And when he smiled she saw he still had all his teeth, a rarity amongst the courts where hunger took its toll of teeth and gums as well as of muscles and skin. Smiling back, Kitty was glad she had all her teeth, too, though it wasn't something that had ever occurred to her before. But she wished her hair was like his – the soft, hay-coloured locks were overlaid with gold where the sun had caught them. It was roughly cut, hacked, really, so that it stood up at the back in a series of ridges and peaks, but you could see his hair was clean, not greasy and nit-ridden.

'Seen all you want? Well, I'm Johnny an' as I said I'm nigh on fourteen. Been on the road since I were ten. Who're you when you're at 'ome?'

'I'm Kitty, I'm twelve, like I said. On the road? Wha's that mean?'

He laughed, then stood up and pulled a bag out from under the bench. 'Means I don't stay nowhere long,' he said laconically. 'Might as well 'ave a bite afore the place wakes up. Like bread 'n cheese, does you?'

'Oo-oh, *yes*!' Kitty breathed as he produced half a loaf and a thick heel of cheese from the depths of his bag. 'I'm rare hungry – all I 'ad yesterday was an ice-cream an' a bite o' cabbage.'

'Right. An' I've a ragin' thirst on me – got a bottle?'

'No . . . but I got a tin.' Kitty delved into her own sack and produced an empty corned beef tin. 'I drinks outer this, mostly.'

'That's grand, better'n a bottle. Why didn't I think o' that?' Johnny looked at her tin with such respect that Kitty felt the first faint stirrings of pride in her thin little bosom. Something she had was worth envy . . . and now he was dividing the bread and cheese! Her mouth watered so hard that she had to keep swallowing.

'Here. Start on that, chuck, whiles I fetch us some water. There's a drinkin' fountain at the back o' this palm 'ouse.'

He handed her the bread and cheese, the bread folded over so that it formed a sandwich. Kitty took a deep breath and a big bite. It was marvellous, the best food she had ever tasted, better even than the stop-me-and-buy-one's ice-cream. But she went slowly, knowing how easy it was to get the cramps in your bread-basket if you bolted food after a long period without anything, and the boy was back with the water before she was halfway through her sandwich.

'There y'are! Tek a drink, then a bite. 'Elps it down, like.'

Kitty was having no difficulty in getting it down, but obeyed his injunction and realised that it made the food go further, filled you up more. She said so, and Johnny smiled.

'Oh aye, you gets to know all the tricks when you're on the road. Don't meet many lasses sleepin' rough, though. What 'appened?'

'Me Mam sent me on an errand, but I were robbed and I dustn't go 'ome,' Kitty said briefly. 'She'd kill me, them trimmin's was worth prob'ly a 'undred shillin's.' It was the biggest sum she could think of, too huge to contemplate. 'She'll owe the milliner, see? Oh aye, she'd kill me awright if she got 'er 'ands on me; she's tried afore.'

Johnny nodded, chomping his bread and cheese.

'I believe you! My ole man tried that, so I 'it 'im over the 'ead with me gran's walkin' stick an' lit out. Ain't never been 'ome since.'

'Where's you from?' Kitty said thickly, through bread and cheese.

'Burly, that's what we call . . .'

'Well, knock me down, ain't that the strangest thing! Upper Burlington Street . . . *we* call it Burly, too!'

Johnny, bread and cheese halfway to his mouth, stopped to stare.

'No! Well I'll be 'anged . . . whereabouts?'

'Paradise Court, that's the second entry on the –'

'We was nex'-door-neighbours, Kit, as good as! I were from Elysium Court, right by you. Elly and Parry, we called 'em. Wha's your last name, then?'

'Drinkwater; me mam's Sary and me da's 'Ector an' there's the twins, Amy an' Bob, and Betty, Eth,

Mo . . . she's Maureen really . . . an' Phyllis.'

'The kids'll all be younger'n me,' Johnny said dismissing them. 'I'm Johnny Moneymor, we was from Londonderry, way back.'

'Oh ah,' Kitty said. Talk of Irish antecedents was common in the courts, though no one ever seemed able to tell you what Ireland was like since they had either left as nippers or never been there at all. 'I once 'eard me da say 'e 'ailed from Connemara. But I's from Liverpool, an' proud of it.'

She didn't quite know what made her say it, she only knew that, as the words left her mouth, they were true.

'Me an' all,' Johnny said contentedly. 'I allus comes back, teks a look and goes again. One o' these days I'll sail from Liverpool Docks aboard a big ole transatlantic liner, an' come 'ome wi' a pocketful o' cash an' a heap o' good things. An' I'll go on deck an' look up at the Liver birds sittin' broodin' over the Mersey, an' know I'm 'ome.'

'I will an' all,' Kitty decided. 'I'll sail from the Docks, jus' like you, Johnny.'

'No way. Lads only,' Johnny said, gazing dreamily into the distance. 'No wimmin aboard.'

'Yes they is!' Kitty contradicted. 'Or I'll put on trowsis an' pertend I'm a lad. I'll go, you wait an' see.'

Johnny chuckled and reached out a long arm. He rumpled her filthy hair, then sat up straight and looked at her very seriously.

'Guess you will. Ever 'eard of the public baths, chuck?'

'Sure. But I don't 'ave no gelt,' Kitty admitted, knowing at once what he meant. 'I's filthy, I know it.'

'Well, what about a dip in the Scaldy?'

Every kid living within a mile of the Leeds & Liverpool Canal knew all about the Scaldy, though it was mainly the boys who bathed in it. It was a section of the canal near the Chisenhale Street Bridge where the big sugar refinery, Tate & Lyle, pumped quantities of hot water they no longer needed into the canal, turning it into a paradise for the local lads. So now, though Kitty knew exactly what he was suggesting, she looked at him doubtfully.

'Me? But it's only lads what swims there, an' besides, me brothers might see me.'

'Oh aye, I forgot. Do they go there at night, then?'

'At *night*? No, course they don't!'

'Then we will, you an' me. I'll snitch a bit o' soap an' we'll get us a penny or two so's you can do your 'air wi' paraffin. I'll nick a dress off a washin' line. Eh, queen, your own fam'ly won't know you!'

'Oh, I don't know,' Kitty quavered. 'I can't swim, Johnny. Kids get drownded in the Scaldy.'

'Not if they're wi' me they don't,' Johnny assured her stoutly. 'I swim like a fish, I'll see you right, Kitty. Only you'll be picked up an' sent to the work'ouse when summer ends, you know that, doncher, unless you cleans up a bit. Wharrer you been livin' on?'

'Cabbages, spuds, stuff outer dustbins,' Kitty muttered, hanging her head. 'I done awright, honest.'

'Well, wi' me you'll do better,' Johnny assured her. 'Are you game, Kit? Want to come on the tramp? I gets through a lorra books, you can 'ave 'em after me, an' you'll eat well, I promise you that, an' you'll sleep soft.'

'I dunno,' Kitty said, terribly tempted. Not only had she missed her friends and familiar surroundings, she had missed the fictional life she plunged into every time she opened a book. 'I come to Penny Lane to 'unt for me friend . . . I only tried six or seven 'ouses so far.'

'Oh ah? An' what'll your friend do for you that I can't, eh?'

Kitty looked at Johnny's sun-tanned face and gilded hair, at the deep blue, laughing eyes. He was the best thing that had ever happened to her, he knew what it was all about, he would help her, see her right – hadn't he said so just now? Beautiful and kind the girl from Penny Lane might be, but she wouldn't want Kitty trailing round after her, being an embarrassment, Kitty acknowledged that now. So she smiled back at Johnny and jumped to her feet, slinging her sack over her shoulder as she did so.

'She won't do nothin', Johnny Moneymor,' she said, and laughed with pleasure at her own sudden certainty. 'Fancy me, swimmin' in the Scaldy when everyone else is tucked up in bed! Lead on, I'll tag along o' you!'

It was one thing to talk gaily at sun-up in Sefton Park about swimming in the Scaldy, Kitty realised later, but quite another to set off through the dark streets, with the gas lamps' hiss the only sound, heading towards home. Every foot of the way, once she got onto home territory, she expected to see a Drinkwater hiding behind a tram-stop, or in a doorway, or under the dark arch of a bridge. But she knew in her heart that she was safe enough. The pubs were long closed, no matter how bad the twins might be they wouldn't roaming the streets at two or three in the morning, and even when Da was at his worst and wickedest, even when Sary was roaring, hitting drunk, they'd not stray far from the Court at this hour. So Kitty padded along beside Johnny, carrying her precious new dress in her sack with a cracked pair of boots slung by their laces round her neck.

'You'll need boots, on the tramp,' Johnny had said, but she didn't believe him; they felt hateful on her feet after weeks of toe-wriggling freedom, and anyway she only ever wore boots in school, because the teachers got nasty if you didn't.

'Not far now, chuck,' Johnny murmured into her ear. 'Want me to carry them boots?'

'No, I'm awright,' Kitty said quietly. 'They ain't heavy, not like a coupla cabbages.'

They were heavier than most cabbages and her neck was tired, but she wouldn't have admitted it for the world. She wanted Johnny to think her strong as himself and as keen on the adventure ahead.

'Here we are,' Johnny said at last. Even in the dark the canal waters shone, reflecting the starry night sky. 'Put your clo'es under the bridge, chuck, an' foller me.'

Kitty didn't have many clothes to take off, in fact only her shirt and her rope. She threw both articles down and tiptoed after Johnny, who had stripped off his own shirt and trousers, shed his boots and socks, and was poised on the edge.

'See the steam?' he asked her as she drew alongside. 'Eh, it'll be lovely an' warm – I can't wait!'

He was in, plopping quietly into the water, then holding out a hand to Kitty. 'See, I'm standin' so you won't get your face wet. C'mon!'

Kitty took a deep breath and joined him. She was smaller than he, the water came halfway up her chest, but it was quite hot and when Johnny handed her a small square of some sort of red, strong-smelling soap, she began to rub it all over her torso with real enthusiasm. It would be so good, so very good, to be clean! Mrs O'Rourke had insisted that before she ate, Kitty should have a good wash. Once or twice, in winter, she had got the tin bath down, filled it with saucepans of steaming water heated on the fire, and handed Kitty the soap with instructions to 'Have a good splash now, child, but don't you be forgettin' to use that soap!' Sary rarely bothered with washing her children but when she did it was under the tap in the yard and she held you there, letting the icy water batter you until you could escape. No pleasure there, only Sary's fingermarks bruising your arms for weeks afterwards, and red slap marks all over you where she'd beaten you into some sort of submission.

'Sit on the bank an' wash your other 'alf,' Johnny told her above the splashing. 'Go on ... I'll parry your 'air.'

He had very nearly been caught nicking the paraffin, had been forced to pay for it, in the end.

'Why doncher go to the Disinfection Office on Burly, they'll do 'er free, there,' the man in the hardware store had suggested rather too loudly, when Johnny had whispered something to him. 'She your sister? Tek 'er there, they'll see to 'er all right an' tight.'

Johnny knew she wouldn't go back to Burly though, not during daylight hours, so the paraffin it had to be. And after he had rubbed the stuff into her scalp until she would have screamed had anyone else done it, and then helped her by holding her head – but not her face – under water to a slow count of five hundred, she thought her hated visitors might really have swum their last this time.

After that, they played, frolicking in the warm and soapy water, admiring the slow whitening of

Kitty's limbs, the dark, clean masses of her hair.

'It's real thick,' Johnny said at one point. 'Your 'air, I mean. An' curly, I reckon. It'll be nice when it's dry.'

'I wish I was a water baby or a mermaid,' Kitty said wistfully as Johnny tried to teach her to swim. She had read about Tom the water baby at school. 'Oh . . . I can stay up, I can swim!'

It didn't last long, but it was a start. 'Five strokes . . . it'll be ten next time you 'ave a go,' Johnny said. 'Race you to the bank . . . walkin', not swimmin'.'

They stayed in the water until dawn began to turn the sky to pearl, then Johnny helped her out and they ran races along the towpath until they were dry, lacking towels of any description.

'Now put the dress on,' Johnny said at last. 'An' the boots. Wish I could ha' got you stockin's, but there, at least you've gorra pair o' boots.'

Kitty had been longing to put the dress on all day, but Johnny had been firm. A clean dress could only be worn by a clean person, he explained, so she had waited. But now the moment had arrived, and in the first milky grey of dawn, she slid the dress down over her head and Johnny did up the buttons at the back.

Kitty looked down at herself. It was a blue and white checked dress, gingham she thought the material was called, and though a little long, it fitted well. She turned to face Johnny, half-expecting some masculine rudeness, but Johnny looked at her slowly and carefully, walking all round her as though her appearance was truly of interest to him.

'You look real good, real pretty,' he said at last. 'Tomorrer I'll git a blue ribbing for your 'air. Put the boots on an' we'll go along to Mrs Bridge's eating place, down by the Albert Dock. She starts at six, it must be near on that now, and she does a lovely lentil an' spud broth. An' you get 'alf a loaf with it, as well as a mug o' tea.'

The two of them wandered slowly down to the docks, Kitty in her new boots as well as her new dress, which was a good reason for their lack of speed. The boots felt strangely heavy and unnatural, but Johnny assured her she would come to appreciate them, in time.

Mrs Bridge had a tiny wooden shack with three tables and twelve chairs, but she gave the youngsters two large plates of her broth for tuppence and sent them to sit by the water to eat since all her chairs were taken.

'Bring back me plates,' she warned them, but comfortably, with a smile. 'Who's your little pal, Johnny?'

'She's Kitty; she's a good kid,' Johnny said proprietorially, as though he had known Kitty for years, if not actually raised her personally. 'We're off on the tramp later today.'

'Oh ah? Where you thinkin' of headin' for, this time?'

'This time we're headin' for Wales,' Johnny said. 'Ain't that right, our Kitty?'

Kitty thrilled to the casual possessiveness in his tone.

'That's right, Johnny,' she echoed. 'We're headin' for Wales!'

Chapter Six

With Nellie and Stuart gone and the Mattesons about to depart, Lilac began to be very dependent on her friends. But Polly was courting, Liza had an evening job serving behind the counter in a fish and chip shop on St James Street, and visiting Marie Springfield meant cramming into her cramped little house and 'minding' the kids whilst Marie's Mam and her sisters went down to their local pub. What was more Ella, the sister who had just given birth to twins, had a rather dubious reputation – she 'walked' Norfolk Street of an evening, folk said – so Lilac was uneasily aware that Nellie would disapprove of too close a friendship with the Springfields.

She had found lodgings, though she did not think she cared for them much. It was a once-smart house in Great Nelson Street, handy, the landlady said, for the library, the art gallery, St George's Hall, and other such refined places of culture. But it was also near Lime Street – Lilac could hear the trains arriving and departing from her lonely room – which made her think wistfully of Nellie.

She had not heard from the handsome Alan Blake, what was more. It was all very well telling herself that she'd not expected to hear, but it did not do much for her self-confidence. It was the first time that any man had virtually stood her up, and to make matters worse Art, who had always danced attendance on her, suddenly seemed to have found better things to do with his time. Had someone been advising him that she would never fall into his arms if he hung about her, but might do so if he withdrew a little, Lilac wondered indignantly. Well, if so, he would presently get a big surprise, for she was doing well enough without him. As for Alan ... if he walked up to her in the street she would pretend she couldn't tell him from Adam, which would teach him a lesson, him and his posh relatives and his big transatlantic liner!

Work was far more absorbing than she had expected, however, and far harder, too. Lilac, who had done extremely well at school and was generally thought of as bright and able, was horrified at the difficulty she encountered in managing her machine. She was afraid of pushing the sacking too far in case the needle went through her finger, the smell of the raw material made her sneeze and her eyes seemed to run constantly. She told herself she was not mechanically minded, but no one else thought twice about taking their machine to pieces when something went wrong and putting it together again so that it worked. Also, the other girls in her room worked at twice the speed and seemed to her to be entirely fearless, and the supervisor, a harsh-faced, tight-mouthed harridan called Mrs Loose, took an instant dislike to her newest employee.

'It ain't your fault you're a bit slow, queen,' Bertha Harris, the loud-mouthed, short-skirted girl on the next machine told Lilac. 'You need to start young at dis job – do as I do, folly me an' you won't go far wrong!

Lilac was used to broad Liverpudlian but she often found Bertha almost impossible to follow, since Bertha's use of slang was entirely individual. Words, Bertha said once in all seriousness, meant whatever she told them to mean ... shades of Humpty Dumpty in *Alice Through the Looking Glass*, Lilac thought, grinning to herself. 'When I use a word it means just what I choose it to mean – neither more nor less.' But she kept the quotation to herself, having already discovered that though the girls in her room could all read, more or less, it was only with great effort and never for pleasure. Books are a closed book to them, Lilac concluded, chuckling inwardly. But they were kind enough, particularly Bertha, and it was through her that Lilac discovered everyone on her assembly line was at least a year younger than her and sometimes more: Bertha herself, talking her strange blend of scouse, pseudo-American slang, Cockney rhyming slang and anything else she could lay tongue to, forever at jazz concerts and dances, bringing home sailors in at least three different shades, astonished Lilac by admitting to being 'Seventeen, come next March.'

'They're friendly and nice, but they're awfully rough,' she told Polly, who grinned and said it was a far cry from the Mattesons and admitted that in the Ellison Fancy Pickle factory, where she worked – and wept as well, since they pickled a lot of onions – the staff on the shop floor were all either young girls still wet behind the ears or old shawlies who had been doing the work forever.

So after Lilac's first week's work, when she had sat in the dying sunlight in her small room and written a cheery letter to Nellie, heated herself up a tin of soup on her small gas-ring, and washed out her cotton stockings and her second-best blouse, she decided to give herself a bit of a treat. She could not go and see Nellie yet because she had not been with the firm long enough to take a day or two off, and though Mrs Matteson and the doctor had urged her to go up to Scarisbrick to see them she thought it was too soon, but it would be rather fun to go round to Coronation Court and see Art's family – his sister Etty had been a friend – and find out at the same time just where Art had got to.

Not that I'm interested in Art's whereabouts, Lilac reminded herself, choosing a light and summery cotton print to wear, for the autumn day was warm and sunny. Since it was Sunday she got some white gloves out of her long drawer and pulled them on. She had a rather nice blue hat which went with the summery dress so she stabbed that in place with a couple of hat-pins and decided on the spur of the moment to go to morning service at St Anne's on Cazneau Street, the church she had attended with Nellie and Aunt Ada when they had lived on Scotland Road. Whilst she was working for the Mattesons she had gone to church with them, but now she could please herself and it would be rather nice to go back, see her friends. After the service I'll maybe go round to the Corry, she planned busily, and after that I'll buy myself a meal at Miss Harriet Young's Dining Room on the Scottie, and after that ... oh, after that can take care of itself!

The service was a bit of a shock to Lilac, after several years of attending the very much smarter church on Rodney Street with the Mattesons. She had forgotten how shabby everything was, including the congregation, and how small. Even the East window, at which she had gazed in awe as a child whilst singing hymns at the top of her voice, seemed smaller and duller, the jewel colours that she remembered paler and less striking.

And though there were several people she recognised, they all seemed to belong to her aunt's generation. The vicar was a younger man than the Revd Charlesworth, with a deep, actor's voice and a great thatch of brown hair in place of Revd Charlesworth's shining pate. He was very polite to Lilac, shaking her hand outside in the porch and telling her it was nice to see a new face in the congregation, but she had not enjoyed the rather sanctimonious delivery of his sermon, every word accompanied by upturned eyes and pious glances, so she murmured something conventional and eased her hand out of his damp clasp as soon as it was polite to do so.

The O'Briens were Catholics, so they would go to Mass, not morning service. Of course, Lilac thought to herself, as she left Cazneau Street, crossed into Rose Place and began to stroll slowly down towards the main road, it's quite possible that I might meet ... someone ... once I reach the Scottie. She turned into Scotland Road, glancing into shop windows as she walked. It was equally possible that the Catholic service might end at the same time as that at St Anne's, so if she continued to walk at her present pace she might presently find herself overtaken by, well, by anyone who happened to have attended St Anthony's that morning.

If I do hear familiar footsteps I won't look round, I'll pretend to be absorbed in the beautiful hats in Miss Denny's, or the gold chains and diamond rings displayed in Murphy's the jewellers, she decided. She by-passed Jim's Fried Fish, which reeked of last night's trading, and the Market Inn, redolent of stale beer and worse, and began to walk a little faster. She could hear people coming along the pavement, she would walk past Young's Dining Room, idly, then stop a little further on and turn back, as though she'd not quite made up her mind where to eat.

She strolled on and presently heard footsteps following her; she was almost sure she knew who made them. She turned to stare fixedly into the nearest window, pretending absorption, her whole attention really focused on the maker of the footsteps, now about to overhaul her, to pass . . .

'Well, if it isn't our Lilac!' The young man stopped in front of her, gently taking her hands in his. 'What are you doing on the Scottie on a Sunday morning, chuck? Not shoppin', that's for sure!'

'Art!' Lilac said with a well-simulated start of surprise, 'Fancy seeing you – I was sure you'd be in the middle of Mass, or off with your pals for a day at New Brighton!'

'Just come out of St Anthony's,' Art said. 'So? What are you doin' here, our Lilac?'

'Attending church, same as you,' Lilac said demurely. 'No point in trailing all the way back to Rodney Street, and anyway, I only went there because the Mattesons expected us to do so. I thought I might pop into the Court, see how everyone is, only it's quite late and the shop windows are fascinating . . .'

'Particularly that one,' Art said. There was a laugh behind the words, almost, Lilac thought indignantly, as if he didn't believe she had been happily window-shopping, with never a thought for where she was!

'Yes, I've always been . . .' her voice trailed away and she could feel the heat start to burn in her cheeks.

'Fascinated by death?' Art said, too smoothly. 'J. Whitaker & Sons, Undertakers . . . that was the window you were starin' in, I believe?'

Lilac began to giggle. Trust her to make a fool of herself and trust Art to rub her nose in it!

'Was I? I was still thinking about the hats up the road . . . not that I wear hats more than I have to. I like to feel the wind in my hair so I thought I'd walk along the river later, down by the pierhead.'

'Well, I'll come along with you a ways,' Art said.

Lilac, glancing sideways at him, saw that he was looking his best in a dark suit and white shirt, with a panama hat in one hand. He really is rather nice-looking, she thought, with a tiny frisson of excitement chasing up and down her spine, then she reminded herself that this was the Art she had known all her life and the excitement died.

'All right. Who's at home today, Art? Your mam and da?'

Art shrugged. 'Dunno; haven't been back meself yet. I'm lodging in Ullet Road now, with Tippy Huggett; remember, you met me there a few weeks back when I'd been round to take a look at the room.'

'Oh . . . then. Yes, I remember.' Lilac, who had assumed Art had been lurking in order to be with her, felt more than a little crestfallen. So he really had been visiting in Ullet Road! 'Well, are you goin' back to the Corry now?'

'Eventually. I have to take me old woman her money or she'd never last the week,' Art said cheerfully. 'But how about a spot of grub first? We could go to one of the canny houses if you like, cheap and cheerful.'

There were a number of small eating houses in the courts, places where the woman of the house was a better than average cook and could earn herself a few pennies by selling the delicious stews and soups which she had been making for her kids and the rest of her family for years, ekeing out a mutton bone with every available vegetable and seasoning the food with pot herbs, grown in half a beer barrel in her back yard or even in a window box.

'I was going to treat meself to a chump chop, potatoes and gravy at Harriet Young's,' Lilac said wistfully. 'They do a lovely steamed pudding too, with candied peel and sultanas. But if a canny house suits you better . . .'

Art took her arm. His hand was warm and firm on her bare skin and she was aware of him towering over her as they set off again, back the way she had just come. I've always liked tall men; what a pity it's only Art, she thought, moving a little closer to him. Eh, but it was good to see him again, good to be chatting easily to her old friend!

'Young's it is! I were pullin' your leg over the canny house, our Lilac, I wouldn't take you somewhere low. I reckon that with Nellie gone you're longing for decent, home-cooked grub, aren't you? But Tippy an' me works wonders when we get goin' of an evenin', wi' a frying pan and a couple of eggs, a few rashers, some cold spuds . . . oh aye, we eat better'n we ever did at home.'

Lilac bit back the words, 'Of course you do,' remembering that Art had never grumbled over his mother's total lack of domestic ability. She glanced up at him though and saw that he was grinning down at her.

'Go on, flower, say it! Me mam's no cook . . . still an' all, we survived, the six of us, so now we've gorra learn to feed ourselves. Here we are!'

He ushered her into the dining room and they chose a quiet table against the wall. Art, with an air of authority, ordered clear soup, chops and steamed pudding for two, then sat back and regarded her with deep pleasure.

'You look a treat, Lilac,' he said after a moment. 'Makin' bags an' sacks suits you.'

'It doesn't,' Lilac said, 'but it's a job. Like the bank is, I suppose.'

Art chuckled.

'It can't be as dull as the bank, queen,' he objected. 'Eh, but there's times . . . still, no point grumblin'. It's the means to an end. Ah, here comes our food.'

The meal was simple but well-cooked and satisfying, and rather to her own surprise, Lilac found Art amusing and even exciting company. He really was handsome, when he smiled you saw his nice white teeth and he smiled often. Lilac became aware that several girls of about her own age kept glancing enviously across at their table and the waitress was putty in his hands, bringing them a cupful of pieces of ice when Art told her the water was warm, coming over a couple of times to make sure everything was all right . . . Lilac knew the signs, it was clear that women liked her companion. And he talked naturally, easily, telling her all the latest gossip in the Court – who was going steady with whom, who had jobs, who was wearing charity clogs – and all the gossip in the bank, too. Lilac made him laugh with her factory experiences and all was going swimmingly when Art took her completely by surprise.

'Don't know if Nellie mentioned it, queen, but I've been offered the chance of a job with Deacon's, over the water in Birkenhead.'

'Birkenhead? That one-eyed town?' Lilac said rudely. 'No point in vegetating there, Art, when you could be here, where the action is!'

'Birkenhead's a big town and it's quite an important job,' Art said equably. 'It 'ud mean a rise in pay and they've agreed to a living-out allowance. I could afford a house of me own – a small one.'

'Really? But you could go across every day, on the ferry. Lots of men do, if they work in the shipyards.'

'True. But since I've moved out of the Corry anyway, I might as well go the whole hog and cross the water.'

'I suppose you could, though I don't see the point,' Lilac said doubtfully. Why was it that she couldn't feel entirely comfortable about Art moving away from Liverpool, even though it was only to Birkenhead which you could see, just about, from Bridgewater Street? 'I suppose Birkenhead may be all right, in its way. Only you'd miss the cinemas and theatres and things, wouldn't you? And the shops and the concerts.'

'No, because if I wanted a night out which Birkenhead couldn't provide, I'd come over on the ferry,' Art said logically. 'It's not a one-way thing, the ferry, queen. Besides, it's like Stu was saying, you've got to look to the future. A feller's career *is* his future – and his wife's, for that matter.'

'Oh, you talked it over with Stu, did you? But he's wed, with a kid on the way, if you were married it would be different, I could understand you wanting to go.' Lilac waited whilst the waitress cleared their plates and put the desserts in front of them, then dug her spoon into the plump and creamy steamed pudding. 'Ooh, I do love a duff, and this one's prime! But since you aren't married, I don't see why you can't stay here.'

'No-oo, I'm not married yet, I grant you, but I'll be married one day, and I've gorra look to that day, or me wife won't get the best of everything, and that's what I want for her.' Art put his own pudding spoon down and leaned across the table. He took hold of Lilac's chin in a firm but gentle hand, tilting it so that she had to look up at him. His face was ardent, his eyes glowed with an expression which Lilac recognised, with some embarrassment, as strong and emotional affection. 'Lilac, as soon as I'm settled in the job, I'm goin' to ask you to move over to Birkenhead and take a chance on me.'

Lilac's mouth was full of steamed pudding and she was jolly sure she had custard round her mouth. What was more, Art's proposal – if you could call it that – had come out at full blast just when one of those silences which fall on an assembled company had occurred. All round her, Lilac saw heads turn, attention fix on her face.

And she had a mouthful of pudding and custard round her mouth. She knew she was scarlet with embarrassment, looking a fool, feeling a worse one. She sat back, pulling away from Art's imprisoning hand, swallowed her mouthful and then, defiantly, spooned more pudding into her mouth and swallowed that, too, before she spoke.

'I'm not moving anywhere,' she said crossly. 'Not with you, Art O'Brien. Haven't I said it enough times?'

'I've not asked you yet, Lilac,' Art said quietly. Lilac, sneaking a look at him, saw that he was red as a turkey-cock, with sweat beading his brow. 'So I'd best not bother, eh? Is that what you mean?'

Lilac stared down at her plate. He was being perfectly horrible today, he had quite spoiled the nicest meal she'd had all week, he'd embarrassed her in front of a great many people and now all she wanted to do was get away from him and have a good cry somewhere quiet, because her lovely day had turned sour on her. Suddenly, she was not at all sure that she wanted to see Art go right away from her, never come calling, never jump aboard an Oceanic when she was already sitting on the slatted wooden seat. Hadn't the sight of him warmed her heart, lightened the darkest day for her? But why did he have to rush everything? Why couldn't he accept that she wasn't ready for marrying or committing, that all she wanted for a year or two was to have some fun before she settled down?

'Well, queen? If you don't want to take a chance on me, then I might as well be off – to Birkenhead or wherever. But if you've still got an open mind, mebbe we could gerron a bus and go to New Brighton, play the pinball machines, paddle in the sea, act like a coupla pals for a bit.'

Lilac looked at him, seeing him waveringly through the hot tears which filled her eyes. Why oh why did she have to answer him now? Why couldn't she just say New Brighton sounded fun and hadn't they better pay the bill and get aboard a bus? But, still convinced that everyone in the dining room was waiting for her reply, she spoke stiffly, as to a stranger.

'Me mind's made up, so no point in pretendin'. You'd best go to Birkenhead and forget me.'

He went white. She had never seen Art's face, or anyone else's for that matter, drain of colour so completely.

'Me, forget you? Queen, I'll never do that. But don't worry, I shan't stay 'ere an' pester you. I'll go.'

He shot back his chair. He'd taken his jacket off whilst they ate, now he put it on again, wildly, with half the collar tucked in and his tie awry. He jerked some money out of his pocket and threw it down on the table. It was quite a lot of money and some of it missed and fell on the floor, rolled and tinkled and fell.

There would still have been time. She could have got to her feet, said she was sorry, caught hold of him . . . but she did none of those things. Scarlet-faced, longing to crawl away somewhere and hide, with the waitress coming across the room looking concerned and all the other customers staring at them, Lilac got down on her knees and began to try to pick up the money.

'Oh Art, honest to God, what a way to behave! Give us a hand, can't you? Don't just stand there!'

Even then all might have been well. If only Art had helped her, or made some joking remark! But instead his words were bitter, a reproach flung at her head with intent to wound.

'Oh, so I'm good enough to grovel on the floor and give you an 'and, but not good enough to marry! That's right, our Lilac, first things first, you get the money – that's what counts, isn't it? That's what you're after, at the end o' the day . . . a feller wi' cash an' a posh accent, who can buy the sorta clothes you want to show off in! I 'ope you find 'im, queen, because I'm not just goin' to Birken'ead, I'm goin' a lot furder dan dat!'

She had not heard his speech turn so broad since they were kids together, and perhaps his words stung all the more for being spoken in the white-hot heat of anger.

Lilac sobbed once, then shouted, 'Go, then! For God's sake go and be done with it!' and saw, through her tears, Art's figure actually heading at a run towards the door.

She sat back on her heels, then stood up, slowly,

the money in her hot hand. She crashed it down on to the white tablecloth and picked up her gloves, then headed for the door. The waitress called after her that the bill hadn't come to as much as the gentleman had left, but Lilac ignored her. She was quite literally shaking, partly with temper, for Art had made her look a prize fool, and partly with distress, for she knew she had behaved very badly and had hurt not only herself, but Art as well.

The door was still swinging from Art's violent exit, so she slid through the doorway and into the sunny street. She looked to the right, then to the left. A good number of people thronged the pavement, men, women, children, but of Art there was no sign.

Lilac hesitated. Should she go to the Corry? To Ullet Road? Where would he go, where would he run? Because he would be feeling really bad, as bad as Lilac felt, and she realised that she felt absolutely horrible, as though . . . oh as though she had lost something very precious, something she really valued, and she shouldn't feel like that, not over Art, because he was simply a friend from her past who had proved that he wanted to be more than a friend. And she wasn't ready for that yet – would never be ready so far as Art was concerned. Would she?

Lilac shook herself and set off along the pavement. Perhaps he had gone to the Corry – should she go along and take a look? But she would never have the courage to go up to Art's old home, not with her eyes all red and her nose the same, very likely. Art's mum was a proper horror, she'd be real pleased to see Lilac, whom she despised and disliked, so down.

But Art was miserable, and so was she; she really ought to try to make amends. She wanted to meet him somewhere quiet and private, where she could apologise nicely without half the world staring, and explain to Art . . . explain that if only he'd spoken quieter, or when her mouth wasn't full of pudding . . . not that her answer would have been different . . .

Oh Gawd, it was no use. They'd meet up in a few days . . . she'd go to his bank on Exchange Flags and ask for him, she'd hang around outside until he came out . . . how could she have behaved so badly to one of her oldest friends? Even if she didn't want to marry him – well not yet, anyway, not right here and now!

Lilac was walking without either knowing or caring where she was going, but the autumn sunshine warmed her and presently she began to feel a little better. They had both been fools, both been unkind. Art should apologise too, there were faults on both sides. And he hadn't taken into account that she had just started a strange job, was living in strange lodgings, that her little family, Nellie, Stuart and the as-yet unborn baby, had moved down south, leaving her to her own devices.

If only . . . if only she hadn't been *quite* so hasty! If only she'd been a little more polite – if it had been anyone but Art she would have thought about his feelings, done her best to let him down gently. Why oh why had she been so thoughtless?

She stumbled along the pavement, indifferent for once to the shops, the passing crowds. It was Sunday, so there wasn't much traffic; she crossed over a couple of side roads, then the main road, then simply walked, whilst inside her mind raged round and round the problem. By the time she came to herself, however, and found she had reached the pierhead, her anger was directed less at herself and more at Art.

She had planned a lovely day and Art had ruined

it. She'd not asked him to propose marriage in front of a roomful of people, and she'd every right to say no, anyway. Why should she marry anyone, she wouldn't be nineteen for another eight weeks . . . Art was selfish and pushy and he'd made her look a fool, it was that she couldn't forgive. But when a voice hailed her, when a hand caught hers, she knew a moment of total delight, of relief so great that her knees went weak. He had found her – they would be friends again, the sunshine had meaning, the blue sky smiled on her!

'Well, if it isn't Miss Lilac! Where have you been? I've searched for you; I wrote but you never answered.'

It was Alan Blake, looking incredibly handsome, incredibly debonair, with his naval cap tilted over one eye and his eyes sparkling with admiration for Lilac in her prettiest summer dress with the little blue hat pinned on to her piled-up, red-gold hair!

Just for a moment Lilac's unreliable heart sank like a stone, then it rallied a little. Here was someone who would appreciate her, someone who would understand!

'Well, Mr Blake! I thought you'd forgotten all about me!'

'You're unforgettable, Lilac. You were unforgettable in a black dress with a little white cap and apron, but in blue you're a vision the heavenly hosts couldn't forget! Where are you bound? For the ferry? How about giving me your arm whilst we talk, then we can stroll down to the dock, see what's going on . . . have you eaten?'

'Yes . . . but it was ages ago,' Lilac said quickly. Unhappiness had given her an enormous appetite, she now realised. She could have sat down to clear soup, mutton chops and steamed pudding again and eaten the whole lot with relish. 'Where were *you* going, Mr Blake?'

'Call me Alan, please. I've every intention of calling you Lilac; it's such a beautiful name, so appropriate – your colouring is as fresh and striking as a lilac bloom in spring! I wasn't going anywhere in particular so I can accompany you on a walk, or a ride, or for a meal. Oh, I'm delighted to have found you again, I never thought I would!'

'If you'd written . . .' Lilac said, but she sounded indulgent rather than angry, even to her own ears. 'Why didn't you write, Alan?'

'My dearest girl, I did! I wrote from New York, as soon as we arrived, then again a couple of days later. When we docked here I went straight round to 39 Penny Lane and a woman I'd never seen before answered the door!'

'Oh dear, you can't trust anyone! She promised faithfully to forward any letters,' mourned Lilac. 'What did your letter say, Alan?'

'Well, I described the voyage and New York, then I suggested we meet at the pierhead at three on Saturday afternoon – a week ago yesterday, that was. So when I saw you strolling along I thought maybe you'd mistaken the day and the date; my handwriting leaves a lot to be desired but you didn't look as though you expected to meet anyone . . .' He put his arm round her waist and gave her a squeeze. Lilac drew back, but not very far. It was so good to be admired by someone, especially someone as nice-looking as Alan, and what was more he had a successful career, a big house, rich relatives . . .

'So what would you like to do, Lilac? Let's celebrate our meeting up like this – was it entirely by chance?'

'It was,' Lilac admitted. 'I won't say I'd forgotten you entirely, but you most certainly weren't on my mind. In fact, I was thinking about someone else altogether.'

He nodded, then took her hand and tucked it into his arm.

'Naturally, a beautiful girl like you has a great many admirers, but I'm out to prove ... well, let's say I'm out to prove that we can enjoy one another's company. I'll hire a cab and we'll go off into the country, to a nice little village I know. There's a woman who does splendid cream teas in her cottage garden; it runs down to the river, and after we've eaten we could hire a boat and go for a row, or walk in the woods, or just stroll through the village, watching the sun set over the hills. What do you say?'

Lilac pretended to consider, but there was no competition, not really. She could go back to her room, boil an egg in her kettle to make herself a meal and cup of tea at the same time, read her copy of *Woman Magazine* which she already knew from cover to cover, mend a hole in her stocking, and go to bed early.

Or she could get into a cab and go off to the country with a handsome young man who was jingling money in his pocket, and have a high old time!

'Come on, Lilac, take pity on me! It's a lovely sunny afternoon, but I've no one to share it with unless you come out to tea with me. Is there anywhere you'd prefer? I only suggested the country and a cream tea because it's such a lovely afternoon.'

'Well, I've some mending to do, and a friend will be coming in later ... oh, all right, I'll come,' Lilac said, having quite a job even to imitate reluctance.

'But I start work at seven tomorrow morning so I've got to be in by ten.'

'Trust me, Cinderella! Hey, cabbie!'

'Well? Whaddya think?'

Kitty looked at herself in the lid of the biscuit tin which Johnny had produced from somewhere and a slow smile spread across her face. She looked ... well, different. Respectable. Pretty, even. Her cotton dress was neat and clean and Johnny had found a white belt and a pair of almost white plimsolls, much better than the boots which had been so heavy she'd developed painful blisters.

The previous day he had borrowed some garden shears from a man cutting a hedge. He had told her to keep very still – she hadn't screamed, even when she felt the metal against the nape of her neck – and he had scrunched cleanly through her curls, chopping away with the shears and a look of great concentration on his face until, apparently satisfied, he stood back.

'There y'are!' he had said triumphantly. 'Lorra girls 'ud give their eye-teeth to 'ave this new-fangled bobbed 'air, you've got it for nowt. What d'you think?'

She had felt cautiously up her neck ... up and up ... to the ends of her hair which now felt like a prickly garden hedge. Her hands came round to the front.

'Me lug'oles show,' she remarked, not sure whether she was voicing a complaint or making a comment.

'Tha's right. You've gorra wash 'em now, queen.'

'Ye-es ...' She felt across her forehead. 'Ooh, it's all bristly, like a bloody sweep's brush!'

'It sticks out a bit, 'cos it's new-cut,' Johnny

said quickly. 'It'll soften down after a few washes. Jest you see.'

A few washes? Kitty was about to exclaim that she couldn't wait years for soft hair when it occurred to her to wonder if Johnny meant she would be washing her hair regular, like say once a month. She opened her mouth to ask him, then closed it again. No point in courting trouble, better to demand a mirror.

'Gi's me shears, den, lad, if you've done,' the hedge clipper said as Johnny lowered the shears down onto the pavement. 'Well, if I ha' knowed why you wanted 'em . . .'

'Yeah, but she looks awright, don't she?' Johnny said, handing the shears back. 'There's a lorra girls 'ud give their right 'ands for nice bobbed 'air, like what our Kitty's got.'

'Mmm,' the man said a shade doubtfully. 'Oh well, I ain't never come to tairms wi' fashions; mebbe you're right.'

So now, staring critically into the shiny tin-lid, Kitty smiled to herself. Johnny might not be a skilled hairdresser – well, he wasn't – but he'd done as good a job as he could. And there was no doubt about it, she looked better. Cleaner. And she did look just like the flappers who queued outside the cinemas and dance halls on a Saturday night. Last Saturday she and Johnny had been in Edge Lane, quite near the Brayton Dance Hall, and they had both remarked on the numbers of crop-headed girls in very short silky dresses hanging around outside waiting for it to open.

'Well? Whaddya think?' Johnny said again, though Kitty guessed that he'd have a pretty shrewd idea of her feelings just from looking at her face.

'It's real nice, Johnny,' she said at last. 'You're right, it's neater an' cleaner an' . . . an' everything.'

'Glad you like it,' Johnny said. 'Then we'll go tomorrer. Awright wi' you? So this arvy we've gorra get our stuff together.'

'What stuff? We don't want me old clo'es, do we?' Kitty said. 'But I've got me sack an' me tins an' that.'

'Kitty, why did I decide to tek you with me, eh?'

'I dunno, Johnny,' Kitty said humbly. She had frequently asked herself the same question. 'Why did you?'

'Because you read, you like books. An' when you're holed up in an 'aystack an' the rain's comin' down like stair-rods you need somethin' quiet to do, which ain't mischief. See?'

'You mean we oughter nick some books?' Kitty said doubtfully. She had always used the free library, but you had to take the books back regular, you couldn't just borrow them for months on end. 'Where'd you do that, Johnny?'

'Nick *books*? Don't ever let me 'ear you say that agin,' Johnny said impressively. 'Ain't you never 'eard of second'and books? Old 'uns? They ain't pricy, an' what's more to the point, if you looks at it right the 'ole country's a liberry. Cos the book you buy for a penny or two in Liverpool you can swop for other books in Crosby, or Southport, or Wales, even. 'Sides, books is . . . oh, they's special, see? We'll buy 'em, like toffs.'

'Awright, Johnny,' Kitty agreed. She, too, thought books were special but she had never queried the supply of tatty old romance and adventure tales which Johnny fished out of his old brown sack. 'What wiv?'

'Money, acourse. Is there anythin' you can do to earn?'

'Prig some flowers an' sell 'em at street corners? Or

I could carry shopping. The shawlies will be shoppin' for Sunday up an' down Byrom an' the Scottie any time.'

'Nah, you ain't strong enough for that, yet,' Johnny said. 'And you'd be bound to meet one o' your fambly. Best get some flowers, though in the country there's flowers to pick for nothin'!'

'You mean you don't 'ave to nick 'em from a garden?'

'That's right. Still, we ain't in the country yet. Go off, then, an' meet me 'ere tonight with some money. We'll get the books first thing in the mornin', then slide off.'

Kitty nodded. They were under a quiet bridge on the canal, with the light already fading and the water the colour of pewter. It was a good tramp to the flowers she had in mind, but well worth it to buy the books Johnny talked of. She just hoped she would get a say in what they bought; Johnny's taste ran to bloodthirsty adventure right now, though he'd read most of the children's classics which Mrs O'Rourke had nurtured Kitty on. But Fenimore Cooper could pall when you'd read ten of them on the trot, as Kitty had.

'Awright? See you later.'

Johnny raised a hand and was gone, swallowed up by the dusk. Kitty, with a sigh, shouldered her nicking sack, took off her plimsolls and slung them round her neck by their laces and set off too, for the long walk to Rodney Street.

Art had made all his arrangements. He'd even got himself lodgings in a pleasant suburb of Birkenhead. He'd explained to his parents that the money would be better and that, should he be unable to visit, he would send his share of family expenses home by post.

I'll keep on helping until I have responsibilities of me own, he would have said, once. Until I've me own wife and kids to take care of. Once that happens, I'll need all the money I earn for them.

But he didn't bother to so much as mention it, since he knew, now, that he wouldn't be marrying. Not now, not ever. He'd known some decent girls in his time, some beautiful, some plain, some full of bounce and go. But he'd only ever been in love with one of them and that was Lilac Larkin. He'd loved her since he was seven, when she'd come to Charlie's wedding in Coronation Court in her pink silk dress with its matching ribbon.

She'd been full of courage, even then. He'd teased her and she'd thumped him, kicked his shins with her little black boots, sworn at him ... he chuckled at the memory. A right tartar, young Lilac. Oh God, what had happened to her to change her so completely? She had become a single-minded little snob, so eager to climb the ladder of social success that old friendships meant nothing to her. Yet how would he go on, without even the hope that one day she'd turn to him?

He was walking down Scotland Road, trying to convince himself that he was making the right move. He and Lilac had had their row weeks ago and she'd not contacted him, given no sign. If only Nellie and Stuart had still been in Penny Lane he could have engineered an accidental-on-purpose meeting but as it was he only knew she was working in Bridgewater Street, at the bag and sack factory. He'd considered hanging about there, but she'd know. He couldn't bear her to know how he ached for her, how he longed to creep round there and beg her to remain his friend for old time's sake, even if she couldn't abide the thought of a closer relationship.

He reached Miss Harriet Young's ill-fated Dining Room. If only he hadn't been such a fool as to put into words what his heart had been saying for the last year at least! Stuart had warned him, but he'd taken not a bit of notice.

'Our Lilac's young and getting her independence for the first time,' Stuart had cautioned. 'Don't try to tie her down before she's ready. If you wait, Art old friend, she'll turn to you. But let her sow a few wild oats first, eh?'

'I thought it was fellers who sowed wild oats,' Art had protested. 'Young ladies aren't like that!'

Stuart chuckled.

'Who said our Lilac was a young lady? She's a modern Miss, a flapper, an ambitious kid ... call her what you like, she isn't going to fit into that old out-dated mould! Take my advice – which you asked for, remember – and let her have her fling.'

But he hadn't, because the job in Birkenhead had seemed such an ideal opportunity, and he was *sure* she'd come down the Scottie hunting for him, sure she'd wanted to see him. And then they'd fought, hurt each other, parted. And she'd not sought him out nor he her, because damn it, even a feller fathoms deep in love has some pride. And now he was leaving, walking up and down the Scottie saying goodbye to the old places, the old ways – his old life, really. And hoping, really hoping, that presently he'd see a red-gold head weaving its way through the crowd ahead of him, or feel a soft little hand catch at his arm, hear her voice with the liquid bubble of laughter in it which he loved so well.

Art walked on. I'll give it five more minutes . . . ten . . .

Chapter Seven

It must have been the cock crowing in the farmyard which woke Kitty. At any rate, something had. But she was wise to country ways now and did not pop her head out of the cosy nest she and Johnny had made last night in the farmer's haystack. Instead, like a dormouse, she curled neatly round, taking care not to knock against Johnny, and began, very, very carefully, to shift the loose hay which they had pulled in after themselves when they went to bed . . . not much, just enough to see through.

They had chosen their stack and made their nest in darkness, which was probably why they hadn't realised quite how near the farmhouse was. Now, through the screen of stalks, Kitty could see the low, grey house, the outbuildings with lichen patching their roofs, the cushions of moss and stonecrop where the slates were cracked and broken. An old farm, she saw approvingly, but inhabited. A cock had crowed, it was clearing its throat for another burst, and she could see a kennel, the black and white sheepdog within raising a head for a moment to listen, before settling down once more, chin on paws.

Kitty, with infinite caution, cleared a slightly better window for herself and gently insinuated her head into the hole she had made. Looking sideways this time, she could see the beautiful countryside, spread out before her like a living map. There was something different about this scene though, something unexpected. Living rough, on the road, she had already learned a lot, and one thing which was important was to know as much as possible about the countryside through which you were passing. Such knowledge, Johnny had impressed upon her, would never be wasted; not in the long run it wouldn't. Accordingly, Kitty looked round her carefully. Above the farmhouse were the humped shoulders of the Berwyn Hills, and below the farmhouse was a fertile valley. Sheep grazed there, and cattle. The road which snaked along at the foot of the hills was, according to Johnny, the road to London – imagine that! The hedges, which yesterday had been bright with autumn's passing, looked colder this morning, as though the first breath of winter had touched them . . . of course! What was different was the frost! Sparkling white in the first rays of the sun, already disappearing from the tops of the wind-bent trees, crisping the last of their burden of brilliant leaves, the first frost of winter had painted the valley, touched even the mighty hills with its crystal breath.

Kitty sat back to think about this newest development. Winter was serious. Johnny said so, and he knew everything. They couldn't sleep rough once winter came, he said. Well, not every night, anyroad. They would have to look for shelter when the weather was particularly bitter and farmers, mean as their meanest guard-dogs, would lock their barns and fire off their blunderbusses at anyone trying to steal a night's shelter in wintertime, when they wanted every last wisp of hay, every stored turnip or mangold, for their own stock.

Yet, looking out on the white and gold, it was difficult to believe that this actually heralded winter.

Or that, if it did, winter could be so unwelcome. No mozzies, Kitty thought gratefully, rubbing a faded mosquito bite on her arm. No milk turned sour in the heat, no pushing through breast-high bracken abuzz with bluebottles all attacking you as if they had a personal grudge against kids, no spending half a day soaking in a tepid river pool, trying to get rid of the fleas which had infested the last barn.

Beside her, Johnny stirred and woke. He put a hand out and touched her arm. Kitty turned and slid back into their nest. She put her face close to his, loving the feel of his breath on her cheek, the warmth of him so close.

'There's a frost; an' the farm'ouse ain't more'n thirty foot away,' she hissed. 'The dog's awake, but no smoke from the chimbley yet.'

'A frost! Well, we ain't too far from 'ome, but we needn't go back yet awhile. Pity we overslep', but we was awful late gettin' 'ere. Best burrow through.'

Kitty rolled onto her stomach and inched her way back to her spy-hole. There was still no sign of movement from the farm but in the red-gold light of the rising sun the windows stared blankly at her. She concluded that the farmer, as well as his wife and six children if he had them, could all be just the other side of those brilliantly reflective panes and she would never know. And Johnny wouldn't take chances, or only calculated ones.

'Aye. Someone's bound to be about soon; I'll go first.'

In the dusky dimness of the big stack she found her carrying bag and looped its rope round her ankle. Then she began to burrow, digging her way through the hard-packed hay like a little mole. It occurred to neither of them that they were also as destructive as moles – that farmers had a good reason for not wanting nests made in the middle of their haystacks, since animals like their hay handled as little as possible – and if it had, it wouldn't have affected their actions. They had to sleep somewhere, after all, they had their own way to make just like the moles, the farmyard rats and the farmers themselves.

Light began to filter in as Kitty's scrabbling hands neared the outside of the stack. Behind her, she knew, Johnny would be filling in. They might sleep here again in a night or two – nothing was likelier, in fact – so they wanted no gaping holes to announce their recent occupation.

She reached daylight and cautiously began to pull the final plugs of hay inwards. She was facing out onto gentler country now, the road and the soft meadows with their bleating occupants spread out below her. Lying here, she could see on the further side of the road a pond, willow trees, a great many hazels and alders and then the beginnings of moorland, with more sheep and a couple of ponies grazing on the thin grass amongst the gorse bushes.

'All clear, Kit?'

That was Johnny, gently nudging up close behind her.

'Aye, norra soul for miles. Out we go?'

'Out we go!'

At this point, speed was essential. The last thing you wanted was to be caught half in and half out of a haystack. Kitty wound herself into a tight ball, pulled the last of the hay to one side and then launched herself. It was a fair drop but she landed easily, like a cat, and turned to see Johnny already out and repairing the stack behind him before dropping lightfooted down beside her. His face was still pink from the warmth of their nest and his hair tousled, but the sleep was beginning to clear from his eyes, leaving them bright and alert.

'Lead on, chuck,' Johnny said. 'Them hazels will do.'

They made for the hazel clump; once in its shelter Johnny leaned against a young tree and grinned at her.

'Well, what d'you say to some brekfuss?'

'I'm 'ungry enough to eat an 'oss,' Kitty agreed. 'What've we got?'

Johnny shrugged dismissively. He must know as well as Kitty did that their carrying bags were more or less empty.

'We'll go to the farm. Clean me up!'

It wasn't easy. They had both managed to pick up a good deal of their bedding, but Kitty worked away, clearing Johnny from head to toe of the evidence. Then he did the same for her, remarking as he tousled her hair until hay-dust and hayseed flew that she could 'do with another 'aircut, an' the sooner the better if 'e'd gorra get the 'ay out of it often!'

'I's no wuss'n you,' Kitty protested. 'Wash your face!'

They both washed, the water, cat-iced round the edges, making them catch their breaths with the coldness of it. Kitty was only glad that Johnny hadn't decided they should bath – he was a demon for cleanliness and insisted that they wash as often as water came their way.

'You right? C'mon, then.'

Back to the farmhouse now, along the driveway, innocence in their shining faces, their neat persons. Not a strand of hay, not a seed. Two children who could have spent the night respectably in a proper bed, asking to buy some milk – Kitty knew Johnny's ways by now – and then finding they didn't have enough money, but would work for it . . . they were on their way somewhere . . .

The dog barked at them and shot out, but it was chained. It was a typical Welsh sheepdog, black and white fur muddy, narrow head buzzing, Kitty thought resentfully, with an urgent wish to sink its white and pointed teeth into a kid's leg. No matter if the kid was clean and fresh-faced, the dog knew where they'd spent the night. Thank God it can't tell anyone, Kitty thought devoutly as the dog lunged at them. Thank God it's tied up an' all!

Johnny knocked confidently on the leaning wooden door. His knock echoed hollowly, as though the room beyond was empty. But it wasn't, they could hear someone moving slowly across the room. Shuffle shuffle, pause, shuffle shuffle.

The door creaked a little ajar. Kitty could only see a large, open-pored nose and one deep-set, suspicious dark eye. The owner of the eye said something in Welsh; it sounded unfriendly.

'Sorry, we don't speak the lingo, but we're 'aving a walkin' 'oliday in Wales,' Johnny said, with just the right mixture of friendliness and deference. 'We was wonderin' if you'd sell us some milk? We're that dry, me an' me sister.'

The door opened a bit further. The man who stood there was enormous, he couldn't stand upright in the doorway but had to do a sort of semi-crouch. He looked slightly mad to Kitty, and she drew back a little, wondering how Johnny could stand there bold as brass and talk to the great, unkempt giant before them.

'Or per'aps you could let us 'ave a drink o' water, if you ain't got milk,' Johnny continued. For the first time in their acquaintance, Kitty heard uncertainty in Johnny's dulcet tones. People usually answered him, if only to lunge forward, clack him round the lug, and slam the door in his face with a shout of 'Git out, you nasty young beggar!' But this man did nothing, he just continued to look at them. It occurred to Kitty that perhaps he spoke no English, in which case they really were stumped.

'Water? A drink? Do you speak English?'

The same thought had obviously occurred to Johnny, for he spoke slowly and with great care.

The big man frowned, then nodded slowly.

'I speak English,' he said slowly. 'Also Welsh. You want some milk?'

'Yes, please. We've got . . .' Johnny fumbled in his pocket, then turned to Kitty, his expression puzzled. 'Kitty, did you take the purse when we left that cottage this morning?'

Kitty prepared to patter out her usual story of lost money but the man shook his head at them.

'Not pay. You work? You would help Maldwyn?'

'Oh, what a good idea,' Johnny said, as though he'd not just been about to suggest it. 'I'd never ha' thought o' that! Yes, Mr Maldwyn, we'll work for our milk, my sister an' me. What's to be done?'

The huge man closed his eyes for a brief moment and a spasm of pain crossed the great, craggy face. Looking harder at him, Kitty saw that one of his huge feet was insecurely wrapped in rough bandages, and that he was not resting his weight on it. She had moved back when he and Johnny started talking but now she moved forward again. She pointed.

'Wha's the matter wi' your foot?'

The giant Maldwyn glanced down.

'Crushed. Caught in tractor . . . pain iss ferry bad.'

Kitty sucked in her breath but Johnny immediately ducked under the man's arm and entered the kitchen.

'Kit, get some water,' he said. His eyes were bright. Kitty could see that he was pleased by a development which meant they could be useful. 'Sit you down, Mr Maldwyn, whiles we see what we can do.'

'Milk cowss,' the man said in a faint voice. He sank heavily onto the chair which Johnny had pushed forward. It was an old basketwork one and slumped sideways under his weight, but you could tell by the legs, Kitty thought, that it had been slumping sideways, without breaking, for many a year. 'Let Patch off 'er kennel; give 'er to drink.'

'Right. Only we'll do something about that foot first,' Johnny said authoritatively. 'You need a doctor, mister!'

The man took no notice. Kitty jerked Johnny's arm. 'Johnny, 'e's passed out! What'll us do?'

'Get them bandages off,' Johnny said. 'Put the kettle . . . oh, no use, the fire's out. Light the fire, Kit. There were chips by the barn door, I seed a big pile. Then 'eat some water.'

Long experience had shown Kitty that if you were given an order you obeyed it at once or took the consequences – which were generally unpleasant – so she rushed across the yard and got an armful of kindling from the barn, then laid it carefully on top of the still-warm ashes in the open stove. She found matches and lit the fire, then since Johnny was unwrapping the strips of torn up sheeting with almost womanish care and gentleness, she went to the back door and stared ruminatively at the dog.

Poor thing! It was growling and scowling, but its water-container was empty and it looked desperately wild. Kitty tried to pick up the empty tin to refill it, but the dog snarled warningly and made a pass at her hand, so she went across the yard to the well she had noticed and staggered back with the half-full bucket which had been standing waiting. She tipped water into the tin and the dog drank deeply, then stood back. Kitty inched forward. The dog was watching her keenly, its bright, light eyes fixed on her face. She went nearer still.

'D'you wanna be unchained?' she asked softly. 'If so, you gorra let me get near!'

The dog moved its front paws in a little dance on the spot. Its long, filthy plume of a tail moved slowly from left to right. It cocked its head and gave a tiny whine.

Kitty knelt.

'Come 'ere, Patch,' she said. 'Come to Kitty, there's a good gal!'

The name was probably the password, she thought afterwards, but at the time she was just so relieved that the dog's animosity seemed to be lessening that she didn't stop to wonder why.

'Patchie, Patchie, Patch,' Kitty crooned in her softest tones. 'Come to Kit, there's a lovely gal then.'

And the dog came. On her belly, slowly, she slid forward until her trembling head was resting on Kitty's bare knee. And Kitty unclipped the rusty chain and fondled the dog and then led it indoors.

'Dog's off the chain,' she said nonchalantly. 'Wonder what 'e gives it for its grub?'

Maldwyn was still out for the count, it appeared. Johnny looked up, shrugged, and returned to his work. He had got all the bandages off save for the last layer, which was black with blood and stuck into place.

'Dunno. Find it something ... that there's got

food in.' He pointed to a cupboard, door ajar. 'I'd best soak this off. Bring some water over.'

Kitty found an enamel bowl and half filled it with water. The fire was taking hold so she pulled the kettle over the flame. Behind her, Maldwyn gave a deep groan and Johnny gasped at the same moment. Quickly, Kitty returned to his side.

'What is it? Are you . . . oh, Johnny!'

To say that the foot was crushed was no more than the truth. The poor, mangled thing lay there, the toes blue, the flesh torn so that she could see the white of bone and sinew.

'How the blazes 'as 'e stuck it?' Johnny whispered. 'Kitty, I'll stay 'ere, you'd best go to the next farm, fast, an' tell 'em to send for a doctor.'

'Which way's the next farm?' Kitty asked practically. 'Can I take the dog? Then they'll know it's awright.'

'Good idea. Look, give it a bit o' bread an' 'ave some yourself, to eat on the way,' Johnny ordered. He was never at a loss, Kitty thought admiringly. 'See if there's cheese ... . only this weren't done yesterday, 'e's been badly for a coupla days, I reckon.'

Kitty, rooting, found a huge cheese and cut three bits off, one for each of them. Maldwyn, who had regained consciousness, was still not up to bread and cheese. He lay in the chair, sickly white, and now and again he sucked in his breath and let it out in a low moan. Even to Kitty's inexperienced eyes he looked in great pain.

'Got it? Then off wi' you. No, 'ang on, let's see what Maldwyn says.'

But Maldwyn wasn't able to understand what they were asking. He would stare at them for a moment and then slowly close his eyes; never a word passed his lips whilst they made tea in his pot, fetched a stool for his foot and propped it up with a cushion which Kitty found in the front parlour.

'Oh, well,' Johnny said resignedly when they had asked Maldwyn in every way they knew whether Kitty should turn right or left outside the farm gate. 'Best get on, Kit. Tell 'em 'e's mortal bad an' they'd best 'urry. I dussen't do owt more'n we done awready.'

Kitty set off. The driveway down to the road was long and the hedges overgrown, but the gate swung smoothly enough on its hinges and she had the dog on her length of rope trotting beside her. She and the dog had shared the bread and cheese, which seemed to give Patch the idea that they were friends. Kitty, who had longed for a dog without any expectation of even knowing one, got enormous satisfaction from the dog's mere presence and when, after walking at least two miles, they came to a neat grey farmhouse with geese strutting in the yard and a man with a full bucket in each hand crossing the road towards them she had no hesitation in hailing him.

'Mister, I've come from the farm up the road a ways; Maldwyn's in a spot o' trouble . . .'

The man stopped walking and set his buckets down, then smiled at her. 'Mornin', lass. What you doin' wi Maldwyn's Patch, then?'

Kitty hadn't realised she had been afraid of the sort of reception she might get until the man was so matter of fact and friendly. Then she had to fight to stop her voice wobbling as she told her story.

'So me brother Johnny's there now, an' me an' Patch come for 'elp,' she ended. 'We think 'e's real badly, mister. 'Is foot's 'orrible, raw an' 'orrible.'

The man picked up his buckets again and motioned her to open the gate. 'Right, I got you,' he said briskly.

'Don't take no notice of them old geese, just stay close. Get the missus I will, she wass a nurse before we wed.' A young man in a worn cap and labouring clothes came out of the byre carrying a long pitchfork and Kitty's new friend raised his voice to a bellow. 'Eifion, get in the motor an' go for a doctor; Maldwyn Efans 'as 'ad a nasty accident. Like to lose 'is foot, by the sound.'

The young man propped his pitchfork against a wall and turned away without a word; presently Kitty heard the roar of an engine and a motor car came round the corner of the building. The young man raised a hand to them, roared something in Welsh, and was gone up the drive. Kitty's companion turned to her and stuck out a hand.

'Dewi Jones,' he said. 'Bronwen'll come ... stay you here.'

'I'm Kitty and me brother's Johnny,' Kitty supplied. 'I'd best start back, mebbe.'

Dewi Jones shook his head.

'No, wait on. I'll fetch out the trap, see, and we'll be at Maldwyn's place in a trice.'

He disappeared into the farmhouse. Kitty sat down on the bench alongside the door and waited, with Patch sitting beside her, leaning against her knee. The geese, which had rushed forward as soon as they saw her but had retreated again when their master shouted at them, began sidling towards her once more, round bright eyes fixed on her face, big orange beaks agape with hisses.

But Kitty was no soft city-dweller, not now, not after three months of country living. Besides, she had Patch. She waited until the leading bird was no more than a foot away, then she leaned forward and slapped it decisively across the chops. The gander, thoroughly thrown off balance, weaved for a moment, then came on again, so Kitty mentally targeted the heart area and kicked out with both feet. She got it right in the middle of its soft, bulging breast with sufficient force to send it staggering, and counted the black bruise from its beak as nothing when the gander, after a long and doubtful look at her, suddenly turned tail and waddled off, taking his numerous wives with him.

'There y'are, queen,' Kitty told Patch, who was watching the geese retreat with great interest. 'A clack over the bloody lug works wonders, whether it's a feller or a goose!'

'I told him to call for me when his ship comes in, and he said he would, and it's this very evening,' Lilac said, feeding a length of material expertly into the hungry maw of her machine and turning it to form the bottom of the sack. 'So if you want to take a look at him, Bertha, now's your chance!'

'I bet 'e's 'andsome,' Bertha said wistfully, zipping round a completed sack and throwing it on to the pile. 'You're ever so pretty, chuck, the prettiest gal in the room.'

'We're all pretty,' Lilac said. ' And we're all different. But Alan *is* handsome, only . . .'

'Only what, chuck?'

Lilac shrugged and zipped her own sack out of the machine, snatching up another piece of material and feeding it in almost in the same movement. In the months which had elapsed since she had started here she had finally become as quick and expert as any other girl in the room and, when she thought about it, was proud of the fact.

'Only I'm not sure I want to marry anyone, or even go steady with anyone! Believe it or not, Bertha, I like me bit of independence and anyway, I've only known Alan a couple of months.'

'A couple of months!' The girl on Lilac's other side, a short, broad-faced girl with slavic cheekbones and slanting, dark eyes, laughed. 'Why, that's a lifetime for someone like our Bertha! You mek it sound like a couple of minutes, queen!'

'Don't tease, Lily,' Lilac said. She had a special fondness for Lily, whose parentage – Liverpool mum and Chinese dad – always made her think of her friend Polly. 'It isn't long; not for me. I'd known Art O'Brien for years, not weeks . . . and I still couldn't make up me mind to marry him!'

'I t'ink it's a pity you didn't,' Doreen muttered. Doreen was dark of hair and eye, bewitchingly pretty, and easily the most spiteful of the twenty-four girls in the sewing room. 'Per'aps we'd of 'ad some peace if you'd gone on goin' steady wi' that O'Brien feller.'

'There wasn't any point, not if he wanted to marry and I didn't,' Lilac said. 'Besides, we were just a couple of kids. It wasn't a – a proper relationship, not like with Alan.'

''Cept you don't want to marry Alan, either, by all accounts,' Lily pointed out. Her machine whined and clattered slowly to a halt. Lily swore colourfully and reached for a new reel of the coarse brown thread. 'Damn, it snapped. I reckon we lose more time re-threadin' these bloody things . . .'

'I might want to marry him,' Lilac said defensively. 'Anyway, I'm going down to London at Christmas to see me sister Nellie and the new baby. Perhaps I'll make up me mind then.'

'Aye, and when you see the lickle gal – what's 'er name? Elizabeth, that's it – you'll see dere's a'vantages to famblies.'

'I know there are, Bertha,' Lilac sighed. She still missed Nellie fiercely, though they wrote a couple of times a week and she rang the small house in Balham at least once a month. 'I expect I'll marry one of these days . . . I just wish . . .'

'What, luv?'

'Don't arst 'er,' Doreen cut in. 'She'll tell you all over again 'ow she can't mek up 'er mind . . . jest don't arst!'

The other girls laughed and Lilac, smiling ruefully, continued with her work. The nicest thing about making sacks and bags, she had concluded weeks back, was that they didn't need a lot of concentration. You could let your mind wander where it willed whilst your hands and your body continued to feed the machine, see to it when it stuck, repair it when it failed and fetch it fresh material when it ran out. All in all, apart from the fact that you were run off your feet half the time and standing all day, it wasn't such a bad job.

'Want more material, Lilac?'

Stubby the warehouseman, only he should rightly have been called a warehouselad since he was no more than five foot tall and only in his teens, came thundering into the room, arms full of sacking. Everyone knew he was sweet on Lilac so there were covert grins, but Lilac just smiled and said she could do with a yard or two, and after he'd left relapsed into her thoughts once again.

Christmas wasn't very far off. Another ten days and it would be upon them. Alan would be home for a couple of days but she wouldn't be able to see him since she was going down to London to visit Nell and Stuart. And Elizabeth, of course. Nellie's letters were full to bursting of Elizabeth, telling Lilac the exact colour of her hair, the brightness of her eyes, the way she smiled.

She would miss Alan, of course. Christmas was a time for friendship, for being with the people you love . . .

Art. She'd not seen hide nor hair of him since that stupid, worrying quarrel. She hadn't *meant* any of the things she'd said and she was sure he hadn't meant the things he'd said, either. Only . . . bad and silly things had got said, feelings had been hurt . . . she'd gone back to the Court a couple of weeks ago, but though she'd seen Mrs O'Brien she hadn't liked to ask. The old devil had looked so sly, like a cat with the cream.

Christmas was a time for making up. She couldn't remember who had said that, but she was sure someone had. So why not make up with Art? Oh, she was going out with Alan, some people might even say she was going steady, but this wasn't about that sort of thing at all, this was about friendship, about love, not about . . .

Love? Did you say love? Oh, but I didn't mean *that* kind of love, Lilac reminded herself hastily, I meant the comfortable sort of love your have for a feller you've known all your life, the feeling that you want to be with him, that nothing you say or do can be wrong, that, together, you could go anywhere, do anything.

Lilac's machine coughed, grunted, stopped. Lilac stared into space. Love? What *was* love, exactly? Wasn't it the exciting, fizzing sort of feeling you got when a handsome young man paid you compliments, taught you to dance the Charleston, kissed you in the queue to get into the Gaiety cinema on Scotland Road or squeezed you in the back-row doubles at the

Smithdown Picture Playhouse? Yes, that was love; it had to be, it was what all the girls talked about, dreamed about – wasn't it?

'Li, yon bugger's stopped! Wake up, queen!'

Hastily, Lilac took the crumpled piece of material out of her machine, straightened it, rethreaded the needle and set it going again.

So if she was right and that was love, what was this dull, gnawing ache? Was it because some part of her simply needed to see Art, to be forgiven by him, to hear his voice?

'Lilac Larkin, that last bloody sack's got no neck, you've sewed clean acrost it! Oh my lor', the gairl's asleep an' dreamin' so she is!'

Lilac frowned and took the sack Mrs Loose was holding out to her. She saw, guiltily, that she had indeed sewn round all four sides. She held it up, then slung it onto the floor at her feet.

'I'll unpick it,' she said wearily, words she had not had to use for weeks and weeks. 'Sorry, Mrs Loose, it won't happen again.'

She could go purposefully into Deacon's Bank, not just wander in and out as she had done half-a-dozen times over the past weeks. She could go in and ask for Art O'Brien, get his address, go over to Birkenhead and see him, tell him she was awful sorry and would he please be friends again?

With the thought, an enormous rush of warmth and comfort engulfed her. The ache, which had been so persistent lately that it had become almost a part of her, miraculously lessened. She zipped the latest length of material into her machine, watched it as it became a sack, zipped it out and threw it on the pile. What a fool she'd been, standing on her dignity, telling herself that it didn't really matter, that if Art cared he'd come to her, not wait for her to come to him. Now that her mind was made up, now that she had decided she would go to any lengths, she felt quite different – warm, hopeful, cheerful even.

It no longer worried her that Art might think less of her for the gesture. Christmas is a time for forgiveness, she reminded herself. I'll take him a present, tell him about Nellie's baby, ask him if he'd like to come down to London with me to see the Gallaghers!

Christmas, which had seemed only moments ago to be rather a hollow mockery, was suddenly decked with bells and bright with holly.

On the Saturday before Christmas, Lilac put on her nicest dress, a fashionable blue shift with a lace collar, and her best silk stockings. She wore her new black court shoes and her camel-hair coat with the black astrakhan collar and cuffs. She had the sweetest hat, also made of black astrakhan, which perched on her newly cut hair and made her look very fetching indeed.

'Miss Dashing Twenties herself!' another lodger remarked as she met Lilac on the stairs. 'Who are you off to impress, Miss Larkin?'

'An old friend who won't be a bit impressed, Miss Dodman,' Lilac told her. 'Old friends don't care much about clothes, but I want to look as if I've tried.'

'Old man friend or old lady friend?' Miss Dodman said with a twinkle. She was in her thirties and therefore, to Lilac, old as the hills, but she was smart, friendly and efficient. She worked in the big library on William Brown Street and she and Lilac often chatted in the kitchen or waiting outside the one bathroom. Miss Dodman frequently told Lilac that with her looks and education she could do better for herself than a factory job. Lilac was sure she was right, but reluctant to chance her luck – unemployment was still rife and a good few of her friends were out of work. So she decided she would ride out the bad times in the factory since no matter what else went by the board, it seemed that sacks and bags would always be needed. She would try for a different, more interesting job when things began to look up.

'Man, actually,' Lilac said. 'See you later, Miss Dodman.'

'Good luck,' Miss Dodman called as Lilac ran swiftly down the rest of the stairs and across the narrow hall. 'Have a nice day, dear.'

Lilac, making her way down Lord Nelson Street, smiled at the well-muffled passers-by, and enjoyed the sting of the cold on her cheeks, for despite the sunshine it was an extremely cold day. She turned left into Lime Street, scarcely giving the station more than a passing glance as she did so. Next week she would be catching a train from Lime Street to go to Nellie and Stu, to meet her adopted niece for the first time, to see the house in Balham, the park where Nellie walked, the trams and trains and theatres, cinemas and dance halls, all the excitements of the capital city. Yet none of it thrilled her as the prospect of meeting Art again did; she could have danced every step of the way to the ferry, except that a tram heading for the pierhead drew up beside her and it seemed downright daft not to jump aboard, climb the stair and sit on the upper deck with the wind making her eyes run whilst the sun warmed her nose into rosiness. From her lofty perch she saw Liverpool go by, the crowds shopping, the windows dressed for the holiday. At the pierhead she got down and went over to the quayside. A ferry was steaming in, people aboard lining the rail. They would be coming over for Christmas shopping – what a day they had for it, too! A pale blue sky, the brilliance of a wintry sun, the city clear of fog and sparkling like a diamond in the chilly, exhilarating salt wind. But she wouldn't change places with the shoppers, not for a million pounds she wouldn't – she was going to see Art and tell him she was sorry!

The young man she had approached in the bank in Liverpool had not been exactly helpful, though.

'Arthur O'Brien? Oh aye . . . he left.'

'I know. I wondered if you could tell me where he'd gone.'

'Hmm . . . was it Chester? I seem to remember some talk about Chester.'

'I think it was Birkenhead, actually,' Lilac said patiently. 'I wondered if you could give me the address of your branch in Birkenhead.'

'Certainly. It's on Hamilton Square; you can't miss it. Big building, on your right as you come up from the ferry.'

She had known all along that she'd have to beard Art in his den, so to speak, but she was disappointed that the young man hadn't made any comment at all about Art's house or his circumstances. Still, he was probably jealous.

People were jostling aboard the ferry now, so Lilac joined them. She found a place by the rail easily, the ferry being comparatively empty now that all the Liverpool-bound shoppers had abandoned ship, and settled to enjoy the short voyage. In the old days she would have explored every inch of the vessel, but now an older and wiser Lilac just stood by the rail, enjoying the motion, the buffeting wind, and the prospect of Birkenhead getting nearer and nearer.

They docked. Lilac and the other passengers disembarked and Lilac set off uphill, first along Woodside, then up Hamilton Street and into the Square itself.

She saw the bank at once, just where the young man had said. It was a big building though nowhere near as big as the building in Exchange Flags where Art had worked. She went through the revolving doors, her heart hammering so hard in her breast that she thought people must be able to hear it, and came out into the bank, all mahogany and hushed voices, dim lighting, respectability. So near, so near!

There were several young men behind the big counter. She went over to the nearest – she had seen at a glance that Art was not one of them – and spoke before she lost her courage. 'Excuse me, might I see Mr O'Brien, please? On a personal matter.'

The young man looked up and smiled dazedly; I knew this hat suited me, Lilac thought absently, and I wasn't wrong.

'Mr O'Brien? I don't think we have anyone of that name here this morning, Miss. If you'll wait a moment . . .'

He left, with several backward glances. Blue always was my colour, Lilac thought, trying not to sparkle too obviously.

There were small conferences and confabulations going on behind the counter. Young men with their heads together, then an older man . . . Lilac began to feel uneasy. She glanced around her, but this was Deacon's Bank, all right, she hadn't made a mistake. Perhaps this was Art's morning off, perhaps they could give her his address so she could visit him at home.

The young man came back with the older one behind him. The older man smiled at her.

'Good morning, Miss. I'm afraid Mr O'Brien has left the bank's employ; he wasn't here very long, which is why Mr Rumbold was unable to help you.'

'Left? *Left*? But he was so pleased ... it was promotion ... he even rented a house ...' Lilac stammered. 'Is he still living here, do you know? Could you possibly give me his address so that ...'

The elderly man stepped forward. He looked a little hot and bothered, a little embarrassed. I hope to God he doesn't think I'm in trouble and trying to find Art to hand him the baby, Lilac thought, horrified. She leaned forward earnestly.

'Look, I'm awfully sorry, I didn't realise Mr O'Brien had left. The truth is we were at school together and I'm getting married in the spring. I would like him to attend my wedding, and since I happened to be in Birkenhead this morning – my fiancé is meeting me here, we're going to buy the ring – I thought I'd just pop in and tell Mr O'Brien to keep the fifteenth of March free. But I could always write, if you'd pass the letter on.'

Two brows miraculously cleared of their troubled frowns; they *did* think I was going to accuse Art of something awful, Lilac thought with a good deal of indignation. But the older man was shaking his head regretfully.

'I only wish we could help you, Miss, but the fact is, Mr O'Brien didn't leave to go to another bank or another branch. He decided he wasn't cut out for a business life and he joined the Merchant Navy. I believe he's assistant purser on one of the big liners, though I wouldn't swear to it. I'm afraid it would be difficult, if not impossible, for us to forward a letter in the circumstances. I suppose you don't know his parents' address, or . . .'

'Oh yes, of course, I know the O'Briens well, but since I no longer live in the city myself I'd not thought of contacting them,' Lilac lied, with a dreadful heaviness descending on her so that it was difficult even to get the words out. 'I'm so sorry to have troubled you. When we've chosen the ring my fiancé and I had better get a cab and go visiting! Thank you for your time.'

She left. Outside, the sun still shone, people still bustled about getting the last of their holiday shopping done. Lilac went and sat down in the Square garden. She felt as though the ground had been cut from under her feet, as though she had fallen heavily, jarring every bone in her body, bruising herself in the process. What should she do now? He didn't live here any more, hadn't lived here for months by the sound of it.

She got to her feet after a few moments thought, however, and headed for the quayside once more.

Right! The time for silliness and holding back was past. She was going to Coronation Court and she was going to find out where Art was and what he was doing if it killed her! Blow her pride, blow her best clothes, blow everything. Let his mother gloat, his sisters sneer; she had an apology to make!

Chapter Eight

Kitty heard the cock begin to crow and got out of bed. She no longer saw the bed as the height of luxury, a thing to be regarded with awe. Now it was just her bed, with blankets to be washed once a month and a pillow whose coarse white cotton slip had to be changed weekly.

In the winter, of course, she had snuggled down each night almost unable to believe her luck. But with summer's arrival she had grown accustomed – accustomed to so many things! A roof over her head, food in her stomach daily, definite jobs to do, tasks to perform.

Johnny was away for a few days though, so right now she should be down in the kitchen, getting on. Maldwyn had explained that he wanted someone to go over to Dublin in Ireland to buy Irish cattle for fattening. Johnny had said he would go when Maldwyn had explained that he could accompany Mr Dewi Jones and his son Eifion and Mr Meirion Davies from further up the valley. Maldwyn would have gone himself, once, but his foot was far from right. He couldn't put weight on it. Kitty doubted that he ever would, and though he got around on his sticks there were a great many things that he still couldn't tackle, might never be able to do again.

Maldwyn was unmarried, so the doctor had asked Mrs Bronwen Jones from up the road if she would come in every couple of days to dress the foot. She did it for three weeks, then asked Johnny if he and Kitty intended to stay.

'For if 'tis so, I might as well show you 'ow to do the dressings, see?' she said. 'No point in me coming 'ere every other day when you and the little girl is on the spot, like.'

So until the foot healed, Johnny and Kitty did the dressings between them, and Maldwyn never grumbled, never cried out, even though there were times when Kitty was sure they must have hurt him.

After Christmas Maldwyn told them he didn't know what he'd have done without them, and said he would pay them a wage for the work they did. They had been sitting round the kitchen table, having finished off a joint of mutton between them, with potatoes from the straw-stacked pile in the back yard and some winter greens, cut with the frost still on them. Johnny looked slowly round the table, then let his gaze stray further, to the fire-bright kitchen, the range with the kettle hissing away on the hob, the doors open so that the warmth of the blaze might offset the cold outside. Snow had fallen for the first time since they arrived, and though it wasn't much of a fall it had laid, spreading a thin white blanket over the countryside, topping the Berwyns with ice which hid the dead bracken and heather.

'You're keepin' us,' Johnny pointed out, bringing his attention back to Maldwyn and the offer of a wage once more. 'We've gorra roof over our 'eads. That'll do us, over winter!'

Maldwyn shook his great, shaggy head. I really must have a go at his hair with the scissors, Kitty thought with some relish. She always offered to cut Johnny's hair but he did his own, squinting into a polished tin-lid and a window-pane to do the back. But Maldwyn's thatch would really present a challenge!

'No, I'll pay you something ... a share, like. Save it up. A labourer is worthy of his hire as it says in the Good Book.'

Maldwyn was a chapel-goer and a deeply religious man, but his religion was a private thing. He never tried to persuade either child to do more than help him to the chapel door, and had told the minister in no uncertain terms that both Johnny and Kitty were devout Catholics and not to be swayed from their faith. Kitty, whose idea of religion was hazy and consisted mainly of the threats her mother had voiced ... if you do so-and-so Father O'Hare will 'alf kill ye ... was happy to go along with whatever Maldwyn said, but Johnny occasionally looked thoughtful.

He had looked thoughtful over being paid, too.

'Does that mean we can stay all winter?' he said finally. 'We'd work 'ard, eh Kit?'

'Ever so 'ard,' Kitty agreed, gazing hopefully from one face to the other. The thought of facing that snow, with no roof, no bed, no bright fire, was as painful to her as the thought of living once again with the Drinkwaters in Paradise Court would have been.

'Stay till you want to go, like,' Maldwyn said. 'No chick nor child of me own do I have ... stay and welcome.'

They had been glad to agree and now whenever Maldwyn got money for his stock or for the milk from his four placid Friesian cows, Johnny and Kitty got some money too, and Johnny put it in an old tobacco tin and hid it somewhere. Kitty didn't ask where and Johnny never told her, but she guessed it would be outside. Maldwyn was kind and their friend, but he was not young. You never knew, Johnny said darkly, and continued to save all their wages in his old tobacco tin.

Whilst she thought about the past months, Kitty had been splashing her face with water and wriggling into her clothes. If Johnny had been here she would have washed longer and brushed her hair harder, but since he wasn't she skimped a bit, salving her conscience with the recollection that since her first task that morning would be to muck out the byre, she would have to wash again anyway after that.

Presently she padded downstairs and put the kettle on. Maldwyn was a hard and honest worker even with his injured foot, but it took him a while to get dressed; as soon as he was able after the accident he had dispensed even with Johnny's assistance. What he did like, however, was a big mug of tea so that he could take a drink as he struggled into his thick homespun shirts and practical working trousers. Accordingly, every morning Kitty went downstairs, riddled the fire and took out the ashes, filled the kettle and made the tea. She carried the big mugful up to Maldwyn's room, banged on the door and put the tea down by the bed. Then she went over to the window and drew back the curtains, letting in the sunlight, or a view of the slanting silver rain, or even of snowy pastures. Maldwyn always sat up and greeted her and gave her his shy, awkward smile.

'Feels like a king I does,' he invariably remarked. 'Nice it is to be waited on now and again!'

He did the same this morning, picking the mug up with both hands and tilting it blissfully to his mouth, his eyes smiling at her over the rim.

'Managing without Johnny, are you?' he asked presently, as Kitty, having admired a brilliantly sunny

August day, made for the doorway once more. 'Eh, I used to enjoy going to Dublin in the old days.'

'I'm muckin' out first, so if you're down before I come back in, don't forget I'll be hungry enough for two,' Kitty said with a grin. 'I don't mind doin' Johnny's chores, so long as I get to eat 'is grub!'

Maldwyn laughed.

'You eat plenty on your own account,' he said. 'A couple more rashers will go in the pan though, since you've said.'

Kitty, skipping downstairs, smiled to herself. There were men who wouldn't want to cook the breakfast whilst a bit of a girl mucked out, but Maldwyn wasn't like that. He'd done everything for himself since his old mother had died ten years back, and was only worried that he might be overtaxing his workers when his lameness made a job impossible. But he managed most things. He could swing a scythe with the best, not that he needed to do so. The local farmers hired harvesters, tractors, anything they might need between them, and then they went from farm to farm come harvest time, helping with the entire crop. As for sheep-dipping, shearing, taking the beasts to market, Maldwyn and Patch between them did wonders. Patch would bring the sheep right to Maldwyn's knee, who with his great size and strength and his sticks could get even a reluctant ram into the dip, or wedge him under one arm whilst wielding the clippers with the other hand.

But he needed the children. Not just for the things they could do without a second thought which would have taken Maldwyn hours, not for the dressing of his foot, which had finished weeks ago anyway. He needs us now, Kitty thought, because he has grown used to us. His previous solitude had been forced upon him but once he got to know Kitty and Johnny he found he was able to tell them all sorts of things – his private worries were shared, his anxieties, his pleasures, even.

Kitty, who had always been garrulous herself, with the Liverpudlian's liking for discussing, in intimate detail, everything which happened to her and her friends, could well understand his desire for conversation. To sit down of an evening in front of the range and talk over the quality of the wool he had cut last autumn and the price he expected to get next back-end, to muse over the advisability or otherwise of letting Patch have a litter of pups, to wonder aloud whether a flock of geese would not be a good idea, or possibly whether they should set the broody hen on a clutch of duck eggs, so that they could have ducks on the pond, was good and necessary to both her and Maldwyn.

The only real problem which had arisen had been books. In towns and cities there were always shops which sold old books, and libraries which would lend, but in the heart of the country books were not available and Johnny needed books. He said he was educating himself for a fine future, but Kitty, who had the books after him, thought he read mainly for entertainment and love of reading.

Then Maldwyn wanted some cattle cake and Eifion Jones offered to take him into Corwen the next time he went. Johnny went along to give Maldwyn a hand – it was in the early days when their friend was not so well-used to his sticks – and came back positively glowing.

'There's a liberry, queen,' he gasped as soon as he was over the threshold, thrusting a pile of books into her arms. 'Maldwyn joined . . . it's a free library . . . and said I could tek 'is share. They've got all sorts, *and* there's an old bookshop. I picked up a copy of

Bleak House for a penny; it's got no cover, but all the words is there!'

'Oh, Johnny!' Kitty said, almost as excited as he. She had grown deathly afraid that Johnny might leave, just to get back to books. 'Oh, ain't we lucky?'

They were. She knew it. Knew it now, knew it then, knew it every time she woke up, knew it as she shovelled the steaming, stinking piles of cow dung out of the byre, as she was doing now. Lucky Kitty Drinkwater, lucky Johnny Moneymor – even lucky Maldwyn Evans, with his neglected old farmhouse and his much-loved animals.

We're a fambly, good as, Kitty told herself as she shovelled. And presently, washing up in the sink with the delicious smell of bacon frying in the room behind her, she caught a glimpse of her reflection in the window pane and thought that her own mother probably wouldn't know her. Short, richly red-brown hair curled loosely around her head, her eyes were bright, her cheeks glowed pink with health whilst her limbs were rounded and strong, her smile self-confident. The girl whose reflection looked back at her from the window pane was a far cry from the skinny waif who had so often felt the weight of Sary Drinkwater's hand, who had stolen food just to keep alive, who had been afraid for twenty-two hours out of every twenty-four.

I'm not the same person, Kitty thought wonderingly, rubbing herself dry on the rough towel. I've forgotten what it's like to be hungry and scared all the time. Sary's Kitty died the night she lost them trimmings. Johnny's Kitty was born soon after. And I know which I'd rather be, which I'm glad I am!

*

A few months later, Art watched the Liver birds getting bigger and bigger as his ship steamed up the Mersey and wondered at his own lack of excitement.

It was over a year since he had sailed down the Mersey on the tide, determined that if he couldn't settle to banking without even the prospect of winning Lilac's love, at least he would have adventure.

But he soon discovered that an assistant purser's life was not for him; there were pretty girls in plenty on the big passenger liner which had employed him, but he thought them affected and insincere. He hated their loud laughs, short skirts, and apparently non-existent morals. Their drawling voices and upper-class accents often defeated him – one cannot keep up a conversation in which one's principal remark is 'What did you say?' – and their humour embarrassed him. But when the female passengers saw that he was young, nice-looking and single there was no stopping their pursuit. He was fair game in a world where women considerably out-numbered men and the bright young things chased him remorselessly.

There were pretty girls on the staff, of course, but an assistant purser was supposed to entertain the passengers, not the staff, which meant he must be extremely polite to the men and let them beat him at deck tennis and cards, and it was soon made plain to him that he was expected to gently flirt with any young woman who wanted to flirt with him. So Art jumped ship in New York and signed on as a deck-hand on a small freighter which chugged up and down the East Coast, transporting anything which needed moving from one place to another.

He stuck it for three months, then signed off at the end of the voyage and worked in a gentleman's outfitters for a while. He got the job because the proprietor was fascinated by his English accent and thought it lent class to his establishment. But he didn't like the subservience of shop-work and this time he gave notice and signed on as a steward on a liner which was Liverpool bound. He was lucky to get the job; unemployment was biting as deeply in America as it was beginning to bite in Britain and Art thought gloomily that if he was going to starve anywhere, he'd as soon it was Liverpool.

And now here he was, standing at the ship's rail, staring at the city as it gradually grew larger and larger and feeling a great lump in his throat and an unaccustomed blurring in his eyes.

Home! He'd been away for nearly twelve months – he had left in December and it was now November of the following year – and in that time he'd grown up a lot. He didn't see himself going back to the bank, he thought he'd go mad with the boredom of it, but he knew for certain that he wanted to be based in the Pool, even if he was never ashore for very long.

He would go to sea; he knew that now. He'd work his way up, take examinations, slog at it, and eventually he would get his ticket. He didn't fancy a liner, though. He rather thought he'd like a coaster or a trawler rather than a passenger ship. He wanted the sea, hard work, and a degree of forgetfulness. He had noticed that when he was working really hard, slogging as he called it, he didn't think of Lilac from one hour to the next, and that was what he wanted – to reach a point when he simply never thought of her. Then and only then, Art thought, would he be free, able to concentrate on his own life.

I want a home and a family, Art dreamed as his ship steamed slowly and cautiously into her berth. I'm an ordinary bloke with ordinary hopes and desires;

a girl who loves me, a couple of kids, a neat little house like Nellie and Stuart's place in a nice little suburban road like Penny Lane ... that would make me happy.

Once, he had truly believed that the only thing which would make him happy would be marriage to Lilac, but now, after more than a year of wandering, he knew better. Happiness did not have to depend on only the other person; if you changed your outlook and attitude, turned your life upside-down and lived very intensely, then suddenly you realised that there was more to life than winning the love of one particular person, even if she was someone who had meant a lot to you.

Accept that she will never be yours and look for second best, Art had advised himself grimly at some stage during the past twelve months. And without even realising it, he had taken his own advice. His broken heart, if you could call it that, was on the mend. Returning to Liverpool meant that he could face seeing Lilac with someone else and still go ahead with his own life.

But as the city got closer, so close that he could hear the street-cries of the vendors on the waterfront, he did feel a little pang. If things had been different, if he'd had a girl – *the* girl – waiting for him, standing on the quayside waving to his ship, jumping up and down with excitement because any moment now they would be in each other's arms, how happy he would be!

Give yourself a chance, O'Brien, Art ordered himself as, bag in hand, he went down the gangplank after the ship had docked. You'll find the right girl for you, even if her name isn't Lilac Larkin. And you'll live happily ever after, see if you don't!

'I'm worried about Li, that's the truth, Stu. In this past year she's had more young men than I've had hot dinners and she hasn't settled with any of them. If you ask me, it was always Art, it's just taken her a long time to see it. And now she knows she wants him, he's gone, and that means she can't settle to anyone else.'

'He'll come back, sweetheart,' Stuart said comfortably, pulling the blankets over his shoulders. He was always first in bed because his preparations consisted simply of a quick wash, an incredibly quick shedding of all his clothes and a dive between the sheets. 'Come to bed, leave your hair straight for once.'

'I shan't be long; five minutes,' Nellie said with considerable optimism. She sat down before the dressing-table; Stuart could see her reflection, the troubled expression on her small, much-loved face, her long white cotton nightgown with the frill round the neck which made her look like a choirboy – or a leg of pork. Stuart had teased her about it several times and now he snorted softly, *oink, oink!*, and saw her smile before reaching for her night-cream.

Stuart loved watching his Nell prepare for the night ahead with as much serious attention as though she would fall to pieces if she didn't follow her familiar routine. Smiling to himself, he watched as Nellie did all the daft, lovable things which women apparently thought necessary before succumbing to the lure of the sheets. She tied her smooth shining hair up in curl papers so that the ends would turn under when she undid them in the morning. She had had her hair cut fashionably short a year ago, much to Stuart's sorrow, and now had to curl it, whereas when it had been long she had just fixed it in various pretty, feminine styles

– a knot on top of her head, a bun at the back, a long roll – which had caused her far less trouble.

After she had done her hair she spread some sort of cream stuff all over her face, then wiped it carefully off again with a piece of cotton wool. Then she sluiced her face with clear, cool water and patted it dry. She rubbed cream into her hands and then pressed her cuticles back with an orange stick and filed her nails into smooth curves with an emery board.

In the little adjoining room baby Elizabeth slept. They had both checked that she was asleep, hanging over the cot and exchanging proud glances at the beauty of their sleeping daughter. She had Stuart's dark hair and eyes and Nellie's fair skin and sweet smile, and something else entirely her own, an innocent mischief which made both her parents her adoring slaves.

Now, having finished her preparations, Nellie stood up. She walked towards the bed, then hesitated as she always did.

'Was that the baby? I'll just make sure she's all right.'

'She's fine; fast asleep,' Stuart said to his wife's back. She did this every night as well. He supposed that she would still do it when Elizabeth was a woman, if she was living under their roof.

Nellie pushed the intervening door open with infinite care. Though they both agreed that Elizabeth was an angel, she could scream and yell like the devil incarnate when woken from a sound sleep. Nellie moved out of sight for a second, then returned, smiling.

'Sleeping like a baby,' she whispered, closing the door gently behind her. She hopped neatly into bed beside Stuart, leaned back on her pillows and reached for her book. Usually they both read for a while before turning the light out, but tonight Stuart did not even bother to take his own book off the bedside table; he guessed that Nellie wanted to talk.

Nellie opened her book. She glanced at the page, then put a finger in it to keep her place and turned to him. 'Stuart, there must be some way of getting in touch with Art! I mean, surely he wouldn't have signed on with a foreign ship? And anyway, ships dock sometimes . . . he must be in England occasionally. I wrote to my friend Beryl and she went round to the Corry and talked to Art's sister Etty, but they've none of 'em heard a word from Art since he left the bank. You don't think something awful's happened to him, do you?'

'No, of course not. But according to Lilac, sweetheart, he did have cause to believe she simply wasn't interested. She said Art proposed marriage and she sent him off with a flea in his ear. She admits she was pretty horrid, and to a man deep in love such behaviour is worse than just horrid. If you'd done something like that . . . deep despair takes some getting over, believe me.'

'I know,' Nellie said feelingly. 'When I thought you'd forgotten all about me . . .'

Stuart leaned over and kissed her smooth, faintly scented cheek.

'Silly puss, as if I could! But anyway, Art will get over it and come back here. Give him time.'

'But suppose Lilac goes and marries the wrong man?' Nellie wailed softly. 'I didn't care for that fellow she was going round with last Christmas, and the new one . . . well Polly says she seems to go for the type of men other women avoid, the dangerous ones who just want a good time.'

Stuart sighed. He was extremely fond of Lilac, he hated seeing her becoming hard-faced, chucking young men over on a whim, seeming more interested in their ability to pay for her fun than in any intrinsic worthiness of character.

'All right. We'll go up to Liverpool for a weekend soon,' he said comfortingly. 'You'll only be happy when you can talk to Lilac face to face; I do understand that. Shall we say the end of the month?'

'Oh Stu, you are kind to me,' Nellie said ecstatically. 'I'll feel so much happier if I can talk to our girl meself, instead of writing letters or trying to make sense over the telephone. Can we go Friday and come back Monday, mek a long weekend of it?'

'I'm sure we can manage that,' Stuart said. He took Nellie's book out of her hand and lay it down on the bedside table. 'Now you'll want to thank me properly, so we might as well turn out the lamp.'

Nellie doused the lamp and in the warm darkness turned to him. Stuart felt her soft arms entwine him, her soft lips seeking for his across his cheek. His heart began to beat faster and he untied the neck-string of the demure nightdress with fingers that trembled, and pulled it down over his wife's creamy shoulders.

'Nellie, Nellie, Nellie,' he murmured as she pressed close. 'Oh, what a lucky devil I am!'

Lilac got the letter saying that Nellie and Stuart were coming to the city for a long weekend just before she left for work one morning. She was delighted, excited, even a little apprehensive, for much though she longed to see them she knew she would have to come clean about a number of things which she hadn't fully explained in letters or over the telephone.

For a start, she no longer worked at the bag and sack factory. She had told Nellie about her new job of course, but not how she had come to get it. It had all come about when she had realised that she had lost touch completely with Art, that the O'Brien family neither knew nor cared where he was, that the authorities merely said his whereabouts were not known to them. Then the iron had entered Lilac's soul. She couldn't get Art out of her mind, she couldn't take other fellows seriously, so she decided the thing to do was to fill her life totally, to find as many men-friends as possible, and to wait.

Accordingly she had told Alan that she was not interested in seeing him again and had deliberately set out to meet the type of man who she felt could give her a good time without trying to tie her down to marriage or a permanent relationship. She went to modern dancing classes at the dancing academy on Edge Lane and became very proficient very quickly, for she was a natural dancer. She also made a new friend who was to show her how to escape from the drudgery of the factory into something far more amusing – something which also paid well, as she was soon to discover.

Her new friend, Charlotte Unwin, was in looks at least the exact opposite of Lilac. Her father, she said, was a Spaniard, her mother Irish, and this fiery combination had resulted in Charlotte having luxuriant black curls, olive-tinted skin and a figure as curvaceous and footsteps as light as any Irish fairy.

The two girls took to each other on sight. Perhaps it had something to do with the fact that Charlotte's young husband had disappeared with a chorus girl from a Cochran review at the Empire Theatre on Lime Street. She told Lilac bluntly that men were not to be trusted, but that didn't mean she was averse to netting another one.

'Only next time,' she told her new friend, 'I'll have more sense than to talk about love or forever; it'll be *what's in it for me?* next time.'

It was Charlotte's suggestion that the two of them might go into partnership and rent a room on a popular thoroughfare where they might teach seamen, as well as others, the intricacies of modern dancing.

'They need patience an' a pretty lass to give 'em confidence,' she said. 'Most of the dancing academies teach girls, but we'd specialise in fellers. We'll be Miss Charlotte an' Miss Lilac an' they'll be queuein' up jest to get in at the door.'

'Sailors? Queueing to learn to *dance*?' Lilac said derisively. 'They'll think we're teaching something very different, you mark my words, and I don't intend to have anything to do with *that* sort of thing.'

Charlotte flashed her Mediterranean smile, then rolled her eyes expressively.

'Oh aye, they may come in for the wrong reasons, queen, but they'll stay 'cos they can see the point o' larnin', if it gets 'em into the arms of girls like us.'

'What do you mean by arms?' Lilac said suspiciously. She had only known Charlotte a couple of months.

'I means jest what I say. Arms as in dancin', not whorin', if that's what you was thinkin'. Listen, are you on? Because in my considered opinion, the pair of us could make a tidy living if we rented the right sort of premises and found ourselves enough pupils. Only we'd have to mek it clear from the start that it was regular teachin' for older people, not for kids an' flappers. There's plenty caterin' for them already.'

'I'm on, for a bit at any rate,' Lilac decided. 'If it works . . . well, we'll see.'

It did work. And not only did they soon find themselves with more pupils than they could cope with so that they had to hire other girls to work for them, they also began to meet quite a different type of customer to the ones they had envisaged when Charlotte first got her bright idea.

And oddly enough, the dancing school really helped Lilac, if not to forget Art, at least to keep his loss from the forefront of her mind. And when she discussed it with Charlotte, her friend admitted that with so much to do and with success so close, she hardly ever woke in the night to weep for her absent husband.

As the school flourished, their fame as teachers of modern dance and as girls in whom beauty and character mingled began to spread. Respectable people, particularly older men, came to learn from them and after a few lessons, often asked one or other girl out to a theatre or restaurant.

Charlotte was choosy, Lilac more so, but they began to have an enviable social life, though there were always some people who raised their eyebrows. Then respectability, which had hovered doubtfully, arrived on their doorstep. At Lilac's insistence they opened the dancing school to young ladies as well as men.

'Never mind if they say it's a marriage bureau, so long as they come to our classes and pay our fees,' Lilac said decisively, when Charlotte complained that one particularly pretty girl had stolen a patron from under her nose. 'We're neither of us interested in permanence, not yet, so we shouldn't worry ourselves when the flappers are prepared to take on men who may interest us only briefly.'

'You're right,' Charlotte sighed. 'George Harris was rich, but he had two left feet and bad breath. Miss Nichols is welcome to him.'

The dancing school, successful though it was, did not keep both girls occupied during the day. Charlotte saw to the books, kept the rooms in good order and trained the staff, whilst Lilac took a job as receptionist at a big hotel, the Delamere, situated in a prime position on Tythebarn Street. She found the work congenial and not too hard. She was offered the job by the proprietress after she'd organised a display of modern dance in the Delamere's ballroom, and she accepted with some trepidation. Factory life had made her believe that she could do nothing else, but in fact the job of receptionist suited her very well. She sat behind a flower-decked desk looking immaculate and smiling a welcome, she did the books, learned to use a typewriter . . . and fought off amorous male customers so tactfully and with such success when she was on the late shift that the proprietress, a harsh-featured woman called Mabel Brierson, told her she was worth her weight in gold and would undoubtedly own and run her own hotel, some day.

So Lilac was beginning to have a very good idea of her own worth, and she did not intend to throw herself away on any handsome young sailor or poorly paid clerk. If it had been Art it would have been different; even thinking about him still gave her a warm and breathless glow, but she was beginning to wonder if her old friend would ever show his face in Liverpool again. Certainly he had never visited The Waterfront Academy of Modern Dance, Props Miss Lilac and Miss Charlotte.

But the letter from Nell put her in a spin.

Her sister knew all about the job as receptionist,

knew that Lilac taught dancing in the evenings, but had no idea what a very successful venture the dancing school was, nor how convenient a place for meeting men with money and time on their hands. And if Nellie had known she would not have approved; Lilac knew that five years ago she herself would have been horrified at the mere suggestion of deliberately setting out to meet fellows, but now it was different. A factory girl only met clerks and deck-hands. A receptionist might never click with a customer. But a dancing teacher . . . ah, that was a different kettle of fish altogether. She and Charlotte had made up their minds to marry for money if they could not marry for love, and because of the school at least they had the choice. Men of all shapes and sizes, men from every walk of life, crossed their paths and were closely scrutinized with a view to matrimony.

'Not that I'd dream of marrying whilst there's a chance that Art and I might make up,' Lilac admitted wistfully. 'Besides, I do enjoy life; I'd rather not marry at all than pick the wrong man.'

'I'm not marryin' again yet, either,' Charlotte confirmed. 'We're mekin' money, and having a lot of fun at the same time. But later, when we're gettin' really old – say when we're twenty-six or twenty-eight – then we'll mebbe need a rich feller!'

'By that time it'll be too late,' Lilac said, chuckling. But Charlotte, though she laughed too, said Lilac knew very well what she meant – and Lilac acknowledged it. One day they would get tired of dancing with every Tom, Dick and Harry, tired of having their feet trodden on and their dresses tugged off their shoulders, tired of theatres, cinemas and restaurants, even. Perhaps they'd get tired of waiting for the men in their lives, too, for whatever Charlotte might pretend, Lilac knew very well that her friend was always scanning the crowded room with the same wistful thought that haunted Lilac herself: will he come? Will he be here, tonight?

'My sister and her family are coming to see me tomorrow and staying till Monday, so I shan't be teaching,' Lilac reminded Charlotte on Thursday evening. 'Mrs Brierson's given me time off . . . we'll have fun, the four of us.'

She knew Nellie would ask awkward questions and Stuart would eye her shrewdly and listen to local gossip and perhaps even put two and two together and make four, but she would still have fun because she loved them all so much, the young Gallaghers. Besides, she was hostess and she loved entertaining. She had moved out of Lord Nelson Street and into a flat on Mount Pleasant when she got the hotel job, and as soon as she had read Nellie's letter she made her plans for the weekend. She would sleep on the couch in her living room so that Nellie, Stu and little Elizabeth might have her bedroom. She had planned meals, entertainment, cosy sessions round the fire in the evening whilst baby Elizabeth slumbered in the next room. It was November, the days shortening, and the weather had passed through every possible phase in a couple of weeks. Rain had fallen, and sleet; they had enjoyed a couple of days of brilliant sunshine; fog, always prevalent in a city so close to a river estuary, had blacked them out for three solid days, and even now, after a pleasant enough afternoon, there was a decided nip in the air as soon as darkness fell – a good excuse for a fire, roast chestnuts, and bread toasted on a fork held out to the flames.

Friday arrived at last. Lilac was at the station fifteen minutes early, with a beautiful teddy bear for Elizabeth and a heart full of affection for Nellie and Stuart. They got off the train, tired, pale, even a little confused, with a very large suitcase and the baby clutching Stuart's shoulder and wailing, and found themselves whisked off in a taxi and welcomed to Lilac's shining flat with a meal in the oven keeping warm and a bottle of wine standing in the sink, keeping cool.

'You're living in style, queen,' Nellie said, sounding pleased yet puzzled. 'My goodness . . . wine!'

'I've a good job and a good boss. The wine came from Mrs Brierson, with her compliments,' Lilac explained. 'What does little Elizabeth eat, Nell? I've done a casserole of beef with suet dumplings for us, it's nice and warming on a chilly evening – but I was at a loss what she would like.'

'She's a young lady now she's had her first birthday, and will have a tiny bit of the stew with some bread and butter,' Nellie said. 'Dearest Li, do you mind if I go through and change her into her night-things and clean her up? She's fractious now, and cross, but once she's clean and fed she'll be a different person – and so will I, because there's nothing so tiring as a grizzling child.'

'You carry on. Stu will help me to dish up and lay the table. We can gossip whilst we work,' Lilac said. As soon as Nellie had bustled from the room with the baby in her arms she turned to her brother-in-law. 'Sit down Stu, this minute. When I need your help I'll tell you what to do.'

'That's nice, because I'm extremely tired,' Stuart said, sinking into Lilac's rocking chair. 'What a pleasant room, my dear, and how cosy you've made it. Let me do something soothing, like boiling a small pan of milk with a little sugar in it for Elizabeth's drink, and we'll talk. I don't mind telling you Nell's been in a real state about you. She thinks you've got too many fellers and you change them too often. She doesn't believe you're really happy. In short, chuck, she still has hopes of you and Art.'

Lilac, pulling a pan of potatoes over the heat, looked thoughtful.

'Nellie always did know me better than I knew meself,' she said. 'I've tried and tried to contact Art though, Stu, and there's no way. Nell is right, I do go out with a great many young men, but there's safety in numbers, they say. This way I can wait for Art without being bored and dull. And I sometimes think I'll wait for ever, rather than give even the thought of him up. If *only* he'd left some sort of address with someone, so I could write. But he's bound to turn up here some day – isn't he?'

'I think so. Us Liverpudlians are queer folk, queen. We're attached to this dirty old city by a strong cord and it tugs us back eventually no matter how far we roam. Look at Nell, she's got a nice home – well, you've seen it – and a lot of friends, yet she can't wait to come back here. Any excuse and she's planning a quick visit. I reckon I can keep her down south for another two years and then it's bring her back or see her seriously unhappy. And I wouldn't want that.'

'What about you, Stuart? You were born and bred here, same as Nell and me. How do you feel?'

Stuart had boiled his little pan of sweetened milk. As Lilac watched he poured it into a mug with a spout and began to run it under the cold tap. 'Cooling her majesty's booze; she can't cope with drinks unless they're blood heat,' he explained. 'Me? I'm the same, love. Just the same. I can't wait to get back.'

*

The weekend flew by, of course. Nellie and Stuart proved to be extremely understanding about the dancing school and were very impressed when Lilac took them round on Saturday evening when the classes were in full swing.

'Your partner can Charleston up a storm,' Stuart said admiringly as Charlotte, long beads swinging, headband low on her dark brow, proceeded to make the wild, wiggly dance look both easy and exciting. 'You have some very superior pupils, Lilac love – that's a First Officer off a liner over there, still in uniform!'

'Who pays the band? They must cost you the earth!' Nellie exclaimed, but Lilac was able to reassure her.

'They don't cost a lot because there's so much unemployment in the Pool. They're all unemployed during the day and they make a bit at night by playing for places like this. They're rather good though, don't you think?'

'Awful good,' Nellie said. 'The trumpeter keeps smiling at you, Li. He seems a nice young man.'

'Oh, that's Spudsy Bishop. I was at school with him . . . well, I wasn't actually since he was at St Ant's, but I knew him pretty well. He was in Art's class, in fact.'

'Oh. Does he . . . do you . . . ?'

Lilac laughed.

'No he doesn't and we don't! I've no time, Nell, and precious little inclination to tell you the truth. I'm . . . I'm still waiting for . . . for . . .'

'Good,' Nellie said, nodding her head decisively. 'You're right to do so. He'll come back, I'm sure of it.'

Lilac took the Gallaghers to the hotel of course, and

the staff were charmed by Elizabeth and pronounced Nellie and Stuart a very pleasant young couple. Mrs Brierson insisted on entertaining them to coffee and biscuits in her suite of private rooms and told Nellie that she valued Lilac very highly.

It was what Nellie most wanted to hear. And when Stuart tactfully took Lilac for a walk whilst Nellie saw to the baby, his first remark was a promise that Nellie should not hear what he was about to say.

'That sounds bad,' Lilac said rather apprehensively. Stuart had gone off visiting friends a couple of times, leaving the girls in the flat together. Newspapermen being the way they were, Lilac guessed that Stuart might have enquired about The Waterfront Academy of Modern Dance and its proprietresses, Miss Lilac and Miss Charlotte.

'I wouldn't say it was bad, chuck, but you must be careful. A feller told me that when you started the dancing school it was widely believed you were running quite a different business from what you advertised – get me?'

'Yes. I *told* Charlotte that would happen but she said so long as the fellers came and saw for themselves, it wouldn't matter. And it hasn't mattered, not really. We're very respectable now.'

'Oh aye, now you are, so I won't reproach you – but you wouldn't want Art hearing rumours about you and perhaps believing them, would you?'

'My God . . . you don't think . . . is *that* why . . .'

Stuart laughed and squeezed her arm reassuringly.

'No, I'm sure it isn't. But two young girls running a business have to be whiter than white, chuck. When you start your own hotel, and Mrs Brierson seems to think you will one day, then your reputation must be above reproach. So bear it in mind, eh?'

'I will,' Lilac said fervently. 'And I'm ever so grateful to you for not saying anything to Nell, because she'd be upset and there was nothing like that, I promise you.'

'You don't have to promise me; I know it. Come on, better turn round and go back to the flat or Nellie will wonder what we've been discussing for so long.'

On the Monday, Nellie and Stuart went the rounds saying goodbye, telling everyone it wouldn't be long before they came home, promising to write. Their train left at noon, so Lilac offered to take Elizabeth out for a walk whilst her parents packed and Nellie was delighted to have the child taken care of whilst she and Stuart were busy.

It was a very cold morning. Elizabeth was warmly wrapped up in a bright red coat and hat, with sturdy shoes on her tiny feet when she set off with her aunt. But she couldn't walk far, and since she had greeted Lilac's suggestion of going down to the docks with great enthusiasm, Lilac ended up carrying her most of the way.

Elizabeth loved the shipping. Down to the pierhead the two of them trundled, then along the docks, Elizabeth now walking, now riding triumphantly in her aunt's arms. She still wasn't talking much, though she could mum-mum and dada-dada with the best, but she could wave, and smile, and crow with delight and she did a great deal of it as Lilac pointed out the big ships, the water, the bustling people on deck.

They reached the deep-water berth where a big liner was about to sail and stood watching the preparations for a bit. Elizabeth jumped up and down, sat on her well-padded bottom, allowed Lilac to lift her up onto her shoulders the better to see what all the noise and bustle was about.

Just before the liner steamed out, Stuart joined them. He took the baby from Lilac and the three of them waved enthusiastically to the crowds on deck, most of whom waved good-naturedly back.

'Wasn't that fun, queen?' Stuart said to Elizabeth as they turned away to return to the flat. 'Now let's hope you've been so active that you'll sleep all the way to Balham!'

Art saw them. He had prowled the city, waited outside the bag and sack factory, even visited the house in Lord Nelson Street where Lilac had lodged, and gone round to 39 Penny Lane. He had had no luck, but then he didn't rightly know if he wanted any luck. He wanted to see her yet he dreaded it – rightly, as it turned out.

He had signed on as assistant purser again, but this time on a much smaller liner, one that crossed the Atlantic less with party-going in mind than business trips. He had been working hard ever since the passengers began to come on board and stopped for a moment when the flow slackened, went over to the porthole in his crowded office for a breath of fresh air.

She was there, within thirty feet of him, her beautiful hair tugged loose by the wind and by the baby in her arms, looking up at the ship as she began to steam out of her berth, waving, smiling.

He stood as if turned to stone. He could only stare, whilst all the unacknowledged, subconscious hopes he'd nursed for the past year crumbled to dust.

They were getting smaller, smaller ... Lilac just

a tiny figurine, the babe a dot in her arms ... and then a man approached them. He took the baby, held it comfortably in one arm, put the other gently round Lilac's waist for a moment. Then the three of them waved and waved ...

'Mr O'Brien, if you've nothing better to do, perhaps you could give me a hand with these figures?'

Art turned away from the scene. There were tears in his eyes, tear-tracks down his cheeks. He rubbed at his face fiercely, trying to calm himself, but the purser, who had reminded him of his duty, was looking down at the pages on the desk.

'Sorry, sir,' Art said huskily. 'Saw someone I thought I knew. Pass the stuff over, I'll get on with it now.'

Chapter Nine

The year that Kitty was fourteen, Maldwyn bought her a proper dress. Before, she'd scrimped and saved out of her egg money or any bit of cash she was paid for anything and kept herself in working clothes, but this time Maldwyn said she should have the dress and Johnny, looking at her critically as they washed up after their meal, agreed.

'You've growed out o' everything you've got, Kit,' he said. 'Kecks is fine for workin' in, but you want a decent dress for market days an' that.'

'I can buy a skirt,' Kitty protested. She looked down at herself and noticed, for the first time, how much leg stuck out at the ends of her trousers and how much wrist from the ends of her shirt-sleeves. 'Anyway, I've gorra skirt, come to think. Won't that do?'

'It iss not good enough for what I've got in mind, lass,' Maldwyn said. 'Look, Johnny'll tell ye.'

He limped off, a huge man, shy as a girl and as gentle as one, too.

Kitty turned to Johnny. 'What's 'e mean? What's 'e gorrin mind, Johnny?'

'It's the farm,' Johnny said slowly. 'Maldwyn wants us to 'ave it when 'e's dead an' gone. You an' me, Kit. I said we didn't expect nothin', that we'd no right, but 'e said we'd earned it. Better'n that nephew of 'is, 'e said, cos Elwyn Ap Thomas don't know one end of a pitchfork from t'other. Elwyn's goin' to be a 'countant, Maldwyn says. Mal 'asn't got no time for 'countants.'

'That's true,' Kitty agreed. 'Cor, fancy 'im wantin' to leave the farm to us, Johnny! But they won't let 'im, eh?'

'Mal says they will. Says 'e'll tie it up all legal an' sign things wi' a lawyer. Wants it to 'old water 'gin any court in the land.'

'Oh. But the dress . . .'

'We'll 'ave to go up to Corwen wi' Mal, an' see the lawyer,' Johnny said patiently. 'Mal says we've gorra look real respeckable, else the lawyer will think 'e's off 'is chump.'

'Oh, I do understand, then,' Kitty said thankfully. 'But there's no 'urry, is there? Mal's got over 'is bad foot a treat, 'asn't 'e?'

'Yeah, but . . . 'ow old d'you think he is, Kit? Maldwyn, I means.'

Kitty frowned. To her an adult was an adult, unless he was bald or had snow-white locks. Maldwyn's grizzled hair was still more dark than grey and his weatherbeaten visage looked just like everyone's face round here.

'Umm . . . thirty?' she volunteered at last, seeing that Johnny honestly wanted to know what she thought and didn't intend to give her a clue.

Johnny shook his head.

'Nope. Older'n that.'

'Oh. Forty . . . no, say fifty.'

'Older'n that.'

'He ain't never sixty!' Kitty said in an awed voice. That was a ripe old age, that was, and Maldwyn got about just as well as she and Johnny would if they had a bad foot.

'The truth is, queen, 'e's seventy-two. That's what

'e told me an' Mal never lies, it's one of 'is things.'

'Seventy-two!' Kitty whistled. 'No wonder 'e wants to mek 'is will, then!'

'Yeah. So you let 'im buy you the dress, an' we can get it all sorted out.'

'All right. I'd like a dress,' Kitty said thoughtfully. 'But give us the farm . . . they'll never let 'im, Johnny.'

Maldwyn took them to a lawyer in Corwen, but left the two youngsters in the outer office whilst he and Mr Brindley Travers talked. There were a few magazines on a table in the outer office so Johnny and Kitty amused themselves by reading, but presently Maldwyn came out again and gestured to them to follow him down the stairs and back into the street.

'English, he is,' he said in a low voice, jerking a thumb towards the door from which they had just emerged. 'Not a nice person, I'm thinking. We'll catch a bus to Wrexham.'

'Where's Wrexham?' Johnny asked as they clattered along the pavement, all three of them in their best boots. 'What did 'e say, Mal?'

'Seemed to think I wass running mad to leave the farm away from family, though as I said, families stick together in times of trial and hardship, they don't go their own ways like that Elwyn has. So I thought, get going Maldwyn or this feller will 'ave the pants off you, and not a word of Welsh to 'is name either! Wouldn't trust 'im with a bundle of hay, let alone my farm. We're lucky though, there's a bus in ten minutes to take us to town.'

'So why Wrexham?' Kitty said as they reached the omnibus stop. 'Do you know anyone there?'

'I do. Man wi' an office on Charles Street, not far

from the hotel . . . the Wynnstay Arms. Feller named Hywel Hughes. A friend, like. Trust him wi' me life, I would.'

'Oh, then that's all right,' Johnny said cheerfully as the vehicle they wanted came trundling up the street towards them. 'Wouldn't like to t'ink I'd put on me best kecks for some English bugger what 'ud cheat 'is own gran'mother!'

Maldwyn chuckled and pushed Kitty ahead of him on to the omnibus step.

'You'll like Hywel,' he assured them. 'Trust 'im wi' me life I would.'

Kitty was collecting eggs. She knew most of the places the hens laid, and in summer, when the hens laid more eggs than they could use, she took them to Corwen Market and sold them to the townsfolk along with butter, cream and a few vegetables or a couple of past-lay hens. Today being market day, she would go into town in the trap with the brown pony, Tilly, between the shafts. Once, Maldwyn or Johnny had always accompanied her when she went to sell, but not any more. She had grown tall on the good farm food and though she was slim she was also tough and capable. She could put up her small stall herself, and sell her goods, and if anyone tried to molest her or take her money it would be the worse for them. Patch always went with her and Patch could give a troublemaker a nasty nip on the ankles if nothing worse.

Besides, Kitty thought, laying the big brown eggs tenderly in her basket, it wasn't as if there ever was trouble at Corwen. Most of the farmers and their wives knew her and although they still tended to speak in Welsh amongst themselves they often included her in their conversations, especially now that she was beginning to be fluent in Welsh. Indeed, often she spoke the language instinctively; Maldwyn spoke Welsh as his first language and she had picked it up almost without noticing, suddenly realising that she understood and could answer in the same tongue.

From the byre, she could hear Johnny whistling. They had milked the cows earlier and Johnny was mucking out whilst she collected the eggs. Maldwyn would be getting breakfast – they took it in turns – and as soon as they'd eaten she would go out to the field, bring the pony in and harness her up to the trap. Maldwyn and Johnny would do all the work about the farm today, including her share, whilst she sold their eggs, chickens, butter and vegetables. Last night she and Johnny had collected the string beans. They had had a good summer and the beans hung thick and heavy, far more than they could eat or salt down. Maldwyn had pulled a basketful of carrots for her, too, and had washed them under the pump. Carrots sold better all bright and clean, though they didn't keep so long – but townsfolk didn't seem to care about things like that.

The little black hen with the torn comb usually laid right at the end of the orchard, so Kitty went that way, pushing through the long, dew-wet grass and singing to herself. September was a good month, and October wasn't bad either – she would have a great many apples to pick and bottle, and store away in the apple loft. At the bottom of the orchard there was a thick old hawthorn hedge, less to keep stock out than to protect the apple trees from the winds of winter, and it was here that the little hen scraped herself a scrappy, twiggy nest and laid her clutches of eggs.

Kitty leaned into the hedge and felt about. Her fingers closed round the eggs ... two, three, four ... and she backed out again, bringing three eggs with her. She would leave one for the little hen, so that she laid there again rather than wandering off and forcing Kitty to wander after her.

It was a bright morning; Kitty crossed the orchard, stopping by a particularly fine bush apple. She tested the fruit, but they still weren't ripe. Nevertheless she picked one and bit; sharp juice flooded her mouth and the crispness of the green-tinted flesh was good. She ate the apple, flung the core into the long grass and then went back to the house. She went into the kitchen and carried the basket carefully over to the low stone sink. Most of the eggs were clean and smooth, but one had chicken-dung all over it. Maldwyn, easing fried eggs out of the pan, grinned at her as she wiped the dirty egg clean.

'Ever made bramble jelly?' he asked. 'I thought we'd go after blackberries tomorrow, then you can sell bramble jelly when we need all the eggs the 'ens lay.'

'I made blackberry and apple last year, but it didn't go too well,' Kitty said, putting the cleaned egg back in the basket with its fellows. 'Do they prefer jelly, then?'

'Yess indeed; no pips, see? If you've false teeth a reg'lar nuisance are berry pips. We could tek our tea with us, go over the 'ills a ways.'

Kitty, agreeing, smiled to herself. Seventy-three Maldwyn might now be, but he was a child in some things. He adored picnics, always insisted on food being carried out to the hayfields in early summer, and later to the harvest fields. And he still didn't seem more than forty or forty-five to her as he limped about the farm, doing his work.

Thinking about his age made her remember the great will-making which had taken place in the market town of Wrexham about a year ago. Maldwyn had been right, they had all taken a liking to Hywel Hughes, a tiny fat gnome of a man, cherry-cheeked and cheerful, who had drawn up the will and had it witnessed by two passers-by. One witness was a soldier, home on leave from the army, the other a bright-faced lad from one of the hill farms at the back of the town. Maldwyn had insisted that strangers should be witnesses because he didn't want his nephew being told before time about the will.

'We don't want no trouble,' he had said gruffly. 'Try and persuade me to change my mind, Elwyn would ... greedy for money, see? No love of the land, no fondness for me, but greedy. Once the deed's done, though, and I'm gone ...'

'We'll 'ave trouble, I'll stake me 'at on it,' Kitty had said privately to Johnny later that same day. 'That old Elwyn, 'e won't lerrit rest, 'e'll come naggin' at us.'

Johnny shrugged.

'Don't matter,' he said laconically. 'A will's a will, see? A legal docyment what you can't overturn, that's a will.'

But right now the pony must be put in the trap, the trap must be loaded, and she must be off. Kitty loved market days, and was delighted when Johnny brought the pony and trap into the yard, all tacked up and ready to go. Johnny was grand, she thought affectionately. He did everything he could to make her life easier. At just seventeen he was tall and gangly, stronger than he looked but still with the boyish grin and the twinkle which had taken her fancy so strongly when they had first met.

'Ready, Kit? Put them eggs aboard, an' the beans, an' you're ready for the off. 'Ave you 'ad your breakfast yet?'

'Not yet. I'll gerrit down me quick, though.'

They ate breakfast, enjoying every mouthful. The tea was a bit weak; Maldwyn said they were almost out of tea and Kitty must be sure to buy some before she left Corwen. Just as she was about to swing herself up into the driving seat of the trap he pressed some money into her hand.

'Buy yourself a bite o' dinner,' he whispered. 'Don't go 'ungry till you gets 'ome, Kitty lass.'

Kitty took the money and gave him a hug.

'You're a prince, Mal,' she said. 'Oh, we does love you, Johnny an' me! I won't knit you another muffler – can't say fairer than that, eh?'

Maldwyn laughed and rumpled her hair. That first winter he had uncomplainingly worn the uneven, holey muffler which Kitty had painfully knitted for him, only admitting how useless it was when she had spent her egg money on a beautifully thick one, on sale at a local clothing emporium. Since then, mufflers had been a joke between them.

'You can make me some bramble jelly, instead,' he called as she swung herself into the driving seat. 'Awful fond o' bramble jelly I am!'

Soon, Kitty and the little brown pony were jogging along the road, heading for the town. She could see over most of the hedges from her lofty perch and was struck, as so often before, by the beauty of her surroundings. To her left the high hills were ablaze with the rich purple of heather and the richer gold of the gorse. The trees were still in full and glorious

214

leaf and when the road crossed a small stone bridge the stream beneath it reflected the innocent blue of a cloudless sky. It was hard to look back down the years – gawd, it was fully three years since she had run away from Paradise Court – and remember her life in those far-off days, the grim, grey hopelessness of it. It was almost impossible to realise that only fifty or sixty miles away – she was still vague over distances – people lived in conditions which she now considered a hell on earth, not even loving one another or taking care of the children of their bodies, but resenting them, beating them, sometimes, she knew, killing them. She often wondered what her mother had made of her sudden flight, whether anyone had searched for her, but had concluded that it scarcely mattered. If her mother had informed the police, the search had never extended to Corwen, or indeed to North Wales. After all, she had never pretended to be anyone other than Kitty Drinkwater and the name had never raised an eyebrow down here.

The road curved round to the left and Tilly followed it, her hoofbeats muffled by the soft road-dust. Presently, however, they met the cobbles of the town and Tilly slowed her brisk trot to a walk. The little grey town was beginning to fill up already, some stalls were set up, others in the process of erection. Kitty made her way to the market yard and tied Tilly to a tethering post. She watered her with a handy bucket, fed her a couple of apples and then began to carry her goods to her table, next to Mrs Dewi Jones's fancier stall.

Customers wandered along, poking, measuring. They exchanged jokes, gossiped, tasted butter or a piece of broken biscuit. Kitty sold a dozen eggs to a woman in an old-fashioned black cloak who asked kindly after Maldwyn and said she'd call one of these fine days and had Kitty seen the travelling fishmonger this morning?

The day jogged on its familiar course. Kitty bargained briskly, laughed a lot, swapped a bag of her string beans for a pot of heather honey. The sun rose in the sky and wasps buzzed round Mrs Dewi and had to be repulsed. They were after Mrs Dewi's plums, her big early Victorias, so Kitty swatted wasps with a folded newspaper and bought some of the plums as a treat for Maldwyn – he only grew the small purple ones – and planned plum jam, or perhaps a plum pie.

The minister came up to her stall and congratulated her on her butter. 'Best in Corwen,' he joked. 'Well, not bad for a stranger, eh, Mrs Ellis-Wynn?'

'Oh, I wouldn't call her a stranger, Reverend,' Mrs Ellis-Wynn said. 'Speaks the Welsh like a native she do.'

And Kitty smiled and sold the last of her eggs and was totally, blissfully happy.

It was growing dusk when Kitty reined up in front of the farmhouse again. Lights twinkled warmly from the kitchen. She could hear the murmur of voices, see movement through the thin checked curtains. She climbed down a trifle wearily, the heavy bag with the money in it clutched in one hand. They would be very pleased, Mal and Johnny, she had done better than ever before, sold out! She knew she should get Tilly out of the trap and rub her down before she did anything else, but she always let the men know she was home. No sense in not doing that; it meant Johnny would come out and help her and Maldwyn would begin to dish up. She had eaten a beef and mustard sandwich and drunk a pint of buttermilk earlier, but that had been hours ago and right now she was starving hungry again.

She looped Tilly's harness round the tethering post and pushed open the back door.

Johnny was sitting by the fireplace. He looked up, startled, when she entered the room. He was white as a sheet and looked ill.

'Johnny? What's wrong? What's happened?'

She knew something was wrong, the whole room reeked of it.

'Oh, Kit . . . come and sit down.'

Johnny was on his feet, coming across to her, concern on his face, his eyes red and swollen. Kitty stepped back.

'Maldwyn? Where's Mal? Why isn't he here?'

But she knew. Knew as soon as she saw Johnny's red eyes and the pallor of him, the stricken expression on his face.

'Oh Kitty, love, Mal's gone. It were a stroke, the doctor said. Not long after you left, queen. Mal's dead.'

After that, everything happened in a sort of fog. The minister came and he, the doctor and Johnny arranged the funeral. The work went on. Patch slunk round the house close on Kitty's heels; they heard her whining in her kennel after they'd gone to bed, so Kitty went down and fetched Patch up to her room. She and the dog curled up on the bed and comforted one another in their loss.

Neighbours came. Maldwyn had been well liked, loved even, for his generosity, his strength which he would lend to any in need, his strong, abiding faith. Everyone offered help to the children but Johnny and

Kitty knew that what they needed was hard work, to get them over this dreadful, sad time.

'I know 'e was old,' Kitty said to Johnny after the funeral and the funeral tea were over. 'I know 'e was jest an ordinary bloke, in a way. But we did love 'im, didn't we, Johnny?'

' 'Course we did; an' 'e loved us,' Johnny said gruffly. 'Mal loved everyone, wanted the best for everyone. Now 'e's gone we gorra do the best we can for ourselves an' the farm.'

There was no word from the relatives, but Johnny got the will out anyway. He and Kitty read it anxiously and agreed that it was clear as a bell; they had the farm.

Then a week after the funeral they had visitors. Kitty and Johnny were sitting by the fire, having eaten a quick meal. They were both very tired, for even with his lameness to contend with, Maldwyn had always done his share and more of the farm and house work.

Kitty got up and went over to the door as soon as the knock sounded. She thought it was a neighbour, popping in to see how they were getting on, but it was not. It was Elwyn Ap Thomas, his wife and his lawyer, Mr Brindley Travers.

They did not wait to be asked in but entered as of right and seated themselves by the fire even whilst Kitty, thoroughly discomposed, was stammering out an invitation to them to sit down.

'Mr Maldwyn Evans came to me to make a will,' Mr Travers said, very dry and precise and cutting across Kitty's words without compunction. 'But he made no will because I persuaded him that it was not in his family's best interests. Since, therefore, Mr Evans died intestate, or without making a will,' he added the last bit with a malevolent glance at the two young people, staring at him, 'the estate and all his possessions go to his next of kin, Mr Elwyn Iawn Ap Thomas, my client. And this means that you young people are guilty of trespass.'

'There is a will,' Johnny said quietly. 'Mr Evans didn't like your attitude, Mr Travers; he didn't trust you, either. So we went to Wrexham, where Mr Evans made his will at the office of another lawyer, a Mr Hywel Hughes, where it was duly signed and witnessed. I have the will here if you would like to see it.'

Kitty had never heard Johnny talk without his Liverpool twang before. She stared at him, astonished, as he turned away and began to fumble in the dresser drawer. Fancy Johnny talking like a toff!

Johnny found the will and held it out to Mr Travers. The lawyer snatched it, read it, handed it to his client, who read it also. Then Elwyn Ap Thomas made as if to hand it to Johnny – and instead, with an exclamation of impatience, threw the document straight into the heart of the red-hot stove.

'A tissue of lies; a forgery,' he said shrilly. 'The fire's the best place for it! Now I repeat what my legal adviser has told you; you are trespassing. We will give you one hour to get out of this house and renounce all claims to it. If you refuse to go, Mr Travers and I intend to call the police.'

His words went unheeded, for the moment at any rate. Before Kitty realised what he intended, Johnny had dived at the fire, shoving his arm into the red-hot heart of it. As he did so he gave a cry of sheer agony . . . and even as Kitty dived on him to drag him away, Elwyn ran over to him and actually tried to wedge his skinny bottom against the boy so that Johnny was forced deeper into the fire.

'Let him burn if that's what he wants!' he shouted. 'He's a liar and a thief – liars and thieves should burn!'

But Patch soon put paid to that. She snarled once and flew for Elwyn. As Kitty dragged Johnny, screaming, away from the fire, Elwyn began to scream in his turn – Patch was attached to his leg. Kitty saw the white teeth begin to redden round the edges and felt only an enormous satisfaction, a dreadful, deep hatred.

Mrs Ap Thomas was crying, stammering something, the lawyer was contenting himself with threats. Kitty got Johnny to the sink and began to pump cold water over his arm: she had heard Maldwyn say it was how he had treated his burns when he'd fallen back and sat, for a moment, on top of the stove.

'Shoved my bum into a bucket of cold water I did,' he had told her. 'Maybe not what a doctor would do, but it worked a treat, lass! Better I did feel in no time, no time at all.'

But Johnny's burns were bad, really bad. Kitty took a look and shuddered. She wouldn't let him take his arm out from under the constant stream, then suddenly he was pulled away from her. Elwyn, his face contorted, was dragging at the boy's shoulder.

'Out I said and out I meant!' he shouted. 'Out of my house and off of my farm or I'll have the police on you!'

Patch was whimpering. Kitty looked and saw that the dog was holding up a crushed paw; blood dripped slowly from it. Kitty looked round for a weapon and found the big iron frying pan. She pounced on it and backed towards the door, swinging the pan in front of her. Johnny, half-fainting, lay slumped against the sink. Patch, whimpering still, limped painfully over to her on three legs, showing her teeth at Elwyn as she passed him. He must have stamped on the dog's paw, Kitty thought, wincingly. But there wasn't much one girl could do against two determined men and a woman who was prepared to allow them to behave the way they had. She could only do her best to get them all out of here without further injury.

'Get back!' she hissed at the two men, swinging the pan. 'I'll send the pair of yez to kingdom come if you try one more dirty trick! We're goin' for now, but we'll be back . . . because this is *our* place, not yours, willed to us all legal. And we won't forget what you done tonight!'

She backed up to the door, opened it, felt the cool night air surge into the room. She dropped the pan, took Johnny's weight on her shoulder, felt Patch pressing close to her legs . . . and they were in the yard, the door of the farm slammed behind them, alone in the dark with a drizzling rain falling and puddles at their feet.

She thought of the haystack at once, of course, and the byre, the apple loft. But she was afraid. If she lay down, if she let Johnny and Patch lie down, God knew what the Thomases might do. Fire the barn or the stack? It seemed highly probable in view of what Elwyn had already done. She could hear from Johnny's sobbing breath that he was scarcely conscious of what was happening. His pain had taken over; all he could think of were the deep burns on his right arm.

'Johnny, love, you've got to reach the stable,' Kitty said urgently in his ear. 'Come with me . . . one foot at a time.'

It took ages, hours it seemed, but she got him to Tilly's stable and slumped him across the pony's back. She could do nothing about Patch's paw right now, but the dog would follow. If they could just get as far as the Jones's farm . . .

It was two miles. Two long miles. Johnny moaned all the way, she spoke to him but he could not answer, he was in some world where pain and darkness held sway. Patch whimpered and fell back, Kitty and Tilly waited, and the dog caught up.

But they made it. They reached the farm. Kitty knocked and the dogs all barked but no one came to the door. It was probably well past midnight, Kitty supposed, so you could scarcely blame them. And anyway, all they wanted was to be kept safe from the Ap Thomases for the time being. A stable would do. A pigsty even.

Kitty got Tilly into a stable and slid Johnny off into the hay. Then she lay down beside him. He was shivering uncontrollably and still moaning, choking on sobs. She put her arms round him and Patch, still whimpering, curled up close. It must have been an hour before Kitty slept, and her sleep was shallow and deeply troubled. And she, who had been so brave and resourceful awake, wept in her dreams.

Morning brought Eifion, the son of the house. He came into the barn, whistling, and stopped short.

'Duw, what the 'ell . . . ?'

'If your Da heard you, you'd cop it,' Kitty said, struggling into wakefulness. 'Eifion, bach, we're in trouble. Patch 'as got a crushed paw and Johnny's burned real bad. Tek a look.'

He looked, shuddered.

'How did 'e do that?' he whispered. 'Burnt near to the bone 'e is. Why aren't you at the farm? Was it robbers?'

Kitty told him. She told him everything. About the will which Elwyn had burned, about the lawyer lying to them, about Elwyn trying to push Johnny deeper into the fire, and deliberately crushing Patch's paw with his heavy shoes.

'Here, better see Mam,' Eifion said, white-faced. 'What wickedness indeed . . . I know nothing about the farm, but what wickedness to burn a will and try to burn your Johnny.'

'Could you fetch somethin' to carry Johnny on?' Kitty said. 'He's awful badly, I doubt 'e could walk.'

But before Eifion could do anything Johnny woke, groaned, pulled a face and got to his knees, then lurched to his feet.

'Gi's an 'and, there's a good feller,' he panted. 'Gawd, me arm's fair killin' me; what 'appened? What did them people want?'

'Never mind that,' Kitty said, shaking her head at Eifion, who had opened his mouth to remind Johnny of the previous night. 'Can you get to the kitchen? Eifion's mam will see to you.'

They got Johnny indoors. Mrs Jones was horrified over his arm, ran for a soothing lotion, for bandages to keep the air off. But Kitty, mindful of Maldwyn's home-remedy, said that she rather thought Johnny would be better to keep his arm as cold as poss-ible because that was what Mal had advised for burns.

'Oh? Yes, I remember Maldwyn saying . . . and deep though they are, they've not yet blistered,' Mrs Jones said. 'Run water, Eifion!'

Eifion ran water and Johnny immersed his arm in

it. He sighed with relief. 'It feels easier,' he declared. 'What's Patch done to 'er foot?'

Mrs Jones looked at the dog's paw, then settled Johnny in a comfortable chair with the basin of water on a table beside him and knelt to Patch.

'Nasty, but it'll mend,' she said at last. 'Fetch me some disinfectant, Eifion, and then fetch your da; milking he is, but he'll come when you tell him there's trouble.'

When the story had been told in gory detail to Mr Jones he looked worried and upset.

'That such wickedness can happen – such evil,' he said. 'It sickens me to my stomach. But what to do? The will's gone, you say? Quite burned up?'

'I tried to get it out,' Johnny said defensively. His face went sickly greenish at the memory of that dreadful moment. 'But the fire was blazin' in the range, I didn't 'ave a chanst.'

'And who else knows about this will?'

'Mr Hywel Hughes, of Charles Street, Wrexham,' Johnny said promptly. 'He drew it up.'

The Joneses looked at one another. Mrs Jones was the first to speak.

'Dewi, was that the Hywel Hughes . . .'

'Aye, that'll be the one. I don't think you should be too hopeful of help from that quarter, little ones. Who witnessed the will? Did Maldwyn not show it to anyone else?'

'Two men witnessed it. A soldier and a farmer's lad. The lad's name was Jones, though I can't recall his first name, but I remember the soldier's name because he was a scouser, like us. John James O'Hare, that was 'is name.'

'Grand. Address?'

' 'E never give it,' Johnny said. 'You don't, not on

a will. So far as 'e was concerned, 'e was jest a bloke in the street earnin' hisself a bob. Mr 'Ughes gave 'im a bob to be a witness,' he added.

'Please, why can't we go to Mr Hughes?' Kitty said, whilst the Joneses wrestled with the problem of tracing a boy named Jones and a man from Liverpool. 'Mr 'Ughes was ever so nice to us, weren't 'e, Johnny?'

'Aye; but he was old, wasn't he? Older than Mal?'

'Yes, he was a bit older. Two classes 'igher in the school, Mal told us. But why . . . ?'

'His obituary was in the paper, see?' Mr Jones said heavily. 'Well known in these parts was Hywel Hughes and well-liked, too. Not like that Travers fellow.'

'His obi . . . 'is what?'

'The feller's died, our Kitty,' Johnny said, his voice flat. 'Ain't there a law against burnin' a will though, Mr Jones? Kitty an' me 'ud swear to it, wouldn't we, Kit?'

'Ye-es, but they could say, with a certain amount of truth, that since you were beneficiaries, or claiming to be under the will which was burnt, then your testimony was scarcely without prejudice,' Mr Jones said, sounding like a lawyer himself. 'Got to find them witnesses you have, or you're going to have a job to prove your claim.'

'Didn't you ever see the will, Dewi?' Mrs Jones said suddenly. 'Maldwyn was a good friend – did he never show you the will?'

Mr Jones shook his head.

'No, and perjure myself I cannot, nor would Maldwyn expect me to do so,' he said. 'He was straight, Maldwyn, straight as a die.'

'And you didn't see hide nor hair of it?' his wife said persuasively. 'You never heard it mentioned?'

'Oh aye, it was mentioned, several times. Maldwyn told me he intended to leave the farm to the boy . . . and to Kitty, of course . . . and I applauded the idea since the young people had worked hard for him. But not a line in writing did I see.'

'Oh well; perhaps you will find the witnesses,' Mrs Jones said, looking hard at the two of them. 'The law's a strange thing – that a lawyer can perjure himself without a second thought but a farmer cannot . . . and if that Elwyn Ap Thomas comes here to live, he'll regret it if it's the last thing I do.'

'He'll sell,' Johnny said sombrely. 'That was what Maldwyn allus said – that 'is nephew cared for nowt but money.'

'It'll take a while to prove, wi' no will to back him up,' Mrs Jones said thoughtfully. 'There's a cousin in Australia and another nephew in Canada – swear to it I will. That'll give you time to find those witnesses, the pair of you.'

'And in the meantime, you've a home here,' Mr Jones said decisively. 'That arm must mend, Johnny bach, before you go searching for anyone. And when you do go, we'll keep Patch safe against your return. They won't want her but she's a grand worker with the flock, grand. Now let's have some breakfast, Bronwen my dear, and later I'll drive into Corwen, have a word with a legal friend or two, see how you stand.'

'We'll never forget what you done for us,' Kitty said, her eyes bright, suddenly, with the tears which she had never shed when she was struggling to bring them through safe. 'Even if we ne'er 'ave the farm, we won't forget, will we, Johnny?'

And Johnny, leaning back in his chair, his eyes dark-rimmed with pain and fatigue, agreed they never would.

Johnny and Kitty stayed with the Jones family for a week. At the end of that time Johnny took Kitty aside to the barn for a serious talk.

'We can't stay, Kit, no marrer 'ow nice they is to us,' he said bluntly, as soon as he had made certain they were alone. 'We're wastin' time, chuck. We gorra find them witnesses.'

'Yes, I suppose ... only isn't Mr Jones's friend doin' 'is best for us? Mr Jones said 'is friend would go to Wrexham, try to see if 'e could tek a look at that Mr 'Ughes's papers an' that, see if there were a record, like. Shouldn't we wait for 'im to say what 'appened?'

But Johnny was of the opinion that time spent waiting was time lost.

'The sooner we git after them fellers the likelier we are to find 'em,' he urged. 'Let's start to tramp tomorrer.'

Kitty felt they were being too hasty, but on the other hand, she felt guilty at eating the Jones's food and sleeping in their truckle beds, especially if they were never going to gain their inheritance and so would be unable to pay the family back for all their kindness.

And Mrs Jones agreed with them that they should be doing something.

'I remember reading somewhere that possession was nine-tenths of the law, and them Thomases will be snugging down an' taking over more with every day that passes,' she said worriedly. 'What's more, if they sells it whilst you're doing your finding out, it 'ud be rare difficult to get the farm back I shouldn't wonder. As for Patch, you may leave her here and she'll be well looked after, I'll treat her like my own. Then you must come back, see, to pick up the dog and decide what to do next.'

This made sense to Johnny, and even Kitty could see the logic of it. What worried her, though, was that she could see Johnny was anxious to be off, not necessarily because of the farm, but because he didn't really think they would ever get their inheritance, and wanted to return to the tramping life while his arm mended at least.

'We will try though, won't we, Johnny?' she asked anxiously as the two of them left the Jones's on a crisp, bright morning, with blackberries all over the hedges and button mushrooms spangling the pastures. 'We won't just give up an' let them 'ave it all?'

'Course we's goin' to try. Only first we gorra pick up our gelt,' Johnny reminded her. 'I took the money Mrs Jones lent 'cos I don't want *no-one* to know we're not penniless, see? If them Thomases ever found out . . .'

'Do you know, I'd forgot the wages?' Kitty said, considerably heartened at the recollection of Johnny's secret hoard. 'That'll keep us in grub for a week or three, eh, Johnny?'

'Oh aye, that'll see us awright. So we'll 'ide up in the old shepherd's 'ut till dusk, then go down and get our gelt, then be on our way.'

'Where'll we go first?' Kitty enquired.

'We're goin' straight to Wrexham to see if we can find that lad, though I admit without 'is name it's a faint 'ope,' Johnny told her. 'And after that it's back 'ome, queen, because wi' a name like John James O'Hare that sailor should be easier to find. My, but ain't it good to 'ave a purpose again?'

And Kitty, striding out step for step with him

through the bright, cold morning, with a thick coat on her back and food in a bag slung over her shoulder, had to admit that it was better to be trying to claim their rights than just sitting at the Jones's farm, feeling thoroughly miserable.

The day spent in the shepherd's hut proved rather more interesting than they might have wished, and that was because, not an hour after they had settled in, they heard someone approaching up the hillside, pushing stealthily through the thickness of dead bracken, making for the hut.

'Git under the 'ay,' Johnny hissed at once. 'It can't be them Thomases, but jest for sure . . .'

They hid under the hay, scarcely daring to breathe. As they lay there, they heard soft little movements outside and then someone – or something – pressed a nose to the crack of the door and inhaled deeply. Then, even as Kitty began to scramble out of concealment, there was a short, sharp bark. A let-me-in bark.

'Oh Patch, whatever are you doing here?' Kitty said, hurling the door open and dragging the dog inside. 'Oh dear, what will the Joneses think?'

'They'll guess,' Johnny said. 'Wonder if she'd go back if we told 'er to?'

'No she wouldn't,' Kitty said stoutly, both arms round the dog's neck. 'She's comin' with us, Johnny. She'll be no trouble, honest to God!'

'Well, it might be best,' Johnny said vaguely. 'I just 'ope no one saw 'er.'

'Nor 'eeded that bark,' Kitty said rather apprehensively. 'I'll tek a look outside I think.'

But when she opened the door and peered down

the hillside, there was no sign of life from the farm. In fact she spent most of the day spying on the Ap Thomases, and very boring it proved. Not until noon did they put in an appearance, and then it was Mrs Thomas, curl papers in her hair and slippers on her feet, slopping out to the yard and across to the byre.

'They 'aven't got the cows in; don't they know cows 'ave to be milked?' Kitty said angrily. 'What's 'appening to 'em? They won't 'ave no stock left.'

'They sold the cattle day after we left; I never said nothin' because there weren't nowt we could do,' Johnny said. 'Best that way, at least the beasts won't be sufferin' from their iggerance.'

'True. Then why did the ole woman go to the byre?'

'Daft Penrhos is workin' for 'em,' Johnny muttered. 'They kep' one cow so Eifion told me.'

'Oh. But Penrhos really *is* daft; 'ow can 'e work for anyone?'

'Dunno. Forget it. 'Sides, they coul'n't git anyone else to go there. Folk think they're 'orrible, even them what sez blood's thicker'n water.'

'Oh.' Kitty withdrew from her spyhole for a moment. 'I wish the sun 'ud go down.'

'It will. 'Ave a sleep, chuck, or you'll not want to walk tonight.'

Kitty thought she would never sleep, but she did; boredom drove her to it. And when she awoke it was because Johnny was gently shaking her shoulder.

'Wake up, queen,' he said, very low. 'You'll 'ave to watch for me. Keep Patch quiet, though.'

Together, the three of them stole down the hillside. The stars were out and a thin curl of silver moon lit the night. The kitchen window was the only one illuminated at the farmhouse and the smoke from the chimney went up straight as a die. Johnny touched Kitty's arm and indicated it.

'No wind. Good.'

He led them round the farm and past the old orchard to a piece of pasture where Tilly sometimes grazed. It was pitted and pocked with rabbit holes and as soon as they reached it, Johnny began to peer at them and to count under his breath.

'One, two, three, four, five . . . turn right. One, two, three . . . turn left. One two three four . . .'

He wove around, finally coming to a halt beside one particular burrow.

'Right. Don't watch me, queen, watch the 'ouse.'

Kitty turned her back on him and stared at the lighted window, but before she had grown bored with the view or tempted to peep there was a light touch on her elbow.

'Gorrit! I've took the lot, no point leavin' none. Come on, let's 'ead for Wrexham!'

Chapter Ten

Gibraltar isn't a very big place, and it is said, by Gibraltarians, that if you stand in Casemates Square at the bottom of Main Street, everyone who is anyone will pass by you in the fullness of time. Art, wandering along with his hand solicitously cupping the elbow of a pretty young lady, was about to test the truth of that saying.

'Hey, Art! Arthur O'Brien, don't you dare walk by me and never a word!'

Art stopped so suddenly that his companion gave a squeak.

'Oh, Art, 'ow rough you are, you jerked at my arm! Who calls to you? Ah, a young man – do you know 'eem?'

'Well, well, well!' The young man, short and broad with curly hair and dark eyes, seized Art's hand and pumped it up and down. 'I never thought to see you here . . . how are you, old feller?'

'Tippy Huggett! What on earth are you doing in Gib?'

Tippy laughed, still holding Art's hand as though loth to let him go.

'Just visitin', same as you, I daresay. I signed on as a deckhand on a cruise ship – the *Mersey Wanderer*; lovely vessel. She's lying offshore even as we speak, so I come over to buy me mam some pretty china. It's said to be cheap here. Art, where in 'eaven's name 'ave you been these past years? Why, only the other week I was ashore in the Pool and I met young Lilac whatsername . . . she were askin' after you.' He seemed suddenly to become aware of Art's companion and his face crimsoned hotly. 'On'y a friend, like,' he said hastily. 'Jest interested, that's all.'

The girl smiled at him, her teeth a flash of white in her dark face. Art turned to her and said something in a foreign tongue. The girl nodded, gave Tippy one last curious glance out of a pair of magnificent dark eyes, then turned and disappeared into the crowd.

'Who were that?' Tippy asked curiously. 'She was very pretty, mind. A friend o' yourn?'

'Local girl; mother's my landlady,' Art said almost absent-mindedly. The burning question on his mind had nothing to do with Hortensia. 'I sail from the port of Gibraltar now, when I'm not working ashore, that is. I haven't been back to the Pool for, oh, ages. What were you sayin' about Lilac? I know she's married, but . . .'

Tippy stared, then frowned.

'She ain't! Well, if she is, it's a well-kept secret. She's Miss Lilac you know, of The Waterfront Academy of Modern Dance on Mount Pleasant; t'other one's Miss Charlotte. They've got a great little business I'm tellin' you, great.'

'But I saw her! Leastways I saw her wi' a babe in her arms, bouncing it up and down and making it wave to the ships. So I thought . . . naturally I thought . . .'

'Oh, the baby! That'ud be her niece, Nellie's lass,' Tippy said knowledgeably. 'She dotes on little Elizabeth they say. But your Lilac's doing well for herself and just about everyone knows her. She's the receptionist at the Delamere Hotel – you know, the big, smart hotel on Tythebarn – and she has that dancing school.'

'And she isn't married? You're sure, Tippy old pal?'

'Certain, sure,' Tippy said stoutly. 'She reckons you are, though. Says that must be why you haven't come back. She keeps her eyes open, asks all over. And since a good few of her pupils at the school are seamen she'd probably hear if you did come back.'

'Dancing! Here's me thinking her a prim little house-wife darning socks and making meat pies, while really she's working in a posh hotel half the time and teach-ing dancing the other half.' Art grinned from ear to ear. 'Well I'm damned! And definitely not married, you say? Engaged, though? I guess she's engaged?'

'Nope. Told me last time I asked that there was safety in numbers and besides, she was waitin' for someone.' He grinned at Art. 'I didn't ask who that might be, old friend, because I thought I knew. And judging from the look on your face, I weren't so far wrong.'

'But we – we had a real bust-up,' Art protested. 'Called each other every name we could give tongue to. And after that I tried to find her and couldn't. Not immediately, of course, while I were still mad, but later when I'd cooled off a bit.'

'No, well, she left the bag and sack factory, see. *And* the place in Lord Nelson Street. I suppose you looked at one or t'other? And she said she did try to find you, haunted Exchange Flags, went over the Mersey to Hamilton Square and asked the clerks in the bank if they could 'elp . . .'

'And I'd gone, o' course,' Art said with a groan. 'I tried the factory and Lord Nelson Street, but I felt an almighty fool so I didn't ask, not for ages. I kept well out of sight and just hoped to walk into her; be accident-on-purpose, if you get my meaning.'

'Well I'll let you into a secret; I heard Lilac even

went back to the Court; yes, she bearded your family in their den, and your mam never liked her you know, then she tried the shipping register and spent all her spare time at the docks, even asked your old friends what 'ad become of you. Only we didn't know either, see, so we couldn't help. But *now* . . .'

'Tippy, tell her . . . oh Gawd, if only I could just up and go, but I've got a responsible job here, I'm with a small concern, I couldn't just let them down. Look, will you take her a letter? No, go round and see her, tell her I'm coming home as fast as I can . . . here, don't you go off, I've got a room up Bell Lane, over a confectioner's shop. Come up there with me, we'll have a bevvy together and a meal and you can write her address down so I can drop her a line. Tippy, you were always a good pal – you've done more for me than you know! She *isn't* married, she don't have a kid . . . and she's waiting for . . . for someone. I can't believe it, you know, I keep thinking in a moment I'll wake up and it'll have been another dream.'

'Well, it ain't no dream and neither am I,' Tippy assured his old friend. 'Look, I don't know your Lilac's address because I'm not in the habit of visiting ladies' flats . . . well, not other feller's ladies, anyway . . . but if you send the letter to Miss Larkin, care of the Delamere Hotel on Tythebarn Street, that'll find her.'

'Wonderful,' Art said. 'I'll never forget this Tippy, never! For as long as I live you'll be me bezzie!'

'I thought I were your bezzie anyway,' Tippy said. 'Even when you didn't write, didn't get in touch, I still reckoned you were me best pal and kinda hoped I were yours.'

'I've been a fool,' Art muttered. He turned left off Main Street and drew Tippy up a steep and narrow alleyway between tall, thin buildings with balconies above their heads. About fifty yards or so up the alley he stopped outside a heavy mahogany door. He unlocked the door with a large iron key and it swung inwards, revealing a tiny square lobby and a flight of stairs.

'Here we are; follow me but go careful, the stairs are steep and pretty dark.'

The two young men climbed the stairs and stopped again on a narrow landing. Art put another key into another lock and flung that door open too.

'My place,' he said. 'It's small, but it does me well enough.'

Tippy looked around. He saw a pleasant room with a double bed on one side and a screen folded back beside it. A long, narrow window was curtained in a good deal of white lace but since it was open, the curtaining was blowing out more or less straight so that Tippy could see the houses opposite, no more than six or eight feet away. There was a square of carpet on the floor, a kitchen section with a gas ring, a low sink and a wooden draining board, and the rest of the room held books, flowers, pictures and ornaments, a small desk, a dining-table and chairs.

'Neat, eh?' Art said with obvious pride. 'Hortensia is a good homemaker and she's proud of the way she keeps my room. Always fussing around she is, getting me bits and pieces.'

'Hortensia?'

'The girl I was with. Hortensia Valilodad.'

'Art! So Lilac was right, you are married!'

Art looked offended.

'I am not! I suppose I could call her my landlady, since her parents own the whole block, but in fact she's just a friend. She's taken me under her wing, cooks for me, cleans for me . . .'

'Sleeps with you?' Tippy said bluntly.

Art looked self-conscious.

'I've been that lonely, Tip, and unhappy, too, thinking that Lilac had gone and married some feller . . . and it's not as if we live together or anything like that, it's just that occasionally . . . and she needs pretty things which I'm happy to give her – I earn good money: if I can bring her a bit of happiness . . .'

'I guess I don't want to know,' Tippy said hollowly. 'But Art, if you're going to write to Lilac, go home to the Pool . . .'

'It won't happen again,' Art assured him. 'I told Hortensia a little bit about Lilac, so when I tell her I'm going home, that Lilac isn't married after all, she'll understand. She's a sweet girl, not like some. All she'll want will be my happiness, I assure you. Now what do you want to drink? The ale's quite good and I bought a loaf and some cheese this morning . . .'

After Tippy had gone, Art lay on his bed gazing at the ceiling and thinking about Lilac. What a fool he'd been to jump to conclusions, not to check that she really was married, had a child. And how could he have forgotten that Nellie had been expecting a baby . . . of course she lived in London, but he should have guessed that she would come back to see her beloved adopted sister. And the man who had put a casual arm round Lilac's waist – now that he thought about it seriously, he realised it had been a brotherly rather than an amorous gesture. It had been Stuart, of course – what a complete and utter duffer he had been! But Tippy had removed his obstinate, self-imposed blindness and now at last he could see!

*

237

'Pig and son of a pig! Take that . . . and that!'

Crash! went the blue pottery vase on the wall beside Art's head, scattering water and spikes of Spanish lilies as it flew through the air. Hortensia, her dark eyes flashing magnificently, her bosom heaving, reached blindly for the next object, and a silver fruit bowl, complete with its usual complement of oranges, grapes and bananas, took wing. Art ducked and winced as it met the window-pane squarely and crashed through it, then winced again as a startled roar announced that the fruit bowl had scored a direct hit on an innocent passer-by.

'Hortensia, listen to me! I never promised . . .'

'You . . . are . . . a . . . dog!'

The ivory paper knife in the shape of a crocodile was lighter than the fruit bowl. In the interests of not utterly thwarting the thrower, Art did not duck and gasped as the paper knife caught him across the Adam's apple.

'Ouch! Hortensia, if only you'll listen for a moment . . .'

'Deceiver! You took my innocence . . . in my mother's house . . . English swine, liar, thrice-cursed!'

She was running out of throwables, Art saw thankfully. Unless she started on the saucepans and the cooking utensils of course.

'Darling Hortensia, we had an agreement . . .'

'Pig! I say you are a pig and a liar! An agreement . . . poh-poh! I spit on our agreement!' she spat. 'You told me you loved me, you said one day . . .'

She started on the saucepans. Art, who had bought them and had chosen cast-iron knowing it to be the heaviest and longest-lasting of materials, began to duck in earnest.

*

Lilac had had a really awful day. The hotel had been fully booked but she had been approached by a regular customer who wanted a bed for a couple of nights. She had juggled and moved people around and at last managed to persuade two ladies that they would be better off sharing a room rather than paying twice as much for a room each. The regular customer was grateful, but the chef, a man of great talent but uncertain temperament, was not.

'I have no spare salmon; it is all very well, Miss Larkin, to say that one can always fit someone else into the dining room, but food can only be stretched so far. First it was thirty-eight, then forty, then forty-four. But forty-five people, if they all mean to have the salmon, will all go a little hungry and will blame me – me, who does the marketing, prepares the food, plans the menus . . .'

'I'm sorry, Monsieur Arrat,' Lilac said sincerely. 'Can you not serve one person with melon in place of smoked salmon?'

'I have no melon,' Monsieur Arrat said sulkily. 'There was none in the market this morning, it will have to be tinned grapefruit, and no guest would choose tinned grapefruit when he could have my smoked salmon nestling in a bed of scrambled egg. Since it is all your fault you had best go and purchase some more salmon before all the shops shut.'

So Lilac, who should have been heading homeward, had to make her way to Byrom Street, to a fishmonger highly regarded by Monsieur Arrat. She bought smoked salmon, added half a dozen fresh eggs so that she might make herself an omelette when she

239

finally reached home, and set off for the hotel once more.

She arrived to more chaos. The chef was satis-fied with the extra salmon but the housekeeper had counted the sheets back from the laundry and found two missing. She had sent a kitchen maid round to Chung's Chinese laundry on Smithdown Road because her chambermaids, who should rightly have gone, finished work at four. So Lilac's first task was to face Monsieur Arrat once again when he discov-ered that his favourite peeler of potatoes, who should have been hard at work on the next day's supply, was missing from the scullery.

By the time she had sorted everyone out, forced the housekeeper, a bad-tempered old woman who should have been retired years ago, to apologise to the chef, gone into the kitchen herself and arranged the wafer-thin slices of smoked salmon in curls, ready for the creamy scrambled egg, she was almost as inclined to scream as the chef had been. And far from going home and throwing herself on to her bed to rest, she was due down at the Academy in . . . gracious, in an *hour*, to take her turn at teaching the latest craze to cross the Atlantic, the Black Bottom.

So when Mrs Brierson called to her as she was crossing the front hall she very nearly pretended to be deaf and continued on her way.

Nearly, but not quite. After all, it was scarcely her employer's fault if things had not gone right. Lilac smiled and turned towards the desk.

'Yes, Mrs Brierson?'

'A letter for you, Miss Larkin. It came care of the hotel, but I think it's personal. Here you are.'

An ordinary brown envelope with handwriting on it. Lilac took it, glanced at it as she went to pop it into her handbag — and froze. She stared down at the well-remembered writing like a bird stares at a snake. It was Art — Art writing to her, after all this time! It had been years, without a word, and now a letter — what could it mean? Good news . . . or bad? Suppose he was writing to her to tell her he was married, with children? If so, she would rather not open the envelope, would sooner stay in ignorance for the rest of her life . . .

No. That wasn't true; not knowing had been the worst part. Very soon she would know and either way, she guessed it would be a relief.

'Miss Larkin? My dear, you've gone quite white! Does the letter contain bad news, perhaps?'

'Bad news? No, indeed. It's a letter from an old friend, a friend I've waited to hear from for these past two years. It's good just to see his writing again to tell you the truth, though I was . . . am . . . surprised that he's got in touch after so long.'

Lilac continued with the movement of pushing the envelope down into her handbag. She smiled up at Mrs Brierson and her employer, clearly relieved by her words, smiled back.

'Well, that's good news, as you say. Good night, Miss Larkin.'

'Good night, Mrs Brierson,' Lilac said, her voice lifting. She hurried out of the hotel and, in the road outside, looked at her handbag longingly. Should she stop and open it now? But the March evening was chilly and besides, she wanted her own room, her own company, when she opened the precious envelope and read the letter she had waited so long to receive. She hurried on her way, suddenly realising that she'd not so much as looked at the stamp or the postmark, all she'd done was stare at the handwriting.

He might be anywhere – he might be in this very city!

But by the time she reached her flat common sense had reasserted itself. If he was in Liverpool he would scarcely have written, he would have called round. No, he must be away somewhere . . . but she would know soon enough.

She reached the hallway, climbed the stairs, unlocked her dôor. She loved her little flat, took a great deal of pride in it, but this evening her eye flicked heedlessly across the potted fern by the front door, the arrangement of daffodils and narcissus in the tall white vase, the pictures in their gilded frames, the soft, Welsh wool rugs. All she wanted was to get the lamp lit so that she might settle down in her chair and read her letter.

She lit the lamp, threw off her coat, plumped down on the scarlet velvet cushion laid negligently on the seat of her chair. She took out the letter, slit the envelope with a trembling finger, and drew out the two lined sheets of paper. For a moment she simply checked that she had not made a mistake, that it really was from Art. She found that she remembered in greatest detail everything about his writing, how he dotted each *i* and crossed each *t*. Yes, she knew it was he, without reading a word. She sighed deeply, happily. Then began to read.

Dear Lilac,

I'm sorry; there, I said it first! I made a God-awful fool of myself that day in Miss Young's Dining Rooms and I've been sorry ever since. It was loving you too much you see, queen – when you love someone like that everything they say is terribly important, terribly serious. So all I could think was that I'd muffed it and lost you for ever. And Lilac, love, if I had really lost you for ever then I didn't want to go on living, didn't care if I lived or died.

I ran away after that. I told myself I was going to be independent of you, make a life for myself without you, but really all I was doing was running away, and there's nothing to be proud of in that. I did come back though. After a twelve-month. I searched all over but you'd good as vanished, or so it seemed. I know now that you'd changed your job and moved away from Lord Nelson Street, but at the time I thought you'd probably met someone else and married them. Daft, eh? And then, when I'd given up and signed on for another voyage, I actually saw you. Down on the dock, with a baby in your arms and a fellow beside you.

I know now that it was Nellie's baby and Nellie's fellow, too, but at the time the bottom fell out of my world. I reached Gibraltar and saw a job advertised, for someone to do the paperwork and accounts for a small shipping line. Sometimes I'd be on board their cruisers – they have two passenger ships – and at others I'd be in Gib, doing the paperwork etc.

I took the job, got myself a flat, began to try to forget. Only I couldn't, not quite. And then I met Tippy Huggett and he told me you weren't married, nor engaged. He said he thought there was a chance for me . . . I was over the moon, queen, over the moon! If I could have I'd have handed in my notice right away and hopped on the first Liverpool-bound vessel I saw, but I've got a deal of responsibility here and I couldn't do it to them, they're decent folk, they depend on me.

Besides, queen, I don't know how you feel! Could you drop me a line, let me know whether there's any

*hope? I'll give you my address at work, since I've
recently changed my lodgings. And if there is a chance
of us getting together again . . . well, I'd move heaven
and earth for you, my darling girl.*

 With love from
  Art

Lilac read the letter through three times, very slowly. The first two times her hands were trembling so
much that the paper fluttered like a leaf in the wind,
but by the third read she had got a hold of herself
and she simply let the flooding, overwhelming joy
take charge. She hugged herself, she kissed the
letter, she thanked God, Tippy Huggett, Art, even
the ship which had brought the letter, the postman
who had delivered it. Then she jumped up and went
over to the kettle standing on the ring and lit the gas
beneath it. She felt absolutely certain that at long last
things were starting to go right. She clutched the letter, her magic talisman, her good fortune, and kissed
it again, noticing that she had, at some stage, shed
tears all over it, which was not the sort of thing she
usually did, being a sensible and down-to-earth young
woman.

But I'm not sensible or down-to-earth, not where
Art's concerned, she told herself giddily. I'm in love,
I'm in love, I'm in love!

Presently the kettle boiled and she made herself
a cup of tea and read the letter again. And again.

Then she sat down and wrote a reply.

Kitty and Johnny stayed in the Wrexham area for
a while, then left, their search a failure.

'Askin' for a feller called Jones is like askin' for a

fish in the sea,' Johnny said disconsolately. 'Every-one's called Jones, jest about. And everyone shops in Wrexham on Beast-market day, every blamed one. We aren't agoin' to find 'im, so we'd best search for t'other un.'

'Yes, awright,' Kitty agreed, not without some reluctance. She no longer feared her parents – she doubted if they would recognise her if they met in the street, nor she them – but she was afraid of the city. Even when she was full-grown with a job and money in her pocket she thought she would never forget the miserable conditions at her home in the Court, nor the hunger which had gnawed at her morning and night, a hunger deliberately fostered, she had come to believe, by her mother. And not only did she remember the hunger, she would never forget the complete lack of love, the hatred even, which her parents had shown towards her.

But then she remembered the other Liverpool, the one of her summer wanderings, when the city had taken her to its warm and generous heart. Liverpool had sheltered her beneath its posh doorsteps, fed her from its rubbish bins and its vegetable gardens, shown her its parks and gardens, its beauty at dawn and sunset, its miles of glorious waterfront. And it was not just the city, it was the people, many of whom had been kind to her. Best and first was Mrs O'Rourke of course; Mrs O'Rourke had quite simply given her a reason for living. Then there was the girl from Penny Lane, the stop-me-and-buy-one boy, the people who gave her pennies for carrying their par-cels or food because they saw she was hungry. There were others; a scuffer, telling her off for loitering in the park because a rich old woman had complained, and slipping her tuppence when no one was looking;

coming back next day with a pair of clogs and a grey woollen cardigan. She'd lost the clogs to a bigger child and popped the cardigan one day when food was scarce, but they'd been given from kindness and she had appreciated it.

And Johnny. When he was scarcely more than a kid himself he'd taken her under his wing, cleaned her up, chopped off her verminous hair, destroyed her filthy rags and given her some self-pride. And he was a Liverpudlian, just like her.

Yet still, when Johnny announced that they would go home now, cross the Mersey, she felt a stab of fear, of very real reluctance. She put a hand on Patch's collar, gaining comfort from the dog's closeness; Patch would not desert her, no matter what. Suppose her mam had set the scuffers on her? Suppose her dad was home and recognised her, beat her up? But it was pretty unlikely; only a ninny would worry about things like that and she was no ninny, she was Johnny's chosen companion, she had all but been the owner of half a farm – and might be again if they could track John James O'Hare down!

'So will we hoof it, or travel like lords?' Kitty asked Johnny as they came out from the barn where they had spent the night. 'Weather ain't up to much.'

Johnny looked up at the sky and sniffed suspiciously. The wind was getting up and the clouds overhead were moving fast. Even as he looked, a faint, misty rain began to fall.

'Hmm . . . what'll it cost on a train, eh?'

They enquired and Johnny shook his head, half sadly but half gladly too, Kitty was sure.

'Nah, we aren't partin' wi' that much gelt! 'Sides, they wouldn't be too keen on lettin' Patch ride, I daresay. We'll do it on foot in a couple o' days.'

'Right. I like to hoof it,' Kitty said loyally. 'And we ain't in that much of an 'urry, eh, Johnny?'

'We'll tek it easy,' Johnny promised, and indeed they both enjoyed the walk.

It was evening on the third day when they reached Birkenhead. They caught a ferry, Patch squeezing between the two of them as unobtrusively as possible, and stood silently at the rail watching the port gradually approach, then disembarked with the other passengers.

'We aren't sleepin' rough in the streets, we'll go to a lodgin' house,' Johnny said authoritatively as they began to move uphill. 'There's doss 'ouses for sailors along the waterfront, we'll go there.'

'I can't, not a doss 'ouse for sailors,' Kitty reminded him. 'Don't be silly, Johnny.'

'Sorry, I forgot. But there's places where we can both go . . . I'll get us a bed, don't worry, queen.'

They found a cheap lodging after several unsuccessful efforts. At the first place the bedding was filthy and stank of stale sweat and urine. Kitty, with wrinkled nose, told Johnny it wouldn't do and the pair of them turned away, followed by screeches from the offended landlord. At the second place they were told they would have to share a bed and tie the dog up outside and though they agreed to do so, when they went into the room every bed was already occupied by at least one person.

'Tell one of 'em to shove up,' the landlord hissed. 'Den slip in beside 'um.'

They were luckier on the third attempt. They were each given a bed-roll of reasonably clean materials – a thin straw mattress, a lumpy pillow and a blanket – and shown into a large room where a number of people already lay sleeping on the floor. Patch, it was agreed, might sleep on the floor by their bed.

'I didn't want to share,' Johnny muttered. 'Not with some of our wages still left, but us'll 'ave to mek do tonight. I'm wore out.'

So the two of them put their mattresses one atop the other, wrapped themselves in their blankets and cuddled up like puppies. And very soon Patch sneaked onto the mattress with them, adding her warmth to theirs. Kitty thought she would never manage to sleep but it had been a long, hard walk through some pretty rough weather. They both slept within ten minutes of their heads touching their pillows.

Next day Johnny decreed they should split up.

'I'll do the docks, you an' Patch do the streets at the back o' the docks,' he said. 'Don't forget – John James O'Hare. Tell anyone what asks there's a reward, that'll fetch 'im out if 'e's around.'

'I'll try the boozers an' the schools,' Kitty volunteered. 'An' the snooker 'alls an' the workin' mens clubs.'

Johnny stared at her.

'Kit, I knew you was a bright kid, but you's bloody brilliant!' he said. 'You'll strike gold afore me I've no doubt . . . where'll we meet?'

'Inside the Shamrock Café on Preesons Row, if they'll let Patch inside,' Kitty said promptly. 'If not, outside.'

When she had lived in the city she had often hung round the Shamrock, wooed by the rich and delicious smells which came from it and also by the friendly way satisfied customers, seeing her wistful face as they came out again, would chuck her a penny or even save her something to eat – a crusty bread roll spread with butter, or a little cake with currants in.

'Preesons . . . oh, yeah, I know it; just off Derby Square, ain't it?'

'That's it; opposite the Victoria Memorial. What time?'

'Oh, say six o'clock. We don't want to go on after dark. If I'm not there on time it could mean I found 'im, though, so 'ang about a bit.'

'What if you're hot on his trail though, Johnny? Or what if I am, come to that? Where'll we meet then?'

'Back at the lodging 'ouse, I reckon. Here, I'll gi' you some cash so's you can git yourself a meal or a bed. But I reckon we'll meet at four.' He raised a hand, turned to go, then turned back. 'You sure you'll be all right, Kit? Sure you wouldn't rather we stuck together?'

Kitty would much rather have stayed with Johnny but she saw his point; Liverpool was a big city and John James O'Hare just one rather insignificant young man. To find him could take weeks, but if they split up and searched separately it could halve their labours.

'Nah, it's awright, this way's surer. An' I've got Patch; she wouldn't let no one 'arm me. See you at six, then.'

At six o'clock prompt, Kitty was walking up Preesons Row. She had met one O'Hare, though he turned out to be Tom and not John, but meeting him had been a lucky chance which cheered her up considerably and made her think that maybe their search would be crowned with success after all.

'An' aren't I sorry I'm de wrong feller, an' you

wit' Irish eyes an' de sweetest smile?' Tom O'Hare said genially, when Kitty had explained her quest. 'But haven't I a brudder, Jamie O'Hare, and a cousin wit' de very name you mentioned? Cousin John's a seaman, too, he may be in port now for all I know. I'll mek some enquiries for yez, sweet'eart . . . tell me where to find you again!'

'Me and my brother are meeting at the Shamrock Café in Preesons Row at six this evening,' Kitty said, making a lightning decision. 'If you've any news, we'd be real grateful if you'd join us there then.'

'Well, unless I get a ship soon me time's me own,' Tom O'Hare said, and suddenly his face looked sad for a moment. 'I'll be glad to do what I can to 'elp, chuck.'

So despite having called in at a dozen pubs and engaged a great many people in what turned out to be fruitless conversations, Kitty was still feeling rather pleased with herself as she reached the Shamrock. She glanced round but there was no sign of Johnny, so she went inside, Patch as close as a shadow, her soft nose touching Kitty's calf.

It was as lovely as she had always imagined it to be. With Johnny's money in her pocket and her nice clean clothes on her back, with her hair neatly bobbed and her body well-nourished, Kitty allowed the waitress to take her to a window table, sure that no one would ever recognise in her the little waif of years ago. She explained to the waitress that Patch was well behaved and would lie quiet, and said she was waiting for a friend. However, as the time began to pass she decided she might as well eat – after all, Johnny might easily have had some luck and be talking to their quarry this very minute. She ordered brown Windsor soup, scrag-end stew and two veg, followed by strawberry blancmange, and she bought a cornish pastie for Patch, who ate very daintily, without crumbs. The meal cost tenpence, and was accompanied by a round of bread and butter and a cup of tea. We should come here every day, Kitty thought enthusiastically, drinking her soup the way Maldwyn had advised, from the side of the spoon and without any slurping, either. We won't get better value than this anywhere, and all three of us have got to eat!

She knew she was eating quickly and tried to slow down, but even so the meal was finished before Johnny had put in an appearance. There was a clock on the wall saying ten minutes to seven; Johnny wouldn't expect her to wait any longer, she would have to leave. But they'd meet up at the lodging house, later. Kitty put her face close to the window and peered out. There was someone out there . . . she hadn't misunderstood Johnny's directions, had she? He had said meet inside and not out?

She half-rose from her seat, then sank back again. It was a child outside, not an adult, hovering as she, Kitty used to hover, sniffing the lovely smells of hot cooked food, thin as a stick and clad in a raggedy little dress which barely covered her bony bottom.

That might have been me, Kitty thought, awed. Poor kid . . . she looked round her. She had eaten her entire meal, but that could be remedied. She beckoned the waitress over.

'Excuse me . . . could I have a – a bacon sangwidge to tek out wi' me? And one of them curranty cakes?'

'That's another fourpence,' the waitress said. 'Shan't be a tick, miss.'

She disappeared and came back moments later with a thick, steaming bacon sandwich and a currant cake. She put them into separate brown paper bags and handed them to her customer.

'There y'are, miss. I 'opes as 'ow you enjoy 'em.'

'Thanks. Goodnight.' Kitty struggled into her coat, touched Patch to rouse the dog, and then, with some reluctance, left the warmth and brightness of the small café for the chilly darkness outside.

For a moment she thought the child had gone, then she saw her again. She was coming across the road like a moth to a flame, and as she passed close by, Kitty spoke.

' 'Ere, I couldn't eat all that lot – like to finish it up for me?'

The child turned towards her and in the glow from the gas lamp overhead, Kitty saw her face.

A thin face which had once been round and rosy, with the blonde hair once tied back with white ribbon straggling unkempt and verminous down to her shoulders.

Recognition was instant and two-fold.

'My Gawd . . . Bet!'

'Well, if it ain't our Kitty! Oh Kit, where've you been? You do look grand . . . is that f'me? Oh, I's so 'ungry . . .'

Betty Drinkwater, for it was undoubtedly Kitty's little sister, almost snatched the proffered sandwich. She crammed it into her mouth, the grease running down her chin, and swallowed it in huge, wolfish bites. Kitty bent over the better to see the child. Tears rose, unbidden, to her eyes and trickled down her cheeks.

'Betty?' she whispered. 'What is it? What's 'appened? Our Mam allus fed you littl'uns proper, it was on'y me what went so short I could've ate road-dirt. Where's the twins? An' the others?'

'Arny were run down by a tram and died in the 'ospickle,' Betty said thickly, through the sandwich. 'Bob ran off a long whiles back. Our Da went off about then . . . three year ago, it'ud be. Mam said 'e might of been killed, but someone told Bob 'e'd gorra lass into trouble out Crosby way. And Mam's real ill, awful ill. I's scared she'll die an' leave me to fend for the kids. I does me best, Kit, but I's allus hungry, allus cold.'

'I remember,' Kitty said feelingly. 'Oh Betty, what-ever can I do? Mam hated me, you know, if she sees me face she'll probably snuff it anyroad, from shock and 'orror – I suppose she thought I was dead, eh?'

'Never said,' Betty mumbled. She was finishing off the sandwich, holding on to it so fiercely that her fingers were almost meeting through the bread. 'Good riddance, she said, and suffin' about serpent's teeth.'

'There you are, then, she ain't goin' to welcome me back, exactly.'

'No . . . I mean yes, she would!' Betty exclaimed. She looked up at Kitty, tears trembling on her lashes. 'Oh Kit . . . please come back, please! I's on'y ten, I dunno which way to turn, honest to God! I jest know they'll all die an' it'll be my fault an' I'll 'a been a bad sister to 'em.'

'Well, I was supposed to be meeting a friend,' Kitty said doubtfully. 'Look, 'ang on a minute, I'll leave a message wi' the waitress just in case 'e turns up. But I'll see 'im later, explain.'

Kitty went back into the Shamrock, asked the waitress to tell Johnny, should he turn up, that she had had to leave but would be at their lodging house before ten that night, and went outside once more.

She took Betty's hand and perhaps it was that which decided her. She had taken the child's hand many times in the past and had always liked the feel of the plump little girl's cushiony palm against hers. But now Betty's hand was just like a claw, whereas Kitty's own hand had flesh on it, and muscles in the wrist.

'You really will come 'ome? You an' the dawg? Jest for a minute, to see our Mam?' Betty said tremulously. 'Oh, Kit, you're real good; I allus knewed you was the best of us. Arny an' Bob were 'orrible to you and when you went they was 'orrible to the rest of us. Arny was wuss'n Bob, even.'

'Shouldn't speak ill o' the dead,' Kitty reminded her sister gently as they made their way across Derby Square and dived down Castle Street. 'Still, you've 'ad a bad time, chuck, I can tell.'

'It weren't too bad till our Da went,' Betty admitted. 'There was food, when 'is 'lotment come, and Mam went on wi' 'er sewin'. But fust our Da went an' then Mam were took bad . . . there won't be nothin' for 'em tonight . . . ' the child stopped dead in her tracks, her expression stricken. 'Oh, Kit, an' I ate that sangwidge!'

'I'll buy a loaf an' some cheese, when we reach the Scottie,' Kitty said hastily, seeing that more tears were about to fall. 'Don't worry, we'll feed the kids tonight.'

Far from cheering Betty up, however, this seemed to bring on a fresh attack of misery.

'You was often 'ungry, Kit, an' I knew you was, an' I never give *you* owt 'cos I were afraid of our Mam,' Betty wailed. 'Mam said you was such a wicked kid, see, an' you was older'n me an' I didn't know, then, 'ow it 'urt to 'ave an empty belly.'

'Well, we both know now,' Kitty said ruefully, feeling that tears were not too far from her own eyes. 'An' we'll do our best to see it don't 'appen again. Come on, queen, step out or we shan't get back to the Parry afore the shops close.'

She meant it as a joke since the shops would not close until nigh on midnight, but Betty took her seriously and scuttled along clutching her sister's hand, scarcely bothering to talk any more.

And presently they reached the Scottie and Kitty pulled Betty into George Lunt's for a large loaf, and a little further up the road into Costigan's grocer's shop for the cheese. But knowing that the money Johnny had given her would have to last, she bargained in Lunt's for a yesterday's loaf and told Mr Costigan that she would take cheese-ends if he'd any going cheap.

'An' I'll tek a couple o' tins o' conny-onny,' she added grandly, 'an' a twist o' tea.' She remembered that her mother often drank tea when she had run out of more alcoholic beverages and besides, milk was good for the kids. It seemed strange to acknowledge that her mother would not have milk in the house because she'd become used to a constant supply on the farm. But the milkman only came round Paradise Court in the mornings and Sary had never patronised him; she used the sweet, thickened condensed milk in her tea and in anything else which needed the addition of milk.

Without being asked, the man in Lunt's had given them a paper carrier bag, so the cheese and milk were piled on top of the loaf and Betty hung onto Kitty with one hand as though she feared to let her go. With her other hand she was busy eating the currant bun the baker had popped in on top of the loaf.

It was strange, turning off Scotland Road into Burlington Street after so long. They passed the fishmonger whose boy had been the start of all

Kitty's adventures – Kitty thanked him from her heart as she went – and then crossed over Titchfield Street, passed a couple of court entrances and there was Paradise Court itself, looking to Kitty's eyes more like purgatory than paradise at that moment.

They went into the Court itself. It was very much smaller than Kitty remembered, and unbelievably shabby. The flags were layered in filth, the one gas-light sputtered fitfully, showing leaning doors, cracked window panes, a broken chair and an abandoned mattress with the stuffing leaking out. As though Kitty's horror was palpable, Patch pressed harder against her leg and gave a small whine. Kitty automatically fondled the dog's smooth head, then stared around her once more.

'Gawd,' she said in an awed whisper. 'Gawd, it's wuss'n I remembered, an' that's sayin' suffin'!'

'Yeah, the welfare lady said it were run-down,' Betty murmured. 'There's almost no one 'ere in work, though, our Kit. It ain't just our Da an' Mam, there's others an' all.'

'What about the Hallorans? An' the Percivals?'

'They left. Moved, I means. It's bad 'ere now, our Kitty. It's the Fletchers what done it.'

'Done what?'

'Oh, brung it low. They're allus in trouble an' they're a big fambly. Mam, Da, a couple o' aunts, an uncle, three big gels, a dozen kids . . . Mam says the gels 'ave sailors in.'

'Oh,' Kitty said, following Betty's example and keeping her voice low. 'It's quiet now, though.'

'Oh ah; they'll be at the boozer,' Betty explained. 'Better come in, our Kitty; that's our Eth cryin'. Poor bitch, she's 'ungry. Ruthie don't holler much; younger, see. Used to it, I dessay.'

Betty stumped up the step and pushed open the creaking door.

'Mind the Drop,' she said. 'They're in the front.'

They were. Two small girls, all thin and ragged, though neither quite as thin as Betty. Eldest always gets it hardest, Kitty thought, then moved forward, doing her best to smile. The lamp was lit but it was sending out some pretty fierce fumes; she wondered if the children could see who she was or could recognise her if they did. Four years is a long time when you're only eight or nine.

Betty took hold of her hand and led her forward; Kitty could feel Betty's pride in her, as though by producing their big sister she had done everyone a big favour.

'Here's Kitty come 'ome,' she said softly. 'Eth, stop snivellin', she's brung food, an' a dawg! Did you 'ear that, Ruthie – we got grub!'

Two ragged heads swung towards her; two pairs of dull eyes brightened. Kitty produced the loaf, the tins, the cheese. The smallest girl, a child no more than two years old, held out her hands, cupped, in a gesture of begging so painfully eloquent that Kitty had to swallow a lump in her throat.

'Bread an' milk,' she said to Betty. 'I'll open the tin, you crumble some bread into – into somethin'. I don't remember Ruthie, she must've been born after I left.'

'I 'member you, Kitty,' Eth said.

She must be nine, it stood to reason she was nine, but you could have thought her five or six. And there had been others, there was Phyllis, and Mo . . .

'Where's Phyllis and Mo?'

'The Welfare took 'em, just after you left; never

257

seed 'em since,' Betty said briefly. 'Mam said they'd be better off.'

'I remember when you was 'ome, Kitty,' Eth said suddenly. 'Mam were allus . . .'

Her voice died away. She looked avidly at the chunk of loaf which Betty was crumbling into three empty bully-beef tins.

'Can someone fetch water?' Kitty said.

Eth got to her feet. Her nose was running and she staggered as she tried to walk. Quickly, Kitty caught hold of her and sat her down again, on the bundle of old newspapers and rags which dominated the room.

'S'awright, queen, I'll go meself. You'll feel better presently, when you've ate.'

She went out to the yard, the kettle in one hand, and filled it at the communal tap. Returning to the front room, she looked hopefully at the grate. No wood, no coal, nothing but long-dead ashes. And it was a chilly evening.

'No fire? Oh well, I daresay it'll go down just as well cold,' she said cheerfully, hacking a hole in the can with a rusty tin opener and mixing the milk with water until it was of a pouring consistency. She made the bread and milk and handed the children the tins. They ate with their fingers, lacking spoons, and with feverish haste. Then they looked at her; they said nothing, just looked.

'Bite o' bread an' cheese?' Kitty said. 'Ain't much else, but I'll go round next door presently, get 'em to boil us a kettle. Then we can 'ave a drink o' tea.'

'Oh Gawd, I forgot! Mam . . . come up an' see Mam, there's a dear, Kitty,' Betty coaxed. 'She's poorly . . . you might know wha's wrong.'

'I shan't, an' the sight of me is bound to mek 'er worse,' Kitty said uneasily. 'Oh, awright then, I'll jest tek a look.' She turned to Patch, sitting gnawing on an ancient bone she must have found somewhere. 'Stay 'ere, there's a good gel.'

Betty lit a stub of candle and they left the two little girls single-mindedly chewing bread and cheese in total silence and climbed the rickety stairs. At the head of them was a tiny landing, with the children's slope-roofed room to their left and the main bedroom to their right. Kitty peeped through the doorway, not venturing to enter, expecting either a storm of abuse or possibly even a missile. But there was nothing. Not even movement.

Encouraged, she ventured further.

Sary Drinkwater lay on her back on the old brass bedstead. She had a pile of rags over her and her hair hung over her face in a wild tangle. She heard the two girls in the doorway and slowly her big, untidy head swung towards them.

Her face was frightful. Her eyes were bloodshot and screwed up against the fitful candlelight, her skin was blotched and purplish, her toothless mouth hung open; saliva ran down her chin and puddled the rags beneath her head.

'Mam, 'ow d'yer feel? We brung food, an' there'll be a cuppa presently.'

'I could do wi' a cup.' Sary's voice was slurred and her eyes seemed scarcely to move, but she had taken in something at least, as her next remark proved. 'Who's your pal?'

Kitty put out a warning hand but it was too late; Betty was in full flood.

'Why, Mam, it's our Kitty, come 'ome to look after us till you're well agin! Doncher reckernise 'er?'

Sary peered, then half-closed her eyes.

'Kitty?' she said in a wondering voice. 'Not Kitty Drinkwater?'

'That's right, Mam,' Kitty said, preparing for flight. 'I jest popped in to . . .'

'Kitty! Me eldest . . . me best . . . Gawd, I thought you'd gone for good, thought you was dead . . . an' you've come 'ome! Oh Kitty, love, things 'ave been that bad for us sinst you left, things 'ave gone cruel 'ard. Oh praise be, she's come 'ome!'

Kitty said gruffly that she had indeed and backed carefully out of the room. Downstairs again she wondered, as she worked on the food, what she was to do. Betty had convinced her that the family were in dire straits, but the interview with her mother suggested to her that things were worse than even Betty knew. Sary Drinkwater was not ill; she was mad. And madwomen, Kitty suspected, didn't get better. Did this mean that she would have to stay here in this vile and abominable place, rear her three sisters and feed them all by her own efforts *and* see to the great, creaking hulk of a madwoman in the bed upstairs?

I'd sooner die, Kitty thought desperately. I can't do it, I'd much sooner die.

But she knew – none better – that death didn't come for the asking, and that duty, that horrible word, had a way of forcing itself upon you. Could she leave Betty, Eth, and little Ruthie to starve? Could she leave them, even, to the mercy of the madwoman upstairs? I had Mrs O'Rourke for a bit, and I managed somehow, she told herself. They've got nothing, and they won't manage, they aren't strong enough.

But others as strong as she and with more reason to stay had just run off. First Da, then Bob. Why should she stay, when they'd deliberately driven her out all those years ago? Why couldn't she give them the rest of her money, spend one night with them and then cut and run, back to Johnny, and the hope of the farm, the promise of the open road and good company?

I'll see what Johnny says, she told herself much later that night, when she and Patch sneaked out of the house and set off across the city in the direction of their lodging house. He'll advise me, tell me what to do for the best.

But Johnny wasn't at the lodging house.

'Seen neither 'ide nor 'air of 'im,' the landlord said. 'Still, you an' the dawg's welcome if you've got the dosh.'

'Not tonight,' Kitty said. She felt numb with fear. What she most dreaded had happened, she had lost touch with Johnny! Then she remembered that they could both read and write. 'Look, can I leave a note for me brother? You'll give it to 'im when 'e does come?'

'Aye, I'll give it 'im,' the man agreed. 'Want a bit o' paper?'

He found Kitty a crumpled sheet and a stub of pencil and Kitty, after much thought, just told Johnny that she'd gone back home to help out and could be found at 8 Paradise Court.

' 'E'll come for us,' she told Patch as they walked back across the city. 'Johnny'll not leave us 'ere.'

She returned to the lodging house after a couple of days. The landlord said no one had been, no one had asked for her. Kitty could only think that Johnny must have found their witness and taken him back to Wrexham or the farm. After she'd gone, the landlord chucked her note on the fire. No use keeping it since he'd forgotten all about it when the lad had come looking. Best put the whole thing out of his mind. Cheeky mare, using him as a bloody notice-board!

After three days, she decided Kitty would have to leave the family to fend for themselves and actually go in search of Johnny. It was clear that their plan had failed in some way and she could not contemplate staying here in this dreadful house. That's what I'll do, tomorrow, she vowed to herself late that night, as she and Patch joined the little girls in the pile of rags and old newspaper which was their bed. Tomorrow I'll give 'em what's left of Johnny's money and split. There's so little I can do anyway ... I'm only one, they need an army of helpers to get them right. Well, I'd better get a doctor to the old woman 'fore I go or she'll pop her clogs and the kids'll get sent to the workhouse or worse – what's worse, come to think? And I'll clean the place up or they'll die of filth and vermin ... I saw a rat in the back kitchen, scuttling across the floor bold as brass, good thing we finished up the bread and cheese!

So she promised herself an escape in the forefront of her mind, but in the back of her mind, where truth lies waiting, she knew she could never do it, never desert them. And when sleep claimed her she wept in her slumber and her sobs woke little Ruthie, who burrowed through the rags and curled up against Kitty's chest and seemed to comfort her a little, for the weeping gradually slowed and stopped.

But Kitty's dreams were dreadful.

Chapter Eleven

Lilac had always been a hard worker, even-tempered and patient, but once she had written to Art telling she was every bit as sorry as he – sorrier – and received a reply which could only be described as lyrical, she was so cheerful, so happy, that even Charlotte remarked on it.

'And not only are you grinnin' from ear to ear day and night,' Charlotte said accusingly one morning, 'but you're singin' and laughin' and gettin' through a huge amount of work . . . it ain't natural, our Li!'

'What's unnatural about happiness?' Lilac said, on her hands and knees polishing the dance floor. 'Anyway, you should be grateful; Mrs Higgins never got a shine like this on it – you can see your face, just like in a mirror!'

'That's what I mean . . . who wants to see their face in a dance-floor? A quick mop-over would have done very well.'

'It needs polishing,' Lilac said, rubbing away. 'To tell you the truth, Charlotte, I've got so much extra energy that I hardly need to sleep at night! I know Art and I won't be able to get together at once, because he's got to arrange for someone to take his place for a couple of weeks . . . that's what we've decided, incidentally, that he'll come here for a fortnight whilst we do our arranging and get ourselves wed, then we'll go back to Gibraltar for a bit, just until Art can arrange something over here. And we're going to have a little honeymoon in New Brighton, because when we were kids Art was always saying that one day we'd go there, and the day we fought and he went off we'd planned to spend the afternoon there. So a honeymoon there will be a long-delayed treat . . . oh, I'm looking forward to that little honeymoon just as much as if it were Venice or Rome we were visiting! After that we'll go back to Gib and he'll start trying for jobs over here.'

'How can you get a good job in Liverpool from Gibraltar?' Charlotte said doubtfully. 'It's hard enough when you're actually livin' here!'

Whilst her friend polished the floor she was rubbing up the window panes, plumping the cushions on the small chairs and dusting the skirting boards.

'Yes, I know, but Art's awful good at mathematics, a real genius. And he's had all that experience now in running a small shipping line, so he hopes perhaps one of the big shipyards – Cammel Lairds or somewhere – will take him on.'

'Yes, I suppose that's possible,' Charlotte admitted. 'But things are pretty bad right now, they say even people in quite good positions are losing their jobs. And you're doing so well, queen – the hotel can't manage without you, the dancing academy needs you – why quit when you're on top?'

'I've already told you; because Art is also doing well, and making good money. And though I really enjoy reception work and I love the dancing school, for Art I'd – well, I'd give it all up.'

'So that's being in love, is it?' Charlotte mused. She stood on one of the spindly chairs and reached up to dust the upper sash. 'And all these months I've been wishing it would happen to me – I must have been mad!'

Lilac giggled.

'I've decided I don't know the first thing about love,' she said frankly. She knelt up the better to consider the matter. 'First I thought it had to be exciting, then I thought it had to be dangerous. Then I decided what I really wanted was security, and love would have to be accompanied by loads of money . . . and then I lost Art and I knew what I wanted. I wanted him, Charlotte, at any price, under any circumstances, I wanted him until I ached with it, until it was all I could think about. So now we've mended our quarrel and are planning a life together, I can't help but be happy. But I don't know whether it's love, or whether it's something quite different, I just know that without Art there isn't much point to my life. Is that love? You tell me!'

'I guess it is,' Charlotte said rather wistfully. 'It's so long since I was in love that I find it quite difficult to remember. I wonder, do fellers feel the same?'

'Art does,' Lilac said contentedly. 'He's just like me; his letters are one long grin . . . if you understand me.'

'I do,' Charlotte sighed. 'Oh, Li, you are so lucky!'

Over in Gibraltar, in his temporary room in Irish Town, Art went through the days in a similar daze of happiness to that which Lilac was enjoying. He had found the perfect flat for a young married couple; it was on Town Range and it overlooked Trafalgar Cemetery in which lay the men who had died at the Battle of Trafalgar many years before. It was a pretty cemetery, with big old trees, beautifully kept gravestones, and it was cool and peaceful even in the warmest weather. Because the new flat was right at the top of an old house it was quite private, which would be better, Art considered, for a newly married couple, and it had recently been modernised. It was near the shops so marketing would not be a problem, but near the harbour, too, and Lilac would be able to catch a bus to Rosia Bay whenever she wanted to spend an afternoon on the beach.

But we probably won't stay here long, Art told himself as he arranged for a year's rental on the flat. We'll be wanting to get back to Liverpool ... I mustn't forget Lilac's dancing school; she and her friend Charlotte have built it up from nothing, it would be a sad shame to let it go. And anyway, once our children are in school she might be glad of a little hobby.

Children! The thought of having a family, living in a neat little house like the one Nellie and Stuart had shared in Penny Lane, was a dream of which Art thought he would never tire. He could just imagine it all, the neat red-brick house with a little garage at the side for his motor car (when he could afford one) and four good bedrooms upstairs, one for the girls, one for the boys, one for he and Lilac and the last one a spare room, for guests. Then downstairs the big, modern kitchen with a gas cooker and an Aga to heat the water. A proper front room, all carpet and cushion covers, a back garden for the veggies and a front one for flowers. Oh aye, he'd got it all planned out, all right.

He didn't want a big family, even though the Catholic faith frowned on birth control. Art had attended Mass on a Sunday and gone to Sunday School, listened to the Father and done his best to be a good person in his own quiet way, but where Lilac was concerned everything else went by the board. He had quite made up his mind that he would be the best husband ever, so there was no point in having kids like doorsteps and ruining Lilac's health and figure. Too many kids keep you poor, Art thought, and I don't want my kids to have what I had – more kicks than kisses – nor to find them turned over to an orphan asylum like Lilac was, if the worst happens and one of us dies. Didn't the good God give me self-control, as well as this great love of Lilac burning in me breast? Well, I reckon we'll have two boys and two girls and then shut up shop. There's something nice and satisfying in a family of six . . . a bit of a squeeze in me new car, perhaps, but we'll fit in somehow when we go off to New Brighton for the day, or across the river and into the blue hills of Wales.

He talked to his employer about a fortnight's holiday; Mr Bassano was willing. His small company was flourishing, he liked Art, appreciated the additional time the younger man put in without ever expecting more money or any sort of perks. What was more, Art was straight, told his employer everything and made sure that Mr Bassano was not cheated.

'Take a fortnight . . . take longer if you need it, Mr O'Brien,' Mr Bassano said generously. 'When you bring your young lady-wife back with you we'll have a grand party to celebrate your wedding . . . but you will come back? I don't know how we managed before you came.'

Art assured his employer that he would most certainly return and began preparations for departure. He moved out of Irish Town into the flat in Town Range and spent happy evenings choosing furniture, pictures and ornaments. Hortensia's farewell fling meant that he had had very few breakables left when he moved out, but he enjoyed buying new ones, anticipating, with each purchase, Lilac's pleasure in the pretty or practical, mundane or unusual.

He was wandering back up through the town one evening, having had a drink with some friends, when he heard his name called. He had been about to cross Convent Place but had paused to watch the guard change in front of the Governor's Residence, and on hearing his name he turned and saw Mr Bassano, waving vigorously. Art stopped and waited for the older man to catch him up.

'Mr O'Brien, I'm glad I caught you,' Mr Bassano panted. 'My old friend Albert Edwards has come to me . . . his purser aboard the *Queen of the Straits* has been taken ill; he's done some juggling around and now tells me that he has a berth for a temporary purser aboard the *Queen* . . . she's a sizeable cruise ship and she sails tonight for Liverpool, she'll be berthed there for two or three days . . . would it help you to clear up your arrangements if I released you for the duration of this voyage? Albert would be grateful, and I daresay we might manage without you for the period in question.'

Art could scarcely believe his ears; a chance to get back to Lilac now, to talk over their plans in person . . . to hold her in his arms for the very first time!

'Me? Go back to the Pool for a couple of days? Oh, Mr Bassano, it would be – I can't tell you—'

'Good. You sail in three hours. Can you be ready?'

'I'll be there in fifteen minutes,' Art gasped. No time to telegraph or telephone . . . but what does it matter? 'This will make things so much easier . . . thank you, Mr Bassano!'

And Art was as good as his word; he was aboard the *Queen of the Straits* in less than an hour and working in the purser's cabin ten minutes later. And that night, when he eventually got to bed, having got his books up to date and his passenger lists sorted, he was too excited to sleep.

Liverpool! He was going home for the first time for ages. Unexpectedly, without a fanfare, no one waiting at the docks for him – and it was the best thing which had happened to him since he was a nipper and had first set eyes on little Lilac Larkin in her pink silk dress!

They docked at eleven in the morning. The waterfront was busy but not unusually so. Art had stood at the rail as they approached the port, devouring it with his eyes. Never before had the Liver birds seemed more welcoming, never before had the city shone so white and gold in the sunshine, the sky such a perfect arc of blue above! He knew he would not be met but to his surprise, on stepping ashore he was greeted.

'Well, if it ain't Art O'Brien!' A hand seized his shoulder and spun him round, another hand seized his. 'How do, whack! Don't say you've forgot your old friend Matt?'

Art gaped.

'Well, blow me down, if it isn't Nellie's little brother! I've not seen you since you went to sea . . . oh, it must be half a dozen years back.'

Matthew McDowell grinned, still holding Art's hand.

'There weren't nothin' much to go back to the Court for, not once Aunt Ada died and Nellie moved out. I say, that's a lovely feller Nellie's got herself, ain't it? I bin dockin' in London these past few years, and it's been grand to 'ave our Nell an' 'er Stuart to visit, a family on the spot, like. But didn't I 'ear you was in a bank or an office or some such t'ing?'

'I was, but I left. I'm at sea on and off ... look, do you remember Lilac?'

'What, the kid our Nell took on? Little Lilac Larkin?' Matt's grin widened. 'I 'member her chuckin' a pile o' spare ribs at your 'ead and kickin' an' swearin' ... eh, grand little kid!'

'Well, I'm going to see her later, but I'd like a bevvy an' a cheese barm first. Come with me? We could go to the Sparling Hotel, it's only just across the road. Have a chat about old times.'

'Well, I dunno ...' Matt said slowly. 'On t'other 'and, I'd like to see young Lilac again.'

This was not at all what Art had bargained for but his doubts must have shown in his face, for Matt thumped him on the shoulder with a friendly fist, accompanying the gesture with a guffaw.

'S'awright, la', I were 'avin' you on! You was always sweet on our Lilac from the time you was little, I do 'member that much! Right, let's go to the Sparly, 'ave ourselves a bevvy or two. You stayin'at the Corry, then?'

Art shook his head.

'Nope. I send money ... but I'm only here for a couple of days, I'd sooner book into a lodging house near where Lilac works, so we can have some time together. We're getting married in a few months.'

'Tyin' the knot, eh?' Matthew whistled. 'Well, good for you, young feller! Lilac were in the bag and sack factory, but our Nellie said something about betterin' herself, hotel work, was it?'

'Oh aye, it were hotel work, and she's done well for herself,' Art said proudly. 'She's the receptionist at the Delamere Hotel on Tythebarn Street, and she's got a—'

'Dancin' school on Mount Pleasant,' Matthew finished for him. 'That's right, our Nell said to pop in there some time, get meself a few lessons in all the latest steps. Well, since it's all in the family, Art old feller, why don't you book in at the Delamere? She'd gi' you special terms, no doubt.'

Art stared, eyes rounding.

'Well, I never would have thought of that! Yes, why not? I'd like to see the look on her little face when I walk in, bold as brass, and ask for the best room in the house!'

'You won't git more'n two words out afore she's hangin' round your neck,' Matt said shrewdly. 'Tell you what, let's 'ave a bob on it, eh? Ten to one she'll be givin' you an 'ug afore you've opened your mouth.'

'You'd probably win,' Art said ruefully as they turned into the Sparling Hotel. 'Look, I'll buy the grub and the bevvies now an' if she gives me time to ask for the best room in the hotel, you can pay me back.'

Art and Matt enjoyed their meeting, their meal – which turned into something a good deal more convivial than a barm and a bevvy – and above all, reminiscing about old times. Art had not kept in touch with the inhabitants of the Court because working in a bank and then leaving the city had isolated him, but Matt knew everyone and everything and was only too happy to pass on all the news.

'I got relatives all over,' he said proudly, as the two of them sat at a window table, sipping their ale and waiting for their food to arrive. 'There's me brother Charlie down south, me cousin Lou in New York and me other cousin, Jessie, in France . . . she

271

married again, you know, a Frog of all t'ings . . . and then me mates are mostly at sea . . . odd, ain't it, that I still get this yearnin' for 'ome, and that 'ome is still the Pool?'

'We all suffer from it,' Art said wisely. 'I've got a good job in Gibraltar, ashore mostly, an' I'll be taking Lilac back wi' me when we're married, but we shan't stay abroad. It'll be Liverpool again for us, just as soon as I can get a decent job back here. Mind, we'll do awright in Gibraltar; it's a good place to be.'

'Oh aye; 'alf the navy an' most of the garrison would agree wi' you there,' Matt said. 'Here comes our grub – eh, you can't beat the Pool for good grub!'

Lilac came on desk duty at lunchtime, having spent the morning sorting out the books, the rooms and the staff. The chef wanted to change the menu; an artist of his calibre, it appeared, could not be content to cook the same food week after week after week. He desired to make a raspberry mousse encased in puff pastry and served with fresh cream for dessert.

'In October?' Lilac said despairingly. 'Why not make it an – an apple mousse? Or a lemon one? At least I could send someone round to the shops for lemons without being laughed at.'

'You meestake,' Monsieur Arrat said, wagging a finger the size and shade of a pork sausage under her nose. 'Or per'aps I should say you underestimate ze wonders of ze rrrrailway.' He always became very French when thwarted. 'Scottish raspberries, Mees Larkin, Scottish raspberries!'

'Oh? Are they in season now? I'm sorry, I didn't know,' Lilac said humbly. It paid to be humble when dealing with an aristocrat of the pastry board, like Monsieur Arrat.

He nodded earnestly, beaming at her and patting the air with one hand as though an invisible child stood before him.

'Zey are in season. And I wish also for ze best beef, in strips . . . 'ow ees eet called . . . ?'

Having sorted out the menus for the week to the chef's satisfaction, Lilac then accompanied a new chambermaid round a bedroom, showing her how a bed was made, how a well-handled feather duster could remove cobwebs from lampshades, picture rails and long net curtains, all without knocking anything askew, and how a little vinegar applied to a mirror and then buffed vigorously with a soft duster could bring an immaculate, smear-free shine.

After that it was cashing up and telephone bookings, after that it was seeing the sewing woman about sides-to-middling some well-worn best sheets so that they could be used for the staff bedrooms in the attics, and after that Lilac had a light lunch on one end of the kitchen table whilst the staff flew around getting ready to serve twenty-eight guests with something a little more elaborate than Lilac's cold beef and pickle sandwiches, and coffee.

She had just finished her ice-cream when Mrs Brierson came into the kitchen, fanning herself with the reservation book.

'Well, if Mr Robeson tries to book in again, Miss Larkin, I hope you'll send him packing . . . or rather, assure him we're fully booked,' she said with a rueful smile, sinking into the chair opposite Lilac's. 'Not only does he complain about everything, but he insists on doing so at the top of his voice in the most public place he can find. And now Miss Jenkins in Room

8 tells me that he made a very strange remark to her when he met her on the landing in her dressing-gown! Have you nearly finished your luncheon, my dear? I've left Miss Skidmore on the desk, but she isn't really qualified ... I felt I must have a break and a cup of coffee or I'd expire.'

Lilac got to her feet.

'I had almost finished,' she said. 'If I may, I'll take my coffee up with me. I'd love to know what Mr Robeson said to Miss Jenkins though I don't suppose we'll ever find out. Thanks for a very nice luncheon, Monsieur Arrat,' she added diplomatically.

The chef, about to serve home-made bread rolls with cream of asparagus soup, nodded distractedly, and Lilac took the reservations book and left the room, climbing quickly up the stairs to the reception hall. She sat behind the desk and drew the account book towards her; best check who had already paid their bills and who still needed reminding.

Her head was bent over the book when the swing-door from the lobby was pushed open. She saw, out of the corner of her eye, a tall figure enter, and so instead of studying the figures she pushed the accounts to one side and drew out the reservations book. She ran her finger down the page ... it appeared they had only three new guests so far today, and as Miss Jenkins and Mr Robeson had both left and the Elgin family had paid and gone soon after breakfast there were still a fair number of the better rooms available.

The man approached across the well-polished wood-block floor. Lilac kept her finger on the new line but looked up at him, beginning the bright, pleasantly professional smile with which she greeted would-be guests.

'Good aftern ... Oh! Oh, oh, oh!'

She was out from behind the desk and throwing herself into Art's arms before he could even open his mouth. She clung like a burr, like ivy to a wall, like a lass to her lover, whilst Art held her gently, then tighter, then tighter still, and kissed the top of her red-gold head and then lifted her off her feet to claim her mouth.

Lilac pressed unbelievingly against him. The warmth of him, the strength, the wonderful familiarity of him – yet they had never cuddled properly before, just the odd snatched kiss, her scolding, him apologising, and the feel of his hand, big and warm, round hers, their sides touching as they walked along the pavement, argued, fought ... made up. She sighed, a great sigh fetched up from her boots, and relaxed, letting happiness, incredulity, stunned belief in the miracle, all wash over her in turn.

He was here! She knew that this must be a dream because really he was hundreds of miles away, on that little rock sticking out into the Atlantic Ocean which was Gibraltar, but yet he was here, in her arms. They were going to get married, he was coming back in a couple of months and they would marry and ... oh dear God, the feel of him, the safeness, the security of his touch!

Art broke the embrace first. He held her away from him, his grey-green eyes scanning her face as though he could never see enough of it, his toffee-coloured hair crisply short as she remembered it, his teeth white against the tan she had never before seen on his normally city-pale face. But it was the face she wanted to see, and the fact that she suddenly saw that he was not only her beloved Art, but also an extremely handsome young man, did not matter. It was a bonus, but one that was simply not necessary. I would love him, she thought with deep contentment, if he was ugly as a pan of worms; when he's old and bent and grey I'll love him still. What a curious thing love is, when just his touch can start a long, slow burn of desire for him within me, yet I don't want to go to bed with him particularly, I just want to be with him!

'Well, sweetheart – surprised?'

'Oh, darling Art – *so* surprised! You said not for another eight or ten weeks, my hair's a mess . . .' she touched the smooth, red-gold mass of it, bunched up on her head in a velvet band, falling on either side of her face in tiny, wispy kiss-curls. 'And I'm wearing the most miserable old dress and ugly old flat shoes.'

'You look wonderful. You'd look wonderful in rags, in—'

'Miss Larkin! Whatever would your fiancé say?'

Mrs Brierson's voice cut across his words, and despite the laugh in her voice they jumped apart guiltily. Lilac's cheeks felt suddenly hot and she saw Art's eyes shift uncomfortably. She turned towards her employer, standing behind the reception desk.

'Mrs Brierson, I'm sorry, I took one look at Art – Mr O'Brien – and everything just went straight out of my head! He isn't supposed to be here for at least a month . . . I still don't know what's happened . . . it's just so wonderful to see him! Oh Art, I'm on duty for another five hours . . .'

Art turned to Mrs Brierson and sketched a tug at a non-existent cap.

'How do you do, Ma'am? You'll be the Mrs Brierson I've heard so much about,' he said gravely, extending a broad, tanned hand. 'I was about to book meself a room in the hotel when this young person rushed round the desk and grabbed ahold of me. Your staff can be very welcoming to a man fresh from a long sea voyage, I must say!'

Mrs Brierson laughed and blushed and shook Art's hand.

'How d'you do, Mr O'Brien,' she said, twinkling up at him. Lilac saw proudly that his looks and charm had quite won her employer's heart. 'I'm sure you really are Mr O'Brien, for Miss Larkin is a most restrained young person as a general rule.' She turned to Lilac. 'In the circumstances, Miss Larkin, perhaps you would like to take the rest of the afternoon off? I'll book Mr O'Brien into Room 6, with the compliments of the management.'

'I can pay me whack,' Art protested. 'I was going to do so, it never crossed me mind . . .'

'My dear young man, Miss Larkin is as good as an extra right hand in this hotel; when you and she come back to Liverpool, if she is still interested in this sort of work, I intend to ask her to take her job back, and how I'll manage for the year or so you'll be in Gibraltar I don't know,' Mrs Brierson said frankly. 'That is why I've been talking to business friends about getting you employment over here . . . but having met you, I'm sure you'll find yourself work very quickly – and good work, too.'

'Oh, Mrs Brierson,' Lilac sighed, still clutching Art's arm as though reluctant to let him go, and beaming at her employer with starry eyes. 'We'll come back as soon as we can, won't we, Art? And nothing would make me happier than to work here again . . . I so love the work, the staff . . . you've been so good to me, made me so welcome, taught me so much . . .'

'Good, that's settled then. Now if Mr O'Brien would just sign the register, I'll show him to his room whilst you get your things together, Miss Larkin. Then if you

277

could bring Miss Skidmore in from the office and tell her to stay on reception until she's relieved we shall be organised. And we'll see you in the morning.'

'Miss Larkin, you're a very fortunate girl; that is the nicest young man I've had under my roof for a long while. And to think you sent him packing years ago – and you could have been happily married all this while!'

'I didn't appreciate him until he went,' Lilac said happily. She had come into the hotel next day to find all the staff singing Art's praises. He was sensible, helpful, he made the girls laugh, and had sent a message to the chef to say that dinner last night had been the best meal he'd eaten for many years. And now to have Mrs Brierson, a woman she respected deeply, telling her all over again how lucky she was to be engaged to Art, put the seal on her pleasure.

'What's more, you're having the day off,' Mrs Brierson said now as Lilac went to slip out of her jacket. 'You've got a great deal of arranging and planning to do; Mr O'Brien explained. He says it will be an early December wedding – such a festive time of year, my dear – so we're doing the reception here, a really first-class buffet, the chef told him what would be seasonal then. And Mr O'Brien wants you to get your dress at Blacklers, I told him they do the most beautiful wedding gowns . . . I've already discussed menus, the guest-list, bridal attendants . . .'

'Is there anything left for me to do?' Lilac said, standing behind the reception desk and looking round her rather dazedly. 'Flowers? My bouquet? Who are my bridesmaids?'

'Well, Mr O'Brien knew you wouldn't want too

much fuss since it's got to be a Register Office wedding, so he thought your niece Elizabeth should hand you a lucky horseshoe, and his sister Etty and your friend Charlotte might be your attendants.'

'Lovely, just who I'd choose,' Lilac said. 'Did Art . . . Mr O'Brien I mean . . . tell you what he gave me, yesterday afternoon?'

'No, dear,' Mrs Brierson said vaguely. She appeared to be making more lists and was running her eye absently down the latest one as she talked. 'What was that, then?'

Lilac held out her left hand, waggling the third finger slightly.

'Look!'

'Oh, the prettiest ring!' Mrs Brierson exclaimed, taking Lilac's slim fingers in hers. 'I declare, that *is* a lovely ring. What is the stone?'

'It's an amethyst surrounded by diamond chips,' Lilac said proudly. 'Art said it was the nearest he could get to Lilac – isn't it pretty? I love it so much! And it fits, so he even got the size right.'

'And have your bought the wedding ring?'

'We're getting that today,' Lilac said. 'I telephoned my sister Nellie to tell her the date and talk about the arrangements – we've booked a wedding car and the Register Office for eleven o'clock – and she and Stuart will definitely bring little Elizabeth up the day before, so we can all be calm and relaxed on the day itself.'

'Wonderful,' Mrs Brierson said. 'You'll make the prettiest bride, Miss Larkin – we at the Delamere will all be very proud of you!'

The day Art sailed he looked down at the dock

and remembered his homecoming a couple of days earlier. Then, not a face turned in his direction, not a hand waved. Now he could see Lilac and Charlotte clutching each other, waving, Lilac blowing kisses. Near them stood Mrs Brierson, also waving and daringly blowing kisses whilst in the background Monsieur Arrat, Miss Skidmore, some of the chamber-maids and the girls from the kitchen clustered, waving hankies and tea-towels and shouting to him that it wouldn't be long before they saw him again.

They had taken him to their hearts because of Lilac, of course. She was such a marvellous girl, no one could resist her. But he was not just a passenger on the ship, he was still the purser, so after waving until Lilac was just a tiny dot amongst all the other dots, he went below and began on the pile of paperwork which sailing always brings in its wake.

He wished he could have had long enough to take her to New Brighton, though. They had almost got there so often, it would have been nice to have arrived home and whisked her across the Mersey on the ferry to the seaside place which had been their childhood Mecca. Odd how the place haunted them – always there, always beckoning, but they somehow hadn't managed to make it. Well, never mind, they would honeymoon there, it had been agreed between them.

He was just finishing his paperwork when there was a slight commotion outside the cabin door and a woman entered, holding a young girl by the hand. She was a pretty, dark-haired woman in her fifties, Art guessed, and the child must be about eight or nine. She held a skipping rope negligently but Art got the impression that for two pins she would have started skipping, there and then, in his neat and tidy office. Young rip, he thought, and then looked properly at the child. Immediately he was struck by the little girl's extraordinary likeness to the young Lilac – she had the same gleaming, reddish-gold hair, the wide blue eyes, the trick of looking down at the ground and then up again through her thick, light lashes. And somehow the same jaunty, devil-may-care attitude, too, though Lilac had been a penniless orphan and this was a little lady with a family rich enough to send her to Gibraltar aboard a cruise ship.

'Ah, purser; my name is Nicholson, Mrs Edward Nicholson. My grand-daughter and I are travelling with you to Gibraltar, where Lucy's father is stationed with the Royal Navy. Lucy's going to stay with him for a few weeks, but unfortunately we have been allocated an inside cabin and I was wondering, since the ship isn't fully booked, whether I might pay the extra and move to an outside one? The truth is, Lucy needs fresh air. She suffers from asthma and finds the cabin stuffy, which has already led to one attack.'

'I'm sure something can be arranged, Mrs Nicholson,' Art said, getting out the big passenger-list. 'Let me see ... ah yes, I've found you: Mrs Edward Nicholson and companion, travelling from Liverpool to Gibraltar. You're on 'B' deck, in cabin three, right?'

'That's right.'

'Well, we've an outside cabin free on 'A' deck. Yes, it would probably suit you and your granddaughter quite well. I'll just lock up here and then I'll take you up to it myself.'

'That's most kind,' Mrs Nicholson said gratefully. 'Although Lucy sits up to dinner with everyone else, she goes to bed straight afterwards and since I like to sit with her for a little while before she sleeps, an outside cabin would be more pleasant for me, too.'

On the way to the cabin Art mentioned, casually, that Lucy bore a remarkable resemblance to his fiancée, a Liverpool girl named Lilac Larkin. Mrs Nicholson raised her brows.

'Indeed? Well, Lucy takes after her father, not her mother ... my daughter Alicia was as dark as I am myself. I don't know Frank Dobson very well, in fact this will be only the second time I've met him, so for all I know your fiancée and he might be closely related.' She paused to glance at the child, now running ahead with her skipping rope, occasionally skipping as calmly and efficiently as though she were still on dry land and not the heaving deck of the *Queen of the Straits*. 'To tell you the truth, Mr O'Brien, there was a family disagreement.' Mrs Nicholson lowered her voice. 'My daughter married to disoblige us, as the saying goes. She had been engaged to a suitable young man ... he was heartbroken when she eloped ... but I daresay he's happy now, with his new wife and little family. And much though I miss my dearest Alicia – it must be nine years since she died – Lucy is a great comfort to me. She is the sweetest, most thoughtful girl.'

'And is she going to live with her father?' Art asked as he waved Mrs Nicholson ahead of him down the companionway. The child was already at the bottom of the stair, skipping in earnest now, the rope banging with smooth regularity against the well-polished floor. 'Is he settled in Gibraltar, for a time?'

'That is the intention,' Mrs Nicholson said cautiously. 'I've been a widow for fifteen years and am about to re-marry. We thought it best if Lucy went to her father for a while, so that Mr Addison and I might settle into our new home. But I couldn't give

Lucy up for ever,' she added quickly. 'We have resolved, Captain Dobson and I, to share her so far as is possible.'

'That sounds sensible,' Art said, throwing open a cabin door. 'Miss Lucy, you've gone too far – come back and examine your new cabin with your grandmother.'

Lucy ran back, beaming.

'Oh, a *window*,' she exclaimed joyfully. 'Oh, isn't this nice, Gran? We'll be able to see the sea and the gulls and have a breeze when it gets hot. Thank you, Mr O'Brien.'

'It will do very well,' Mrs Nicholson said, having taken a good look round. 'Could you arrange for one of the deck hands to bring my traps along here? I'd like to settle Lucy in by bedtime.'

During the days that followed, Art saw quite a lot of Lucy Dobson. She was a lively and intelligent child and it was soon obvious that whilst her grandmother adored her, she was no longer of an age to play games for hours at a time with her little tomboy of a granddaughter. Art, however, was glad of someone to amuse and came out of his office daily to play deck quoits, to teach Lucy new skipping games, to play cards in the evenings and to advise on a fancy dress when the weekly fancy dress ball loomed.

He was on his way to meet Lucy when the storm blew up.

It came from nowhere, the way storms at sea so often do. One minute it was calm enough beneath a lowering sky, with leaden clouds chasing one another across the horizon. The next moment a low rumble of thunder was followed by another and another, by lightning flashes, forking from the highest heavens deep into the sullen, surging sea. Then the rain came, great shining rods of it, bouncing off the suddenly boiling surface, hitting the deck so hard that the spray leapt head-high, forming puddles and lakes on the tennis court, running in rivers around the hatches on the foredeck.

Art watched from a convenient shelter and wondered just where Lucy had got to. She was an adventurous kid, she'd already been extracted from the engine room with a ruined cotton dress, and dissuaded forcibly from trying to climb the funnel. She loved the kitchens and pottered round there, helping with anything that she was big enough to do, hindering quite often, though always without any evil intent. If we'd been a sailing ship she'd have been balancing on the yard, darting in and out of the lightning strikes, Art thought rather balefully, for he had grown extremely fond of Lucy and rather resented her grandmother's casual acceptance of her charge's various adventures.

Art had arranged to meet Lucy on deck for a game of boule, a diversion which was proving popular amongst the younger element on board, but clearly she had realised that there would be no deck games until the storm abated and so had remained below. He was about to leave his look-out when he saw, dancing along the deck with her skipping rope dangling behind her, Lucy's small figure. She looked even smaller than usual with her clothing and hair drenched through, but she grinned at the sight of him and waved the wooden handle of her rope.

Art dived out of hiding and was soaked before he'd gone more than three yards. He gestured furiously to Lucy – the ship was heaving and tossing, it wasn't safe on deck, he realised, even if you didn't count the lightning and thunder.

'What?' Lucy shrieked across the short distance which separated them. 'What do you want? It's *lovely* out here – Gran wouldn't book us tickets on a big ship with a swimming pool because I can't swim yet and she said she'd never have an easy moment, but this is almost as good—'

Behind her, Art saw the wave coming. A great green monster, as high as the ship's rail, it raced towards them faster than an express train and every bit as dangerous. He waved his arms, shouted, began to run ... and saw the wave hit the ship, curl above the rail, and come crashing down on the deck, several tons of green water, sharp with salt and weed, pebbles and sand.

He saw Lucy taken. That was it, she was taken, just as though the wave had curled a great green hand round her skinny little person and scooped her over the side and into the ocean. Art grabbed a lifebelt, heaved at the warning bell with all his strength, heard it begin its clangour ... and scrambled over the rail. For a moment he stood poised – he heard voices behind him and roared a brief explanation, 'Kid overboard!', as loudly as he could against the elements. Then he saw in the water below him, just for an instant, a frightened white face, a swirl of red-gold hair – and he dived.

He reached her. Somehow, he didn't quite know how, he got hold of her, floated on to his back, forced her into the lifebelt, got her up on his chest and began to turn back towards the ship. The sea was running high still, and now that he'd got Lucy in a firm grip he was hanging on to her and the lifebelt, concentrating on keeping afloat, hoping to be seen because if they weren't there could be only one end to Lucy's latest escapade.

They were seen; a rope came snaking over the side, more lifebelts were thrown, they were lowering a boat. Lucy had been shuddering with cold, he thought her unconscious, but suddenly she turned her head and grinned weakly at him, looking so like the small Lilac that he could only grin back, knowing he should be angry with her but wanting only to see her safe, up on deck with her grandmother crying and cuddling her, regretting, at last, her lackadaisical stewardship of this most precious cargo.

He got her into the boat; the two men on board hauled her over the side and dropped her on to the bottom-boards, then turned to Art. But the boat had drifted too near the hull and they had to leave him to tread water for a moment whilst they worked desperately at the oars to avoid being crushed against the echoing steel plates. And Art, whilst they struggled, found himself fighting a force which was stronger than the arms of the men in the boat, stronger than Art himself; he was being drawn back and down by the currents which swirled around the ship's hull.

For a moment longer he fought it, not realising why he was gradually moving away from the boat, despite his attempts to get aboard. He saw Lucy, on her knees, holding out her small hands to him, her expression desperate. He even heard her voice, clearly, above the storm.

'Mr O'Brien . . . Art! Come to Lucy, swim to Lucy!'

Then the sea sucked him down. He fought it maniacally, struggled to rise to the surface as his lungs began to burn with the effort of holding his breath. Then he was dragged deeper, deeper yet, the sea no longer gleaming green around him but black, black.

He realised what was happening to him, knew that he was powerless to prevent it for one brief second before he spiralled down into the lightless deeps beneath, his breath gone, water in his lungs, his body squeezed by the pressures of the depths into the likeness of a rag doll.

His last thought was that he would never take Lilac to New Brighton now.

Chapter Twelve

It was all over the national dailies that he was a
hero, that he had died saving a child. Nellie read it
idly, standing in the kitchen with a cup of coffee in
one hand, waiting for the wash-boiler to reach heat.
No sooner had the dreadful news sunk in, however,
than she was out of the room and on the telephone
to Stuart at his office.

'Stu . . . have you seen today's *Times*?'

'No, not yet,' Stuart said. He worked in a newspaper
office, so presumably, Nellie thought, he had enough
to do writing for his own paper without reading other
people's. 'Why? Is there something we should pick
up?'

'No . . . Stuart, c-can you come home? It's Art
O'Brien, Lilac's fiancé. Of course there might be two
of them, but he was acting purser on the *Queen of the
Straits*, I'm sure that's what Lilac said. He – he's been
drowned, Stu, saving a little girl's life.'

'Drowned. Art? Oh, dear God, and he and
Lilac . . .'

Stuart's voice, which had been indulgent, absent-
minded, only interested, she could tell, because he
thought there might be a story in it, sharpened into
dismay. He had been fond of Art, Nellie knew, but
he loved Lilac, as she did.

'That's right; he came home to plan their wedding.
Oh Stu, this will kill her – I must go to her! Can you
come home right away?'

'I'll leave at once.'

A different tone yet again, crisp, stern. Nellie
could picture him hurling himself down all those
marble stairs, through the revolving doors and out
across the pavement to the nearest tram stop.

Nellie had been using the telephone in the hallway,
sitting on a low chair, so now she stood up, replaced
the receiver on its stand, picked up *The Times* and
walked into the kitchen. Elizabeth was sitting up at
the kitchen table, doing a wooden jigsaw. She had a
summer cold and every now and then blew her small
nose noisily into the hanky attached to her wrist by a
length of wool. She looked up as Nellie entered.

'What's 'a matter, Mam?' she said thickly. 'Your
eyes is red.'

'Mam's sad,' Nellie said. 'Someone we love is . . .
is not well. I've rung your Da at the office and he's
coming home. We're going to have to go to Liverpool,
queen.'

'Liverpool?' The child's eyes brightened though
the lids were heavy still. 'To Auntie Li?'

'That's right, sweetheart. We're going to see Auntie
Li.'

Elizabeth promptly got down from the table and
set off across the kitchen.

'Wait, Miss Impatience; where are you going?'

'To pack me things,' Elizabeth said. 'I'm going
to be Auntie Li's flower-girl, in a bootiful pink dress!
Can I take dolly Gwen and Red Ted?'

'Oh my God,' Nellie said. The room dipped and
swayed; she clutched the sink for support. 'Oh, my
God! Oh my baby, my poor baby!'

She sank into a chair and put her face in her hands,
then began to cry; for Lilac, for little Elizabeth, for all
the pain that this cruel death would engender. Art

was beyond tears, beyond pain, yet she cried bitterly, helplessly, for him. He had been so young, so full of hopes and dreams, and they had all been lost in one moment of gallantry, one foolhardy, wonderful moment in which he had saved a life and lost his own.

Nellie was still sitting in the kitchen when Stuart's key grated in the lock. He burst into the house, ran down the hall and, as she got stumblingly to her feet, he snatched her into his arms.

'Oh my love, my poor darling,' he murmured against her hair. 'Get some things together, we'll go by train, we can be with her before dusk.'

'Stuart, you're the best,' Nellie said huskily. 'Look, read the report whilst I pack. I'm sorry I didn't do it earlier, it was the shock, I suppose. All I could think of was the wedding, and . . . oh, Stu, my poor baby!'

She burst into tears again and headed for the stairs. Stuart started to follow her, then turned back and began methodically to tidy the kitchen, pulling the kettle over the heat and setting the teapot ready. Above his head, he could hear Elizabeth prattling away to herself in her small room. Some people might have assumed that when Nellie spoke of her poor baby she meant little Elizabeth, robbed of her chance to be a flower-girl at her aunt's wedding. But Stuart knew his wife better than that. It was Lilac, a young woman in her twenties, for whom she wept, because Lilac, in every sense but one, was indeed her baby.

Lilac sat behind the reception desk. Her face was perfectly white, but her smile, though a little stiff, sprang into being every time a guest came through the front door and approached her. She was calm and collected, because she did not believe the newspaper reports; how could she? She and Art O'Brien were going to be married, she wore his ring, had bought her gown, had planned her trousseau and her honeymoon, had even reserved the best bedroom at the largest hotel in New Brighton.

Staff came and went; Mrs Brierson was as pale as Lilac, but she wept; Lilac did not weep. Why should she, when she knew the whole report to be some horrible mistake, when she expected that any minute Art would come bustling in through the door, to seize her in his arms, kiss her with little kisses, tell her what a sensible lass she was not to be taken in by a sensationalized story?

Presently Monsieur Arrat came up from the kitchen. He looked different; she tried not to stare because it was rude, but his eyes were red, his nose positively glowed and his lower lip trembled. He told her there was a light supper set out for her downstairs and said she should go down to the kitchen now, she'd been on duty long enough.

She stood up and nearly fell. She wondered just how long she had been on duty – she didn't usually get so stiff that her legs failed her. But she walked across the hall behind Monsieur Arrat, pushed open the green baize door and began to go down the stairs. She was halfway down the flight when the blackness came up to meet her, like icy water creeping slowly up her body, devouring her. A terrifying numbness accompanied the blackness, an all-devouring chill which swept over her. She tried to clutch at the bannister rail to save herself, tried to call out . . . then fell, swooping headfirst into the ice-cold dark.

Monsieur Arrat caught her before she hit the ground. He had been standing a few paces ahead of her and he simply held out his arms and swept her against his chest. All day he had been lamenting, crying, declaring that he could not work when such a terrible sadness had afflicted one for whom he had so much respect, but now that they needed common sense and practicality more than anything, he shed his affectations and became a tower of strength.

'I'll take her to one of the empty rooms,' he said, in almost accentless English. 'Poor child, she's coming to terms with the unbearable; that takes some doing. Someone must stay with her and when she comes round I will bring her supper up on a tray. With a whisky and hot water, I think.'

'I'll sit with her,' Mrs Brierson said. 'Sadie, go round and fetch Miss Charlotte; tell her what's happened – I'm sure she doesn't know or she'd have been round before now – and Phyllis, make me a couple of hot water bottles for her bed.'

The girls scuttled off to do her bidding and Mrs Brierson saw Lilac tucked up in bed and beginning, drowsily, to come round. She held Lilac's cold hand, murmured soothingly to her and presently despatched a maid to tell Monsieur Arrat that they would have the supper tray in ten minutes, please. Then she settled down to wait for Lilac to acknowledge her whereabouts.

Lilac opened her eyes. Outside the window she could see the sky, deep blue with dusk, but someone had lit the gas and a faint golden glow suffused the room in which she lay. She moved restlessly and realised someone was holding her hand. Her heart bounded joyfully in her breast – she had known Art was coming to her, he was here, he was holding her hand, sitting by the bed. . .

She clutched the fingers in hers and it was Mrs Brierson bending over her, saying something about a supper tray. Behind Mrs Brierson, Charlotte hovered, pale, red-eyed. Lilac shook her head at the mention of a supper tray, thoroughly disorientated, unable to remember with any clarity what had happened to her or where she was. After all, if she was still at the Delamere, what was Charlotte doing? Charlotte belonged to another life, her dancing academy life, she would not be at the Delamere! After a moment or two, however, Lilac sat up on one elbow and looked around her. She saw she was in bed, in the hotel, with hot bottles behind her knees and at her feet, with her employer sitting beside her holding her hand, whilst a great, echoing emptiness filled her aching head.

She looked helplessly across at Charlotte, wanting to ask her what had happened, why she felt so ill, but the words would not come. Slowly, she slid down the bed again. She turned her head away from Mrs Bierson and Charlotte and closed her eyes, but she was powerless to prevent the tears from squeezing out under her lids and trickling, slow and cold, down her cheeks.

'Lilac, my dearest child, my own dear girl, what a tragic, wicked waste, your dear boy gone and you far away, unable to do anything about it. Come to Nellie, dearest, tell Nellie!'

Warm arms enclosed her, a warm cheek was pressed to hers. The cheek was wet with tears, the hands clutching hers were trembling. She could feel Nellie's passionate sorrow, the love which enfolded her as Nellie hugged her tight.

'Oh, Nell, it isn't true, say it isn't true,' Lilac begged. Her voice was odd, harsh and croaking. 'He can't be drowned, not my Art, not my dear old Art.'

'You know it's true, love,' Nellie whispered. 'He's a hero, he saved a kiddy's life . . . but that don't help, not when he's gone.'

'Oh, but it's a mistake, it must be! We're going to be married, we're going to New Brighton for our honeymoon, we'd planned it in our letters, he came all the way from Gibraltar for two days just to talk about it! He can't, he can't be drowned.'

'He's dead, queen,' Nellie said gently. 'But you're alive, and you've got to go on living. Come on, sit up and have some of this nice supper what chef prepared.'

'He's dead? My Art really is dead?'

'That's right, queen. Look, a cup of thick soup, some bread – chef's homemade – and a glass of whisky to help you to warm up, all set out so lovingly . . . they're that fond of you, Li, that. . .'

'You're telling me that the newspapers got it right? That it was my Art who dived off the ship and saved the little girl and then got sucked under by the currents round the hull? My Art who drowned?'

'That's right, Lilac love. I've never lied to you, have I? And I'm not lying now. Art's gone and you've got to come to terms with it.'

Lilac nodded slowly and lay back against her pillows. The ache in her breast wouldn't go away, she supposed it never would, nor the hollowness in her mind. Could a person live with such pain, such loss? She asked Nellie whether it was possible and Nellie looked at her with such understanding, such loving sympathy in her big, expressive eyes!

'A person can try, queen,' she said quietly. 'A person has to try.'

If it hadn't been for her iron determination to get her family straightened out, Kitty didn't think she would have survived that first month. Patch helped, just by her constancy and affection – just by being there, when Kitty knew very well that
the dog was pining for the countryside – but it was a terrible four weeks for Kitty, after three years of clean air and comfort on the farm. Poor Patch, too, was a country dog, terrified of city ways, city traffic, city people. But dogs are resilient and when they love they put their hearts and souls into it. Patch had loved Kitty from the moment the girl had let her off her chain and fed and watered her when Maldwyn was unable to do so. She had stuck closer to Kitty than a burr, always at her heels, only going off with Johnny or Maldwyn when they needed her to round up stock or bring cows or sheep in off the mountains.

Now, living in a city slum with food scarce and kicks ten a penny, she still stuck to Kitty. She grew gaunt and nervous, though Kitty did her best to see the dog was as well fed as circumstances allowed, but Patch never wavered in her affection and concern for her young mistress. And Kitty, no matter how tired she was, no matter how much she longed for a sit-down, took Patch down to the waterfront or up to the park night and morning and threw a stick for her so that the dog got plenty of exercise to keep her muscles in trim. What was more, Kitty begged bones from the butcher, scraps, rag-ends of meat or fish, and saw, somehow, that Patch was always more or less adequately fed.

The family fared equally well; that was to say they were mainly fed. Betty was a big help, carting the two younger ones around with her, using an old pram to carry shopping home and thus earn pennies. But once Sary's initial joy over Kitty's return cooled a little, Kitty often saw her mother staring at her with a horrible sort of calculation in the mean, bloodshot eyes. And the doctor had proved adamant. He would not come to the Court unless he was paid in advance.

So after a month of trying to improve her mother's physical condition, Kitty somehow lugged her parent, by tram and on foot, up to the centre on Brougham Terrace where free medical treatment was handed out, if you didn't mind the waits, the queues, and being treated by many of the medical staff as though you were nothing better than ignorant and unimaginative cattle who were lucky to be examined and should not expect to also be addressed.

They saw a young doctor, a man who examined Sary Drinkwater thoroughly, but with a sort of sneering distaste which annoyed Kitty very much. At the end of his examination he sent Sary off in the care of a nurse who would weigh and measure her and turned to Kitty.

'You the daughter?'

'Yes,' Kitty said equally baldly.

'Hmm. She drinks to excess, of course.'

'Yes.'

'Eats all the wrong food, too . . . fried potatoes? Bread and jam? That sort of thing?'

'When she eats at all,' Kitty said. 'What's 'er food got to do wi' anything?'

'My dear girl, it has everything to do with her state of health! She's overweight, flabby, I daresay she seldom walks . . .'

'She don't 'ave the strength,' Kitty said bitterly. She was disliking this young man more with every moment that passed. 'What I want to know is, what do I do about it?'

'Do? Why, stop her drinking and start her eating properly. She needs milk, meat, fresh fruit and vegetables of course . . . hey! Where are you going?'

'I'm goin' to find if there's a doctor in this place what can talk sense,' Kitty said furiously, turning to glare at him. 'Me Dad left 'ome three year ago an' we don't get 'is 'llowance no more; me brother flew the coop soon after. There's me an' three little sisters, I ain't gorra proper job, I picks up what I can . . . 'ow the 'ell d'you expect me to find food like that for me Mam?'

The doctor looked a little abashed, then rallied.

'I can only advise,' he said pompously. 'She's got where she is today through her own faults, you can't expect me . . .'

But he was speaking to a closed door. Kitty had slammed out.

Getting Sary to see another doctor was hard, but Kitty did not intend her time to be wasted. She bullied her mother into joining another queue and said grimly that unless Sary behaved she would find herself minus an elder daughter by morning. Sary gave her an evil look but consented to join the queue and presently they were ushered into another small, bleak consulting room. To Kitty's relief the second doctor was older, and, if wearier, very much more practical.

'She's had some sort of debilitating fever which has affected her mind, I fear,' he said to Kitty, smiling down very kindly at her. 'She isn't mad, as you feared, but she has lost touch with reality a little. If you can keep her away from alcohol and see that she drinks

297

fresh milk and has something like cabbage or carrots most days, I am fairly confident she will recover. I'll have a tonic mixed up in the pharmacy, but fresh air, exercise and the best food you can manage will do her more good than any medicine I can provide. Now, my dear, what are your circumstances?'

Kitty explained.

The doctor nodded and frowned.

'I really think your smaller sisters should go to the Father Berry Catholic Children's Home on Shaw Street. They will be well-treated, well-fed, and that will enable you to see to your mother as best you can.'

'But they ain't orphans,' Kitty protested. 'They've gorra mam an' a dad; and me, acourse.'

'They have no one to support them,' the doctor explained. 'Your mother is ill and likely to be so for several weeks yet, your father has gone, and you're . . . what, fourteen?'

'Fifteen,' Kitty said. Being a practical young woman she could see the truth in his words. 'Right. 'Ow do I gerrem into this place?'

So the deed was done, with the doctor's help. Ruthie might not have understood what was happening to her but Eth did, and the look of relief on her small face when she was taken into the home and warmly welcomed, when she watched as Ruthie was picked up and cuddled by a fat nursery-maid and was shown the clean, warm clothing she would wear, went a long way to convincing Kitty that she had done the right thing. What was more the little girls were reunited with Kitty's other sisters, Phyllis and Mo, who had been at the Home for over a year and were very happy there.

Kitty told the girls that this was not a permanent thing, that they would only be cared for until

Sary Drinkwater was able to take them back. But in her heart she could not see Sary ever again being sufficiently responsible to take care of her children. Even when Sary's health improved she was clearly not a happy woman and the future seemed to hold no charms for her.

'Me dad leavin' must of cut 'er up more'n I'd ha' guessed,' Kitty remarked to Betty on a day when their mother refused to leave her bed. 'Poor Mam, she really must of liked the old soak.'

'Well, I didn't,' Betty said. 'Mam was always me favourite. She were awright when she were well, was me Mam.'

Despite missing the two younger girls, coping was easier once it was just Kitty, Betty and their mother, with Patch as moral support. Easier in one way, that was. Sary, who never seemed to take the slightest notice of her children, was told that the younger ones had been taken to someone who would feed and clothe them whilst she was too ill to do so, and accepted the explanation without more ado. Betty wept for a couple of nights and gave Kitty long, pained stares ... she was presumably thinking that she had done her best to keep the family together yet this big sister had handed the little ones over without a murmur ... but Kitty herself really missed Eth and Ruthie and felt guilty into the bargain, until she had visited them a couple of times after they had settled in.

The orphanage was a plain place, and practical, but the children were fed and neatly clothed, well taught, and if not loved, at least cared for in a responsible manner. Eth was soon seen to be in her element as the staff took her in hand, and Ruthie had been happy from the start, not only enjoying the food and the clothes, but revelling in the constant attention. Kitty, horribly aware of her own shortcomings as a provider, was glad to see the little girls growing sturdier with each visit, and soon stopped blaming herself for letting them go. The alternative was too horrible to contemplate, for even after a month her mother seemed little improved and the work Kitty managed to get scarcely fed the three of them. It would never have stretched to five.

'What did you do when you wasn't 'ere, Kit?' Betty asked, one chilly evening as the two of them and Patch snuggled down in the pile of rags. 'Was you very un'appy all alone?'

'I weren't alone, chuck, I were with a pal,' Kitty said slowly, a hand buried in the thick ruff of fur round Patch's neck. 'We was in the country, me an' me pal, on a farm. I 'spec' we'll go back, one day.'

'A farm? Wha's a farm?'

'Oh Betty, you know very well! Pigs an' cows an' that. Medders, fields . . . honest to God, kiddo, you must ha' seen about farms in books!'

'Oh, books,' Betty said. 'I can't read good.'

'I'll teach you if you like,' Kitty said. 'You goes to school, though.'

'Oh, aye, but only when I 'as to. I'll be 'appy when I can stay 'ome wi' you an' our Mam.'

Kitty did not reply. She knew very well that Betty sagged off school as often as she could but she simply could not take on the task of forcing the younger girl to attend classes. Besides, when school was in it was easier for Betty to get the odd job – fetching shopping for the old or the idle, wheeling the pram down to the docks for broken boxes which she could sell for firewood, lugging coal or potatoes home from the market – whereas in holiday time every kid was out there trying for work.

'Kit?'

'Yes, chuck?'

'Tell me about your farm.'

'Well, it's at the foot o' the Berwyn range – them's mountains. They're real lovely, are mountains. Blue an' misty sometimes, clear an' 'ard agin the sky others, spread wi' all sorts o' greens in the spring an' purples an' pinks in 'igh summer when the 'eather's out.'

'Mmm, sounds real lovely. Is that where you got your Patch from?'

'That's right. One mornin' me and me pal 'ad been sleepin' warm in an 'aystack . . .'

She told Betty about their arrival at the farm, Maldwyn's injury, his kindness to them. And when the child slept she went on thinking about the farm – and about Johnny Moneymor.

What had happened to him – more important, what did he think had happened to her? Had he found the witness to the will, taken him back to Wrexham, fetched a lawyer to confront the thieving Ap Thomases with their lies and treachery? Had he searched for her, Kitty? Somehow, she was sure he had, but it was too late. No one could search for ever and if he was still prosecuting his claim then he would have to be in Wales, and if he had been successful and had won, then he would have to be on the farm, taking care of things, protecting his property. Their property.

Because of course Johnny knows that I know where the farm is, whereas all he knows about me is that I used to live in Paradise Court but swore I'd never return there. He didn't get the note, that's for sure. So he might hunt for me up and down the Scottie, but likelier he'd go to Penny Lane because he knew

I had a friend there, or he'd hunt through the docks and the area he told me to search. The one place he wouldn't look is the Parry, so I'm safe enough here.

But that was silly, because she wanted her pal more than almost anything, certainly more than she wanted this collapsing house or her mean-eyed mother. But she couldn't just leave them to manage without her, not when she knew very well that they wouldn't. See them right first, she told herself meaninglessly, because seeing them right was an impossible task. See them right first, and then go your own way.

But thinking about the farm, and Johnny, was an escape from the bitter poverty, the ugly dilemma, in which she found herself. The apparent friendliness which Sary had shown at first had soon dissipated; her mother would have used violence against her, save that Kitty was clearly the stronger and fitter of the two. I'm more of a gaoler than a daughter, Kitty thought bitterly, for she hid her money away from Sary, never allowed her a penny to herself. If she did, she knew very well it would all be splashed out on drink, and that she dared not allow. And not only did she keep Sary short of cash, she also kept her either in the house or accompanied her outside it. Her mother would steal to get alcohol, and on the only occasion she had managed to get herself as far as the Black Dog unaccompanied she had also got herself very drunk indeed. Kitty guessed she had begged drinks, and supped the dregs in glasses, and because she hadn't drunk for so long, Sary had speedily become incapable. It had taken the combined strength of Kitty and her younger sister to drag the screaming, cursing hulk which was Sary Drinkwater out of the gutter and back to the house in Paradise Court.

'Nex' time we'll leave you lie,' Kitty had hissed breathlessly as they dropped Sary unceremoniously on the bottom stair. 'I'm warnin' you, Mam, there 'adn't berrer be a nex' time!'

But it was no life for any of them, Kitty thought now, as the dog's warmth mingled with that of the two girls and made the bed almost comfortable. And what'll we do when the weather worsens? Even now she was always tired, always hungry, always worried. September and October had been relatively mild, but now it was November, and when it grew really cold she doubted her ability to keep them warm and fed. Sary was clearly far from well and cordially hated her gaoler-daughter, even though everything Kitty did was for her ultimate good. But you can't teach an old dog new tricks, Kitty thought, stroking Patch's silky ears. Her mother had always been a violent woman, a heavy drinker. Nothing would change that now, except for old age and infirmity, and Sary was only thirty-eight, though she looked and acted sixty.

But it was no good thinking like that or she'd never sleep. Kitty curled up with an arm round Patch's neck and directed her thoughts back to the farm. Wouldn't it be marvellous to wake up in her own little room, with the mountain range glowing with sunrise outside her window and the heather's purple deepening to brown? Downstairs a big log fire, outside the clean, fresh mountain air, the winter-pale grass, the trees with their bare branches dusted with frost.

Some kids are so lucky, she thought drowsily, her mind eased and gentled by her recollections. Some kids have all that from birth, it's as natural to them as city streets and hunger are to kids like Betty, to women like me Mam. Why, if things had been different . . . .

She sat bolt upright, ignoring the cold air which her sudden movement had brought swirling into their nest. If things had been different . . . well, why should they not be? Why should she, her mother and her sister, to say nothing of Patch, not set out on the road, as she and Johnny Moneymor had done? God knows they could not be worse off than they were at present, and at least if they were in the country they would have fresh air to breathe, fresh water to drink, and the clean fields and meadows to walk in. Patch would be better – she worried more about the dog than about the rest of the family since she had brought Patch to this dreadful pass – Sary and Betty would be better and she, Kitty Drinkwater, would probably be able to earn them a living of sorts.

Even if the Thomases are still at the farm, I can earn my living in the country, Kitty thought. I can milk a cow, clean a byre, drive a pony and trap, sell at a market . . . her skills, which were non-existent in a city, suddenly began to mount up to something worthwhile when you thought about the country. Why, I could keep house for a bachelor farmer, she thought excitedly, remembering how Maldwyn had painstakingly taught her to cook, to make and to mend, to clean and polish. Oh yes, of course, why hadn't she thought of it before? It was in the country that their future lay, Mam's and Betty's as well as hers and Patch's. She would talk to them about it the very next day!

'Go off, 'oofin' it? Wi' winter comin' on? You're mad!'

Sary Drinkwater heaved a huge shoulder up in the air and burrowed further down under her filthy bedcovers. The gesture said louder than words that she did not intend to budge from her bed unless she was forced. Kitty gritted her teeth and caught hold of the dirty blanket. She tried not to notice the tiny movements of bugs in the matted wool; they'd die off when the weather worsened, she told herself – so long as we don't follow suit, she added, with grim humour. She heaved and the blanket slid half off the bed.

'Get *up*, Mam,' she said sharply. 'The doc told you fresh air an' exercise. We're goin' for a walk to the country, me and Bet, an' you're coming' with us.'

'No – I – ain't!' Each word was accompanied by a heave on the blanket and Sary was still a strong woman. 'You goes, the pair of yez, an' good riddance I say!'

'We will go,' Kitty threatened. She turned and stormed out of the room, with Betty and Patch close on her heels. At the bottom of the stairs she turned to her sister. 'What'll we do, Bet? I can get work in the country, I've got friends there, but there ain't much I can do in the city! Shall us go, you an' me?'

Betty heaved a sigh and shook her head.

'She'll die if we leave 'er,' she pointed out. 'She'll be up the boozer a-beggin' bevvies – or stealin' 'em – afore you can say scuffers. We'll 'ave to sit it out till she's gorrer full senses back.'

Kitty sighed and nodded, biting back a sharp retort that their mother would be a fool even if she had her full senses, as Betty called them, returned to her tomorrow. But she did try to make her point.

'Mam lives for the booze now, flower,' she said gently. 'I dunno as 'ow I can stay for ever, an' with Mam that's what it'ud be.'

'I know; but Mam was good to us when she were 'erself,' Betty said. 'Not to you, Kit, you've gorra right to go, I know it, but she were awright to the rest of us.'

'You wouldn't go to the children's home, like the others, I suppose?' Kitty said without much hope. 'They'd feed you there, an' that.'

'If I did that Mam wouldn't even try to git better,' Betty observed shrewdly. 'She'd sink like a stone, I tells you.'

'Yeah; you're right. Well, we'll go on tryin' for a bit, then,' Kitty said wearily. 'See 'er through the winter. Best tek the pram down to the docks, see if you can find some broken boxes to sell. I'll bide 'ere wi' Mam and try to think it through.'

She was still thinking, without getting anywhere at all, when there was a tentative knock on the door.

Johnny! Kitty thought; he's found me! And she flew across the room and hurled open the front door.

'Oh, Johnny, I's . . .'

It wasn't Johnny. It was a buxom, smiling girl a few years older than Kitty herself. Kitty recognised her as one of the Fletchers who now lived in what had once been Mrs O'Rourke's neat house. She smiled rather diffidently; the three big daughters, and this was one of them, were always friendly and cheerful, and though the males of the family did roar out songs and a few curses when they came back from the boozer, though the females seemed to have rather a rapid turnover of gentlemen friends, Kitty thought the Fletchers were a cheery crowd. At least they were a change from the rest of the inhabitants of Paradise Court, who tended to keep themselves to themselves and clearly considered, despite Betty's strictures, that it was the Drinkwaters who had brought the Court low rather than the arrival of others.

"Ello, chuck,' the girl said. She had thick yellow curls, bright blue eyes and a wide, friendly grin. Her front teeth had a little gap between them which somehow made her look younger than she probably was, more Kitty's age. Kitty could tell that the yellow curls came out of a peroxide bottle and that her pink cheeks also owed something to artifice, but she admired the older girl nevertheless. 'I t'ought it were time we interdooced ourselves, seein' as we're neighbours, like. I'm Marigold Fletcher, an' you'll be. . . ?'

'I'm Kitty Drinkwater,' Kitty said. She held out her hand. 'How d'you do?'

That was what they said in books, but Marigold looked taken aback for a moment, then seized Kitty's hand in a warm and friendly grip.

'Ow do, Kitty,' she said heartily. 'I come to ask 'ow's your mam?'

'Poorly, thanks,' Kitty said gloomily. 'I were tryin' to get 'er to come for a walk . . . jest a bit of a way at first, the doc say she oughter 'ave exercise an' fresh air . . . but she won't budge from 'er pit.'

'Eh, dat's a shame. I brung 'er a rice pudden', still 'ot. Think she could swally a mouthful?'

'She could, I'm sure,' Kitty said, holding out her hands for the pudding basin the girl had been holding behind her back. 'Ooh, you are good, you are kind . . . it's been queerin' me 'ow the 'ell I were to get 'er a meal today . . . gelt's runnin' low to tell the truth.'

'Yeah . . . well, I wondered if you'd like to do a bit o' work for me,' Marigold said. She dimpled beguilingly at Kitty. 'I been an' got meself a room on Grayson Street – for me business, like – but the fellers don't know where to find me. If they come 'ere, our Daisy an' our Vi'let will oblige, but the fellers from the dock won't bother to search me out, see? An' someone told me you wrote lovely, so I bought a pad an' a pencil an' I thought you could write me

some lickle notes, like? I'd pay, acourse,' she added
hastily.

'Be glad to,' Kitty said joyfully. A job where she
could stay and keep an eye on her mother would be
ideal. 'Gi's the paper, I'll do some right away.'

'Good. An' will you deliver 'em for me? Down at
the docks where the big ships come in? I'm fed up
wi' walkin' up and down meself, so I'll pay you two
bob a day so long as you write out twenty or thirty
and deliver the same number. What say?'

'Well, aye, but who do I deliver 'em to?' Kitty said,
rather mystified. 'I wouldn't know your friends from
Adam, would I, eh?'

Marigold giggled and the pink in her cheeks deepened.

'Well, I'd like to say officers only, but I reckon
I might do meself in the eye that way, eh? So 'ow
about any feller off of a ship what's just docked?'
'Ah, I see,' Kitty said. Now she understood – Marigold wanted sailors to pay her for . . . well, whatever
it was that sailors paid bad girls for . . . but she didn't
want to walk the streets herself, not now she'd risen
to the heights of renting her own room. 'But Marigold,
suppose the fellers thought it were me what was
toutin' for business? What then, eh?'

'Just given 'em some lip an' keep the dog by
you,' Marigold advised after some thought. 'You'd be
awright, the fellers like . . . well, they like a woman
wi' some flesh on 'er bones, you're a kid, really.'

'It's worth more'n a couple o' bob a day, though,'
Kitty said pensively. 'I'd 'ave to get someone to sit wi'
me mam, else she'd start knockin' back the gin before
you could say mother's ruin. If I 'and them papers to
twenty fellers . . . .'

'Oh ah, I see what you mean, but I won't git

twenty customers from twenty papers,' Marigold said quickly. 'Oh, you 'ave to put yourself in the way of a dozen, mebbe more, blokes to get one or two customers.'

'I daresay. But once they knows where you are you won't need me, so I gorra mek the money whiles I can,' Kitty pointed out righteously. 'Five bob a day an' you're on.'

'Five bob! Gawd, you'll 'ave me flat on me back in the gutter at that rate,' Marigold protested, though still so good-naturedly that Kitty guessed she was willing to pay more. 'Say four an' a tanner?'

'Five bob,' Kitty said placidly, sensing her advantage. 'Can't give up me time for less.'

'Right. Five bob, then. Start tomorrer?'

'Start now; gi's the papers,' Kitty said with her usual practicality. 'I'll keep on till you've got enough steadies, then I'll 'ave to find summat else. Where's the copy?'

'Ain't got one,' Marigold admitted. 'I thought you'd do it better'n me. Just say that it's Marigold, now available at Number 20 Grayson Street. Prices reasonable.'

'Hadn't you better say you're teachin' French or something?' Kitty said, starting to write the message on the first sheet of thin paper of the pad Marigold had thrust into her hand. 'Ain't this agin the law?'

'Well, goin' wi' a feller's agin the law, but you can write teachin' French so long as they don't b'lieve you,' Marigold said generously. 'I don't want no fellers wi' brains in their 'eads a-bangin' on me door.' She giggled. 'If you see what I mean,' she finished.

'Look, I can't do a good job standin' 'ere,' Kitty said presently. Trying to write with a stub of pencil on the thin paper, with the pad balanced on her rather inadequate knee, just wasn't possible. 'You go orf, Marigold, an' I'll bring 'em round later. When does you move into Grayson Street?'

'Move, whaddyer mean?'

'Well, when do you start to live there?'

'Live there? I ain't goin' to live there, chuck, I'm just a-goin' to carry on me business there,' Marigold explained. 'So I'll be at number twelve if you want me.'

'Oh! Right,' Kitty said. She waited until Marigold had gone into her own house, then closed the door thoughtfully. She now had a well-paid job for a short while; she must make the most of it and decide what to do when it finished because she was icily determined not to simply give in and stay at the Court with Sary and Betty.

'I'll do me best by 'em both,' she told Patch as the dog sat at her feet, watching her pencil copy out page after page of Marigold's message. 'But I won't give up me life to 'em, it ain't fair and I won't do it.'

Patch sighed and laid her head gently on Kitty's knee; Kitty smoothed the silky fur and sighed too.

'It ain't fair on you either, Patchie,' she murmured. 'But we'll be all right; there's gorra be a way out, there's jest gorra be!'

The job was all right, though tiring and slightly risky. It turned out that she often had to conduct the customers to Grayson Street, since sailors in need of a woman in a strange port aren't prepared to buy street maps. They would sooner pick up some floosie actually on the spot, even if she didn't have much more to offer than a cheap five-minute gallop and a wall to lean against.

However, Patch lessened the risk considerably. Some men she liked, in which case she trotted quietly at Kitty's heels through the darkening streets, never needing more than a word now and then. But some men she disliked, and Kitty soon grew to realise that Patch was a far better judge of character than she was herself. A smart young man with well-brushed clothing and hair Brylcreemed flat to his scalp might be the very one to take a grab at Kitty, thinking to save his money and get what he wanted by stealing it – Kitty was still not at all sure what went on between Marigold and her customers, but she did know it wasn't for her – but Patch soon put a stop to any such thoughts, let alone actions. She would get between Kitty and the man and her hackles would rise up all along her back until she looked the way Kitty imagined an angry wolf would look. And she kept up the most ominous grumbling growl all the time, too, only ceasing when they reached number 20. The only man to decide she couldn't hurt him had been badly bitten, far too badly to want to continue to defy the growling, stiff-legged Patch, so Kitty thought that her personal safety was assured whilst she and the dog were together.

The money she earned from Marigold was good and Mrs Fletcher, a woman as good-natured and easy-going as her daughters, had agreed to keep an eye on Sary whilst Betty and Kitty were out, so things began to improve a little for the Drinkwaters. Food was more plentiful, Sary's health began to improve, Betty positively blossomed.

Spring came and Kitty saved her money and bought herself a cotton skirt and jacket and her mother a lightweight shawl. Betty had a new dress and Kitty got a neighbour to mend the door of number 8 and spray the walls and floor with disinfectant. Sary cooked for

311

them sometimes and Betty attended school now and then.

'I can see the day when I can leave 'em to their own devices ain't that far off,' Kitty told Patch, as the two of them paraded up and down the waterfront with their papers. Kitty, having been eyed askance by both senior officers and policemen on several occasions, had taken what Marigold thought was a really brilliant step. She had gone to the Shamrock Café, where she was still a customer from time to time, and asked them if they would like advertising leaflets drawn up and handed out down at the docks, since she was already performing this service for a young gentleman who gave lessons on the ukelele. The proprietress, who had noticed Kitty as a decent young girl who though plainly dressed always paid her bill promptly, agreed, so now Kitty was paid twice over for her services and if questioned by authority, could always show the Shamrock's menu, innocently printed on pretty pink paper.

She had begun to make good money from her two jobs, and was saving up so she could leave Bet and Sary with some money. She was planning this one day when she went to eat her carry-out, sitting on a bollard by Wapping Dock, and discovered that she wasn't hungry.

This was a rarity. Kitty stared at the bacon sandwich and the apple and then at Patch, who was watching her hopefully.

'You're welcome to it, old gel,' Kitty said, breaking the sandwich into pieces and feeding them to the dog. 'Now as I come to notice, me throat's awful painful, it don't feel a bit like swallerin' food. I could do wi' a drink though.'

She got herself water from a dock-tap, then resumed

her slow saunter alongside the shipping, but as the day progressed, so did her feeling that all was not well with her. The sore throat was bad enough but presently she became aware that while other people were buttoning their coats against the wind, she felt so hot that she had removed her own jacket and tied it round her waist by its arms. That wasn't natural, not even on a mild March day – I reckon you're gettin' a cold, Kitty Drinkwater, she told herself accusingly. Well, you can't afford to be ill, not wi' Mam comin' on well an' Marigold doin' so nicely. She'll get someone else to find fellers for 'er, and then where will us be?

She got herself home and into the pile of rags; her mother had proper bedding now, decent stuff, but she and Betty were saving their money. Kitty was still hoping she would be on the road before too long so spending money on bedding would be a waste.

Next morning she didn't know how to get up; her throat was raw, it hurt her to breathe, and her eyes felt as though someone had cooked them overnight for a joke. She staggered downstairs, saw Betty off to carry parcels from Paddy's Market to the buyer's homes, made her mother tea and porridge, watched her eat it and somehow got herself over to the Fletcher's.

'You look flushed, dearie,' Mrs Fletcher said. 'Ow's your mam?'

'Think I gorra cold comin', but me mam's grand,' Kitty said with satisfaction. 'She's beginnin' to look more like herself. Still . . . keep an eye on 'er, Mrs F.'

'Be in there as soon's I've 'ad me breakfuss,' Mrs Fletcher promised. 'See you later, Kit.'

Kitty went to Marigold's room first, as she always did. Marigold answered the door in a rather dirty dressing-gown with her beautiful golden curls done up in papers and her face as red as a beetroot. 'Don't bring no one back today, chuck,' she said hoarsely. 'I ain't quite meself; I feels rare bad.'

'Me too,' Kitty said ruefully. 'Reckon we've both got 'ead-colds.'

She decided to go round to the Shamrock for some more menus but she never reached it. She began to feel odder and odder; the sky kept dipping and dancing above her head, the tall buildings shrank one minute and grew like grass the next. She sat on the kerb and put her head on Patch's shoulder and had a little weep because she felt so poorly, then she tried to get up and move along. Someone was telling her to move along, she could hear a voice but she could see nothing, only a sort of patchy red and black.

Presently the patchiness turned black altogether and she slumped forward into the road, unconscious.

Frantically, Patch grabbed her by the sleeve and tried to drag her back to safety, then she barked and barked and barked. Someone came along, saw Patch and the girl in the gutter, leaned down and stroked the dog. Patch sniffed cautiously. This was a good girl, a nice girl, a girl she could trust with her beloved Kitty. Patch wagged her tail and sat down, handing over responsibility. And the nice, good girl took one look at the hot and feverish little face, pulled Kitty clear of the roadway, then telephoned the nearest hospital.

'A young girl's collapsed on Preesons Row, just outside the Shamrock Café, opposite the Victoria Memorial,' she said crisply. 'Please send an ambulance at once; I'll wait with her.'

And very soon the ambulance came clattering round the corner and the young lady got into the vehicle, then jumped out again. 'Can you not take the dog? It's our only hope of identifying her,' she said to the ambulance men. 'If not, I'd better stay with it and make my way to the ward on foot.'

'We'll tek the bloody dog,' the driver said as the other men stared at one another. 'Why not? It won't be aboard for more'n a few minutes.'

So the ambulance rattled off to the Isolation Hospital, because the ambulance men knew scarlet fever when they saw it, and Lilac Larkin sat by the swaying bed and stroked Kitty Drinkwater's hot, dry little hand and held onto the dog's collar so it wouldn't be flung about by the motion of the ambulance and wondered just what she had let herself in for this time.

'You shouldn't oughter 'old 'er 'and, Miss,' the ambulance man said presently. 'Scarlet fever's infectious; a killer, if you don't mind me sayin' so, Miss.'

'I'm not worried,' Lilac said, and the ambulance man assumed that she had had the disease and did not fear a recurrence. It did not occur to him that such a pretty, well-dressed young lady simply might not care if she lived or died.

Chapter Thirteen

They tried really hard, at the isolation hospital, to find out who Kitty was so that they could get in touch with her relatives, but Kitty put them completely on the wrong track by telling them, when she was at her worst, that her name was Kitty Drinkwater and she and Patch came from a farm a few miles from Corwen.

'Can you give us the name of the farm, or the village, even?' the ward sister said persuasively. 'We need to get in touch with your people, dear, so that we can try to prevent the disease from spreading through your family. And it would help us if we knew how you'd contracted the illness.'

She was rather taken-aback when Kitty announced that she'd doubtless got it from a sailor. And then Lilac, without meaning to, cast fresh confusion on Kitty's story.

'She may have come from a farm in Wales once, but now she hands out leaflets for the Shamrock Café,' Lilac explained, laughing at the nurse's bemused expression, and showed the older woman a menu which she had found in the pocket of Kitty's light jacket. Perhaps fortunately Lilac knew nothing about the other leaflets, the ones advertising the services of Marigold, and Kitty, even in the darkest days of her fever, said nothing to give anyone a clue.

Patch was not allowed in the hospital, though.

Not even Lilac's most persuasive arguments could work that particular magic. 'She'll respond to her dog,' Lilac said hopefully. The ward sister sniffed. 'She'll come round and speak to it, the way mothers do for their babies,' Lilac stated. The ward sister sniffed louder.

So Patch lived in Lilac's room when she was in it, and behind the reception desk at the Delamere when she wasn't, and fretted for her little mistress, though she was sufficiently sagacious to know, somewhere in her mind, that Kitty was being taken care of. She knew partly because she was an intelligent animal and partly because, when Lilac returned from hospital visiting, she often used Kitty's name over and over, whilst looking deeply into Patch's worried eyes. So Patch was satisfied that, if she stuck close to Lilac, she would end up reunited with Kitty.

Lilac spent all her spare time at the hospital. Not actually on the ward because that was not allowed, the disease being extremely infectious, but on the other side of a broad pane of glass, through which she could see and even speak to, the small patient. From the moment she had seen Kitty lying in the road a chord had been struck somewhere within her – a sense of fellowship, perhaps, or a vague recollection? She had looked at the small, hot face, the abundant red-brown hair, and felt that she had seen Kitty before. What was more, Kitty needed her – needed her as badly as, several months ago now, that other little girl, Lucy, had needed Art O'Brien. Art had risked his life for a child and lost; she was scarcely risking her life, but at least she was doing something for the kid, doing her best, in fact. And since no one else had come forward, her best would have to do.

So whenever she wasn't working, Lilac sat and talked to Kitty through the pane of glass until one day, one wonderful day, Kitty's heavy lids lifted and the fever-bright eyes stared straight into Lilac's. Lilac saw Kitty's lips move, but could not make out, through the glass, what the other girl was saying. She ran for the nurse, who went into the room, but came back shaking her head and saying that the child was talking gibberish.

'She said something about the girl from Penny Lane . . . you don't come from Penny Lane, do you, Miss?'

'No-oo. But I did, once, or rather my sister did,' Lilac said thoughtfully. 'Now I wonder . . . I thought I knew her, there's something just at the back of my mind where I can't reach it . . .'

'Never mind, at least she's spoken,' the nurse said. 'Likely she'll pull through after all.'

And that was Lilac's first intimation that the staff had previously thought Kitty a lost cause.

It was wonderful to come round to white sheets, cleanliness, sweet air and no responsibility, but to glance sideways and see the face she had so longed to see within feet of her – that really did make Kitty wonder if she had died and gone to heaven! But presently a nurse came in with some foul medicine which she tipped ruthlessly down Kitty's protesting throat and Kitty realised she had been ill, was still ill, and must have imagined that face, for when she looked sideways at the pane of glass it was empty; only the reflection of the nurse with the medicine, the bed and Kitty herself rewarded her glance.

'What's your name, love?'

'Kitty Drinkwater.'

'Where d'you come from? We know about the farm, chuck, but not the exact address.'

Kitty felt a spasm of fear; she should not say, she might get Johnny into trouble if folk thought she was laying some sort of claim on the place. She frowned; her head still ached horribly and the skin had peeled off her forehead and cheeks, leaving them sore and dry-feeling.

'I . . . don't live there any more.'

'Where d'you live, then?'

'Off the Burley; number 8 Paradise Court.'

'Do you mean off Burlington Street?'

'Yes, that's right,' Kitty said, already slipping back into the feverish world of sleep she had so briefly emerged from. 'Wi' me sister Bet.'

'Right,' the ward sister said. 'I'll get a health visitor round there later in the day. We'll soon get it sorted out.'

'Well, you're gettin' better,' someone said the next day. It was one of the nurses, sounding cheerful but a bit surprised, as well. 'Be on your feet in a week or two. Then you'll be allowed to see your friend.'

'Friend?'

'Aye. The pretty one what comes and sits behind the glass; don't say you've not noticed 'er!'

So the face was not a dream, then. Someone was there, someone pretty. Could it be Marigold? Or Betty? But deep inside herself she didn't believe it was either of them. It was – it had to be – the girl from Penny Lane.

Nellie had heard, by letter, all about the little girl with scarlet fever and it had worried her deeply. It was all very well for Lilac to say she thought she remembered the child, that Kitty was so alone, that she was only allowed to sit behind a sheet of glass until the danger of infection had passed, it sounded reasonable enough put like that. But Nellie was afraid that Lilac had simply lost her will to live and was looking for a way out. Lilac had never had scarlet fever as a child so she could easily contract it now, and despite the marvels of modern medicine scarlet fever often proved fatal, particularly if the sufferer caught the disease when already at a low ebb both physically and mentally.

So now she sat in her kitchen watching the bread prove and keeping an eye on the clock whilst the oven reached heat and wondering what Stuart would have to tell her when he got home. For Stuart had applied for a job in Liverpool at last and it was a job after his own heart, furthermore. Deputy editor of a reputable evening paper, with the sort of responsibilities which he had been used to taking on in London. So today he had caught the milk train from Euston and would be in Lime Street – Nellie felt a great surge of envy – in good time for the interview.

Prejudiced though I am, Nellie thought now, getting up and putting the loaf tins on her kitchen table whilst she swung open the oven door a short way and prepared to face the blast of heat, I think my dear Stu stands a good chance. He's covered most of the work, he's a scouser born and bred and understands other scousers in a way an outsider would find impossible, and he's so bright and sensible . . . oh surely he'll get the job? Then we can go home at last!

He had said he might ring if he had time, but otherwise he would just jump on a train, and since she'd not heard it was either that they were going to inform the applicants by post or, worst and most unbearable of all, that he hadn't got it and would have to keep looking. Nellie sighed and slid the bread into the oven, closing the door with her usual excessive caution, though she had never flattened a loaf yet. She'd decided not to pester God with any more prayers or promises – she had popped into church every time she passed ever since Stuart heard he'd got an interview, for a few words with the Almighty – but she couldn't help herself having a little extra dig now.

If he gets it, God, he'll be givin' pleasure to so many people, she remarked in an offhand way, more as a chatty aside than a prayer as such. All them folk on the newspaper, my Stuart knows 'em all, he understands 'em . . . if you've got any influence at all . . .

She stopped short, horrified at herself. Either pray or don't, Nellie Gallagher, she told herself. Just don't hint He couldn't if He would! And then, since the loaves were safe in and Elizabeth would be at her nursery school for another couple of hours, she slid to her knees and said a few words of apology for her doubts, a few words of thanks for Elizabeth and Stuart, a reminder that Lilac was a good little soul and needed her family round her at this sad time . . . and then she signed off, got to her feet and went to fetch the beeswax to polish the dining table and chairs.

Waxing away, her face pink with effort, Nellie began to go over in her head all the good reasons for returning to Liverpool, not just her own good reasons but Lilac's, too.

Lilac could see more of little Elizabeth, Nellie thought now, staring unseeingly at the table, gleaming like a dark lake beneath her ministrations. Nellie was still sufficiently besotted with her only child to believe that the mere sight of little Elizabeth would improve anyone's outlook on life. Why, the child adores her Auntie Lilac, having such affection must make a difference – and I could start to introduce her to young men . . .

Nellie had spent two weeks in Liverpool trying to help Lilac to pull herself round after the tragedy – though Lilac had been wonderful, full of courage and good sense – and had seen the Academy of Modern Dance in full swing. Had Lilac wanted to meet a nice young man, the dancing school offered unrivalled opportunities, but though unfailingly polite and as cheerful as was possible in the circumstances, no one could have failed to notice Lilac's total disinterest in the opposite sex. Clearly, finding Lilac another young man was going to be a formidable task and one which might never succeed. But reviving Lilac's interest in life – Nellie smiled at the mere thought of Elizabeth's smooth hair and wide, enquiring eyes – might just be possible when her little niece was present.

Having polished the dining table until she could see her face reflected in it, right down to a tiny spot on her nose, Nellie put away her duster and the beeswax and decided to treat herself to a little outing. She would fetch Elizabeth from nursery school and take a nice walk to Tooting Bec Common, where they would watch little boys sailing boats on the pond or large girls, in school uniform, walking across the grass, shouting, teasing.

I'll pack some sandwiches, Nellie thought, bustling through to the kitchen to check her bread, and a bottle of home-made lemonade, and we'll have a little picnic, Elizabeth loves a picnic. And just for a bit I won't think about the job, or worry about Lilac's state of mind, or fret about my baby being brought up away from home. And whilst I do our carry-out I can plan what to make Stuart for his tea, because he'll need feeding up, poor love, after the sort of day he's probably had!

In the morning the weather had been rainy, uncertain – typical April weather in fact. By the time Nellie set out though, the sun had decided to break through and the wind had dropped to a gentle breeze.

Elizabeth was, of course, last out of the gate. Nellie had often pondered on why it was that when she met Lilac out of school in the old days, Lilac had always trailed far behind the other kids; now here was her little Elizabeth doing just the same. But her daughter was with two or three others, all chattering and cheerful, surrounding the teacher who was young and pretty, clearly loving her job and her company, too.

Nellie saw Elizabeth scanning the waiting parents and nannies – for it was quite an expensive nursery school – without anxiety, though with some interest. Sometimes Nellie called for her daughter, sometimes another mother picked Elizabeth up when she called for her son, Simon. But today Simon had long gone so Elizabeth would realise that she was to be Mummy's sole companion this afternoon.

'I like that best,' Elizabeth had assured her solemnly on an earlier occasion, when Nellie had asked if she missed Simon. 'I have other children in school all day, I like it to be just you an' me.'

Nellie had been enormously pleased; now she waved as Elizabeth broke away from her teacher and came gambolling across the playground towards her.

'Mummy, mummy . . . oh Mam, is that a picnic?' she squeaked, apparently guessing that a covered basket with a bottle sticking out of it indicated treat time. 'Oh, can we go to the common?'

'Would you like to?'

Nellie caught the enchanting child up in a tight embrace from which Elizabeth was slow to struggle free; she loved cuddling, could never get enough of it.

'Oh, yes, please! One day, when I'm bigger, I'll have a boat to sail on the pond, won't I? One day I'll be tall enough to swing on the swings without you to push, one day . . .'

'One day you'll be pushing me on the swings,' Nellie said, setting Elizabeth carefully down on the pavement and straightening her short camelhair jacket and the grey skirt which she wore beneath it. It was a short skirt, but not so short as some of the mothers; my legs are too thin to show off me knees, Nellie protested when Stuart suggested she should try the really daring skirts. But it wasn't the main reason: short skirts were for girls, and Nellie was very conscious of herself as a woman.

'Did you bring me scooter?' Elizabeth said anxiously. 'Oh, I could scoot to the common in a minute . . . in a second, very likely!'

'No, I didn't bring it, because you can't scoot on grass,' Nellie said. 'Besides, you don't want to be watching your scooter all the time we're eating our tea, do you?'

The handsome red scooter had pride of place in Elizabeth's affections right now, though she was passionately keen to own a tricycle. Simon had a tricycle and it meant that when his mummy took them to the park Simon was usually miles ahead of them. Nellie, noting this fact with some concern, for even in a quiet place like Balham the traffic worried her, had privately decided that a tricycle would have to wait until Elizabeth was at least six.

'No-oo,' Elizabeth admitted. 'Sides, when I'm scootin' we can't talk much and I can't hold your hand.'

'True,' Nellie said, squeezing the small and probably grimy fingers securely clasped in her own. 'So let's step out; what shall we do first? The boating pond or the swings or our picnic?'

'Pond,' Elizabeth said decidedly. 'Then sarnies, then swings.'

Nellie wondered whether to correct the slang, then decided to leave it. Elizabeth isn't a little southerner, she's a little northerner, and if she sounds it so much the better, she thought defiantly. She and Stuart did their best to speak standard English, but in the comfort of their own home and each other's company they frequently lapsed a little.

It wasn't far from the nursery to the start of the common. They crossed the High Street, went under the railway bridge and there they were, though they still had quite a walk across the green grass before they reached the more interesting bits.

'Shall I tell you what we did in school today?' Elizabeth said presently, as they walked. 'We made sandpies in the sand-table first. Simon made a little sand-cake with the red mould and then he tried to eat it and Miss Millicent said it was dirty and Red-face said dogs widdled in sand and Miss Millicent said . . .'

'Darling, who's Red-face?' Nellie said patiently. She was endeavouring to stop her daughter from nicknaming, with very little success so far.

'Sara Boyle. She gets angry so quick, Mam, and

her face is often red. She hits the little ones and . . .'

'Yes, all right, only you should call her Sara, darling, because that's the name her mummy gave her. I hope you don't eat sand?'

'Only sometimes,' Elizabeth said sunnily. 'Not every day.'

Nellie tried to turn a snort of amusement into a cough. She blew her nose ostentatiously whilst Elizabeth continued to dance along beside her.

'Where was I, Mam, before you interrupted? Oh yeah, you said to call Sara Sara, only there's two Saras you know, Red-face and Sara, so I . . . poor Mummy, that's a really nasty cough!'

Nellie squeezed her daughter's small paw again.

'I love you, queen,' she said. 'Hey-up, here's the boating pond . . . and the old feller wi' the beard's sailing away already!'

The two of them leaned on the round concrete rim of the boating pond, watching the yachts – tall, elegant ones with painted hulls or gleaming woodwork, small, busy ones floating along, seizing as much of the fitful breeze as they could – and of course the owners, mainly small boys except for the elderly man with the nautical cap, the blazer and the white beard.

'I call him Cap'n,' Elizabeth whispered. 'Cap'n Whitebeard.'

Nellie turned away to hide another of her reprehensible giggles and got the feeling that she had just interrupted someone staring at her. It was an odd feeling, but unmistakable. Of the small group of people clustered around the pond on her right, one had been fixing her with a gaze . . . she glanced across, then away. A man, probably about her own age, had appeared to turn his eyes hastily back to the water, to where a small yacht was turning clumsily as its tatty sail suddenly picked up the wind and filled to a bulging cheek of plenty. He had a small, none-too-clean boy with him and he bent down and directed the child's gaze towards the small yacht.

'See 'er take the wind, Tommy? She's on'y small but she's cheeky ... see the way she snatched the wind off of that big, white yacht?'

Tommy leaned over the parapet and beat the water with one hand. The small yacht, heading for him, hesitated as though in doubt over the advisability of its actions, then sailed stoically on. It came to harbour in the man's capable hands, then was taken out, dripping, and seized by the child.

'Awright, Uncle Joey,' the boy shouted shrilly. 'You stay 'ere, I'll go rahnd the uvver side, send 'er over to you!'

'Will do, me ole mate,' the man said. 'Orf you goes!'

As soon as the child had left him he turned to look at Nellie once more, and found her eyes already fixed on his. He coloured, then dropped his gaze to the water, then seemed to change his mind and looked straight across at her, grinning. He half-raised a hand in a salute, then began to stroll the short distance between them.

Nellie thought about moving away, then changed her mind. The man did look familiar, but she couldn't quite bring to mind where she had seen him. It was possible that it could have been in France, of course, when she had nursed during the war, but there was something about him ... he had come, she was suddenly sure, from further back in her past, so she must have met him in Liverpool, because she had lived there all her life until going to France.

'Miss . . . oh cripes, if I 'aven't gorn and forgot your name, Miss,' the man said. 'Doncher remember me? Joey Prescott what found your little sister – if she was your sister – that time she ran away dahn the Wapping Dock in Liverpool? You 'ad a bruvver Charlie – that I *do* recall – an' 'is wife was 'avin' a baby. Your sister was called Lilac . . . Now that's not the sorta name a feller can forget!'

'Why, Joey Prescott!' Nellie exclaimed joyfully as light dawned. 'How could I have forgotten you, after what you did? I was so grateful, but we never exchanged addresses – and if you came to the Pool again you never looked us up.'

'War broke out soon afterwards,' Joey reminded her. 'My ship was torpedoed twice, I was lucky to escape wi' me life the second time. Well, if this ain't rich . . . 'ow about you an' the little lady joinin' me an' young Tommy 'ere for a nice cuppa? I'd be 'appy to treat you both to a bun, an all.'

Nellie laughed but shook her head regretfully.

'It's awful nice of you, Joey, but we've got our tea with us; Elizabeth was really looking forward to a picnic – Elizabeth's my daughter, by the way. I'm Nellie Gallagher now, not Nellie McDowell.'

'I see . . . yes, come to think, there was a sailor who glared at me that night – dark chap, curly 'air – you married 'im, did you?'

'Oh! No, that was . . . no, I didn't marry him, my husband was a war correspondent in France; now he works for the *London Evening Telegraph*. And Lilac was engaged, but . . .'

Joey Prescott whistled.

'Little Lilac, engaged! It don't seem possible, but then it don't seem possible that I'm out o' the Navy an' workin' for the Merchant line, fust mate on a coaster! I done the paperwork nights, an' got me ticket five year back.'

'Did you get fed up with the Navy?' Nellie asked. She watched Tommy, who was showing Elizabeth how to set the sails of his small yacht. Elizabeth was lying on the parapet on her tummy, small fingers deft on the tiny ropes, obeying Tommy's laconic instructions to the letter and completely absorbed, Nellie could tell.

'Fed up? Yeah, I guess I did. Wanted a bit o' stability in me life, wanted a wife, a family, that sort o' thing.'

'So you're married, too?' Nellie glanced down at Tommy. 'But the little boy said . . .'

Joey looked back towards the yachts and the water, at the sails filling and flattening as they caught and lost the breeze.

'I'm not married now, my wife died six years ago,' he said quietly. 'She'd just 'ad a baby – I lost 'em both.'

'Oh, Joey,' Nellie said softly. 'That's a dreadful thing. I am so sorry.'

'Oh, I'm awright now,' Joey said. 'Time takes the sting away, jest like they tells you it will. I was desperate for a bit, but . . . you learn to live wiv it.'

'Yes, but it's hard,' Nellie said. 'Lilac's fiancé was drowned at sea six months ago. She's still very unhappy.'

'The poor kid,' Joey said. 'Cor, an' to think I've been goin' up to Liverpool a couple of times a month this past year and never thought to try an' find the pair of you! Mind, I did just after the war, I went up and dahn the Scottie, popped into the Court . . what was it called . . .'

'Coronation Court,' Nellie supplied, laughing. 'We moved out of there years ago. Now tell me, what are you doing on Tooting Bec Common in the middle of the week?'

'My ship's 'avin' a bit of work done,' Joey said. 'So I got me a few days free. I take it you're livin' in Tooting Bec?'

'Balham. Not far away.'

Joey nodded.

'I've got a room in Tooting, just for when I'm in the Smoke, but I'm savin' up for a place in the country somewhere. Then, when I retire, I'll 'ave somewhere nice to go. Is Lilac wiv you dahn 'ere? I'd like to meet the kid again.'

'No, she's still in Liverpool. She's a hotel receptionist during the day and she teaches dancing in the evenings. She's quite a little businesswoman . . . but so unhappy, Joey.'

Joey nodded, his expression sombre.

'Yeah, I know what she's goin' through. Wish I could 'elp . . . tell you what, give me the name of the 'otel and drop 'er a line, tell 'er I'll nip in for a chat next time I'm in the Pool.'

'That would be kind,' Nellie said. 'But why not come over to Balham, meet my Stuart and have an evening with us? We'd love it – Stuart would really like to meet you, we talked about you so much when Lilac was younger.'

'Well, I will,' Joey said. 'Fanks, Nellie! Tell Lilac I was askin' for 'er.' He turned to his small charge. 'Come on, old feller, time we got ourselves that cuppa.'

'Wait a minute, Joey; why don't you and Tommy share our picnic? I'm sure it'll stretch that far!'

'That would be grand,' Joey said. 'And then Tommy

and me, we'll walk you back across the park an' treat you to a cuppa an' a spiced bun at the Flora-Dora tea-rooms. And I'll write your address on something so we don't lose touch again.'

'That was a very nice man, that Mr Uncle Joey,' Elizabeth said to her mother as the two of them began the walk home. They had had their picnic, then their cup of tea and their spiced bun, and then they had waved goodbye to Joey and his small friend and set off. 'I liked him very much, Mam. He knows Auntie Lilac too, doesn't he?'

'Yes, though he hasn't met her since she was seven years old.' Nellie was struck by a sudden recollection. 'Elizabeth darling, do you remember Auntie Li telling you the story of when she ran away from the Culler? A kind sailor rescued her and took her home to Uncle Charlie's place and she saw Auntie Bess's new little baby – the baby that's your big cousin Henry now. Well, that sailor was Mr Prescott when he was in the Navy.'

'Then he *is* my uncle,' Elizabeth said joyfully. 'I told Tommy he was, only he wouldn't listen – boys!'

'He isn't really your uncle . . .' Nellie began cautiously, only to see her daughter shaking her head sadly.

'Oh, well, no, but a *relative*,' Elizabeth insisted. 'He's the nicest uncle I've got, and I don't have to call him Mr Thingummy after all! I just hope he tells Tommy! Tommy's just his landlady's son you know, not a real relative at all.'

'I thought you liked Tommy,' Nellie said. She was beginning to see a distinct similarity between her headstrong adopted sister and her small daughter and found the resemblance worrying. 'I thought you got on very well.'

'Yes, he's nice,' Elizabeth conceded, hopping along the pavement on one foot and swinging rather heavily on Nellie's hand. 'But even if he's nice that doesn't mean he can always be right, does it, Mam?'

'Well, no. But Joey isn't related to us at all, darling, he's just an old friend from long ago.'

'He's my uncle,' Elizabeth said in a tone which brooked no argument. 'My *unrelated* uncle. From long ago.'

Stuart was very late home indeed, but he came up the short path to the front door with such a light step and his key rattled so briefly in the lock that Nellie, who had been watching for him from their bedroom window, positively flew down the stairs and across the hall, arriving just as he entered the house, her face alight with anticipation.

'Well? Oh Stu, darling, you must be worn out! Elizabeth's in bed and asleep, your dinner's in the oven keeping warm – I did you a beef stew with suet dumplings because the longer it cooks the better it gets – and there's a lemon mousse for afterwards. Well, aren't you going to tell me what happened?'

'Guess,' Stuart said, smiling down at her. 'Just guess, Nellie Gallagher, who cared so little that she went off out this afternoon when I was frantically ringing to give her the news!'

'Oh Stu, darling! Oh, I waited until nursery school came out and then I picked the baby up and took her to Tooting Bec Common for a picnic and . . . you got it! You did, you did, and we'll be going home at last! Oh, aren't you the cleverest, the best . . .'

'Well, yes, I think I'm pretty damned good,' Stuart said with a conspicuous lack of modesty. 'There were eight of us – eight, sweetheart, imagine that – and every one a local man and most of 'em very nearly as experienced as me. One or two were the wrong side of forty, one was more or less my age, a couple younger, the rest late-thirties. I think we all interviewed quite well, but it was the fact that I'd done the nationals that told in my favour in the end I think.'

'That and your lovely, intelligent, trustableness,' Nellie said, hugging and laughing and kissing the side of his neck. 'Come and feast on beef stew an' dumplings, me lovely feller!'

'And what did you do with yourself today?' Stuart asked presently, when he had taken the first edge off his hunger, and sipped the wine which Nellie had anxiously bought, kept at room temperature and served in their best glasses. She had not dined either, preferring to wait for him, so they shared a pleasant candlelit dinner, with both of them glowing with achievement, though most of Nellie's glow was vicarious.

'Well, after you'd left at the crack of dawn, dearest, I sat down and wrote a nice long letter to Li. Then I got the babe up and got her breakfast. She was a little difficult, still cross because you'd not taken her to Liverpool with you, crosser when she found she'd have to wear her waterproof and her pixie hood because she says she can't skip in a waterproof ... and she didn't like it at all when I said that was all right, since she wouldn't be taking her rope to nursery. It rained quite hard until nearly noon, you know, unless you were too busy to look outside.'

'I arrived like a drowned rat, but I was early so I

went straight to the gents and tidied meself,' Stuart admitted. 'We all had the sense to do that except for the snooty one who came from Crosby and travelled all the way by cab! He got wet running between the cab and the office and stayed like that until he dried off . . . wouldn't crowd into the Gents with the rest of us – very infra dig! Go on though; what did you do next?'

'Oh, Stu, my life is so dull compared with yours! Well, I baked the bread for the week, and I prepared the vegetables for tonight, did the housework . . . waited for the telephone to ring . . .'

'We didn't know until three o'clock,' Stuart admitted. 'It was a series of interviews, and even when we knew I didn't have a chance to phone for an hour, they were taking me round from office to office, introducing me to people. It was fun, I enjoyed it. Everyone was dead friendly, honest!'

'Yes, well; it's home,' Nellie said. 'And then, as I told you, I picked Elizabeth up from nursery and walked to the common . . .'

'I've got a ravishingly beautiful secretary called Iris,' Stuart said wickedly. 'Miss Holmes I'm supposed to call her, but I prefer Iris . . . I bet she'll pander to my every whim.'

But if Stuart had expected an outburst of jealousy he was disappointed. Nellie's face lit up with a huge, beaming smile.

'Not the Iris Holmes I worked with in my last year in nursing! Can it be the same one? She's got deep blue eyes, set with a sooty finger they used to say, and black hair, lovely creamy skin . . . oh Stu, is it really old Iris?'

'You're supposed to drag me off to bed to take my mind off the woman, not claim acquaintance,'

Stuart said, drinking the last of the wine in his glass and reaching for the bottle. 'What an annoying wench you are, Nellie me gal! But fancy you knowing Miss Holmes – it really is a small world, isn't it?'

'Liverpool is,' Nellie said contentedly. 'And it's our small world, Stu – won't it be wonderful to go back?'

They sat up until the early hours, talking. The salary was generous, a car would be provided, telephone and travel expenses paid. Stuart had asked about the availability of housing and was told that there was plenty available; they would be able to pick and choose a property at a price they could afford.

'I thought we'd buy, not rent, this time,' Stuart said as the two of them sat by the fireside, Nellie curled up on Stuart's lap gazing at the flames and no doubt seeing her city in the glowing embers. 'How about trying for something nice and neat on Hawarden Avenue, or Gresford Avenue come to that, in that area, anyway? It's near our old haunts, but you'd get the garden you're so set on and you'd be a sight nearer your Lilac than if we moved out of the city itself.'

'I wouldn't mind one of them big houses on The Boulevarde,' Nellie said wistfully. 'We could have our Lilac to live with us; not that it 'ud do, I know that. But I'd dearly like to have her under me eye until she comes to terms with losing Art.'

'That may take a lifetime, sweetheart,' Stuart said gently. 'And living with us wouldn't be the answer, I promise you that. Sometimes the happiness of people you love is nigh on unbearable.'

'But we wouldn't flaunt our happiness,' Nellie

said uncertainly. 'We'd be tactful, wouldn't we?'

'Nell, when our Elizabeth does something funny or clever, could you stop that great big grin spreading across your face? When I come in tired and you welcome me with a kiss and stories of your day, do I not relax, lean on you, show my love? To try to change, to hide our feelings, would ruin the best thing we've got, believe me.'

'All right. I agree then, that we can't ask her to share our home. But once we're back . . .'

'Oh come to bed, you little plotter! We'll talk about it over and over these next few weeks, I have no doubt. I'll give in my notice tomorrow and work my month, then we'll be off! I'm as excited as you, I promise you. There's a little pub near the offices . . . no, don't hit me, I'm to be allowed all sorts of indulgences because it is I, Stuart Gallagher, who got the job and will be bringing you triumphantly home!'

Towards the end of the month Stuart took a couple of days off which were owing to him, so that his small family might begin to plan their move, and on the first of these he offered to take Elizabeth to nursery so that Nellie might begin to get all her china washed, wrapped in newspaper and stacked neatly into the big tea-chests the removal company had lent them.

'Oh thanks, Stu,' Nellie said gratefully, lifting the delicate, rosy-petalled cups and saucers down from the dresser and carrying them over to the sink. 'It'll be a weight off my mind when these are packed away, because I expect there'll be a good deal of upheaval and they are so pretty and precious.'

So Stuart set off with his small daughter scooting

along beside him and chattering like a magpie all the way.

'Yesterday I told everyone in my class that I were going to move back to Liverpool and some of them . . .' Elizabeth dug her toe into the pavement and scooted well ahead, then turned her head to shout. ' . . . Some of them said horrid things!'

'Did they? What?'

'Well, Simon said could he have my scooter, which was unkind, wasn't it, Daddy? And Annabel said she would sit in my seat and Simon would love her best.'

'Stupid person!' Stuart said at once. 'You'll be taking all your things with you, naturally.'

'Will I? Oh, good,' Elizabeth said, clearly relieved of a secret worry. 'But not me friends, Daddy?'

'Well, no. But you'll make new friends, you see. Very easily and quickly, because Liverpool people are the friendliest people in the world.'

'Are they? Really? Friendlier than Londoners?'

'Oh yes, much friendlier,' Stuart said, thinking of journeys on the underground railway when no one spoke to anyone else except to complain if an elbow got them round the ear. 'Well you know Aunti Li, and Mummy, and me . . . we're all friendly, aren't we?'

'Yes, and I are,' Elizabeth said. She had stopped her scooter so that Stuart could catch up but now she indicated it rather impatiently. 'Could you take my scooter now, Daddy, so we can talk? It's hard to talk and scoot, my puff runs out and my squeak starts.'

This frequently happened, so Stuart picked up the scooter and took his daughter's small hand in his. 'Righty-ho, sunshine,' he said breezily. 'Talk away.'

'Oh, thank you. Right. Well, I want to know whether that Uncle Joey Mummy and I met in the park is a really-truly uncle or just a pretend uncle. That Tommy – he wasn't Uncle Joey's real . . . well, Uncle Joey wasn't his real . . .'

'Hang on a minute, queen,' Stuart said, perplexed. 'I'm not following you. Which Uncle Joey? Which park? When?'

'Oh days an' days ago,' Elizabeth said in a rush, having given the matter some thought. 'On the day you went to Liverpool and lefted me behind.'

'Oh yes, Mummy said you'd gone to the common. And you met a man called Joey? Mummy didn't mention it.'

'I spec' she forgot. He said do you 'member me, and he said did you marry that chap you was with and Mummy said no she married you, an' who did Joey marry, and *he* said his were deaded an' he wasn't sad no longer.'

'Gosh, so Mummy knew him before she married me,' Stuart said, staring down at his small daughter. 'An old friend, then! What else did this old friend say?'

'Oh, he talked and talked, and Mummy talked and talked. And Tommy and me sailed his boat and we had ice-creams and little cakes and melonade which fizzed up our noses . . .'

'Lemonade, not melonade,' Stuart corrected automatically. 'Did Mummy say what his last name was?'

'Can't remember. But I know who he is . . . he rescued Lilac when she ran away . . . oh yes, he's a sailor.'

A sailor! A cold knot of apprehension began to tighten in Stuart's stomach. He was pretty sure that the father of Nellie's first child had been a sailor; if she'd met up with him again by chance, and he knew his Nellie too well to think she would plan such a thing, then no wonder she hadn't mentioned the fellow to him! She must have been hoping that the child would forget all about it too, never think about the bloke again, and nor she would have, had it not been for the double coincidence of his having a day off and Elizabeth's conversation turning to friendship and relatives.

'So what happened, love? What did Joey look like? Was he nice?'

'He was very nice,' Elizabeth said solemnly. 'Not as nice as you, but really nice. He had a brown face, light brown hair, blue, round eyes, he was same tall as you, trousers, shirt . . .'

'Yes, I know what you mean,' Stuart said, since Elizabeth was going puce with the effort of description. 'And he had a little boy, Tommy.'

'Yes, but he weren't Joey's, not really,' Elizabeth insisted. 'He was *my* uncle, not Tommy's.'

'I'll ask Mummy,' Stuart said soothingly. 'She'll tell me whether he was your uncle or not. But don't you have enough uncles, sweetheart? I'm afraid I can't provide any, but Mummy has several brothers. And you've scores of cousins.'

'Ye-es. But Joey's especially nice,' Elizabeth repeated with deep conviction. 'Oh, there's Simon . . . I'll go and tell him I'm taking me scooter to Liverpool with me . . . bye-bye, Daddy, see you later!'

Stuart waved until she and Simon had disappeared into the school, then turned his footsteps homeward with a heavy heart. He knew jealousy was a destructive and pointless emotion which could only harm him and those he loved. Why could he not believe Nellie when she said she had never truly loved another? Why was it so hard to be sensible, to ask outright about Joey just to set his fears at rest? He resolved to ask the moment he stepped through the front door, but knew he would not do it, knew it would fester within him until it became obvious from his attitude that something was wrong. Then Nellie would have to prise it out of him . . . and no matter how harmless the explanation, there would always be that little, niggling doubt . . .

But he was wrong this time.

He got back to the house and there was Nellie on the front step, talking to a man in a sports jacket and flannels. The fellow was tanned and fit looking; Stuart's heart began to bump. Could this possibly be the Joey his daughter had spoken of? And if so, just what was he doing on the doorstep, renewing acquaintance with his, Stuart Gallagher's, beloved wife?

Stuart could feel his hands forming fists, his temper beginning to build, as he flung open the gate and took the little path in a couple of swift strides.

'Nell? Who the devil . . . ?'

'Stuart, you'll never guess who's come calling! Do you remember me telling you how Lilac ran away from the Culler when she was little, and was rescued by a seaman who took care of her for me? Well, it's him – Joey Prescott! We met on the common a couple of weeks ago, I came home full of it, only when you arrived back from Liverpool to say you'd got the job it just went clean out of me head!'

All the jealousy, all the fears, all the stupid, niggling doubts, disappeared. Stuart gripped the other man's hand and shook it heartily, a big smile forming.

'Well, Joey Prescott – it's like meeting a living legend, old feller, the times I've heard the women clacking on about how you saved our Lilac from a fate worse than death! Nell, love, what are you doing on the step – come in, Joey, come in ... did Nell explain about me?'

'Talked about nothing else,' Joey said. 'I 'ear congratulations are in order? Though it's a bit late to congratulate you when you've been married 'alf-a-dozen years! I come over now because my ship's sailing in a few days so I thought I'd pop rahnd an' see whether Mrs Gallagher 'ad writ to Lilac abaht me callin' on 'er when I'm in Liverpool.'

Stuart led their guest through the house, hesitated outside the front room, then grinned at Joey and shook his head. 'No point in pretending we live in there; we live in the kitchen, and if I know Nell that's where we'll find the kettle singing away. But see that photo on the mantel? That's our Lilac, taken last year; quite a change since you saw her last, I daresay! You can see she's turned into a beautiful young woman. And now I'll just get the rum and some glasses, and we'll have a tot to celebrate this reunion.'

Joey stared hard at the photograph, then followed Stuart out of the sitting-room and into the firelit kitchen.

'That's a lovely picture of a lovely girl,' he said approvingly. 'This room's a treat, ain't it? You can tell Mrs Gallagher's a real 'omemaker. I 'aven't 'ad much 'ome life, so I loves a real kitchen.'

'You call her Nellie, and me Stuart, old fellow, and don't forget, we know all about you, me as well as the girls,' Stuart said, fetching glasses for the rum. 'They've told me about you over and over, believe me. You ran away from a London orphan asylum when you were twelve and went to sea. Nellie watched Lilac like a hawk when she hit twelve in case she had the same idea, but she managed to leave the Culler in a more conventional fashion.'

'That's right; I lived in the Metropolitan Orphanage, to the east of Aldgate pump. We all 'ad brahn suits an' big boots, daily lectures on the importance of rememberin' we come from 'ardworkin' people – the deservin' poor rather than idle layabouts drinkin' their money away. No one told us where they got this money from, mind. No wonder I split!'

'Poor little boy,' Nellie said softly, beginning to make tea in the big, brown pot. 'Stu was a Culler boy – did you know that?'

'No . . . you never said, the other afternoon on the common. We was talking rather more abaht the past, though.'

'Here, a toast!' Stuart said. He handed Nellie a small drink and Joey a rather larger one. 'To absent friends – particularly our Lilac!'

They drank. 'And you really will visit our Lilac whilst you're in the Pool?' Stuart said.

Joey nodded. 'Oh aye; always intended to see 'er again one day. Mebbe I'll tek 'er on the ferry . . . I don't suppose Nellie said nothin' abaht it, but I lost my wife six years ago, so I know what young Lilac's goin' through.'

'No, she didn't,' Stuart admitted. 'I'm really sorry, old fellow.'

Joey sighed and raised his glass.

'She was a good gel, my Annie,' he said. 'But I've got some rare 'appy memories; they'll do me, for now.'

Chapter Fourteen

They didn't know how to tell Kitty. Matron, an awe-inspiring figure in a dress and apron so stiffly starched that they would have stood up quite unaided, said that someone who knew her well would be best, so Sister called Lilac into her office for a quiet word.

'Miss Larkin, we've had grave news of Kitty Drinkwater's family. I fear her mother and sister are both in hospital. Mrs Drinkwater isn't expected to live and the child, Betty is very ill indeed.'

'My goodness – what's happened?'

'They were taken to the David Lewis Hospital after they fell into some sort of a cellar . . . I'm not too clear on the details but I imagine the mother was the worse for drink. Apparently the cellar was full of something, coal dust, rubbish, I'm not sure what, which all but smothered the pair of them.'

'How did they struggle out?' Lilac asked. 'I suppose a cellar has stairs, though . . . or were they too injured to help themselves?'

'I imagine so, but fortunately a neighbour heard cries for help and managed to rescue them both, though not before considerable damage had been done.'

'What a dreadful story,' Lilac said with a shudder. 'I suppose Mrs Drinkwater must have fallen against the cellar door and brought the child down as she fell.'

'I don't think the cellar had a door; the health

visitor was shocked by the state of the house, and is strongly recommending to the authorities that the landlord must demolish the whole building, but that's no help to the Drinkwaters, of course. And in the meantime, what do you think? Should we tell Kitty?'

'I think,' Lilac said, 'that you had best start at the beginning, Sister, and tell me the whole story. Up to this moment all I knew was that you'd discovered Kitty's address and were sending someone round.'

'That's right. A health visitor went round, only to find the house deserted. Neighbours told her that as soon as Kitty was out of the way Sarah Drinkwater got herself up to the public house on the corner and began drinking again. The family next door heard the woman return home. Then they heard an argument, then a clatter followed by appalling screams which were suddenly cut off. Fortunately one of the older girls had visited the house and suspected what must have happened. She and the others managed to get a rope round the mother and hauled her out first, then realised that the child was still down there under . . . well, under the rubbish. They got her out, but they said she was blue . . .'

Lilac shuddered.

'Poor little soul. But she'd not developed the fever, at least.'

'Malnutrition had taken a sad toll of her health even before the accident, and now because of her breathing difficulties there is some doubt over her recovery,' Sister said. 'The mother is a big woman, her weight, crushing the child . . .'

Lilac shuddered again. 'Poor little kid. She wasn't fit before the accident, then?'

'No, indeed. Kitty is well-nourished so I'd guess that her time on that farm near Corwen stood her in good stead, but the other child was quite neglected. The health visitor spoke to the authorities and learned that two other children had been taken away from Mrs Drinkwater a couple of years ago, and that Kitty had taken two more little girls into the Father Berry Home only weeks before the accident, explaining that she could no longer feed and support them. It's very sad, but with unemployment affecting more and more people, and with slum housing conditions the way they are, I fear we can expect to see a good deal more disease and death amongst those forced to live in such places.'

'Yes, and the ones who go under are those who don't know where to go for help and have no idea of their entitlements,' Lilac said, trying not to let her emotions show in her voice. 'They're the ones who suffer. They hide away, sure they're in the wrong simply because they can't cope. There are good and caring parents seeing their children grow ill and weak . . .' her voice broke and she stopped abruptly.

'Ye-es, in many cases I would agree with you, but Mrs Drinkwater wasn't a good or caring parent,' Sister said firmly. 'She disliked Kitty and used to beat her; the child had a broken arm, cracked ribs . . .'

'What? She beat her children? I know it happens, but . . . how did you find out?' Lilac said. 'Did Kitty tell you?'

'Not exactly. But the signs are there for anyone to read – a self-set arm doesn't mend quite straight, one of the ribs had actually pierced the skin. It happened years ago, but we could see she'd been maltreated. So when she was more herself Nurse asked her how she broke her arm and so on and Kitty said frankly that her mother had done it when annoyed. And the neighbours said that Mrs Drinkwater gave the children almost nothing to eat and let them fend for themselves, though they seemed to think that Kitty had only lately returned to the house, which is no doubt the reason for her present good state of health.'

'What a wicked woman!' Lilac said, appalled. She thought she knew a good deal about life in the courts, but in Coronation Court there had been friendship and kindliness and a deep sense of loyalty as well as poverty. She remembered men fighting their wives and occasionally hitting their children, but not hitting to deliberately break bones. 'Kitty's well out of it, then.'

'I agree. If the woman was to recover ... but I don't think that is likely to happen. And the family next door, though well-disposed to Kitty and the younger girl, have troubles of their own. One of the older girls and two of the children have taken scarlet fever and are being nursed on another ward here. But I mustn't digress; what I called you in to discuss was how much we should tell Kitty.'

'I'm inclined to think she should be told nothing, until their problems are resolved one way or the other,' Lilac said after a moment. 'There's no sense in worrying her needlessly. Should the subject arise, however, it may be necessary to tell her how things stand. In the meantime I'll visit the sisters at the Father Berry Home – I was in an orphan asylum myself a few years back, it wasn't all that bad, we were fed and clothed. Only ... you like to know you aren't forgotten.'

'That's very good of you, Miss Larkin. You don't think perhaps Kitty may resent not having been told later, when she's better?'

'I think perhaps she can deal with resentment then more easily than she can deal with worry now,' Lilac said, again after thought. 'I may be wrong, but that's how I feel. She wouldn't be allowed to visit the other hospital, would she?'

'Indeed not.'

'Then there can be no harm in leaving her ignorant for a little longer.' She smiled at Sister and rose to her feet. 'If I may, I'll go along and have a quiet word with Kitty, tell her I'm off to the Berry Home, and then I'll catch a tram up there and tell the children that Kitty's improving fast. I won't mention their mother or the other girl unless one of the children asks outright, and I'll see how much I think Kitty can take.'

'I wouldn't want you to tell an untruth,' Sister said doubtfully. 'But I'm sure you'll manage to satisfy them that all is well without actually . . . thank you for your time, Miss Larkin. Perhaps we may have another chat later in the week.'

Lilac left Sister's office and went along to the ward. Kitty was sitting up in bed reading a book. She had chosen, or had had chosen for her, Lilac was not sure which, a book for very young children with very large print. Sensible, since she was still weak and lethargic and doubtless finding it difficult to focus – or concentrate – for long. She was following the adventures of a lively rag doll, but looked up and smiled as Lilac sat in the visitor's chair on the other side of the glass.

'Afternoon, Miss,' she said. Lilac could just catch the words. 'I'm ever so much better today – I 'ad an egg for me dinner!'

'Well done,' Lilac said, smiling. 'Would you like me to bring you some books when I come tomorrow? I'll choose more tales with big print, which will be easier for you until you're rather stronger.'

'They 'ave to stay on the fever ward, though,'

Kitty warned. 'You can't tek 'em 'ome with you . . . better leave it a while. Johnny, a friend of mine, 'e'd be shocked to 'ear they burns the books after a while.'

'It's to prevent the spread of infection, though,' Lilac said, 'so he mustn't be shocked. Kitty, my dear, I'm going to visit the Father Berry when I leave here and Sister tells me you've sisters in there. Would you like to send them a message?'

'You? Visit the Father Berry Home?'

'Yes, indeed. I was at the Culler Orphan Asylum myself for many years. My sister Nellie, too. If you'll give me your sisters' names . . .'

'Course. But I wish someone 'ud get a message to me sister Betty for me; she's at number 8 Paradise Court, off Burlington Street. I gits scared, 'cos me old woman can be 'ard to tek care of, an' Bet's only a bit of a kid really. You see, they'll be took care of in the Berry 'Ome, I know that; Mam an' Bet is on their own.'

'I'll get a message to her,' Lilac said steadily. 'I'll see it's passed to her even if I can't see her myself.'

'You would? Oh Miss . . . thanks,' Kitty said eagerly. 'You are real good.'

'It's no trouble, anyone would do the same. Now what do you want me to say?'

Kitty lay down her book and frowned at her white fingers on the cover.

'Say . . . Kitty's in 'ospickle but she'll be jest fine soon, an' back wi' Bet soon's she can. An' say I's awful sorry to 'ave left 'er in the lurch, an' is there anything she needs real bad,' Kitty said at last, all of a rush. 'An if they're mortal 'ungry, Miss, could you lend 'em a few coppers? I'll pay you back when I git outer 'ere, honest to God.'

'Don't worry about it any more. I'll see they're fed and as comfortable as they can be,' Lilac said. 'I bet you think they'd be better off in hospital, like you!'

'Well, they would be,' Kitty said frankly. 'I's shamed for you to see that 'ouse, Miss, but there's no 'elp for it.'

'Yes there is,' Lilac said. She leaned close to the glass, so that Kitty could hear her without possibility of a mistake. 'Kitty, your mother and Betty *are* both in hospital, getting the best possible care. After you were taken ill there was an accident. Betty was helping your mother upstairs and somehow they stumbled and ended up in the cellar. It was a nasty fall but they're being given every attention. They're in the David Lewis Northern Hospital.'

Kitty's furrowed brow cleared.

'Oh, thank Gawd,' she said fervently. 'Oh, Miss, you don't know 'ow you've relieved me mind! I 'ad visions of 'em starvin', the pair of 'em, like I thought about me dear ole Patch till you said you'd got 'er safe. I spec' me Mam were drunk an' they fell down the Drop . . . it's a wonder they weren't smothered. Who gorrem out?'

'Your next door neighbours, whose name escapes me for the moment. Kitty, dear, if you would like me to do so I can go and visit your mother and Betty when I come back from the Home, and see how they are.'

'Oh Miss! Give Betty me love an' tell 'er to bear up . . . tell 'er I'm gettin' well, an'· she must, too.' She looked anxious for the first time since Lilac had broken the news. 'She will get better, won't she, Miss?'

'I see no reason why she shouldn't,' Lilac said stoutly. 'She's had a dreadful experience, but she's in good hands. Anyway, Kitty, I'd better be off because I'm on the evening shift at the Delamere so I've got quite a lot to get done this afternoon!'

Kitty agreed and waved her off and Lilac made

her way along the corridor and out into the fresh air.

It was not a nice day. It had started off with rain, light and drizzly, but now a yellowish fog hung over the city, with not a breath of wind to stir it. Lilac got a large silk handkerchief out of her coat pocket and looped it round her mouth and nose. It made breathing easier but it didn't do much for seeing. However, she found the small confectioner's shop she was looking for without much trouble, went in and bought a pound of toffee, and then walked a little further along to the tram stop. She didn't have long to wait before the tram she wanted inched to a stop beside her, but already by then the fog was penetrating her handkerchief and she was glad to climb aboard and sit down in the relative warmth. 'The Father Berry Home, on Shaw Street, please,' she said to the conductor when he came to collect her fare. 'When did this fog come down? I've been hospital visiting and when I went in it was just dampish.'

The conductor rattled her out a ticket and considered.

'Let me see ... sudden-like, it were,' he said. 'Must 'ave been an hour or more ago. Wind dropped away to nothing the way it does an' the fog began to pour in from the river. If it stays thick like this Gawd knows what time I'll git 'ome tonight.'

'Same for me,' Lilac said rather gloomily. She settled back in her seat as the conductor moved off down the tram. What a nuisance that she was committed to so much to-ing and fro-ing with the filthy yellow fog so thick! She knew from past experience that the trams got later and later, omnibuses simply ceased to run, people grew irritable and lost their way, and when darkness fell the traffic crawled, their headlamps unable to pierce the fog but merely lighting up the blanket so that seeing through it was even more impossible. Still, a promise was a promise, and she had made it clear that she would at least take a peep at the invalids in the David Lewis.

It took almost twice as long as usual to reach Shaw Street. Lilac hurried up it and along to the Home. She knocked, explained her errand, was admitted. She was a little surprised to be told by a friendly nun that she was not visiting two children, but four.

'Phyllis and Maureen have been here almost two years; they're a great support to their sisters,' the nun said. 'I daresay Kitty forgot that they were already with us when she asked you to visit. But come into the sitting room and I'll send the girls down to you.'

The four little girls who came into the superintendent's sitting room were not at all like Kitty to look at. They were all fair and blue-eyed, with round, rather blank faces. They had none of the sharpness of their elder sister, nor her ready smile, though when Lilac explained who she was, said that their mother had had a fall and was in hospital but that Kitty, also in hospital, was feeling much better and asking for them, and got out the toffee, divided into four small, brown bags by the kindly nun, smiles peeped for a moment.

'When I was your age I would have been mobbed for that toffee,' Lilac said as she handed it over. 'Have you got pockets?'

Four small heads nodded. Each child stuck a chunk of toffee in one cheek and the rest of each bag disappeared into the capacious pockets of their pinafores.

'I'll give Kitty your love,' Lilac said gently. 'And I'll come back and see you next week. When she's well enough she'll come herself, of course.'

The children watched, expressionless, as Lilac headed for the door. They did not ask about their mother, nor about Betty. Lilac was thinking them dull and unsympathetic when, just as she took hold of the handle, one of the children nudged the one next to her.

'Thanks, Miss,' the two of them said in chorus, and one added, 'Tell 'er we're awright, would you, Miss? Tell our Mam to get well an' all. An' tell our Kit as 'ow Eth's takin' care of the kids in 'ere.'

'I will,' Lilac said warmly, and made her way down Shaw Street and back to her tram stop, feeling that she had judged them rather too harshly. They looked stupid, they appeared indifferent, but that was what an institution did for you if you didn't exert your personality, and those poor little kids were probably still stunned by what had happened to them.

Outside, the fog caught at her throat and stung her eyes, making her reach into her pocket for the silk handkerchief. She fumbled in the narrow opening, but the handkerchief wasn't there. Cross with herself, for she remembered now that she had jammed it in carelessly when she climbed aboard the tram, she retraced her steps, but it wasn't in the street nor on the steps of the Father Berry Home.

Shrugging, Lilac turned back towards her tram stop. It was a nuisance, but she didn't need the handkerchief to get back to the Delamere safely, she could turn her coat collar up and keep her chin tucked down and she would still be able to visit the hospital and be back at the Delamere in plenty of time for her shift.

The trouble was, it was just not possible to get a tram on Shaw Street – or on Islington Square for that matter – which would take her straight to the

David Lewis Northern. She would have to change. And whichever way you looked at it, this was no weather to be hanging around at a tram stop whilst time ticked by and your shift got nearer and nearer.

Liverpool's pretty compact; if I go by tram as far as the Old Haymarket and change onto a Vauxhall Road one, then I can easily nip through to the hospital, do my visiting and then walk to Tythebarn Street, Lilac decided. Once she got in the general area of Exchange Station, in fact, the hotel and the hospital were quite close. But the fog was horribly thick and the tram, when it came, was the wrong one. Lilac squeezed herself aboard, wedged between two bad-tempered shawlies with enormous shopping baskets, and stood, peering out at the swirling yellow fog. She realised she was aboard the wrong vehicle when someone announced they were on Great George Street, so she pushed her way crossly out of the vehicle and waited for a tram going in the opposite direction.

She was lucky; a tram sailed up almost immediately and she climbed aboard, but the fog was getting thicker by the minute and to make matters worse the conductor was clearly new to this particular route, so whenever the tram slowed and stopped every passenger gave his or her opinion of their whereabouts.

'Dis is Renshaw Street – sure an' d'you t'ink I don't know me own social club? It's dat big buildin' . . .'

'Renshaw? And 'aven't I bin stoppin' off at Meece's o' Ranelagh Place to buy me taffy an' lickerish since I were a nipper; I can smell it, we're alongside Meece's.'

'Rubbidge, we're just agin de Regal cinema!'

'We come down Ranelagh Place minutes ago, dincher reckernise Lewis's? I reckon this must be Lime Street.'

'Nah, we'd 'a' smelt de trains ... we're well past de station; we'll be on St John's Lane be now.'

'Well, we ain't at the terminus yet,' the conductor said with a brave attempt at humour. 'Reckon we'll all know if we gets there!'

Various furious comments told him, in no uncertain terms, that if they found themselves at any terminus he could just take them all back where they belonged, so the conductor got off and consulted the driver as to their exact whereabouts. He then climbed back aboard again and gave them his driver's opinion.

'E can't see no more'n you can,' he said. 'Next crossroads, e'll stop an' I'll nip down, see if I can spot a road-name.'

So it was in this slow and unsatisfactory fashion that Lilac made the cross-city journey, eventually getting down at Exchange Station, hoping that it really was that station and not Lime Street, with her fellow passengers grumbling mightily as they were borne off into the increasing gloom.

Lilac, coat collar turned up, hands dug deep into her pockets, the moisture already beading her hair and her breath wetting the edge of her collar, checked that it really was Exchange Station, got her bearings and looked for the subway which would bring her out in St Paul's Square, within easy walking distance of the hospital.

The subway was horrid; usually it would have been crowded with people making their way from the station to the small streets which were crammed between the station itself and the docks, but tonight it was almost deserted. Lilac, still with her chin buried in her coat collar, passed a woman with a grizzling child, a tall man with a brightly striped muffler wound round his face, and a seaman with a kit-bag over one shoulder and a bulging paper carrier in his hand. The fog hadn't actually penetrated the subway but the walls ran with water and the smell and general aspect of the place was vaguely sinister. It struck Lilac for the first time that the subway could easily have been a sewer; all it lacked was rats.

However, she emerged into the fog again, crossed the road and began to walk up what she devoutly hoped was East Street. She knew it was when it crossed the railway lines; just here the lines massed, all of them meeting before plunging into the station, and she was able to walk alongside them, one hand on the bricks, until the road ended in a blank wall.

'Old Leeds Street,' Lilac reminded herself beneath her breath, turning left as she did so. She only had to follow the buildings now and she would be in Back Leeds Street which led directly into Leeds Street – not a lot of imagination had been used when naming streets in this area, she thought with an inward smile – which led, in its turn, to King Edward Street, where the hospital was situated.

The fog, if anything, was thicker down here, nearer the docks. But she found the hospital by keeping her wits about her and clinging to the wall, and was glad to enter the foyer, looking round affectionately at the familiar place, for it was here that her Aunt Ada had been cured of the flu, when Lilac had first met Stuart.

The woman behind the desk might have been the very one who had smiled so sweetly at them then, but this one, on being told of Lilac's errand, looked grave.

'I'd best call Sister,' she said. 'If you'd not mind waiting, Miss?' She indicated a hard chair set against the wall. 'I won't be more than five minutes.'

She was as good as her word and presently returned

with a ward sister rustling along behind her. 'Sister West, this is Miss Larkin, a friend of Kitty Drinkwater, who's in the Isolation Hospital. She's come to see Mrs Drinkwater and Betty, on behalf of the other girl.'

The ward sister did not smile, but she gave Lilac a direct and friendly look and held out her hand.

'How do you do, Miss Larkin? I'm afraid I've bad news for you. Mrs Drinkwater died earlier in the afternoon. Betty is sleeping; she's very weak. Would you like to come up to the ward?'

Lilac hesitated.

'I've never met . . .' she began, but Sister West shook her head.

'It's all right, the mother's body is already in the hospital mortuary. But the child . . . perhaps if you could tell her Kitty's well . . . the only time she speaks is to her sister, trying to explain how she came to let her mother leave the house, as though a bit of a thing like her could have prevented . . . but there . . . if you would follow me?'

Lilac followed. There seemed little else she could do.

The children's ward was a long one, and most of the beds were unoccupied at this time of the afternoon.

'Unless they're confined to bed they're having tea,' Sister explained in a low voice. 'Betty's in a side-ward. This one.'

She opened the door and went in; hesitantly, Lilac followed.

The child lay, so small and flat that she scarcely rippled the covers, neatly in the middle of the narrow white bed. Her skin was a strange, bluish-purple colour, her breathing ragged and stertorous. She was so thin, Lilac saw, that her bones seemed in danger of breaking through the skin and the hand lying on top of the covers was little better than a claw.

But Sister was bending over the bed.

'Betty, dear, a lady has come to see you – a lady who has been to see Kitty, too. Kitty knows all about your fall, she doesn't blame you in the least . . . but I'll let Miss Larkin have a word.'

She moved aside, then pulled a chair up to the bed. Lilac sat obediently down on it, and leaned nearer to the small, still figure. She glanced up at Sister, who nodded encouragingly.

'She can almost certainly hear,' she murmured. 'Do what you can, my dear.'

Lilac took the small, cold hand in hers and chafed it between her palms.

'Betty? Kitty's so sorry you're ill and says please get well, just as she's getting well, so you can be together again,' she murmured. 'She quite understands about the fall . . .'

The pale lips moved, the head stirred just a little on the pillow.

'It . . . were . . . the Drop, our Kit,' the child breathed. 'She were so strong an' 'eavy, there weren't nothin' I could do.'

'No, you did wharrever you could,' Lilac said at once. 'You did real good, our Bet, I couldn't 'ave done berrer meself.'

She didn't know what made her say it nor why she spoke with the thick accent she had used as a child, but Betty heaved a sigh which Lilac was almost sure was satisfaction. 'Oh, Kit, I loves you,' she said, her voice so faint that Lilac had to lean even closer to hear the words. 'But I does ache!'

The child took another deep breath, as though to say something more, then expelled the breath gently.

She did not breathe again.

When Lilac left the hospital an hour later she was in a very low state of mind. That poor little kid could never have made a full recovery, would always have been ailing, and her circumstances were such that she would have had to enter an institution. But even so . . .

A life snuffed out because of a selfish, drunken mother and an uncaring father, Lilac mourned as she stepped out once again into the thickness of the fog. If you're a foundling, like me, at least you aren't burdened by those who ought to support you but instead seem to do their best to undermine you and bring you low. Even if I'd not had Nellie's support I'd have been a good deal better off than the Drinkwater kids.

Art had been burdened by an uncaring father and a downright nasty mother, Lilac remembered, stepping out into the road once more, but he'd turned out lovely, had Art. Caring, strong and honest. As different from the other O'Briens as chalk from cheese. But despite her resolve to turn the loss of Art into something which would strengthen her and make her into a better person, it was still too new, too raw, to be anything but painful to think of him.

It would not always be thus, though. Nellie had assured her of this, said that one day Lilac would be able to remember Art with love and affection and enjoy the memories, as one would enjoy remembering a childhood long gone, or one's wedding day or first dance.

'Time really does heal,' Nellie had said in her soft voice, giving Lilac a strong and steady glance.. 'It'll heal your hurt too, queen, I promise you, though it'll seem impossible for a good few months yet.'

And Lilac, remembering Nell's first love and the child she had borne, knew that the older girl spoke from experience and admired her more than ever, remembering her bravery at the time and her unfailing cheerfulness.

Presently, she realised she must have turned in the wrong direction when leaving the hospital, or perhaps she had unthinkingly left by a different entrance, for all of a sudden there was a change in the steady thickness of the fog, a feeling of space before her, and a sound she knew but could not immediately recognise, a soft slapping, chuckling, a gurgling ... Lilac stopped short and stared around her, considerably dismayed. It was water, that was what she could hear, so somewhere not too far away, unless she was much mistaken, was the edge of the dock! Darkness had fallen some time ago; she realised she had not so much as glanced at a clock during her time in the Northern Hospital, but now, when she looked up, she could not even see a glow above her. The fog was completely blanketing the street lamps, always presuming there were lit lamps near her, of course.

Standing still, with the fog beading her coat and hair with moisture, she realised that she could have turned a couple of times without realising it, and that the dock need not be directly in front of her but to the right, the left, or even behind. It was a horrid feeling, for the place seemed to be deserted and though Lilac could swim she did not much fancy her chances in the chill of the fog, especially when muffled in her coat and boots.

But she could not stand here for ever, waiting

for something to happen. She felt forward with her foot, found firm ground, stepped, felt forward again, stepped . . .

It would have taken a long time and she still might have ended up in the water, but she was saved by a commotion ahead, a little to her right. She could hear voices, a bumping sound, cheerful shouts: the dock was no longer deserted, she could even see a figure, dimly outlined, not more than a few feet from her.

Lilac started forward, beginning to smile.

'Oh, excuse me . . . I'm lost, I came out of the hospital and must have turned in the wrong direction . . . could you possibly guide me back to the road? I would be so obliged to you!'

They were sailors, still in uniform – deckhands, probably. Half-a-dozen of them. A couple of them looked at her incuriously, then shook their heads – could they be foreign, perhaps? But they were not, as they soon proved.

'Hello, chuck – lost, are ye? Right, folly us!'

One man took her right arm, another her left. They turned resolutely right, walking as though they could see through the fog, though Lilac, dragged bemusedly between them, could still see nothing.

A third man, slightly behind them, spoke in a thick country accent, his voice slurring a little.

'Thee's got a right shapely boom on thee, lass; Ah wouldn't mind an 'andful o' that!'

Best ignore it, Lilac was thinking, when the man gripping her right arm spoke sharply.

'Gerrout, Tam, finders keepers; Alf an' me 'as fust go.'

Lilac tried to tug herself free of the men, without success, so she began to struggle.

'Ay up, gairl, we'll pay ye all fair an' square,'

the man on her left said. 'We're jest ashore, see –
got plenty o' gelt. Ow much d'you charge? I reckon
it'll be five bob each, eh? Got a room?'

'No I have not,' Lilac said furiously. 'I told you I was
lost in the fog and lost I was! I'm not street-walking,
I'm a respectable woman!'

'You're a nice gairl – ain't they all?' the man on
her right said consolingly. 'But the money's good –
why, you'll tek 'ome fifteen shillin' jest from the t'ree
of us; can't be bad, eh?'

'You'll wake up in gaol after I've been to the police
. . .' Lilac began, then felt her captors veer abruptly
to the right. A narrow alley loomed, she could just
see the walls on either side. Oh God save me, she
thought as they dragged her, kicking vigorously and
telling them at the top of her voice that they were
making a mistake which they would suffer for, they
don't believe me, they're going to . . . to . . .

Desperation lent Lilac strength. She tore herself
out of the grasp of the two men, swerved to avoid
the third, and was away, running heedlessly now, no
longer fearing that she might plunge into the dock, no
longer fearing anything but pursuit and what the men
whose voices, shouting to her, were growing fainter
with every step she took, might do.

She was beginning to believe she had escaped,
that she really was free of them, when she heard
footsteps. A man's tread, she was sure of it. She
stopped short, staring blindly around her. She saw
ahead of her a tall building with golden light spilling
out of a doorway . . . she ran full out, her breath
sobbing in her throat, a hand pressed to a stitch in
her side, and just as she got close to that golden light,
just as she began to feel herself safe, she cannoned into
someone.

'Whoa, lass, whoa! You're in a hurry ... what's up, gel?'

A face loomed above her own. An intelligent face, the mouth curved into a slight, enquiring smile, the brows rising.

'Oh, oh, some men ... they're chasing me, they think ... they think ...' Lilac stuttered. 'Don't let them get me!'

'You poor gel ... come on, come into the 'otel, you'll be safe enough in there.'

The man pushed her gently in through the open doorway and Lilac, still trembling and with her legs beginning to feel as though they belonged to someone else, nearly fainted with shock and relief.

It was the Delamere! In her mad panic-stricken flight she had actually run to her destination!

She turned to the man standing beside her, a hand still on her arm.

'I'm very grateful,' she said awkwardly. 'I hadn't realised where I was ... I'd been hospital visiting and I got lost in the fog ...'

'You're soaked, you've been terrified, an' someone's nigh on tore the coat off your back,' the man remarked. 'Eh, your legs is black an' blue! Where's the receptionist, you need a clean-up before you goes on anywhere else.'

'I am the receptionist,' Lilac said with a watery giggle. 'I was on my way to work when those men attacked me. I expect I'm late, and Mrs Brierson probably thought as it was quiet she'd go down for her dinner. Thank you very much sir, for your help, but I'd better get behind the desk now and start work.'

'That you won't, ducks,' the man said decisively. He crossed the foyer in a couple of strides and banged the bell on the desk. 'You'll want to straighten up first

'. . . you're covered wiv mud an all, you know!'

Lilac, still trembling with reaction, glanced down at herself and had to fight back the tears. She was filthy, not just her coat but the dress beneath it as well, her stockings, her shoes . . . and glancing in the mirror behind the desk she could see that she looked an absolute fright – her hair hung in wet witch-locks around a pale face on which scratches and a big blue bruise had appeared.

'You're right,' she mumbled. 'I'll have to sit down for a minute, too, before I can start work.'

One of the maids, coming to answer the bell, glanced across at Lilac and then stared.

'Oh, Miss . . . what 'appened? I'll get Mrs Brierson at once, she'll see to you.'

The man got a chair from behind the counter and made Lilac sit down on it. Then he knelt and began to take her shoes off. It was quite a hard task since the shoes were thick with mud and Lilac's feet had been trampled on in the mêlée so that blood was caked round her torn stockings and black bruises were beginning to appear. As he worked he said conversationally: 'You're Lilac Larkin, ain't you? I reckernise you from your photograph.'

'Yes, I am. But . . . but . . .'

'I'm Joey Prescott; I met your sister Nellie down in Balham . . . didn't she write?'

Lilac stared at him; yes, she recognised him now, he had changed scarcely at all, he even had his tiny little moustache, though she supposed he must look older – it had been fifteen years after all. She smiled at him, the colour beginning to creep back into her cheeks.

'Of course, she said you might come to Liverpool, but . . . oh, Joey, isn't it strange? The first time we met you rescued me and now you've rescued me again! Thank you so much. I don't know what I'd have done if you'd not caught me – gone on running until I dropped, I imagine.'

'You poor kid,' Joey said. 'Ah, 'ere comes the marines!'

It was Mrs Brierson, looking very concerned.

'My dear Lilac, Ethel says ... my goodness, you are in a state! Did you fall? Your poor little toes ... you've been knocked down in the fog, everyone drives too fast these days, you're lucky to be alive!'

'It wasn't ...' Joey began, but stopped at a warning glare from Lilac.

'I'm only cut and bruised, Mrs Brierson,' she said. 'If I can just have a hot wash ... oh goodness, my clothes!'

'Exactly; you're in no state to sit behind the desk, my dear, even if I were to allow you to do so, which I most certainly shall not. Look, the hotel's half empty, I'll give you a room and lend you a nightgown so you can get a good night's sleep, and in the morning we'll hope the fog has cleared so you can go back to the flat. Only ... are you sure I shouldn't call a doctor?'

Lilac laughed and stood up, albeit shakily.

'No, really, I'm just shaken up.' She turned to Joey. 'I'm so sorry, I should have introduced you; Mrs Brierson, this is an old friend of mine, Mr Prescott. Joey, my employer, Mrs Brierson.'

The two shook hands solemnly, then Joey cleared his throat.

'I was comin' to see Lilac, take 'er out for dinner,' he said rather awkwardly. 'But I'd like a room for a night or two, if you can manage that.'

'Aha, a customer! But it isn't fair, Joey, after you've brought me in here and helped me that you should

'. . .' Lilac began, to be shushed at once by her employer.

'Your friend's welcome to stay, dear. Special rates for friends and family, eh? Now Lilac, I'll give you Room seven because it's near the bathroom and you're going to need a good, hot bath. And Mr Prescott, Room twenty-two is free, that's on the third floor and next door to another bathroom.' She paused discreetly. 'Is it just the one night?'

'I'm not sure,' Joey said. 'Lilac might prefer me a bit further off!'

Lilac began to disclaim, but Mrs Brierson took her arm.

'Come along, my dear, you're in no state to stand here arguing! I'll get Eva to bring a tray of supper to your room presently, unless you'd rather put my thick dressing gown on and come down to the kitchen?'

'I'd like that; can Joey . . . Mr Prescott, I mean . . . come down as well?' Lilac asked. 'We've got rather a lot to talk about.'

Mrs Brierson gave Joey a quick, hard glance, then her face softened and she smiled.

'What an excellent idea; Mr Prescott, what do you think?'

'I'm more at 'ome in a kitchen than a posh dining room,' Joey admitted, returning the smile. 'Shall we say in 'alf an hour, give Lilac a chanst to get 'erself smartened up?'

'Half an hour it shall be; I'll warn the chef. Now off with you, Miss Larkin. I'll ring for George, he'll show Mr Prescott to Room twenty-two.'

Joey spent five nights at the hotel, and every spare moment with Lilac. When she was working he amused himself, walking Patch for miles along the docks, taking her on the overhead railway right out to Seaforth to run on the sands. Patch took to him at once, and revelled in the exercise after putting up with the very much shorter walks which were all Lilac could manage. When he wasn't walking the dog he looked round the shops and visited the museums and art galleries, informing Lilac with a grin that he had never known improving one's mind could be so pleasant.

On the second evening he went with her to the hospital and talked to Kitty, who was no longer infectious but very weak and lethargic still. The death of her mother and sister had put her back, there was no doubt of that, but Lilac could see that Joey was good for her. He made her laugh with anecdotes about Patch and his museum-visiting, he taught her how to tie various nautical knots, and he told her she was good company so he intended to visit her again. Having met Lilac's protégée, he then felt it incumbent upon him to buy her puzzle books, jigsaws and other amusements, and to invent games which could be played by someone propped up by pillows and with a short attention span. Kitty pulled a long face when he told her his ship sailed next day.

'Never mind, I'll be back in three or four weeks,' he said comfortably, when she turned her head into the pillow. 'You'll be out of 'ere by then, you can come and walk Patch wiv me – miles, we cover, ole Patchie an' me.'

As for Lilac, she found herself looking forward to her off-duty times with real enthusiasm, when Joey would buy her fish and chips and walk her along the docks, or take her riding the overhead railway so he could show her the big ships and explain about them, or just sit in a café drinking coffee and catching up with each other's lives.

And for the first time, Lilac found herself able to talk about Art without breaking down.

'It's because I've been in the same situation, so I knows 'ow it 'urts,' Joey said wisely, when Lilac commented on the way she felt. 'My Annie was a lovely gel, I wish you could 'ave met 'er, you'd 'ave got on a treat. But she's gorn and now I can look back on the good times and be glad I 'ad them, to remember 'er, see? I've made myself forget the bad times. She didn't want to die, see? She fought against it; them's the times you've gotta forget or you'd go mad.'

She understood. She told him, low-voiced, that she dared not let herself imagine Art's death, the pain was too bad. He nodded.

'Aye; thank God, littl'un, that you didn't 'ave to watch it. You just tell yourself it's over, the bad time, that your feller's at peace.'

She cried, then. Little, heart-tearing sobs, her head buried in his shoulder. And he was good, rocking her in his arms, telling her to cry out the pain, to let the tears bring her ease.

When the time came for him to leave he said he'd call in again, if she'd like him too.

Lilac nodded hard; to her own surprise she was too full to speak. He had been so good, he had helped her in a hundred different ways, yet he was almost a stranger . . . one meeting, fifteen years ago, and he had got closer to her than almost anyone else, save for Art and Nellie.

'He's lost a lover too,' Nellie said, when Lilac told her how she felt about Joey. 'He understands in a way most of us can't, even those of us who've . . . who've known sadness. He's coming back again, I hope?'

Lilac smiled and nodded. 'Yes, in about a month. I wouldn't be able to face Kitty otherwise. She says he reminds her of Johnny Moneymor, the boy who took her into Wales. There's no higher compliment than that!'

Chapter Fifteen

Kitty looked around her, at the bright summer day, at the clear blue sky above, even at the buildings opposite the Isolation Hospital, and thanked her stars that she was coming out of it on her own two feet, even though Lilac was insisting on hiring a taxi cab to get her home.

And not to Kitty's own home, either. She was to go to Lilac's flat as, Kitty supposed ruefully, she no longer had a home, not any more. After her mother's death there had been no one to pay the rent at the house in Paradise Court, and in any case the authorities had announced that it was to be demolished. That left her homeless . . . perhaps it had been that as much as her sudden loss which had brought about the relapse but, thinking about it now as she crossed the pavement on her shaky legs, with Lilac's warm hand on her elbow, Kitty suspected that it had been guilt.

When she had been told that Sary and Betty had both died her first feeling had been of the deepest and most dreadful guilt. Betty had managed before Kitty had come on the scene, that was what she kept thinking. Bet was only a kid and none too bright, but she had somehow kept what was left of their family together, she had even kept their mother alive despite her heavy drinking and the illness which hung over her as a result. Then along came Kitty, capable Kitty, and within a matter of months the kids were in a home and Sary and Betty were dead.

Kitty had stared at the ceiling for two days, ignoring what went on round her, waiting for death to smite her as she surely deserved to be smitten, wracked with grief for poor little Betty, who had tried so hard, who had actually loved the drunken hulk that was Sary Drinkwater.

It had taken Joey to point out the obvious – that they hadn't died of scarlet fever, brought home by Kitty, which was something to be thankful for. She could scarcely blame herself for contracting the disease, since she imagined she had caught it off Marigold, who had been in and out of the Isolation Hospital around the time that Kitty was at her worst. Marigold had recovered – Kitty was very glad of that – and was probably back at work already. Joey pointed out as well that it was because of Kitty's hard work and presence that Sary and Betty had lived as long as they had; it was only in her absence that they had been unable to keep going and had died.

'You stayed, 'orrible though that place was, an' did your best for 'em, when it would 'ave been easier to 'ave give 'em money and scarpered,' he said bluntly. 'You're a good gel, young Kitty, an' don't you forgit it!'

It made Kitty feel a good deal better, though she did not blame herself unduly for Sary's death; it had been only a matter of time, she knew that. But Betty – ah, her sister was different. She had *earned* a life, Kitty thought confusedly from the depths of her weakness and guilt, but she had not lived to enjoy what she had earned. And that was wrong, wrong!

Then Joey told her about his Annie, how she'd contracted a horrible disease called meningitis which had killed her and their little baby. He told her of his deep feelings of guilt because he'd been at sea, had only returned in time to watch them die . . . ·Kitty had held his hand and cried, then, not for herself but for Joey's young wife and her own young sister, who had deserved better but who would not have dreamed of laying blame.

When Joey went the guilt and depression came back for a bit, but Lilac talked to her, restored a sense of perspective and a degree of self-esteem, reminding Kitty that she had other little sisters who would be proud and happy to spend time with her when she was out of hospital, reminding her – as if she needed reminding – that she had a debt to pay to Johnny, as well.

'He was a good pal to you, and though you never meant to leave him in the lurch, it happened,' she reminded Kitty. 'When you're well you'll have to get in touch with him, dear. Think how glad and grateful he'll be that you're alive and well, even if you never get that farm!'

But now Kitty crossed the pavement, her knees wobbling from the unaccustomed exertion, and stood on the kerb, breathing in the salt air with a blissful smile on her face. It was good to be out of doors again, good to be free of the hospital smells, disinfectant, doses, boiled cabbage. She smiled at Lilac, who was stepping into the road to hail a passing cab.

'Here's the cab; hop in, Kitty,' Lilac said cheerfully. 'We'll be home in a jiffy.'

Kitty got into the car and sank thankfully down on the soft leather seat.

'Phew, who'd ha' thought walkin' down a corridor and acrost a pavement could be so tirin'?' she gasped, leaning thankfully back against the cushions. 'I reckon I'll be good for nothin' for a coupla days, Miss.'

'That's all right; Patch will look after you,' Lilac said. 'I told her you were coming home today and she got so excited! She's a remarkably intelligent dog you know.'

'I does know,' Kitty said, contentedly watching the city go by through the side window. 'It's been ever so good of you to keep 'er for me, Miss, I won't forget it.'

'She's been good company; but now I'll have you, as well,' Lilac said. 'Isn't it odd, we exchanged a few remarks in a hat shop goodness knows how many years ago, yet even then I felt that you would be a friend, one day. And here we are, going to share a flat!'

'Only till I can gerrout and work,' Kitty said flatly. 'I've gorra get some money so's I can find Johnny and I can't let you do any more for me, Miss.'

'And if you persist in calling me "Miss" when you know very well my name is Lilac, I won't do anything at all for you,' Lilac said roundly. 'What's the matter, Kit? You called me Lilac in hospital without your tongue falling off!'

'Oh aye, but in there it were different,' Kitty said awkwardly. 'Oh Mi ... Lilac, I mean, look at me bloody legs!'

With boots on, and a short, full skirt, Kitty's thin little legs did indeed look pathetic, like a couple of pipe cleaners. Lilac patted her skinny knee consolingly.

'Yes, legs like a canary but a heart like ... like a lion,' she declared. 'Don't worry yourself, Kitty, you'll be strong and stout again in no time. And in a couple of days you can meet my sister Nell, because they'll be settled in their house by then, and she'll help me to feed you up and get you fit for this work you talk so much about.'

'I gorra work, for me own sake,' Kitty said, looking almost pleadingly up at the fair, smiling face so near her own. 'If I find Johnny an' 'e's awright wi'out me, I's still goin' back to the country, see? There's all sorts I can do there. But I'll need some cash, an' me full strength.'

'Good for you, then,' Lilac said. 'Just don't try to run before you can walk, there's a good girl. I'm going to enjoy taking care of you. Why, as soon as we get home you're going to have a proper dinner – roast beef, roast potatoes, cabbage – and then I'll pop you into bed with a nice cup of hot milk and some arrowroot biscuits and you can sleep off your exertions until morning.'

Kitty smiled, but inside herself she sighed. She did not know how to tell Lilac that she needed, above everything, to have a bit of independence after weeks and weeks of being babied and bullied and bossed by every ward maid and nurse at the hospital. She didn't want coddling, weak though she might be, she wanted the challenge of peeling her own spuds, boiling her own kettle, even shopping for her own milk and biscuits.

I were always better at lookin' after folks than bein' looked after, she thought rebelliously. 'I'll have to tell 'er, sooner or later, or I'll bust.

'Here we are, my dear,' Lilac said as the taxi cab pulled up alongside a large block of flats. 'Let me give you a hand – the driver will bring your bag up.'

Kitty's bag was full of the stuff which Lilac had brought her; nice things, pretty things, useful things. But not chosen by Kitty, nor paid for by her. I'll never stand it, Kitty thought desperately as Lilac insisted on helping her up every one of the twenty-four stairs to her flat. I'll go mad cooped up here, dependent agin, 'stead o' gerrin' out there an' copin' for meself.

Nevertheless, by the time they reached the flat she was glad to sit down and found herself quite unable to eat the excellent meal Lilac had cooked. But the welcome from Patch made up for her sudden weakness, for Patch was beside herself with joy. She tried to climb onto Kitty's lap and was gently pushed off, for Kitty was not used to such displays of affection and was very soon weeping, her arms round the dog's neck, her tears liberally bedewing Patch's thick neck-ruff. And Patch wriggled and whined and gave little yaps and licked and licked, her golden-brown eyes shining with devotion, her every movement proclaiming her love. Kitty found all her annoyance with Lilac for coddling her, all her guilt over Sary's and Betty's death, fading away to more manageable proportions. Patch loved her no matter what – and Patch reminded her more than anything else could have done that there really was another Kitty, another life, waiting out there for when she was well enough to go in search of it. So she would do just as Lilac said, get herself strong and fit once more. And then – ah then, she would find out what had happened about the farm, what had become of Johnny, if it took her the rest of her life!

Kitty had moved into the flat with Lilac at the end of May. It was nearing the end of June before she announced her intention of leaving, and then she did it not to Lilac, but to Nellie.

She had grown fond of Lilac's beloved sister and made a great fuss of little Elizabeth, but in fact she told Nellie her plans because it had struck her that Lilac's loving care was as much for Lilac's sake as it was for Kitty's own, and Nellie confirmed this.

'She lost her fiancé in a tragic accident at sea; they were to be married in a matter of weeks,' Nellie had explained. 'Stuart got the job in Liverpool soon afterwards, but Elizabeth and I couldn't leave the house in Balham until it was sold and then we had to find ourselves another house, organise the move and so on. Oddly enough, I thought I was coming home to take care of her, but Lilac's grown competent and self-reliant and doesn't need me the way she once did. In fact, my dear, it was you she needed – someone to take care of, to cherish. You've done her a great deal of good and if you feel that the time has come to act a little selfishly and move out, perhaps you'll be doing her even more good. There's a young man who seems fond of her . . .'

'Joey Prescott,' Kitty nodded. 'He's ever so kind but I don't know whether he's sweet on Lilac. She gets letters most weeks, he rings the hotel, but 'e 'asn't come up again yet. Joey said somethin' about a trip to New Brighton, but she said it were too soon.'

'New Brighton! That's where . . . she was right, it is too soon,' Nellie said decidedly. 'But Kitty, my dear, where will you go? You are very much stronger, you've got a good colour, you've fleshed up nicely, but jobs are hard to come by and both Lilac and I would hate to see you grow thin and pale again.'

'I said I'd git work first, but I won't, I'll go to the country,' Kitty said at once. 'Johnny an' me, we lost each other in Liverpool, but I know where he'll be, if he's able. It's a long story, but after I ran away from 'ome after I lost them trimmin's . . .'

She told Nellie the story and Nellie, making pastry on Lilac's kitchen table, looked doubtful.

'And you're hopeful that he found the witness

to the will and got the farm? My dear, of course it's possible, but if he had wouldn't he have tried to find you?'

'He would, of course,' Kitty agreed. 'But how? First I were in me mam's house in Paradise Court, the one place I swore I'd never go near no more, then I were in the Isolation 'Ospickle. I reckon he's give me up, but I ain't done for yet. Me and Patch 'ere, we know our way 'ome.'

'Tell Lilac, then,' Nellie advised. 'She'll help you, I know she will.'

Kitty could not explain, not even to Nellie, that she neither needed nor wanted help. In some part of her mind she believed that she would only find what she wanted alone, by her own efforts. So one overcast morning, when Lilac had gone happily off to the hotel, leaving Kitty to do the housework and cook a meal, she packed her bag, wrote her friend a note, and left. She and Patch trotted down the stairs, out of the front door and along the pavement without a single backward glance; their attention was fixed on what lay ahead – the grey ribbon of road which would wind slowly onwards until it reached the place they longed to be.

Footing it wasn't the fun it should have been with just the two of them and no Johnny, but even so, they enjoyed themselves. Once they were clear of the city Patch really perked up. She ran ahead, she loitered, she rushed into meadows and snuffled along river banks. But she kept an eye on Kitty and was at her side in an instant when someone approached.

The first night was spent in a garden shed, the pair of them curled up on a pile of old sacks. Kitty, who had spent the past months under a roof and sleeping between sheets in a proper bed, was surprised at how good it was to find herself a makeshift meal and sleep on sacking. No doubt it would pall after a night or two, but right now, it felt good. On the second day she got a job, of sorts. She passed a farm where they were haymaking and went into the field. Without a word she picked up a pitchfork and joined the line, turning the hay, whilst Patch disappeared and came back after an hour or so with a rabbit hanging limply from her mouth.

The farmer's wife let them share her midday meal and took the rabbit in exchange, she said, for allowing Kitty to sleep in the hayloft. And next morning, early, she invited Kitty in for a bite and asked if she would give a hand with the poultry before going on her way. She had a lot of poultry and wanted the sheds where they roosted cleared through so Kitty cleaned, disinfected, brushed, barrowed . . . and was fed again, and thanked, and sent on her way.

On the seventh day they had barely set out from their latest barn when they heard thunder grumbling and growling in the distance. The Welsh hills, for they were nearing their destination, were lit from time to time by flashes of lightning. But Kitty and Patch plodded on through the downpour, with their hearts set on reaching the farm. They got there just as the storm grumbled off into the distance and a pale and watery sun lit up the scene. Patch and Kitty, by common consent, reached the gate and just stood, staring. There was the house, its tiled roof steaming gently as the sun gilded it with long, golden rays. There was the barn, there were the haystacks, the sheep in the fields, their fleeces steaming too as the sunshine touched them with warmth. And behind, there were the humped shoulders of the Berwyn range, green with new bracken and gold with gorse, and the rowans and birches overhanging the pond, every leaf sparkling with raindrops.

'Ain't it just beautiful, Patch?' Kitty murmured, her hand on the dog's ruff. 'Oh, how'll I dust go up to the door? If that man answers the door . . . oh, Patchie, I dussen't!'

But it was as though her body took over, since her hand reached out and swung the gate open, then latched it behind her. The two of them walked up the drive, Patch staying close, seeming to know by instinct that even on this familiar ground, Kitty needed her constant loving presence.

The front door was shut, of course. Country folk didn't use the front door. Kitty and Patch went round the back, seeing the familiar yard, the shippon, the byre.

A man was working in the byre, cleaning out after the day's milking. He was tall and strong, but he wasn't Elwyn Ap Thomas nor the poor half-wit who had worked for him. Kitty couldn't remember seeing him before and once more she hesitated. Johnny had been stringy and gangly, but very strong; was it likely that he would employ another young man to work for him? But it was possible – she had worked hard, perhaps Johnny could not manage alone? If he had the farm, that was, and she would never find out if she didn't move from this spot!

Resolutely, with a hand trembling on Patch's collar, she walked forward. The man came out of the byre, saw them and stopped short. Kitty stopped too, just for a minute. And then she was running, her arms held out, running and running, with her mouth stretching into a huge smile and words babbling from her lips, as wildly and foolishly as the words were babbling from his.

'Johnny! Oh Johnny, Johnny, Johnny! Oh, how I've missed you!'

And Johnny lifted her up and hugged her so hard that her babbling ended in a breathless squeak and then he put her down and hugged Patch and rocked the dog from side to side and called her his old love and his favourite dog. And then he put Patch down and grabbed Kitty again and held her tight, and the raindrops in her hair ran down and wet his checked shirt and she felt safe and comfortable in his arms.

'Oh Kit, I searched and searched, why didn't you come to the lodgings? I were late at the Shamrock but I went back two or three times over the next day or so around six . . . oh Kit, I've been desperate!'

'I left a message with the landlord,' Kitty said against his chest. 'I went back to the café, too. I were wi' me Mam and me sister, they was starvin', Johnny, and . . . oh, so ill and 'elpless. And then I got scarlet fever and they put me in the Isolation 'Ospickle, but I come as soon as I could.'

'Course you did, chuck . . . that bloody landlord though – I arst an' arst if 'e'd seen you . . . I lit out o' here at Christmas an' spent three days searchin'. Never thought to go up to the Court, though, seein' as you was so scared of meetin' your folk.'

'Oh Johnny, if only I'd ha' known! But I couldn't ha' left 'em, they wasn't fit to be left. In fact, I never did leave 'em. They died, Johnny.'

'Through no fault o' yourn, Kitty love,' Johnny said at once. 'That I do know. And ain't Patch fit an' 'ealthy? Oh, it's grand to see the pair of you, grand! Come in the 'ouse, I'll cook you a bite; I'm 'ungry an' all.'

They went into the kitchen. It looked neglected, dust lay thick, but the fire burned up bright and the pantry-cupboard was well stocked. Kitty's fingers itched to get going with a scrubbing brush, a duster, lots of hot soapy water, but it would have looked rude so she sat down and watched as Johnny joyfully fried bacon and eggs and made a pot of tea.

'Now . . . tell me about this place,' Kitty said when they were settled at the table with the food in front of them. 'What 'appened, exactly?'

'Well, I found John James O'Hare, but 'e was 'eadin' for the ferry, to go over to Birken'ead, so I 'ad to follow, acourse. That's why I weren't at the Shamrock by six. In fact, I lorst 'im, 'ad to spend the night prowlin' the area where 'e'd disappeared, but I picked 'im up again next mornin' and managed to 'ave a word. John James O'Hare's a real nice feller, queen. He'd got a week's leave from 'is ship but 'e agreed at once to come to Wrexham wi' me. We caught a bus, an' when we got to the lawyer's, guess what?'

'What?' Kitty said. Stuart had told her that any decent solicitor worth his salt would have had a copy of the will, but agreed that it might take force to shift the Ap Thomases, and also warned that if they had sold the farm on, it could be difficult to oust the new owners without a lengthy legal battle. But she would not have said any of this for the world, not with Johnny sitting opposite her, eyes shining, fair hair on end, proud of his story and longing to surprise her.

'They 'ad a copy of the will all along! If only we'd gone to 'em, Kitty, 'stead o' wastin' our time searchin' for that Jones boy! Still, it come out all right in the end.'

'You mean the Ap Thomases jest moved out?' Kitty said. 'Without a fight, even?'

'Well, it warn't quite so simple as that! But they was tryin' to sell it, see, so our solicitor – Mr Huw Hughes, Mr Hywel's son – said we'd 'ave 'em for fraudulently disposin' of ... I can't 'member the right words, but you know the kind 'o thing. They might not ha' budged for that, e'en so, but then the neighbours came.'

'The neighbours? Mr Dewi and Mrs Bron, you mean?'

'Aye, but not only them, Kit! The people you met in the market, the Morrises, the Evanses, the Llewellyns ... people what was kind to us, but I didn't think would ever *do* anything. They come up the road in a big crowd, wi' me in the middle, an' we walked right into the farmyard an' Mr Huw flung the back door open wide so' they 'ad to listen. An' the minister ... 'e fair thundered at ole Ap Thomas ... they all came. Kind o' shamed the Thomases into goin' ... Elwyn's missus wailed an' wept like a founting, said she'd 'ad no part in it, but it din't matter, they went. An' everyone 'elped me to move back in.'

'And you got the stock back?'

'Oh aye, Mr Huw made ole Elwyn cough up for the beasts. Bought stock at the Christmas market in Corwen ... you'll be pleased wi' them, our Kitty, they're prime! An' ever since, I been workin' as 'ard as I could, and a-prayin' you'd come back. Mrs Bronwen kep' sayin' you'd come, but it were a long time ... 'ere, 'ave some more bacon!'

'When you came to Liverpool, what did you do?' Kitty asked, accepting half-a-dozen rashers of crispy bacon. 'Where did you look?'

'I looked everywhere, then I put advertisements in the papers, wi' a box number, only there waren't no replies. I don't suppose you read the papers much, eh?'

'Not much,' Kitty said, remembering those hungry, desperate days. 'No money to spare, see.'

'Aye, that's true. I stayed three days, then I 'ad to come back or we wouldn't 'ave 'ad a farm, but I were near out of me mind wi' worry. Only I 'ad a feelin' you'd not let me down. And ·'ere you are, large as life an' twice as 'andsome!'

'Yes, 'ere I am,' Kitty agreed. 'I were lost without you, Johnny, an' that's the truth. If it 'adn't been for Patch I dunno what I'd ha' done.'

'Like me, you'd ha' soldiered on. Oh Kitty, love, it's blamed good to set eyes on your funny little face!' He leaned across the table, his eyes slowly travelling across her face. 'Ain't you growed pretty!' he said suddenly. 'And ain't you growed tall an' all, come to that! You're a big girl, our Kit.'

'You're a big feller yourself,' Kitty said contentedly. 'Not bad lookin', either.'

He grinned bashfully, then leaned back again and shovelled bacon into his mouth. 'When we split up we was a pair o' kids, but now ... I reckon we oughter make this partnership official, don't you?'

'Dunno what you mean,' Kitty said suspiciously. 'Don't you trust me, Johnny Moneymor?'

'Course I do, but ... aw hell, our Kit, you're not a kid and neither am I! If we stay 'ere, together, there'll be talk ... don't you see what I'm gettin' at?'

'No,' Kitty said bluntly. 'Tell me.'

'We ain't brother an' sister; right?'

'Right. But no one round 'ere thinks we are, does they? We come clean wi' Mal ages ago.'

'That's right. So why don't we mek it official?'

382

'What the 'ell d'you mean?' Kitty said in an exasperated tone. She could feel her cheeks beginning to grow warm. 'Don't talk in riddles, Johnny.'

'Well, what I means is ... no, that ain't quite ... we oughter tie the knot, put our 'eads in the noose ... dammit, our Kitty, we oughter git married!'

Kitty stared at him across the table. He was so tanned and fit, his hair sun-gilded, his eyes bright and clear – he could not possibly want to marry her, of course, he just wanted to set people straight.

'Git married?' she said faintly. 'You don't want to do that!'

Johnny got up from the table, crashing his chair onto the floor behind him. He came round and lifted her out of her own chair, so roughly that he knocked her knee on the table-edge, causing her to give a squeak of pain. Holding her tightly against his chest he spoke into her hair.

'Kitty, you don't know 'ow bloody mis'ruble I been, nor 'ow worried, nor 'ow pointless it all seemed without you! There weren't no fun in it, not jest for me ... for two pins I'd ha' chucked it all up and teken to the road again! And I aren't agoin' to work 'ere an' see you go off an' marry some yokel like Eifion, just acos 'e's got more courage than what I 'ave. I – I *needs* you, queen, an' I 'opes you needs me.'

'Well, I does need you,' Kitty said. 'But we ain't in love, are we, Johnny?'

'Dunno. I jest likes you best of anyone.'

'Oh Johnny, that's just 'ow I feels,' Kitty said blissfully. 'I'd love to marry you, if you really want to marry me.'

'That's settled, then,' Johnny said. 'We'll get the Reverend to read the banns an' that. Mrs Bronwen will be pleased; she says ·we's made for each other.'

He stepped back a little from her and when she looked up at him he smiled, the old, dancing, mischievous smile that she loved so well and had missed so much. 'Close your eyes, Kit.'

Obediently, and wondering what was about to happen, Kitty closed her eyes. For a moment nothing whatsoever happened, and then she felt Johnny's lips gently fasten onto hers and they were kissing, and Kitty, who had never kissed anyone, found that she really liked it and could do it just right, or she supposed she must be doing it right since Johnny made a contented little mumble against her mouth and tightened his arms round her, squeezing her so hard that she felt she really ought to protest.

Only somehow, she was too busy – and happy – for a protest to make much sense.

Lilac was eating her breakfast, sitting in the spring sunshine with a cup of coffee and some toast and marmalade, when she heard the post plop through the letterbox.

She wasn't waiting for a letter, particularly, but curiosity drove her up from the table and into the hall. There were three letters, two personal ones, both handwritten, and an official one – a gas bill, she could tell. She returned to her meal, scanning the envelopes. One from Polly – that was nice – and the other was from Kitty. Kitty had written a couple of times in the months since she left, but the letters had been guarded, almost deliberately careful, as though she was keeping something from Lilac. Perhaps now she's going to tell me what it is, Lilac thought hopefully, slitting the envelope open with a buttery knife. She's such a dear little soul, I do want her to be happy, but I can't force her confidence if she's keeping something secret. I ought to go and visit her, her thoughts continued, but somehow I'm always so busy . . . and I don't know that Johnny Moneymor she's in partnership with . . .

She unfolded the letter. It was longer than usual, she saw with approval, and started off in a sprightly fashion.

Dear Lilac,

For a while now, Johnny and I have been talking about getting married. I expect you'll think we're too young, and don't know each other well enough, but when I got back here, Mrs Bronwen Jones, our neighbour from up the valley, said it weren't right us living in the same house, and I guess she knows better than most what's right, she's strong chapel is Mrs Bronwen.

I thought it would be best to do it right away, but you can't – did you know that Lilac? You have to have permission and that, if you isn't twenty-one – I'm sixteen acourse. So Mrs Bronwen said we oughter have a girl live in, and I got young Alwenna Evans from Corwen, she sleeps with me in Mal's big old brass bedstead and she helps with the housework so's Johnny and me can get on with the farm work.

But we can't stand it no longer, Johnny and me. We want it to be just us, just Johnny and Kitty, and Wenna's a nice kid but she don't like the country all that much, she misses living in a town and being with other girls her age. And there's feelings, Lilac, what I can't explain too good, but we both feel them, so we went and explained to the reverend and he agreed that feeling like we do, it were marriage or nothin, so we're going to do the ·deed and would like you to come to the wedding, with your Nellie, your Stuart and your Elizabeth, of course.

I wondered if you'd bring your Joey to the wedding, Lilac? I'm mortal fond of Joey; everyone seems to like him. But that's up to you of course. Wouldn't want you to feel I was interfering.

I didn't say nothing before because I were ashamed of wanting Johnny, I didn't think I ought, since we'd not known each other for years, like some people do when they wed. But we talked to the reverend and he said it were natural, and that the only thing was I were a bit young, only he said I knew me own mind – which I does – and better to marry than burn, which sounds very strange, but it was what he said.

Johnny reckons we've waited plenty long enough – it's nine months since I came home to the farm – so we won't wait no longer. The date is set for 14th April, so if you come down the day before, Lilac, that'll be wonderful. You can stay here, all of you – it's a big old house, lots of spare rooms – and after, there's a dinner of course and then Eifion's going to give an eye to the stock and we're having a honeymoon in Llandudno, just a few days. Please say you'll come, and please ask Nellie and the others for me, since there won't be many guests, only local.

I hope you aren't cross at us getting wed, Lilac; you'll always be me best friend, you were so good to me, but Johnny's different. I want to spend the rest of me life with him and that's the truth. Reckon I love him.

With kind regards,
    Your loving Kitty

Lilac read the letter through once, then again. She chuckled several times, and then, to her horror, found she was crying. She mopped furiously at her eyes and chided herself; she wasn't losing Kitty, Kitty had never been hers to lose, the girl was clearly deeply in love with this Johnny Moneymor and though she was very young it was better, as the reverend said, to marry than to burn. And besides, working together on the farm as they did, anything other than marriage would be unnatural since they liked one another so well.

I'm twenty-three years old and I'm not getting married, Lilac found herself thinking as she put away her breakfast things and got ready to go round to Nellie's to show her the letter and pass on the wedding invitation. I was in love once, of course, deeply in love, but after I lost Art I simply stopped thinking about marriage.

Joey Prescott's intelligent, reliable face flickered into her mind. Joey wanted to marry again, she knew it, though he didn't talk about it much. They were good friends, she enjoyed his company, looked forward to his visits to the Pool but she never considered him a . . . a suitor. Kitty had only met him that one week, of course, and she'd liked him well enough to ask him to her wedding. But then she clearly thought that Joey meant more to her, Lilac, than he did. He was just a friend, just someone she could talk to, just a feller who came around every couple of months to take her out, have a laugh, talk over old times.

Lilac glanced out of the window, then chose her scarlet coat ·with the matching tam-o'-shanter. It was chilly, the March wind was whipping at the bare branches of the trees, so she might as well wrap up warm. She was off today since it was a Saturday –

Mrs Brierson usually tried to see that Lilac's weekends were free – so she could catch a tram up to Nellie's place and they could talk over the wedding there, with a whole day in front of them.

Lilac stuffed the letter into her pocket and picked up her scarlet wool bag, slinging it over one shoulder. A wedding! She hadn't been to many but the ones she had attended had always been fun. She would enjoy meeting Johnny and seeing dear little Kitty settling down happily ... a honeymoon in Llandudno, that sounded nice, she must remember to ask Kitty when she replied to her letter whether she was having bridesmaids and if she would like Elizabeth to hand her a lucky horseshoe: the child had been disappointed once ...

All the way to Nellie's house in Halkyn Avenue Lilac kept finding her annoying eyes filling up. It was the wind, she decided, only on the tram she could scarcely blame the wind. She remembered Joey's last visit, when he had invited her down to London, saying they'd make a weekend of it; how she had repulsed him, telling him that whilst she enjoyed his company she didn't intend to give people cause to gossip. He had been hurt, he had gone very quiet ... but Joey was so good-natured, he'd been his usual happy self next day.

That had been five weeks ago though; he'd not been up to the Pool since. He'll come, he's probably waiting for better weather, Lilac told herself. After all, his ship's bound to come into the docks sooner or later, and then he'll come hammering on my door, with his big white grin and his steady gaze and his warm, safe hands.

He usually came once a month, regular as clockwork. She would just mention it to Nellie, see what her sister thought. As for asking him to Kitty's wedding, though, she couldn't possibly do that – that really would give him ideas!

When she reached the house Nellie was spring-cleaning. She had her hair swathed in a blue and white striped duster and a large paintbrush in one hand. She was, she explained, whiting the kitchen ceiling.

'Where's Stu?' Lilac asked suspiciously. 'And Elizabeth?'

'They've gone to Elizabeth's dance-class,' Nellie said serenely, climbing back on her stepladder. 'Put the kettle on, love, and we'll have a nice cup of tea when I've finished here.'

'How long will you be?' Lilac asked. She never did her own decorating, she used the man who kept the hotel in trim, but now, watching Nellie wielding the big, floppy brush on the ceiling, she itched to have a go. 'Is there anything I can do to help?'

'Would you like to have a go at keying up the surface of the old paint on the back door?' Nellie said diffident-ly. 'There's a bit of sandpaper . . . you just sort of make circles, then when I put the fresh paint on it'll stick.'

'Oh. Right,' Lilac said. 'Had I better wrap something round my hair, our Nell? You aren't half free with that whitewash!' She indicated the line of tiny white specks which had just appeared ·on the draining board.

Nellie laughed.

'Did I do that? Yes, perhaps you'd better cover up a bit. There's another duster in the drawer to the right of the sink, and you can borrow me old overall, it's hanging behind the door.'

Shortly, properly dressed and equipped with sand-paper to rub with and a feather duster to get rid of the debris, Lilac began on the door. She rubbed away industriously, whilst above her Nellie sloshed around with the whitewash, occasionally apologising as the spots flew through the air. By the time the kettle boiled both girls were absorbed, but Lilac left off for long enough to make the tea and then Nellie climbed reluctantly down from her stepladder and the two of them settled themselves at the kitchen table, Nellie sweeping off her duster and shaking her hair down as she did so.

'Whew, it's hot up by the ceiling,' she remarked. 'It don't half make your arm ache an' all.'

'And it makes you pale,' Lilac said with a giggle. 'Your face is white as a sheet, Nellie Gallagher!'

'I feel more scarlet than ... oh, am I covered in whitewash?' Nellie said, standing up to peer at her reflection in the small mirror beside the sink. 'Gracious, me face is covered, I'd better fetch a flannel ... only I'm going to have that cuppa first, I'm really dry.'

She sat down again and picked up her cup. Lilac waited until her sister had slaked her thirst, then fished Kitty's letter out of her pocket and spread it out on the table.

'Heard from Kitty this morning,' she said. 'She and Johnny are getting married, they want us all to go to the wedding. Have a read.'

'Getting married? Those children?' Nellie picked up the first page and scanned the neat lines of writing. 'Good gracious, so they are!'

'We'll go, won't we?' Lilac said, when Nellie lay the pages down again. 'I'm so fond of Kit, and you're the same. I'd hate to miss her big day.'

'I love a wedding,' Nellie agreed. 'Yes, we'd be happy to go. I daresay Stu will book us in at a hotel, rather than putting on poor Kitty when she's preparing for her wedding. What about Joey, queen? D'you think he'll come?'

Lilac picked up her cup and left her chair, walking over to the teapot where it stood on the draining board.

'I'm just pouring meself another cup,' she said. 'Joey? Oh, I wouldn't think he'd be interested, would you? He only met Kitty three or four times, when she was in hospital. Besides, he can't pick and choose where he goes, he has to fit his life ashore round his sailings.'

'Heard from him lately?' Nellie asked casually as Lilac, with her fresh cup of tea, returned to the table. 'It seems a while since he was in the Pool.'

'No, he's not written for a while. Nor visited, come to that,' Lilac said equally casually. 'I wonder if he's got as berth aboard a different vessel, one that doesn't touch the north-west, though I should have thought he'd write and let me know.'

'Oh, perhaps he's busy,' Nellie said. 'Want a biscuit, chuck? There's a bag of ginger nuts just inside the pantry door. Get 'em out whilst you're on your feet, would you?'

Lilac fetched the biscuits and sat down again with a thump. She opened the bag and fished out two biscuits, took a bite out of one and handed the other to Nellie.

'Lovely, my favourite,' she mumbled. 'Nell . . . is Joey cross with me?'

'Oh, Lilac love, you sound just like a little girl; I do love you! You come straight out with things sometimes . . . it's awful nice, that.'

Lilac put her biscuit down.

'He is cross, isn't he? Oh Nell, it's been nearly six

weeks . . . I miss him, really I do, but he wanted me to go down to London . . .'

The story poured out; how Joey had seemed to Lilac to be getting a bit possessive, had actually suggested she go down to London with him for a weekend. How she'd told him she didn't want people gossiping about her, how he'd gone a bit quiet, then seemed his usual sunny self. Only he'd not written since, nor visited, and she was worried, she wouldn't hurt him for the world . . .

'Have you written and told him so?' Nellie asked. 'But of course, you'll have done that.'

'No I haven't,' Lilac said at once. 'It was his turn to write to me, I couldn't write just out of the blue, it wasn't as if I'd said anything nasty, I only said what you'd have said . . . that I couldn't spend a weekend with him and cause talk.'

Nellie looked across the table at Lilac and raised her eyebrows, but she said nothing.

'Oh, Nell, don't look at me like that! You'd never . . . you wouldn't want me to risk my reputation . . . I mean think what people would say . . .'

The silence stretched. Lilac picked nervously at a patch of whitewash on the table.

'Nell? What's the matter?'

'Lilac, love, if Stu had asked me . . . whatever he'd asked me I'd have said yes, because I loved him so much. And I believe you're very fond of Joey.'

'Oh . . . fond! That's a bit different, surely, from wanting to chuck me cap over the windmill for him?'

'Perhaps it is; I'm not sure. Tell you what, flower, suppose I said if you had a choice, to – well, to sleep with Joey or never see him again, what would you choose?'

Lilac stared at the older girl.

'*Sleep* with him? I can't believe me ears, our Nell! Surely you wouldn't expect me to behave like that – you've brought me up to behave meself!'

'I hope I brought you up to be generous and loving – and to know your own heart as well as your own mind,' Nellie said gently. 'What would you do, Lilac love?'

Lilac got up from the table and carried her cup over to the sink. Without turning to face Nellie she said indistinctly, 'I dunno; it ain't a fair question, our Nell! I were going to marry ·Art, remember. I don't reckon Art 'ud think much of it if I . . . if Joey an' me . . .'

Tears were near. Nellie got up as well and took her cup to the sink, then put her arms round Lilac and gave her a hug.

'Perhaps it weren't a fair question, queen. But it made you think, and that's all I was trying to do. Now let's get on with this decoratin', or I shan't have made the dinner by the time Stu and the babe get home!'

Chapter Sixteen

Lilac stayed with the Gallaghers all day. She played with Elizabeth, helped Nellie to decorate the kitchen, walked round the garden with Stuart and admired his display of purple, white and gold crocuses, the snow-drops under the apple tree and the spears of daffodils and narcissi pushing up through the dark earth.

No one mentioned Joey, though the wedding was much discussed. Elizabeth, Nellie announced, would wear a primrose-coloured silk dress – it was bound to be warmer in a month – under her rust-coloured coat, just in case it wasn't. Nellie herself would have a new dress, to be worn under her own best coat – beech-leaf green – with a new hat, colour to be decided.

'What'll you wear, love?' Nellie asked her young sister, but Lilac just shrugged and said she'd prob-ably buy something new since it wasn't often she got invited to a wedding.

Nellie smiled and said if her help was needed there was nothing she liked better than a shopping trip and Lilac said with more enthusiasm than she'd yet shown that she would definitely get Nellie to go with her, because two heads were better than one when it came to choosing pretty clothes.

'I'll run you home, queen,' Stuart said when they'd had their tea and Lilac stood up to go. 'We'll all come, get some air.'

Nellie, however, declined the treat.

'You know I'd like to come,' she said with feigned

regret. 'But the place is such a mess and tomorrow's Sunday, I'd like to get it cleaned up before then. So I'll stay now, then we can go out for a ride in the country tomorrow afternoon.'

'Oh . . . thanks Nellie, but I shan't be coming round tomorrow. I've . . . I've been invited out . . . just to dinner . . . by one of the guests.'

'Well, that's nice,' Stuart said genially, shooting a quick, rather worried look at his wife. 'Umm, anyone we know?'

'No, I don't think . . . it's a Mr Albert Evans, he's very nice, not married or anything,' Lilac said quickly. Her cheeks, Nellie noticed, had gone very pink. 'I've been out with him once or twice before, he comes over to Liverpool regularly, every few weeks. He's got a – a small business in Sir Thomas Street and another one in Manchester. Sorry I forgot to mention it before but it completely slipped my mind. I'll see you all next Saturday, if not before.'

'Right, love,' Nellie said cheerfully, kissing her sister's hot cheek. 'Have a lovely time with your friend.'

'He's not really my *friend*, just an acquaintance,' Lilac mumbled. 'You'll probably have far more fun driving out into the country, only I did promise . . .'

'It doesn't matter; I love you to have fun,' Nellie declared. She gave Lilac a friendly push. 'Go on, queen, Stu might let you get the car out of the garage and drive it as far as the gate if you hurry.'

Stuart, however, popped back a moment later, ostensibly to fetch a torch to light Lilac down the path. He grabbed one off the sideboard, then turned to Nellie.

'What's all this, then? I thought you said she was really fond of . . .'

395

'Shush! Talk later,' hissed Nellie. 'Go *on*, Stu, little Elizabeth has ears like a donkey. Drive carefully, I'll see you soon.'

Stuart, with a doubtful backward glance, left. Nellie waited until she heard the car cough into life, until she heard its engine disappearing down the road, then she took off her apron and walked through into the front hall.

The telephone stood on a small, round table, with a chair conveniently near. Nellie hesitated. Ever since Joey had come calling six weeks ago, in some distress, he had been ringing her whenever he was in port for a progress report. It was painfully clear that he was head over heels in love with Lilac, but he was very aware that Lilac was still telling herself she had buried her desire and ability to love a man in the grave with Art.

'I'm not gettin' any younger, Nellie,' Joey had said plaintively last time he had rung. 'I don't say I mind waitin', I'd wait for years, like, but 'ow do I know that at the end of the wait she won't turn to someone else? Someone not so patient wiv 'er?'

'Art nearly lost her through being impatient and trying to force her hand,' Nellie had said worriedly. 'Me and Stu are so fond of you both, Joey, that it would break our hearts if the same thing happened. Look, you're right to keep away from her, it's the only way to make her look at the situation. I believe she'll begin to miss you a bit, then she'll miss you badly, and by the time you come calling again, she'll see her feelings for what they are.'

'What are they?' Joey had asked. 'Damned if I know, gel!'

'They're stronger than she believes,' Nellie had replied. 'Strong enough to have her admitting how she feels when it's tell or lose you. Oh Joey, be patient, I'm sure it'll work out all right in the end.'

But now, standing by the telephone and gnawing her lower lip, Nellie wondered, for the first time, whether she was doing Joey a real disservice by advising him to stay away. She didn't believe Albert Evans existed, Lilac was a real little chatterbox as far as admirers were concerned, but she did believe that, if pushed, Lilac might jump in the wrong direction.

However, it was a week since Joey had last rung and if her calculations were right he should be back in London right now, in his lodging house. The house wasn't on the telephone, but she could ring the shipping office, see if she could get a message to him. On the other hand, sending a message seemed rather extreme. She could drop a line, ask him to telephone her.

She was moving away from the telephone when it rang, sharply, making her jump. She grabbed the receiver from its rest and held it to her ear. 'Liverpool 22212, Mrs Gallagher speaking.'

'Hello, Nell; it's me, Joey. Are you awright to talk?'

'Joey! I was standing right by the telephone, wondering how to get in touch with you ... no, it's all right, there's nothing wrong, in fact I think it's rather good news. Kitty Drinkwater's getting married, and we've all been invited to the wedding – you as well. Lilac's worrying about you, Joey, and getting awful het-up. The wedding's on the fifteenth of April – any chance?'

'How important is it?' Joey's voice had lit with hope, Nellie could almost see the smile on his face. 'If I come, I mean.'

'I believe if you come to the wedding, you'll be able to suggest that the two of you set a date,' Nellie said.

'Her first reaction, I think, was that Kitty was much too young, which she is, of course. And I think it occurred to her that she was going to miss a lot by her determination not to marry ... she's been very quiet all day.'

'An' you mentioned me?'

Nellie chuckled.

'I did. Joey, can you come to the wedding? It'll be in Corwen, North Wales.'

'I'll make a point of it,' Joey said. 'I'll come, no matter what 'appens, though I'm due a few days arahnd then. Tell you what, I'll drop Kitty a line but I won't say nothin' officially to you.'

'Lilac doesn't know you and I are in touch,' Nellie said. 'Better keep it that way.'

'Yes, acourse. Right, then. See you on the fifteenth!'

Nellie replaced the receiver slowly and walked back into the kitchen. Suppose she was wrong? Suppose the worst possible thing would be for Lilac to arrive at the wedding and find Joey there too? But it was no use worrying, she'd done it now. They would just have to wait and see.

Kitty woke and rolled over. Outside the window the sun shone, sending long golden beams through a gap in the curtains. Beside her, Patch stirred too, then stretched, sat up, and vigorously scratched her ear.

'I 'opes as 'ow you ain't got fleas, old gal,' Kitty said absently, tugging at the ruff round Patch's neck. 'We can't give you a bath today – we're gonna be too busy gettin' wed!'

The girl from Corwen, Alwenna, had not shared her bed, not last night. She had gone home, to prepare for the wedding. Kitty had told dear Mrs Bronwen that she wanted to spend her last night as a Drinkwater in her own bed, in her own room, and Mrs Bronwen, having given her a long steady look, had agreed it seemed sensible.

'After all, girl, if you'd ha' wanted to do wrong what need of a double bed when there's the whole farm at your disposal?' she said, with her usual practicality. 'I'll see to it that there's no talk. Not that they'd dare say a word against you, not wi' me an' mine to contend with!'

So Kitty rubbed Patch's ears absent-mindedly and was grateful for the sunshine and imagined Lilac, Nellie and the others in the hotel on the main street, waking to the country sounds of cocks crowing and cattle lowing instead of to the blast of ships' sirens and the constant noise of traffic.

In the next room she could hear Johnny whistling as he dressed and sloshed water about. She sat up and prepared to swing her legs out of bed, wondering whose turn it was to milk the cows but deciding she would get up anyway. There were bound to be a hundred tasks which needed their attention and the wedding was at two this afternoon. Then there was the wedding breakfast, and after that she and Johnny were going off for their short honeymoon in Llandudno.

'We'll wed in the afternoon so we can get the work done, then we can enjoy ourselves,' Johnny had said. 'Mrs Martha's bringin' the grub over in 'er wagon at about noon an' your posh friends will be arrivin' soon after. I like that Joey, mind. A feller after me own 'eart.'

'Yes, Joey's grand, and the others ain't no posher'n what we are,' Kitty had said, looking contentedly round the glowing farm kitchen. 'Oh Johnny, didn't

Joey love the farm? I can't wait for Lilac an' Nell to see this place, as well. I loves it, I does!'

Joey had arrived the day before yesterday. He had brought with him two presents, a green parrot which talked and a hand-embroidered tablecloth of such beauty and intricacy that even Johnny had been impressed. He had insisted that Joey stay with them rather than in town, once it had been revealed that Lilac didn't actually know Joey was coming.

'It's a surprise,' Joey said, looking rather hunted. 'I wanted to tell 'er, but Nellie said a surprise would be best.'

'Nellie knows Lilac better'n she knows 'erself,' Kitty had observed. 'Don't worry, Joey, it'll be awright.'

But right now the Day had arrived at last, their Day, and here was she, dreaming on the edge of the bed instead of getting up and getting going on the thousand and one things she had to do.

Kitty padded across the room and pulled back the curtains. Sunshine flooded in and through the open window wafted the familiar smells of a well-kept farm: hay, beasts; the tang of stables and byres came to her nostrils and over and above everything else the fresh country smell of meadow, brook and tree.

'You up, Kit? Don't forget, I'm milkin' this mornin', but you're cookin' us a decent breakfast. Joey's down-stairs, tryin' to get the parrot to stop swearin' an' carryin' on.'

Johnny's voice came hollowly through the door. Kitty padded over and opened it. She grinned at him, then stood on tiptoe to give him a quick kiss.

'Mornin', Johnny! Glad Joey's makin' 'imself at 'ome. So this is it, eh?'

'That's right. Want me to put the kettle on as I go through? Then you can wash in 'ot water.'

'No, it's all right, I'll have a cat's lick an' a promise now, then fettle meself up good before the others arrive. I wonder what me sisters will make of this place, eh Johnny? I reckon they'll love it.'

'They can come an' stay next summer,' Johnny said magnanimously. 'Give us an 'and wi' the 'ay 'arvest. Do 'em good to 'ave fresh country air.'

'It would. I wish we could 'ave 'em 'ere all the time, but it ain't on; still, we're doin' okay. One of these days . . .'

'One of these days we'll 'ave kids of us own,' Johnny said practically. 'Your sisters will make their own way, chuck, same as you an' me.' He took her shoulders in his hands and swayed her towards him. 'Gi's a kiss, pretty Kitty.'

Kitty complied and for a moment they stood there, she in her worn cotton nightgown and Johnny in his homespun shirt, corduroys and socks, totally relaxed and at ease in each other's embrace. Then Johnny sighed, moved his mouth from hers, gave her one last squeeze and let her go.

'Best get on,' he advised. 'Us'll be sharin' the same bed in the 'otel tonight an' the big brass bedstead when we come 'ome, Kitty – we'll 'ave the rest of our lives for kissin' and cuddlin'.'

'Yes, I know. It's goin' to be grand, ain't it, Johnny?'

He nodded, smiling down at her.

'Aye, grand. Don't forget me breakfast, I's starvin' already and I ain't started the work yet!'

Lilac had spent the night in her hotel room alone, with the Gallaghers next door. She had dreamed about weddings, about loss, about sadness, and had woken with a heavy heart and dark-rimmed eyes. She had borrowed Nellie's scented talcum and tried to disguise the shadows, but without very much success – and what did it matter, anyway? She was only going to see country folk, no one she knew.

They were taken to church in the trap, Johnny having already left whilst Kitty, splendidly apparelled, waited nervously in the front room with Mr Dewi Jones, who was going to give her away. By the time they arrived the church was packed, but a pew had been reserved for them by a tall young man in a dark suit who saw them coming out of the corner of his eye and stood courteously to one side to let them slide past him to reach their seats.

Lilac went to pass him and stopped short.

'Joey! Oh Joey, it's so nice to see you, I wondered why you'd not been near us . . . are you all right?'

The surprise was total – she had refused to pass on the invitation in case he got ideas, but probably Kitty had written to him separately. And seeing him, dark-suited, handsome, smiling down at her as though they had never had a cross word – and they hadn't, really come to think – gladness was her principal emotion. She smiled up at him and took his hand in hers, and when he would have pulled it away she wouldn't let him . . . it was so very nice to see him again, such a marvellous surprise . . . she sneaked a glance at Nellie, next to her, but Nellie was finding her place in the Order of Service and showing little Elizabeth how to find the hymns and taking no notice of Lilac at all.

People were rustling behind her, turning. Lilac, too, turned. She could see Kitty's small sisters in the pew with some farmers from further up the valley and smiled at the four little blonde girls, giggling together over an open hymn book, though she doubted whether the two smaller ones could actually read.

There was a commotion in the porch, then Kitty came floating up the aisle on Mr Jones's arm. She looked slender and beautiful, and a good deal older than her sixteen years. Her dress was white satin with lacy panels and a small, upstanding collar, and someone had arranged her hair with a coronet of flowers around it.

Lilac smiled at her and Kitty smiled back; a blissful smile, Lilac thought enviously. And then Kitty's eyes moved ahead once more and Lilac saw the expression in them soften and change as they fell on her bridegroom, his yellow hair slicked down, his dark suit immaculate, and his head turning, his eyes anxiously searching for Kitty.

Joey squeezed her hand. She looked up at him, enquiringly, and Joey leaned down towards her.

'Doesn't Kit look a picture? You can tell she's goin' to be so 'appy.'

Lilac nodded. She felt pretty happy herself, right now, but that was a transitory thing; Kitty's happiness, she suspected, would be a way of life, a permanency. Love was like that, you might be miserable on top, over some small or large thing, but you had the happiness beneath all right, just waiting to break through. When you had someone of your own, that was.

The bride and groom were at the altar now, about to make their vows. Kitty looked so different, Lilac thought. Slim and regal in her lace and satin even though the gown had been lent by Mrs Ada Morris from up the valley, with her bright, red-brown hair coiled up into a knot on her head and a wreath of tiny white flowers holding her veil in place, she would have graced any wedding in the land. No one would have recognised the starved little waif with her bare feet and filthy, oversized shirt in this beautiful, healthy young woman who kept glancing adoringly up into her groom's countenance. Even if she'd not known before, the wedding would have made it plain to Lilac that Kitty and Johnny were deeply in love.

'With this ring I thee wed; with my body I thee worship; and with all my worldly goods I thee endow.'

Johnny's voice, rich and deep and shorn of its usual accent for the occasion gave the words their full meaning and more. Lilac glanced at Joey and he was looking down at her, with such an expression in his eyes! She knew, at that moment, that Nellie had been right; if you loved a man you didn't worry about your reputation or the rights and wrongs of it, you just wanted to belong to him, to make him happy. And suddenly she knew that she loved Joey and wanted him as Kitty wanted Johnny. But how could she be so shallow, so fickle? She had loved and wanted Art, his death might never have come about had he not come home to be with her for a couple of days ... how could she even think about loving someone else?

And then, as though the thought had triggered her memory, she found herself remembering in detail her dream of last night. Earlier it had just been a vague, confused recollection but now it all became clear.

She had been walking along the Scottie in the dream, with Art strolling beside her, he a lad again, she a lass. They were talking idly, of this and that, enjoying the sunny day and each other's company. And then, down the road towards them, came a young sailor with a rolling gait and a wickedly twinkling eye.

'Art ... that's Joey Prescott, you know, the feller I told you about,' the young Lilac said excitedly. 'Oh, 'e's a nice feller – 'e rescued me, you know, when I run away from the Culler. I've gorra speak to 'im!'

She ran forwards and as she ran she grew up, so that by the time she reached Joey and held out her arms to him she was Lilac now, not Lilac then. And beside her was Art, grown up too, and he was smiling as well, smiling at Joey.

'Nice to meet you, Joey,' he said. 'You'll take care of 'er for me, won't you? She's a rare 'andful, but I wouldn't want 'er no different.'

The two men clasped hands and Art turned to her and she saw, in his dear, familiar face, the truth, just for one marvellous moment.

Art had always wanted the best for her and he wanted it still, wherever he was. He was no longer able to take care of her himself so he was handing the job on and doing it willingly.

She had turned to Art, wanting to thank him for her freedom, but instead she woke up, and outside her window the birds were singing and it was Kitty's wedding day and the dream had gone, leaving her bereft.

But now she had remembered, and all her stupid doubts and fears meant nothing. She felt as gay as the blackbird carolling away on the chestnut tree by the porch and as light as a puff of thistledown on a breezy day.

It was all right! She was doing the right thing, she knew she was. Art would be with her always, but not as a reproach for happiness or a spy for good behaviour. He would be, as he had always been, her friend.

The wedding march swelled out; Lilac looked at the faces of the young couple coming down the aisle, wreathed in smiles, and she felt hot tears rise to her eyes. But even as she mopped them carefully away with her small, scented handkerchief, even as she smiled mistily up at Joey and clutched his hand, she knew they were the right sort of tears: she was weeping, not for what might have been, but for joy.

'You awright, sweet'eart? Not upset 'cos I'm 'ere, when you didn't expect to see me?'

It was said in a whisper, but Lilac heard every word.

'Upset? Oh no, dearest Joey, I'm so happy and relieved, I can't tell you. And Joey?'

'What, Lilac?'

'I'm coming back with you when you go – to London, I mean. And I'm not going to let you leave me ever again.'

Joey squeezed her hand and then carried her fingers to his lips and kissed them.

'With my body, I thee honour,' he whispered. 'I love you, Lilac Larkin!'

KATIE FLYNN

A Liverpool Lass

arrow books

Acknowledgements

Many thanks to the people who helped me to understand and untangle the Liverpool of today from the Liverpool of yesterday. Please forgive me if I've missed anyone out, but here are some of them:

Rosemarie Hague, who shared her memories of the thirties with me, and her friend Mrs Lil Pearson, who remembered Liverpool between the wars. John Cross, who put me in touch with Richard Brown, whose warm and lively recollections of times past will colour a great many books, and Heather Cross, who put up with John and I gabbling on and eating her out of house and home.

The staff of the Local History section of the Picton Library, who know their stock backwards and were most helpful.

The staff of the International Library at the Picton, and Rhys Bebb Jones and his staff both at the Holyhead and Moelfre libraries on Anglesey, searched their shelves and came up with just what I needed. My thanks to them all.

In memory of Richard Brown, a true Scouser.
who was born and bred in the city of Liverpool
and knew it like the back of his hand.
His wit and humour and his rich vein
of reminiscence were of inestimable value
in the writing of this book.

Prologue

1905

It was a wild and rainy night, the sort of winter's night to stay indoors, and it seemed as though most of the inhabitants of the great maritime port of Liverpool had decided to do just that. The mean and narrow streets which led up from the docks, the crowded slum-courts, even the docks themselves, were deserted save for the figure of the girl in the plaid shawl.

The girl hurried along, occasionally glancing up at a streetlamp, aware that there was a lightening of the sky to the east of the city which would presently herald the dawn. Her shawl was soaked, her feet in their too-large boots squelched with every step, yet she made her way through the streets without pause or hesitation, clearly intent on her errand. She skirted puddles when she came to them, avoided the rubbish-laden gutters, but wending her way through the maze of small streets presented no problem. Hunching her shoulders against the driving rain she darted down alleyways and across broad thoroughfares, never pausing until she reached a ette. area of the city where she seemed, at last, less certain.

Here, where the street lighting was better, where there were tall trees at intervals and a street-cleaner had kept the gutters clear so that the rain tinkled merrily along towards the drains, she hesitated for the first time. She glanced up at the street sign above her head and nodded slowly, reading the legend *Rodney Street* and approving it in some way. Then she began to walk slowly along the pavement, looking curiously at the great houses as she passed them. Here were whited steps, an occasional potted aspidistra in a gleaming window, velvet curtains and soft white nets. Here there would be maids to scrub the steps, a servant to answer the door, even a chauffeur, if the family possessed one of the increasingly popular motor cars. Affluence was apparent here, even in the driving rain with the sky darkened with clouds and the houses wearing a shuttered, defensive look.

Presently the girl stopped outside one of the largest and most imposing houses in the street. It had a railed off basement area, a short flight of steps and a brass plate affixed to the pillared portico. The girl stared up at the windows as though she expected a face to appear between the dark curtains but seeing she was unobserved, she climbed the steps, one, two, three, four, and slid noiselessly into the shelter of the portico.

Once out of the direct malice of the weather the girl drew a bundle from her shawl and laid it on the tiles at her feet. Then she reached up, standing on tiptoe to do so, and lifted the great brass knocker, letting it fall three times with sufficient force to be heard clearly, even above the buffeting wind.

She listened for a second and then, apparently hearing sounds of arousal, she took off the long plaid shawl and with a gesture both hasty and tender, she wrapped it warmly round the tiny shape at her feet and then pattered down the steps and onto the pavement, a thin, dark dress affording her almost no shelter from the still falling rain. She had been quick before but she was quicker now, dashing heedlessly through the puddles, skidding round the corner and out of sight long before the big front door creaked open, long before the child within the soggy shawl began to mutter as it missed the girl's warmth and nearness.

The man who opened the door was clad in a long grey dressing gown made out of an old blanket; he scowled dreadfully as he glanced into the street, then he saw the shawl-wrapped child at his feet and started forward as if to go in pursuit of whoever had rung the bell, calling over his shoulder as he did so:

'Nellie, hurry yourself, some wicked gairl's left a child on the step! Oh, which way did she run, the minx, which way? Fetch a constable, Nellie, for I won't have it, she shall be caught! Rouse Mrs Ransom, Nellie!'

But no one saw the girl, shivering and shawl-less, making her way back through the wet and windy city, and long before day dawned or anyone had missed her, she had slipped once more into her bed.

'It'll be some servant girl who'd managed to conceal her shame and knew from the plate on the door that this is Culler's Orphan Asylum,' Mrs Ransom said sourly, as Nellie unwrapped the long plaid shawl, then a thick piece of white blanket, to reveal the child within. 'I don't know what the world's comin' to; no respect, no values.'

'It's a dear little girl,' Nellie said softly. 'Oh ma'am, look at that hair, it's so fair it's almost silver – we oughter call her Sylvia!'

Nellie was a plain little creature with her light-coloured, stringy hair, skinny limbs and pale face, but there was sweetness in the line of her mouth and determination in the jut of her small chin. The large, clear eyes which she turned towards the older woman had a direct and honest glance and her voice was low and pleasant, though she still retained the accent of her native Scotland Road.

The matron was a big woman, bulging out of her

flannelette nightgown and the thick coat she had thrown on for warmth. She had a heavily jowled face with a jutting chin and small, calculating eyes. Now, she scowled down at skinny little Nellie, her maid of all work. Old Arthur Davies, who did any rough work which the orphans could not manage, had gone grumbling back to bed as soon as Mrs Ransom appeared.

'Sylvia! That's a heathen name. She'll get a decent, plain name, like the other foundlings. Let me see … we've got an Ellen, a Mary, a Sarah …'

'There's a name on the shawl,' Nellie said, gently folding the blanket around the baby once more. 'It's in joined writing, though; I can't mek it out.'

The matron screwed up her tiny eyes until they almost disappeared behind the mottled shelves of her cheeks. She bent forward, heavy jowls prominent, and picked up the shawl, sniffing at it as though she were indeed the bloodhound she momentarily resembled.

'It's clean,' she said grudgingly. 'Smells of some sort of flower, and it's a good quality silk, too, thick and soft. Stolen, no doubt. And the name's been embroidered; must've cost a pretty penny.'

'Yes, but what is the name?' Nellie said anxiously. She herself was no foundling, she was Nellie McDowell, only daughter of Dolly and Cedric McDowell, deceased, with three older brothers and two younger ones living with relatives in Coronation Court just off the Scotland Road. Nellie knew that if the baby was known to be a foundling she would have the fact thrown at her head a dozen times a day for many years, but if she had a proper name of her own it would be easier for her to refute any insults and to tell herself that one day someone would come for her.

'It's *Larkin*,' Mrs Ransom said, her brow puckering

afresh as she deciphered the tiny, handstitched letters. 'That's an odd sorta name; I just knew it were nicked!'

'Perhaps that's her last name,' Nellie said hopefully. 'You'll have to give her a first name, Mrs Ransom.'

Mrs Ransom was sniffing once more at the smooth, expensive plaid. Suddenly she raised her head and nodded portentously, a smile dawning.

'Lilac!' she said. 'It's lilac, that's what it is!'

And Nellie, who was no fool, saw her chance and jumped in at once.

'Oh Mrs Ransom, you are so right – Lilac Larkin! Why, that's the prettiest name, yet you gorrit straight off! And Mr Hayman's always sayin' each lickle child should have an individdel name ... oh, he'll be tickled with that name! Lilac Larkin! Why, it sounds quite the lady!'

Mrs Ransom, about to explain that it had been the flower scent on the shawl to which she referred and not the child, opened her mouth and shut it again. It was true that Mr Hayman, the main benefactor of the orphan asylum, had impressed upon them the importance of finding each foundling an individual name. He had done it because Mrs Ransom, in an absent-minded moment, had named several of her girls either Ellen or Mary because it was easier to remember, but it annoyed Mr Hayman that there were now such a number of Ellens and Marys amongst the hundred or so girls within these walls. Boy orphans went two streets away, to Hope Street, where the home was run by a married couple, Mr and Mrs Dunn, and apart from glimpses in the street and in church, the children from the two homes seldom met. Despite the fact that the Dunns had charge of the boys, and boys are said to be more difficult than girls, the boys' home had a better reputation. Mr and Mrs Dunn were strict but fair, they managed better, and what was more the Dunns put more

5

thought into the naming of boy foundlings than Mrs Ransom did with her girls.

'Yes, Lilac Larkin will do,' Mrs Ransom said, therefore. 'Of course, the child's mother might repent, come back ... but I doubt it. Not with a fatherless child and a theft on her conscience.'

'Yes, ma'am,' Nellie said, eyes downcast but with unholy satisfaction shining in them nevertheless. Long experience of Mrs Ransom had taught her that the older woman could be handled, if one was careful. She swept the baby, blanket, shawl and all, up in her arms but was arrested by a cry from the matron.

'Nellie McDowell, just what do you think you're doing? Put that child down at once and tek the shawl off of it!'

Nellie unwrapped the baby gently and saw the small face begin to prepare for grief once more. Mrs Ransom saw it too and spoke hastily.

'There, take the child, then, but leave the shawl; it's too fine for a foundling's bedcover and besides, it's still damp. Take it ... her ... to the nursery and find it a corner. I'll speak to Mr Hayman after church on Sunday.'

Nellie picked up the child again, wrapped this time just in the piece of blanket, and the incipient wail was almost comically checked, as though in this skinny rabbit of a thirteen-year-old girl the baby could already sense an ally.

'Right, ma'am,' she said humbly. 'I'll heat some milk to quiet her first, shall I?'

'Milk and water,' Mrs Ransom said, not harshly this time but hastily nevertheless. 'Better start as we mean to go on.'

Nellie gave a little bob, the child still clutched to her flat bosom, and left the room. As soon as she was out of earshot of the matron's room she addressed the baby lying quietly in the crook of her arm.

'Well, and aren't you my pretty, then? You're my first foundling, for 'twas me who named you, even though old Ranny thinks 'twas herself! Be a good gel for Nellie, Lilac, and you shall have milk, and no water added, not tonight, for you've had a hard time of it, you poor crittur.'

The baby sighed and snuggled and Nellie's heart contracted with pleasure; after her parents' death she had been brought here because her aunt could only cope with the boys, but how she had missed them, Charlie, Hal, Bertie, Fred and Matt! But Charlie, Hal and Bertie had been big enough to be useful, and Fred and Matt were the twins, just babies. It was only Nellie who, it seemed, was too much trouble, only Nellie who was sent away from the warmth of Scotland Road and the bawdy, hungry life of the court to be brought up amongst strangers.

'You'll 'ave a full belly and you'll get schooling, and they'll tek you into service because you'll be trained up right,' her Auntie Ada had said on that long-ago day when six-year-old Nellie had first been brought to Rodney Street. 'I know it seems 'ard, queen, but you'll thank us when you're growed.'

'We'll come and see you, our Nell,' Charlie, the eldest, had said reassuringly. 'When we're workin' at the docks we'll come and tek you on outings in the charrybang, and gi' you jam butties and a toffee stick. We won't forget our Nellie.'

They came, a time or two, every year. Stiff-faced, adam's apples bobbing, hair slicked down with water. But Mrs Ransom didn't let her little girls go out with young fellers, even if the young fellers swore blind they was the little girl's brothers, and even Charlie and Hal

7

got sick and tired of sitting in Mrs Ransom's dark, overcrowded sitting room and trying to find something to say which they wouldn't mind Mrs Ransom overhearing.

Last time they'd come they had reminded her she would be working herself in a couple of years and then she could come back to the court and see them, and Auntie Ada and the twins.

'We'll 'ave a hooley for you,' Charlie said. 'Do you 'member when our Mam taught you to sing "Only a bird in a gilded cage"? I've gorra mouth organ now, I can play it real well, we could do a nice duet.'

But here she was, skivvying for Mrs Ransom, not due to go into proper service for another couple of years at least and maybe longer, since she did her work well and never complained. The twins would be big boys now, getting on for eight years old, and the others were young men.

Nellie reached the kitchen door and swung it open. It was dark and cold and Nellie knew that when she lit the gas blackbeetles would leg it for the darkest corner and would scrunch beneath her cold bare feet if she wasn't careful. The room smelt of gas, the coke-burning range, stale food and old meals. She had to lie Lilac down whilst she lit the gas, but when the light slowly bloomed she looked round almost with contentment. She had someone of her own, now, to love! They had taken her away from the lads, stolen her home – which had only been one room when all was said and done, but what a deal of laughter and love had dwelled there – and given her into slavery with Mrs Ransom. But now she had little Lilac and no one would take her away. Not likely!

'Nellie loves you, Lilac,' the girl murmured as she poured milk into a pan and set it on the stove to warm.

'Nellie'll look after you, don't you fret. Oh, you'll be quite the little lady, Lilac Larkin!'

Nellie and baby Lilac became all but inseparable as time went on. Lilac was not claimed and everyone at the Culler, even the nursery staff, were too busy to object when the little maid of all work found time, energy and love for the new foundling.

Nellie even took the baby to church with her, though the rule was that only children over five should attend the services. Smaller children grew bored and fidgeted, wailed or even talked, to the despair of accompanying staff. But Nellie seemed able to keep Lilac quiet and content just by holding her, so on Christmas Day, when the service was brightened by the giving of small gifts from other parishioners to the inhabitants of the Culler, Nellie was allowed to take her place, with the baby in her arms, along with the other twelve-to fifteen-year-olds attending morning service. Churchgoing children were split up according to age into two groups, and they went either to morning or evening service, following a rota kept by Miss Hicks, one of the least popular members of the teaching staff.

So on this particular Christmas morning, Nellie set off with the others. She wore a tickly brown dress, too short in the skirt and too long in the sleeves, a white calico pinafore, a brown cloak and a big brown felt hat which came so low over her eyes that she had to tilt her head to see under the brim. Clothing at the Culler was a communal business: you were given, fresh from the laundry, a dress which approximately fitted you but not the one you had handed in for washing the previous month, and hats and cloaks, though supposedly

9

one's own, were also treated in a cavalier fashion and simply seized by anyone wishing to go out.

But baby Lilac wore a soft, much washed cream-coloured woollen shawl and a long gown which was almost new and smelt sweetly of soap, and she snuggled happily against Nellie's scratchy cloak and slept deeply, her cheeks a healthy rosy pink, her big blue eyes demurely closed.

Because it was Christmas the church was packed, but the Culler pews were reserved, girls to the left, boys to the right. Bitter experience had told Nellie that the Culler boys were best avoided; full of mischief, said people who liked them, whilst those less charitable – particularly those who lived near the Dunns' establishment – called them Dunn's devils and worse.

However, she had no choice on this occasion but to sit on the end of a row, since Miss Hicks had bidden her to do so, adding, in a hissing undertone, that should Lilac start to cry Nellie must take her out at once, whether it was before or after the distribution of the Christmas boxes.

But Lilac was good, though she woke up when the singing started. She was probably woken less by the carols, Nellie thought indignantly, than by the efforts of Mr Dunn's devils. They certainly were not a musical crew; voices which were totally flat, others which creaked and soared unevenly, others still which roared in the bass, made the noise from their pews hideous and Nellie suspected that they were doing their best to ruin the service for everyone else. She didn't blame them for that, particularly, but she did hope they wouldn't make Lilac squall, for though the baby was good, and Nellie had thoughtfully provided herself with a bottle of sweetened water which she had stuck into the pocket of her pinafore, there was always the chance that strange and discordant sounds might upset the child.

But Lilac just lay in Nellie's arms blinking her big eyes and moving her mouth occasionally in a reminiscent sort of way, as though she was savouring, in memory, her breakfast milk. And they got through four carols, three lessons, a couple of psalms and were settling down for the sermon before the accident – if it was an accident – happened.

The boys were quiet, apart from scraping the floor-tiles with their boots, coughing, whispering sibilantly one to another and occasionally sighing or giving a stifled snort. And then, out of the blue, there was a brief scuffle from the pew opposite Nellie's and a large glass olly rolled slowly across the aisle. It was a prince amongst marbles, streaked with red and blue, a winner which anyone would have been proud to own. It trundled unerringly across and came to rest right by Nellie's boot.

And behind the marble came a boy, one of Dunn's devils, and behind him, bent on destruction, came Miss Hicks, who must have seen the marble's journey from her own pew further back and was determined to make the owner suffer.

Nellie told herself afterwards that she acted instinctively, out of a deep-rooted fellow feeling for another orphan. Lilac appeared to give a convulsive heave and a kick and her shawl dropped down, right on top of the marble. Just as Miss Hicks reached for the boy's shoulder, Nellie bent and retrieved the shawl, ignoring the fracas and smiling into Lilac's small, fair face as she adjusted the garment.

Miss Hicks let go of the boy and gave Nellie a push, trying to see if the marble still lay at her feet. Nellie exaggerated her stagger and her shoulder struck her next-door-neighbour, who bumped into the girl next to her, creating a domino effect which made the last girl in the pew give a rebellious squeal as she was thrust rudely against the wall.

'Did you pick up that marble, Nellie McDowell?' Miss Hicks whispered vengefully, whilst the boy hovered, bending down to see if his property was amongst the girls' boots and the church hassocks. 'If you did ...'

'Ssshhh,' hissed the congregation, including some of the bolder orphans, and Miss Hicks grabbed once more at the boy's shoulder, giving him a hard shake as she did so.

'Stand up this minute, you wicked boy, and ...'

The boy obeyed with startling suddenness so that his head struck Miss Hicks in her thin chest. She gasped and stepped back, and Nellie caught the boy's bright, dark eye. A wordless message passed between them: Do you have it? Yes, I do. Then the dark eye flickered into a wink, a grin tilted the corners of his mouth so briefly that no one but Nellie could have seen, then the boy dropped his gaze and spoke, not to Nellie but to the teacher.

'Sorry, Miss. I was only lookin' for me olly, like. It's gone, anyroad.'

'Ssshhh!'

The boy turned to go back to his own pew and Miss Hicks, with a furious glare at the people who were shushing her, turned back too and marched noisily across to her own place. She sat down and Nellie tried to concentrate on the sermon whilst still wondering what her present from the congregation was to be.

When the sermon was done the presents were given out and proved to be a small bar of Fry's chocolate for each child. Nellie's mouth watered for the rest of the service but she knew better than to try to sample the

12

treat. Nothing would give Miss Hicks more pleasure than confiscating the chocolate. So Nellie bided her time and at last the service was over and the orphans began to spill into the aisle, boys and girls together for once in an undisciplined crush.

The boy was near her, Nellie sensed his closeness, saw out of the corner of her eye his thin, intelligent face. He was at her elbow and for a moment she was afraid he would make some sign which would be seen – and correctly interpreted – by the dreaded Miss Hicks. But she wronged her new friend. He jostled carelessly past her, and she felt his hand slide under the shawl whilst he still feigned ignorance of her nearness. Coolly and carefully, Nellie slid the blood alley into his hand. For a moment their fingers mingled, hers small, cool and hesitant, his lean and calloused, probably dirty, certainly warm and self-assured. And as the marble changed hands something was pressed into Nellie's palm, something hard and oblong and wrapped in shiny paper. Nellie knew without looking that it was the boy's chocolate bar. Without thinking she turned towards him, meaning to say there was no need, that he must take it back, but he had gone, melting into the throng of Dunn's devils, just another member of that alien race, boys.

She and Lilac shared the chocolate after dinner, the baby chumbling on the tiny piece that Nellie held for her. And then, for the first time, she smiled straight up into Nellie's face. an innocent and gummy beam, as though to reward her for her generosity.

Nellie's heart turned over. Lilac was the little sister she had never had, and Nellie would make sure that no one ever sent Lilac away to live amongst strangers. What was more, Lilac should never want, not whilst Nellie was there to see she was treated right.

And that boy, that Dunn's devil, had warmed Nellie's heart by his kindness in giving her his chocolate when there was no need, she'd been glad to rescue the marble. She had liked his face, too, liked the way he grinned and the quick, neat way he had taken the marble from her. Now that it was too late she wished she had asked his name, but it didn't really matter. She would keep her eyes open and perhaps she would see him again, some time, and thank him properly for the chocolate.

It had made Nellie's Christmas just perfect, though: Lilac's first smile and the exciting affair, known to her ever afterwards as the Boy and the Marble, to say nothing of two whole bars of chocolate! She was in a good mood all day and sang about her work, even though the longed-for visitors from Coronation Court had not arrived by bedtime.

She dreamed of them, though. In her dreams Charlie, Hal, Bertie, Fred and Matt trooped through the front door of the Culler, their arms laden with small gifts for her and Lilac. And always, hovering nearby, was a dark-haired, bright-eyed lad with a marble grasped in one grimy paw ... and no bar of chocolate of his own.

Chapter One

1912

Nellie was twenty and Lilac six when Nellie first took the younger girl back to Coronation Court where she herself had spent the first half-dozen years of her life. She was fiercely proud of Lilac, knowing she was prettier, cleverer and more loving than other children of her age, but when she took her home and watched her mixing with children who were not orphans, she discovered that Lilac had a will of her own and a great deal of determination, too.

It all started when Nellie decided to take Lilac to her brother Charlie's wedding. Nellie was earning a little money now, for she was properly employed by the orphan asylum, though her wages were tiny compared with what she might have earned working at one of the factories or even in domestic service, had she risen to the lordly position of parlourmaid. But working at the Culler meant she was still with Lilac, and that suited Nellie just fine. What was more, having money of her own meant not only that she could see Lilac was treated right, but could also afford a wedding present for Charlie and Bess, so that Lilac could join in the pleasure of giving. And she was on good terms with the present cook – cooks at Culler's seldom stayed long owing to Mrs Ransom's meanness – who had promised her what she described as 'some bits of ham and mebbe a lickle cake or two', so her own popularity, and that of Lilac, was assured. Aunt Ada had never reproached her for not bringing her wages home – she could

15

scarcely do so when she had turned Nellie over to the asylum all those years ago – but she did appreciate a small gift, especially of food. Her husband, Uncle Billy, had been ill with consumption for as long as Nellie could remember, and had been unable to work in a real job for years, though he was a clever wood-carver and made beautiful little stools, chairs and small toys; anything, in fact, which could be carved on his lap.

So now the two of them set off, both equally full of anticipation. For the first time in her short life, Lilac had a dress which was not made of brown serge and covered in a coarse white pinafore. Nellie had been grimly determined that the child should not have to wear the Culler uniform for the wedding and by buying cheap and working hard on the garment herself she had managed to do Lilac proud. It was clear that the child regarded the pink silk dress which Nellie had saved so hard for as almost too good to wear, and walking along the street now her free hand stroked the skirt continually. She kept touching the white lace collar too, as though to make sure it had not disappeared, and every now and then she bent down to straighten her white stockings – which were perfectly straight – showing her pleasure so openly that Nellie was downright glad she had chosen to dress her Lilac fine. She had skimped on her own outfit, though the grey and white striped skirt, the lavender-coloured blouse and the neat black boots were better than most managed in these difficult days. She knew that the rest of the family would have had to save hard to get themselves geared up for the wedding. Aunt Ada worked in a local grocer's shop, long hours for small pay, and helped to run a stall in Great Homer Street market on a Saturday night, but she got damaged goods cheap and was clever with her needle so she and

Uncle Billy would look pretty smart. Uncle Billy would get his good suit out of pawn and Aunt Ada's Sunday hat would be redeemed at the same time, and trimmed with fresh flowers so that everyone would believe it was new. Shirt collars would be chalked to hide the wear, socks would be darned, shoes relined with cardboard, and the McDowell family would show a brave face to the world. Aunt Ada's two daughters were both working now, Jessie married to a clerk in a shipping office and Lou engaged to a sailor on the New York run. Both lived away from home, Jessie with her husband of course and Lou in the big house where she worked as a kitchen maid.

Charlie worked at the docks as a holdsman, a trusted member of his gang. When unloading a ship he had to bring the cargo up and fasten the winches securely, making sure that each load was properly stacked. When they were lading he had to stow the goods neatly, using the space economically and making sure that, when unloading commenced, the easier stuff was available to be moved first. When he had a ship his pay was good, and because he knew his job and his gang were all seasoned dockers he was usually in work. Indeed, even when ships were scarce and half the dockers unemployed, Charlie usually managed to find himself a job of sorts. He would walk to the smart suburbs – Everton, Crosby, Seaforth – and dig gardens or muck out stables, clean windows or strip down engines, for he was a keen amateur mechanic and was saving up for a motorbike. A tall, tough young man who could hold his own in any company, he was popular with workmates and employers alike, and dearly loved by Aunt Ada and Uncle Billy, but once he and his Bessie were married they would move out of Coronation Court and get a room of their own. Aunt

17

Ada would miss his sturdy, commonsense companionship, and she would miss the money he brought in so regularly.

Hal was a seaman when he was in work. At various times he'd shipped as assistant cook, deckhand and stoker on a steamer, but he was unemployed at the moment and waiting for a berth. He'd done a few days at the docks, working alongside Charlie in the holds, but he preferred the more reliable pay of a seaman. Bertie was a porter at Lime Street station, sometimes with money to spare because of his tips, at other times talking bitterly of emigrating to America and making his fortune, because a feller couldn't hope to make enough to marry on as a porter. Nellie knew that her aunt was glad Bertie couldn't marry his young lady, a 'mary ellen' called Unity who sold fruit from a stall in Great Homer Street. Bertie said she was a good girl – she was certainly very pretty, with waistlength reddish brown hair and eyes which exactly matched – but it was rumoured that mary ellens were no better than they should be and it was true that Charlie said he'd seen Unity down at the docks more than once, with a different feller each time. But that didn't mean she was bad, surely? Nellie hoped not, since she was sure that Bertie would be broken-hearted if he and Unity never wed.

So when the Saturday of the wedding actually arrived Nellie and Lilac set off hand in hand in their nice new clothes with the July sun on their shoulders, Lilac swinging on Nellie's hand and chattering nineteen to the dozen, for the smaller children rarely left the orphan asylum save for the walks to and from church on a Sunday, and a wedding was a most tremendous treat. Lilac, in her wedding finery with their present – a brass-handled hearth brush – safely stowed away in Nellie's bag, danced along the pavement without a care in the world, all lit up with excitement and with a thousand questions on her lips.

'What's that? What's them?' she kept demanding as they made their way through the streets, and Nellie was delighted to inform her when she could. And besides, it helped Lilac's short legs to cover the distance when they were talking and laughing.

'That's Lime Street Station, where Bertie works,' Nellie told the child. 'Cor, you should see the trains in there, Li! Great big old puffers ... one day us'll get aboard one and go off, shall us?'

'Can we go now?' Lilac said wistfully. They still had a long way to walk and already she would have liked a bit of a rest. She wished they could have taken a tram, she knew Nellie caught one occasionally, but she also knew it cost a lot so she didn't mention it and when Nellie said no, they couldn't go on a train today because they didn't want to be late for the wedding, did they, she walked on stoically, only reminding Nellie that she had been promised a look at the sea the next time they had an outing.

'When you're bigger we'll go down to the docks, tek a look at the big ships,' Nellie promised recklessly. 'We could catch the ferry and go over the water to Woodside, it's ever so pretty there. Why, we could even go to New Brighton, to the real sea, chuck!'

Considering the amount of persuasion Nellie had had to employ to get Miss Maria, the infant teacher, to let her take Lilac to the wedding, she shuddered at the thought of the struggle which would be necessary before anyone would allow her to take the child on the ferry across the Mersey, but she knew that Lilac was worth struggling for. The little girl was so bright and intelligent, she could not bear to see her become dull and easily led, as some of the orphans were. Sometimes Nellie thought the children might have been better off left to live in poverty and to die young rather than to be transplanted to the artificial life lived in the orphan asylum with no one to love you, no one to care about you. But then she remembered that some orphans made good, and decided that Lilac would be one of them, so that was all right.

'When will I be bigger? Tomorrow? Next Sunday?'

Nellie laughed and squeezed the small hand so confidingly placed in her own.

'Not as soon as that but sooner than Christmas,' she promised. 'We'll cut through St John's Gardens, shall we? Ever so nice them are, specially in spring, and even now there'll be flowers and trees and that, and then we're in Byrom Street and that's ever so near the Scottie.'

They cut through the gardens, enjoying the scent of roses as the sun fell warmly on the open blossoms, and soon enough they were walking up Scotland Road and Nellie was beginning to see people she knew, landmarks she recognised, not just from her recent trips but from when she had lived here as of right. She had been coming home now for four years, ever since she had been considered old enough to undertake the journey alone, but this would be Lilac's first visit.

'What's that, Nellie? Up them steps.'

'That's Paddy's Market, where your dress came from.' Nellie did not add that the dress, in its early days, had lacked the lace collar she had carefully stitched onto it and had been big enough to contain two orphans. But she had spent long evenings up in her small attic room cutting and stitching and altering, adding the lace, the ribbons, the tiny pearl buttons which fastened the bodice. 'No time to tek a look now, queen, but some day ...'

They did look, though, as they passed. Barefoot ten-year-olds dressed in rags sat on the steps selling newspapers. A big black man in seafaring clothes pushed cheerfully past the boys, his arms full of chamber pots, some floral, some plain, one with 'Milton Hotel' printed in blue on its bulging white side. A woman, elderly, black-clad, draped in a shawl, climbed the steps, her shopping basket crammed with what looked like cabbages. Even out in the street you could hear the noise of bargaining, shouting, laughter, smell the food being served in Scouse Alley, where you could sit up to a scrubbed white table and get a full roast dinner for a tanner and a wet-nelly – a barm-cake drenched in warm treacle – for a ha'penny. Lilac sniffed approvingly and pointed out that she was hungry but Nellie just shook her head, smiling down at her.

'Hungry? You don't know wharrit means, chuck! At least you're fed at the Culler, even if it's mainly plain stuff.'

Lilac thought this over, then announced: 'I'm hungry for something which isn't plain, then. I'm hungry for something sweet and sticky and – and bad for me.'

The poor little sod's spent six years eating borin' food which she's been told is good for her, Nellie reminded herself. It was hard on the foundlings, though the Culler's Orphan Asylum was all they knew, but Nellie could still recall her mother's scrag-end stews and treacle pudding, and her famous conny onny butties, with the condensed milk spread thick on the bread, a promise of which brought good behaviour from all her kids under the most trying circumstances.

'Tell you what, queen, if you're good today I'll bring you to the market next time we gets our legs loose. Will that do?'

'Oh Nellie, I do love you,' Lilac said, hugging Nellie's hand to her pink silk chest. 'I'll be ever so, ever so good!'

'And I love you,' Nellie said, very gratified. 'What's more, I'll bet a quid to a shillin' there's jam butties and cake and all sorts waiting in Aunt Ada's parlour, to say nothing of what's already on the tables in the court.'

Aunt Ada's parlour was also her kitchen, the family wash-place and the twins' bedroom, but today, because of the wedding, it would be all set up nice, Nellie knew, the same as the court would be. A court was common property to the twenty or so families who lived around it, but a wedding breakfast was a communal feast and almost always took place in the court since the guests could scarcely cram into the tiny houses. Today Nellie knew the court would have been scrubbed and whitewashed, there would be flowers and white paper cloths on the tables borrowed from the church hall and food arranged down the middle. There would be a barrel of ale, lemonade for the kids and tea for the old shawlies who didn't care for liquor. A wedding was a big event in any community and everyone would have added what they could to the feast. Mr Finnigan worked for a local butcher and he would get Aunt Ada a couple of pig's cheeks and some trotters; Aunt Ada would stew them with onions and they'd be fit for a king. Bessie's Dad, Arthur Melville, would have bought the ale and lemonade since the hooley was being held in Coronation Court where there was a lot more room than in the Melvilles' back-to-back in Conway Street. Because of this the Melvilles would contribute generously to the breakfast and buy all the ale instead of sharing the cost with the groom's family, probably thankful to have been spared the orgy of cleaning and preparation necessary before one could hold a wedding. And the signs of the approaching nuptials would have been evident for weeks, Nellie knew; indeed, when Charlie had come

22

bashfully to the Culler to invite her to the wedding he'd apologised for the splashes of whitewash in his hair.

'Been doin' the walls and ceilings,' he had said gruffly. 'We've painted the windowsills and doors a good strong blue – Hal nicked the paint off of the docks when he had a day's work a month or so back – Ada's borrowed Mrs Hecharty's new curtains, they're blue silk with birds on, her Frankie brought 'em back from his China trip, and we've chose a big roll of oilcloth; red, it is, with a white and yellow pattern; the twins will fetch it Saturday morning.'

'Eh, I reckon it'll look a treat,' Nellie said admiringly. 'What's your Bessie wearing?'

'Dunno. I'm the groom, aren't I? The bride doesn't tell the groom what she's going to wear,' Charlie said reproachfully. 'She's a smart lass though, my Bessie; her mam's good with her needle, so she's making her something special.'

But now, fast approaching the court, Nellie felt a tug at her hand.

'Is that it, Nell? Is that where the wedding is?'

'That's it, queen,' Nellie said softly. She felt so proud she could have burst. Charlie had even whitewashed round the entrance to the court, he had painted the edge of the paving stones and put a couple of big old jars with bulrushes in them on either side. From within came the excited sounds of people preparing for a happy event; children called, a dog barked, someone shooed the dog away, someone else appeared in the entry.

'Come in, our Nellie, just in time! Bring the littl'un and you can have a word with Auntie before we mek for the church. Come on, kiddo, you tek my hand.'

Hal, in a shiny blue suit with a white shirt and a red tie came out onto the pavement. Behind him hovered another man, someone Nellie had never seen in her life before, yet for a moment he looked familiar. He was of medium height, with black hair which curled like a fleece all over his head, tanned skin and dark eyes which held her own steadily. Nellie smiled at him – he was clearly a guest – and suddenly realised that he reminded her of the Dunn's devil who had given her chocolate for his marble years ago. But this young man was quite a lot older than the Dunn's devil would have been, it was just a fleeting likeness.

And now Hal was making friends with Lilac, telling her what a pretty girl she was and admiring her dress and Lilac, who had shrunk back against Nellie's skirts at this unaccustomed approach from a member of the opposite sex, suddenly seemed to decide he was harmless. She smiled at him and put a small paw confidingly into his. Hal smiled back, then put his other hand on Nellie's shoulder and kissed her cheek.

'Our Nell, you look a picture,' he said roundly. 'I'll give this young lady a buttie whilst you have a word with Auntie, see if there's owt left undone, then we'll mek for the church together. Unity's with her sisters; they left earlier.'

'Thanks, Hal, only don't go feedin' Lilac, I don't want her to get her dress mucky. Show her the weddin' presents, she'll like that,' Nellie said. The second young man was still looking at her – staring, almost – and she began to wonder if she had a smut on her nose, or if she should have worn a hat. As Hal turned to go into the court he caught the young man's eye and turned back to Nellie for a moment.

'Oh, Nell, this is David Evans, he's got a berth aboard a coaster trading from Holyhead up and down the west coast of Scotland. We berthed together before. I'm leaving with the *Moelfre Maid* when she sails tomorrow: Dave's mate, I'm cook.' He turned to David Evans. 'Davy, this is me sister Nellie and her gel,' he said. 'Come on, Lilac, let's go an' tek a look around.'

'Hello, Nellie,' David Evans said. 'There's nice you and your littl'un do look; well, I hope to see you later. Perhaps we might have a bit of a dance together when the hooley starts.'

Nellie murmured some appropriate rejoinder. So he was Welsh – that accounted for the lilt in his speech, the coalblack curls and sparkling dark eyes. But what on earth did the mate of a coaster and Hal have in common? She supposed, doubtfully, that David must only recently have risen to such heights and then, as she turned towards the house, she felt his eyes on her, almost burning on the back of her neck where the hair was lifted to show the fresh whiteness of her nape. She risked a quick glance back and he was still staring at her, with a sort of hungry intentness which made her feel hot all over. Suddenly she felt quite sure that whatever had caught his attention it was not a smut on her nose nor her hatless state. But she moved on, knowing that no nice girl would allow a young man to see that she had noticed his hot glances, let alone felt intrigued by him. Crossing the court she saw Lilac, hand in hand with Hal, going to view the wedding gifts. She looked happy and natural and indeed the sight of the court *en fête* seemed to have made a great impression on her – and no wonder! Nellie was glad to see that even the dustbins, which usually made the air ripe all summer, had been banished for this special day, and the flagstones which floored the court were scrubbed to show their original white and smelt of carbolic. The twins, armed with leafy branches, were keeping the flies off the food already set out on the long tables and Bertie came out of the house with a tray piled with glasses and mugs. He saw Nellie and whistled.

'Our Nell, I never see you look so gear! You're a pretty judy, you'll turn a few heads!'

Nellie dodged past him, receiving another kiss on the cheek and a rumbustious hug which rumpled her blouse and made her gasp and laugh. Before entering the house however, she checked that Lilac was all right without her. Hal, having done his duty by the child, had gone off to talk to his friend, but Lilac was clearly being well looked after. Nellie saw the child shyly take a leafy branch offered by Matt and start to wave it rather dangerously over a plate of scones. Freddy shouted a warning and Matt shifted her to a covered dish, informing her that it contained spare ribs which, when the hooley started, he would personally let her taste. Other children wandered over: a small, square boy with a frown and a cowlick of hair dangling over his forehead went and helped Lilac with the switch, and they started to talk.

Relieved of her most immediate worry and keeping her gaze firmly turned from the fascinating young Welshman, Nellie made her way up the narrow stair to the stuffy room under the eaves where Aunt Ada and her two daughters were getting ready. All three women were dressed, but Ada was pinning a wide straw hat on her neatly brushed hair, Jessie was wailing over a recently discovered hole in her white wedding gloves and Lou was trying to darn the glove whilst her sister waved her hand about and said it must be mice because it were all in one piece after our Ellen's hooley.

'There's no mice in my house ... ' Aunt Ada was beginning, when she saw Nellie's reflection appear behind her in the glass. She turned abruptly, the hat tilting absurdly over one eye, and nodded approval. 'Nell, you're lookin' your best. You tek the prize, chuck! Look at her, girls!'

Nellie looked at herself in the glass. Her shining fawn hair, freshly washed, showed the chestnut and gold gleams of summer and her usually pale, triangular face was flushed with excitement. Her grey-green eyes, fringed with thick, brown lashes, were wide and bright, the whites touched with blue, pristine as sheets on the line. I'm almost pretty, she thought with astonishment, I really am almost pretty! Perhaps David Evans was looking at my prettiness – now there's a thing! Even her figure was improved by her best clothes. The lavender- coloured blouse showed off her small, high breasts, her waist looked tiny clipped in with the broad black belt, and the swell of her hips was accentuated by the gathers of the grey and white striped skirt.

'She's a credit,' Jessie said. 'Our Mam always said the Culler would do right by you, our Nell, and she was right. You're a credit, that's what.'

'Well, thanks, both,' Nellie said. 'Have you seen little Lilac, though? She's down in the court, wi' the twins, keepin' the flies off the spare ribs.'

The three women peered out of the small window. Aunt Ada drew back first.

'She does you credit, luv,' she said approvingly. 'I 'ope she knows what she owes you, our Nellie. That dress musta cost a pretty penny.'

'I got it from Paddy's market for tuppence. Then the lace collar was threepence, pearl buttons a ha'penny, silk ribbon penny ha'pence for three yards,' Nellie said proudly. 'She's a pretty kid, though; them curls is natural. And she's nice, Auntie. A good little kid.'

'Tell you what, why don't we let her give the bride the posy, and the 'orseshoe for luck,' Jessie said suddenly. 'Matt an' Fred, they don't want to do it, they'll be pleased if your littl'un would.'

And Nellie, agreeing that Lilac would hand over the posy very prettily, felt that she could have burst with pride.

By the time the wedding was over and the newlyweds had returned to the hooley in the court, Lilac had decided she was in love with Matthew McDowell and would undoubtedly marry him when she was a lady. She told him so and he laughed, but he looked pleased, she thought, and the flush which warmed his lean, tanned cheek made him even more attractive.

'Me and Nellie are sort of sisters, but if I married Matt we'd be proper sisters,' she told another friend, the small, square boy with the frown as they sat on the whitened doorstep eating spare ribs, Lilac muffled up in a huge apron of Aunt Ada's so that she didn't spill grease on her finery. 'How old are you, anyway?'

'I'm seven; me name's Art,' the small boy said gruffly. 'Matt's fourteen; he won't want to marry a kid like you, when you're fifteen he'll be ... he'll be ... ' he struggled vainly with the sum for a moment, finally ending, '... he'll be ever so old! You oughter go for someone younger, sconehead.'

'He won't! And you shouldn't call names and anyway I wouldn't marry *you* for a sack of rubies,' Lilac said furiously. '*And* you're fat, sconehead.'

'I am bloody not fat, I'm just strong. You'se a toffee-nosed snob, you are.' Art put on a squeaky, effeminate voice. 'Oh, what a pretty little lady!' His voice went back to its usual nasal growl. 'Toffee-nosed kid, and you'se is on'y a foundling! No mam, no da, you'se a real gutter kid!'

'I am not! Nellie's my sister ... I do have a mam and

a da, only they aren't here right now. My mam's a princess and my da lives in the big house with the pillars. I am *not* what you said!'

'And I never asked you to marry me,' continued hateful Art as though she had not spoken. 'I'd rather marry a tinker's cat, I would! Look at you, all wrapped up in an old apron; if the sun shines on you would you melt?'

Lilac tore off the apron and dumped her plate on the step. She got to her feet and threw the greasy bones straight at Art's head, following that up with some brisk kicks to his shins with her small and shiny boots.

'You're a big fat old pig,' she shouted. And then, in imitation, albeit unconscious, of something someone had said earlier: 'How d'you like the trut', me fine bucko?'

Art took a swipe at her; it was a half-hearted swipe and it missed its small, enraged target, who had quite forgotten her claims to ladyhood as she lashed out with her boots and shouted any insult which came to her tongue, and you learned a thing or two from the other kids at the Culler.

'Shut your face, Lady Muck,' Art said, when she paused for breath. 'And pick up them greasy ribs off of our clean flags.'

Lilac turned away, tears of temper running down her cheeks – and walked right into Matt. He caught hold of her pink silk shoulders and then tilted her chin so she had to look up into his face. He had a lovely face, thin and brown, with laughing grey eyes and very white teeth. His hair was soft and dusty-fair and he was wearing a white shirt and long dark trousers. Lilac fished a tiny white handkerchief out of her dress pocket, blew her nose and then knuckled her eyes briskly. Only babies cried as she well knew, and she didn't want Matt to think her a baby!

'What's up, chuck? Been quarrellin', have you? Did you spill them bones on our nice clean flags? Better pick 'em up before someone puts a foot on 'em and goes arse over tip.'

' Ye-es, it was me,' Lilac said, unwilling to admit that she had actually thrown them at Art but unwilling, also, to tell a fib. 'I'll pick them ... oh!'

Art, without a word, was grubbing down at her feet, collecting the bones.

'It were my fault, Matt,' he said gruffly. ' Teasin' her I wuz. I'll clear the mess, you get the gal a nice buttie – there's tinned salmon, someone said.'

' Thanks, Art,' Matt said. He put a brotherly arm round Lilac's shoulders and led her over to the table. 'Here, a salmon sarny; now you come and sit with me and Fred and eat it all up like a good'un. Then you shall have lemonade.' And, once she was settled: 'Now queen, what was that all about? Art's not an arguefier, not as a rule he ain't.'

Lilac hesitated. She could scarcely say they had squabbled over Matt himself and she found that she did not want to admit she had been almost boasting of her intention to marry him.

'Um ... I was rude and called him fat,' she said at last. 'And he was rude and called me a foundering. He said I had no mam or da. But,' she added, impelled by honesty, 'I started it.'

'And will you be friends, now? You threw the ribs an' Art picked 'em up, so you should be friends.'

'I will if he will,' Lilac said readily. 'He isn't fat. He was nice till we quarrelled.'

'Course he ain't fat and he's a nice kid, too. And you do have a mam and da, you just don't know where they is, right now.' Matt, who had sat himself and Lilac down on a long bench against someone's windows, turned and shouted. Art came out of the house and smiled shamefacedly at them as he made his way across the crowded court. 'Art, come and shake the littl'un's hand and mek friends. Today's special, don't forget.'

Watched by the twins and several other wedding guests, Art and Lilac solemnly shook hands.

Davy Evans stood in the court eating a ham sandwich and guarding a pint of ale and thinking about that girl.

Nellie McDowell, his friend Hal's sister. Wasn't it odd now though that Hal had never mentioned a sister particularly, that he could remember? Brothers, yes, and the step-sisters, Hal's Aunt Ada's daughters, but never a sister of his own ... and so young, too. Jessie and Lou were both in their late twenties, Jessie married to a clerk, Lou engaged to a young blood who was on the New York haul and, according to Hal, probably had a fiancée in every port. But Davy was sure he'd never heard a Nellie McDowell mentioned.

He'd met Jessie and Lou before. They were nice girls, but no one in their right minds would find them pretty! Buxom, yes. Well set up, perhaps. But pretty? Not in his eyes, anyway.

But that little Nellie! He'd seldom felt more attracted to a girl on sight – just his luck she was clearly married, and with a child, and looking no more than a child herself. Mind, it might be as well, Davy reminded himself; he had responsibilities – but they had never stopped him admiring pretty girls and trying to get alongside. It didn't do to mess with married women,

Davy knew that well, but he'd watched her in church, whilst the service was taking place, and there was no man with her. She sat with the child, they shared a hymn book, she clearly adored the little girl, making sure the child's kneeler was in the right position, finding the place for her in the prayer book and generally attending to all her wants.

She had such a lovely little face! Her eyes were big and clear, opening wide when she had looked up at him, and the little white teeth of her, biting her full lower lip anxiously, wondering if she had a smut on her nose to make him stare so; he had read the thought in her eyes as they met his. She had not yet acknowledged her own beauty he knew, she thought nothing of the tiny waist, the swell of hips and breast, the budding femininity of her which was the more attractive because it was so unconscious of its power.

I could write a poem to her, Davy thought, taking an enormous bite out of his ham sandwich, then opening the bread up to smear more yellow mustard onto the pink meat. A poem about the colours which streak her shining hair, the soft fawn of hay and the clear gold of wheat, the brown of limpid river water under a summer sun, the glowing auburn of a burnished chestnut. And her skin, pale as milk with the flush of a dawn rosebud in the cheek, and her brows, tender arcs above those clear and brilliant eyes!

Was she married, though? No one had said so. Women did have babies out of wedlock but he didn't think, somehow, that Nellie was the type. Indeed, I would have sworn she was as virgin as the child Lilac herself, he thought, surprised at his own persistent worrying at a point which should be academic, since he had responsibilities and lived far from here and besides, she had not looked at him once since their first meeting. Now she was doing her duty as a daughter of the house, handing food, pouring ale, seeing that the children – and there were a good number of them – were fed and had lemonade in their cups. Presently, when everyone's hunger was satisfied and the musicians arrived, they would begin the dancing, and then he would dance with her, married or single, because he guessed she would be as light on her feet as a feather, would lie in his arms like swan's-down, like a cloud, like a dream.

Across the court from him, Nellie stood on tiptoe to kiss Charlie. Flushed, laughing, she turned from her brother to kiss the bride, having to duck her head to avoid the enormous brim of Bessie's wonderful hat, decorated with what looked like a still-life of flowers and fruit. Nellie, kissing and laughing, was flesh and blood, not a cloud or a feather, Davy saw. But she still had such sweetness, such a shy yet easy way with her ... ah, the girl of his dreams was Nellie, the sort of girl he would be so proud to call his own, should he ever win her!

Not that he could think about marriage, as things stood. But nothing lasted for ever, one day his family responsibilities would surely end and allow him some life of his own?

But there was the child ... oh, dammit, there's a mystery here, Davy said desperately to himself, and I shall find it out! I will not sit back and watch and envy as others take her hands, put their arms round her waist!

The musicians arrived: two fiddle players, a man with a mouth-organ, and a big woman whose mighty breasts trembled and shook as she sang *Bless this House* and *Mother of Mine*. Then the fiddlers tuned up, the man with the mouth-organ blew a few faint notes, and Charlie seized Bessie and began the dancing.

Davy went straight to Nellie.

'Miss ... er ... '

'McDowell, but you'll call me Nellie,' the girl said shyly. 'You're a friend of our Hal's, ain't you?'

'I am indeed, Nellie. Will you do me the honour of letting me have this dance?'

'Oh, yes ... just let me settle Lilac.'

They danced and danced as the warmth softened and the light with it. When it was too dark to see properly to dance they sat on the flags or on the benches or the doorsteps and sang all the old tunes to the fiddlers' playing. Davy sang solo several times but Nellie, chuckling, said she had no voice to speak of and could not hold a note and listened to him with a softened look on her face and held the child Lilac, asleep, in her lap.

There was more food then, and Bessie and Charlie went up and changed out of their wedding finery, to walk round to their newly painted, newly furnished little house. It was only part of a house really, Ada told Davy and Nellie, but it would do right well till the babies came. And Nellie blushed and Davy whispered in her ear that he would want to walk her home himself, but he knew she was at home, so ...

'We don't live here, Davy,' Nellie said. 'We live in Rodney Street, me and Lilac.' She took a deep breath and looked up at him, anxious once more and troubled, he could tell. 'Did Hal never tell you? When Mam and Da died I was one too many for Aunt Ada so she sent me to the Culler Orphan Asylum. I work there now, to be near Lilac, but I come back when I can to see the boys and Aunt and Uncle.'

'And ... and Lilac isn't your sprog, then?' Davy asked, too dumbfounded to be tactful. Nellie blushed deeper and laughed and shook her head.

34

'Oh Davy, you couldn't have thought Lilac was mine, she's so golden-haired and beautiful! No, she's a foundling; I've always taken care of her. We're better'n sisters, I always say, and we'll be together like sisters, I'll never leave her. Well, fancy you thinkin' me a married woman!'

'Believe it I could not,' Davy said earnestly. 'Yet what else could I think, when Hal introduced you as his sister Nellie and her girl? Oh, Nell ... can I walk you home when the hooley's over?'

'I can't ask you; it'ud be miles out of your way,' Nellie said uncertainly. 'What's more, I'll be in enough trouble, comin' in so late, without someone seein' I've a feller with me. But mebbe it won't matter, since cook's leavin' the kitchen window a tiddy bit ajar for me.'

'I'd walk a hundred miles to be with you,' Davy whispered. He put his lips gently against the soft place between neck and shoulder and kissed the tender skin. 'Nellie, from the moment I saw you ... '

'Oh Davy, me too! But I'm just a skivvy at the Culler, you know, they don't pay me much, and I've got Lilac to look after and ...'

'What do I care, girl? I've got a family, too ... old parents, a brother who isn't quite ... quite like other lads his age. But we can enjoy one another's company. Let's start walking now, if it's a goodish way. I'll carry Lilac and we'll have a bit of time to talk.'

He glanced around the court. Several people were asleep in the soft summer night, lulled by the music and by the comfort of full bellies. The bride and groom had long since gone, the twins were snoozing in the doorway of their home, Ada and Billy, Jessie and Lou, had all disappeared. Bertie and his Unity were cuddled up, singing softly, Bertie keeping time to the music with one hand tapping his knee. Hal had borrowed the mouth organ and was experimenting with it, one moment capturing the air, the next making it squeak and groan comically.

'You'll really walk with me? You are good,' Nellie sighed. So Davy took the sleeping child from the girl's lap and held her comfortably in one arm and put the other gently round Nellie's slender shoulders and the three of them set off, out of the lamplit court and into Scotland Road, where even at this time of night there were people wandering about because of the oppressive heat in the small houses and also, Davy guessed, because they had taken too much ale to sleep easy in their beds.

'You'll have to tell me which way to go,' Davy said presently, as Nellie turned a corner without warning and very nearly left him behind. 'The moon's bright; it makes the gas lamps look silly, but I don't know the city that well, save for the dock area.'

'I only know the bit between Rodney Street and the Scottie,' Nellie murmured. 'But even by night I don't think I could lose meself.'

And she was true to her word, leading them without hesitation through the city streets until Davy saw Lime Street Station looming and got his bearings.

'Do you know your way back to the docks from here?' Nellie whispered when at last they stood against the side wall of the Culler, with the kitchen window happily unlatched and now standing open. 'Which dock is the coaster lying in, anyway?'

'She's in Wapping Basin, we've loaded coal,' Davy whispered back. 'I go to the end of the road, then where?'

'I ought to go with you, send you,' Nellie said softly, giggling. 'First you see me home, then I see you home!

No, go to the end of the street and you'll see the cathedral, the bit they've built, dead in front of you. Go down St James Road – it's all mucky from the building – and then cross it and take Nile Street until it fetches up on St James Street. When you reach the goods station go down beside it and you'll see the docker's umbrella. Just turn right and follow that and you'll be at the basin in no time.'

'The docker's umbrella?'

She laughed softly at his puzzlement.

'It's what Charlie calls the overhead railway. It goes right along, from Seaforth to the pierhead. I'm going to tek Lilac on it one of these days, for an outing.' She patted his arm. 'Got that? St. James Road, the cathedral, Nile Street, the station. And then the overhead railway right along to Wapping Basin. Goo'night, Davy, and thanks.'

She began to gently rouse the child, taking her from Davy and standing her down on the gravel path. Lilac yawned, knuckled her eyes, stared around her and then, on Nellie's murmured instructions, held her arms up to be helped through the window, but when Nellie went to lift her Davy touched her arm, detaining her.

'That's a cold way to part, Nellie McDowell,' he whispered. 'Won't you give me a kiss, girl?'

She blushed rosily, he could see it even in the cold moonlight, then held up her cheek. He put his arms round her, the child leaning drowsily first on one and then on the other, and pulled her close, then began to kiss her. First her cheek, then her chin, nose, eyelids, brow ... mouth. He felt the softness of her lips tremble at his touch, felt her body swoon towards him, then gently put her away from him. Time enough for that, time enough.

'Goodnight, Nellie. When shall I see you again?'

She looked up at him, dark-eyed in the moonlight.

'I don't know; when Hal gets married?'

He laughed softly, and, unable to resist, kissed her mouth again, a quick moth's touch.

'No, I don't think I can wait that long, girl! I'll write to you, tell you when I dock in the 'pool next. Can I come here, to the Culler?'

She drew back, shaking her head.

'Oh no, they wouldn't like that at all! Write to me and I'll write back, we'll arrange something. Goodnight, Davy.'

She turned from him, lifting the child through the window and preparing to follow. Davy took her small waist in his two hands and lifted her high, chest-height, then sat her gently on the sill. Dimpling at him, she swung her legs decorously over the sill and dropped onto the floor. Davy saw that she had beautiful legs, slim and strong, with pretty ankles. He leaned on the sill and blew her a kiss but she shook her head at him, gesturing him back, then lowered the window soundlessly and snibbed the catch across.

The last Davy saw of her before he began his own walk home was the gleam of her smile, the flutter of a waving hand. Then she was gone and he was alone once more.

Chapter Two

'Take off that ridiculous ribbon, Miss! No, don't dare to scowl at me like that ... come up here!'

Miss Flora Hicks, who taught the nine-year-olds, stood in front of the class, a piece of chalk in her right hand, a switch in her left, and glared at Lilac Larkin – who glared right back, standing defiantly up in her seat, her eyes sparkling.

'I won't tek the ribbon off! It's *my* ribbon, Nellie give it me, it's to keep my pigtail tidy!'

Miss Hicks tightened her mouth, then crossed the room in three or four long strides. She looked downright dangerous, Lilac thought apprehensively, with her mean face blotched with red and her mouth turned down at the corners and tight as a trap, yet why should she, Lilac, be afraid of her teacher? She had done nothing wrong, it was just because she was new to the class that old Hicksy was picking on her. And she'd tell Nellie, that she would, and then old Hicksy would be sorry!

Right now, however, Miss Hicks did not look sorry for anything – not even for her small victim. She grabbed Lilac by the brown serge shoulder and shook her briskly, then snatched the offending pink ribbon from the end of the child's long, red-gold plait, scrumpling up the smooth satin and shoving it viciously into the pocket of her long black skirt.

'You'll wear brown ribbon, the same as everyone

else,' she said grimly. 'I might have known – it all started when you gadded off to a wedding with that servant-girl, and her no better than she should be – I might have guessed it would mean trouble, defiance, lack of respect. And after the wedding it was "can she come here, can I take her there," until you got thoroughly above yourself. Well you might have got away with behaviour like that in Miss Maria's class, but not here, Miss. It'll be no tea for you tonight, and early bed.'

Lilac didn't care about her tea, which was always uninspiring bread and thinly spread rhubarb jam, nor about going early to bed, but she cared about her ribbon. She steeled herself for trouble.

'I didn't know I wasn't to wear it,' she said. She had meant to sound apologetic but the words somehow came out defiant. 'I want my ribbon back, now, then I'll put it in *my* pocket.'

Above her, the teacher smiled nastily. From her lowly position Lilac could see straight up the woman's large, cutaway nostrils. It was not a pretty sight and nor was the curl of her lip when she heard Lilac's words.

'Oh, you will, will you? Well that's where you're wrong, you stuck-up little brat!' She gave Lilac a hard shove. 'Get back to your seat and put your hands on your head. Stay there until I tell you to move.'

Commonsense and self-preservation told Lilac to do as she was told. Unfortunately, she did not listen to either, since she was now in a furious rage herself. She had done her best for a whole term to learn to live with Miss Hicks and to fit in with the rest of the class, but it was so different from life lived in the infants, with kind Miss Maria and Nellie always on hand! She liked reading and doing sums, but she did not like being bullied and shouted at and reviled day after day, and

Miss Hicks was about to find out just how little she liked it.

Stumbling back to her seat she sat down, put her hands on her head and then said clearly, 'Please may I have my ribbon back, Miss Hicks?'

'No. You won't see that again,' Miss Hicks said calmly, but with a gloating note in her voice. 'Don't let me hear another word about the ribbon, Lilac, or you shall get six strokes of the cane on either hand.'

'If you don't give it back,' Lilac said, voice trembling, 'then you're a thief.'

It had been quiet in the room whilst the altercation went on, but for a moment you could have heard a pin drop. No one, Lilac was sure, so much as drew breath. And then Miss Hicks flew across the room, her black skirt flapping round her skinny ankles, her big feet in their stout and sensible boots clumping hard on the floor, and dragged Lilac out of her chair. She tried to turn her over the desk but Lilac, divining her intention, squiggled and wriggled and fought, and in the end took the cane wherever Miss Hicks could place it, which was in vicious cuts across her arms, legs and one cheek whilst Lilac tried to snatch the piece of ribbon she could see just showing in the teacher's skirt pocket.

It was a good deal more than a dozen strokes later that the woman thrust her pupil back into her seat and moved away from her.

'May that be a lesson to you,' she said in a thick, shaking voice. 'Children, get on with your work.'

Nellie was setting the tables for tea and singing softly to herself as she did so. The work at the Culler Orphan Asylum was hard, but towards teatime there came a lull when tables were laid, bread cut, jam served out into dishes and milk and water in tall jugs placed at the head of each long table. Nellie enjoyed setting tea, knowing that very soon Lilac would be out of her class and on her way through for the meal. Of course it had been nicer when Lilac had still been in the infants, but when she left it and came into the school proper there had been no particular objection to Nellie's insistence that she, too, should move on.

'You've been a great help with the little ones,' Miss Maria had said wistfully. 'I always hoped you'd stay ... you're such a hard worker, Nellie my dear. But I mustn't be selfish.'

Nor had she been. She had told Mrs Ransom that Nellie McDowell was a pearl beyond price and advised the matron to keep her at all costs, even if it did mean a change around whenever Lilac Larkin was moved up the school.

Mrs Ransom was not a sympathetic or an understanding woman, but she did know upon which side her bread was buttered. Nellie had taken considerable pains with herself this last year, ever since she and Lilac had gone home to Coronation Court for Charlie McDowell's wedding. She spoke more carefully and seemed anxious to tone down the nasal Liverpudlian accent which she had heard – and indeed, used – almost all her life.

It had occurred to Mrs Ransom that Nellie would make a considerable impression on anyone who might be thinking of endowing the orphan asylum. To produce a servant girl who was pretty and fresh looking, who worked harder than any other member of the staff and who had a pleasant speaking voice ... well, Mrs Ransom was sure Nellie could charm a good deal of money out of benefactors' pockets, if only she could be prevailed upon to talk to the people who mattered.

And Nellie could be prevailed upon to do just that, in return for what amounted to a promise that she might remain with Lilac until the younger girl was old enough to leave the Culler. Indeed, at a recent board meeting Nellie had served the tea and Henry Harrison, a very important member, had praised her pleasant manners and stumped up a money-order to buy much-needed text books for the younger children.

So here was Nellie, setting the tea and singing *Danny Boy* and telling herself that she was thinking of Lilac and how they would read together before bed, while all the time she was really thinking about Davy Evans and the *Moelfre Maid*.

A year had passed since that memorable night when Davy had lifted her through the kitchen window and she had only seen him three times since, but they wrote letters whenever they could and she thought about him almost all the while. He was cleverer than she, as clever, possibly, as she believed Lilac would become – what other child of seven could read as well as a nine-year-old and do sums that baffled even older children? – and he spoke two languages, Welsh and English, and was learning French in his spare time, what there was of it.

She knew so much about him now! He was the son of elderly parents, his father was bedridden and his mother was a saint. She must be, to cope with his father and also with his brother Dickie, who had been born to Mrs Evans when she was fifty years old. Dickie was slow, Davy told her. Simple. He needed a good deal of help just to get through each day, but they loved him very much and he was so loving back that it was a pleasure to do things for him.

Davy and Nellie were courting, of course, though no one knew. Well, perhaps Lilac guessed, because she was a shrewd little creature, but no one else had any idea. Even Hal, who knew Davy liked to come into Liverpool so he could visit a lady-friend, did not know precisely who the lady-friend was.

It wasn't that they tried to keep it a secret, either. But for now they were neither of them in any position to marry, Davy with his family and Nellie with her Lilac, so they must be content to get to know one another, and very pleasant they found it, strolling by the river in the autumn dusk and then walking inland, arms entwined, with the smell of roasting chestnuts in the air and a frost nipping at your nose and sending the bright leaves tumbling down from the trees in St John's gardens.

Because she was writing to Davy, who wrote in a fine, sloping hand, Nellie began to pay more attention to her own handwriting. She and Lilac worked together, evenings, to make their writing better, and Nellie found that, in reading stories to Lilac and reading Davy's letters to herself, her reading improved, too. And then there was that first exciting meeting, to be relived in bed at night, when it was growing cold in her attic and the bed trembled to her shivers until she managed to get some warmth out of her thin blanket. Later, when the cold became almost unendurable, she and Lilac would share Nellie's truckle bed with all the blankets piled on top of them and that was lovely and snug, with their arms round each other and the child's sweet breath on her face.

The only trouble was that it was strictly forbidden, so Nellie had to sneak Lilac out of her dormitory and up to the attic, and then down again next morning, when she got up in the chilly pre-dawn dark, but though the other children certainly knew, no one told. They all had their little secrets, Nellie supposed, and were content to allow others to make the best of things so far as they were able.

Nellie's second meeting with Davy had been just before Christmas. They wandered round Lewis's, a wonderland of coloured lights, tinsel and Christmas trees with cottonwool snow, and bought each other a gift: socks for Davy, gloves for Nell. He called her Nell, said Nellie wasn't right for her, kissed her beneath the mistletoe, cuddled her up warm against his rough serge dufflecoat and told her about his family Christmas. A goose, cooked to a crackling golden brown, a pudding all aflame, after dinner a walk along the shore to pick up driftwood for the fire, then home for tea – ham from the family pig slaughtered at the backend of each year, baked apples stuffed with sultanas, and a fruit cake, rich and soggy. Games round the fire, an aunt playing the piano whilst the family sang the old songs until it was time for bed.

Just being loved by Davy had made her Christmas marvellously merry; she thought of the Evans in their cottage and knew Davy would rather be with her – had he not said so? She and Lilac laughed about everything: the non-existent presents for the children, save for coloured texts handed out by the board of governors, the meagre dinner with a tiny slice of overcooked bird and the thin gravy, the pudding which was nearly all bread and suet.

Besides, after that they went back to Coronation Court and had their tea with the family, and Charlie's Bessie felt queasy when the pudding came round and Charlie blushed and they all made jokes and even Nellie realised at last that Bessie was pregnant, and promised to knit a nice woolly coat for Baby McDowell.

Thinking of Christmas and the kiss under the mistletoe made Nellie think about Davy's last visit, an

April visit when he had brought Lilac a beautiful hoop and taught her to bowl it along the pavement with a little stick; how the three of them had laughed over the antics of that hoop with Lilac in charge, how it had reeled like a drunk, dizzying slowly along the pavement until it tipped into the gutter, spinning round slower and slower until it dropped with a clatter.

Davy had been in Liverpool for two whole days, and each evening she had managed to see him. They had watched the Punch & Judy outside the St George's Hall, shouting encouragement to the Toby dog, the Crocodile, anyone. They had gone to the Gem, Nellie's first visit to a picture house, and watched Mary Pickford and Owen Moore in a film called *Caprice*, whilst holding hands in the dark. After a while Davy put his arm round Nellie and she leaned her cheek on his shoulder. In the interval they ate cream ices and bought salted peanuts to take home to Lilac, who was denied the treat because she was too young, Miss Maria thought, for evening outings.

And now it was summer again, the July weather proving warm and pleasant. And Davy would surely be docking in Liverpool soon, to load his coaster, and they would meet, and kiss ... her whole body shivered with delighted anticipation. How she loved him, how she longed for his presence, that slow, delightful smile, the way his hair curled tightly, the nice shape of his head ...

A bell rang sharply somewhere and Nellie, abruptly restored to the present, made for the kitchen to collect the last jug of watered milk. Tonight, she thought, Lilac and me will practise our times-tables and then I'll read to her from *Simple Susan* and we can do a bit of writing if I can find some spare paper, somewhere. Tomorrow I must be nice to the postman, just in case there's a letter, and smile at the paper boy, because he sometimes finds us scraps of newsprint without writing on. And at the weekend we'll go back home, me and Lilac, to see if Bessie's had the baby yet ... I'll take my knitting ... oh goodness, school's out ... run, Nellie!

'Mrs Ransom, I'm real worried; Lilac never come for her tea and one of the girls said Miss Hicks had kept her late for ... well, for something she done wrong. So I went to the classroom, only to see, like, but there was no sign of Lilac. When I found Miss Hicks she said she'd sent her to bed, but young Mary Bliss said as how Miss Hicks had laid into Lilac with her stick, marked her right across her poor little face, and the child's disappeared, Mrs R, really she has. I told Miss Maria and we've searched high and low, but she's not in the house!'

Nellie heard her own words tumbling one over the other in her haste and worry, heard her accent thickening, and was simply past caring. She just knew that something awful had happened to Lilac and all because she, Nellie, had been too busy mooning over a young man to take immediate alarm when Lilac had not appeared at tea-time! She might love Davy Evans – well, she thought she did – but she could not love anyone more than she loved Lilac and now the child was missing! But Mrs Ransom's large face did not reflect the worry that Nellie assumed she would feel.

'She'll have hid away somewhere, to lick her wounds,' she said. 'What do the other children say?'

'They think she's run off,' Nellie said. 'Miss Hicks hits awful hard, Mrs Ransom; I should know!'

'She's nowhere to run,' Mrs Ransom observed with unconscious cruelty. 'She won't have gone far.'

'She might have ... I'm going to look,' Nellie said. Her hands flew to the strings of her apron and she began untying them and then heaved the garment over her head. 'It's warm out, I won't need a coat.'

'Check the cloakroom,' Mrs Ransom said suddenly. 'See if her coat's there. If it's gone I suppose you'd better search.'

Nellie nodded and left the room, but she ignored the long corridor down which the cloakroom was to be found and made instead for the front door. She knew Lilac wasn't in the house and she knew, also, that if the child had run away there was somewhere she could run. To Coronation Court. Oh, the authorities were always on about the scandal and disgrace that the courts brought to the city, saying they should be pulled down because they bred disease and pestilence and encouraged ignorance and unnatural practices. But they seemed not to notice how warmly the people of the courts felt for one another, how closely they clung!

Lilac had noticed, though, and remarked on it. Hand in hand with Nellie, as they made their way back to the orphan asylum after Nellie's Sunday afternoon off, Lilac chattered wistfully about the place and the people they had left, as though Coronation Court was infinitely superior to Rodney Street. Nellie had tried to tell her that at least she was getting a good education from the teachers at Culler's, but Lilac had said she'd sooner go to a ragged school, like Matt and Fred, especially if it meant she could live in the court.

As she was about to go out of the front door, Nellie heard her name called. She turned and saw Lilac's friend Emmy waving to her. Emmy was a placid child with a long ginger pigtail and right now she was putting her finger to her lips and beckoning Nellie.

'What is it?' Nellie said rather sharply as soon as she was close enough. 'I'm off out to see if I can find Lilac.'

'She ran down the street, she were bawlin' her eyes out,' Emmy said plaintively. 'She mighta took me ... I wouldn't mind a-going outa here. I'd like to go to sea an' all.'

'To sea? She said she was going to *sea*? Why on earth ... except that I've promised to take her there one day, only somehow time's so short and I do like to go back home when I get a few hours off ... thanks very much, chuck, now you'd better go to the playroom or you'll be in trouble with your group leader.'

'Shan't, we're all in the same group,' Emmy said. ' Tell Lilac we're on her side when you see her.'

'Of course,' Nellie said, comforted by the younger girl's words. It was nice to know that Lilac was popular, despite being in a class with girls who were mostly a year older than she, and some nearer two. 'See you soon, Emmy.'

Coatless, she slipped out of the front door and began her search.

When Lilac had slipped out of that same door an hour earlier she had been all but blinded by tears and positively seething with humiliation and rage. That Miss Hicks had hit her ... she had been smacked often enough, smacked across the legs and arms, occasionally across the face, by members of staff who were impatient or spiteful or just plain careless, hitting any child to stop them in their tracks. But she had never been attacked with a cane and felt the real pain of it searing through her soft flesh. She looked down at the raised pink weals on her legs, then fingered her cheek and felt the wetness of what she imagined to be blood. She speedily realised that it was just her tears, however, and gulped back the sobs, feeding her fury instead by telling herself that she would find a policeman and tell him to arrest Miss Hicks and put her in prison for hitting little girls!

And all the time she was thinking, she was walking, stumbling along in the hateful brown uniform with her long, red-gold tail of hair lacking a ribbon and coming unplaited with every step. And presently she stopped short and looked around her and realised that almost without meaning to do so, she was already well on her way to being a truant. She was in a strange street, one she could never recall walking down before.

She had not been walking particularly fast, but she had been paying no attention whatsoever to her surroundings. Now she slowed even more and looked curiously about her. On the opposite side of the road was a large, municipal building; she read the legend 'Public Baths' over the door and as she walked slowly along the pavement, smelt soap, hot water and – regrettably – people's unclean feet. Next came a big, grassy graveyard, with the stones in the older part all atilt and blackened by time and the church to which all this grass belonged looking benign in the late afternoon sunshine. At the place where her road met a wider one down which trams and motor cars roared, she looked up at the plate on the end house and saw she was in Cornwallis Street. Which way, which way? She had told Emmy she would run away to sea, but she had really meant ... just what had she meant? To run to Coronation Court and Matt, who would be kind to her and would come back and hit Miss Hicks on her behalf?

Perhaps. Or perhaps she had just meant to frighten everyone, give them something to think about. Mr Hayman, who was the most powerful person in Lilac's small universe, was always going on about sparing the rod and spoiling the child, but Lilac was quite sure that he would not be at all pleased if she ran away and she rather hoped that his displeasure might take the form of hitting Miss Hicks very hard with the ivory handled cane he always carried. She spent several pleasant moments picturing Miss Hicks, with her skirt kilted up, running madly down the road, leaping and roaring every time Mr Hayman's cane struck home. Which was how she came to cross the busy main street, because she saw a gap in the traffic and dived for it, without even considering whether this was the way she wanted to go.

And having crossed over, it seemed only sensible to continue in the same direction, along Blundell Street, with a lovely smell of trains which Lilac immediately recognised from her encounters with Lime Street station coming from the goods yard to her right, whilst very soon another strange smell assailed her nostrils, first a really horrible stench and then a sweeter one. A factory? Yes, but manufacturing what? There was a navy blue sign above the rooftop with writing on ... *Queen's Soap Works*, it said. Why should soap stink though, Lilac asked herself, wandering on.

But presently she saw that it behoved her to walk briskly, as though she knew exactly where she was going, for a large boy of ten or so in ragged clothes with the filthiest bare feet Lilac had ever seen came up to her and addressed her with a horrid leer.

'Ello lickle judy; does your muvver know you're out? Wharrer you doin' in vese parts, hey?'

Deep inside Lilac, a little warning bell sounded. She drew herself up and looked at the boy with as much hauteur as she could muster.

'I'm going to see my Auntie Ada, and you'd better look out, or I'll call a copper,' she said briskly. 'My Uncle Billy's a pleeceman, so just you slope off!'

The boy laughed but he obeyed her injunction and Lilac, her heart beating a little faster, continued to walk along Blundell Street until she came out on a wider road yet and was about to continue further when, above her head, she heard a fearful racket. Looking up, she saw the overhead railway which Charlie had called the docker's umbrella. The train and its carriages came crashing and clanking along and went off into the distance ... all the way to Seaforth, Lilac told herself, remembering Nellie's words, and there are children on board no older than me – oh, aren't they the lucky ones?

Having gazed her fill at the overhead railway she walked along until she saw, on her left, some tall gates. They were open and without intending to go where she was not allowed, yet doing so anyway, Lilac wandered through them when the gatekeeper's attention was elsewhere and found herself – wonder of wonders! – gazing at her very first dock. She saw, right opposite her, water, hundreds of water, she told herself rapturously, water which licked against the brick walls and the ships' sides and the mooring posts, water which sparkled and chuckled and purred as it moved ... it must be the sea, Lilac thought, devouring it with her eyes. Oh, this must be the sea, and she had run away to it, just as she had threatened!

By now her hair had come mostly unplaited, so Lilac finished the job off with her fingers, smelling the strange salt smell of the sea and feeling the wind tugging at her hair, filling her with a sense of adventure, of her own smallness in this great universe that she had so recently discovered. She decided that she would live here always, sleeping under the docker's umbrella, begging or stealing food from one of the shops or cafés she had passed, possibly even working for someone –

Charlie was a docker, perhaps he needed someone to give him a hand?

Sitting on a bollard, however, she began to feel rather lonely, and when a young man came and sat on the bollard beside her she smiled at him and asked him whether he was a sailor or a docker?

'I'm a seaman from the SS Ocean Queen,' the young man said. 'What the 'ell are you doing 'ere, luv? I know they 'ave funny little ways in Liverpool, but ain't you a bit young to be on the game?'

'What game? I'm not playing anything,' Lilac said indignantly. 'I was going to see my aunt only I lost my way and then I saw the railway – my brother Charlie calls it the dockers' umbrella – and then I saw the sea and I came over to have a look … you don't have any pennies, do you? I haven't had my tea.'

The young man looked closely at her and Lilac looked closely back; he was seeing a small girl in a dull brown dress with a calico pinafore over it and tangled red-gold hair streaming down her back. If he had been a regular scouser he would probably have recognised the Culler orphan asylum uniform but fortunately, Lilac realised, he was from away. His voice was sharp and clear with a sort of whine to it and he made the word game sound like gyme. In her turn Lilac stared at him, seeing a sturdy young man in seamen's clothing – a dark blue jersey and trousers – sitting on the bollard with his legs drawn up a little so she could see a neat patch on one navy knee. He was looking at her curiously and Lilac saw that he had a round, humorous face with blue-grey eyes and a wispy moustache. When they had both taken each other in he grinned at her and raised his mousy eyebrows comically. Lilac grinned back.

'Know me again, gel?'

Lilac laughed.

'Oh yes, anywhere,' she said joyfully. 'Do you have any pennies? I could pay you back perhaps, one day.'

'That's good, because you don't look like a beggar's brat,' the young man said. He slithered down from the bollard and dug in the pockets of his narrow trousers, producing a handful of small coins. 'Want some fried fish and taters? I was goin' to git meself some; we can share.'

'Yes please,' Lilac said ardently. She trotted beside him as he strolled out of the fascinating dock area, taking his hand to cross the wide and busy stretch of the main road. 'Oh, I do love fried fish!'

'Me too, though you'd think, bein' at sea so much, I'd git sick of fish. Now did I tell you my name? I'm Joey Prescott and I'm from London, in case you 'adn't guessed. I 'ails from the Isle o' Dogs.'

'I'm Lilac Larkin. I'm from Rodney Street, right here in Liverpool,' Lilac said readily. 'Where's the shop for the fish? Is it far?'

'Nah, not far, Lilac. That dress what you got on – looks like some kinda uniform.'

Lilac shot him a suspicious glance, but he smiled blandly back and because she liked him she nodded, sure he meant her no harm.

'Yes, that's right. It's the Culler. That's an orphan asylum, but I'm not an orphan, not really. My brother Charlie says I've got a mam and a da all right, it's just that I dunno where they are right now.'

'There you are, then. And just where's this orphing asylum when it's at 'ome?'

'I *told* you: in Rodney Street,' Lilac said with what patience she could muster. This young man was obviously none too bright! 'Where's the fried fish shop?'

'In Canning Place. Fact is, sweet'eart, I dunno where

54

Rodney Street is – d'you know Canning Place, or South Castle Street or South John Street? Are they near Rodney Street? If so, we might walk rahnd there, take a look at this orphing asylum.'

'No. Well, that's to say I don't know, because I don't know where any of those places are, I only know the Scottie and Rodney Street,' Lilac said rather untruthfully, since she knew the way between the two quite well. 'And I don't want to take a look at the Culler; I've run away from it, you see. So if you don't mind, I'd rather stay with you.'

'That's all very well, but what abaht when the old *Queen* sails? What'll you do then, eh?'

'I could come on board with you, help you to ... to do whatever you have to do,' Lilac said hopefully. 'I'd like that.'

'Ho, would you? But the crew's men, not gels!'

'We could cut off my hair and you could buy me some trousers. Then they wouldn't know I was a girl ... I could be your cabin boy,' Lilac said, with vague memories of the stories Nellie read her and the tales Charlie and Hal told jostling together in her tired brain. Because she was tired, a part of her quite wanted to give in, let Joey take her back to Rodney Street. After the fried fish, though, not before.

'No, it won't do,' Joey said, after a pause during which they recrossed the busy street and slowed by a tram stop at which several people waited. 'We'll ride on a tram I think, littl'un. Give our legs a bit of a rest.'

So Lilac sat proudly in the tram with her new friend, chattering away as though she had known him all her life, and rode in style past a great many of the huge, fortress-like docks – Wapping, Salthouse, Canning – before alighting alongside a huge and imposing building which Joey told her was the Custom House.

'The fried fish shop's really on South Castle Street,' Joey said, taking her hand as they crossed the pavement. 'But it's only a step from here: can you smell it?'

Lilac, sniffing, said she could and presently, with watering mouth, she found herself in a small, whitewashed room crowded with rough wooden tables and wielding a determined knife and fork over a plate of the best fried fish and potatoes she had ever dreamed of devouring.

'You're right; best fish in the 'pool', her new friend said, eating almost as vigorously as she. 'What do you have for your dinners at that place, then, Culler's?'

'Bread and rhubarb jam,' Lilac said thickly through a mouthful. 'Pass the vinegar, Joey!'

Nellie was worn out and terribly worried by the time dusk had fallen and she had still seen no sign of Lilac, but at least she knew, now, that she was heading in the right direction. She had followed the trail like a bloodhound, asking everyone she passed, 'Have you seen a kid of about seven, with red-gold hair, wearing the Culler uniform?'

It was astonishing the number of people who did not know the Culler uniform, though less astonishing when you remembered, as Nellie did, how rarely the children went far from the vicinity of Rodney Street, and because it was a street largely used by the medical profession the children did not see shoppers or, indeed, shops. There was Philip Stern the pawnbroker, of course: a fascinating window for small noses to press against, and Mrs Rhoda Broughal's hats, but other than that it was a dreary procession of brass medical plates on most doors as surgeons, laryngologists and dentists vied discreetly for customers.

Even the twice daily church attendance on a Sunday did not mean a long walk, since Mrs Ransom, with a fine disregard for firmly held convictions, saw the entire orphanage off to Catholic Mass at the cathedral on the corner of Warren Street in the morning and to evensong at St Luke's on Bold Street in the evening. As both churches were a very short walk from Rodney Street, the long crocodile of brown-clad children making their way to church was not a common sight to the majority of Liverpudlians.

But even so, a good many people had noticed the child with the red-gold hair, and Nellie was able to chart Lilac's progress down as far as the docks. Then she simply lost the trail. She went up and down the road which ran alongside the docks asking, asking, but had no luck until she had gone right along to the pierhead. Here she met a fat woman with three small children who said she recalled seeing just such a child in a fried fish shop on South Castle Street. She was with a seaman, they looked like father and child to the fat woman.

'Father and child?' quavered Nellie. 'Oh, ma'am, I had better hurry!'

Thoughts of the white slave trade made her feet patter along at top speed, but when she reached the fried fish shop and enquired for Lilac of the weary, red-headed man behind the counter, sweating and swearing as he dipped fish in batter and threw it into the hot fat, she was once again too late.

'They've gone, chuck,' he said, wiping beads of sweat off his brow with the back of a freckly hand. ' The feller asked me de way to Rodney Street, but de lickle lass said as 'ow they'd go to the Scottie instead and visit her auntie.'

'And did they go towards Rodney Street or the Scottie?' Nellie asked, hope stirring. It did sound as though Lilac had met a young man who meant her no harm, not if he was trying to get her back to Culler's. 'Did you notice?'

But the red-headed man had not even seen them leave and an appeal to the assorted customers waiting to be served or eating their food brought no more information forth. No one had noticed the little girl with the red-golden curls once she and her companion had got up from the table.

Nellie had eaten nothing since her dinner at noon and it was now nearly ten o'clock. She was footsore and thirsty and beginning to be healthily cross with Lilac. If Nellie had told the child once not to talk to strangers she'd told her a dozen times, and yet look at her! First moment she got away she got herself picked up by a young man and when he tried to take her home as he ought she confused the issue by talking about the court on the Scottie Road! For the first time, Nellie felt a tiny thread of fellow-feeling for Miss Hicks – Lilac could be a real little monkey!

So instead of setting off at once, possibly in the wrong direction, Nellie bought a paper of fried potatoes and a china mug of tea. She leaned against the wall – the tables were all taken – and ate and drank quite slowly, and when a man got up to leave she slipped into his seat and allowed the warmth and the food to be absorbed slowly into her cold and hungry body.

So it was half-past ten before she left the fried fish shop, and as she reached Canning Place she had the biggest piece of luck so far. She was turning into Mariner's Parade to cut through into Paradise Street and there, walking jauntily along the narrow pavement and whistling to himself, was Davy Evans!

Chapter Three

Nellie took one long, astonished look and then, with a sob, she ran straight into Davy's arms and felt them close joyfully round her.

'Nellie McDowell, what on earth are you doing here? Oh, dreaming of you one moment I was, and the next you're in my arms! But you're crying ... my darling girl, whatever is the matter? Tell Davy, let me help.'

Nellie took a deep breath, tried to detach herself from Davy's warm embrace – cuddling in the street was for little sluts who knew no better, she had been taught – and then sank gratefully back onto Davy's lean, strong chest.

'Oh Davy, I've never been so glad to see someone in me whole life – Lilac's gone and run away, she's with some feller ... '

He put her back from him, a frown creasing his brow.

'Lilac's run off with some feller? Cariad, it's dreaming you are! Lilac's a little girl, she wouldn't ...'

Despite her anxiety, Nellie gave a watery giggle.

'Oh dear, was that how it sounded? She ran off because a teacher whipped her, and then it seems she fell in with some feller – he's a seaman someone told me – and they had a fish supper together and now ... and now they've gone again and I've lost them and I'm so afraid for her ... and I'm furious, too, that she could be so silly and thoughtless after all the times I've told her and told her ... oh, Davy, what must I do?'

'Blow your nose, wipe your eyes and let me put my coat round you; you're shivering like a leaf,' Davy said firmly. 'A seaman, eh? I wonder if he's got a bed in the sailors' home? I booked in late and missed supper so just going down to Castle Street I was, to get a meal, when I ran into you – or rather you ran into me.' He watched whilst Nellie dried her eyes, blew her nose and then snuggled into the jacket which he had slipped out of as he spoke. ' There, is that better?'

'Yes, much. But Davy …'

'No buts. We'll have to check that she hasn't gone back to Rodney Street before we do anything else, or do you think she'll make for Coronation Court?'

'I don't know, and I'm worn out and …'

'Don't fret, you've walked quite far enough for one night. I'll call a cab.'

'I've got n-no m-money,' Nellie shivered. 'I just r-ran out as I was.'

'Did I ask for money? Hey, cabby!'

Davy told the cabby to take them to Rodney Street and once there, he waited in the cab whilst Nellie checked on Lilac's whereabouts.

Realising that her own absence might have been remarked by now, Nellie went to the back door and the cook let her in, round-eyed with astonishment over what she described as 'all the goings-on'.

'We've had a dozen runaways before, but none so much trouble,' she said roundly. 'Why Nellie, it was you everyone was worried about, you they reported as missing to the constable! They had to send Arthur all the way to the police station at the top end of Warren Street, and him a-grumblin' that gairls always landed on their feet like cats, and they'd no cause to mek an old man walk miles when he'd just had his tea! You've always been a reliable worker you see, Nell, so not even Miss Hicks could believe you'd run off too, they thought you'd been took by some Man!'

'Well, tell them to un-report me,' Nellie said crossly. 'I'm perfectly all right, I shall spend the night with my family, in Coronation Court. I'm hoping that Lilac may have fled there. And you may tell Miss Hicks,' she added grimly, 'that she and I will have words if and when I get my Lilac back safe.'

Back in the cab once more, she took Davy's hand in hers and spoke with the utmost earnestness.

'Davy, I have to go to the Scottie, but if you'll tell the cabby to stop at the sailors' home then you can get out there and I'll go on alone. I'll be quite all right, honest!'

'Oh yes, and I can see myself explaining how I let a young girl go off in a cab by herself, and me sleeping the sleep of the just in the sailors' home,' Davy said sarcastically. 'No, I'm with you, cariad. Just sit back and we'll be at the court in no time.'

Meanwhile Lilac, in blissful ignorance of the search which was going on and never giving a thought to poor Nellie's worries, was sitting on another tram which was rattling gamely down the Scotland Road. Beside her sat Joey, peering out and exclaiming that if he'd known her relatives lived near Paddy's Market he'd have brought her back earlier.

'Never miss a visit to the Market when I'm in Liverpool,' he said wistfully. 'Got some good stuff dahn there, and the grub's a treat an' all.'

'Me and Nellie's going there to buy our presents for Christmas,' Lilac said. 'I've been saving all year – I've got thruppence and our Nell will give me some more nearer the time, she says.'

'Who's Nell? Someone else in the Culler?'

'No, Nell's my sister! She's a big girl, not little, like me. She takes care of me and buys me things – I love our Nell best of everyone in the world, I love her even better than our Matt.'

Joey shook his head.

'You're a reg'lar one, you are! First you're an orphan, then you've got brothers, then you've got a ma and pa except you don't know where they are and now you've got a sister Nellie and someone you love called Matt. Who's Matt when he's at 'ome?'

'Oh, a sort of brother, like. I think we should get out now … cripes, look at all the people about although it's the middle of the night!'

They climbed down off the tram and stood for a moment on the pavement. A chancy wind had got up and housewives doing their shopping had their shawls wrapped tightly round them against the night's chill. Above their heads the gaslights flickered uneasily in the sudden gusts and Lilac seized Joey's hand firmly in her own. It was strange how darkness changed things – her dear Scottie Road looked quite different and faces which, in daylight, would have seemed smiling and kind looked somehow sinister now as their owners bustled from shop to shop, waiting for the owners to reduce their prices as closing time drew near.

'Well, which way?' demanded Joey as his small guide simply stood there, looking about her.

Lilac, about to tug him off towards the court, had a sudden, uneasy feeling that her welcome there might not be so assured in the middle of the night as it had always been by day. Suppose Aunt Ada, who had a sharp tongue, bawled at her and sent her packing? Matt would know, and he would think she had been a fool to run away so late, he would say she should have come to them at once, not leave it until the last moment like this. And then there was Uncle Billy, quietly coughing in his corner; he might not be pleased to see a child he had only met a few times ... and she had told Joey lies, she found she did not want Joey to learn that she really was an orphan, that she had no claim to any of the brothers and sisters she had told him about.

'Umm ... I think we'll try Charlie first,' she said therefore, suddenly remembering that Charlie and Bessie had a lovely little house of their own now, and a spare room as well. Surely Charlie and Bessie, who were always so nice to her, would not turn her away? Why, Bessie was expecting a baby and always made a great fuss of Lilac, said she was a pretty crittur and that Nellie was the best sister a girl ever had. Yes, it would be better to try Charlie's first. He and Bessie lived in a landing house just off Victoria Square and Lilac found her way there easily enough, tugging Joey along behind her.

'I can't leave you outside,' Joey said when they reached the large block of houses, divided up by floors into different homes. 'Whereabouts is their flat?'

'Flat? It's a house, only all on one floor, with other people's houses over and under,' Lilac explained. 'See those little iron steps? We go up them, then along the balcony. It's number five.'

The housing block was humming with life despite the lateness of the hour. People were calling out to each other, children hung around the balconies in small groups, playing, shouting, and adults came in and out of their homes. Lilac noticed in the incurious way of children that a good deal of attention was being

lavished on number five, but she was now only interested in how she would be received when they arrived,
so hurried up the steps and along the balcony, not
bothering to stop and ask what was happening –
indeed, for all she knew this might be normal behaviour at night for the block.

She reached the doorway of her destination. Yellow
light flooded out into the darkness and the kitchen was
full of women. For a moment Lilac stopped short,
dismayed. Had she got the number wrong? Where
were Bessie and Charlie? And what was that awful
noise?

She stepped into the room. A woman looked across,
began to order her out, to tell her to play with the other
kids, and then seemed to realise that she was a stranger
and had a man with her, as well. She came over to the
doorway. She was a tall, loose-limbed woman with a
mop of untidy yellow hair and a face upon which the
ravages of drink had already made their mark. But she
seemed in charge here and spoke directly to Joey, taking no notice of Lilac.

'Evenin'! What might you be wantin', me fine
bucko? If it's Charlie you're after, then isn't he down
de boozer where all de fellers should be at such a time?
Mrs Matlock is with Bessie an' her mam's there too and
they say she's doin' fine.' A loud shriek from the room
Lilac knew to be the young McDowells' bedroom made
her break off and glance over her shoulder. 'Need 'ot
water yet, our Iris?' she called. 'I'll be wit' ye in a
minute, dere's a feller here wants Charlie.'

'I can't take the child to the pub,' Joey objected. 'Can
she wait here, with you, whilst I have a word with
Charlie? She'll be no trouble.'

Lilac would have preferred to go with Joey to the
boozer, but the truth was she was horribly tired after

her exhausting day and wanted nothing so much, right now, as a rest. So she squatted down in a corner of the kitchen and tried to become invisible. The tall woman sighed, then nodded reluctantly.

'Right y'are. Stay there quiet, chuck.'

She left the room. Other women, chattering, curious, came and went. Lilac's eyelids began to droop but presently she saw that she had been forgotten and, when another shriek from the direction of the bedroom made her skin prickle, she decided she simply must discover what was going on. After all, if Bessie was ill she might be glad of Lilac to stay the night and get Charlie's breakfast on the morrow.

So she walked nonchalantly across the room and slid unobtrusively into the bedroom.

The room was brightly lit with an array of candles on the washstand and mantelpiece. Bessie lay, naked but for a thin shift, with her dark hair curling damply across her sweaty brow, in the middle of the bed. A woman crouched on the bed in front of her, pushing at her knees, which were bent up and open in a manner which Lilac thought both strange and somehow obscene. There was something very odd about Bessie's stomach, too. She had always been a buxom girl but now her stomach looked enormous. It was pointed and sweaty and seemed to have a life of its own, a life which the woman pushing against Bessie's knees seemed to acknowledge, for now she bent her head, braced herself against Bessie's white knees and shouted, ' The 'ead's showing; you've gorra give a rare old push now, queen!'

Bessie's face was gleaming with sweat and red with effort. As Lilac stared, half fascinated and half repelled, Bessie gritted her teeth, tucked her chin into her chest, and pushed until veins stood out on her forehead and there was blood on her lip where her teeth had driven in. She had hold of a piece of knotted sheet and was pulling on it as though she was playing tug-of-war with the woman holding the other end. Lilac recognised Bessie's mother, Mrs Melville, and saw that she was crying. Lilac found that she was crying too, just a little, because it was hurting Bessie, you could tell, and even as she thought it the great, heaving tug and push ended in a grunt and a little shriek. And as Bessie began to relax the woman took her hands off Bessie's knees and dived between her legs and Lilac saw that something lay on the sheet, something which looked uncommonly like a dark ball.

The woman seized the ball-like object and turned it gently and Lilac saw that it was the baby's head; now she could make out the small, pursed face, streaked with blood and wet, and as the woman gently and smoothly pulled the rest of the baby appeared, not too fast but not too slow either, and Bessie gathered herself and pushed again, grunting, panting, and the baby was born!

There was a little murmur from the women round the bed; gladness for the young mother, her travail at an end, pleasure in the sight of the babe, pink and alive, beginning to cry as the midwife slapped it to make it take that first, crucial breath.

'What is it?' Bessie asked weakly, raising her head. 'Where's my Charlie?'

'It's a lickle lad; your old man's in the kitchen; I'll fetch 'im,' someone volunteered, but the midwife, seeing Lilac's round-eyed face in the doorway, said, 'No, I'll need you here; send the kid.'

Lilac needed no encouragement. She turned and rushed along the narrow corridor and back to the kitchen. The door was open and she bolted into the room.

'It's come, the baby's here!' she shouted. 'Where's Charlie? Where's our Charlie?'

Charlie and Joey must have been on the balcony for Charlie came at a run through the kitchen, tousling Lilac's hair in passing.

'Joey 'splained,' he said briefly. 'You can kip down on the couch in the front room, just for tonight.'

Joey, coming in behind Charlie, caught Lilac's shoulder when she would have followed, and pulled her to a halt.

'No you don't, leave the gel alone,' he said severely. ' That's no place for the likes of you. Nah then, you awright wi' Charlie?'

'Oh, yes,' Lilac said thankfully. 'You're *very* kind, Joey, but Charlie will take care of me now.'

'He's a good bloke,' Joey agreed. 'My, but you're a little liar, aren't you? Bruvver, indeed!'

'He's almost my brother,' Lilac said, aggrieved. When she thought of the lies she could have told – she could have invented a whole family and told the gullible Joey that she was on her way home from some posh boarding school instead of admitting to the orphan asylum – she felt he was being unduly fussy to carp over a tiny lie about relationships. 'And anyway, it would have taken me ages to explain, it's such a long story!'

'Oh, sure. And the way to 'ell is paved wiv good intentions,' Joey pointed out somewhat obscurely. But he put a warm hand round the back of her neck and then bent and dropped a kiss on her upturned face. 'Little blighter – I wouldn't mind if you was my sister!'

He turned on the words and made for the balcony door. Lilac rushed after him.

'Oh Joey, won't you stay here as well? Where are you going? I do like you so much – I wouldn't mind if you was my brother, too!'

Joey laughed but shook his head.

'I can't stay 'ere, sweet'eart, I'm booked into the Sailors' for the night. The *Ocean Queen* sails on the tide tomorrer and you'll have to go back to your asylum, you knows that, don't you? But be a good gel and one of these days, when I'm in the 'pool, I'll come a-visitin', in me best, and tek you on the ferry to New Brighton. You can tell 'em you're courtin' a young feller from the Isle of Dogs named Joey Prescott and they'll give you leave like a shot!'

'Oh, but Joey, when? When will you be in the 'pool again? Don't go, don't ...'

But he had gone with a wave of the hand, striding along the balcony, stepping over small groups of children, clattering down the iron stairs. She could see him in her mind wending his way through the still-busy streets, whistling, grinning at passers-by. Kind Joey Prescott. She would never forget him.

'Oh, Davy, whatever are we to do? I could've sworn she'd be at Aunt Ada's but they've seen neither hide nor hair of her. I'm that worried ... d'you think I'd best go back to the Culler again?'

'No; if she's back, she's safe, if she isn't you'll want to go on searching,' Davy said.

They were standing in the entrance to the court as they had stood, Nellie remembered, on that long-ago wedding day – was it really little more than a year? – when they had first met. Perhaps it was thinking about the wedding that made Nellie suddenly say, 'What about our Charlie, though, Davy? Got his own place he has, not too far from here. Him and Bessie asked me and Lilac round for our tea a few weeks ago. Lilac thought the new house was the most beautiful home in the world; she was made up to be invited. Do you suppose ...?'

'Well, it's awful late, but we might as well try,' Davy agreed. 'Do you know it's past midnight, Nell? Will anyone be awake?'

'We'll rouse them, though our Bessie isn't sleeping so good now she's got so big with the baby,' Nellie said. 'Oh, I pray we find her there!'

But in fact they did not have to intrude on the young McDowells to discover Lilac's whereabouts. The streets were thinning of people, the market stalls were closing and the shops were closed by the time they reached Victoria Square.

'It's that block; number five, and all the lights are on! I wonder ... ' Nellie was beginning, when a seaman came lightly down the stairs from the second-floor flats. Nellie put a detaining hand on his arm when he would have passed them.

'Oh, excuse me, have you come from number five? I wonder if you've seen a little girl ... '

The young man's face, which had seemed ordinary enough, split into an enormous grin and promptly became beautiful.

'Don't tell me – you'll be Nellie, and you're searching for a golden 'aired little angel by the name of Lilac Larkin! She's safe and well and snoozin' on Charlie's sofa right this minute. I met her dahn by the docks earlier this evening and when she got tired of gaddin' rahnd she tole me about Charlie and Bessie and I brung 'er 'ere.'

'You found her? Oh, how can I ever thank you?' Nellie gasped. 'She's as dear to me as my own child ... well, I've had her in my care ever since she was tiny and a prettier, brighter kid you'd go a long way to find! Oh, what's your name – there must be something we can do to thank you!'

The young man coloured and grinned sheepishly first at Nellie and then at Davy.

'I'm Joey Prescott, and it was nothin', she's a nice kid, but she could've been in trouble if she'd met the wrong feller; you want to try to make her see that.'

'Oh, she won't do it again,' Davy said easily. 'She'll do as she's told now, specially for Nell here.'

Joey nodded, but still looked doubtful.

'Mebbe so, but I doubt it, and I know what I'm talkin' abaht. I was a foundling, left on a doorstep, and I ran off to sea when I was twelve. Now Lilac, she's got you, Miss Nellie, from what she said, but she's already had a taste of freedom; can't guarantee she won't take to it, like.'

'We'll cross that bridge when we come to it, thank you kindly,' Davy said. He spoke rather formally and Nellie gave him a sharp glance. Could it be that Davy was jealous? But that was just absurd! And it was rude, too, when you considered what Joey had done for Lilac.

More warmly than she might otherwise have done, therefore, she turned to Joey and spoke.

'You may be right; Lilac certainly didn't give me a thought when she ran off this afternoon and she could easily have fallen into the wrong company. I'll keep my eye on her, don't you fret, and many thanks again, Joey.'

'And now I'll walk you home,' Davy said, when the young man had disappeared into the darkness. 'Not that you'll want to wake everyone at the Culler, I don't suppose. Look, I know a lodging house not far from here; I've had a room there a couple of times, we can stay there for what remains of the night and pick Lilac up first thing in the morning. But do you want to pop up to number five now and make sure they keep her with them until then?'

'I'd better,' Nellie said rather reluctantly. She felt

foolish, barging into her brother's home at this hour, but as it turned out she was made very welcome by the new father.

'Nellie, give us a hug!' Charlie said exuberantly as soon as she stepped into the kitchen. 'See this little feller? He's Henry Charles McDowell, after me and our Hal; want to have a hold of him?'

So Nellie held her little nephew and they had a cup of tea and then, since it was getting on for two in the morning, she and Davy left.

'I can't face going back to the Culler right now, I'll tell them I spent the night at my aunt's,' she said as the two of them crossed the square. 'Where's this lodging house, Davy? You're sure it's respectable?'

'Would I take you anywhere else? Here, down this alley and across the road at the end. We'll be there in two shakes, then you can have a nice hot wash and sleep until breakfast time.'

Very early next morning, Lilac awoke in her borrowed bed and stared round her, quite unable to imagine where she could be. Every morning of her entire life so far she had awoken in the Culler; first in the nursery at the very top of the house with Nellie in her tiny slip of an attic room nearby, then in the long dormitory for the seven- to nine-year-olds. Never, in all that time, had she spent a night away from the orphan asylum – until now.

And now there were sounds coming from Bessie's kitchen and somewhere a kitten was mewing dolefully. Lilac looked over at the window; there were lovely curtains drawn close, but she could see round the edges of them that day had definitely dawned. In fact it might be quite late, but what did it matter? No Mrs

Ransom to scold, no Lizzie Brandreth to tip her out of bed and shout at her for being late, no Miss Hicks to glower across the long breakfast table, her fingers no doubt itching to pull Lilac's long hair.

No Nellie, either, though. Nellie, who loved her, would be worried by her non-appearance, probably she would have gone round to the police station and asked if they had a missing child called Lilac Larkin anywhere on the premises.

Nellie loved her. Nellie would cry.

On the thought, Lilac scrambled out of bed. It was all very well to think of herself as a runaway, but she had always known, in her heart, that she would have to go back. Back to bread and scrape and watered milk, back to brown hair ribbon and scratchy underclothing. Back to bossy girls, boring girls, spiteful girls. But also back to Nellie, whose skin smelt sweetly of soap and water and whose hair shone from brushing. Back to Nellie, who had surrounded and encompassed her with love and caring all the days of her life.

She had not undressed last night so did not have to dress now, which was fun after seven years of constantly undressing each night and dressing again each morning. Her hair was a shocking tangle, though. She poked ineffectually at it, then decided to borrow a brush from either Bessie or Charlie, whoever was up and about – and someone was, she could hear a subdued clatter coming from the kitchen.

She opened the front room door and let herself out, with a quick, valedictory glance at her 'bedroom'. It was rather a stiff room, with a new second-hand sideboard, a new second-hand carpet and several new second-hand chairs. But the sofa on which she had slept so peacefully was one which had belonged to Bessie's Gran and the blanket Charlie had thrown over her had been crocheted by Aunt Ada especially for Charlie's new home. Lilac stole back and folded the blanket neatly, then went and drew back the curtains. It was still very early, a milky mist hung over the houses opposite and wreathed around the patchy grass between them. But there was a warmth behind the mist which she could almost feel – it was going to be another sunny day.

She made her way to the kitchen and it was Charlie clattering softly, Charlie taking the milk jug out of the bowl of water where it had been left to keep cool overnight, pouring some into a cup, getting the kettle off the fire and wetting the pot, making Bessie a nice cuppa, he said. He bustled round the kitchen in his trousers with his top half bare and his beard beginning to darken his chin. He was not going down to the docks today, he explained, though it would be business as usual tomorrow. He had drawn back the curtains and put a brush over the oilcloth and he had finished off yesterday's milk and the white jug stood ready for when the milkman called in the square below.

'When you hear someone shout "Milko!" run down, chuck, and get 'im to fill the jug,' Charlie said, carefully pouring tea into a pink cup. ' Tuppence worth, tell 'im, there's two pennies on the dresser, and say the baby's come and it's a boy, name of Henry Charles.'

'Yes, all right. Shall I make Bessie some toast?' Lilac asked, and Charlie said he was sure his wife would be very grateful, and would she like to make some for him at the same time and some for herself, too, if she'd a mind.

'What about the baby ... I mean what about Henry?' Lilac said, but Charlie thought Bessie would find up something for the baby; he went red and looked down at his bare feet when he said it and Lilac wondered why people didn't talk much about babies and then remembered where the baby had emerged from and stopped wondering. Only, had she dreamed it? Nell said babies came from God and were brought to earth by angels first and then by big white birds. It sounded unlikely – but not as unlikely as what had happened last night in Charlie's big brass bedstead!

Still, it didn't do to ask too many questions, people hated that, so Lilac sawed uneven chunks off the loaf with the bread-knife and then speared the slices on a fork and held them out to the open stove-front. The bread toasted and she pattered through to Bessie's room with it.

Bessie was sitting up in bed with a shawl round her shoulders and the baby nestled close to her bare skin. When she saw Lilac she sort of snatched at the shawl and the baby was hidden, but then Bessie smiled and relented.

'I'm feeding him,' she said, half proud, half shy. 'Want to see 'im suck?'

'I'll get the jam,' Charlie said and left the room, and Lilac perched on the bed and watched the tiny baby against his mother's breast and laughed when Bessie pulled him off with a pop like a cork coming out of a bottle and put him over her shoulder to bring up his wind.

But at the back of her mind lurked the thought that today, retribution must be at hand. She knew she could not stay here, she would have to go back to Rodney Street, and then what would happen? She asked Bessie, who stopped smiling down at the baby and looked seriously across at her.

'Well, chuck, you never give a thought to our Nellie when you run off, did you? Didn't you guess 'ow she'd worry?'

'All I thought was ... that I wanted to run away. Look at my poor leg, Bessie.'

Bessie gave a cursory glance at the fading pink weals; it was clear that she thought a few blows from a cane a poor reason for running off and leaving Nellie in the lurch.

'So what, chuck? Everyone gets whacked, sometime. No reason to forget your best friend, is it? No reason to send our Nellie half mad with worry.'

A pang of something very like remorse made Lilac give a small gulp.

'Will she not love me any more?' she enquired anxiously. 'Will she leave the Culler?'

'Oh, she'll love you all right, but 'ow many times has she told you not to talk to strangers? And what did you do?'

'Oh but Bessie, Joey wasn't a stranger, he was nice, honest he was. Really nice, like Charlie and you are!'

Bessie smiled but she still looked serious.

'Sometimes, chuck, a feller's nice for to get you in 'is power. If Joey had been a diff'rent bloke you coulda been in deep trouble. So you must listen to our Nellie and think before you leave her.'

'But if Joey had been nice just to get me in his power I wouldn't have liked him. And I didn't leave our Nellie, I left the Culler,' Lilac argued. 'I wouldn't leave Nell, honest I wouldn't.'

'But you did, and there's no arguefying with that,' Bessie pointed out, shifting the baby from her shoulder to her breast once more. 'You're gettin' to be a big gairl now, chuck, you must think of others and not just of yourself.'

That silenced Lilac, because she knew very well that Bessie had hit the nail on the head. She had not given Nellie – or anyone else – a thought. All she had thought about was herself, her humiliation, her pain, her rage.

In fact even now all she was really thinking about was how she would be treated back at the Culler. What the other children would say, whether they would praise or blame, how she would tell her exciting story in the dormitory, after lights out. Punishment, she realised, she was relying on Nellie to avert.

'Well, Lilac? You goin' to think of our Nellie, another time?'

Lilac hung her head.

'I will, honest I will. I do love Nellie, honest I do!'

'Actions speak louder than words,' a dour voice behind her said. 'So this is where you've run to!'

'Nellie!' squeaked Lilac. She turned and threw herself into Nellie's waiting arms. 'Oh Nell, I'm so sorry, I'm so *very* sorry! I hate them, all of them, but I love you more'n anything! And I won't do it again – not if you don't want me to.'

'I hope you mean that,' said Davy, appearing at Nellie's shoulder and grinning wryly at Lilac. 'Oh, what a deal of trouble you've caused, bach! You've had Nellie and me searching the streets, questioning people ... up all night, just about.'

'I'm sorry, Davy – how did you know I was runned away, though? Did Nellie write? No, there wouldn't have been time ... Davy, stop laughing and tell me!'

'Never mind that now,' Nellie said severely. 'How many times have I told you not to talk to strangers? As for runnin' off the way you did, goin' off with young Joey Prescott, takin' food from him ... well, you deserve every one of them stripes Miss Hicks handed out, queen.'

But even as she spoke Nellie was hugging her, smoothing the tangled hair back from her forehead, her eyes overflowing with tears and love.

'I didn't mean to be bad,' Lilac sighed, hugging

76

Nellie as hard as she could. 'I didn't think ... and Joey was awful nice ... how d'you know about Joey, Nell?'

'Met him; asked him if he'd seen you,' Nellie said briefly. 'Oh Lilac, I was that worried; thank God Joey found you and kept you safe for me. Don't you ever do that to me again, queen. No more runnin' off without a word, understand? Next time, *if* there's a next time, which I hope and pray there won't be, come to me first.'

They left Davy when their ways divided and Nellie and Lilac walked slowly through the streets in the morning sunshine, heading for what Lilac knew would be recriminations at best and real trouble at worst. She tried to tell Nellie how it had been, what had made her act the way she had, but somehow, with the weals beginning to fade and the memories of Miss Hicks' assault fading too, it was difficult to tell Nellie just why she had flown out in such a rage that she had never even told her dear Nell what she intended.

What was more, she soon realised that Nellie was not quite herself. She was pale and abstracted. Several times Lilac got the feeling that Nellie was answering more or less at random and that she had not been attending too closely. And this was simply unbelievable, because in all her seven years, Nellie had paid closer attention to Lilac, to her desires and feelings, than anything else.

She's still angry with me, and no wonder, Lilac thought dolefully as they walked. She can't forgive me – I don't deserve to be forgiven. But in her heart, of course, she neither believed this nor thought it. She had done wrong and repented, all her previous experience of Nellie told her that she would be taken back into favour at once, if not sooner!

'Will they be very angry with me, Nellie?' she asked at last, after a longer-than-usual silence. 'Will they beat me again? Will they lock me in the cellar and only give me bread and water?'

This roused Nellie from her abstraction in a most satisfactory way.

'No they will not!' Nellie said roundly, eyes flashing, cheeks turning pink at the mere suggestion. 'Not if they want to keep me, that is! No, I shall tell them you're sorry – and you must tell them so as well, mind you, Lilac – and then you may be forgiven. They'll want you to promise never to do such a thing again of course,' she added. 'But you've guessed that, I daresay.'

'I'll say I'm sorry,' Lilac murmured. 'I'll say I won't do it again, too. Can I say that Miss Hicks may not cane me again, either?'

This seemed fair to her, and she saw Nellie's mobile mouth twitch into a quick smile and then hastily firm itself up again.

'I'll speak to Miss Hicks,' was all she said, however. ' They'll insist on some sort of punishment, probably staying indoors for a week and doing extra tasks, but that won't hurt you.' She saw Lilac's astonished and outraged expression and smiled grimly. 'It'll do you good. You're growing spoilt and wilful, queen, and it's partly my fault. You must learn your place.'

Lilac nodded glumly and they walked on, still hand in hand, but presently Lilac put her arm round Nellie and gave her a squeeze.

'Do you love me, Nell?'

And Nellie, as Lilac had known she would, stopped

in her tracks and picked Lilac up, big girl though she was, and gave her a kiss and a loving hug.

'Oh queen, you know I do!'

Chapter Four

1914

It was the sound of footsteps outside the dormitory window which woke Lilac, and this was odd, because she was a sound sleeper as a rule. Perhaps it was because the footsteps were trying so hard not to be heard, stealing along with only the faintest patter, but whatever the reason, Lilac suddenly found herself awake and alert, her eyes straining towards the faint light from the window.

Who could it be, stealing so quietly past the Culler? There was a war on, suppose it was a German spy, come to get them? But a spy, Lilac reasoned, would scarcely waste time on an orphan asylum with the docks so near – no, it was unlikely to be a spy.

Because it was getting near Christmas the children got up, now, whilst it was still dark, dressing by candlelight, shivering in the unheated dormitories and the long, cold corridors, quite eager to get downstairs to the dining hall even when the breakfast porridge was burnt or their morning drink more water than milk. But there was something in the hush from the house which told Lilac that it was still early, that the bell would not be rung for a while yet.

So why was she awake? To be sure the footsteps had woken her, but that was no reason not to return to sleep once she had convinced herself there was no danger, so why did she not just snuggle down again and go back to sleep until morning? Was there something special about today, apart from being awake when everyone else still slumbered?

And then she remembered. No one could be certain when Lilac's real birthday was, but Nellie had decided that since to all intents and purposes Lilac's life had started on the day she arrived at the Culler, her official birthday would be the second of December.

And today was the second, Lilac remembered, and felt excitement course through her. Not that the Culler made anything of birthdays, not with sixty inmates all of whom had got themselves born at some time or other, but Nellie never let the date go by without a gift, however small, and a treat of some sort. They had been twice to Lewis's, a favourite outing, so that Lilac could gaze enviously at the beautiful toys and clothes. Once they had taken themselves off to Bold Street to drink coffee and eat a squishy, delicious cake in Fuller's, served by real waitresses in frilly aprons. Another time Nellie had taken Lilac to the Royal Studio, where either Mr Brown, Mr Barnes or Mr Bell, they could not tell which, had sat her before a country scene with a bunch of artificial roses in her hand and taken her photograph. Nellie had a copy of the photograph on her wash-stand and Aunt Ada had one on her sideboard. Lilac liked to look at the photograph and imagine that one day her rich relatives would see it and demand to be told the name of that beautiful child who was so like the baby stolen from them years ago, but other than that she felt slightly cheated by the photograph. The main gainers had been others and not Lilac Larkin!

But today Lilac was nine years old and despite the fact that the country was at war with Germany, Nellie had promised it would be a specially good birthday. Davy would be in the 'Pool, on leave from his frigate, for he had joined the Navy on the outbreak of war, and there was to be a special Christmas pantomime staged at the Royal Court theatre opposite Queen's Square so that troops who would not be in Blighty at Christmas should still have something seasonal before they were sent abroad. It was Davy's excellent suggestion that he should treat Lilac and Nellie to a seat in the stalls as his own particular birthday present.

And Nellie, not to be outdone, had said that on the Saturday afternoon, when she was off, just the two of them would do something nice. Not Davy, since he would be working aboard his ship all day, though he would join them in the evening for the theatre trip, just Nellie and Lilac. Like old times, Lilac thought to herself; she was not jealous of Davy, that would have been silly because she knew she was the most important person in Nellie's life, but she did like to have Nellie to herself on her birthday.

' Tell you what, we've talked about it often enough,' Nellie had said the previous evening, when she was supervising Room nine's undressing. 'Tomorrow we'll go for a trip on the overhead railway! We'll tek the tram up to Seaforth and come back by rail, then we'll have a fish supper at the pier'ead, make a day of it.'

'Oh, Nell,' Lilac gasped. 'Oh, I can't wait! You are so lovely to me!'

'I've always wanted to do it meself,' Nellie confessed. 'All the big ships ... you can see 'em best of all from the railway – better than from the top deck of a leckie, even.'

Electric trams were no longer quite the novelty they had been for Lilac, since Nellie and she now caught the tram quite often when they went home to Coronation Court. Nellie had found a way to supplement her small income, and the extra money made it possible for them to ride on the trams from time to time. She had always been a good knitter and now she was being paid to knit for the troops by a rich lady who was on the board of governors of the Culler, so in the evenings, whilst she supervised baths and bed, Nellie stood with the wool tucked under one arm and the needles clicking away like mad whilst her work gradually grew.

'There isn't much money in it,' she told Lilac. 'But every little helps.'

Nellie never said so, but Lilac knew that a good deal of the money went on Lilac herself, and she guessed that Nellie put the rest away towards her marriage. Davy was so nice, so handsome, and so extremely attentive! And he was beginning to talk about taking a couple of rooms somewhere off the Scotland Road, so that Nellie could be near her brothers whilst he was at sea. Even Lilac could see how much he liked Nellie; he bought her little presents, spent all his spare time with her when he came to the city, and was quite willing to send Lilac off to the cinema or to take her to Coronation Court so that he and Nellie could spend some time alone. In fact Lilac thought it might only be a matter of time before the three of them had a nice little house somewhere ... and goodbye to the horrible Culler, she told herself now, warm in her bed, cuddling her arms round herself ecstatically at the thought.

So what a day this was to be, then! No wonder she had woken at the patter of footsteps ... and this made her wonder anew who was outside the home at this early hour and what they were doing. Had someone dumped a baby, the way someone had dumped her, nine years ago to the very day? Well, if they have I'm not going down, Lilac thought smugly. Nor will Nellie, because she's got me to look after, she wouldn't want another baby. But she sat up on her elbow, nevertheless, and stared across at the nine narrow beds with the nine humped up shapes of nine sleeping nine-year-olds.

What a lot of nines, she thought. If I was to go to sleep again I'd spoil it, it would be ten sleeping nine-year-olds … just let me take a quick look …

She swung her legs out of bed and clutched her skimpy cotton nightdress around herself, then made for the window. Nellie always closed it in the wintertime since everyone knew that darkness was bad for the young and the cold air worst of all, but now, with infinite caution, Lilac moved the heavy sash upwards, then knelt on the floor and poked her head out. Below and to the left of her was the portico; was there a wild figure running off down the street, or a would-be burglar effecting an entrance to the lower windows? But so far as she could see there was nothing and nobody, only the dark sky with the stars twinkling frostily, a puddle in the road reflecting the sky and telling her of earlier rain and the salty breeze which blew from the Mersey bringing a tantalising breath of the tidal river and the great open spaces of ocean beyond.

She was still kneeling there, almost mesmerised by the sweetness of the pre-dawn wind and the brilliance of the stars, when she heard something outside the room, just a tiny thread of sound but still something. Her heart, which had been thudding quietly away down there, gave a sudden bound; burglars! She knew there was nothing much to steal at the Culler, but there was always her pink dress, let out and lace-trimmed and many-times washed, which Nellie kept in her own chest of drawers upstairs. And the little red cloth coat with the black velvet collar and cuffs which Nellie was cutting down for her to wear, come Christmas. Suppose someone had heard rumours of these riches? Suppose even now some old shawlie from the slums was making her way up the attic stairs, intent upon stealing that pink dress and red cloth coat to sell in Paddy's Market on the morrow?

Lilac stood up and gently lowered the window into place. If she left it open ten to one Maudie, who suffered with her chest, would wake and start to wheeze and cry. Then Lilac would be in trouble twice over, once for daring to be awake when everyone else was sleeping and once for letting air in.

She padded barefoot over to the door and opened it a crack. Sure enough, there *was* someone stealing up – or down – the attic stairs, she could just hear the faint, well-remembered creak which the second stair from the bottom always gave when trodden on. The conviction that someone was after her clothes increased. She would have to raise the alarm or at least rouse Nellie!

Accordingly, she tiptoed out of the dormitory and across the corridor, then stared fearfully up the attic stairs. She thought she caught a glimpse of a slender figure just before it disappeared round the corner. It had not looked like an old shawlie, but mary ellens were fond of their personal finery, suppose one of them, and they were reputed to be bad girls, had heard rumours about Lilac's dress and coat?

Her clothes, Lilac felt, raised her from the lowly position of a foundling to someone who mattered, someone who had relatives to be visited and friends who were not at the Culler. If she lost them ... Horrified by the mere thought, she set off up the attic stairs, carefully missing the creaking one, and arrived on the little square landing with freezing feet and an uncomfortably bumping heart.

Nellie's door was slightly ajar. Still on tiptoe and dreading what she might see, Lilac approached it.

Through the crack between door and jamb, Lilac could see Nellie sitting on her bed. She was just sitting, with her chin in her hand, gazing abstractedly at the wash-stand. It was a tiny slip of a room, not a room at all really but a partitioned-off piece of the attic, and it was easy to see that Nellie was alone. And easy to hear, Lilac suddenly realised, that Nellie was crying.

And she had been out; her shoes had clearly just been kicked off and were wet, had left wet marks across the boarded floor. And she was only just unty-ing the strings of the brown capelike garment which the Culler provided for members of its staff.

So it had been Nellie whose footsteps had disturbed her sleep, Lilac realised rather resentfully. And just why was Nellie crying, when it was her little Lilac's ninth birthday and she should have been full of excite-ment at the thought of the treats ahead of them?

She could have gone in and comforted Nellie, but that would have meant letting Nellie know she had been seen and besides, Lilac really did not want to know why Nellie walked around at night and cried. Perhaps she has a belly-ache, Lilac decided. If she's got a belly-ache she won't want my cold feet in her bed. So I'll go back to my dorm, I think, and try to go to sleep to make morning come quicker.

With that thought, Lilac swung round and pattered off down the stairs, making so little noise that she could scarcely mark her own progress. Back in her room she got into bed and curled herself into a small ball, wrapped her freezing feet in her nightdress and pulled her blanket well up round her ears. And presently she fell asleep and slept soundly until the rising bell sounded.

'Did you sleep well, Nellie?'

Lilac's blue eyes fixed themselves ingenuously on

Nellie's grey ones. It was the nearest she meant to get to asking about what had happened in the night and it was immediately obvious that Nellie did not intend to come clean.

'Yes thanks, queen. Well, if me eyes are a bit reddish it's because … ' She had come into the playroom with her hands behind her back and now she brought them forward. Before Lilac's delighted gaze she saw the red cloth coat – completed down to the last stitch. And it looked … oh, marvellous, beautiful, just what Lilac most wanted!

'Oh Nellie, you are kind! I do love you … can I wear it to the pantomime? You won't make me wait till Christmas, will you? I might easily *die* if I had to wait till Christmas!'

'It's for your birthday, I got you something else for Christmas,' Nellie said. She held the coat out enticingly. 'Want to try it on?'

'Yes please, Nell dearest.' Lilac struggled into the sleeves, then stood docilely whilst Nellie straightened, buttoned and finally turned her towards the window. 'It looks good doesn't it, Nell?'

'Yes, I think so, but look in the window-glass, you'll see your reflection in that,' Nellie said. 'And we'll find a mirror somewhere on the way to Seaforth so's you can see better what it's like. Come to think there's a mirror in the milliner's down the road, you can see it through the window. We'll go that way, then you can see yourself properly.'

'It looks lovely,' Lilac said, having scrutinised her reflection narrowly. 'What'll you wear to the theatre, Nell? It should be something special.'

'Well, I've my brown cloak, that'll do,' Nellie said at once. 'We can't have two new coats, queen!'

'No, I suppose not. And it is my birthday,' Lilac said.

'I'd better not wear my new coat for the docker's umbrella though, Nell. Don't want to get it all covered in smuts.'

Nellie laughed.

'I was going to say that; you're a thoughtful kid,' she said. 'Best get your cloak, then. We'll be off in half an hour.'

The tram ride was fun, though they sat inside because it was very cold now, the wind bringing tears to Lilac's eyes when she faced into it.

'No weather to be at sea,' someone said, and Lilac saw Nellie's glance shoot apprehensively over towards the docks. Lilac knew vaguely that Nellie worried about the war and about Davy, but she never said very much and so far as Lilac could see, if you were in a ship it didn't much matter whether it was a little coaster chugging up and down the west coast of Scotland selling Welsh coal or a frigate with guns dodging enemy shipping, you could still get drowned if the weather was wrong.

She loved the trip on the overhead railway, though. The train rattled along, signals clanked, and they were able to look down on the busy dockyards and see the great liners and the little coasters and all the other bustling marine life which filled the port in wartime.

There were a lot of uniforms about. Nellie looked wistfully at the sailors in their blues but she didn't say much. She never did, Lilac supposed. She stood up once or twice, when the train slowed, and tried to see whether she could spot HMS *Milligan*, which was Davy's new ship, but there was so much shipping that it was impossible to pick one vessel out, particularly since they did not know it by sight.

'Davy said she had a taller funnel than some,' Nellie said distractedly as they peered into the Canning dock with its closely packed vessels looking as though one could have crossed the dock, jumping from ship to ship, and remained dry-shod. 'But they all look alike to me.'

'Never mind, Nell, we'll see him tonight,' Lilac said placidly. Nellie had bought her a bag of pink and white humbugs and she was sucking them slowly, to make them last. Her cheek would have a pattern on it, she decided, where the latest sweet had clung to the soft flesh of her inner cheek.

'Yes. Course we shall.' The train swung inland and stopped and Nellie stood up. 'Come on, chuck, that's our ride over, this is the pier'ead. Want a dish of cockles, or bangers and mash? It's your birthday!'

And if her happiness had a hollow ring, if there was anxiety in the pale face, then Lilac ignored it. After all, it *was* her birthday and should not be spoiled because Nellie had a belly-ache.

'Well, but why hasn't he come, Nell? He said he'd come ... why didn't he meet us outside the Culler, like he said?'

The two girls stood outside the Royal Court Theatre, watching the early evening crowds surge around, good-humoured, loud-mouthed. Someone was playing a mouth-organ to amuse the people waiting to go in, a pretty girl smiled at them over her basket of apples and oranges, a man held a fistful of coloured balloons, another sold paper bags of hot roast chestnuts, yet another had hazel-nuts dipped in toffee and coloured cocoanut candy threads which he thrust into paper cones and sold at two for a ha'penny.

'I suppose he's needed on board ship,' Nellie said anxiously. 'Oh Lilac, love, you aren't the only one who wishes he'd come! I'm right worried, really I am.'

'So am I, because we'll miss the beginning if we don't go in soon,' Lilac pointed out. 'And it *is* my birthday treat. Why didn't Davy give you the tickets in case he had to be late?'

'He did,' Nellie said slowly. 'He posted 'em, I've got 'em in me purse. But this was Davy's present, queen. I'd feel guilty to go in without him, wouldn't you?'

'No I wouldn't,' Lilac said decidedly. 'I've never been to a pantomime, I want to see all of it! Oh come *on*, Nellie, do let's go in. Davy will find us – you haven't got his ticket as well, have you?'

'No, he kept his own. But Lilac, love … '

'Oh please, Nell! Please, please let's go in! Davy will come soon, but we'll miss the beginning.'

'All right,' Nellie said. Her voice was flat. She took Lilac's hand in her own cold one. 'I suppose it's only sensible.'

'Yes, it is. Davy would say go in,' Lilac said, trotting eagerly ahead and pulling Nellie after her. 'Why, he may be in already for all we know.'

He was not in the theatre, but the two girls settled down in their seats and Lilac got out her bag of humbugs, sadly depleted but still worth investigating, and stared around her.

There were a lot of smartly dressed people, many of them children no older than herself, and the seats on which they sat were covered in red velvet whilst an exciting smell filled the air, though Lilac could not entirely identify it. Perhaps it owed something to ladies' perfume and something to the rich smell of cigar smoke, perhaps there was a hint of heat from the big gaslights which illuminated the place and another sort of smell from the folds of the red velvet curtain which hid the stage, but whatever it was it was strange and exciting and made Lilac's heart beat faster and her breathing come in little jerks.

Then the curtain rose on fairyland and Lilac forgot Davy and Nellie, she forgot the Culler and Coronation Court and lost herself in the bright life of the people on the stage and the wonderful jokes and music, the colours and the voices, the breathtaking beauty of it all.

Nellie had bought them oranges for the interval and that was another smell to add to the others, a sharp, exciting sort of smell which went with the delicious, tangy taste. Oranges had never before come Lilac's way, but she enjoyed every mouthful. And then the curtain went up again and once more she was spellbound.

It was the longest evening of Nellie's life, easily the longest. She did not know how she sat through the pantomime, though like Lilac, she had never seen such a thing before and in different circumstances would have loved every minute of it.

But she had gone out to meet Davy last night and he had not come, and he had never failed her before. Something must have happened ... how could she bear it, if something had happened to the *Milligan* and thus to Davy? And she was disappointed in Lilac, too. For the first time, it occurred to Nellie that her darling was spoilt and selfish – and whose fault was that? Why Nellie's own fault, of course, because no one else had spoiled Lilac, no one else had given her everything she could manage to give her, had seen she had little treats, trips out, even a share in Nellie's own family.

Of course it wasn't fair to judge Lilac for wanting

desperately to see the pantomime, nor in not wishing to wait for Davy outside. Indeed, it was as well they had not waited, since they would probably have forfeited their seats and missed the entire performance. But Lilac had not been in the least interested in Nellie's worries after the pantomime had ended and had even demanded, during the eating of their fish supper, that Nellie should listen to her and not keep staring at the doorway.

And when they got back to the Culler, Lilac went on chattering about the pantomime and about her lovely evening and Nellie sat and knitted and waited for the child to go to bed and although she supervised the nine-year-olds, as she always did, anyone could have seen that her heart wasn't in it, not tonight.

But Lilac didn't seem to notice Nellie's abstraction nor the fact that her eyes would keep filling with tears. Oh dear God, Nellie was praying, don't let anything bad have happened to Davy because I do love him and ... oh God, I do need him! Keep him safe, don't let anything bad have happened!

And after Lilac had gone to bed Nellie sneaked quietly out of the house, though she had no right since her time off ended at ten o'clock. But she could not have gone meekly to bed, not without at least making a push to find out where Davy – and the *Milligan* – was.

It was a cold night again, colder if anything than the previous one. Nellie wore her thick cloak and muffled her head in a big woolly scarf and walked all the way down to Canning Dock, and there she asked everyone who came through the gates whether they had seen HMS *Milligan* or knew what had happened to her.

'Late, is she?' a portly, grizzled sailor said, scratching his head and tilting his cap to do so. 'No wonder, a deal of shipping there is, wantin' to get into port, and others wantin' to prevent 'em. What's she carryin'?'

'I don't know,' Nellie said faintly. 'I think she just keeps the others safe ... in the convoys, that is.'

'Oh, aye? A frigate, she'll be. Well, she'll be in soon, no doubt.'

Nellie waited down by the dock until she could see that the rush of men coming ashore had slackened to an odd one or two and then she walked back to the Culler. She realised, belatedly, that as a sailor's young woman she had no rights, would not even be informed if Davy had been killed in action. That news would go to his old parents, on Anglesey, who might have heard Davy speak of her but probably did not know her name, let alone her address.

Oh God, what should she do? Tomorrow I'll go to Coronation Court whilst the children are in church, she decided, and talk to Hal and Bertie. I can't burden Charlie with any more worries, he's got enough of his own. Bessie was thriving and the children were well but Charlie was talking about joining the Army and everyone was against it. Nellie thought life was hard enough without having to leave your wife and baby, but Charlie felt it was his chance to see the world and a bit of life; she only hoped that the matter would be resolved by the war ending, though it did not seem as likely now as it had earlier in the year.

She let herself in through the kitchen window, took off her shoes and rubbed some life back into her frozen feet with a rough towel, then tiptoed up the stairs. She was tempted to peep at Lilac, but remembering the child's indifference to Davy's absence earlier she hardened her heart. She went straight to her own room and lay down on the bed, but not to sleep. She was going over in her mind what she must do. And before the bell had rung to rouse the children, before the sky had done more than lighten a little in the east, she was up and dressed, a small bag packed.

Nellie went down the stairs and out of the back door, clutching the folds of her old brown cloak around her. She had her savings in her bag and a new, chilly determination filled her. She would go to Davy's parents and beg them to tell her what had happened to their son, explain that he and she were courting, intended to get married. Davy had talked a lot about his home, perhaps more than he knew, so she should have no difficulty in finding it. He talked about Amlwch, the nearest big town, and had said there was a railway station there. But perhaps the sailor was right and Davy's ship had merely been delayed, in which case no harm would have been done, for she was sure Davy would have taken her home to meet his parents before they married. And if Davy's ship was missing, if he had been killed, then at least she would know, at least she would no longer have to suffer this agony of uncertainty.

Waiting for the ferry down at the pierhead, for the train which would take her to Amlwch left from Rock Ferry on the other side of the water, Nellie thought, for the first time, of Lilac. Would the child worry? Would she fret for Nellie? Well, if she does it will be the first time, Nellie realised sadly. She ran away and I was worried sick, now I'm running away – perhaps a little worry will do Lilac good, make her a nicer, more thoughtful person.

The ferry drew up alongside, jarring against the wooden landing stage, and Nellie watched whilst the gangplank clattered down and people began to surge forward. She joined them when most were already aboard and was impressed despite herself by the casual, matter of fact attitude of other travellers. Mostly, she supposed, they were going to work in Cammell Laird's or some other shipyard, but they were well used to the short voyage and stood talking in small groups or hurried downstairs to the saloons, leaving Nellie to lean over the rail and watch the shore come gradually nearer.

Once she disembarked she only had to walk up Bedford Road and there she was at Rock Ferry Station. Nellie bought a ticket and got on board the waiting train, settling herself in a third class carriage, taking a corner seat so that she could watch the scenery and try to take her mind off her worries. There was a tinted photograph above the seat opposite and whilst she waited for the train to move, Nellie examined it.

It showed a quaint fishing village, a beach, a rocky curve of bay, and the legend beneath read: *Moelfre fishing village, Anglesey*. Nellie stared and stared at it. One of those houses might be Davy's house, she thought. And I'm going right there, to Moelfre fishing village! Oh, this has to be a good sign, a sign that everything will be all right. Oh please, God, I've never asked you for much, not for meself, just for Lilac now and again. But please God, let Davy be all right, let me find him safe at home when I get to that little fishing village! Oh God, I love Lilac ever so, but I think I love Davy in a different way, so take care of 'em both and let me find Davy safe when I reach Moelfre!

It was a long journey, but Nellie had started early. Soon after two o'clock she found herself on the station plat-form at Amlwch, looking hopefully round her. It was several miles to Moelfre and she knew it would be best to arrive at the village whilst it was still light, but unless there was a convenient bus she would have to either spend some of her small store of money on a cab or walk.

A porter came across the platform and stopped by her, seeing her apparently waiting.

'Can I 'elp you, Missie?'

'Oh … I want to get to Moelfre; is there a bus?'

The man shook his head.

'Not now, Missie, last one's gone. Goin' to see a friend, are you? Well, seven miles it is to walk, too far with the evenings drawing in early, but Ap Owen and his missus come off your train, they go near the village, mebbe they'd give you a lift?'

'Oh, would they? I'd be very grateful,' Nellie said thankfully. 'Would you ask Mr Ap Owen how much he would charge to take me?'

'He won't want your money,' the porter said comfortably. 'Glad to do a good turn he'll be; besides, there'll be stock in the cart, but I daresay you won't mind that. Bide you here a moment, Missie, we'll soon have you fixed up.'

He was as good as his word. Nellie and two sheep shared a farm cart whilst the farmer and his wife sat in front, chattering away nineteen-to-the-dozen in Welsh and occasionally breaking into awkward English for a moment to ask Nellie if she 'wass all right now, and quite comfortable, then?'

Nellie looked curiously around her as the cart drew away from the station yard. The town square was a pleasant place with an ancient towered church to her left and a large public house, the Dinorben Arms, to her right. There were several roads leading off the square and she was amused and rather startled to see, in the middle of what looked like a main thoroughfare, a large outcrop of rock, and outside the hotel a goat grazed and brown hens scuffled in the dust near the imposing station entrance. Nellie reflected that she had come a long way from Liverpool ... imagine an outcrop of rock on Scotland Road or a goat cropping the grass outside Lime Street Station!

At first, the road along which the cart rattled was lined with dwellings but very soon the houses petered out and they were in open country. The road became narrow and winding, climbing up hills and swooping into valleys, the meadows and fields quiet and the trees leafless in the December chill. They passed through a village of grey stone houses with gardens still bright despite the lateness of the year and then, on her right, Nellie saw a mountain rearing up into the sky, its sides pocked with evidence of some form of mining.

Seeing her gazing, the farmer's wife gestured towards it.

'Parys Mountain that is, where they used to dig out a deal of copper in times past. And them's the ochre pools – not that you can see 'em too well from 'ere. You want to ask your friends to take you there, 'tis a strange sight.'

Nellie strained her eyes, but could only make out the glint of water far off.

'And this is Pensarn; not far now,' Mr Ap Owen remarked as the cart clattered into another small grey village. 'Smithy's open, I see. Just 'ave a word with Huw I will.'

He pulled the horse up and climbed laboriously down whilst the sheep shoved and bleated and Nellie stared over the side of the cart into the flaming heart of the smithy where a short, swarthy man in a filthy leather apron stopped whacking at a red-hot horseshoe for a moment to answer whatever query Mr Ap Owen had addressed to him. As he spoke the smith gestured to the wall behind him and the farmer walked over and took down a workmanlike looking hayfork which hung there, then returned to the cart, climbed up, clicked to the horse and they were off once more, with Mrs Ap Owen balancing the fork across her ample lap. The couple began to talk in low voices, not that they needed to lower their tones, since they were speaking in Welsh.

Nellie, who had not until now considered that she was in a foreign country, suddenly wondered what on earth she would do if Davy's mother and father spoke only Welsh; heavens, that really would be difficult! But it was unlikely; Davy spoke such good English that it was hard to realise it was not his first language.

'Not far now,' Mr Ap Owen said presently. 'Drop you at the top of the village, we will; only a short walk down it is but not too good for a horse and cart, like.'

'Thank goodness it's still light,' Nellie said presently as the farmer pulled his horse to a standstill. She struggled out of the cart, helped by the strong arm of Mrs Ap Owen. 'Thank you very much indeed for your kindness, I'll tell the Evans family how good you've been.'

'Not at all, not at all,' Mr Ap Owen said. 'Off you go, my dear, you'll be there in five minutes or less.'

Nellie, bag in hand, went briskly down the steeply sloping lane. She passed low stone cottages to left and right, turned a corner, crossed a humped grey bridge over a stream whose banks were lined with stooped, bare- branched trees, stopped for a moment to stare at the first waterfall she had seen, and then, turning back to the road, she saw on her left the fishermen's cottages and the Crown and Anchor public house whilst on her right was the beach, a curve of grey, fawn and greenish stones with boats pulled up above the wintery silver of the sea.

Nellie stopped for a moment and stared, letting her gaze wander from the cottages crouched a few feet from the shingle up the slope of the cliff, to where she knew Davy's home was. When she wrote to him she sent her letters to the post office which, he had told her, was just a front room in the public house, but since he had talked of walking down to the post office to fetch the letters, she knew that his home must be on the street she could see climbing the hill, and because he had also said his back garden overlooked the sea, it must be on the right side of the street and not on the left.

Nellie began to walk past the fishermen's cottages, then past the public house, then up the road, Stryd Pen, where Davy must live. She felt excited, frightened and apprehensive all at once, looking searchingly at the terraced houses, which were more substantial than she had imagined. They were roofed with blue-grey slate and had deep porches and tiny windows set into the thickness of the walls and each one had a small front garden choked with the remnants of autumn.

The houses were not numbered but in any case Davy had never mentioned a number. Should she simply walk up to a door and knock, ask if this was the Evans's home? And then, staring up at the next house, she saw something which banished all her doubts. A very old ship's lantern hung to one side of the porch. Davy had showed her that lantern, told her it was a present for his father, who would enjoy lighting it up on dark winter nights when Davy was home, to guide him back to the cottage when he'd been down to the Crown and Anchor for a pint.

Nellie went over to the door, raised her knuckles to rap, and hesitated. It was awfully rude to just wish oneself on someone at this hour of the evening; would old Mrs Evans realise how desperately she needed news of Davy? But a mother would understand, surely? Nellie knew that if someone was worried about Lilac, she would do everything in her power to reassure them.

And anyway she had little choice. Moelfre was far too small a village to find a boarding house, at least in mid-winter, willing to take her in. It would have to be as she had planned it – she would have to tell Mrs Evans who she was and explain her errand.

Without giving herself any more time to think about it, therefore, Nellie took hold of the knocker and brought it down decisively on the wood of the door.

Chapter Five

The door opened inwards. Against the golden light
which flooded out into the tiny square of front garden
with its tangle of winter-bare shrubs Nellie could barely
make out who had opened it save that it was a woman.
And her first words were not much help since they were
in Welsh, though Nellie could hear the interrogative
tone and guessed that the woman was asking her what
she wanted.

'I'm sorry to trouble you,' she stammered, therefore,
'but are you Mrs Evans? And is Davy Evans your ... '

With an exclamation the woman pulled the door
wider and gestured her in.

'A friend of my Davy is always welcome; come in
with you and warm yourself ... Duw, it's bitter cold out
there, girl!'

'Thank you,' Nellie said. She walked into the room,
aware as she felt the warmth of firelight and lamplight
how cold she was. She looked around her, at the flames
licking up the chimney, the rugs on the well polished
boards, the gleam of a Welsh dresser laden with ornate
and rosy china, at dark oil paintings in gilded frames
on the bulging, whitewashed walls. A homely room ...
and in a chintz-covered armchair pulled up close to the
fire an old man, bent and as bald as an egg, was eating
something from a round blue dish. He looked across at
Nellie, gave her a brief and toothless grin, then returned to his meal.

The woman who had invited Nellie in turned to the

old man and spoke loudly, in Welsh. Nellie guessed that her presence was being explained even as she was pressed gently into one of the easy chairs.

'Sit you down, girl. Da don't speak no English ... I suppose you've had no news of Davy? They wrote and told me he was missing after the *Milligan* went down, but there's always hope, that's what I say ... though they were in the Baltic sea and it's cruel cold out there.'

'Missing?' Nellie quavered. 'Oh, dear God, and I've prayed for him every night and morning, I've begged for his life ... does missing mean there is hope, then?'

'Hope cannot die,' the other woman said. She looked attentively at Nellie. 'Tell me, cariad, just what were you to Davy?'

'We were to be married,' Nellie murmured. Scalding tears were chasing each other down her ice-cold cheeks and there was a low, nagging ache in her back. 'Oh, Mrs Evans, we were to be married!'

'Married?' Mrs Evans, Nellie saw through her tears, was staring at her with curious intentness. She was as dark as Davy, with a gentle, very youthful face and black, bright eyes, widening as though with shock and then narrowing to stare. Nellie noticed that her hands were gripping each other so tightly that the knuckles were white and she thought again how like Davy she was with her black hair, though her curls were softer, falling beside the oval of her face like two bunches of grapes. 'You poor scrap of a thing, to come all this way just to hear news like that! He had promised marriage, then?'

'Well, not in so many words; we'd been courting for more than a year though, and he was looking for a couple of rooms so we could set up home together when we could afford it. I knew he'd be away a lot but what did that matter? When he was home we could be together.'

'True. He'd not told us, you see – his Da and I. But doubtless he meant to bring you home here some time?'

Mrs Evans's voice was quiet, yet there was pain in it, and resignation, too. Almost as though she had expected sadness.

'I don't know, but I suppose so. He talked about you both …' Nellie rubbed her eyes and then looked narrowly across at the woman she had taken to be Davy's mother. 'I got the idea you were old and ill … are you Mr Evans' second wife? For now that I look close, I can see you're not much older than Davy.'

'Call me Bethan,' Mrs Evans said. 'Cariad, I'd best tell you the truth though I hate to give you pain. It's not Davy's mother I am but his wife. His mother is bedridden, she keeps to her room all winter, though when Davy is home … when he was home … he would carry her down in summer to sit outside in her chair. However, she's very deaf and his Da only speaks Welsh so won't have understood a word of all this, which is two people easier in their minds for ignorance. They worshipped Davy, you see, and he was very good to them. Sometimes I thought he only married me to have someone here to take care of them whilst he was away.'

Nellie shook her head. She must be going mad, she thought that Davy's mother had just said she was not his mother but his wife, but everyone knew that Davy was going to marry her, Nellie McDowell, and live with her in Liverpool when he was not sailing the seas.

'The kettle's boiling,' Bethan said. 'A nice cup of tea now, that will help you to get things straight. It's worse for you than for me, Nellie, because I've got something to mourn – seven good years – whereas you had only the promise of bliss to come. And I always teased him, see? Said he had a girl in every port and half-believed it. Because he was beautiful, was Davy.'

Was. Then it was true, Davy was dead. Bethan said so and you only had to look into her face to know that she would never lie, not even to comfort.

'Yes, he was beautiful,' Nellie echoed. 'He couldn't have married me, then? Not even when I told him ... '

She stopped short. Bethan, who had been pouring water from the steaming kettle into a fat brown teapot, stopped as though she had been turned to stone. Then, very slowly, she completed her task, stirred the pot, went across the room and disappeared into a low doorway, coming back presently with a jug of milk and two pink tea cups. She made the tea and put a cup right into Nellie's hands, then sat down in the chair opposite and fixed Nellie with her dark and brilliant gaze.

'Not even when you told him that you ... that you were going to have a baby? Is that why you came so far, Nellie, and look so pinched and pale? Are you carrying my Davy's child?'

And Nellie, worn out, cold, frightened and terribly alone, simply nodded and put her cup of tea down, struggling to her feet.

'Yes, I think so. I'll go now. I'm sorry to have troubled you, I only came for news of Davy. If I'd known ... '

'Sit down, Nellie! You shan't stir from here tonight. You can sleep with me, I've got a double bed upstairs, we'll go up after I've put Father to bed for the night – he sleeps down here, on the box-bed in the wall. I can't get him upstairs, see, though when Davy was home – or Dickie, of course – one of them would help me to get him into a proper bed. Then tomorrow, when you're rested and are over the shock, we'll talk.'

'There's nothing to say,' Nellie said wearily. 'But you are so good! – I'll leave first thing tomorrow, then.'

'And you with Davy's baby in your belly and me with nothing ... *nothing* to remember him by? You shall not leave, you have as much right here as I – more, perhaps, since Davy and I could not make a child no matter how hard we tried!' Bethan came across and knelt on the floor in front of Nellie, putting her warm arms up round the younger girl's shoulders. 'Davy didn't know? He longed for a son you know – or a daughter, come to that, but he mostly spoke of a son. He would not want a son of his to suffer in any way and what's more, he'd want him brought up here, in Moelfre, with the Welsh coming easy to his tongue and his good relatives around him. Ah, how I wish the babe were mine! Indeed, for all people need know, he could be mine, and this cottage and the fishing boat, the cows in the top meadow and the pigs in the sties, the bit of money the old'uns have saved, it could all be his, Nellie, if you'll stay with us.'

'I'm too tired, I don't understand,' Nellie said, but the warmth and the tea at which she sipped was renewing her strength minute by minute. By morning, she thought, I will have accepted that Davy is dead, that I am going to have his baby and that this girl – Bethan – is his rightful wife. 'All I want now is to sleep.'

'And so you shall, cariad,' Bethan promised. 'But when did you last eat, girl? So pale you are, like milk!'

'I don't feel hungry, though I've not eaten since yesterday,' Nellie said vaguely. 'I had fried fish and a drink.'

'I baked today so we've new bread in plenty; and there's an apple pie – we've several fruit trees out the back. A slice of apple pie will do you no harm, whilst I settle Father.'

She brought the apple pie and another cup of tea. Nellie ate, staring into the flames, though she was aware of Bethan helping the old man out of his trousers and thick fisherman's jersey and into a nightshirt. Then Bethan opened a cupboard and a bed came down out of the wall and she assisted the old man into it. They talked all the while in Welsh, the old man saying little but Bethan's voice purring quietly on, as full of affection as though this was her own father and not that of her dead husband.

At last she turned to Nellie.

'So you managed to eat it all. Good. Now let me show you to your bed. I'll stay down here whilst you undress, then come up later.'

Nellie followed her hostess wearily up the short flight of narrow wooden stairs. A tiny landing at the top had three doors, all crooked at the top because of the sloping roof. Bethan threw open the right-hand door and ushered Nellie into a sizeable room. There was a brass bedstead, a stout table with a jug and ewer on top, and a huge, old-fashioned wardrobe and dressing table. On the wall framed texts and a couple more dark oil-paintings could be seen by the light of the lantern Bethan carried, and the small window set into the depth of the thick old wall was curtained with crisp cotton and had a diamond-patterned cushion on the broad sill, making it into a perfect window-seat.

'Here we are; pop your things off. Got a nightgown? No? Well, no need of one, anyway, you'll be warm enough – it's a featherbed of course – and two blankets. We've another room as well as the one Mother sleeps in, but the bed there isn't aired, or I'd offer that instead of a share of this one.'

Nellie, swaying with tiredness, pulled off her blouse, kicked off her shoes, and wriggled out of her long skirt. Her cloak was downstairs, hanging up behind the door just as though she was a proper visitor to the cottage instead of an intruder, the woman who had, albeit unknowingly, stolen Bethan's husband from her. Bethan had left her, but she had also left the lantern and turned down the bed. Nellie looked at the fat featherbed and the long bolster and then just climbed wearily onto the coarse linen sheet and pulled the blankets up. She had not even extinguished the lantern, but then Bethan would need to see when she, in her turn, came up to bed.

Lying there, with sleep hovering, it suddenly occurred to Nellie that she was in Davy's bed. Oh, the pain of it, the sudden, startling sense of actual physical deprivation! The fact coming home suddenly, cruelly, that she had lain in his arms for the last time, had known his sweet kisses and the easy strength of his lovemaking for the last time. Never more to hold and be held, never more to be Davy's beloved, nor he hers!

She had been in his bed before, from the very first time when they had lost Lilac and he had taken her to the lodging house and slipped into bed with her, promising to do nothing that she would not like. The trouble was, she liked it too well, had needed no persuasion to lie with him again whenever they had the chance. And they had made the baby together, though Davy had not known what he had done, and she had been frightened when she knew for sure she was pregnant in case he was not pleased, tried to abandon her and the unborn child, chose to turn from her.

As if he would have! She knew, now, that Davy had loved her in his way, even though he had been married to another woman. But she could not believe Davy had loved Bethan, or he would never have pursued Nellie and taken her virginity from her. Though thinking

back, to the things he had said, the way he had behaved, Nellie concluded sadly that Davy might well
have thought there was no harm in having a wife in
Moelfre and another in Liverpool.

Poor Davy. After all, two wives meant a doubling of
responsibility as well as a doubling of pleasure. And
he, who had meant well by both of them, Nellie was
sure, had gone down with his ship, seaweed in his hair,
fish nibbling his chilling flesh, all the thoughts and
hopes and fears, all the longing for a son, come to
nought.

Except that it hadn't come to nought, since she was
pregnant. She had recently felt a faint fluttering within
her, as the captive minnow flutters against the imprisoning palm, and knew it was the baby moving.
Later, perhaps, she would be afraid again – of the birth,
of the responsibility for the child, of her own helpless-
ness when it came to earning money, providing a
home. But right this minute she was not afraid. She
would manage, somehow. She would bear her son – or
daughter, if so it proved – and bring the child up right,
not to lie or cheat, because Davy, bless him, had lied to
her and cheated Bethan, but to be honest and kind and
true. She would find a way to earn money sufficient for
the two of them and she would raise the baby to be
proud of his Welsh father, to love his heritage.

But this exalted frame of mind did not last long. She
turned her head on the pillow, and caught a faint
masculine scent, something of Davy still on the bedding, some indefinable something which spoke of his
recent presence. Nellie had not seen him since September; had he been with Bethan in the last few weeks?
Jealousy, raw as a whip, flicked over her. And then
came despair and loneliness and fear.

When Bethan came to bed a few minutes later she

put warm arms round Nellie and rocked her sooth-ingly, as though Nellie was no older than Lilac.

'Poor Nell, poor Nell,' she crooned. 'Go to sleep now, go to sleep, and we'll talk it all out in the morn-ing.'

Nellie stirred in her arms.

'I want Davy,' she sobbed. 'I want him so badly, Bethan!'

'So do I, cariad,' Bethan whispered, her voice break-ing. 'Oh, so do I!'

'How did you sleep, Nell? You poor little thing, you were still sound off when I got up to see to Mother and Father so I let you lie. They've both had breakfast, Father's outside on the bench watching the fishing boats prepare for sea and Mother's nicely settled, read-ing a magazine the lady from the post office sent over. Later, you must come in and have a word with Mother; she's a brave old lady. She's lost her favourite son and Davy's brother, Dickie, is at sea too, and he's a trifle simple, so of course she worries about him more, but you'd never know it. Crippled with rheumatism she may be, but she's always got a smile and a cheery word. Now no hurry, girl, but we have to talk, and it had better be out of doors that we do our talking, I'm thinking. Still, take your time.'

It was a cold, bright day. Nellie, who had slept like a log, had only woken when Bethan's cheerful voice had called her name, forcing her into wakefulness. Now, washed and dressed, hair neatly brushed into a bun on the nape of her neck, she went into another bedroom to be introduced to old Mrs Evans and found her as Bethan said, a tiny, wizened hazelnut of a woman, all bent and doubled up with rheumatism, but with a bright, affectionate smile for them both and a welcome for Nellie, though she seemed to be under some misapprehension since she greeted Nellie as though she and Bethan were related.

'Any member of our dear girl's family is welcome here,' she said. 'Stay as long as you can, little one.'

As they descended the stairs, therefore, Nellie looked a question at Bethan, who understood at once.

'Easier, see, to say you're my sister, come to stay for a day or so,' she said. 'I wouldn't give them pain for the world. That was what I told Father last night, when I put him to bed; better stick to that story, I'm thinking.'

'Ye-es. Anyway, I'll be gone soon enough and it won't matter,' Nellie said, following her hostess across the pleasant kitchen and into the small scullery beyond. A full copper steamed on a range and the low stone sink was full of sheets, soaking in hot water. Bethan went across the room, rolling up her sleeves as she went.

'Laundry for the big house,' she said briefly. 'You won't mind if I get on? You could make us both some tea and cook some porridge, I daresay, for I've not yet had my breakfast.' She turned and smiled warmly at Nellie. 'Might as well make use of you whilst you're here, girl ... there's a spare apron on the back of the door.'

Bethan herself was dressed in warm blue wool with a white calico apron tied round her. Nellie, in the grey dress she had worn for the journey, was suddenly conscious of her travel-stained appearance, for she had had no choice but to put on the clothing she had worn yesterday since her bag only contained clean underwear and a warm jacket.

'You'll have to tell me where things are,' she said now, tying the apron round herself and walking over to take down a shining copper pan from the array on the wall-hooks. 'Do you make porridge with water? Or do you use milk?'

'Milk, since we keep a few cows in the meadows at the top of the cliff,' Bethan said over her shoulder. She heaved a sheet out onto the washboard and began scrubbing vigorously, suds up to her elbows. Under her vigorous pummelling tiny, many-coloured bubbles flew up and burst when they touched the wooden draining board, or landed on the hardpacked earth of the floor, for the scullery was a lean-to, built on at some stage but not properly floored.

'And where do I find the porridge oats?' Nellie said next, pouring milk from a big blue jug.

'In the brown crock in the larder.' Bethan jerked an elbow at a door in the wall. 'Did you sleep well, cariad, in spite of everything?'

'Yes, like a log,' Nellie said, surprised to find that she spoke no more than the truth. She remembered lying in bed weeping, with Bethan weeping too, in each other's arms, like sisters. Well, perhaps we are sisters, she thought defiantly now. Davy would have liked us to be friends, I'm sure. 'Can I help you with that sheet before I start to cook?'

'No, I can manage well enough, I promise you. I mangle in the back yard, though, and that's awkward work. You can help with that, presently. But right now if you cook the porridge I'll finish here and then later on I'll make a cake. We keep hens, of course, but they never lay as good in winter as in summer, so we have to use our eggs careful like, but they cost no more than a bowl of scraps and a dipper of corn twice a day. And we'll have fish for our dinner; Freddy Mackerel has gone out to the fishing in Father's boat so he'll bring us back some of his catch and the money for the boat later.'

'Is he buying the boat?' Nellie asked, stirring oats into a pan of milk and water.

'No, he rents it. It all helps, but we'll miss Davy's money. Though there's a pension, and Davy paid into a club – we'll get that in time.'

'I'll pay me way until I leave, I won't be a charge on you,' Nellie said, suddenly embarrassed. She had no right here, no matter how hard she tried to gainsay it!

'No need. The old folk are well off by most standards and I do some washing, some field work, clean up at the big house once in a while, grow vegetables out the back, and sell flowers done up in bunches when spring comes. We make butter and cheese when we've milk to spare and sell it at the market ... we do very well, better than folk in the city, I daresay.' She turned from the sink, lowering her voice, though she had already said that Father spoke only Welsh and Nellie had seen him through the window, sitting out at the front in the winter sunshine, watching housewives and children making their way up and down Stryd Pen. Later, when the day got going a bit, Bethan said he would go down to the stained wooden seat by the fishermen's huts and join other old men to gossip and eye passersby, and the comings and goings of boats in the harbour. 'When we've eaten we'll go for a stroll along the cliffs; I want to ask you something.'

'Well, I'll have to start walking back to Amlwch to catch the train home soon,' Nellie said. But she didn't mean it and knew, somehow, that Bethan understood that the words were said because they were expected rather than meant. 'Unless there's a bus?'

'Not till market day, but ... ah, the porridge looks cooked. Let's eat.'

And later, walking up the cliffs with the fresh, exciting sea breeze in her face and strange sights all around, Nellie and Bethan talked from their hearts. Nellie told Bethan all about Lilac, the child who had been as good as her own child since her arrival at the Culler, and Bethan told Nellie how she and Davy had longed for a child – she even admitted that a baby would have cemented their marriage in a way nothing else could.

'For though I loved him, I think he had no thought of marriage until his parents grew so infirm and Dickie such a worry to him,' she admitted as they strolled, arm in arm, up the steep incline to where the rolling meadows waited. 'And with Davy gone I've got nothing, Nellie, save memories of a happiness which may have been false. Now you've got your little Lilac, a job, a family ... so if you stay here and give birth to Davy's baby and we pretend the child is mine, how much better for us both it would be!'

'Oh, but people would know, everyone here would know, you'd find yourself with few friends, there would be gossip ... '

'No, I've thought it all out! And be honest, girl, if you go back with a child or even with a big belly the orphan asylum people won't like it. They'll turn you over to one of those places for bad girls and you won't last long there, you aren't bad enough! But if you let me have the baby then you can go back to your job, and Lilac, and pick up your life where you left off.'

'But the people here ... '

'Trust me! Didn't I say I'd worked it out? I've already said you're my sister, now I'll say you've come to see me through my time and I'll put a cushion under my smock – first a tiny one, then larger, larger – until you have the baby. The days are growing shorter with winter coming on, you won't need to be seen about much. Indoors we'll say you feel the cold and hang you about with shawls and extra clothing, outdoors you can wear that brown cloak of yours. Honest to God, girl, no one will even think we're playing games, why should they? And Davy's baby will inherit, just as he would have done had things been different, for I know my Davy too well to think he would have turned his back on his own flesh and blood. Oh Nell, is it cruel to say what can you offer, compared with all this? And you'll still have Lilac! And you'll be here until the birth and after, I'll take care of you, see you want for nothing.'

Nellie stared; Bethan had indeed thought it all out. The plan seemed foolproof, and yet …

'Bethan, surely that won't work, because the people close to you would know the child wasn't yours, wouldn't they? Where *do* you come from? Do you have no relatives of your own who might question you suddenly producing a baby?' Nellie asked curiously. 'You sound a bit different from the way Davy sounded, too.'

'Oh a bright girl you are and no mistake,' Bethan said, her dark eyes shining. 'There's clever that little baby will be with you for its Mam and our Davy for its Da! From Cardiff I am, another big city – another port. That's how I met Davy, out walking down Tiger Bay with my girlfriend Sally and her brother Bill. A big family are the Eliases, two brothers and ten sisters I had, so glad to get shot of a girl were Mam and Da. They liked Davy right well; six months we knew each other and then for two weeks he courted me, begging me to be his wife, so we wed and I come back here. I wrote a few letters, but my Mam never replied – too busy getting shot of the others, I daresay – and very happily I settled down, considering I was a city girl and you can't get much more country than this!'

'So your plan is that when the baby's born I'm to go back to Liverpool, and Lilac, and forget I ever had a baby? Bethan, I don't know whether I can! Already I feel a closeness for this baby that I don't feel for Lilac, dear to me though she is.'

'No, indeed, not to forget your baby! An aunt you will be, and a frequent visitor, I hope … just not a mother twice over, Nell, for you have your little Lilac, waiting. You owe her something, and all your owings to the baby I will pay and willing, eager! Oh Nell, I've lost Davy and all I have now is the old people and them more pain than pleasure if the truth be told. Let me have the baby and I'll look after it so well … oh, Nellie, you don't know how I'll love that little baby.'

And Nellie, looking into those dark and passionate eyes, knew that she would agree with Bethan's plan, that she must leave her baby. All unknowing, I stole Davy from her, and I am going to have the baby which should have been hers, Nellie told herself. She's right, I'm in no position to give the baby the things Bethan can give it and I have a responsibility for Lilac, too. So I'll stay here until the baby is born and then I'll go back to the Culler and take up my old life and no one the wiser.

She wrote to Lilac that afternoon and posted it next day; just a note explaining that Davy had been killed and she was staying with his parents for a few weeks, until they had got over the shock. Lilac was only nine and would scarcely understand her motives, but at least she would see that Nellie was going to come back as soon as she could, though the staff at the Culler, Mrs

Ransom in particular, would be very angry with her. But they won't know anything, and they'll probably give me my job back, Nellie told herself optimistically. And if they don't I'll get another job, because I'm good at my work, that no one can deny.

So the two girls settled down together and grew fond of each other and Nellie learned a few words of Welsh and chatted to Davy's father and went up to the bedroom and talked to Davy's mother. But she never forgot that she was supposed to be a city girl from Cardiff who spoke no Welsh – that at least was true – and she saw, with great surprise, that their story was accepted by everyone.

So Nellie helped Bethan in the house and used the big old mangle in the back yard and wore a droopy shawl indoors and her cloak outside. She watched as Bethan put a tiny thin cushion under her smock, then a larger one, then a larger one yet, and the more she got to know Bethan the easier it was to think of parting with the baby, for Bethan was good and generous, never stinting the two old people of love or care, working like a black for them, rarely thinking of herself. She deserved at least the solace of Davy's child, Nellie told herself, and remembered, when she walked down the long garden which ended in the cliff, threading her way between the winter cabbage, the potato clamp with the straw sticking out at the bottom and the bare-branched fruit trees, that all this would belong to her baby one day, that it was his inheritance. And by giving him up, I'm really the one who is giving him all this, she told herself, and it eased the little, niggling ache in her heart.

And as the winter days drew out the two girls talked about Davy and about the baby, and in bed at night, when Bethan slept, Nellie thought about Lilac and wept for her loss, not of Lilac, who would be waiting for her, but of the baby, who would never know the sacrifice she had made for it, never know that she was its mother.

Lilac awoke on the day after her ninth birthday with no conception of what was about to befall her. She ate her porridge, noticed Nellie was missing from her usual place behind the urn, decided it must be that bellyache which had made Nellie so abstracted the previous day and went in to her class as usual.

By teatime, however, the whole of the Culler was in an uproar over Nellie.

'She's a good gairl,' the cook kept remarking. 'She's never gone off ... something's 'appened to 'er.'

'She must have gone to Coronation Court,' Lilac said enviously. 'Why didn't she take me?'

'What? Gone to the court with a bag full of clo'es and 'er best winter cloak on 'er back? She's gone off, that's what she's done.'

Lilac glared at cook and went up to Nellie's room to check. Here, she stared in real dismay at the empty clothes rail, the empty hooks on the back of the door. Her hopes rose when she checked the chest of drawers, for Nellie's aprons and uniforms were neatly folded there. But in the long drawer at the bottom of the chest lay the pink dress and the red cloth coat with velvet collar and cuffs, and at the sight of her best things Lilac's heart constricted in her bosom. Nellie really had gone, then, and without a word. She had quite deliberately left, sloughing Lilac and the Culler as a snake sloughs last year's skin.

And with Nellie's going, Lilac's pampered existence at the Culler came to an end. Lilac had taken for granted the fact that Nellie saw to her clothes, so that every small garment was always clean and pressed, mended and matched. Now, she had to do as the others did – accept any brown dress and white pinafore that seemed likely to fit her out of the laundry bag, iron it with one of the heavy flat irons warming on the range down in the kitchen, and after so many days wear, put it in the dirty linen basket at the end of her dormitory and go to the laundry bag for a clean one.

She got her own supper, and it was always bread and scrape now, because there was no Nellie to save her bits and pieces. She was in class until teatime and then she went straight to the playroom with her peers. No extra reading lessons sitting beside Nellie on the bed upstairs or in the housekeeper's room. No cosy chats over crumbly biscuits and hot milk, no trips down to the post box with the teachers' private letters, no loving cuddle before she went to sleep at night, watched by nine envious pairs of eyes.

Lilac had been a foundling all her short life, but she had never felt that this was a disadvantage because in the background, taking care of her, looking out for her, seeing to her every want, had been Nellie McDowell. Nellie had provided Lilac with a ready-made family too and it was a real jolt when Lilac was boasting about Bessie and Charlie and the baby to hear someone mumble slyly that it was about time she realised that Charlie was Nellie's brother and not hers, because foundlings didn't have brothers.

Lilac felt heat rise to her cheeks. She turned on her heel and walked across to the opposite side of the playroom; an unfeeling snigger followed her.

And Miss Hicks, of course, was in her element. She made sure that Lilac felt the full weight of her dislike, a thing she had scarcely dared to do overtly whilst Nellie was so useful a member of the staff, and so well-liked by Mr Hayman, what was more.

In her heart, Lilac felt that she was being served out by her unhappiness because she knew very well that she had not behaved properly towards Nellie; when Davy had not arrived at the Royal Court Theatre Nellie had been distressed and unhappy but she, Lilac, had been too interested in the pursuit of her own pleasure to comfort the older girl. What was more, looking back down the years for the first time in her short life, Lilac realised that she had always been a taker, never a giver. Oh, she had loved Nellie, but she had never done anything for her, not if it inconvenienced herself! I could have helped in a lot of ways, she realised now, when it was too late. I could have given Nellie a hand often, when she was up to her eyes in work, but I never did. I never even thought of it.

When Nellie comes back, though, I'll show her I'm sorry, Lilac's thoughts continued. I'll do all her work for her, I'll save my pennies to buy her presents and I'll go to bed without being nagged and I won't keep reminding her about taking me to New Brighton, or to the museum. I'll ask her what she'd like to do, instead of just choosing my favourite at once. Oh, but I wish she'd come back soon!

Sometimes she thought about Davy and wondered if he and Nellie were happy together, for she had concluded that Nellie must have gone to Davy. She had not gone to Coronation Court. Lilac slipped out one afternoon three weeks after Nellie had left, and visited the court, only to find Aunt Ada, Uncle Bill and the rest as ignorant of Nellie's whereabouts as she.

'Where's the feller live, chuck?' Charlie asked when Lilac told him she believed Nellie must have gone to Davy. 'We could write, or go there, see if she's all right.'

But Lilac, who had never taken much notice when Davy and Nellie were talking, could remember nothing, not even whereabouts in Wales he lived, far less the name of his village.

'Doesn't Hal know?' she asked miserably. 'I was sure Hal would know.'

But Hal was not around to ask. He had joined the Navy when Davy did and been posted to foreign parts. Aunt Ada wrote, but no one knew how long it would take for Hal to receive the letter or even if, because of the war, he would ever receive it.

Aunt Ada took her back to the Culler so that she could talk to Mrs Ransom about Nellie, but that did not save Lilac from a beating. As Miss Hicks joyfully cut at Lilac's smarting palms she reminded her, with every stroke, that she would have to mind them all, now.

'No more outings, Miss,' she said breathlessly, between blows. 'No more special treatment. You're just a wicked girl like other wicked girls, and you'll be treated as such.'

And Lilac, cold and alone in her bed, cold and lonely in classroom and playroom, knew at last what Nellie had been to her. Salvation, that's what she had been, but Lilac hadn't known it. When she comes back ... she kept thinking. Oh Nellie, when you come back how happy I shall be!

After three months everyone told her that Nellie had gone for good, would never return. On bad days Lilac believed them and wandered around like a little ghost, but most of the time she was warmed and encouraged by a deep inner certainty. She had been disloyal, she had been selfish, she had been uncaring. But Nellie was generous and true. She would be back, Lilac was sure of it.

It kept her going through the darkest days that

winter and when the first signs of spring appeared in the gardens of the city and Nellie had not reappeared Lilac was still buoyed up by that inner certainty.

Nellie would return and claim her and find Lilac a changed person, then the two of them would pick up their lives where they had left off in early December. She clung to the thought as dreary day succeeded dreary day, as the evenings lengthened, the trees budded, the daffodils burst into flower.

Because without Nellie, she knew now, her life was not worth living.

Chapter Six

When she had first arrived in Moelfre and agreed to take part in Bethan's little deception, Nellie had never really thought anyone would be fooled into believing that Bethan and not herself was pregnant. Was that why she had agreed to it? Yet as time went on, as Bethan faithfully copied the swelling of Nellie's stomach on her own sturdy form, it became clear that not only would it work, it should, if all went well, be the means of securing the baby's future in the only way Nellie could see clearly.

Because Bethan had been true to her word. Nellie went round the village in her enveloping cloak and she carried the baby well, her pregnancy scarcely showing until the child was due. She was introduced as Bethan's sister Nellie, come to see the other girl through her time, and no one questioned the truth of it. After all, they didn't know Nellie, had never seen her until she was introduced as Bethan's sister. They had no reason to suspect that she was with child, far less that Bethan was not, when they could see Bethan getting larger week by week and could discern very little difference in Nellie's slender figure.

But the birth of a first baby was notoriously difficult; Nellie was worried that she might have a bad time which would mean calling the doctor in to help with the birth, but Bethan reassured her.

'Haven't I birthed half-a-dozen of Mam's babies, and me only a baby myself when I started?' she said bracingly, when Nellie admitted what was worrying her. 'But if I do need help then we'll swear the doctor to secrecy – he comes over from Amlwch, after all, it's not as if he were a local man.'

By this time Nellie had the feel of the community enough to realise that the town seven miles off was foreign ground to most of the Moelfre people, so she held her peace. And besides, it was difficult to worry or be uneasy as a hard January turned into a mild February and the fishing boats went bobbing off onto a silver-blue sea under a great arch of sunfilled sky.

On the day that the baby was due, however, Nellie went off by herself for a long walk and when she got back she could see Bethan had been crying. Missing Davy, no doubt, Nellie thought, and prepared the tea for the old people – Bethan's creamy homemade butter, some honey from the hives which squatted down by the stream in the village and yielded sweet heather honey in spring, and the homemade Welsh cakes which Bethan had taught her to make. When she had made the tea and seen the old people satisfied she and Bethan went for a walk together, partly to help Nellie to start the baby, for walking was good, Bethan said authoritatively, and partly so that they could talk without reservation.

They went along the beach until the rocks barred their way and then up onto the cliffs where already shy spring flowers grew in sheltered spots and the grass was greening up so that the cows had to be carefully watched or they would overeat and bloat themselves.

'Bethan, what's the matter?' Nellie said presently, for Bethan was clearly abstracted, fixing her eyes on the horizon with such a sad look in their depths that Nellie could have wept for her.

'Matter? Oh Nell, you're as dear to me as any sister, but I didn't want to put more worries on you with your time so near. I've not told Mam or Da, but there's been another of those wretched letters from the War Office; Dickie's ship, the *Linda Blanche*, has been blown up by an enemy submarine and Dickie is posted as missing.' Bethan sniffed and wiped her eyes, which were brimming with tears, with the heels of both hands. 'You never knew him, love, but Dickie was the gentlest of creatures, he would not hurt a soul. It pains me to think of his death but we mustn't tell the old people, promise me?'

'I never would. The truth is, they may never need to know,' Nellie said gently. 'Mother is very poorly, isn't she, Bethan?'

'Yes, she is. And Dickie couldn't write, so they won't expect a letter from him. Oh, Nell, what a wicked world this is!'

That evening, Bethan brought out a photograph of Dickie and Davy just before they went away. Davy looked heartachingly familiar, but the picture showed Dickie as a shy youngster with a diffident look and soft, floppy dark hair, standing down by the harbour screwing his eyes up against the evening sun. He had been eighteen when the photograph was taken but, to Nellie's eyes, he looked considerably younger, and very vulnerable.

'If the baby's a boy, we might call him David Richart, after the boys,' Bethan suggested that night as they climbed wearily into bed. 'Or we could call her Bronwen, after Davy's Mam.'

'You name it,' Nellie mumbled, pushing her head into the softness of her pillow. 'I'd rather you did, honestly.'

'We'll see,' Bethan said, and presently Nellie fell asleep.

She woke in the dark of the night to find white moonlight falling on the bed and a wind getting up so that streaks of cloud hurried across the bland face of the moon.

Bethan was crying. Crying softly but continuously, her shoulders shaking.

Poor Bethan; she's lost so much, Nellie thought, and put her arms round the other girl. She soothed and cuddled and crooned and presently, Bethan's sobs turned to hiccups and then her breathing smoothed out and became deep and even.

Soon, both girls slept.

The baby started at five o'clock on a Saturday evening. Nellie felt the first warning surge in the small of her back as she sat over her tea of herring and fried potatoes and caught Bethan's eye. Bethan gave a gasp.

'The baby ... I think I'm starting, Nell,' Bethan said, quickly reverting to her role as mother-to-be. She turned to her father-in-law and spoke to him in Welsh, presumably saying the same thing. 'Should I get upstairs, now, then?'

'Not yet, girl,' Nellie said, smiling at Bethan's face, in which false anguish and very real excitement mingled rather oddly, she thought. 'We'll get the dishes done and the breakfast laid as usual; won't do you no good to pamper yourself!'

It was ten o'clock before the pains got bad enough to bring sweat out on Nellie's brow, but even then she could not give in. The girls had agreed to keep the old people in ignorance of just how imminent the birth was so that there might be no well-meaning interference.

'The pains have ebbed, so it'll likely be a while yet, Mam,' Bethan shouted to her mother-in-law. She spoke in Welsh but translated for Nellie. 'Nellie will wake you when it's born. You stay snug; this'll be a Sunday night baby I wouldn't be surprised.'

But she delivered Nellie at six the next morning,

hanging the baby by his feet to get the first startled breath into his lungs, then cuddling him against her breast to muffle his strong, indignant shout. The baby turned blindly into her and Bethan held the child towards Nellie, looking down at the weary young mother with a most gentle and loving smile.

'Now haven't you done awful well, then?' she whispered. 'Oh Nellie, love, he's perfect – a good few babies I've seen but never one as perfect as this.'

Nellie smiled back at her and felt the tiredness and the pain and the fear all drain away. Speechlessly, she held out her arms and Bethan, without hesitation, put the baby in them.

'He is beautiful,' Nellie whispered. 'Isn't he the most beautiful thing you ever saw? Ah, look at those tiny hands ... oh Bethan, he's Davy the second!'

Bethan nodded, an expression of blissful devotion already on her face whenever she looked at the child. She had warm water ready and now she poured it into the basin, took the birth-smeared boy and dunked him briskly, lathered him, rinsed, and wrapped him in a clean white shawl. Then she put him into the cradle waiting at the foot of the bed.

'Too soon to feed him it is,' she whispered. 'Can you get out? Supposed to be looking after me, you are!'

And somehow, Nellie managed. Between them they got the meals, saw to the child, weaned him from Nellie's milk onto a bottle. Nellie's breasts ached but Bethan bound them and kept her for three days without the tea she fretted for and Nellie's milk dried up and her son, named David Richart, after his uncle and father, took to the bottle and throve.

He was a grand baby from the start, black-haired and dark-eyed, yet placid as a cow save for when he was hungry. The girls spoiled him, but Nellie never forgot that he was to be Bethan's child and Bethan, though she never spoke of it, never forgot it either. She did all the hardest, dirtiest jobs, scrubbed nappies, dug the garden, laid and lit fires, even carried the baby round the village on her hip no matter how heavy her shopping or laundry.

Richart, as the baby was called, had been born at the end of March. By June, Nellie knew she must leave, or she never would. Bethan sometimes mentioned her going, but mostly she reminded Nellie that the boy would be here waiting for her, that she must visit often – and that Lilac missed her.

'Your family, too,' she said one bright morning, when she was planting early potatoes whilst Nellie nursed the baby and looked on. 'They'll want to know what's happened to you. Will you tell them our story – that you came to find Davy and found me, instead? And that you looked after me whilst I had Davy's son?'

Nellie winced a little but nodded sturdily, with the baby's warm weight close to her breast, a constant reminder of what might have been.

'Yes, I'll tell them. And if they don't quite believe me, that won't be my fault. Bethan … I'm going now; today.'

The words hurt her, even shocked her, but she knew she had made the right decision when she saw the relief in Bethan's dark eyes. Poor girl, she had doubtless wondered how on earth she would get rid of Nellie, if Nellie simply made no move to leave.

'Right now? Oh, Nell!'

Bethan scrambled to her feet and flung earthy arms round Nellie's neck. For a moment they clung in silence, then Bethan took the baby gently and held him close to her own breast.

'You've packed all you need? You're sure? Don't forget, my dear, you'll always be welcome here.'

'I will write,' Nellie said slowly. Her arms felt cold and empty, and there was an ache in her breasts. 'But I don't think I'll come back. I don't think I'd dare ... it's better not. Take care of him. And take care of yourself, too.'

She went back to the cottage and said goodbye to the old man by the fireside and the old woman in the bed upstairs. They had grown fond of Nellie over the months since December and she of them, but she could not speak enough Welsh to tell Father how touched she had been by their warm welcome, though she did her best and Bethan translated her words.

Mother was easier, with her stilted, correct English; she understood Nellie's fumbling for the right words, but reminded her that the gratitude was all on their side; where would they have been, when Bethan's time came, had Nellie not stepped into the breach? And isn't he a fine fellow then and the image of our dear Davy?

'You must find yourself a nice young man, cariad,' Mrs Evans told her in her thin, sprightly voice. 'Good with the babies you are; go you off and get a sweetheart and make babies of your own; you'll never regret it for nothing like children, there is, to warm a woman's heart.'

On the carrier's cart with her small bag beside her, Nellie watched the countryside go by and thought how beautiful it was and how fortunate young Richie was to live here. But she suddenly realised that, for her, the city was what counted. She would never forget Moelfre or the cottage or the people, she would never forget Richart, but in truth the last six months or so had been an episode, a tiny fragment out of another life. Now she was going back to the place she loved, the people she loved. Had she and Davy married they would have lived in the city, he would never have tried to take her off to Moelfre, she was sure of it. She had enjoyed her stay there more than she would have believed possible, but it had been a waiting time, not real life at all. And now she was on her way home, back to reality – Lilac, the Culler, the Scottie Road!

It had been a hot day and the evening promised to be equally airless. Nellie got off the ferry at the pierhead and toiled her way through the sultry streets to the Culler. Rodney Street looked just the same; smart, somehow closed up, but that was because most of the houses belonged to doctors whose surgeries were shut. She reached the asylum and hesitated at the front steps. She should go round the back, but if she did then she would see the kitchen staff before she saw Mrs Ransom and that would never do; the matron had a very definite idea of her own importance. So for the sake of peace, it would have to be the front door.

Nellie climbed the steps and stood on tiptoe on the redded tiles to reach the great brass knocker. Even with her fingers round it she hesitated, feeling the perspiration trickle down between her breasts, whilst a flush burned from her neckline to her forehead. Who would answer? What would their reaction be to Nellie Mc-Dowell, who had fled for no apparent reason, turning up again at five o'clock on a sultry summer's evening and asking for her job back? But if she did not knock she would never find out. Resolutely, she brought the knocker down three times.

'Well, Nellie, we've filled the position. What did you expect us to do? You've been gone near on six months, gairl, and there's a war on. We were lucky to get anyone, the women are off to France to nurse the wounded, giddy as mayflies and about as much use, no doubt. But we've managed despite your behaviour which I don't hesitate to say was disgraceful. In fact I'm surprised you've got the face to stand there and suggest we tek you back.'

Nellie looked across the old-fashioned mahogany table at the fat, creased face and narrowed eyes of her erstwhile employer. She had known Mrs Ransom long enough to realise that the older woman had every intention of taking her back, but wanted her pound of flesh first; she wanted Nellie on her knees, begging, and this Nellie had no intention of doing.

Accordingly, she stood up, bag still in hand, and began to turn towards the door.

'Very well, I'll leave. I'm sorry to have troubled you,' she said formally, keeping her voice firm and steady. 'As you say, it won't be difficult for me to find work the way things are at the moment; indeed, I might go off to France meself, I'd like to help with the war effort.'

'Ah now, I didn't say as we wouldn't use you,' Mrs Ransom said hastily. 'For old times' sake ... you are a Culler girl, after all. Then there's Lilac ... '

Despite her resolve not to make things easy for Mrs Ransom, Nellie hesitated. She turned back.

'How is Lilac? I missed her, but my duty was with my cousin.'

Mrs Ransom let the disbelief linger in her eyes whilst they scanned Nellie's slim figure searchingly, making it plain that she believed Nellie to be no better than she should be, that she thought the cousin just an excuse for Nellie to go off, possibly with a young man. And she wasn't all that wrong, either, Nellie remembered ruefully, but she kept her expression innocent, her eyes unguarded.

'Well, Mrs Ransom? How is Lilac?'

'Well enough. She'll be glad to see you. We heard nothing but Nellie, Nellie, Nellie for days – weeks – after you went.'

'Then I'll go through, if I may, to the playroom. She'll be there?'

'Well, we can't have ... you won't have your own room, but if you'd care to share ... '

Lilac was rolling bandages in the playroom with a dozen other girls her own age when the door opened. She had no inkling of who stood outside yet her eyes flew to the door and suddenly she was on her feet, across the room in a couple of bounds, and in Nellie's arms.

'Nellie, Nellie, Nellie! Oh, where've you been, oh I do love you ... I worried and worried ... oh Nellie, hold me tight!'

'You've grown,' Nellie said presently, putting Lilac back from her and smiling her dear, familiar smile. 'You're quite the young lady now! Matron tells me you never got my letter.'

'No, we got nothing. Oh Nell, where've you *been*? Don't ever go away from me again, I'll always be good, I'll never be unkind or thoughtless to you again! Did you go to find Davy, Nell? Was he all right?'

Above her, she saw Nellie's eyes turn sad, her smile fade. She knew, then, that Davy was not all right, that Nellie had not abandoned her to enjoy her own life but had been dragged away.

'No, queen. Davy was killed. I was with ... with his mother and father, taking care of them. I've told everyone else that I was with me cousin, but you'll have guessed the truth. I stayed until someone else came who could take over, then I come home.'

'Oh, poor Nellie,' Lilac said. She hugged her friend tightly, then made a discovery. 'Nellie, there's more of you!'

'Country living,' Nellie said briefly. She pulled away. 'You'd best get on with them bandages; there is a war on, you know.'

'Where are you going?' Lilac said suspiciously. 'I'll come with you … I'll bring the bandages, keep on working.'

Nellie laughed but held out her hand.

'All right. I've not got much stuff, but what I have got I'm going to unpack. Mrs R says me uniforms are still in the chest of drawers, the new girl's too big for 'em it seems, so I'll get meself changed and then I'll supervise washing and bed.'

She was as good as her word, but although Lilac clung close, could not take her eyes off Nellie, kept touching her, taking her hand, hugging her, she was aware that Nellie had changed in some deep and subtle manner which perhaps would be obvious only to those who loved her. She seemed taller and more substantial, but that would just be because Lilac had not seen her for so long. No, the change which counted was a change which went deeper, and hard though she tried Lilac could not put her finger on it. By next day though, she felt she had an inkling. It was as though a layer of lightness and laughter had been peeled off Nellie's personality, leaving the serious side of Nellie nearer the surface than it had been before. And she sensed not only seriousness but a remoteness, a slight chill, which was not at all like the Nellie she knew and loved.

But it did not worry her, because Nellie had come home again, and that was all that mattered to Lilac.

Nellie put up with the Culler for a month and then, after a visit to Coronation Court, she took Lilac to one side.

'I can't stick it, not after having had me freedom for a bit,' she said frankly. 'Too many rules, chuck, too much silliness. Mustn't talk in our rooms at night – why not, for heaven's sake? Me and Clara,' – Clara was the new girl – 'we're young women, not kids, so why shouldn't we have a word after a long day's work? And no lights allowed after eight – it's all right now, with the light evenings, but there'll be a time when I need a light to finish me work and then old Ranny will start laying the law down. And why mayn't we sing in the kitchen? Daft, that's what, to make up silly laws and try to see grown women stick by 'em. And then there's the food: you're gettin' cheap rubbish and it's no use old Ranny saying about rationing; it's just an excuse not to feed everyone decent. The old cook would have had a seizure if she'd seen what that poor woman downstairs is given to feed a hundred kids. What's more there's too many of you kids to one class, now that so many teachers have gone. You can't learn proper when you're in class with five-and six-year-olds, to say nothing of the older girls.'

'Well, Mrs Ransom says we have to put up with the food situation for the sake of our brave lads, and she says the teachers have gone to the war, so we shouldn't grumble about big classes, either,' Lilac pointed out rather self-righteously. She had mourned the tiny helpings of food and the cumbersome classes herself, but had accepted the explanation. And fancy Nellie called the matron old Ranny, like the kids did! But Nellie shook her head.

'No, luv. I dunno where the money goes which used to pay the teachers and buy sufficient food, but it isn't to the tommies. Reckon Mrs R. is feathering her nest; reckon she always did, only I never noticed before. We're off, you and me.'

'Where to?' Lilac asked excitedly. It was clear from her face that she would go anywhere with Nellie, no question.

'That's what I've brought you out here to tell you.' It was evening, and the two girls were walking along beside the docks in the reddening sunshine. 'Poor Bessie's lost without Charlie, she's that lonely, and she never was much good as a manager, and now she's got two little kids to rear. She's moved back into the court, she was sharing with Aunt Ada and Uncle Billy, but now he's gone to his rest, poor soul, she says why don't you and me move in with 'em?'

'Oh Nellie, I'd love it; I could go to school with Ethel and Art and we could play out, of an evening. But what'll old Ranny say? And what would you do, Nellie? You couldn't come back here to work or we might as well not leave.'

'Course not. I'm going to work at the hospital, learnin' to be a nurse. They need girls real badly now and I've always wanted to nurse, 'cos I like looking after folk. And I told Bessie you'd give a hand with the littl'uns and help Aunt Ada about the house when you weren't at school. So we'll give it a go, shall us?'

Lilac was doubtful, for she knew how useful Nellie was and guessed that Mrs Ransom would be reluctant to back down and let the pair of them leave, so Nellie might have been out of luck save for one thing; she had always been a favourite with Mr Hayman. Consequently, when she told Mrs Ransom that there should be more food available and more money to buy ingredients, Mrs Ransom felt obliged to listen.

'I want Lilac to learn to cook properly,' Nellie said. 'Not just how to make one herring feed six. And I want her to get a bit more attention in class, too. She's bright, but she's being held back now because she's in a class with the littl'uns. If we join the rest of my family in Coronation Court then she'll get a fair crack of the whip.'

'And if I say no?' Mrs Ransom said coldly; she paid Nellie a pittance and had no desire to lose her star pupil, Nellie could see it in her mean little eyes. But Nellie had the measure of her.

'If you say no then I'll go straight to Mr Hayman,' she said calmly. 'I suppose I ought to go anyway, but ... '

Mrs Ransom stared viciously at her for an unnerving sixty seconds, then, when Nellie's gaze never faltered, turned away, speaking over her shoulder as though she simply had no more time to argue.

'Very well. Leave at the end of the week and take the child. I'll find a reason which will satisfy the Board.' She turned back, almost smiling, as though at the last minute she was anxious not to give Nellie any reason for carrying out her unspoken threat. 'And Lilac is bright, I'll give you that.'

She was. Nellie realised that Lilac was bright enough to have her suspicions about the changes in Nellie, but not yet bright enough to understand that the person who had left her for six long months had been a girl, and the person who had returned was a woman. A woman who had lost her man and borne a child, and lost him, too.

So when the week's notice was up Nellie packed – two bags this time – the girls said their farewells, and they set off for Coronation Court.

Lilac should have hated Aunt Ada's untidy, over-crowded house after the relatively sheltered life of the asylum, but in fact she revelled in it. When they arrived the heat of the summer was at its height and she and Nellie slept in the raw, with the window of their small room wide to catch every passing breeze, but even so the smells coming in from the dustbins and from the other houses were ripe and sickening. Lilac had to work hard, too, because with Nellie off to the hospital to work, Bessie and Aunt Ada tended to call on her for most things. Looking after Bessie's little ones, Henry and Nathan, and giving an eye to Bessie's tiny new baby, Millie Miranda, took up a good deal of time, and learning to cook with Aunt Ada and to sew with Mrs Billings down on the Scotland Road took up the rest. Nellie was grimly determined that no one was ever going to reproach her for taking Lilac away from the Culler, so life became a series of lessons for Lilac.

Not that Lilac resented this, because she did not. The way out and up is through education, Nellie told her severely. Polish up your writing so it's clear and neat, keep practising reading until you can manage even the biggest words in the papers and you're on the right road.

She didn't say where the right road led, but Lilac saw that she meant it led to a better life and that suited her just fine. Months ago, when Nellie had first left her, she had decided to be rich one day. To marry well, to have a spanking red motor car, a large house with lots of servants, and a steam yacht. And being an intelligent child, she used her eyes whenever she went out and ticked off in her own mind what she most wanted from life. She saw, too, that a good many people, who must want these things as well, somehow managed to fall by the wayside, for Liverpool contained a great many very rich people as well as numberless poor ones. So you had two choices, to stay down or go up, and she agreed with Nellie that up was best, and if you had to be good at things to go up then good at things she would be.

But she realised, too, that being very pretty indeed would help her. Already there were children at the Penrhyn Street School, which she attended with other girls from the area, who were using their looks to better themselves, or at least to make money. One of the girls, Doris, who was the same age as Lilac, would go behind the high brick wall with really big boys, for a ha'penny. And Maybelle, even prettier and only a year or so older, spent a lot of time cruising up and down the docks, earning money from the soldiers and sailors she met there. Lilac was not sure what she did to earn the money, but Maybelle assured her that being pretty meant you did better than a penny a go, and a penny a go seemed riches to Lilac.

When she tried to get Nellie's opinion of these means of bettering oneself however, Nellie said firmly that Doris and Maybelle were bad girls and that she, Lilac, would do things properly and come off better than all of them in the end.

To make sure of this, Nellie paid for private mathematics lessons for both of them. Because Art had been a good friend to Lilac since Charlie's wedding, and now helped her with her work as well as keeping an eye on her out of doors, Nellie prevailed upon the tutor, a pale young man called Claud Norton who suffered from asthma and terrible acne, to let Art attend the lessons too. And Claud was happy with the arrangement, especially since Art turned out to be a mathematical genius, so that their sessions, Claud said, were the most rewarding ones he taught.

And Lilac made friends, lots of them, and brought them home to the court to play in the relatively safe area within the walls. It might be smelly in summer and icy in winter, but at least the courts were not through ways, so there was little traffic, either on wheels or afoot, which meant the children were safer than on the open streets.

What was more, in Coronation Court Lilac saw and recognised not only poverty but quite often, the cause. Because of the war there was less unemployment, but some men and women still drank to excess, hit each other, beat their children, ruined their own lives and the lives of those around them. There was fecklessness, too: women who had never been taught to market frugally, eke out a little meat with a lot of vegetables, cook cakes and make soup instead of buying them. Such women were spent up by mid-week so their children went hungry three days out of the seven, and all for the want of management. Some men were just as bad; they would spend their spare time in the pub or lying in bed instead of finding another means of making a few pence. They bought new boots and chucked out the old because they were too idle to mend the soles, they spent a couple of day's wages on impressing their mates instead of putting the money into the teapot on the mantel.

Nellie had a lot of small boxes into which she and Lilac put spare money. Some for clothing, some for shoes, some for Christmas and birthdays, some for trips and treats. Her friend Annie's mum, working in the munitions factory in Cazneau Street, earning good money for the first time in her life, might laugh at them as she spent, spent, spent, but Mrs O'Grady wouldn't be going to the theatre come Christmas or to the seaside next July. The posh coat she'd bought from Cheap

Jack's down the Scottie would be in pieces in a twelve-month whilst a coat of good material, lovingly altered by Nellie, would be outgrown but never outworn.

So Lilac was learning – faster perhaps than even she knew. And enjoying every moment of it.

As for Nellie, she too was learning, for she found that, having managed to numb the pain of losing Davy and parting from her son, she had somehow numbed her capacity to feel other, gentler emotions. She loved Lilac but no longer agonised over her and could only feel vaguely sorry for Aunt Ada's loss, though she knew that Aunt Ada missed her family badly. For they had all gone now, the young people as well as poor, crippled Uncle Billy. Bertie had gone for a soldier and so had Matt and Fred, though they were strictly speaking under age still. They all wrote home, their letters which had once been full of hope and excitement now reflecting only homesickness and a longing to leave the horrors behind them and return to Merseyside once again. Hal was at sea, on HMS *Laurentic*; she was a troop carrier for the Canadian Expeditionary Force, beating across the Atlantic and docking in Liverpool every couple of months. Hal did get home therefore, but seldom came back to the court for more than a word or two when he was home on leave. He had married to spite his family as the saying goes, a blowsy, feckless girl called Liza. Bessie said Liza was no better than she should be and besides, she never washed, but Hal seemed happy enough. Charlie was in France, Jessie was making parts for ship's telegraphs in Birkenhead and Lou had joined the Women's Forces and was stationed in Calais where she worked with the Army Service Corps.

So Nellie's new job, as a trainee nurse in one of the many hospitals springing up all over the city, was a great help to her, taking her mind off her own worries, making them seem as trivial as, in fact, they were. She was soon a valued member of the ward, the nurses realising she was keen and intelligent. She worked long hours and never grumbled, never took her mind off her job, went home to work again on Lilac's reading and writing, knitted gloves and socks for the troops, was always to be found doing the dirtiest jobs with the least fuss.

And it brought its own reward, as so often happens. Nellie, numbed with tiredness, seeing that no matter how she might suffer others suffered infinitely more, hardly ever thought of Davy. And if, sometimes, she woke and lay with her eyes closed and imagined that behind her lids was a light and airy room with a long, low window, that outside the window there shone the silver sea, the black, fanged rocks, the bite of grey shingle, if there was a small figure paddling in that sea, digging in that shingle, then she never let it make her unhappy. The baby was Bethan's ... he would be six months now, eight months, a year, more. Sitting up, crawling, staggering uncertainly to his feet ... walking, talking! Calling Bethan mam, and the old folk nain and taid.

But it was a dream, another life, nothing to do with Nellie McDowell, who scraped her hair into a bun and scrubbed up and then went through to the wards to help the overstretched nurses with the dressings, carting the dirty stuff away in buckets, wheeling in the tea-trolley, always smiling determinedly, pushing her own worries into the background, always happy, the tommies said approvingly. They did not – could not – know that this Nellie was just a hollow shell, stumbling through life somehow, waiting for her wounds to heal even as they waited to be made whole again.

And in the meantime she loved her work and made friends, in particular Lucy Bignold, who had married her sweetheart in September 1914 and been widowed only two months later. Lucy worked hard too, but everyone knew why she threw herself into nursing. No one knew about Nellie's loss, yet she and Lucy seemed drawn to one another and grew close. Both, Nellie reflected, needed to forget the past, to turn over the book of life and start work on the new page. So she too threw herself whole-heartedly into her work and began, at last, to forget.

But she was still not happy. In the back of her mind was the ache of her loss; first Davy, then the child. She was so alone. Lilac was a comfort, she was her beloved daughter, yet she was not a part of Nellie, not flesh of her flesh, and she was too young and self-centred to enter fully into Nellie's feelings – indeed, she was too young to confide in. Besides, one day she'll marry and go and I'll be alone again, Nellie thought sometimes as she scrubbed floors and burned dressings and helped the nurses to move an injured man from his back to his front or from his front to his side. Oh I wish I could fall in love like all the other girls do!

But it was as though, within her, some young and vital part had been frozen into numbness by Davy and the baby. She did her work with enthusiasm, but at home she seemed to lack the zest which had at one time characterised everything she did. She wrote to Bethan and got notes in reply reassuring her that the child was well and happy. She taught Lilac to cook and to keep house and went with Aunt Ada to put flowers on Uncle Billy's grave. She knitted for the troops and for Charlie's littl'uns.

And then, one cold day in January, she went onto

the ward to find a new intake had been brought in during the night.

Lucy, bustling into the changing room, waved to her as she changed into uniform, and then came across as Nellie was struggling to tie her white apron strings behind her.

'Here, let me do that. The new patients are part of the crew of the *Laurentic*; she was torpedoed a couple of nights ago, in the Channel,' Lucy said briefly, tying the strings of Nellie's apron and straightening her frilled collar.

'The *Laurentic*? Oh dear God, my brother Hal's aboard her – Lucy, is he here?'

'My dear, I'm so sorry, I didn't know. You'd best go straight to Matron and ask. There were a lot of casualties, some of them in bad shape, so some may be on other wards. Go on, I'll explain to Sister.'

Nellie hurried off and found Matron, rushed off her feet because of the number of injured – the *Laurentic* had been a troop carrier – but still sympathetic and as helpful as she could be.

'My dear child, how dreadful for you,' she said, patting Nellie's hand. 'I'll check my lists.'

To Nellie's bursting relief Hal had been in the hospital, though not on Ward Five, where she nursed. He had minor injuries and had been discharged in the early hours of the morning.

With that worry off her mind, Nellie returned to her own ward, but because the wounded were all sailors instead of the more usual soldiers, she found herself thinking about Davy all over again. One man had been so badly burned that they did not think he would survive and she knelt by his bed trying to get him to suck weak tea through a feeder, until she was called by Sister to take the tea-trolley round.

'Some of these boys are in bad shape, so it's been a busy night and you'll be rushed off your feet today,' Sister said. 'I expect Matron told you that our tommies have been moved into Ward Seven, because these chaps need pretty intensive nursing. There are exposure cases, and burns ... all sorts.'

'Were many killed?' Nellie asked sadly. 'It seems so wrong to be glad that my brother was saved when so many are in such pain.'

'I don't know,' Sister said guardedly. 'They don't tell us things like that. Take the tea round now, there's a good girl. The dressings-round will take time today, so we might as well get on as fast as we can.'

Nellie walked down the ward, pushing the tea-trolley. Tired eyes followed her, save for those who still slept. The ward was a big one with thirty beds, not an officers' ward but one for other ranks. Today, though, there would be all sorts, she realised that. She began to hand out cups of tea, trying to keep her eyes on the man she was serving, not to let her gaze wander further down the ward. Some of these men would be Hal's friends, she realised suddenly, and that might mean they would have known Davy, too – might even have sailed with him. Because at the outbreak of war Davy and Hal had shipped together, on the ill-fated *Milligan*, though – thank God – Hal had changed ships before the sinking of the frigate.

She approached the next row of beds, wondering whether she might make it known that she was interested in anyone who had known Davy Evans – and stopped short. A man was staring at her from under a bandage which hid all his hair and most of his forehead. One arm was plastered and he had a chest wound which had been treated and dressed. She could see a bright, dark eye, bloodshot and puffy, a nose with a gash across the bridge, a black beard…

She knew him without a second's doubt. She gasped out his name, her heart beating so hard that it threatened to leap from her breast.

'Davy! My God! But you were reported missing more than two years ago, oh my dearest, I thought… we thought…'

She was on her knees by the bed, holding his uninjured hand, such a variety of emotions pounding through her that she could not have given a name to any, save that of a sense of incredulous relief which ran like a flame through her mind.

'Nell! My dearest girl!' He spoke stiffly, and she saw he had lost two of his strong white teeth, that his lower lip was deeply cut. Her heart bled for him, all his faults were as nought, the deceit, her pain, what did they matter now that Davy was safe?

'Do they know …at home?' Suddenly, common sense returned with a rush. She stood up, releasing his hand, albeit reluctantly. 'Oh Davy… I'll get you tea. You'd best have milk and sugar, you'll need building up I daresay.'

He laughed but when she held out the cup he shook his head, the one eye dancing in a way she remembered well.

'You'll have to help me; I can't change my position for this accursed bandaging.'

She knelt by the bed again, holding the cup to his lips. He sipped, then turned his head slightly.

'You won't know, of course, but Nellie, I'm a married man, father of a little son. My wife's a dear girl, takes the best possible care of my parents … and of our little Richart. I'm sorry I never got in touch, but I knew you'd been told I was missing believed dead and I thought it best... ' he touched her hand, a tentative movement. 'I loved you, Nellie, that's God's truth, but when I found I had a son... '

She looked at him. A tissue of lies? Half-truths? She would never know just exactly what had happened, what Davy had been told, but what did it matter, after all? She had wanted Davy's rightful wife to have the child she longed for, had that changed just because Davy was alive? Of course it hadn't, but it seemed...oh, cruelly unfair! Bethan had it all, Davy, the baby...

'Nell? Say you understand! Say you don't hate me for it! I loved you, in my way I love you still, but I had to choose, see? And if you could see our lad ... just like me he is, dark, laughing... oh, you'd love him, you'd forgive me! Bethan – that's my wife's name – she said you'd got in touch after the *Milligan* went down, and somehow when I returned it seemed kinder just to let things lie. She didn't realise that you and I had...had anything between us, of course; and I've not told her. I would have, if it hadn't been for the boy – and Bethan is very dear to me. I'm sorry, cariad, that you had to find out this way ... but surely you've a sweetheart yourself by now, Nellie? You're far too pretty to be all alone, I bet every fellow in this hospital would give his eye-teeth just for a smile. What's his name?'

'His name?' She pinned a coy smile on her lips, shaking her head at him. 'None of your business, Davy Evans, and you a married man! Yes, I've a sweetheart, he's...he's in France. His name's...Matthew.'

She said the words almost fiercely, making him a present of guiltlessness, cutting herself free of him in the doing, though she was only aware of it later, in her own bed. She finished giving him the tea, put the cup

145

back on the trolley, continued with her round. She worked hard all day, she dressed his chest wound and looked at his chart; one eye would never see again but the other was uninjured. He would be on the ward for a few weeks, then home to convalesce, then back to another ship.

It hurt her that Bethan had never told her the truth, though, had deliberately let her go on believing that Davy was dead, so she talked to him one afternoon, asking him just when he had got in touch with his wife and put her out of her misery.

He told her how it had happened. He had been picked up by an enemy ship and had ended up in a prisoner of war camp. He had written to his wife but she had never received the letter, and then his captors had decided, since he was a countryman, to let him work on the land. He had escaped and made his way home, arriving only six months before.

'Of course Bethan was stunned; for weeks she cried every time she set eyes on me, but it was joy, see? She's settled down now, though. She used to have her suspicions about me – and they were true, Nell, as you know – but no more. We're a family now, the three of us, and Bethan's goin' to have another one, so soon we'll be four. So pleased, she is! Oh, but I wish you could see Richie, Nell! He's the image of me, but far prettier, my Mam says.'

So Bethan had not known, not whilst Nellie had been on the island. That was a comfort. And when Bethan had known, she had not told. But what would have been the point? Only more pain for all of them. Better let it lie, better pretend that there had been no baby, no friendship between her and Davy Evans' wife. As for the new baby, she could never grudge Bethan the child of her own she had longed for, and she knew the older girl well enough to know that Richie would never suffer, never know he was not Bethan's own flesh and blood.

'And does Bethan know you're here, in hospital? You'd best let her know you're alive, because the sinking of the *Laurentic* will be reported in all the newspapers, she's bound to read it.'

He looked smug. She could see how he had changed, matured. Had the war done it, or fatherhood? Not that it mattered, he was a different man as she, she realised suddenly, was a different girl. Now she could turn away, now she could begin to write on that clean, white page!

'That was the first thing I did; I got one of the night-nurses to telegraph. What's more, she'll come to me as soon as she knows, so with a bit of luck you'll meet her ... she might even bring Richie!'

Nellie smiled, murmured something conventional, moved away from the bed, but inside she was in a turmoil. She did not want to see Bethan with Davy and she dared not see Richie at all. She finished her duties in a dither of apprehension – what should she do? Where could she go? And that evening, when she and Lucy were walking down to the tram-stop, the solution presented itself.

It was a cold, crisp evening, the pavements covered with a light fall of snow so that the two girls had to watch where they trod. Lucy lived in a smart part of the city but they caught the same tram though Lucy stayed aboard longer than Nellie. The tram rattled up, full to bursting already, and on an impulse Nellie told Lucy that she would not get aboard since she felt a walk would do her good. After a moment's hesitation Lucy, too, stepped back.

'We'll walk together,' she said. 'There's something

I've been meaning to talk to you about all day, this will be my first real chance.'

'We've been awful busy,' Nellie owned, pushing her woolly mittened hand into the crook of Lucy's elbow. 'Go on, fire ahead.'

For answer, Lucy pulled a crumpled sheet of newsprint out of the pocket of her grey coat.

'Read that,' she commanded.

It was an advertisement for nurses and VAD's, needed in France in the front-line hospitals so that they might be trained up in the hospital's ways before the spring offensive started.

Nellie read it, then pulled Lucy to a standstill, staring at her friend with bright eyes. It looked like the perfect solution, the escape she so desperately needed.

'Lu ... are you going? Can I go, too?'

'Oh, Nell, if only you would! Sometimes I want to get away so badly ... from John's parents, from my own, even from Liverpool, because that was where we were happy. Nell, it's been two years, two and a half, and the time has come for me to forget. It'll be easier away from here. But what about Lilac? And Bessie, and Aunt Ada? How would they manage if you came to France?'

'They'd manage,' Nell said. 'Look, Lu, there's something I've never told another living soul ... '

And walking through the frosty darkness, with the stars twinkling overhead and the salt breeze off the Mersey touching their chilly cheeks, Nellie told Lucy everything, about Davy, Moelfre, Bethan and the baby. And about her own inability to shake free of them, her inability to want to do so, until this moment.

'Now that I've seen Davy again, seen him as a husband and a father, I know that the last link between us is broken and I want to have space to discover what Nellie McDowell is really like,' she said. 'I'm awful sorry to leave our Lilac a second time, but she's got a life of her own which she enjoys and one of these days she'll leave me; it's what happens. I'll find a way to explain that she'll understand ... and I shan't have to face seeing Bethan with Davy, and meeting the child again. How soon can we go?'

'We're due a week's leave, probably more, from the hospital here,' Lucy said. 'We can ship to France a week after that. Look, we're both on earlies tomorrow, if you decide to go through with it ... '

'I shall,' Nellie said firmly. 'I've never been more sure of anything in my life.'

She said nothing to Davy; a small revenge, but a sweet one. He might wonder where she was, what she was doing, but it would be difficult for him to question the other nurses without giving the game away, and that he would be reluctant to do, particularly if Bethan and the boy came. He had known that Nellie believed him dead, after all, and had been happy enough to let her go on believing. Less trouble for everyone, he had said. Ha! For her it had been months – no, years – of heartache. But that was over, behind her, now she was looking forward, not backward.

She had expected telling Lilac to be hard, but the child had made it easy for her. She was eleven now, quite a little woman, she understood that nurses were needed at the Front and applauded Nellie's decision to go to France.

'Everyone in school has brothers fighting or sisters over there,' she said, with a child's eye view of war. 'I shall miss you terribly, dearest Nell, but I'm ever so proud of you. I'll write twice a week and send you sweeties ... you've done things like that for me all my life, now I'll do it for you.'

Nellie did not kid herself that Lilac's self-sacrifice was all that deep. The child worked hard and played hard, she would miss Nellie, but not nearly as much as she had missed her when she was at the Culler. Aunt Ada adored Lilac, Bessie trusted her and treated her like an equal, which, intellectually at least, was no more than her due. Art alternately bossed and adored her, the littl'uns thought her wonderful. Nellie knew that despite the red-gold curls and blue eyes, Lilac Larkin was a tough little nut and competent beyond her years. The streak of selfishness which Nellie had once recognised with such dismay was still there, though it was manageable now, less headstrong. Lilac would go for what she wanted and she'd get it, but she wouldn't trample others underfoot in the doing, Nellie told herself. Nevertheless, when she and Lucy got on board the ship that was to take them to France she waved to the small, rapidly diminishing figures of Aunt Ada, Bessie and Lilac, and wondered if she had done right. After all, there was no denying that she was leaving Lilac for the second time in the child's eleven years. It did not seem fair, somehow, that Nellie's new start should mean that Lilac suffered. But I simply have to get away, else I'll never find myself, she thought, and there's others beside our Lilac to be thought of; young fellers who need my help even more than she does. Besides, I'm not so swollen-headed as to believe that Lilac will be lost without me. She'll do very well, she'll probably be glad to have one less person to boss her around. In fact she might well feel she's better off.

So Nellie went below and she and Lucy sorted out

their belongings and then got into their bunks, and Nellie told herself over again that Lilac would have a wonderful time whilst she herself was working to help the injured in France.

It helped to ease the niggle of guilt, if not to erase it.

Chapter Seven

1917

The hospital had started life as a sizeable chateau, then when the wounded began to come in and the accommodation was insufficient, bell-tents were erected for the nurses' quarters. Huts were built to make more wards, more and larger tents arrived and by the time Nellie and Lucy reached the place it was as large if not larger than the hospital they had left.

'We're nursing more frostbite, pneumonia and trench-foot than wounds right now,' Sister Angus told Nellie and Lucy when they arrived on their ward that first morning. 'I don't have to tell you that nursing illnesses caused by extreme cold, in a draughty tent, isn't ideal, but all I can say is we do our best. They've promised us more huts as soon as they can be built, but until then we on Ward Twelve must do the best we can in the tent. You'll be on days for a couple of months at least, so I'll get Platt to take you round and introduce you to your patients. This is an officers' ward, you'll find the men intelligent and helpful, but you've both been nursing in Blighty so you'll understand all that. If you need anything or don't understand something, feel free to come to me at any time. My bunk is at the end of the ward, if I'm not visible I'll be in there, catching up with the paperwork.'

'I like her; I think we're very lucky,' Lucy said as she and Nellie got the steriliser going a couple of hours later and began to boil bedpans and bedbottles. 'Imagine if she was some old battleaxe! It would be hard on the patients as well as us, but you can see the men like her, and find her sympathetic.'

Sister Angus was a slender woman in her early thirties with dark red hair and a faint Scottish accent. She smiled a lot, revealing a deep dimple in her right cheek, and although she made it clear that both 'new girls' would be expected to pull their weight, she made it equally clear that she did not expect miracles of them.

'You get a half-day off each week and a full day once a month,' she said cheerfully. 'When we're rushed off our feet – which means when the spring offensive starts – I'm afraid time off rather goes by the board, but if possible you'll get what's due to you. As for leaves, it's supposed to be a week in Blighty every six months, but that's rarely possible. Most of my girls go home yearly, however – not that you'll be interested in going back to Blighty yet, I daresay!'

'Definitely not,' Nellie said firmly. 'We've only just arrived. Someone said you settle in to a strange place better if you don't have leaves for a while.'

'That's true, I believe. And you know the rules, of course – no fraternising with the men outside the premises ... no fraternising with them *on* the premises either, but for some reason it really irritates the authorities to see nurses and officers walking round the town together.'

'I shan't want to walk with anyone,' Nellie said at once. 'We've come out here to work, haven't we, Bignold?'

'Yes, of course,' Lucy said, shooting a startled glance at Nellie. 'But I suppose there is some recreation, isn't there, Sister? No one can work *all* the time.'

'That's true, and of course there are various things for you to do when you aren't on duty. You'll find out all about it when you get to know the other nurses;

there are twenty-eight of you sharing that big sleeping tent so I daresay it won't be long before you're fully in the picture. Now, back to your duties; we're still doing a dressings-round, though as I said the majority of the men aren't suffering from wounds, but the ones right at the end of the ward are all trench-foot victims. They have to have their feet massaged with warm olive oil every morning and evening, then they're wrapped in cottonwool and oiled silk, with big fishermen's socks over that. Have you nursed trench-foot?'

'We've nursed frostbite and pneumonia and bronchitis, but not trench-foot,' Lucy said. 'But we'll soon pick it up, Sister.'

And they did. Nellie particularly enjoyed nursing trench-foot because if the condition didn't clear then the boys were Blighty-bound and if it did, if one day when you pinched or prodded the patient felt what you were doing, if you saw a tiny little pink flush begin to appear, then very likely his feet would be saved and he would be able to walk again.

It was harder work than nursing in England however, partly because there was no respite. No going home for an evening with your family, no chatting with the conductor on the 'leckie' as you went to and from the hospital, no stretching out your toes towards a real fire as you relaxed over hot soup and new-baked bread. There was rationing in England all right and Nellie's sweeties had always been saved up for Lilac, but here it was the monotony as much as anything else which got you. And although the kitchen staff did their best it was a bit of luck if you got your hot meal when you came off shift, and the food was not inspiring, either. The choice, the nurses said sarcastically, was between stewed tea or stewed bully beef – provided you wanted one or the other you would not be disappointed.

Nellie had always been slim but she got slimmer, though it was a healthy sort of slenderness. Nurses were expected to move quickly and she became adept at the gliding walk which was as fast as a run without actually being one, adept, too, at always finishing her work, however arduous, on time so that the staff coming on duty could take over with the minimum of effort.

The patients made it all worthwhile, though, because they were so touchingly appreciative of the efforts of the girls who nursed them. The girls ordered them about, heaved them up and down in bed, teased them, gave them nicknames and perhaps they even loved them a little bit. Certainly the young men frequently imagined themselves in love with dark-haired Lucy, dimpled Sarah, sweet-faced Nellie. But, Sister said wisely, it would not last. They would go back home and in the comfortable ordinariness of their lives they would soon forget the 'angels' who had been so good to them when they desperately needed help.

One bright but chilly afternoon a month after their arrival, when both Lucy and Nellie had a few hours off, they decided to walk into the hills behind the hospital. They needed some time to themselves, a complete change, a breath of fresh air in every sense of the words. They borrowed scarves and extra stockings and put on their stout rubber boots and set off, with quite a sense of adventure, for after all, this was abroad, though one tended to forget it in the very English atmosphere which prevailed at the hospital.

'I keep hoping that Officer Baby will have a visit from his Mama,' Lucy said as they crunched up the snowy lane which led to the open countryside. 'He's crippled with rheumatism, he's lost the toes on his right foot from frostbite, yet he never complains, he's always got a joke and a grin for us. And he's only seventeen.'

'Twenty according to his papers,' Nellie reminded her. 'Who spilt the beans about his age, anyway?'

'The fellow in the next bed; they were at school together, apparently, only Jameson was two years ahead of Officer Baby, and of course when he came onto the ward he couldn't resist telling Nurse Symonds and she spread the word. I'm not sure who it was tied the baby's feeding bottle to the foot of his bed, where everyone coming up the ward could see it, nor who found that old teddy bear, but the chaps thought it awfully funny, and it's good for them to laugh. Poor Officer Baby, though, it took him weeks to live it down!'

'He hasn't lived it down yet,' Nellie said, chuckling. 'What makes you think his Mama might visit him, anyway?'

'She wrote to Sister and said she would come over as soon as she could, but the weather's been so bad. And Sister won't say a word, just in case ... but she hopes his Mama might take him home with her, see if she can do something about the rheumatism before it's too late. Dear God, the men who keep youngsters like Officer Baby in freezing cold, flooded trenches for forty-eight hours at a stretch in this sort of weather ought to be shot! What on earth is the point of it all? The Germans won't take the wretched trenches, they don't want them! Oh Nell, I hate this war!'

'It makes you realise that if women ran the world how very different things would be,' Nellie agreed. 'Only ... well, think of Sister Andrews!'

Sister Andrews was the sort of nurse that the younger girls all dreaded, a martinet intent on the appearance of her ward being perfect, which led to an almost unbelievable indifference to the comfort and well-being of her patients. In the name of tidiness she would wake a weak man who had just fallen into his first sleep for a week in order to straighten his sheets or change his pillowslips. She would dismiss a nurse from the ward to 'go and change at once!' in the middle of a dressing-round should the nurse in question get a spot of blood on her apron. She would allow a member of staff to serve the men with cups of tea and would then find the girls work to do so that they were unable to assist patients who could not drink unaided until the tea was long cold.

'She's the exception that proves the rule,' Lucy admitted. 'If she ruled the world ... well, it wouldn't be our sort of world at all. I say, look ... what's that?'

To their left a long slope ended in a leafless hedge and in its shelter crouched a small, white animal. Even as they watched it apparently decided they were harmless and came towards them, then stopped and sat up, long ears pricked, eyes bulging with curiosity.

'A white rabbit, just like the one in *Alice*! No, it can't be, white rabbits are tame and you wouldn't get a tame rabbit right out here. Oh look at him, sitting up and staring at us – isn't he sweet?'

'He'd make a delicious pie,' Lucy said wistfully. She did not care for bully-beef. 'But of course it's a rabbit, I remember reading somewhere that they change their coats when it snows, or they do in some countries, anyway. Look, there's another!'

'Oh, aren't they nice? I wish our Lilac could see 'em,' Nellie said wistfully. 'Kids oughter live in the country-side, don't you reckon, Lucy?'

Lucy was replying when a deep young voice behind Nellie said jubilantly, 'If dat isn't a scouse accent I'll eat me 'at! Hello, gairls, meet a feller as comes all de way from Mairseyside, just like the pur of yez does!'

Nellie turned sharply, unable to stop her heart giving a jump of pleasure at the sound of the voice. She thought she had largely succeeded in losing her Liverpudlian accent but clearly to another scouser it stood out like a sore thumb and she found she was glad of it, glad to be so easily identified. Most of the VADs had quiet, unaccented voices and the officers by and large spoke standard English, but it was just lovely to hear someone talking scouse, and Nellie could not help her pleasure showing as she turned towards the young man who had spoken.

He was a thin young man with very dark eyes set in deeply shadowed hollows in his tanned face. He wore the uniform of the convalescent home up the road, and over it a faded Army greatcoat. His boots had once been shiny no doubt but now they were scuffed and cracked and his hat was on the back of his head, perched rather than worn on the soft, ebony hair. He had a lean, intelligent face, a jutting chin and, right now, a sweet, wicked smile.

Nellie, turning towards him, found that she was smiling naturally at him, as though she had known him all her life. He reminded her of someone – was it Davy? But that was nonsense of course, the only resemblance between them was that both were dark. Davy had been tough and self-assured, ardent, amusing company. This young man wore suffering in the deep-set, dark eyes, and the lines on his face were lines carved there by bitter experience. Yet she felt suddenly happy, as though this chance encounter, combined with the fresh air and the deep, untouched snowfields, had given her back a little of the youthful carefreeness which she felt she had lost.

'Hello whack, and where do you come from?' she said, deliberately using a thick Liverpool brogue. 'I'm from the Scottie, me ... me pal hales from Seaforth –

158

ever so posh, aren't you, queen?'

The young man laughed and held out a hand.

'I'm Stuart Gallagher, born and bred in the 'Pool but working for the *London Evening Messenger* as War Correspondent ever since this lot started,' he said. 'Got myself a splintered kneecap, which is why I've fallen behind me pals.' He gestured further up the hill and Nellie saw five young men standing in a small group pointing to the snow around them, shaking their heads, obviously arguing about something. 'We're going tobogganing; care to join us?'

His accent, now that he wasn't fooling about, was if anything less pronounced even than Nellie's and she hesitated, glancing uneasily at Lucy. After all, she had been the one to assure Sister they would not break the rules – but that did not mean she could not respond to an introduction!

'Hello, Stuart. I'm Nellie McDowell and my friend is Lucy Bignold; we work at the hospital, on Ward Twelve,' Nellie said. 'Lucy, do you think we ought to go tobogganing?'

But if Lucy had misgivings as to the rights and wrongs of tobogganing, she showed no sign of it. She was wearing her grey uniform scarf wrapped round her dusky curls and the cold had brought the roses blooming in her cheeks, had made her dark eyes sparkle like stars. She nodded vigorously, giving Nellie a poke in the back.

'Tobogganing, Nell! I've always loved it, but I know what you're thinking and this isn't walking with an officer in the town, now you can't say it is, can you? And though we told Sister we wouldn't do that, we said nothing about sliding down hillsides ...' she turned and stared at Stuart Gallagher. 'Only where's your toboggan?' she enquired, tilting her head and looking suddenly so pretty that Nellie could have slapped her. Lucy didn't have a Liverpool accent, people in Seaforth were too posh for that; it was Nellie whose voice had attracted the attention of the young officer, she just hoped that Lucy wasn't going to think ...

Nellie's thoughts stopped short, appalled. Whatever was the matter with her? She could not possibly be jealous of her dear Lucy and this pleasant but ordinary young man whose main attraction was that he came from her home city and had recognised her accent.

For a moment she stood rooted to the spot, thoroughly ashamed of her unworthy thoughts, but then she looked at him again, and decided that it was about time she looked at a man and saw a man and not a patient. Finding Stuart attractive, in fact, was a sign of how she was improving, pulling back to being a normal young woman again.

'My toboggan is here,' Stuart said, having clearly not noticed Nellie's sudden stillness. He produced a battered tin tray from under his greatcoat. 'See? A nice dinner tray, but Sister won't notice and we'll put them back before they serve supper. So are you with me, girls?'

'Might as well,' Nellie said with an assumption of indifference which would not have fooled a child of three. 'But how will it work ... are we all going to share that little tin tray?'

Stuart laughed and took an arm of each girl. Nellie told herself that she should have drawn back, but there was nothing in the least amorous in his grip and it was clear that their support was a help to him as he limped up the lane to the gateway where his friends had congregated. And not only that, it felt good to have her elbow held by a strong hand once more, wonderful to feel that frisson of excitement which the attentions of an attractive man, no matter how casual those attentions might be, brought in its wake.

'We've got a tray each,' Stuart told her. 'You stick with me, Nurse Nellie, and I'll put Nurse Lucy in the charge of Sid Fuller. That way, you'll both arrive at the bottom safely. These others, they're just foolish lads, they'll probably overturn you in a snowdrift so deep that you won't be dug out for weeks!'

Stuart was as good as his word. They found a long hill with a smooth, virgin snow-slope and toiled up it, keeping well to one side. At the top, Stuart adjusted his tray, sat Nellie on it with her knees hugged up to her chin, and knelt behind her, with one leg stuck out at an angle because of the bandaging, he said.

'You won't mind, Nell, if I put both arms round you? Only I don't trust you to steer and I don't fancy falling off the back of this tray once we get under way. Are you comfy? Right then, off we go!'

Halfway down the hill Nellie was screaming and laughing all at once, clutching Stuart and begging him to hold on tight, and having the most marvellous time. At the bottom they tipped up, arms and legs entangled, and Stuart helped her up and brushed the worst of the snow off her grey cloak and took her hand to pull her up the hill once more.

'Did you like it?' he asked rather unnecessarily, since Nellie's snowy face was pink with bliss. 'Have you never sledged before?'

'No, never – and it's the most wonderful thing I've ever done,' Nellie said. 'Can we have another go?'

'We certainly can, and if you feel you know me well enough, I'll sit on the tray this time and you can sit between my legs. Kneeling plays hell with my kneecap, or what's left of it.'

It was better, snuggled against Stuart's thin chest, with his arms straining round her just as though they were lovers and not merely acquaintances, yet Nellie somehow knew that this was a game, that Stuart did not have the slightest intention of taking advantage of their proximity. So for the whole of that sunny, snowy afternoon the six officers and the two nurses forgot there was a war, forgot wounds and dressings and pain and the terrible things which man did to his fellow man, and became children again. Indeed, Nellie played like a child for the first time, since childishness had not been encouraged at the Culler, where Mrs Ransom was determined that her girls should learn early that life was a serious business.

When the sun began to go down and they knew their time was nearly up they staged a snowball fight, making the snowballs big and soft so they didn't hurt and falling over with laughter when a particularly telling shot was scored. Nellie's hair came out of its bun and hung all round her flushed and laughing face in damp little tendrils, Lucy's curls were white with thrown snow, Stuart's hat was battered and worn peak behind. Nellie saw, with almost frightened tenderness, that the tension had quite left his face and that the lines were smoothed out by laughter. For the first time it occurred to her that there were worse things than being wounded or killed in battle. Perhaps going constantly into danger, reporting what you saw but not able to take an active part in the fighting, could be, in its way, worse.

The eight of them walked back to town together, then separated on the main road, the girls turning left, the men right. Stuart and Sid lingered though, for a moment's quiet conversation with the girls.

'That was jolly, wasn't it?' Stuart said quietly to

Nellie. 'You've not played in the snow like that before, have you?'

'No,' Nellie admitted, shaking her head. 'I never had the chance to play like a kid when I was one, but ... oh, it was the best thing I've ever done!'

'We'll do it again,' Stuart promised. 'Look, Nell, can I write to you? Because in a few weeks I'll be at the Front, getting ready to report the spring offensive, and unless I'm wounded again I might not get back to the coast for months.' He glanced further along the lane, to where his companions were tactfully waiting, eyes fixed ahead. 'Sid's a grand fellow, he'll want to keep in touch with Lucy, I bet. What about it? Can I write?'

'Of course; I'd like it very much,' Nellie said shyly. 'Give me your address and I'll write to you, as well.'

'Grand.' Stuart fished in the pocket of his greatcoat and drew out a stub of pencil and a crumpled piece of paper. 'Fire ahead, then ... Nurse Nellie McDowell ...?'

Nellie told him her address, then he wrote down his own name and the address she should use. He tore the paper carefully in half and gave her his details, then tucked the rest of the page into his pocket.

'There we are, all sorted, and I'd take a bet that Sid and Lucy have just exchanged addresses too,' he said, grin- ning at Nellie. 'Will you have an afternoon off again next week? Care to risk having tea with me? Well, why should- n't we make it a foursome, you and Lucy, me and Sid?'

'We would have to since nurses aren't allowed out alone, but only in pairs or small groups,' Nellie pointed out. 'Only we really aren't supposed to speak to offi- cers, Stuart.'

'Hmm, I forgot. The American nurses are positively encouraged to go about with us; much healthier, I think. Still, in the circumstances it might be more politic to meet somewhere quiet. Remember the copse we passed a while back?'

'What's a copse?' Nellie asked. Stuart squeezed her hand lightly, then touched her chin with the point of his finger. She felt her cheeks redden but pretended not to notice, continuing to look questioningly up at him.

'What a townie it is! A copse is a small wood, just a cluster of trees.'

'I don't mind being a townie,' Nellie observed. 'Lucy used to live in the real country, out at Crosby, before she came to work in the hospital. She knows all sorts that I don't. But I know more about the city, you see.'

'I shouldn't tease you,' Stuart said remorsefully. 'You girls do such a wonderful job, and most of you only kids … do you remember the copse, though?'

'Yes, I think so.'

'Well, Sid and I will hang about in those trees in a week's time, from about two o'clock. If you can't come that's too bad, but if you can it would be … well, it would be fun. I know a little farmhouse where they do real cream teas … you look as if you could do with feeding up.'

'We could all do with it,' Nellie pointed out. 'You're too thin, Stuart.'

'Nonsense, I'm a strapping fellow!' Ahead of them, Lucy turned and beckoned imperatively. The sun had quite gone from the sky now and the grey of evening was giving way to darkness. 'Oh, you'd best go, my … Nell, I mean. Try to come, next week!'

Nellie nodded, squeezed his hand, turned away … then turned back. She looked hard at the lean, quizzical face which was not handsome or fascinating but which seemed so familiar, so reliable. Then she stood on tiptoe and pressed her cheek to his for a fleeting second before running off down the road to join Lucy.

'What was all that about? Nellie McDowell, you're a dark horse,' Lucy exclaimed. 'I've known you a good while now, but I didn't know you could laugh like that, or play in the snow like a child! If you ask me, this afternoon has done you more good than a couple of days in bed!'

'It has,' Nellie said fervently. 'Just being with – with them – helped me to forget the war altogether for a few hours. And I've never played like that in my whole life – it's wonderful to … to romp, and not to have to wonder what's for dinner, or whose wounds need dressing, or how I'll manage if my pay's held up again.'

'I know what you mean. I liked Sid most awfully, too. As much as you liked Stuart, and you needn't pretend that it wasn't him who made your afternoon so wonderful because I know better. He's a grand young man and Sid Fuller's another. Do you know, Nell, this afternoon for the first time since John was killed, I looked at another man and found I wanted to know him better? So Sid and I are meeting next week. And I bet you're meeting Stuart, too.'

'Yes, I am,' Nellie said quietly. All this time they had been walking up the long road which led to the hospital. 'The only thing is, I never wanted to have to wait and worry over a man again, and if I go on seeing Stuart that's just what will happen, until the war ends.'

'I know. But that's living, Nell. What we've been doing, you and I, is denying life, and you can't do that and be happy. You have to risk pain and loss to gain happiness, that's what I think.'

'I expect you're right. Anyway, we'll meet them again next week. Meeting someone twice doesn't commit you to anything.'

'No, of course it doesn't,' Lucy said stoutly. But her smile was full of mischief as they turned into the hospital foyer. 'We're dedicated nurses who want no truck with young men!'

'Our Nellie's been sledgin',' Lilac observed as she and Art made their way through the dirty slush which was the city's idea of a heavy snowfall. It had been white enough for an hour, then the traffic had started again and very soon the snow was being churned up and melted so that grey slush lined every roadway. 'It sounds great fun, Art. Wish I could go sledging.'

'Get a letter, didya? She all right?'

'Yes, she's havin' a good time, though the work's terrible hard. But she and Lucy went into the country and slid down the steep hills on a tray ... can you imagine our Nellie on a tray!'

'She's only lickle,' Art pointed out. 'Norra lot bigger'n you, young Lilac.'

'She's old, though,' Lilac pointed out indisputably. 'She doesn't want to go getting rheumatiz, playing about in the snow.'

'We could tek a tray and go up Aughton Street, there's a good steep slope there, then we could sledge down,' Art said. 'Why go to school? Mam'll say we 'ad a sickness if we ask 'er.'

'Oh, I don't know, Art. Our Nellie's awful partickler about school. She says it's me only chance to do better, to get an education. Only ... it 'ud just be for a day, right?'

'That's right, just a day.' Art grinned coaxingly. 'Come on, queen, let's give it a go, eh? I'm goin' anyway, but I'd like it better if you'd come too; I'd be real made up, Li.'

'You would? Honest? Wouldn't you have more fun with other lads?'

Art shook his head positively.

'No way! With you and me, it 'ud be real fun.'

Lilac thought about school, which was boring because she was so far ahead of her class thanks to Mr Norton, and then she thought about Nellie's description of zooming down the hills on her tray. It sounded such fun, Lilac thought wistfully, and fun was much harder to come by now that Nellie was in France. And Nellie had only been sledging with Lucy, which was all very well, but nowhere near such fun as sledging with Art would be. She still pined after Matt from time to time, but he was grown-up, fighting in the army, a thousand light years away from the lad she had once admired. Art, on the other hand, was right here. He was taller than she now, and very strong. His cowlick of brown hair still overhung his brow though, and sometimes he caught her fingers in his and held them very tight and a most peculiar feeling came swooning down into Lilac's tummy and arrowed into the very heart of her.

'I'll come, then,' Lilac said out loud. 'We'll skip school and go sledging, Art!'

The farmhouse tea was a great success. The two young men did not meet them as arranged exactly, since when the girls arrived at the copse they found a horse-drawn cab awaiting them and as they walked cautiously up to it Stuart jumped down.

'Ah, you've managed to get away; hop in, then,' he said briskly. 'Sid and I decided to convey you to the farmhouse in luxury – what do you think?'

The cab, with thick straw on the floors and isinglass

in the windows, may not have been the height of luxury, but it was warm, comfortable, and faster than walking. A happy quartet arrived at their destination, paid off the cab and took their places at the table which the young men had reserved.

Conversation might have been a little stiff at first, but Nellie recounted how she and Lucy had been forced to scamper through their duties and to bribe another nurse to finish off for them with a packet of chocolate which Lucy's mother had sent her, and this amused them and broke the ice. And the farmhouse parlour was too pleasant a place for shyness or formality. A great log fire burned in the grate, a black and white cat snoozed before it, there were soft rugs on the floor and Stuart insisted on showing their fat French hostess how to make a decent brew of tea in her tall tin coffee pot. He talked in broken French, which made them laugh, the Frenchwoman talked in even more broken English, which made them laugh more, and the tea was excellent. Home-made bread thickly spread with butter and honey, a homemade cake with chocolate topping and then cream poured over it, the famous tea made in the tin coffee pot and thin slices of pink ham with a jar of the nicest pickle Nellie had ever tasted.

'I'm so full I might quite easily burst,' Lucy said at last, when the table had been cleared of everything edible and the four of them were leaning back, replete. 'I don't know how I'll manage to get back to the hospital – you chaps will have to bowl me along like a hoop!'

'We'll walk it off,' Nellie said stoutly. 'What a pity this farm's in a valley though, and not high on a hill; if it was we could sledge down to the coast on the lady's best trays!'

Great amusement, until Nellie was helped into her coat by Stuart and Lucy was helped into hers by Sid, and the four of them set off into the icy dusk, only to find that it was slow going with the thick snow underfoot and the dusk increasing every minute.

'We'll be in dreadful trouble if we're late,' Nellie said nervously. 'We aren't supposed to go far from the town and they'll never believe we could get lost in the snow.'

'We'll sneak you in somehow,' Stuart said when Lucy explained that there would be someone on watch for them in the foyer. 'If you're in your rooms surely there won't be any questions?'

'Our room is a tent with twenty-six other girls in it,' Nellie pointed out. 'Oh well, we must put our best feet forward and try not to be awfully late.'

They did, and perhaps they were lucky, perhaps the fates do smile, sometimes, on young lovers, even if they would have denied vociferously that that was what they were. Outside the hospital foyer Stuart snatched Nellie into his arms and hugged her convulsively, then kissed the corner of her mouth with such tenderness that Nellie found herself fighting back tears.

'Goodnight, dear Nell. Take care of yourself, and write to me whenever you get a moment,' he commanded. 'I've written the address of my paper on this old envelope because if I pass my medical – and I shall – I'll be off in a few days. They're sending me to Blighty for a spell, to London in fact, but I'll be back, I promise.'

'You stay safe in London if you get the chance,' Nellie whispered against his shoulder. 'Thanks for – for everything, Stu.'

'Thank you, Nell.' Another quick, convulsive hug

and he was turning away. 'Go on, run in.'

She ran, fighting an absurd desire to burst into tears, for it was absurd, she had only met him twice, they were virtually strangers!

The foyer was deserted. She and Lucy shot across it and into the changing room. They were smoothing down their uniforms and back on the ward before Sister arrived to tell them to take the dressing trolley round.

Chapter Eight

The cold winter which swept across the continent in 1917 did not stop when it reached the Channel, it came right on to England. In the small room she shared with Bessie and the kids, Lilac shivered awake, to break the ice on the water in the bucket downstairs before she could wash or put the kettle on. But she did not miss the Culler, not even when she was caned in school for making off during her dinner break, nor when they ran out of coal and she and Art went thieving down at the railway depot, where the great stock of coal for the trains was always a temptation. They were chased by a night watchman and nearly caught, Lilac went flying on the frosty pavement and skinned both knees and one went septic. Anxious not to have the expense of a doctor, Aunt Ada applied fomentations so hot that Lilac wept piteously, but even so, she regretted nothing and would not have changed Ada's harsh medical treatment for the more professional approach which matron might well have taken.

She missed Nell horribly, of course, but they wrote often and she was buoyed up by the fact that now she, like most of her schoolfellows, had someone 'over there', fighting for their country.

She was very happy at her new school, too, though she had been puzzled, at first, over the family's refusal to let her go to St Anthony's, with Art. In the end Art told her the reason himself, his eyes sparkling with mischief.

'We's cat'olics, and youse is dirty proddies,' he said cheerfully. 'Can't 'ave a proddie bein' taught by the good nuns!'

'I'm *not* a proddie; at the Culler we went to the coggers in the mornings and the prods in the evenings,' Lilac said indignantly. 'I can choose which I want, and I'll be a catholic, like you, Art.'

'No you can't,' Art said. 'Well, Ada's a proddie, anyroad, and you'll 'ave to foller her.'

Afterwards, Lilac found she was quite glad to be a 'proddie,' as Art put it. She and Art always walked to school together, she only having to go one street further on to reach her own place of education, and it was soon borne in upon her that much as Art loved St Anthony's, there were things about the Penrhyn Street school which he secretly envied. There was the lovely, modern building, the excellent play area and gymnasium and the young and enthusiastic teachers, some of them only about Nellie's age. The games were better, the teachers were warmly interested in their young charges, and altogether Lilac thought she had the best of the bargain though Art stuck to his contention that there was no school to equal St Anthony's.

It was not only school which Lilac enjoyed, either. Aunt Ada was strict and would not let her play out as much as she would have liked, and Bessie needed all the help she could get with three children under five, but within the confines of Coronation Court – or the Corry, as she soon learned to call it – she had more freedom than she had ever enjoyed at the Culler.

For the first time in her life she was able to go snowballing in winter, because who could enjoy snowballing on a strictly conducted walk? And anyway, the streets were soon cleared of snow in the city centre, whereas in the parks and quite often in the court, the snow was allowed to lie. And there was sliding – the children always made a long slide from one end of the court to the other, carefully marked with a line of rags so that no adult took an inadvertent trip. In spring and summer there was trekking off on expeditions with her friends, sometimes slipping out with Art to help him find old boxes down at the docks which he might carry home and split up into kindling to sell at a penny for two bundles, stealing a free ride on a leckie after school and then using the time you'd saved to saunter along and window shop. All these things had the charm of novelty for a child reared in an orphan asylum. In the Culler food had been dull but plentiful enough, clothing automatically provided, walks few and strictly supervised, play very limited. There had been nothing to do half the time, unless you counted kitchen work or cleaning, and Lilac hated domestic chores.

So of course Lilac's leisure was used to the full, insofar as she was allowed by Aunt Ada and Bessie.

'Art's gone to the canal, to see if he can pick up some more boxes,' Lilac would say wistfully. 'Can I go, Auntie?'

And though for a long time the answer was nearly always no, Lilac was sure that once Aunt Ada realised how sensible she was she would change her mind, give Lilac her head a bit, so she put up with the refusals, sure they would turn to agreement in time.

'I need you here, queen,' Aunt Ada would say. Or 'Nellie wouldn't think much of me if I let you go off with them young roughs,' or even, 'When you're older, chuck.'

And then Charlie got his Blighty one.

It had rained all morning but by two in the afternoon

the sun peeped out and the breeze freshened to a boisterous wind.

Lilac had peeled the potatoes for supper and now she was sitting in the window, mending a great rent in Nathan's blue coat and listening to the conversation going on between the two older women. Bessie was frowning down at the letter in her hand, a letter she must have read at least fifty times since its arrival the previous day, whilst Aunt Ada spat on the toe of her black laced boots and then polished vigorously with a rag. Every now and then she held the shoe up in a ray of sunlight which came through the low window and admired the shine she was creating.

Lilac sewed grimly on and wondered when it would be politic to say something. It was Saturday and the girls all went out on a Saturday afternoon if they possibly could. Her particular friend, Sukey, would wait for her as long as she could, but if Lilac didn't put in an appearance she'd guess she was being kept in and would go off with the others. Usually, Auntie let her go off on a Saturday with Sukey, but today was different, because of the letter.

'By the time you get this I'll be in Blighty, in the Alder Hey Hospital, so mind you come and see me as soon as you can,' Bessie read aloud for the hundredth time, her brow furrowing with effort. 'And don't you worrit yourself; this time there won't be no comin' back.'

'There you are, then,' Aunt Ada said, apparently satisfied at last with the shine on her first boot and starting on the second. 'Get yourself ready, our Bess; you don't wanter be late, do you?'

'Oh, I'm all but ready,' Bessie said. 'No, but Ada, what does it mean? Does it mean 'e's been wounded real bad? Honest to God, I'm scared stiff of what I'll find when we get there.'

'Look, he writ 'imself, didn't he? So there can't be much wrong with 'im. 'Sides, they'd 'a said. Now come along, gairl!'

'Auntie, can I go off with Sukey? I've finished Nat's coat, the seam's tight as a tick, not a bit of light showin' through,' Lilac said quickly. 'I'll be home before you are ... or did you want me to come to the 'ospital?'

Aunt Ada and Bessie exchanged glances. Lilac could see the Great Idea forming.

'Well, queen, we was goin' to tek you, but seeing as 'ow you've 'ad your eleventh birthday, an' we trust you, you can tek the kids outer our way. I'll gi' you a penny or two, then you can get 'em some fades if you're going to the market, they usually 'ave bruised fruit goin' cheap.'

Lilac, taking the money, resigned herself to pram pushing all afternoon. Not that it was so bad; Sukey was an only child and liked kids. What was more she was an only child because her father, a catholic, had walked out on her protestant mother after the most colossal family row. He had gone to sea and jumped ship somewhere, never to return. So Sukey lived with her mother's family and went to the Penrhyn Street school but had cousins and friends at St Anthony's, just as Lilac had. It had given the girls something in common, and it was a bonus that Sukey also loved Bessie's kids and enjoyed helping with them.

'You're sure you don't mind, chuck?' Bessie said as she helped Lilac put Nathan and Millie, the two younger children, into the old pram. Henry was a big boy and usually walked alongside, holding onto the pram, though when he grew tired he would consent to being hoisted aboard with the younger kids. 'The trouble is, if Charlie needs to be a bit quiet ...'

'It's all right, honest. I like walkin' with 'em,' Lilac

said hastily. She had seen how tears were forming in Bessie's big brown eyes and didn't want to precipitate a bout of wailing and lamentation. How strange, she thought, to love someone and want him back, yet be driven to tears in case the very wound which brought him home might be a bad one. She really could not understand grownups!

'Well, so long as you're sure. I'll give your Daddy a kiss from each of you,' Bessie said. She kissed the little ones and made a lunge for Henry, who drew back hastily, already unwilling to sacrifice his masculine image to a mother's urge to cuddle. Besides, they were standing out in the court now, on the steaming paving stones, preparing to go their different ways – anyone might see! 'Thanks, our Li, you're worth your weight in gold to me an' Auntie.'

'Give Charlie a kiss from me, too, an' say I'll see 'im when I'm allowed,' Lilac said at once. She remembered Charlie with real affection, he had always been good to her. 'Bye, then! Wave to Mam and Auntie, kids.'

The children waved vigorously as their mother and aunt set off for the tram stop, then Lilac began to push the pram towards Tenterden Street, where Sukey lived. The pennies were hot and heavy in her hand so she slid them into the pocket of her skirt. She waved to Sukey, standing on the corner ahead, and as she drew closer, patted the pocket to make the pennies chink together.

'Auntie give me some pennies for fruit,' she said. 'They've gone to the 'ospital to see Charlie. Wonder how soon they'll let 'im come home?'

The two girls in their faded jerseys, dipping skirts and patched boots, made their way along Scotland Road towards the Rotunda. It was a popular walk with their age-group and they knew they would meet other pram-pushing girls once they arrived at the theatre. Besides, the broad pavement was good for hopscotch and tag, so long as you didn't fall. It gave the littl'uns a chance to get out of the pram and run about a bit without the danger of being run over by traffic.

'They won't let 'im 'ome that quick,' Sukey said knowledgeably. She had numerous relatives fighting in France. 'A Blighty one is always bad. Did he come 'ome as BS, BL or red label?'

Lilac knew all about patients being graded as Boat Sitting, Boat Lying, or Special Attention, but now she could only shrug.

'Dunno. Our Charlie never said, see? Just that he was in the Alder Hey, and not to worry.'

'Oh. Well, you'll know soon enough,' Sukey said comfortably. 'At least he'll 'ave good weather to get better in by the look of it.' A few days earlier there had been an unseasonable snowstorm but now the snow had all melted away and the sunshine of late April fell warmly on their heads. 'Flossie Arbuthnot's mam's 'avin' another baby – me mam says her Dad'll be livid when 'e comes home.'

'Why?' Lilac said, as much out of politeness as anything. Flossie did not interest her in the least, far less Flossie's mother.

'Why, 'cos Flossie's dad's not the baby's dad, silly,' Sukey said. She leaned over the pram and wiped a trail of mucus from the smallest child's face with the hem of its stained dress. Bessie, though a loving mother, was not always a careful one. 'There's always babies like that in wartime, my mam says.'

'Oh?' Lilac retorted. 'Art's gone to play down by the river, 'cos the tide's out. He's gone with that Fred … wish I could go, too. It's all sand, he says … real nice. But I got landed with the kids, as usual.'

Both girls knew that Art was unlikely to invite a mere girl to join him and his friends. His genuine friendship for Lilac could not, she thought, be called in question, but nevertheless he was beginning to look askance at her entire sex, thinking them cissies and a pretty useless bunch, on the whole.

'Never mind. Perhaps, when Charlie's 'ome, he'll look after 'em,' Sukey said comfortingly. 'Fellers do, when they've been wounded.'

'Our Dad's been wounded,' Henry said, as though the remark had reminded him. 'I 'ope 'e's got both arms, else 'ow'll 'e play "a leg an' a wing" with me and the kids?'

'Wanna walk,' whined Nathan. 'Li, I wanna walk like our Henny.'

'You can't get down till we reach the theatre,' Lilac said. 'Then you can have a good run around.' She turned back to Sukey. 'They're good kids though, a lot better'n some. Oh, there's Kathy and Sara ... they're looking at the pictures of the actors and that. Let's hurry.'

They belted the pram along, skinny legs going like clockwork, and skidded to a stop alongside their friends.

'Hello, you two! What's on, then?'

'It's a murder play, wiv a lorra blood,' Sara said with relish. 'Her what plays the lead, she's ever so lovely, pale an' sad lookin', some'ow. And the murderer looks real wicked – come an' see!'

The visit to the fruit market on Great Nelson Street proved only partially successful. Because of the munitions factory which had been built on Cazneau Street, where the market had once been, it was only half its pre-war size and anyway it was a poor time of the year for fruit, with last year's crop all but over and the new season's fruit not yet arrived. But the girls got a handful of wizened apples and a few weary looking oranges – fades indeed – for their penny and came away moderately satisfied. With their heads together over the pram, gossiping like two old shawlies and occasionally exchanging remarks with their charges, they made their way back along the Scotland Road until they reached the corner of the street where Sukey and her mum shared the family home with a dozen others.

Here they stopped for a final gossip before parting.

'Goin' to come out tomorrer?' Sukey asked, swinging on the lamp standard and staring reflectively at her boots. 'If you don't 'ave the kids we could walk down to the pier'ead, or up Abercromby to look at the posh 'ouses.'

'Dunno. See what Auntie says. But I'll see you Monday, anyroad.'

Lilac waved until Sukey was halfway down Tenterden Street, then, pushing the pram more slowly now after her long afternoon, she continued up the crowded pavement a short way until she reached the entrance to Coronation Court.

'Is it dinnertime?' Nathan asked plaintively. He was a skinny little chap but fond of his food. 'I's hongry, Li!'

'Me too,' agreed Lilac. 'Want an apple, Nat? You too, Henry?'

She passed over two rosy, much-wrinkled apples. Nathan began to eat his at once but Henry bit out a half-moon and held it out to his sister, letting Millie suck and chumble enthusiastically at it.

'You're a good brother, our Hal,' Lilac said, rather touched at the little boy's thoughtfulness. 'You're ever so like your Dad – Charlie always thought of others first, Nellie often said so. Here, you can have another apple all to yourself this time.'

'Fanks, Li,' Henry said thickly. 'Are vey back yet – Mam an' me Auntie Ada, I mean?'

His words came out jerkily as Lilac hurried the home-made pram across the uneven pavingstones, but she was saved the necessity of replying by Bessie, who erupted into the court from the small house, grabbed Henry, gave him a hug, kissed the babies and then pounced on Lilac and hugged her too. It was immediately plain that Bessie was in the grip of two conflicting emotions, joy and sorrow, for though she smiled there were tears in her eyes which presently spilled over and ran down her cheeks.

'Oh Li, love, we've seen 'im! Ever so cheerful 'e is ... but Li, he's lost 'is leg! They'll give 'im a wooden one ... I kept saying, "what's to become of us, what's to become of us?" and then 'e told me ... Li, our Charlie's a hero!' She bent over the pram and snatched Millie out of it, hugging the child to her breast, still shiny-eyed and pink-cheeked from emotion. 'Millie Miranda, your daddy's a hero!'

Aunt Ada appeared in the doorway. She looked pale, though she was smiling.

'Bessie, get them kids indoors,' she said sharply. 'I'll talk to Lilac. Foller me, chuck.'

So whilst Bessie cleaned up the children and fed Millie, Aunt Ada and Lilac prepared a meal and Aunt Ada told Lilac what had happened.

'Seems Charlie saved 'is officer's life,' she said briefly. 'But they both lost a leg, see? And the officer, 'e's a man of property up in the Lake District, wherever that may be, 'e's offered Charlie a home and a job for life ... there's a cottage, a garden ... and all Charlie will 'ave to do is mind the gates of the big 'ouse and drive the officer when 'e wants to go about. So they'll be off when Charlie's fit enough to leave Alder Hey.'

'That's nice,' Lilac said doubtfully. She could read something in Aunt Ada's face which she did not understand. 'Is it the country, Auntie?'

'Yes. It'll be better for all of 'em, chuck,' Aunt Ada said. 'Our Charlie saved that feller's life, no doubt about it, an' now he'll reap his reward, an' Bessie and the littl'uns too. So that's all to the good.'

But Lilac thought that pleased though Aunt Ada must be, she was a little sad as well, and was ashamed of her own feelings.

That evening, when they had eaten their meal and put the children to bed, when the three females were sitting round the dining table going over, once more, what Charlie had said, Lilac thought she knew why Aunt Ada seemed quieter than usual.

Charlie had always been her favourite and when he and Bessie went, Aunt Ada would miss him. And it was not only him, of course. Hal and Bertie, Fred and Matt, had all left home now. Even Aunt Ada's own girls were gone, for Lou was abroad and Jessie married and living away. Nellie was in France, Uncle Billy was dead ... it'll only be Auntie and me, Lilac realised, and despite herself, her heart sank.

What price freedom now, then? Once Bessie and the kids had gone, Aunt Ada would need Lilac more than ever.

Aren't I ever going to get me leg loose? Lilac thought sadly as she made her way up to the room she shared with Bessie and the kids. And I thought it was tough having to take the kids out with me when I'd rather have gone alone ... that'll be nothing like as bad as having to take Aunt Ada everywhere!

'Lilac? Are you comin' out? We're goin' to the canal.'

Art's voice, echoing round the court, brought Lilac's head popping round the front door. She looked uncertainly back over her shoulder, then resignedly shook her head.

'Better not; Auntie isn't too brave.'

'What's the marrer with 'er?' Art said, but he lowered his voice. 'She ain't sozzled, is she?'

Not being too brave was sometimes a euphemism for drunkenness and Lilac scowled at him. Drinking was something of which to be ashamed, and Aunt Ada had always been loud in her condemnation of those who took too much liquor.

'Sshh; course not,' Lilac said reproachfully, 'She's got a touch of stomach-gripes, that's all. And her head aches. I'd better stay with her, in case she needs something.'

It was three months since Bessie and Charlie had left and the August heat was stifling. The thought of the canal was tempting, but it seemed mean to go off and leave Aunt upstairs in the stuffy bedroom with no one to make her a cup of tea when she felt better, or hold her head whilst she retched over the chamber pot. On the other hand, if she had fallen asleep ...

This hope was scotched when Aunt Ada appeared at the head of the tiny, narrow staircase. She swayed, clutched the bannister, then spoke.

'You go off, chuck. I'm best left now. I'll sleep once the 'ouse is quiet.'

'Oh! Well, if you're sure ...'

'I'm sure.' Aunt Ada managed a pale smile at them both. 'You take our Lilac out, Art. It'll do her good to get some fresh air. She shouldn't be stuck 'ere with an old woman all day.'

A real gentleman would have told Aunt Ada that she was not old, but Art was only Art.

'Right, Mizz Threadwell, I'll keep me eye on 'er,' he said briskly. 'Come on, chuck, and mind you do what I say!'

Lilac wavered; what good could she do here, after all? Aunt Ada probably would be better left. She could sleep, like she said. There were spuds peeled and a cabbage sliced, though no meat, yet. Lots of people didn't ever taste meat, she had been told, but it was different for them. All the young people sent money, even the boys. The shillings mounted up quite nicely ... but Aunt Ada had gone back into the bedroom and she, Lilac, had not asked her for a tanner to buy a pig's trotter or half a pound of scrag. Still, she'd done her work and her shopping could be done on the way back, so why shouldn't she go with Art?

'All right, I'll come,' she said. She untied the enormous apron which reached her toes and hung it on the back of the door. Despite the fact that she had no money she knew that Aunt's credit was good, so she would get someone to let her have a pig's foot on tick. There was a nice butcher just past the library on Collingwood Street; she could try him.

'I'll need to stop at Fletcher's, to see if I can get a pig's foot on tick, on the way home,' she said as the two of them set off. It was a sunny afternoon and the gang, in this instance, turned out to be Art himself, his pal Fred and a little lad known as Nips who never seemed to grow and suffered from some sort of skin disease which made adults eye him warily. 'Can I get Sukey? She'd like to learn to swim ... leastways I reckon she would.'

Art sighed but agreed; clearly he was in a good mood this afternoon, so she should make the best of it. Accordingly, she ran the short distance down Tenterden Street and rattled on the door. Sukey's mum answered it, a big white bowl in the crook of one arm. She was beating a batter and only paused long enough to grin at Lilac and turn to shout over her shoulder, 'Sukey, your pal's 'ere!'

Sukey duly joined the expedition, bringing with her a shabby piece of towelling.

'Wharrer you want that for?' Art said rudely, when he saw it. 'Gairls don't swim!'

'They bloody do,' Sukey said stoutly. 'I bin swimmin' since I was a nipper.'

Art grinned at this blatant lie but said nothing more and the children mooched happily along through the warm and dusty streets. Now that she was actually outside, Lilac stopped worrying about Aunt Ada; what was the point, after all? Grownups did not confide in kids, not even when the kids were sensible ones, like herself. If Auntie was ill then they would have to spend some of the money the boys and Nellie sent on paying a doctor to make her better, that was all.

Presently they drew level with the blacksmith's forge, a place which would normally have brought them to a halt as they inspected the great, patient horses waiting their turn, the smith in his stained leather apron hammering away and, best of all, the great roaring fire. But on such an afternoon as this the smithy repelled with its heat and with the flies that danced round the horses' patient heads, so they skidded down Burlington Street, crossed busy Vauxhall Road, avoided death-by-tram by a whisker as one of those mighty vehicles came rocketing down the centre of the roadway, and continued across Houghton Bridge, dropping onto the towpath on the further side.

This was all new ground to Lilac. She looked up at the great buildings towering above the water, wondering what they were; warehouses? They looked grim, the red of their bricks long blackened by the industrial smoke.

'That's the sugar refinery,' Art said, following her glance. 'Look at the water, see it steam? They puts out 'ot water ... nice when the weather's cold but right now I wants a cool dip, so we won't stop 'ere, we'll go on a bit.'

They went on along the towpath until they reached a wider stretch where Art apparently considered the location suitable for their purpose. They stopped and the boys stripped and jumped into the water, clearly following a well-accustomed routine. Sukey and Lilac took off their dresses rather more reluctantly, but left their knickers in place. No nice girl would ever take off her knickers, Lilac was sure of that – she was not too sure that a nice girl would consider swimming in the canal, but on a hot afternoon such as this she was willing to take a chance – and besides, Nellie need never know and Aunt Ada had not seemed nearly so fussy, lately, over what her young charge did.

The water was wonderfully cool on her hot skin when she sat down on the edge and paddled her feet. It wasn't too deep, Art said, so she slid the rest of the way ... and it came well up her chest, nearly causing her to die of fright when she thought, for one awful moment, that it was going to go over her head. She screamed a bit and so did Sukey, and the boys smacked the surface of the water and laughed at them and soaked them ... and finally, Art put a grimy hand under Lilac's chin and told her to 'Take your perishin' feet off of the bottom, gairl, and give yourself a chanst!'

And after watching Nips, who was unconcernedly sculling himself along in the water, Lilac, obediently making frog-like motions with her hands and feet, found she was swimming, actually swimming! Art could scarcely believe it, and when he did he was proud of her, Lilac could tell. He grinned and shouted out to passersby and suddenly the canal was a magic place, the water her element, one of which she would never tire. She splashed and shouted to Art to watch this and frogged her way from one side of the canal to the other. She turned onto her back and splashed with her hands and feet and did not sink. She dog-paddled, and that worked too – she felt marvellous, a real success at this strange, unfeminine sport.

Sukey could not swim, did not want to swim. She refused to take her feet off the bottom, shrieked when they tried to force her to do so and swore colourfully when she slipped and the water splashed her face. Nips, Art and Fred did not jeer too much, because Sukey was extremely strong for a girl and could land a good punch. Besides, they did not feel that girls should swim – Lilac was almost unfairly favoured by fortune, they seemed to infer.

And presently, cooled down delightfully, wet hair dripping deliciously all down her shabby dress, Lilac linked arms with Sukey on one side and Art on the other, and the five of them retraced their steps.

'Now you can swim, we'll tek you to the free pool, on Burlington Street,' Art said as they made their weary way up the Scotland Road once more. 'Doin' anythin' tomorrer, Li? After Mass?'

Lilac knew he meant after he had been to Mass, so she shook her head ... then abruptly remembered the pig's foot.

'Oh, Art, I never went to Fletcher's! Oh, and Auntie won't be too pleased with spuds and cabbage and no meat at all. I'd better go back, I suppose.'

Art raised a brow. He looked tough and cynical, Lilac thought admiringly.

'Your Aunt Ada won't be eatin' tonight,' he stated roundly. 'Come to our mam's, Li, she'll feed you.'

'Oh, but what about Aunt Ada? Surely she'll want something?'

'Not when she's been sick as any dog,' Art said, not unkindly but practically, as it turned out. 'Can't eat when you've been throwin' up, that's one thing I *do* know.'

'I'll see how she is,' Lilac said rather guardedly, 'But someone's got to eat the spuds and the cabbage, I suppose. Come to that, I could get a pig's foot anyway, for tomorrow.'

She said goodbye to Art outside the house and went in cautiously. No one had put the potatoes on and the fire was so low that she doubted whether she could cook the food, anyway. She stole up the stairs and peeped in on Aunt Ada. The older woman was asleep, lying on her back and snoring gently. Lilac cleared her throat, but her aunt never so much as moved.

As she made her way down the stairs once more, it occurred to Lilac that this was not the first time her aunt had been ill since Charlie and Bessie left. Was it possible to be sick in your stomach because you were unhappy? If so, she would have to cheer Aunt Ada up somehow, or neither of them would ever get a square meal again. And in the meantime, since the fire was almost out and the evening warm, she rather thought she'd accept Art's invitation and take her spuds and cabbage round to Mrs O'Brien.

She checked once more that Aunt Ada was sleeping and then set out, with the potatoes and cabbage all in the one pan. She knocked a little timidly, for Art was the eldest of a large family and she found them rather intimidating. Mr O'Brien rarely put in an appearance but Mrs O'Brien, a fat and untidy woman with a reputation for spite, usually took pleasure in reminding Lilac of her orphan status and generally put her in her place. But today, however, since she was bearing gifts ...

Art came to the door, grinned at her and seized the pan.

'What's all this, chuck?' he said loudly. 'No need to bring nothin', you're welcome as me pal!'

'Your mam might as well have 'em,' Lilac said practically. 'Our fire's gone out and there's enough here for two or three. Poor Auntie Ada's still sleepin', so I thought I might as well come round, and you might as well get the benefit of all me spud-bashin'.'

'I told me Mam you was swimmin' already and she scarce believed me,' Art said, pushing Lilac ahead of him into the dark, overcrowded little room. 'Here's Lilac, Mam, she's brung veggies.'

'Oh, *very* nice,' Mrs O'Brien said, in the tone of voice which meant quite the opposite. But she grabbed the pan nevertheless and put it onto the hob. 'And 'ow's your auntie ... not that she is your auntie 'cept in a manner o' speakin'.'

'She's poorly,' Lilac admitted. 'If it goes on, we'll have to get the doctor.'

'Oh? The doctor, for Mrs Threadwell, is it? Oh yes, of course, she'll see a doctor, whilst the rest of us mek do with the pharmy on Leeds Street.'

'Oh well, the pharmacy would probably do,' Lilac said, relieved at the suggestion. Not that Mrs O'Brien had meant to be helpful, she quite realised that. The older woman was just being spiteful, as usual.

'She'll be fine by tomorrer,' Art said comfortably. 'Come and give us a hand to set the table, will you?'

It was not only set the table, of course. It was wipe

noses, clout heads – some of the heads had nits, Lilac saw – and generally help Art to subdue his younger brothers and sisters into some semblance of order. And the cabbage and potatoes which Lilac had meant for two of them were made to go round everyone … eight without me, Lilac realised.

But there was a scouse to go with the vegetables and plenty of bread to sop up the gravy; Mr O'Brien was a docker and well-paid when he was in work and Art picked up odd jobs from time to time. Furthermore, Mrs O'Brien helped out at the fruit market sometimes and Art's younger brothers nicked odds and ends when times were hard.

It was a filling and pleasant meal but as soon as she'd washed the dishes Lilac said she must be off and despite some nasty cracks from Mrs O'Brien about their food being good enough but their company not worth staying for, she left as fast as she could.

Aunt Ada was still sleeping; Lilac stood looking down at her for a moment, and then sniffed suspiciously. There was a funny smell in the room, a faintly medicinal kind of smell. Did that mean that Aunt Ada had seen sense and gone out and got a bottle from the pharmacy? Or she might even have seen a doctor.

And when Lilac took her aunt a cup of tea last thing, before she sought her own bed, she decided she was right, for there was a bottle standing on the far side of the bed, she could just about make it out.

It relieved her mind that Aunt had been so sensible, and presently she went off to bed, well pleased with her day.

September came, and Lilac returned to school. Aunt Ada was well again, in command. But despite the shillings which the boys and Nellie sent, it seemed it was impossible for her to buy Lilac the clothing she needed for school.

'Not even new secondhand?' Lilac said despairingly, when she had been told, in school, that a girl of nearly twelve needed longer skirts and bigger knickers, 'for decency's sake, Lilac,' her teacher said frankly. 'I know not new *new*, Auntie.'

'Sorry queen. I don't know where the money goes, I'm sure,' Auntie Ada said. She sounded rather guilty, Lilac thought. And it was strange, too, because her aunt had always been a good and careful manager. Lilac could remember many a time when Bessie had been given a telling-off for not making the money Charlie sent go round. 'Next time our Nellie sends, I'll put some aside for clothes.'

Christmas came, with letters from Nellie and the boys and little presents, too. It was lonely in the little house in the court, when every other window was lit and every other house bulged with people. Charlie wrote and invited them to his place, Jessie wanted them to go down south to her place, but Auntie just set her mouth and said they couldn't afford it, not this time, and wasn't it only right and proper that her kids should come to her?

'But Charlie can't, he's needed by his boss,' Lilac reminded her aunt. 'And Jessie's that busy up at the big house … '

'Oh aye, they're all too busy to come to us and we're too busy to go to them so we'll ha' to mek do,' Aunt Ada said. 'We'll have a quiet day, our Lilac, jus' the pair of us.'

It was quieter than either of them had expected since on Christmas Day itself Aunt Ada felt under the weather before the dinner was even prepared, let alone cooked, and stayed in her room. She wouldn't let Lilac in to minister to her, calling out in a thick, hiccupy sort of voice that she'd got 'some 'orrible old disease, and wouldn't want no one else a-catchin' of it.'

She was all right Boxing Day, quite pleasant, in fact, though a bit unsteady on her pins. She and Lilac cooked and ate the dinner which Lilac had not had the heart to prepare the day before, then they played cards with the new pack Matt had sent all the way from France, and ate the first layer of a box of chocolates contributed by Nellie. On the next day she had a drink with her dinner, just something to warm her, then they walked down to the docks and looked at the big ships and talked to one or two others, walking like themselves in the brisk winter afternoon.

Lilac began to think that things were going on very nicely, that Aunt Ada's strange sickness was clearly gone, and that they might enjoy the rest of the holiday after all, since school did not start again until after the New Year. But on 27th December it suddenly grew very cold, and it was at this unpropitious moment that she discovered they had run out of coal so they couldn't have a fire.

'Never mind, I'll tek some money from the teapot and go and buy a bag of coal,' Lilac said, when Aunt Ada announced she had used the last shovelful. 'Art will come with me, help me to carry it.'

Aunt Ada muttered something … and it was then that Lilac discovered there was no money in the teapot. She stared hard at its dull tin interior for a moment, almost unable to believe her eyes. Food and coal money had always been stowed away in here as soon as the shillings came in from the boys and Nellie. What on earth had happened to it? Although they had had a small joint of pork for dinner on Boxing Day, there had been no extra expenses. A nice bread pudding had been served, and there had been the chocolates ... oh no, Nellie had sent the chocolates ... so just where had the money gone?

Auntie muttered about winter prices and rationing and how hard life was for a widow-woman on her own and then took herself off and after a thoughtful moment, Lilac took herself off as well, only in the opposite direction. She went across to the O'Briens' and knocked.

'Is Art about?' she said when Art's small brother Joshua came to the door.

'No, chuck, 'e's gone to see Fred,' a voice called from behind Josh's square, squat figure. It was Mrs O'Brien, mellowed, it seemed, by Christmas spirit. 'D'you know where Freddy lives?'

'That's all right, Mrs O'Brien, I'll find him,' Lilac called back. 'Thanks very much.'

She knew where Freddy lived all right, but had no interest in finding both boys together. Art was a tower of strength, but only when he was away from his mates. With them, he was just as bad as any other lad. So what I must do I must do alone, Lilac told herself, heading determinedly up Scotland Road. Fortunately, she remembered an expedition with Art when he had pointed out to her the goods depot on Old Haymarket, and the close proximity of the coal-heap to a brick wall – a perfectly climbable brick wall what was more.

'We get us onto that wall, one hands up lumps and t'other shoves 'em in the bag,' he had explained. 'Eh, coal scrumpin's not bad, not 'ere.'

Girls, it had appeared, held aloof from coal scrumping expeditions, though they warmed themselves freely enough at the stolen fires. But actually nicking the stuff was a mucky business, best left to boys ... when boys there were. Lacking Art, it seemed that Lilac must simply do her best herself.

She reached the coalyard in mid-afternoon. It was very cold, her breath hung round her face in a misty halo and the smell of trains, the sulphur of smoke, the axle grease, the peculiar odour of the coal itself, hung heavy in the damp air.

She walked round the goods yard, taking notice but pretending to be playing some girlish game. She had a length of rope and skipped with it, threw it into the air and caught it, cast it onto the ground and jumped in and out of the loop it made. And all the while the dusk was deepening and presently the sky was almost as dark as the earth and it was the hour which is said to be neither dog nor wolf, a time when a small silhouette, seen for a moment against the dark sky, can easily be just a trick of the dusk.

Lilac tucked her skirt into her knickers and shinned up the wall without fuss. Sitting astride it, she looked around, a quick, furtive glance. She saw no one ... but there was the coal, a huge glistening heap of it, just waiting for someone to start nicking!

The only trouble was, she was alone. She could steal the coal but to whom should she pass it? Which meant she must stuff it into her clothing and then try to get back over the wall with it – or she could throw some good pieces down onto the pavement and then follow, filling the sack she had brought.

The trouble was, she might throw coal over and someone else might nick it, or be hit on the head with it of course. Or someone might nab her whilst she was collecting the stolen coal and drag her off to the nearest police station and hand her over to the rozzers.

The wall was high and the lumps of coal very much larger than Lilac had anticipated. She picked up a piece, using both hands, leaning right down from the wall, then tried to straighten. She found she could not; the coal was too heavy. She put it down again, breathlessly, and picked up a smaller piece. Better. She hefted it shoulder high, went to throw ... and froze. A man, in uniform, was walking along in the shadow of the wall. He was humming a tune, looking down at his feet ... oh God, don't let him look up, Lilac prayed. Don't let him notice me!

God heard, or at least the man continued to stare at his stout boots. Once he was out of sight Lilac counted ten and then began, as gently as she could, to drop the coal onto the pavement. It was getting darker all the time and after a while she realised that she would not be able to carry any more, even if she could see to pick it up, which was getting more and more doubtful. She slithered down off the wall, her hands blackened by coal dust, her, legs and skirt by contact with the wall. She felt around for the sack, found it, began to push pieces of coal inside.

When it was full she straightened her aching back and tried to sling the sack onto her shoulder. She was reminded of the pictures in boys' comics of men in black masks with sacks marked 'swag' slung over their backs. But she could not even lift the bag off the ground, so that was another challenge to ingenuity.

Now and then someone passed, but when they did Lilac just slumped against the wall with her head down and no one seemed to notice her.

When she had half-emptied the sack she tried again and to her joy, found she could just lift it. But there was all the rest of the coal – it broke her heart to leave it after all her hard work. Still, she could come back later and reclaim it, she decided, heaving her sack up in her arms and beginning to stagger back the way she had come.

It was a good walk back to Coronation Court and by the time she was halfway, Lilac was having to stop every few yards. She got home in a state of collapse, wheezed across the paving and clattered the coal down in a heap at the front door. She shoved the door open and staggered into the room.

Aunt Ada was nowhere in sight. The fireplace was empty, of course, the plates from their dinner still on the table. There was someone moving about upstairs, she could hear an occasional thump, but that was all.

First, get some kindling and light the fire, then put the kettle on, Lilac ordered herself. When the kettle's boiling go and tell Aunt Ada that she can come down and get warm, then have a sit-down, then go back for the rest of the coal.

There was kindling at the back of the stove. Lilac fished some out and began to arrange it, wigwamlike, in the grate. She had no matches, but surely there should be some on the dresser ... she knelt up but could see none. Blow, no luck there. Better see if Auntie knew ...

There was a knock on the door and before she could get off her knees, it opened and Art appeared in the doorway.

'Hello, chuck,' he said cheerfully. 'Our Josh said as 'ow you'd been round after me. Is there ... Hey-up! What've you bin doin'?'

'Me? Oh, just buyin' a bag of coal from the coal-merchant on Great Howard Street,' Lilac said casually. 'Wondered if you'd walk down with me, that's all.'

Art gave a disbelieving snort.

'*Buyin*'? I weren't born yesterday, young Lilac,' he observed. 'No one never got that dirty a-buyin'. You've been nickin', ain't you?'

'We-ell ... yes. From that goods yard you showed

me, Art,' Lilac said all of a rush. 'Auntie had run out of coal, we couldn't even have a fire and it's awful cold … she's not too well again.'

'My word,' Art said slowly. 'You went nickin' by yourself, Li? Bet you didn't bring enough 'ome for 'alf a fire.'

Wordlessly, Lilac pointed at her bulging sack. Art whistled.

'You're a rare 'un,' he said at last. 'You're a great gairl, Lilac Larkin! Here, I'll light that for you.'

He set light to the dry kindling, then sat back on his heels and watched as Lilac gently put some of the smaller pieces of coal onto the blaze. She waited until the fire seemed to have taken hold, then put the kettle on.

'I'll give Auntie a shout in five minutes, tell her … oh my Gawd!'

With the words, her eyes had gone instinctively to the clock over the mantel. Except that it was not there. A cleaner patch on the whitewashed wall was the only sign that it had ever been there, in fact.

'What's up?' Art said. 'You 'membered something?'

'The clock … it's gone, someone must have stole it,' Lilac whispered. 'Oh Art, is Auntie Ada all right, do you suppose? Oh, she might of been murdered in her bed!'

Art looked at where the clock had hung, then he looked at the stair. Then he looked long and hard at Lilac. Then he spoke, almost reluctantly, it seemed.

'She's popped it, 'asn't she? You know that, doesn't you?'

'Popped it? What, at Cummins, on Great Homer Street? Why would she do that?'

'Why did you nick the coal?' Art said practically. 'No money.'

'Ye-es, but she didn't buy coal, nor food, not that I

can see,' Lilac said, frowning. 'There's no food on the table, Auntie hasn't even cleared our dishes from dinner, and the fire wasn't lit now, was it? What else would she want?'

Art gave her another of those long looks. Infuriatingly, he looked sorry for her, as though he knew something she did not.

'Well, now, why don't you go up and ask 'er?'

Lilac shook her head.

'Can't. I got a whole heap more coal, waitin' for me to pick it up. It's on the paving beside the goods yard. I'll ask Auntie in the mornin'.'

'You ask 'er now,' Art said. He still sounded sorry for her, as though he only half wanted her to go upstairs. 'It's better that you know, queen.'

Lilac stared at him for a moment, then turned and marched up the stairs. She was down again in two minutes. Tears had made two clean paths through the coal dust on her face.

'Oh, Art! She's ... she's ...'

'She's been boozin,' Art said, as though he'd known it all along. 'Never mind, queen, she'll be awright come mornin'. Now, d'you want me to come an' give you an 'and with that coal?'

They went back and got the coal and afterwards, Lilac realised it was both the beginning and the end of something. It was the end of any sort of family life because once Aunt Ada knew that Lilac knew where the money went, she let the child go very much her own way. And it was most definitely the beginning of freedom.

Aunt Ada never tried to stop Lilac doing things or going places again. Apart from anything else, she needed the money Lilac began to bring in and was all too often in no state to forbid her to do anything.

When Lilac got back from fetching the rest of the coal that evening she found Aunt Ada downstairs, trying to sober herself up. She was drinking strong tea and she smiled at Lilac as the door opened ... then looked startled.

'Wha's 'appened, chuck? Are y'awright?'

'I had a fall,' Lilac said rather stiffly. She walked stiffly too, because she'd tripped when the man chased them, sprawling onto the pavement amongst the chunks of coal, barely managing to get away. In fact, had it not been for a leckie, charging down the middle of the road, she was pretty sure both she and Art would have been caught.

But they were not. Instead, they hung onto the back of the tram like grim death, not letting go until they were well clear of pursuit.

'And we still got the coal,' Art remarked, as they limped into Coronation Court very late that night. 'Poor old Lilac, you won't forgit today in an 'urry!'

'A fall?' Aunt Ada repeated. 'Let's 'ave a look.'

She told Lilac to bathe her torn and bloodied knees in warm salty water and later, when one knee went septic and yellow bubbles began to appear, she applied blisteringly hot fomentations to the wound. But she never asked what Lilac had been doing – because she must have guessed – and she never even suggested that Lilac should stop going off with Art.

All through that cold and snowy winter, Lilac and Art kept both families supplied with coal and various items of food. They nicked what they could and earned money to buy what they couldn't nick. Art made it clear that their partnership was a business one, and they did very well for themselves, considering.

They haunted the docks after school and collected broken boxes, which they split into bundles of kindling. They sold some and kept some.

Then they collected rags. First you had to clean yourself up and go touting for rags somewhere posh, Seaforth was a good hunting ground, up Penny Lane, across to Knotty Ash. Then they sold the rags, which were sometimes quite decent bits of clothing, to traders in Paddy's Market.

After that there was 'carrying'. Boys usually did that, but Art graciously allowed Lilac to lend her muscle-power and the two of them would stagger home with heavy baskets, rolls of wallpaper or oilcloth or whatever a shopper might need to have transported. And a couple of kids were a lot cheaper than hiring a van or taking a taxi.

And Lilac really enjoyed it. She had not enjoyed being cold and hungry, but now that she earned – and spent – the money, at least she was not often very cold or very hungry. She tried to remonstrate with Aunt Ada when that person drank to excess, but Auntie always said it was just Lilac's imagination, that she only took a little nip now and then to keep out the cold, and that Lilac could be sent back to the Culler for telling lies if she ever said she'd seen her aunt the worse for drink.

So apart from schooling, Lilac ran wild and enjoyed every wicked minute. Art remarked, once, that Nellie would have a fit if she could see her precious Lilac now and for the first time for ages, Lilac took a good look at herself in the window pane, and was appalled by what she saw. She had grown long and thin, her clothes were all far too short and tight and her lovely hair, seldom washed, hung in tangles to her shoulders. Her skin was not perfectly clean and sometimes she felt suspicious movements in her hair and had to rush for the paraffin and the steel comb. She did the best she could, but with soap a rare commodity and hot water getting rarer, since when she was at school Aunt Ada frequently let the fire go out, it was not easy to keep clean.

Never mind, when spring comes I'll wash hard, every day, Lilac thought, turning away from the window pane. What's more, when spring comes I'll take Auntie up to the Lake District to visit Charlie, he'll talk some sense into her, get her off the drink.

But spring was slow in coming and Lilac had an education to get – for she never lost sight of her hopes for the future – and money to earn. So though she was sorry for Aunt Ada, and often angry over the waste of their money, she enjoyed her freedom very well and put up with the fact that freedom, in this case, equalled neglect.

Chapter Nine

'Right, girls, everyone ready? Let them in then, Nellie.'

Nellie, standing nearest the door, gulped, nodded and swung the double doors open. Outside, they waited in the chilly spring evening, the wounded who had walked, stumbled, dragged themselves back from the dressing station which, until barely forty-eight hours earlier, had been a bare five miles from the front line.

For it was March 1918 and the big Push, so eagerly awaited by the Allies, seemed to have turned into a disaster, a rout. The German army had moved forward, easily over-running the first positions they reached, and then they had surged on, full of power and confidence, and the weary, ill-equipped allied troops had had no choice but to run or be captured.

Hospitals like the mobile one in which Nellie, Lucy and many others served had been moved up from the coast to within a few miles of the Front in early March, before the offensive began. The people who plan wars were confident that they would be safe there, and more useful once the inevitable flood of wounded which always followed any offensive had to fall back. The generals envisaged wounded men being treated quickly and probably returned to the attack, Nellie thought bitterly as the men dragged themselves wearily across the wide green lawn of the chateau which had become the hospital's new home. No British general ever thought of defeat – and precious few considered the lives of their men, either. But the doctors who ran the hospitals had obediently moved their staff and quarters close to the line though several had voiced worries over the proximity of the enemy to their hoarded medical equipment and precious, overstretched staff.

But the Germans had made the first move and within twenty-four hours of the reverberating crash of the guns beginning, men began to pour in, wounded, desperate ... some just running as they had seen their trenches, outposts, lines disappear beneath a wave of Huns.

It had been terribly frightening, even to hardened souls like Nellie and Lucy, used to the rumble of the guns, the whistle and crash of mortar shells, the tremendous whooshing roar of descending bombs. But treating men who had come straight from the battle, on foot, some with clothing torn off in the blast, others with limbs missing, gaping wounds – and with the knowledge that the enemy were advancing all the time – that was enough to make the strongest soul blench.

A few hours after the first German break-through, the hospitals were also in retreat. Nellie, Lucy and their friends were crammed into lorries, equipment was mostly abandoned though everyone tried to take with him or her some useful tools, and any wounded man capable of walking was ordered to do their best to follow and try to catch up with the retreating hospitals wherever and whenever they set themselves down.

And now they had reached comparative safety at last and set up their tents in the grounds of a very large chateau. Once more they were within a mile or two of the coast and comforted by this, they had set to earlier in the day and had begun to transform stately salons and bedchambers into wards, and smaller rooms into emergency sluices or kitchens ... even dressing-rooms.

Some of their equipment arrived and more was coming from the coast but for now mattresses were put on floors, a room was roughly equipped as an operating theatre, and the girls greeted the arrival of their stained and disgusting old bell-tents with real relief. And now they were trying to sort out their patients; mostly weary men in the last stages of collapse, with dreadful wounds, who had come straight from the front or had been turned out of the departing hospitals to do their best on foot to reach safety once again.

Nellie, nearest the door, had been told to remove bandaging and dressings so that the wounds could be treated, but looking at the sea of faces outside she realised that this could not be a prolonged and careful business. She told the men to form a line and then, as the first one approached her, holding out his arm for inspection, she said briskly, 'What's your name, tommy?' and as he opened his mouth to reply she slid the scissors under the bandages and snatched the dried and encrusted dressing off.

The boy – he was little more – gave a hoarse shriek, abruptly stifled. He swayed and Nellie patted his arm, her eyes full.

'Well done,' she muttered. 'Straight over to the M.O., he'll prescribe and tell you where to go next.'

The second man in the line stood before her. He had seen what she had done – been forced to do – and was sickly pale, his lips tightly set. Nellie snipped and snatched; the man grunted and beads of sweat broke out on his filthy brow. Nellie felt her own brow damp, her hands shaking. But it was no use, if she didn't move fast some of these men would collapse before their wounds had been seen, let alone dressed. She reached for the next dressing, tore it off, dropped it on the floor and gestured the man past her.

'Next,' she whispered. Behind her, she heard the M.O. giving instructions to the nurses doing the dressings, heard the clatter and murmur as the troops moved slowly through the hall. She had no idea what would happen to these young men once their wounds had been dealt with – she could see what looked like several hundred men waiting – and these were just walking wounded, men who were considered capable of getting themselves to safety. There were many others who were being dealt with by the rest of the staff, men whose wounds would prohibit their being moved on ... and what if the Germans suddenly appeared? What would they do then? There were terrible tales of what the Germans would do to English nurses, to young injured tommies, and their air force had already proved that they didn't care much for the rules of war by bombing the hospitals whenever they got the chance despite the huge red crosses on their roofs.

But it was no use fretting; Nellie worked on solidly, trying to chat to some of the soldiers, joking with the ones still capable of talking back, trying not to allow the aura of fear and depression to push her deeper into the slough of despond. But it was uphill work; these were men who believed themselves defeated. She made a cheerful remark to one, something about his leg meaning he'd be back in Blighty for a spell and he said: 'We'll all be back in Blighty pretty soon, Sister – the Germans, too. Nothing can stop them. They're invincible. You should have seen them bearing down on us – all I could do was turn tail – me, who's fought the Hun and the trenches and our own dam'fool generals since December 1914!'

It halted her; she looked into his dark, bloodshot eyes and read conviction there ... and passed him on down the line, turning to the next man. Soldiers were wrong, sometimes. She prayed that this one was wrong.

'Nell, are there many still to come? We're going to run out of dressings pretty soon, someone will have to go to the stores for more. And it's midnight, we've been working since seven, I'm sure we've dealt with more than a hundred wounds. They said it was only a hundred, didn't they?'

Nellie turned and smiled at Emma, a pretty VAD in her early twenties whose good spirits were much prized by the other girls. But today even Emma had clearly had enough. It was, Nellie thought, the horror of not knowing what was happening as much as the tremendous numbers of wounded. They knew the Germans had broken through, knew the Allies were in hot retreat for the first time in their soldiering careers ... was it the end, then? A week ago their hopes of victory had been high, but now it seemed defeat stared them in the face.

'Is that what they said, only a hundred?' Nellie shook her head to clear it and then smiled across into Emma's fair and cherubic face, blanched now with exhaustion, shadowed by fear, smiled also at Lucy, steadily working away next to the younger girl. 'Well, there are a good few more still to come, and I'm sure I've ripped off at least three hundred dressings already and probably more, so you go down to the stores, Em, and take your time. I'll slow down a bit whilst you're gone, that will stop a bottleneck forming round the dressings table, if necessary I'll move over and help Lucy for a bit, just until you get back.' She turned to the M.O., sitting at the table between them. 'Will that be all right, Dr Dunning?'

'What ... ? Oh, for the nurse to fetch more dressings. Yes ... surely. Are we nearly at the end of the line, nurse?'

Dr Dunning was not much older than Nell and he

looked desperately tired. Nellie craned her neck to look through the doorway, blocked with men leaning against the door-jambs, all but asleep themselves as soon as they stopped walking.

'Not many more, sir,' she lied. 'We'll be finished and in bed before the sun comes up.'

'There's a weariness in all of us that's never been there before,' Nellie said three weeks later as she and Lucy were tumbling into their beds and hoping for a few hours uninterrupted sleep. 'I've had a letter from Li and another from Stuart and I've not had time to read either.'

Lucy, sitting down on the bed in all her clothing except for her apron, for it was still cold despite the advance of spring, thrust back the covers and rolled inside, heaving the sheets up round her shoulders.

'Stuart? And you've not read it? What's the matter, Nell? Are you ill?'

Nellie laughed, getting briskly into her own bed.

'No, not ill, Lu. Just totally exhausted. All I think when I get a letter now is, 'well, he was alive when he wrote it', and then I pray a bit that he's alive somewhere, still, and then I go on working.'

'Or go to sleep,' came a mumble from beneath the covers.

Nellie laughed.

'Or go to sleep,' she agreed. 'Oh, Lu, tell me tomorrow will be better.'

But no reply was forthcoming. Lucy slept.

After no more than two hours of sleep, Nellie was awoken by an orderly calling at the door of the tent – and by the drone of aero engines overhead.

'Wake up, girls,' the orderly was shouting. 'Get into the hospital, it'll be safer than the tent ... air-raid warning!'

It was remarkable how swiftly you could wake and dress with the whistle of descending bombs all around and only a flimsy tent between you and the alien night. Neither Lucy nor Nellie had undressed properly, so it was only a matter of moments before they were running across the garden which separated them from the chateau, clutching a blanket each, with their aprons unfastened but at least in position.

They burst into the hospital and found the place in darkness. Other girls equally breathless surrounded them. A chattering, as of anxious sparrows, filled the air. What was it, what had happened, were the Germans here already? A convoy of wounded had clearly just arrived, there were stretchers on the floors, on tables, up and down corridors. Makeshift beds were everywhere and they reached their ward just as the windows were lit up by an appalling explosion, so that for a moment the room was light as day. Sister saw them and hurried between the beds.

'Oh girls, thank goodness,' she gasped. 'Can you start getting the stretcher cases into bed? I'm doing my best, but what with Matron ordering all lights to be extinguished and this sudden influx of new cases, I'm afraid we're not making much headway.'

'Right, Sister,' Lucy muttered. As the older woman hurried off she turned to Nell. 'Twenty hours on duty, two hours sleep ... whatever next, I wonder? Death, by the sound of things out there – well at least we'll die working!'

They did not die because the hospital was not hit, though the railway station in the nearest town and a casualty clearing station were both annihilated. And a couple of days later Nellie, walking wearily across the foyer after a long and difficult shift, was stopped in her tracks when someone addressed her by name.

'Nellie McDowell, are you going to walk right by me? When I've travelled thousands of miles just to see you? Come here and look me in the eye and say you've forgotten me!'

One glance was enough. Nellie forgot she was tired, dirty, wearing a stained apron. She just flew across the foyer and found herself clasped in a pair of strong arms, lifted off her feet, then soundly kissed.

'Stuart!' Nellie said shakily as their lips reluctantly parted. 'Oh, my love, I thought I'd never see you again ... you look very well and fit – what on earth are you doing here?'

'Never mind that for a moment – are you going off duty? Then you must come out with me, somewhere quiet, where we can talk.'

It was against all the rules, all the regulations, too. A nurse was not allowed to go out with a man unless she was chaperoned by at least one other nurse and preferably more. Nellie, with her heart beating nineteen to the dozen and a warm glow suffusing her entire being, never gave rules or regulations, far less chaperons, a thought. She let Stuart put his arm round her shoulders, she slid her own arm round his waist, and thus entwined, they went out of the hospital, across the chateau grounds and into the small town.

'A meal first,' Stuart said. 'I'll see if I can persuade the innkeeper to bring the food up to my room.'

Nellie could not believe this was happening. Was she dreaming, perhaps? She had thought about Stuart, longed to see him, worried that when they did meet he might have cooled towards her, and now he was here and all her doubts had proved false. She looked at him, loving the leanness of him, the tanned face, the lines, even, which came with the constant strain they were learning to live under. They reached the inn and the proprietor agreed to bring a meal to Stuart's room. It was a pleasant room, with a big double bed, a sofa, a round table and four chairs. When the meal – cold meat, crusty bread, butter and beer – was on the table, she examined him closely and knew he was doing the same with her. He had nice teeth and his dark eyes sparkled. He had a cleft chin and an amusement crease in one cheek. His hands were sensitive and strong, she loved just watching him carve the beef, slice the bread.

'Nell, my love, what's been happening to you? I'm on my way to a posting, I'll let you know where I'm going as soon as I know myself, but you look so tired and pale.'

She told him. About the frightening retreat, the slow consolidation, the apparent turn in the fortunes of war, though no one trusted such turns, not any more. Too many bad things had happened. He listened, not interrupting, eyes steady on her face. When she finished he leaned across the table and took her face in his hands.

'My little love, I wish I could have spared you this! But I do believe this is the beginning of the end, truly I do. I can't tell you much – I don't know very much – but I believe the worst is over and that it won't be too long before there's peace. But Nell, darling, even when peace comes, I shan't be free, not at once. Nor you, I daresay, but you should get home before me. Will you wait for me?'

'I'd wait years,' Nellie murmured. 'Oh Stuart, I've been so afraid that you'd forgotten me, or perhaps that you'd meet someone else.'

'Someone else? The girl's run mad,' Stuart said. He got up and walked round the table, then lifted her out of her chair and settled her comfortably in his arms. 'I love you now, I loved you when first we met, I'll love you till the day I die. Kiss me!'

They kissed. Nellie's heart nearly burst with bliss and for the first time for many weeks, she felt safe.

'Nellie? Will you stay with me?'

She knew what he meant. They looked deep into each other's eyes whilst Stuart's hands gentled, persuaded.

'Oh, I shouldn't, I know I shouldn't! Suppose ... the hospital needs me, suppose something bad should happen like ... '

He put a hand on either shoulder and shook her gently from side to side. He was smiling.

'You can safely leave that side of it to me, my love. Will you trust me?'

She did not speak but he read the answer in her eyes. He picked her up in his arms and carried her over to the bed, laid her gently on the covers.

And, presently, they loved each other.

Summer came, and things improved. At first there were fewer wounded, then they began to get prisoners of war on the wards, German youngsters with wide, worried eyes, boys scarcely into puberty. The men who came into the mobile hospital were no longer despairing, sure of defeat. The tide had turned and their spirits had turned with it; they joked with the nurses, talked about what they would do in the peace, longed openly for their return to Blighty, not as just a vague dream but as something which was soon to become a fact.

On the fourth anniversary of the first day of the war

Lucy and Nellie were lying on the grass outside the chateau, in bright, warm sunshine, writing letters. Nellie had plucked a long blade of grass and was ruminatively chewing the sweet stem whilst she considered the page before her and Lucy was scribbling away, dipping her pen into their shared inkpot every few moments, sometimes chuckling, sometimes serious.

'Done!' Lucy exclaimed at last, throwing down her pen. 'Do you know I write to four officers now? I like them all, but I'm not in love with any of them – isn't that sad?'

'What about Sid? Is he one of them?'

'Ah, Sid and I hope when the war ends we'll meet and get to know one another properly, like you and Stuart ought, because you can't love someone you've only met two or three times, can you? Until then I'll continue to write to anyone who writes back to me. But it's a bit of a chore sometimes, when the weather's brilliant and I'd like a country walk instead. Who are you writing to? Stuart?'

'No, I wrote to him earlier. Lilac. I told her all about Stuart coming here, and that he's going back to Blighty for a new posting, and I suggested she might like to write to Matt, particularly now that we've heard about Fred's death. She was always fond of Matt, and he misses Fred horribly – they're twins, you know. I've been so busy, I write to so many people, but I've been a bit worried once or twice by the tone of her letters ... and Aunt Ada never even adds a line any more. Li seems to be out half the time ... I don't know, I'm just uneasy, I suppose. It won't hurt her to write to Matt, it might settle her down a bit. And then there's Charlie; he's invited them to visit him a dozen times but there's always some excuse. It's not like Auntie; she always did adore Charlie. And as to whether or not I'm in love with Stuart, I think I love him and I think he loves me, but we only had those few meetings with you and Sid, and when he came here it was just for one evening. I shall spend time with him when the war's over, like you say, but right now it's our Lilac who needs me most.'

'Well, you might get some leave in the autumn,' Lucy said drowsily. 'The casualties are definitely slowing down; why, Ward Six, the one the German kids are on, has got half-a-dozen empty beds. Can you imagine it? Empty beds!'

Nellie had capped her pen and laid down the page, but now she picked the pen up again, unscrewed the inkbottle top, dipped, and began to write once more.

' *Lucy has just said she thinks the pressure on us is easing*', she wrote. ' *If this continues it may be possible for me to get some leave in a few weeks.* '

'What've you written now?' Lucy asked drowsily. 'I hear your pen scratching away again!'

'Oh, I just said we thought it might be possible to get leave in a few weeks,' Nell said, blotting her postscript and folding the thin sheets of paper. 'Wouldn't it be odd if Stuart met Lilac whilst he was waiting for his ship to sail? He's bound to go abroad again, don't you think? He suspects it will be Egypt, though he didn't say why. He said he might be in the 'Pool for a while, though, waiting for his ship to leave.'

'Yes, you did mention it,' Lucy said. 'Nine times or so ... or was it ten? And talking of times, what time is it?'

Nellie glanced at her fob-watch.

'We've nearly half an hour before we're back on duty,' she said. 'I'm almost inclined to have a lie-down too, like you. Only I rather want to have a word with Lillian, on Ward Six.'

'Oh? Why?'

'Well, have you been into the ward lately? I went in yesterday and it was an education, believe me. There are little boys – kids – suffering from wounds, shrapnel, the lot. Oh Lu, do you remember Officer Baby? Well at least he could have been taken for eighteen or so, but these are boys of no more than thirteen or fourteen and they look what they are, kids! How can the Huns throw kids into battle? And they aren't even allowed to write home to tell their mothers they've been hospitalised, let alone that they're still alive. It's downright wicked. So I've been helping Lillian by writing letters to their mams when I've a free moment.' She gestured to the small pile of sheets before her. 'I got eight done before I wrote to Lilac,' she added proudly.

'It *is* awful, to send kids into battle, but they says the Huns are desperate.' Lucy said temperately. 'First their push shoved us back, then the Yanks came in and our combined push shoved them even further back. Now it's just nose-to-nose stuff again … a killer if you ask me, when everyone's tired. I suppose when the Hun hierarchy need somone to replace men who've died, the teutonic mind sees no harm in sending kids.'

'Well, I think it's wicked and evil; I hope to God no Englishman would do such a thing. And now, of course, there's this awful 'flu. Some of the Germans in Ward Six have had it, haven't they? And someone told me it's raging in the American lines.'

'Yes, and it's in Ward Eight, too. They try to keep flu victims away from other people, but several have died.' Lucy sat up and reached for the pile of letters which Nellie had just pointed out to her. 'Mind if I read one? I take it you're writing in English? Gosh, I never knew you could speak German, Nell!'

'Nor I can,' Nell said with a giggle. 'Sister gave Lillian a letter to copy and Lil passed one on to me, with some addresses. I copy the little paragraph in German, then add my own bits in English. If you want to help, I'm sure everyone would be delighted.'

'Mm hmm. Only you'll get called Hun-lovers,' Lucy said absently. 'You know how horrible they were to Annie when she fell for that German officer and started writing to his mother.'

'Scarcely; Lucy, these kids are babies, honest! But I don't care what anyone says, not when it comes down to it. I'll do what I feel is right. And if that sounds smug I'm sorry.'

'You don't sound very sorry,' Lucy said. She heaved herself to her feet.'Right, I'll do my share, and now let's just walk as far as the pine wood. I so love the smell of the pine needles and the peace and quiet.'

'Good idea,' Nell said. She got to her feet, brushed loose bits of grass off her long grey skirt, slung her folded apron onto her small pile of possessions and linked arms with Lucy. 'I wonder what Egypt's like? Hot, I suppose.'

'I believe the women are extraordinarily beautiful,' Lucy said wickedly. 'How will he let you know if he is going to Egypt, anyway? I'd have thought the censor would have snipped that out, quick as quick.'

'Of course, which is why we devised a code earlier on. I'll probably get a letter when he arrives, but until then I simply worry that … oh dear, it's better not to think about it, let alone talk. Let's change the subject – will you come up to Ward Six with me to deliver my letters before we go on duty?'

'Yes, of course I will. What better time to offer my services?'

The two girls reached the rickety old gate which led

into the pine woods and Nellie swung it wide, then rubbed moss off the palms of her hands and stopped to breathe in the soft, pine-scented air and to enjoy the cool shadows of the trees.

'Isn't this lovely? When I go indoors smelling of the pines and grass and wild flowers the boys look so wistful. Yesterday young Foulkes asked me what perfume I was wearing and when I said it was just fresh air he begged me to bottle some for him!' Nellie scuffed the pine needles under her feet and took her friend's arm once more. 'I wonder what Lilac's doing right now? Wouldn't it be odd if she and Stuart met?'

'Very very odd,' Lucy said. 'Mind you, funny things do happen, specially in wartime. Look at us meeting Stuart and Sid, when they weren't even patients of ours and we scarcely ever left the hospital.'

'That was fate,' Nellie said decidedly. 'And there's no real reason why fate shouldn't throw Lilac and Stuart together, you know. Then they could both write and tell me the other one was fit and well. Still, no use dreaming, it's time we turned back if we're to visit Ward Six before we go on duty.'

'Do you know, Auntie, that four years ago today the war started? Four years! I'm nearly thirteen, so four years ago I was just a baby, living at the Culler. Do you want some more spuds?'

Rationing had been introduced to try to see that everyone got a share in what little was available, but so far as Lilac could see, with or without rationing the people in Coronation Court were learning to live on potatoes, bread and thin air. And what was more, in order to get even a little money, for Aunt Ada had her own uses now for the shillings which came from abroad, Lilac simply had to earn whenever she wasn't in school.

Not that she minded. Since the winter, when she had first realised that her aunt drank to excess, she had started picking up a penny here and there and by now, with fruit and vegetables available once more, she was managing quite well, all things considered.

It was a shame that she so often went scrumping and nicking by herself, of course, but sometimes Sukey went too and anyway, you got more when you were the only one burrowing into a floursack like a very large weevil, or spooning sticky margarine out of the wooden tub in the warehouse and into your nicking bag.

Now Ada and Lilac were sitting at the table, with a plateful of meatless scouse in front of them. But it was tasty, because Lilac had boned a bone off the butcher and it was filling because of the spuds. Lilac had gone out to a house she knew of last night, on Everton Heights, and dug secretly, like a little mole, in their big kitchen garden. First she'd had to scale a wall, then wriggle between the jagged glass cemented into the top of it – she'd caught her skirt and scratched the back of her thigh, careful though she had been – and then it was just a matter of sneaking on all fours between a long avenue of black, red and white currant bushes to reach the maincrop potatoes.

She'd filled her bag gleefully, thinking the owner paid back for the pain of the deep scratch, knowing that he would probably never realise someone had been into his garden. Why should he? The row was already half lifted, she'd done no more than shorten it by a foot or so. And now here was Aunt Ada, staring vacantly down at her plate, ignoring the big, floury potatoes which Lilac had worked so hard to obtain. And she could not have had a drink for at least two days because the overseas money was late and the last lot had run out. And I won't hand over a second time, Lilac thought crossly, remembering how she had nearly bust a gut carting heavy shopping bags to get money for a scrag-end stew, and how Aunt Ada had disappeared with her hard-earned sixpence – and returned without the scrag but with another wretched bottle.

'Here, Auntie, let me give you some spuds,' she said now, raising her voice a little. It was strange, she thought, how their roles had become reversed. Now it was she who managed their budget, she who fetched food home. Auntie was still ever such a good cook, but she hardly ever made the effort any more. She would rather put up with Lilac's hit and miss culinary efforts than come out of her stupor of alcohol and misery to do a bit of work.

'Oh … no thanks, queen. I aren't hungry. I feels downright queer.'

Oh, not again, Lilac moaned silently, inside her head. Not another bout of the madness that drink brought, when her aunt saw maggots the size of shire horses munching the bedroom wallpaper, or the axeman in the black mask and scarlet tights … or had that been the devil? Aunt Ada had begun seeing things a month previously, and Lilac had honestly been thankful since it had stopped the drinking dead in its tracks – that plus the fact that the money was late again.

Still, Aunt could have drunk meths – people did – and she hadn't, so perhaps the giant maggots really were a blessing in disguise. Only now that she thought about it, Aunt looked as queer as she said she felt. She was waxy pale except for two round scarlet patches on her cheeks and there was sweat shining on her brow and her hands, lying in her lap, plucked and twisted and shook like sheets in a strong wind.

'Have you … well, have you seen anything nasty?' Lilac said baldly, after a moment during which she examined her aunt's small, rather bloodshot brown eyes closely. The madness usually showed first in the eyes, which rolled around the room a lot and stared and started from their sockets. Right now, Ada's eyes were half-closed, the lids puffed and heavy.

'Seen anything … oh, that! No, queen, I told you that was the end of that, for me. I aren't lettin' meself go down that road,' Ada said with more feeling than she had shown for some time. 'Didn't I tell you? No more drink; I'm on the water-wagon from now on.'

'Sorry,' Lilac mumbled. It was true that Ada had promised, and it was the first time such a promise had been made, too. Only Sukey, who was in on the secret of Aunt Ada's bad habit, had been sceptical. She said people meant to stop, only they couldn't, not always they couldn't.

'If I eat, I'll chuck up,' Aunt Ada said suddenly. 'Oh, how the room's turnin' round!'

Lilac did not reply but dug into her own meal, and presently Aunt Ada staggered from her place across to the horsehair sofa and collapsed on its uninviting expanse. She sighed heavily, then sat up.

'Queen, I'm goin' to … I'm going to … '

She was. Lilac, clearing up with wrinkled nose and a stout square of flannelette sheet, decided it was no use reproaching her aunt. No doubt she had intended to keep her promise, but Lilac knew from personal experience that it was a lot easier to say you'd be good than to stick to it. A couple of weeks ago, when the barrow boy down Juvenal Street had chased and caught her, shaking half a pound of plums from their stowage place in her knickers, she had vowed, as he walloped her, that she would never steal again.

Huh! And how would she exist without stealing, anyway? Aunt Ada could exist without drinking, or at least without drinking booze, but she'd be in queer street pretty damn' fast without nicking.

She picked up the bucket of dirty water and went and emptied it down the privy which all the families in the court shared. Then she went and cleaned out the bucket at the communal tap and rinsed out her square of flannelette sheet, wringing it vigorously and then hanging it across one of the many rope lines which criss-crossed the court.

It was a lovely day. Hot sunshine poured down on her head, making her feel at peace with the world. She decided to forgive her aunt for getting at the booze and went back indoors to suggest a walk down to the river.

'I dussen't move an inch, queen, or my head'll likely come off an' roll across the bleedin' floor,' Aunt Ada mumbled bitterly. 'Oh, what've I done, dear lord, to feel like this when I 'aven't 'ad a drop for t'ree weeks, four days an' seven hours? What've I done?'

'Plenty, I daresay,' Lilac said pertly, hoping to win a response, if not a smile, but Aunt Ada only groaned and made rumbling noises in the back of her throat which sent Lilac running for the bucket again. She got back in time, but Ada had lain down again, whey-faced. Her eyes were closed and she kept them so, determinedly.

'Gawd, I'm bad; I need 'elp,' she said presently. 'Oh, I feel like death, queen, like death.'

'Yes. Well, I'll mek you a cup of tea,' Lilac said. Long experience had taught her that the women of Coronation Court believed tea would cure most feminine ailments. 'There's water in the kettle, you can be sippin' a hot cuppa in two ticks.'

She had actually made the tea and was letting it brew, a hand tapping experimentally now and then on the teapot's worn brown side, when the knock came at the door. She shouted something indefinable – at the mere sound of a voice a neighbour would enter – and the door creaked open.

'Ello, our Lilac; want to come out, down to the river?'

It was Art, scruffy as ever, smiling uncertainly at her.

Lilac smiled back, equally uncertainly. Of late Art had not been his usual self at all. His insistence that because he was almost a year older, he must therefore be a superior being had begun to annoy her, and his unwillingness to let her 'tag along' seemed a rare insult when you considered that at one time she had been his preferred playmate.

Everyone, even Sukey, had tried to explain that boys usually felt this way about girls as they got older, but Lilac thought it was no excuse. He was so rude, now, accusing her of following him around when she was doing no such thing, telling her she was 'just a daft mare', making nasty cracks at her expense, denigrating her abilities as a cook-housekeeper, telling vulgar jokes which she didn't understand. He even said she was no swimmer, though he knew very well she could keep up with him – even do better – in the water.

What was more, he jeered at her in his new, raucous voice which kept wobbling from temporary bass to cracked soprano, and whenever he thought himself unobserved he rubbed grease on his bony chest, to encourage hair to grow he told Lilac.

'I don't see why you bother,' Lilac said, sniffing. 'What good does hair on your chest do?'

Art looked taken aback; clearly he had not

anticipated that particular question. Then he recovered himself and smirked, giving her a knowing look and shooting out his chest, thumping himself meaningly above the heart.

'Taint *just* the 'airs, it's other things,' he growled. 'Trust you not to know, though - you're only a kid!'

So when he came to the door and actually proposed that she might like to accompany him on a stroll down to the Mersey, Lilac was secretly gratified. She glanced doubtfully back at Aunt Ada, however. Auntie would not bother to forbid her - but should she be left? She looked ill and was definitely unhappy. But whilst making up her mind to refuse the treat despite it being, apparently, a sign of Art softening towards her again, Lilac had poured the tea and carried it over to the sofa. She bent down, intending to remind her aunt that the tea was made, when a sound gladdened her heart. Small, bubbling snores were emanating from between Aunt Ada's pallid lips. She was definitely asleep! And everyone knew that the best thing for any sort of illness was sleep, so her duty was clear. Get out of the house, leave Auntie warm and quiet with a cup of tea to hand should she awake, and go down to the river with Art.

'All right, I'll come,' she said therefore. 'Why the river though, Art?'

'Tide's out; thought we'd go rakin', 'Art said briefly.

Raking! It was a favourite pastime in summer, ever since Art had found the old cockle-rake abandoned above the tideline. You didn't find cockles in the Mersey mud - if you found some and tried to eat them, Lilac thought, they'd probably kill you stone-dead - but you found other things. She'd had a right pretty brooch out of the mud only last year, and there were lengths of timber, sometimes hardly rotted at all, bits of rope, the odd copper ... it was always fun, seeing what you could find in the mud. 'Right, I'll come,' she said with alacrity therefore. 'Bags I first go with the rake.'

'Second; you're a girl, an' only a kid,' Art said automatically, but Lilac did not start a row. It was a lovely hot day and besides, Art did own the rake, so it was only fair that he should have first go.

Side by side, therefore, they strolled out of the court and into the Scottie. There were few people about despite the lovely weather and the two children wandered along until they came to Mrs Brister's canny-house, where you could get a bowl of soup and a hunk of bread for a penny.

'I'll buy us dinners,' Art said. He fished in his pocket and produced some coppers. He had a job from time to time now, helping at the smithy, for with every fit man fighting in France and a great many women either nursing or doing war work, a strong young chap like Art could usually find himself some sort of employment, especially when the schools were out.

'Thanks, Art,' Lilac said, receiving her bowl. She should have told him about the scouse, perhaps, but she'd hardly eaten anything after Ada had been sick and anyway, it would have damaged Art's masculine pride to be refused when he offered a meal. Besides, it smelled good; golden lentils and grated carrot thickened the soup, made, Lilac knew, from the bone broth always simmering on the back of Mrs Brister's fire. She spooned it in until it got cooler, than tipped the bowl up and drank, wiping it round afterwards with a heel of brownish, homemade bread.

'Awright for you?' Art asked, still half-condescendingly. But Lilac, determined not to take offence, just nodded. He was mugging, after all, and it wasn't often someone treated her to a meal.

And presently they reached the river and saw the smoothness of the black mud and the little snake which was the deep channel, way out.

'Tek your shoes off,' Art ordered. 'Leave 'em up here, no one ain't gonna steal 'em.'

That was almost certainly true, Lilac thought ruefully, tugging off her cracked old boots. Nellie would have had a fit if she could have seen Lilac now, with her too-small, faded clothes and worn, patched boots. But one day I'll have lovely clothes and nice food, Lilac reminded herself, tucking her droopy skirt into the top of her knickers so that she wouldn't get her clothing mucky. If I find anything worth selling today there's no way I'll hand the money over to Aunt Ada, either. This time, I'll get me something to wear when school's back in.

'Comin'? Gerra move on then, gel!'

'All right, all right,' Lilac said crossly. She leaned against the big, cast-iron bollard nearest her, pulled off her boots and shuffled them into its shade. Art grabbed at a chain and began to swing out over the mud, then plopped off, sinking to his ankles. He looked back at her, grinning.

'Skeered, are ya? Frightened to git all mucky, eh?'

Lilac ran across the short stretch of planking which separated her from the edge and hurled herself onto the chains. Hand over hand, her body squiggling with effort, she, too, swung out over the mud and plopped down. Art stood back, hefting the rake.

'Good gairl,' he said. 'You can have a go in a minute.'

He began to rake and Lilac dug her toes into the squirmy mud, feeling for anything more solid. Something moved and she bit back a shriek, ploughing her foot forward. A rake was best, but sometimes, if you were lucky ...

It was a hot Sunday afternoon. People strolled across the floating bridge and alongside the docks but they took no notice of two muddy kids, playing by the river. And slowly, as the afternoon wore on, Art and Lilac forgot that one of them was almost a year younger than the other. They became friends once more, with no competitiveness to drive them, no new maturity to get between them. They dug in turns, squabbling amicably over their finds, and got further and further from the shore, nearer and nearer to the gleam of widening water. Art was collecting beer bottle tops to flatten on the tramlines so he could get Nestlé's chocolate out of the vending machines down at the pierhead. He had a good haul, besides some ha'pennies and pennies he had found, in addition to various bits of wood, a flatiron and half an old tyre. He was dreamy and talkative; his old self, in fact.

Lilac, taking her turn with the rake, had found her share of treasures. Bottletops, which she would try to flatten into penny-sized pieces as Art did. Coppers, with the old Queen's head on one side. Two little green crabs, still alive, which scuttled round and round the bully-beef tin in which she had placed them. They would be freed when the tide came in, but until then they were booty, just as the bottle tops and the coins were.

'My turn,' Art said presently, when Lilac had scratched up a large white stone, a bit of cork and a lovely length of rope. 'I got a seashell here once, a real good 'un.'

He took the rake and Lilac jammed her bully-beef tin into the mud, piled the odds and ends beside it – they were already sinking, but who cared on such an afternoon? – and began to dig with her toes, moving further away from the shore as she did so. It crossed her mind after a few minutes that the mud was deeper here, that it was over her knees, that the bottom felt gritty and sharp, but then she felt something interesting and stood on one leg, trying to bring the object up with her other foot by curling her toes around it.

Behind her, Art shouted something. He sounded cross, perhaps even alarmed. Lilac, still standing, storklike, on one foot, tried to turn round, lost her balance and fell forward. She saw the smooth blackness of the mud grow rapidly nearer, with its dimpled, blancmange-like surface, and then she was in it, her hands flailing, she was sinking, tipping sideways ...

'Help! Art, I'm going down!' she shrieked, and began to struggle and fight. She splashed mud into her face, opened her mouth to shriek again, and found it invaded by the slippery, foul-smelling stuff. Her eyes were blurred with it, her limbs slowed, her breath could not come, would not come! She sobbed, tried to struggle, held her breath until all she could see was red and black. Then it was too much effort even to move, the mud was too thick, too stifling, stinking ...

Someone was pulling at her, tugging her free from the mud's insidious grip. From somewhere far off she could hear what sounded like a cracked sobbing, a voice im- ploring her not to sink any furder, for God's sake. And then she heard Art swearing like a stream of dirty water, interspersing each foul word with breathless, cracked pleas for God to 'give us an 'and, then, or she'll be a goner, an' I just couldn't bear that!'

She heard his voice break, the gasps of effort, and then the mud released her with the most horrible squelching sound. One of her arms, the one Art had been tugging, felt as though it had been worked loose from its socket and her chest ached as though every rib was broken but she could breathe at last, she opened her mouth and felt air rush into her squeezed and painful lungs. She gasped and spat feebly, then began to sob. Oh, she ached all over, and she had nearly been drowned. She could have died, easy!

'Honest to God, our Lilac, I thought you was a goner! Jeez, our Li, I was so skeered ... You okay now? 'unky dory? Lean on me, gairl, get your breath, then we'll get outer here.'

'Oh, Art,' Lilac said as soon as she could speak. 'I nearly died ... where's my crabs?'

Art tutted; he sounded just like Nellie, loving but disapproving, Lilac thought feebly but with deep content.

'I kicked the can over, but the crabs is fine,' he said briefly. 'Come on, let's get back to the pier'ead. Tell you what, it's a bar of chocolate for two soon's we're on firm ground again. Cor, I thought I'd never git you out – we'll celebrate.'

Somehow, with Art almost carrying Lilac, they reached the chains under the floating bridge. Art pushed and shoved Lilac aboard, then swarmed up himself. Fortunately, perhaps, it was early evening and the wooden platform was deserted. Everyone must be having their tea, Lilac thought rather enviously. As soon as they reached firm ground however, they both collapsed on the wooden staging, but after a moment Lilac struggled up on one elbow and stared across at her companion.

'Art! Cor, you're *filthy!* I ain't never seen anyone so filthy before.'

Art sat up too.

'You wanter see yourself,' he observed. 'You little nigger minstrel!'

Lilac looked down. She was completely, totally, black. She put a tentative hand up to her head to find her hair was caked with mud. She put her hands to her face ... more mud, slithering on her cheeks where her tears must have cleared some slight passage but thick elsewhere, already trying to dry out in the warmth from the sinking sun.

'Oh, Art! Auntie'll kill me ... I'll die if anyone sees me!'

'They wouldn't know you from any other nigger minstrel,' Art said, grinning. 'Oh, hey-up, don't you start a-cryin' agin, we'll clean you up in a moment, soon's I've had a bit of a rest, like. I had to pull like merry 'ell to get you clear of that mud, you know. Nearly cracked me back.'

'You saved my life,' Lilac said in a small voice. 'I wouldn't be alive now if you hadn't cracked your back. Thanks ever so, Art.'

Art's filthy, mud-speckled countenance flushed a little. He lowered his head and stared down at his muddy bare feet.

'Oh well, you'd ha' done the same for me,' he said gruffly. 'Come on, let's find a street tap.'

They found a tap by one of the docks and cleaned themselves down as best they could. Then they washed each other's hair and stuffed their chilly feet into their boots, the only garments not saturated in the sticky, rich estuary mud.

'Do I look better?' Lilac asked doubtfully as they walked, dripping, along the Scotland Road. 'There's a funny smell, ain't there?'

'It's you,' Art said with cruel frankness. 'You went deeper than me, our Lilac, down to where it really pongs! Good thing it's Sunday, there's not many people about.'

'It's an 'orrible smell,' Lilac moaned. 'Auntie won't

have me in the house, you know, not smellin' like this. Oh, and my back hurts and hurts, as though someone was tryin' to break me in two.'

Indeed, it was not only her back that ached; she had vicious, stabbing pains in her stomach. Cramps, she supposed vaguely. And by the time they reached the court, the backache had settled into a real pain that throbbed through her, making her want to simply lie down on the paving stones and try to ease it.

'Tell you what, Lilac, when you was sinkin' in that mud ... when I thought I wasn't a-goin' to git you out ... know what I thought?'

'No? What?'

'I thought as life wouldn't be no fun if you died on me,' Art said, sounding shamefaced. 'You're only a kid, and a gel at that, but ... I likes you more'n I thought I did.'

Lilac took hold of his hand and pulled him to a halt. She stared straight into his eyes. Despite the pain, despite the aches, despite even the rich and foul smell, she suddenly felt a most wonderful feeling spreading like a warm glow throughout her body. She looked at Art, starry-eyed. How ... how very *nice* he was; she would like to spend the rest of her life being pulled out of the mud by Art! But what about the way he had behaved towards her until today?

'But what about the gang? You said ... you said ...'

'Them? They ain't nothing at all, they don't matter a toss to me,' Art said. 'Lilac, I reckon I love you, that's why I've bin a bit sharp-like with you lately.'

It sounded reasonable to Lilac. In fact it sounded as though Art felt just as she did. With the glow doing strange things to her, spreading and spreading, invading even the tiniest nooks and crannies of her small person, she took Art's hand in hers, then held it to her cheek.

'You saved my life,' she whispered. 'I reckon I love you as well, Art.'

And she meant it. She had thought she loved Matt, once, but never had she felt this extraordinary feeling before, a sort of melting, darting warmth which made her conscious of her whole body – and made Art's muddy figure shine like a knight in armour.

'Right. We'll get married one day, then, shall us? You're only a kid now, but you'll grow bigger. An ... and you're ever so pretty, Lilac, easily the prettiest gal in the Corry.'

'There's only a few of us in the Corry,' Lilac said, fishing hopefully. Surely she had read somewhere that when a boy loved a girl, he paid her compliments? 'Would you say I was prettiest in my class?'

'Prettiest gal in Scotland Road,' Art said, giving the full title. 'If I'm sharp with you agin, our Lilac, just you remind me of this afternoon ... your 'air's got a lovely colour when it's noo-washed.'

'Better'n mud,' Lilac observed. 'You're all right too, Art. Reckon you'll be handsome when you're a man.'

This rather tepid praise seemed to please Art, who gave a blissful grin, even as Lilac was wishing she'd phrased it differently.

'Oh, Lilac ... oh, I wish we were somewhere different, somewhere quieter. Guess I'd give you a kiss.'

Lilac, taken aback, stared. Then she put her hands on Art's shoulders, stood on tiptoe, for he was taller than she, and kissed him, quickly and inexpertly, on the chin.

'There,' she said triumphantly. 'Thanks, Art. I'll never forget today.'

'Nor me neither,' Art said huskily. 'Come on, let's 'urry; me mam'll have the tea out – you might as well come in for it. It's funny, I feel as if I want to be with you all the time, see you're all right.'

'That's nice, but I'll see to Aunt Ada first,' Lilac said. 'It won't tek me long, though. You go home, I'll be round in a cat's wink.'

They reached Coronation Court and Art disappeared into his own house, no doubt to prepare his mother for a guest, whilst Lilac, with her clothes drying uncomfortably on her small person and her long hair dripping all down her back, entered her own front door.

Now that Art had gone she was once more aware of the sharp pain in her middle, but as she crossed the threshhold she stopped short, a hand flying to her mouth.

The room was small and darkish, but even through the gloom she could see a man standing by Aunt Ada's sofa, a man she had never seen in her life before. And her aunt lay back, her skin a curious bluish grey colour, strange sounds emanating from between her loosely opened lips.

'Oh my Gawd ... what've you done to Aunt Ada?' Lilac said shrilly. 'If you've hurt 'er ...'

The man turned. He was dressed in a long khaki coat and brown, shiny boots and he looked as anxious as Lilac felt. All at once her fears that he might have hurt Aunt Ada melted away. He had a good, strong sort of face – this man, she felt sure, meant no one any harm.

'I've done nothing, Lilac, I found her like this,' the man said.'You are Lilac, I take it? Nellie asked me to look in but no one answered the door so I put my head round it and saw ... this.' He gestured to the room and to Aunt Ada, flat out on the horsehair sofa. 'I've only been here a couple of minutes but it's clear to me she's very ill. Can you fetch help?'

'I think she's sozzled, probably,' Lilac said cautiously. She did not want to get involved with doctors or their bills unless it was absolutely necessary. 'She boozes sometimes because she's lonely, I think. How d'you know our Nellie?'

'We met in France; in fact I went and saw her again only two weeks ago. I'm Stuart Gallagher,' the man said. He smiled and a long dimple appeared in one thin, brown cheek. Lilac discovered that he had very dark eyes and black hair which curled across his forehead. He reminded her a bit of Davy, and she had liked Davy! 'Look, luv, it's not the booze, she's really ill. Can you get a blanket from somewhere, she's shivering, and fetch a doctor or a neighbour who knows a bit about sickness. I think it may be a dose of the 'flu that's sweeping the country.'

'I'll fetch Mrs O'Brien, she's Art's Mam,' Lilac gabbled, scared by even the mention of 'flu. A kid in school had caught it and died! 'Shall I make some tea? I'll pull the kettle over the fire, it'll be boiling in a brace of shakes!'

'Right, but get the blanket before you go. I'll watch the kettle.'

Lilac bounded up the creaking stairs like a young tornado, grabbed a thin blanket off the bed and tore down again.

'Here y'are, Stuart,' she gasped. 'Now can I go an' fetch Art and his mam?'

Without waiting for a reply she went to the door and simply shrieked; Art came running, his face enquiring.

'What's up, chuck? Is Ada angry about you gettin' muddied?'

'She's ever so ill,' Lilac gabbled. 'Can you help, Art? There's a feller, a pal of our Nellie's, telling me what to do and lending an 'and.'

'I'll fetch me mam,' Art said stoutly. 'You stay out 'ere Lilac, I'll fetch me mam in a flea's blink.'

But Lilac had fled back indoors, arriving just in time to help Stuart to raise Auntie's head so that they might try to trickle some tea between her lips.

But she would not drink, or rather could not, for once Lilac saw her lips move and her tongue slide forward, as though the liquid was welcome, but then it ran out of her mouth again and soaked into the blanket that Stuart had wrapped round her.

'Is she … very ill?' Lilac said presently, 'She don't seem to know we're here, and she can't drink, though it seemed for a minute as though she might.'

The young man shot a quick glance at her.

'Yes, I'm afraid she's very ill. I think someone ought to get either a doctor or an ambulance. I believe it is the 'flu and that means the best place for her is hospital.'

Whilst they talked, Stuart had been moving around the room, damping a cloth in the water bucket, taking it over to the sofa and wiping Aunt Ada's gaunt, yellowish face. Then he propped her head up on his arm again and told Lilac to try the teacup once more and this time a little - a very little - tea actually seemed to dribble into the sick woman's mouth, and a convulsive swallow and a murmuring cry seemed to indicate that it had gone down.

'That's better,' Stuart said. 'Ah, I think I hear someone coming. Mrs O'Brien, did you say?'

But it was not Mrs O'Brien who panted into the room but Art.

'Mam says I'm to fetch the doctor, she's got the littl'uns 'alf-way undressed for bed,' he said. 'Got some chink?'

Stuart blinked and began to put Ada's head back on the hard sofa arm.

'Chink?'

'You'll have to give Art some money,' Lilac explained. 'He'll go at once and be ever so quick, but you won't get a doctor to come to the Corry without you pay 'im first.'

The young man laughed, then dug his hand in his pocket. He drew out a sovereign and put it into Art's grubby fist.

'Sorry, Art, I should have realised ... and you really had better hurry, or there won't be much point in your going at all.' He waited until Art had hurried out of the room and then turned once more to Lilac.'Your Aunt's shivering, yet she's awfully hot, so I think we ought to try to get her temperature down; I'll take the blanket off and undo her blouse and then we'll bathe her forehead and neck with cold water until the doctor gets here.'

'Sure, Stuart,' Lilac said eagerly. 'Oh, aren't I glad you're here to tell me what to do!'

The doctor came and ordered an ambulance which took Aunt Ada off to the nearest hospital. After she had gone, still without regaining consciousness, Stuart stood in the small room, looking thoughtfully across at Lilac. Art stood beside him. Lilac's aches and pains, which had almost disappeared whilst she was rushing round after Aunt Ada, began to nag at her again. She looked at the two males standing shoulder to shoulder watching her, one no more than a kid really, like herself, the other a young and handsome man, and wondered what would become of her with no Aunt Ada to lend her respectability? How long would it be before her aunt came home from hospital? What should she do until then?

'Well, Ada never noticed you'd been in the mud, I dare-say,' Art said suddenly. 'Unless she reckernised the pong, that is.'

And with the words, it all came flooding back into Lilac's mind. Her horrible misadventure, the smelly mud, how dirty she still was, how stiff her clothing, how mucky her person and her hair. And she hurt, she hurt!

Lilac gave a muffled sob and collapsed onto the sofa. The horsehair pricked the sensitive skin at the backs of her knees, but she was past caring. She folded both arms round her middle and learned forward, groaning.

'What's the matter, Lilac?' Stuart said. 'What's all this about mud? Now that I come to look at you ... well, what a sight! Art, is there a bath?'

'Aye. A tin one, in the yard by the privy.' Art pulled a sympathetic face at Lilac but she was past caring. Troubles seemed to flap around her head like bats; why had she not been a sensible girl and said 'no' to Art's suggestion of mud-raking? 'Shall I bring it in, Stuart?'

'If you would,' Stuart said politely. 'Will your mam still be busy, do you suppose? Because if not, I could use a bit of help.'

'She's got five young'uns to feed and bed down,' Art said gloomily. 'I'll give you an 'and.'

Stuart looked at him narrowly.

'By the look – and smell – of you, Lilac isn't the only one needing a bath,' he said frankly. 'I'll poke the fire up and shove the pair of you in the water.'

Art bridled.

'Not me you won't,' he said firmly. 'She's the filthy one, I'm only a bit dirty 'cos I heaved her outa that mud.'

'I've got a dreadful belly-ache,' Lilac said sullenly.

'I think my insides are going to fall out. It's because Art pulled and heaved at me the way he did ... I can't get into the bath.'

But Stuart jollied her along, heated water, made her drink a cup of tea whilst they waited for the bath to be filled. And though the pain did not go, though she still felt quite sick with it, she managed to stifle her groans. She thought Stuart quite the nicest and best-looking young man in the world and desperately wanted him to like her, too. He was unlikely to feel fond of someone who made a dreadful fuss!

The bath full at last, Lilac reluctantly pulled her dress over her head. She was wearing tattered knickers but nothing else. Stuart got the blanket that had not gone off in the ambulance with Aunt Ada and warmed it by the fire.

'You can dry on that, once you're clean,' he said. 'Come on, into the water.'

Art had been banished since he refused to bath too, so Lilac, still clutching at her agonising stomach, got into the tin tub and sat down. For a moment it was really lovely, as though the hot water was a healing force in itself, but then Stuart threw her the soap and as soon as she began to wash the pain returned two-fold. Wave after wave of it, frighteningly severe.

'I think I've got the 'flu, like Auntie,' Lilac whimpered. 'I'm going to be sick, I am, I am!'

'Hold on!' Stuart ordered her sharply. 'I'll fetch the bucket.'

She retched a couple of times into the bucket but only managed to produce what looked like dirty water. Then she sat back in the bath again, tears running down her cheeks. Oh, she wanted so badly to have Stuart for a friend and all she could do was whine at him and be sick!

'Good girl,' Stuart said kindly. 'Use the soap ... oh here, I'll do your hair.'

He rubbed the soap vigorously into her long hair, then rinsed her with the tall enamel jug full of fresh water. It was cold and for some reason this gave her a whole new series of pains, sharp, darting pains, driving into her lower stomach and back. She gasped but said nothing more until he wrapped a thin towel round her head.

'All right? Want to come out? I'll hold the blanket for you.'

She climbed out stiffly, a mass of acute discomfort. Stuart held the blanket, wrapped it firmly round her shoulders. Doubled up with the pain, she managed to get to the horsehair sofa before collapsing.

'I should have got the doctor to you, I would have if I'd known you'd been face down in Mersey mud,' Stuart said. 'Here, get close to the fire, it'll help to dry you.'

Lilac got to her feet and shuffled nearer to the fire, then felt something running down her legs. A strong feeling that it was probably her insides prompted her to look down. She gasped and collapsed into the chair Stuart had put out for her.

'Oh Stuart, there's blood on me leg! Oh, the pain in me belly's awful, I'm bleedin' to death, I must have been worse hurt in the mud than I knew.'

Stuart flicked the blanket back and looked at her pale and skinny legs. 'You aren't ...' he began, then stopped abruptly. He looked at the watery blood running down the inside of her calf and then looked up at her. He cleared his throat, then used the blanket to wipe the blood off. More trickled down and the pain, sharp as knives, dug into the sides of Lilac's stomach. She whimpered again, clutching her middle protectively, squeezing her knees together as though by so doing she could prevent her guts from descending, which was what she most feared. All that pulling and tugging had obviously done awful damage internally – she was probably dying!

She voiced the thought aloud; Stuart snorted, then rumpled her hair apologetically. His face was pink and his eyes kept darting around as though they wished they were somewhere else.

'Look, queen, what's happening to you is perfectly natural, though painful, I'm afraid. Did Nellie ever talk to you about ... well, about things that happen to ... to growing girls?'

'No, I don't think so,' Lilac said, considerably mystified.

'What about Aunt Ada? Didn't she ever tell you about ... oh hell and damnation, sit still a mo, I'll see if Mrs O'Brien's free yet.'

He left. He was gone a long time. Lilac sat and hugged her stomach and wondered what on earth he was on about. But soon all she could think of was the pain and her loneliness. By the time Stuart returned she was in tears.

He opened the door and came across the floor. He had a cup in his hand and was carrying it carefully, as though anxious not to spill a drop.

He saw her tears and his own expression softened.

'Poor kid, what a time for it to happen! Look, flower, just get this down you. It'll help, honest. You'll go to sleep and feel fine in the morning, Mrs O'Brien says. And she says to tell you that the pains are the start of ...' his face was very red and his eyes were looking – staring, really – down into the cup. He handed it to her and half turned away '... the start of your ... your monthlies. Okay? Now drink up.'

'Oh. All right. Only I don't want to fall asleep here,' Lilac said, trying to think where she had heard that expression before. Monthlies? It sounded vaguely familiar ... if only the pain would go away she might be able to think what he meant. 'Shall I go upstairs before I drink it in case I fall down asleep that very minute?'

He laughed, openly and naturally this time.

'Goodness, it's not that strong, you drink it down here and then I'll see you into bed.' He fished in the pocket of his coat and produced what looked like a bundle of rags and a length of string. 'Mrs O'Brien gave me this for you to ... er to wear ... you'll know how to use it, I daresay. And don't worry, because you aren't going to be left alone, I'll kip down on the sofa until morning.'

Lilac stared at the bundle of rags, then up at Stuart. She could not think why she might need the rags, but it scarcely mattered, because she had just realised she was in love for the second time in one afternoon. She looked lovingly at Stuart. He's the best person in the whole world, she decided. She lay the rags down on the sofa and drank the liquid in the cup, which was hot and sweetly medicinal and smelt of the stuff Aunt Ada liked too much, then smiled up at the young man hovering over her.

'There, all gone! And will you really stay all night? Until morning?'

'On my word of honour, I'll still be here when you get up. And then we'll have to talk about what to do with you until Auntie's well again.'

'Thanks ever so, Stuart. I'll go off now, then.'

He came up the stairs with her. Already the terrible pains had eased to no more than a deep, twanging throb. She sat on the bed and he handed her the pad of rags.

'Don't forget to use these, love, or you'll mark your bed.'

Lilac took the rags and, when he had left, regarded them with disfavour. She knew she should put them on, she had seen Bessie with the same sort of pad several times, but somehow it had never occurred to her that one day she, too, would need the wretched things. She examined the rag pad and presently, saw how it worked. She adjusted it around herself, feeling foolish and self-conscious, thoroughly glad, for once, that she had the room to herself.

She climbed into bed and settled down. As she began to relax it suddenly occurred to her where she had heard that expression - 'monthlies.'

She had heard Nellie blame her pallor on her monthlies, and Bessie explain that she did not wish to heave the sack of coal indoors because she had her monthlies and they were hurting ever so.

And with that she remembered something Nellie had once said. About a girl being careful how she behaved, especially after she'd started her monthlies.

'Why then, Nell?' she had asked curiously.

'Because then a girl isn't a girl any more, she's a woman,' Nellie had said, smiling at her. 'Then she can have a little baby of her own.'

And now it had happened to Lilac herself, the moment of true growing up had arrived! Lilac sat bolt upright in bed.

'I'm a woman!' she said, speaking aloud in her excitement. 'I'm a real woman, like our Nellie and our Bess. Why, I can even have a baby!'

It was a startling, not altogether welcome thought.

Presently she snuggled under the covers once more. Downstairs, Stuart would be sleeping, curled up on the horsehair sofa with a blanket over him. How strange it was that he should have realised she had reached womanhood before she had known it herself. Still, if she had to share this exciting, frightening knowledge with anyone, she would as soon it was Stuart. In the morning she would tell him so, thank him for explaining to her what had happened to her body. If he had meant it, that was. If he really had kipped down on the shiny horsehair sofa.

Should she check? She could sneak halfway down the stairs and peep, although the stairs always creaked she had a shrewd suspicion that after the sort of day he had had, Stuart was unlikely to be woken by a mere creak or two. But then she pulled the blanket back up round her ears and snuggled down. She had no need to check, she knew Stuart was there, that he would keep his word.

She slept.

Chapter Ten

On the day following Stuart's eruption into her life, the three of them – for Art insisted on coming too – made their way to the hospital where Aunt Ada had been taken.

At Stuart's insistence they caught the tram as far as Great Crosshall Street and then walked. Down Tythebarn, along Pall Mall and into Leeds Street. Walking briskly along Pall Mall the children picked their way between the passengers entering Exchange station, and then spent an enjoyable few minutes watching the trains. Then they went under the huge bridge on Leeds Street, and Lilac shuddered with delicious terror at the thought that the bridge might give way when they were halfway under and the trains might come thundering down and kill them.

Who would I save first, Art or Stuart, she wondered, hurrying along between them. Art was nice most of the time, but he could be horrible, rough and rude. Besides, everyone saved the man they loved first, so she would, of course, save Stuart. She imagined flinging herself at him with a wild cry ... 'Run, Stuart, I'll hold up the bridge whilst you escape!' and then seeing Art's round, reproachful eyes fixed on her as they died together ... that would be romantic, now she thought about it. To sacrifice your life for one man and die in another's arms. Cor!

She glanced sideways at Stuart in the dimness under the bridge. He was looking troubled; she guessed he was wondering what to do with her should he be called away before Auntie improved. She glanced at Art. As luck would have it he was giving one of those awful, juicy snorts and wiping his nose on his sleeve. Oh dear. No contest, Lilac thought rather smugly. Art was no gent, though it did occur to her that he might well have caught a chill lugging her out of the mud which would account, at least in part, for the snort.

They emerged into the sunlight and, looking to their right, could see the hospital ahead of them. It was dauntingly large, a great mass of grimy brick surrounded by railway lines, which was no doubt why it was so dirty. Poor Aunt Ada, shut up in there, Lilac thought with genuine sympathy. But it wouldn't matter to her where she was, provided they made her well again.

'Isn't it ugly!' she said however, swinging on Stuart's arm. 'What's it like inside?'

'Not too bad, but you'll see for yourselves in a minute,' Stuart said. 'It was built by a great philanthropist in the last century, a chap called David Lewis, so it may be a bit old-fashioned, but it's one of the best for treatment they say. I was brought here once when I was a kid but I don't remember much about it now. Except that they made me well again, of course,' he added.

'David Lewis? I thought that was a theatre,' Art said. 'I *know* it's a theatre, I bin scrumpin' fruit off of the barrèr outside there, I seen the people go in an' out, all dressed fine.'

'He built that too, I guess,' Stuart said. 'The hospital's usually called the Northern, but really it's the David Lewis Northern Hospital. Probably he built the theatre because he thought Liverpool folk needed somewhere to have a bit of fun as well as somewhere to go when they were sick.'

'And wasn't Auntie lucky, that they took her to the

best hospital there is!' Lilac said. She gave Stuart the benefit of her most dazzling smile. 'I 'spect that was your idea, Stuart. Oh well, she'll be out before the cat can lick its ear.'

Stuart looked at her, started to speak, then seemed to change his mind. He stopped just before the great, dark entrance and checked his charges with his eye. 'Do up your collar, Art,' he said, speaking perfectly pleasantly but somehow managing to make it plain he expected to be instantly obeyed. 'Lilac, don't look so anxious, it won't do to worry Mrs Threadwell. Come on, then! I don't know which ward she's on, but I'm sure there will be a receptionist who can help us.'

Inside the hospital it was quiet and yet it bustled with nurses and people going purposefully about their business. Some of the nurses smiled at the small party, others hurried past without giving them a glance. Stuart went to the desk where a middle-aged lady in a dark dress sat, writing in a big book. He cleared his throat.

'I wonder if you could help me? We're looking for a Mrs Ada Threadwell.'

'Oh yes? When was she admitted, sir?'

Lilac thrilled to that 'sir'. If Art and I had been alone no one would have called anyone sir, she thought. In fact, if I'd asked, or Art, we'd have been lucky to get an answer!

'Yesterday afternoon; latish.'

The lady produced an enormous ledger and opened it, then ran her index finger slowly down the long line of names. The lady's nail was the cleanest thing Lilac had ever seen, even cleaner than a teacher's. Her hair was smooth, too, her face calm and benign. Lilac found herself relaxing in such undemanding company. She had known several nurses and associated them with red, work-worn hands and tired faces and it occurred to her that if being a hospital receptionist meant having clean nails and sitting behind a desk reading from a big ledger, it was a job she would very much enjoy.

'Ah, here it is. Mrs Ada Threadwell, Ward Eight.' The receptionist looked up at Stuart and then at the two children. 'I wonder, sir, whether it might be wiser not to go into the ward with the children? It's an influenza ward.'

'It's all right, we were with the patient yesterday; this young lady is Mrs Threadwell's niece,' Stuart said. 'But perhaps Art should wait outside.'

The lady gave them directions to reach Ward Eight and they set off down a long, shining corridor with narrow windows overlooking the street they had just left.

'I *am* a-comin' in wi' you,' Art muttered hoarsely as they traversed a corridor at right-angles to the main one. 'I ain't skeered ... two kids in our school died of it, though.'

They found Ward Eight and went in through the swing doors. A starched nurse approached them, rustling. She looked coolly at the children but her expression warmed a good deal for Stuart. I knew he was handsome, Lilac thought triumphantly. Even the nurse has noticed!

'Good morning, sir. Can I help you?'

The ward was long and dull, the beds identical, the patients anonymous beneath the tightly tucked covers. Lilac scanned what she could see of them and could recognise no one.

'Mrs Ada Threadwell? She's right at the far end of the ward – she's still very ill, sir. I doubt she'll recognise you.'

Lilac opened her mouth to say it would be a miracle if her aunt recognised Stuart, then shut it again.

Fool that she was, if she let on that she and Art had only known Stuart a day themselves and that Auntie would not have known him from Adam, someone, some interfering busybody of a person, would whip them away from him before you could say 'knife.'

They went over to the bed the nurse had indicated. Aunt Ada lay there, propped up by pillows. Her face was no longer waxy pale, there was a faint flush on her cheeks and her lips, which Lilac remembered fearfully as blue-tinged, were a normal colour. Her breathing was hoarse but steady and presently, her lids flickered open and she looked at them – and the shadow of a smile crossed her face.

'Well, if it ain't our Lilac,' she whispered. ''ow are you managin' without your Auntie?'

'Oh fine … Aunt Ada, guess who come callin' when you was took bad?' Lilac gabbled, taking her aunt's hand and holding it firmly in hers. 'This is Stuart, the young man our Nell talked about … he got you into hospital and he's taken care of us … can you say hello to him, Auntie?'

The tired eyes found Stuart's and held them for a moment and the slight smile warmed.

'Thanks,' was all she said however and Stuart, smiling too, jerked his head at Art.

'All right, we don't want to tire Mrs Threadwell, so if you two will just wait for me in the corridor, I won't be a moment. But we've some arranging to do, your aunt and I.'

Art and Lilac, without voicing any objections, scurried out of the ward. It was very odd, Lilac thought as they pushed through the swing doors and into the corridor, how nicely Stuart said things, never ordering you about yet managing to make you eager to do as he asked, anyway. Even Art, known to be a cantankerous soul, didn't stop to argue with Stuart.

Once in the corridor, the two children faced one another.

'She was awful ill, wasn't she?' Lilac said. 'But she's ever so much better now, don't you think, Art?'

'She was ill all right,' Art agreed. 'But she'll get well, she looks grand already compared to yesterday. Besides, old people don't snuff it from flu; it's kids what die.'

This piece of information heartened Lilac considerably, for though she had noted the improvement in her aunt's colouring, it was a shock to see her lying quietly in bed, so weak that even a few words tired her.

'Course, I knew that,' she said. 'But I daresay it'll be a day or two before she's out, won't it?'

'Oh aye. Good thing you've gorra pal to stand by you.'

'Yes, Stuart's so good,' Lilac agreed, only to see Art turn a hurt and scowling face towards her.

'Him! He'll be gone soon enough. It was me I meant – and me mam and that.'

'Yes, of course, I'm sorry,' Lilac said. 'But Stuart won't leave me there alone, I'm sure.'

'Course he won't,' Art said stoutly. 'Because me mam'll 'ave you to stay at our place when 'e goes. She said.'

'That's nice.' Lilac tried not to remember the crowd of mucky little kids who were Art's younger brothers and sisters, the dirty house, the idle way fat Mrs O'Brien behaved towards her large brood.

'Yes, she's awright, our mam. I say, Lilac, what's a philan ... phinath ...'

'Oh, you mean what Stuart said that David Lewis was? It's a feller what builds big buildings, plans 'em and that,' Lilac said airily. 'Sometimes they call 'em artitecks ... somethin' like that, anyway.'

'Oh, I see,' Art said. 'Hey-up, 'ere comes Stuart!'

Stuart visited the hospital for the last time on the day he got his sailing orders. By now, Aunt Ada was sitting up and taking notice. She was taking milky drinks, eating soft things like porridge and rice pudding, and was clearly hauling herself back to full health at a remarkable rate of knots.

'She's got the constitution of an ox,' the ward sister told Stuart when he asked how long her patient would have to remain in the hospital. 'She can stay two more days just to be on the safe side, but considering the state she was in she's made a remarkable recovery. Because that flu kills strong men and healthy, well-nourished women who've never touched a drop of alcohol in their lives.'

Walking home after the visit was over, Stuart wondered aloud why the ward sister thought Aunt Ada had been in a bad state. He glanced at Lilac's face as he spoke and thought she looked a trifle pink, but they were walking fast ...

'Lilac dear, does Mrs Threadwell have any problems that I should know about?'

It was the nearest he felt he could come to asking a question which could be taken very much amiss. But Lilac looked up at him with those blue, brilliant eyes and answered easily, spontaneously. And why should he doubt her, after all?

'Problems, Stuart? Well, a touch of rheumatism in her knees now and then, which is why I usually scrub the kitchen floor over, but otherwise she's sound as a bell.'

'Well, that's good,' Stuart said. 'And she'll be out the day after tomorrow. Can you manage until then, love? Because I'm sailing on the tide tomorrow, about eleven o'clock. In normal circumstances I'd stay until Mrs Threadwell was able to move back into the house again, but in wartime there are only a certain number of sailings and I dare not miss mine.'

'Then you really are going?' Lilac said wistfully. 'Oh well, thanks ever so much for everything, Stuart. I'll write and tell Nellie how good you've been ... you'll come back?'

'Nothing would keep me away,' Stuart promised, thinking at once of his Nellie, her steady grey eyes, her clear, pale skin and the bell of light brown hair which framed her small face. And of the sweet way she had surrendered to him, the feel of her arms round his neck and the sudden, convulsive movements of her as her passion mounted. For she was a passionate and generous lover, despite her shyness and lack of self-confidence. She was not the first woman he had slept with but she was the only one, he thought now, that he would never forget. And it was nothing to do with their lovemaking; scarcely a day had passed since their first meeting that he had not thought of her, wanted her. 'As soon as the war's over and I'm in Blighty again ...'

Lilac smiled and hugged his hand to her chest for a moment. Stuart tactfully withdrew from the embrace as soon as he could. The child clearly did not realise that her breasts were forming. He supposed he ought to tell her that she should not allow men to touch ... but how could he possibly do such a thing? For all her burgeoning figure she was still very much a child.

'So you'll be all right?' Stuart persisted. 'Until Mrs Threadwell actually arrives home, might it be better if you stayed with Mrs Rafferty, next door? She's a kind old soul ... or there's the Briggs at No. 3, or even Art's mam, I suppose.'

Stuart had not taken to Art's mother. Mrs O'Brien was an idle slut who gave her kids more slaps than kisses and saw no shame in being fat when her children looked – and probably were – half-starved. What was more she had a vicious tongue and had ruined many a reputation. After the shortest of meetings, Stuart realised that Mrs O'Brien was jealous of Nellie because she had bettered herself by becoming a nurse, and thought it unfair in some way that Lilac was bright at school and bidding fair to be a beauty. If she got her hands on the child he was convinced tears would follow – and they would not be Mrs O'Brien's tears.

'Ye-es, only I know Art's Mam best,' Lilac pointed out. 'Can't I stay in the house, Stuart, just for one night? I'll be all right, honest.'

But Stuart felt Lilac should be with someone else and if she insisted that she felt more at home with the O'Briens, then the O'Briens it would have to be. Besides, as she said, it would only be for one night, she could not come to much harm in that time.

Yet when they reached the court and he saw Mrs O'Brien slopping round in a worn pair of clogs which had been given to one of the kids by the local policeman, he hesitated. Perhaps the kid would be better alone ... after all, what harm could come to her in one night? And she was a pretty young girl; he had seen the look in Mrs O'Brien's eyes when her gaze lit on Lilac and he had recognised calculation as the prevalent emotion there present. A pretty young girl would always be at risk where women like Mrs O'Brien were concerned. No, Lilac had best spend the night in her own home ... and Mrs Threadwell would be back soon enough.

Next morning, Stuart said his goodbyes, shook Art's hand, gave Lilac a chaste kiss on the brow and humped his kitbag and his notebooks and pencils round to the docks, comfortably aware that he had done his very best for Nellie's Lilac.

Lilac went around in a daze for the rest of the day. What happiness was hers, for had not Stuart actually said nothing would keep him from her side? He had, she remembered it clearly. *Nothing would keep me away*, he had said, and there could be no clearer indication, surely, that he was as fond of Lilac as she was of him?

Of course, he liked Nellie – had liked Nellie – before he met Lilac. But Nellie, whilst a dear sister, was no beauty. Nellie was small and plain, Lilac reminded herself, whereas she herself was strikingly beautiful, or would be, once she was full-grown. Why, when she had taken Stuart's hand and deliberately held it against the swell of her breast he had gone pink with pleasure ... oh, but he was the best, the handsomest ... she could hardly wait for him to return to her side once more!

And if the thought of Nellie and the pain she must feel over the loss of Stuart's love did cross her mind, it was quickly dismissed. Nellie would meet someone else, might already have met someone else, but in any case, it was scarcely Lilac's fault if Stuart loved her best.

After Stuart had left Lilac had a good cry, then tidied the house and folded the bedding from the couch neatly and lay it upstairs, on the bed which had once been Bessie's. After that she made herself a hot drink of Bovril and ate a small piece of bread with it, then went shopping for a piece of meat of some description. Stuart had given her some money and she intended to make a nourishing stew for her aunt. What was more she had gone out earlier and stopped a passing milkman, who had poured a pint of lovely, creamy milk into her tin jug. Sister Fox at the hospital said rice pudding was good, so Lilac intended to make one over the kitchen fire since she did not want to pay for the use of the baker's oven.

Walking along Scotland Road with a sharp wind nipping her bare ankles, she decided to go to the nearest butcher first. Reggie Foulkes was a bachelor, a big fat man with round red cheeks and what Aunt had described as 'a way with the children.' He had always had a soft spot for Lilac, frequently saving her bones to stew up for soup or a slice of slithery, purple calves' liver. When she first started marketing for her aunt Mr Foulkes had told her how to cook the liver, even buying her a big onion to enrich the gravy. If he had any meat to spare, for despite rationing shortages were so severe that even with coupons and money you might be unable to buy meat, Lilac knew he would sell her some. Besides, he was nice and anyway it was sensible to keep in with him by spending her money there when she had any to spend.

By the time she reached the shop the queue stretched across the front of the pawnshop next door but she joined it anyway, accustomed to having to wait to buy food. She whiled away the time by planning what food she would eat if she could have anything she liked and by talking to Lizzie, a girl who lived a couple of doors down from her in the court. The two of them discussed school, jobs and the other girls, but eventually they reached the doorway, then found themselves actually inside the shop at last.

'Mornin', Missie,' Reggie said as she reached the head of the queue at last and padded across the thick sawdust on the floor towards the big wooden chopping block at one end of the counter. 'How's Mrs Threadwell today? Better?'

'Much better thanks, Mr Foulkes. She's comin' home tomorrow,' Lilac said. 'Any chance of some stewing meat? She needs building up they say at the 'ospital.'

'Have you got your D.7? Any coupons left?' Mr Foulkes said jovially. 'Give us de card, chuck.'

Lilac handed over the two meat ration cards; because meat was so short and so expensive, she and Auntie seldom used their coupons so there were some left. Mr Foulkes nodded and clipped, then handed the cards back.

'Right y'are, me dear. Dere's a grand marrow-bone for you, and a nice big chunk of skirt ... know 'ow to cook it?'

'Yes. For ages, with carrots, onions and a turnip, if I can get one,' Lilac said promptly. 'And water, of course.'

'Don't forget the salt, chuck,' the woman behind her said. She licked her lips. She was short and jolly and came from Cazneau Street. She kept a small sweet shop there; Lilac knew her well though she had not frequented the shop much since Nellie went abroad. 'Eh, that'll mek a meal fit for a queen that will.'

'Aye; and 'ancock's is sellin' carrots to kids,' another would-be meat buyer pointed out. ''e's a good bloke, old 'ancock. Says dere ain't no oranges for de kids no more, so dey can 'ave de carrots. Nip along dere, chuck ... and don't forgit de spuds.'

Lilac had more than once taken a ha'penny down to

Hancock's on Byrom Street and bought a couple of bright, freshly scrubbed new carrots from the proprietor. They were wonderful, tasty and crisp, a real treat when you seldom saw fruit. Apples would be in later, hopefully, but with the war entering its fifth year people were beginning to believe it would never end, so folk tended to hoard food. Most of the apples, Lilac thought wistfully, would be dried or bottled by provident housewives and Aunt Ada had never pretended to be that good a housekeeper.

'Thanks very much, Mr Foulkes,' Lilac said politely, as her newspaper-wrapped parcel was handed over. 'I'll go to Hancock's now, then.'

She was lucky at Hancock's, too. She was given four fine big carrots and a small turnip for her money, though Mrs Hancock had no onions for her.

'Try William Jones, on Great Homer Street,' a customer whispered as Lilac turned away. 'They 'ad onions, earlier. And they'll likely 'ave spuds an' all.'

Wearily, Lilac retraced her steps and dived down Wilbraham Street, emerging quite near the greengrocer's shop. The afternoon was wearing on, and she had not yet made herself anything to eat ... should she take Art's mother up on the invitation to eat there, this evening? After all, it was not the same as staying there overnight; surely Stuart would quite see that after a busy day shopping and cleaning, it would be better for her to eat with the O'Briens?

She queued again and secured four large potatoes and two onions and was about to leave the shop when it occurred to her that it might be a nice gesture to take Mrs O'Brien something. Not the stew ingredients which she had so carefully bought, but something. She looked around her. The man behind the counter, in his grey overall with a stained apron over it, looked at her impatiently. The queue was long and no doubt he wanted his tea. It would have been nice to take Mrs O'Brien some potatoes but she had already had all she was entitled to in that line; what should it be? Finally, she asked the man behind the counter.

'This is for my aunt's dinner tomorrow, is there anything I can 'ave for tonight? Me mate's mam is givin' me a meal.'

The man cast round him and seized a big, rather nibbled looking cabbage.

'This'll do; tuppence,' he said briefly.

Lilac handed over the pennies and hooked the cabbage under one arm. Auntie's shopping sack was already too full and besides, there were caterpillars clearly visible on the outer leaves of the cabbage. Lilac did did not want them in her bag, burrowing into her lovely clean carrots.

She hurried back along Wilbraham Street and then into the Scotland Road. The sack was heavy and the cabbage seemed to weigh a ton. She was very relieved when she saw Art idling along the flagstones ahead of her.

'Hoy! Art, gi's a hand,' she shouted.

Art turned, then grinned.

'Wotcher, wack,' he said. 'Cor, what've you got there?'

'Shopping,' Lilac said briefly, and then, as Art took the sack from her, she added, 'The cabbage is for ; our mam; is it all right if I come to tea?'

'Course,' Art said. 'She'll like the cabbage. Want to stay over?'

Lilac shook her head. Stuart had been adamant that she should spend this one night alone, though he was quite will-ing for her to get Sukey round, or even Lizzie, if she was nervous.

'No, it's all right, Art. I'm goin' to get the place redded up for Auntie.'

Art accepted this and presently, helped her to un-load her sack of food into the rickety sideboard in the living room, then watched as Lilac brushed her hair, rinsed the cabbage and potato stains from her hands and finally, turned towards the court once more.

'Me mam don't set much store by washin',' he said as they crossed the flags. 'But your Nellie does, don't she?'

'Yes, she does. And Aunt Ada,' Lilac said.

'Hmm. You looks better for it,' Art admitted. 'Wish our Etty 'ud try it.'

'I expect she will, when she's older,' Lilac said. Ethel was Art's ten-year-old sister. In a neighbourhood not renowned for the cleanliness of its children she was known as 'mucky Etty', and Lilac had observed on occasion that the child's hands were so black that she could have been wearing gloves. To say nothing of the tiny movements in her thick, greasy mop of hair, nor the fleabites on her skinny arms. 'Girls care more, when they get on a bit.'

'Mebbe.' Art moved ahead of her, to push open the half-shut door of his home. 'Mam, we've gorra visitor!'

Mrs O'Brien was sitting in a collapsed chair, her legs spread so that her skirt formed a basket. She was en-gaged in pulling to pieces what looked like tiny white cylinders and putting the contents into her lap, then tossing the dismembered cylinders onto the floor at her side.

'She's fag-endin',' Art said, seeing Lilac's surprised look. 'You can git a bob for a decent pile of 'bacca, eh, Mam?'

He sounded proud of his mother's foresight and economic ways.

'Aye, that's right, chuck,' Mrs O'Brien said absently. She looked up at Lilac, her gaze flat and uninterested, then she caught sight of the cabbage. 'Well, now, what've you got there?'

'It's a cabbage, for you,' Lilac said, holding it out. 'Art said I could come over for me tea, so I thought ...'

Mrs O'Brien heaved herself to her feet and reached for the cabbage. She smiled at Lilac, showing small and surprisingly white teeth, though there were several gaps through which Lilac could see the fat scarlet cushion of her tongue.

'That's nice,' she said. 'I gorra pot of water on the stove now; I'll put this in, with the spuds.'

She picked up a large, rusty knife from beside the hearth, dealt the cabbage a blow which split it neatly in two, and then before Lilac could say a word, popped it into the blackened pot on the stove and reached for a lid.

'Oh, Mrs O'Brien, there was caterpillars ...' Lilac began, but Mrs O'Brien had returned to her task of retrieving tobacco from the fag-ends and did not look up.

'Caterpillars? Oh well, the 'ot water'll kill 'em orf,' she said placidly. 'Get the pots on the table, Art.'

Art obeyed and Lilac helped, casting occasional looks around the room as she did so.

Mucky Etty was already sitting up to the table, feeding a fat, dirty baby with what looked like bread and milk. She grinned cheerfully at Lilac when she saw her looking, then shovelled another spoonful of food into the baby's mouth.

'Just givin' Freddy 'is pobs,' she announced cheerfully. 'Wotcher, Li. You goin' to sleep over 'ere tonight, then?'

Lilac shook her head, trying not to glance disparagingly at the flyblown living room, the naked toddler under the table playing with Art's collection of bottletops, the baby perched on Mucky Etty's inadequate knee grizzling for more food.

'No, there's too much still to do at 'ome, before Auntie can come back. But Art asked me to tea ... I brought a cabbage.'

'You're sleepin' there alone, then, tonight? That feller of Nellie's gone, 'as 'e?'

That was Mrs O'Brien. Lilac opened her mouth to answer but Art, standing nearby, gave her arm a sharp pinch.

'Stuart, d'you mean?' Art said. His tone was casual, as though what he said hardly mattered at all. 'Sailin' tomorrer, on the tide.'

'Ah, I see. And I daresay Miz Threadwell's comin' 'ome tomorrer, too?'

'That's it,' Art said. 'Come on, Lilac, you put round the eatin' irons.'

It was an odd meal. Lilac could not make out why Art had lied, but she realised he knew his mother – and the rest of the family – a good deal better than she did. So she went along with the fiction that Stuart would be returning to No. 11 later that evening and ate her tea, caterpillars and all, with as much enthusiasm as she could muster. Which, since the cabbage was by far the largest single item in the stew and water the main ingredient, was quite hard work.

What was more, she was disturbed by the way Mrs O'Brien kept looking at her. Speculatively, as though she thought ... what exactly did she think, anyway? That Lilac might have lied about Stuart? Well, she had, but it couldn't be that. She looks, Lilac finally decided, as though she thinks I could do something for her, but isn't sure I will.

The children were friendly, though. The little boys clambered all over her and asked for stories and Mucky Etty said wistfully that if Lilac ever grew out of that nice skirt and blouse ...

Lilac, who was wearing her oldest things because lugging a heavy sack of provisions did not do much for your clothes, widened her eyes a little but assured Etty that when she was done with them she would pass them on.

Etty looked round the room like a hunted convict, evidently saw that her mother was safely out of earshot and leaned closer to Lilac. A strong, ammoniac smell made Lilac's eyes water, but she smiled encouragingly at the younger girl.

'What is it m ... Etty?'

'Don't tell 'er when you've done with 'em, else she'll 'ave them off me and down to Uncle's before you can say knife. Just tip me the wink, see?'

'Right,' Lilac agreed, nodding. It was true that Aunt Ada, when she had been desperate for drink, popped the clock, her own best coat, a variety of hats and even once a sack of coal that Lilac had painfully gleaned, but to pawn the poor, patched clothes on a child's back? For the first time it occurred to Lilac that perhaps it wasn't entirely Etty's fault that she was so mucky. Lilac had noticed, when she and Etty washed up the pots after their inadequate meal, that there was very little hot water and no soap or scouring material. And the children, even Art, had eaten the tasteless mess doled out onto their plates as though it was food fit for a king.

'Oh, Lilac!' Etty's filthy little face shone. 'Oh, you are kind – no wonder our Art finks you're the cat's whiskers!'

The conversation had to finish there as Mrs O'Brien came back from visiting the privy in the yard. Lilac hastily got to her feet.

'I better go, now,' she said rather awkwardly. 'Thanks for the tea, Mrs O'Brien.'

'No need to go yet, chuck,' Mrs O'Brien said. 'Best wait for Stuart.'

'She can't. Gawd knows what time 'e'll get back,' Art said stoutly. 'C'mon, gal, I'll see you 'ome.'

They walked side by side but in silence across the court until they reached number eleven, then Lilac opened the door and peered rather anxiously inside. She did not know what she feared, she just felt that she did not want to be left alone in the dark, or semi-dark, of the low-ceilinged little room.

'Art ... can you come in for a bit, just while I light the lamp?' she said hopefully. 'I'll be fine once it's lit, honest to God.'

'Course,' Art said, following her in. 'Here, I'll light it if you show me where the matches are.'

'On the mantel,' Lilac said. 'There's a candle some-where ... ah, got 'em!'

Triumphantly she handed Art a stump of candle and one of the fat, red-tipped sulphur matches which Aunt Ada always kept behind the clock. 'Can you manage?'

'Course,' Art said again. He scraped the match briskly along the roughness of the black-leaded grate and quickly applied the flame to the candle. Then he held the candle out to Lilac.

'Hold this whiles I do the lamp,' he said. 'Is there oil in it awready?'

'Yes, I think so,' Lilac said. 'I'm sure Stuart would have filled it before he went. Art, why did you ... ?'

'I thought it best,' Art said, understanding at once, without further explanation, just what Lilac meant. 'Me mam ... she can be funny, sometimes. I 'eard 'er talkin' to Miz Butterworth from the back-to-backs on

259

Chaucer Street. Seemed to me you're best in your own place.'

'She doesn't like me much, I know,' Lilac began, but was swiftly interrupted.

'Like? Like's just what she *do* do, that's the trouble. I reckon she'd tek advantage of you, chuck. Still, Ada's back tomorrer, eh?'

'Yes, tomorrow,' Lilac echoed. She looked around her, at the room already growing cosy in the lamplight. It no longer seemed cold or sinister, it seemed like home. 'Well, I'll go up now, I reckon. I'll take the lamp with me and tomorrow, early, I'll light the fire for Auntie.'

'You do that. Tell you what, I'll come over an' give you an 'and,' Art said. 'Mam'll be busy with the kids, she won't miss me.'

'And tomorrow you must have tea with me an' Auntie,' Lilac said. For the first time, perhaps, she looked closely at Art. He had grown tall without her noticing, and lean, too. Did he get enough to eat? It seemed unlikely, after her experience earlier that evening in the O'Brien household. 'We've gorra beef stew!'

Art licked his lips and swallowed. He also reddened a little and pushed back the obstinate cowlick of hair which would fall forward over his eyes.

'Well, I will,' he said. 'Tara for now, chuck.'

'She's coming now, dear. I've written out a list of what she may eat, how she may behave, just until she's herself again. But she's very much better, as you can see.'

Lilac and the nurse were standing in the corridor, watching Aunt Ada walking towards them. Her aunt looked much better, Lilac considered. Her hair was neatly combed into a bun, her face had filled out a little and the lavender blue jacket and grey skirt suited her.

'Stuart bought me the clothes in yesterday,' Aunt Ada had told Lilac earlier that morning, as she prepared to leave the hospital at last. 'That's a good lad our Nellie's found for 'erself, queen.'

Lilac had nodded and smiled, but she had to bite back the words, 'He's mine, not Nellie's!' because she knew Aunt Ada would never understand. Or not yet, at any rate. For now she must allow the fiction to continue that Stuart was Nellie's beau.

But right now Aunt Ada, carrying her dark coat over her arm, was coming quietly towards her, smiling.

'Eh, luv, it's good to be on me feet again,' she said as Lilac took the bag from the nurse and bade Aunt Ada 'lean on me.' 'Now I've come through it I'll be sensible, you see.'

It was the nearest she was likely to come, Lilac supposed, to a promise not to drink again, but it was enough for her.

'It near killed you,' she said sombrely however, as she and her aunt went out through that imposing entrance once more and onto Leeds Street. 'I was that frightened, Aunt Ada – but I'll tek good care of you, like I told Stuart I would.'

'You're a good gairl,' Aunt Ada said. She stopped for a moment and leaned against the wall, a hand to her breast. 'Eh, I'm not so fit as I thought I was ... let me get me breath!'

'I've got a cab; Stuart gave me the cash,' Lilac said importantly. 'He's there ... see?'

She half expected Aunt Ada to reproach her for wasting money, but after only a few steps her aunt was well aware that she was tiring.

'You're a good gairl,' she said again. "'elp me in, then, chuck.'

Lilac had never driven in a cab before and enjoyed the experience; they whisked through the streets like lightning, much faster than a tram and so much quieter! Looking at her aunt's gaunt face and closed eyes as she leaned back against the cracked leather, Lilac thought that it was a good job they hadn't tried to get a tram. The din of metal wheels on metal track, the shouts of driver to conductor, the occasional sharp crackling as the overhead arm picked up a sudden surge of electricity, all combined to make the tram a noisy ride. This, Lilac told herself, gazing through the clean windowpane, was luxury indeed, nipping quietly down side streets and across intersections, free as a bird on the roadway with nothing save the driver's whim to choose your route.

Presently, however, they turned onto Vauxhall Road and got held up by a queue of traffic caused by three trams, nose to tail ahead of them. The driver slowed and stopped and Aunt Ada leaned towards Lilac.

'D'you remember me sayin' as I were never the worse for drink, our Lilac?'

Lilac nodded, one eye on the driver, but he was cut off from them by a glass panel and in any case his attention was on the road ahead.

'Yes, Auntie, I remember.'

'Well, it weren't true. Now and agin, I've had a drop more'n I should. I were lonely, see? No Charlie, no Bessie, me daughters gone, the boys abroad … even Nellie far away. So I took a dram or two, to cheer meself up.'

Lilac nodded uncomfortably. Why could grownups not just leave things alone? If it was over, let it be over.

No sense in talking about it. But Aunt Ada clearly felt differently.

'But no more, chuck. That's it, I'm on the waggon for the rest of me life, that I am. I'm rare ashamed of the way I be'aved, but they told me, in 'ospital, that if I wanted to see sixty I must mend me ways, so I mean to do just that. Not another drop shall pass me lips, our Lilac!'

'Good,' Lilac mumbled, very embarrassed. 'School starts tomorrow though, Auntie. D'you want me to have a day or so off?'

'No indeed, chuck. You go back to school and I'll start a-mekin' an 'ome for you again and before we know it the war'll be over and our Nellie will be back ... and that Stuart feller. And the others – Matt, Hal, Bertie, Cha ... well, no, not Charlie, 'e's in the Lake District with our Bessie an' the littl'uns, but the rest'll be back. Till then we'll manage, you an' me.'

The trams ahead gave a jerk and the cab began to move forward. Lilac patted her aunt's knee.

'And until then, we'll tek care of each other,' she declared. 'Art'll help an' all.'

After that they chatted inconsequentially of other things until the cab drew up in the court. Very grown up now, Lilac paid the cabbie, carried her aunt's case into the living room, then came back and helped Aunt Ada in as well. Her aunt gazed round the room, tears coming to her eyes.

'Oh, Lilac, luv, you've lit a grand fire, an' the clock's back on the mantel and that dinner smells so good,' she declared. 'Eh, and I've been a bad auntie to you ... I'm that touched!'

She sank down on the horsehair sofa and looked round her, then leaned back with a happy sigh.

'Eh, there's no place like 'ome, they say, and 'ow true

it is! What do you say to a cuppa tea? I could drink the well dry!'

'The kettle's on,' Lilac said happily, pulling it over the fire. 'I'll wet the pot presently … I found the pawn ticket and got the clock out when Matt's money came. Stuart paid the rent and gave me money for food, but I said we'd pay him back when the war's over. I made a cake, too – fancy a slice?'

Presently neighbours began to trickle in to congratulate Mrs Threadwell on her narrow escape from death, for the influenza was killing hundreds. They were poor people but each one brought something – a few pieces of coal for the fire, a handful of potatoes, a bit of greenery, an egg for the invalid's breakfast.

Mrs O'Brien did not come but Art did. He looked self-conscious and slightly uneasy, too.

'Me mam sent this,' he said, plonking a shop-bought spongecake on the table. 'Sorry she can't come 'erself, it's 'er day for gettin' the fag-ends from the Rialto, but she'll pop in tomorrer.'

'That cake come from Art, not from 'is mam,' Aunt Ada declared when the boy had gone. 'Bless me if he ain't sweet on you, our Lilac!'

'Yes, he is,' Lilac said with no false modesty whatsoever. 'But he's only a boy, Aunt Ada.'

Aunt Ada chuckled and reached out for her cup of tea. She held it to her lips and sipped noisily, then stood it down and wiped her mouth.

'Oh aye, and you're only a gairl, chuck! When'll we 'ave our tea, eh? That stew smells right good!'

For a whole week everything went very well indeed. Rather to Lilac's surprise, Mrs O'Brien did come round to see Auntie, and made herself very pleasant and useful, too. She did shopping whilst Lilac was at school and put the dinner on the fire and once trudged down to the coal merchant's with Aunt Ada's old pram and came back with a sack of coal.

Lilac guessed that she helped herself to the odd lump of coal and a few potatoes or a handful of rice or flour, but the main thing was, she stopped Aunt Ada from overreaching herself. Lilac, working away hard now because the chances were she wouldn't be in school all that much longer, thought that she had been unduly critical about Mrs O'Brien and that the other woman had a kind heart under her dirty and hardbitten exterior. What was more, she had seen how the O'Briens lived. If it made life easier for the kids, if it meant that Art and Etty and the others got a bit more to eat, then why shouldn't Mrs O'Brien have a few spuds or some coal for fetching and carrying?

After a week, Aunt Ada was supposed to go up to Brougham Terrace to see the free doctor there, and since the tram journey was a long one they set off early – too early, as it turned out. They caught a tram already full of people making their way to work and although the passengers shunted further along the slatted wooden seat so that Aunt Ada might sit down, for she soon began to sway when on her feet for long, Lilac stood all the way. The tram rattled and roared down the Scotland Road, getting first hot, when the door was closed, and then cold, when passengers alighted or boarded. As it swayed along William Brown Street Lilac peeped out at the Free Library and decided she must walk up this way some time and see whether they would lend books to someone of thirteen. She had long exhausted the small school library and seldom got up to St John's market, where she might have bought secondhand.

Brougham Terrace was off the West Derby Road, a district that Lilac did not know very well, but the conductor shouted 'Brougham, Brougham Terrace!' and several people began to queue to disembark. Tenderly, Lilac helped Aunt Ada to her feet, then down from the tram's high step. They reached the clinic before it was open and, in company with a great many other would-be patients, had to wait about outside on the pavement, which was all right until a misty, chilly rain began to fall. Aunt Ada grew pale and silent and Lilac wished they had paid their money and gone to the regular doctor, or even got him to call at the house, but it was no use regretting their action now. So they waited, Aunt Ada looking worse with every minute that passed, until someone suggested she sat on the step, which restored her colour a trifle.

At last a stout young woman in a dark green overall with a white apron over her arm came along and opened up and everyone surged inside, Aunt Ada leaning heavily on Lilac's shoulder. The old shawlie who had suggested that Ada sit on the step nudged Lilac.

'Which doctor d'you want to see, chuck?' she whispered. 'Find 'is name on the door, then sit outside of it, close as you can get ... there's benches. Go on, 'ustle!'

The new patients were milling around, waiting to be told what to do, so Lilac manoeuvred her aunt onto the bench directly outside the door with the name 'Doctor Aloysius Jones' written on a card above it. Thus they were the first to be seen when the doctor eventually arrived. Lilac had not met Dr Jones before but he had looked after Ada in hospital and greeted her with a friendly smile.

'Ah, Mrs Threadwell, how well you are looking! And feeling, I trust?'

'I feel quite fit, thanks, doctor. I can't stand for long, mind, but I'm gettin' stronger by the hour,' Auntie Ada said. 'Our Lilac – that's me niece – treats me like a queen, an' never a bad word between us.'

'Good, good. Now let's take a look at you.'

After the examination the doctor pronounced himself satisfied, though he gave Aunt Ada an evil-looking tonic, to be taken after meals.

'See she has nourishing food, gets plenty of rest, and spends time in the fresh air as she grows stronger,' he told Lilac. 'Keep her spirits up, don't let her get depressed, and before you know it she'll be her old self again.'

'I'll be better than me old self,' Aunt Ada whispered as they made their way out of the clinic, smiling their thanks to the old shawlie who was still waiting, puffing away at an ancient, curly pipe and grinning at them toothlessly round the stem. 'I'll be like I was when Charlie was 'ome!'

On the way to the tram-stop though, a uniformed man approached them. He was grey-haired and worried looking and he asked Lilac's name and demanded to know why she was not in school.

'I've been taking my aunt to the clinic at Brougham Terrace,' Lilac said with dignity. She was annoyed that this man, clearly a school attendance officer, should think she was sagging when she had asked the teacher's permission to accompany her aunt. 'I'm Lilac Larkin from Miss Rudd's class at Penrhyn Street School and if you don't believe me you can ask her; she'll tell you I don't sag from school!'

The man smiled almost apologetically.

'Sorry, luv, but we 'ave to be careful. There's too many kids skippin' classes 'cos they've found a way to earn a bob or two.'

'A bob or two,' Lilac said scornfully when their tram

had come and they had boarded it. 'I'll only be in school another year, then I'll be out earnin', quick as you like. Anyway, if I were saggin' I wouldn't take me aunt along, would I?'

'Oh, you!' Aunt Ada said affectionately. 'When we've had our dinner, queen, you can write to letter to our Nellie for me, tell 'er I'm ever so much better, the doctor says so!'

'Right,' Lilac said, still simmering over the injustice of being accused of sagging when on a perfectly legitimate excursion. 'I'll go back to school tomorrow, then – unless you need me, of course. And I suppose the next time you come to Brougham Terrace, you won't want to take me along, for fear I'll be in trouble at school.'

'Don't worry, luv,' Aunt Ada said. 'I 'aven't got to go for another coupla weeks, if I'm more meself by then I'll probably manage without you.'

Lilac sniffed. She was beginning to enjoy looking after her aunt, and could see why Nellie liked being a nurse, but it was a fact that school examinations were fast approaching and time lost would probably affect her results. The attendance officer had not frightened her, but he had made her realise that she had best stick to her books whilst she could, or risk failure.

'We'll see,' she said darkly, however. 'You aren't strugglin' alone to that place, Aunt Ada!'

Chapter Eleven

'It's over! Nellie, wake up, I'm telling you it's over! The war's over!'

Nellie could hear the voice and she knew, vaguely, what it was saying, but she was tired, too tired to try to make sense of it, far less believe it. She turned her head into the pillow, its roughness softer than thistledown after the past twenty-four hours.

'Go away,' she muttered. 'I don't believe it.'

'What can I do to convince you? Nell, darling Nell, can't you hear the bells?'

She must have been hearing them even in her sleep, but now she listened consciously. Sweet and far away, the chimes rang out over the countryside. And it was not only the sound of the bells, there was a dearth of other sounds. Slowly, groggily, Nellie sat up in bed. She could not hear the guns!

'Nell? It's true, honest to God, the war's over, they've signed an armistice and we're at peace. At peace, Nell! We can go home!'

Nellie opened her eyes. Lucy was kneeling by the bed, her thin face eager, her dark eyes shining. When she saw Nellie was actually with her at last she leaned over and gave her a big hug.

'Oh Nell, isn't it wonderful? No more fighting, no more killing ... no more wounds, even. And we can go home, all of us, not just poor little lads with no legs or arms, not just fellows with great gaping chest wounds or bad gas cases but everyone, all of us!'

Nellie blinked up at her, tears beginning to form in her eyes. It might be over, but at what cost?

'We'll all be boat-sitting or boat-lying, even if we've managed to keep all our arms and legs,' she whispered through the sobs that fought to close her throat. 'We'll go home, Lu, but we'll all be red-labels, every last one of us. This has changed everyone who took part in it – and for what? Who won, really? Frightened children, babies whose mothers are dead, kids whose fathers aren't even a memory, women who've lost everything. They aren't going to be singing and ringing bells, drinking French champagne and pinning on medals. They're finished, over. And us with them.'

'Nellie, love, you shouldn't talk like that,' Lucy began uncertainly, just as a voice outside the window roared, 'La guerre – fini, fini, fini!' 'Oh Nellie, love, you can't say that – you can't believe it!'

'Why not? It's God's truth – if there is a God,' Nellie said quietly. 'There may be no more wounded, Lu, but the place is full of people who've got this terrible Spanish 'flu – seven died during my shift last night, in two days' time most of the men I said goodbye to an hour ago will be dead. And do you think this – this miserable mess, these terrible five years, won't be branded on all our souls? Do you think, just because we won, we're going to get off scot-free?'

'Oh Nell, Nell,' mourned Lucy. Tears were chasing each other down her pale cheeks. 'Just tell yourself no more killing. Then you'd better go back to sleep, you poor kid.'

Nellie nodded wearily and retreated once more beneath the blankets. But not to sleep. In their own family, Charlie and Bertie had been badly wounded and Fred and Hal were dead. Drearily, she thought of them, the thousands and thousands of soldiers, sailors and airmen, poets, tailors, clerks, young men with brilliant minds, with kind hearts, with nothing save an urgent desire to serve their country. Dead, all dead. All swallowed up by the inefficiency of generals, the ineptitude of their officers, the cruel cold, the clinging mud.

And now this Spanish 'flu which killed with a swiftness and efficiency which made the huns look amateur. Was this how God treated the young men who were only trying to do their duty? They had got through it, the fighting had stopped, but why should that save them? So swing your scythe, Death, bring them low! Harvest the hopeful and the helpless, the guilty and the innocent, leave no poppies blooming on Flanders field!

And watch the widows, the mothers, the helpless children, mourn.

'There's goin' to be a big party in the Corry,' Etty told Lilac when the two of them met the day after Armistice Day. 'They'll all be comin' 'ome, me Dad, me Uncle Reggie, all of 'em. Your Nellie an' all ... the fellers, too ... what's their names? Big blokes they are, your Charlie's bruvvers.'

'When's the party, then?' Lilac asked suspiciously. 'They can't all come home right now, can they? It'll take a while, Auntie says.'

'Sat'day,' Etty said briefly. 'Got a dress I could lend? Or a skirt an' jumper?'

'Yes, I'll lend you something,' Lilac said. The two girls were standing on the flagstones by the entrance to the court, but now she turned and began to walk slowly across to number eleven. It was a cold day, but clear, the frost skimming the paving stones so that they sparkled when the rays of the sun struck them. Not that there was much sunshine in the court, but on the

Scotland Road, where people in their best were hurrying along to the pubs to start celebrating, the afternoon sun was beginning to melt the frost.

'Can I come an' see?' Etty asked eagerly. 'Oh, Li, you're ever so kind to me you are, much nicer than me mam.'

'Not now, Et, I've got to get me aunt's tea,' Lilac said kindly. 'Come round when you've 'ad yours, all right?'

'Right. Art's workin' at the market today, so we'll 'ave somethin' *worth* 'avin.' The child licked her lips reflectively. 'Art's all right,' she said as Lilac turned away. ''e's a good bruvver, is Art.'

Lilac, letting herself into the small house, smiled at Aunt Ada, sitting on the sofa with the fire burning brightly and holding a slice of bread impaled on a sharpened metal corset rib towards the fire. This toasting fork was Art's invention and very efficient it was too, provided you kept a bit of rag wound round the blunt end of the rib, to protect your hand from the hot metal. The smell of toasting bread was delicious and Lilac flung her bag of books down on the table and collapsed on the sofa by her aunt, sniffing appreciatively.

'Oh, Auntie, that smells good! Do we have any butter?'

'No, but pork dripping's better, I say,' Aunt Ada said, hissing her breath in as she turned the toast and scorched her fingers. 'Fetch us the salt, there's a good gairl.'

Lilac went through into the little lean-to with the sink and the cupboard and the big, brass tap. She got the screw of salt out, then picked up the teapot, carefully spooned in a tiny amount of tea, and returned to her aunt.

'Here we are, Auntie! Ooh, I do love dripping toast!'

'There's baked apples for afters,' Aunt Ada said, handing Lilac the first piece of toast. 'Matt's money arrived, so I got two on me way back from seein'

Granny Stamp. One of the mary ellens sold them cheap … she was that excited because the war's over.'

'They look lovely,' Lilac said, peering at the round Glaxo tin settled amongst the smouldering coals. The apples were gleaming golden brown already, their skins splitting, the smell of them mingling with the smell of the toast. 'Did you put a bit a sugar in? And a clove?'

'Course I did,' Aunt Ada said, pretending to be huffy. 'I been bakin' apples on the fire before you was born, chuck. You comin' to this street party tomorrer?'

'Can't,' Lilac said briefly. 'Not till late. I'm workin', aren't I?'

With the war devouring more and more men – the age for conscription had gone up to fifty-one earlier in the year – there was a great dearth of women willing to do domestic service. Why should they, when they could do men's jobs and earn four or five times the money? So Lilac had taken a Saturday job with an elderly Jewish couple living on Rachel Street, which ran between Cazneau and Great Homer Street. The house seemed like a mansion to Lilac and it was not a particularly arduous job, either. Lilac enjoyed it as much for the opportunity to see how other people lived as for the wage of half a crown which she received each Saturday evening.

When the job was first suggested, Lilac knew very little about the Jewish religion and could not understand why the Coppners should want a girl to clean, prepare a cold meal, and light the fires and the gas mantles on a Saturday. Why could they not get their maidservant to do it? But Ruth, the maidservant in question, explained it all.

'We're all Jewish, me too,' she said, sitting in the rocking chair in the small, cozy kitchen at number five, Rachel Street. 'Our religion says we must not work on the Sabbath and though some families turn a blind eye to the servants, that isn't the Coppners' way. They believe in the spirit of the law and not just the letter, so they employ a gentile to do it for us on a Saturday.'

'But Sunday's the Sabbath,' Lilac pointed out. She was on her hands and knees, brushing coal dust from the stove-front. 'I may not know much, but I do know that!'

'Not for Jews it isn't,' Ruth assured her. 'Our Sabbath starts at sunset on a Friday and goes on until sunset on a Saturday. So later on I could light the gas mantles, though now it's getting dark earlier, we'd rather you did it before you go.'

'Oh!' Lilac said. She sat back on her heels the better to digest this information. 'So no Jews work on a Saturday? But Uncle's a Jew, and he was open when I went past this morning.'

'Oh aye, but he's just going to sit behind his counter, someone else will do all the work whilst Uncle watches to make sure he isn't being cheated,' Ruth said. 'Can you light the fire in the main bedroom now, chuck? There's kindling and coal ready.'

But now, Aunt Ada began to spread dripping on the second piece of toast whilst Lilac tipped the heavy, blackened kettle so that the steaming water fell into the warmed teapot.

'Eh well, if you must work you must,' Aunt Ada said. 'I'm mekin' a cake for the party and there'll be dancin' an' all sorts.'

'Not much fun with no fellers to dance with,' Lilac pointed out. 'Still, I'll come as soon as the Coppners have finished with me.'

'That'll be fine, then,' Aunt Ada said. 'Now if you're

really goin' to lend mucky Etty a dress you'd better look something out.'

As there was rejoicing in the streets, so there was rejoicing in the Coppner household, for Abraham Coppner, the son of the house, was with the West Lancs Pals, pushing their way into Germany by now, no doubt.

'But alive,' Mrs Coppner said when Lilac asked about him and when he was expected home. 'Away for a good bit yet, yes? But alive, bubeleh.' ·

Lilac, busily dusting, lighting fires, cooking a big pan of potatoes and putting a chicken casserole into the oven – they had a real gas oven which seemed marvellous to her – heard the street party down the road start, but contained her natural impatience to be off until she heard the lamplighter pedalling his bicycle along the narrow pavement. When he came, she usually went, so now she checked that all the gas mantles were lit, the fires burning up bravely and the food almost ready. She went and told Mrs Coppner that she was about to leave and Mrs Coppner, who was fat and rosy with a hooky nose, bright, beady dark eyes and a kind smile, opened the fringed silk purse which hung from her waistband and handed Lilac a big, shiny half-crown.

'Good girl, thank you for your help,' she said. 'Ah … a little extra to help you celebrate and to make up for missing your street party.'

And to Lilac's complete astonishment she handed over another half-crown, every bit as shiny as the first.

'Oh thanks, Mrs Coppner,' Lilac said breathlessly. 'See you next Saturday, then.'

She went into the kitchen and Ruth was there, also smiling.

'Something for your party,' she said. 'I made them myself ... yesterday, of course.'

'Oh, Ruth!' gasped Lilac. A bag of honeycakes was pressed into her hand. 'Oh, you are so good to me!'

'You do your work well and you're always cheerful,' Ruth said, smiling. 'Have a good time at your party – see you next week.'

Lilac slipped out of the back door, across the tiny yard and out into the jigger which ran along between the house-backs. It was dark here, but she turned left into the entry and could see the first gas lamps blooming in the street ahead of her. The lamplighter was old, his bicycle a model so ancient that you could hear him coming half a mile away. Lilac greeted him and he grinned toothlessly at her, stopping his bicycle at the next lamp-post and reaching up with his hooked stick to tug the little chain and turn the light on.

'Wotcher, young'un,' he wheezed. 'Eh, I'm late tonight and no wonder ... there's folk everywhere, dancin' in the gutters, swingin' from me lamp-posts ... I'll be lucky to finish by midnight.'

'Have a bun,' Lilac suggested, holding out the bag. 'Go on, they're awful good.'

The lamplighter took one and bit, then beamed. He held the bun up in the air in a salute.

'Here's to victory!' he mumbled. 'Fanks, chuck.'

Usually Lilac wandered home rather slowly through the dusky streets because there was so much to see. What was more, she usually spent a bit of money on her way home – a treat or two for Auntie, some- thing nice for herself. But tonight there was the party – and the sight of other parties in almost every small street and court she passed made her eager to reach the Corry.

She arrived at last and stood in the entrance for a

moment, just staring. It reminded her of Charlie's wedding day, long ago, when she had been a tiny girl and Nellie had brought her here for the first time. She remembered everything so clearly! The oil lamps and candles provided by everyone living in the court to illumine the festivities, the long tables borrowed from the church hall with white paper spread out over them, the food, the excitement, the best clothes ... here it all was again. She remembered Davy, dark and beautiful, with his smiling mouth and twinkly eyes and Charlie, so young and proud, with Bessie pretty and plump in her pale dress and big hat.

And Nellie. Smelling of soap and cleanliness, soft-handed, low-voiced, blushing when Davy teased her, playing with Lilac, talking to her cousins. And Matt. Dear Matt! She had fallen in love with Matt then, just as she had fallen in love with Stuart, now.

She looked appreciatively round the court. Families who were as familiar to her as though she had known them always, the cask of ale everyone had put money towards, the pile of apples from Hester, who was a mary ellen and often contributed fruit to local gatherings.

She walked into the court slowly, smiling at everyone. She put the bag of honey-cakes down near the rest of the food and turned to find Aunt Ada. She could not see her, but then there were so many people about, singing, shouting, dancing on the central flags. She saw Art, holding a glass in one hand and talking to someone. She called his name and he came over to her.

'Ello, our Lilac! You bin workin'? Me an' all, but I got back afore you. Come an' 'ave some ale.'

'In a minute; I just want a word with Auntie ... where is she, Art, d'you know?'

Art shrugged, looking around him.

'I 'aven't seen 'er for a whiles,' he said vaguely. 'Probably indoors, 'avin' a rest. It's tirin', a party.'

The door stood open. Everyone's door stood open. Lilac went into the black cave, crossed the room, fumbled for the matches to light a lamp or a candle. It was odd seeing the light all outside and none within, but Auntie would have taken her lamp to illumine the party, as everyone else had done.

Scrabbling along the mantel, Lilac found the matches and the candle. She lit a match, scraping it smartly along the iron grate, then held the candle high. The room was deserted; Aunt must have gone up to bed, tired out after the celebration.

The fire was out, though. A pity, because Lilac could have done with a nice cup of tea. Still, she could go back outside, with Art and the other youngsters, and see if someone had a kettle going. Better check Auntie first, though. She might want something, though it was far likelier than she was snuggled down and fast asleep.

Candle in hand, Lilac mounted the steep and narrow stair. She pushed open the door of her aunt's room. Ada was in bed, the covers pulled over her, only her greying head clear of the blankets. There was a rather unpleasant smell in the room, a heavy, sickly sort of smell. It brought a crease between Lilac's brows because it reminded her of something, though she did not quite know what. She stole forward, not wanting to wake Aunt Ada yet anxious to check that she was all right.

The older woman lay on her back. Her face was suffused and by her mouth was a pool of something wet and dark. Lilac gasped and her heartbeat speeded up. Aunt Ada was ill! She leaned further forward and pulled down the blanket. The edge caught against

278

Ada's lank, greying hair and her head rolled sideways, jerkily. Lilac gave a muffled scream and stepped back, heart really pounding now, as though she'd been running a race. Something was badly wrong, the way Auntie's head had moved you'd have thought ...

'Auntie? Auntie Ada, it's Lilac; are you ill?'

No answer. No snoring, no sighing, no breathing, even.

No *breathing*?

Lilac touched her aunt's face. It was cold. She pushed the blankets down further and saw that the stain on the pillow and on the mattress was an ugly puddle of vomit.

She backed away from the bed. She was telling herself that Auntie was ill and needed help, that she must fetch someone at once, to take Aunt Ada back to hospital.

But in her heart she knew that Ada was dead.

It was a terrible thing to have happened, and it could not have happened at a worse time. With the party scarcely over, Lilac was arranging – or trying to arrange – a funeral.

Art was a help and Mrs O'Brien was good, but oddly enough it was the Jewish Coppners who really arranged the funeral in the end.

'A good girl you've been; a faithful little servant,' Mr Coppner said, stroking his long, grey beard. 'Now you are in trouble – Ruth told us – so we will do what we can to help you.'

And despite being Jewish, Mr Coppner knew a lot about such things. He went and saw the doctor who had done the post mortem on Aunt Ada, and told Lilac, sadly, that she had died because her airways had become blocked.

'She wasn't used to drink, you see,' he explained. 'She'd not touched a drop for weeks and weeks. Then someone gave her glass after glass of strong ale, she felt ill, vomited, choked ... and died.'

'Who gave her drink?' Lilac asked, stony-faced. 'She'd been so good, she was gettin' well ... she was all I had in the world till our Nell comes home.'

'Who?' Mr Coppner shrugged. 'Who knows? Some well-intentioned neighbour, perhaps. What's done is done, child. Now is the time to make all tidy and start to arrange your future.'

There was a service in the church on the corner of Wilbraham Street and the Scottie, then a funeral procession to Anfield Cemetery, where Ada was to be buried. Lilac, who had often played in Stanley Park with never a thought for the cemetery on the opposite side of the road, trudged along through the chilly November mist and wished that she was a heedless kid again, running on the grass with Art whilst Nellie looked on and smiled at their antics.

'Mrs Threadwell paid into a burial club, so that will cover the funeral expenses,' Mr Coppner assured Lilac. 'I think, in the circumstances, that it might be better not to have a wake.'

Lilac was happy to agree. The thought of feeding all the people who attended the funeral was frightening, but fortunately no one seemed to expect it and after the committal they all went off to their own homes, leaving Lilac with the Coppners, Art and Mrs O'Brien.

Mrs O'Brien was looking totally unlike herself in a clean black coat and hat and shiny black boots. She wore a large mourning brooch and had scraped her greasy hair into a bun at the back. Mr Coppner had ordered a cab and offered the O'Briens a lift home when he saw Art and Lilac standing beside one another by the graveside. Mrs O'Brien, smiling and nodding and patting Lilac's arm whenever she got the chance, agreed with alacrity.

'We'll tek good care of 'er,' Mrs O'Brien said when they reached the entrance to the court. 'What else is neighbours for, I'd like to know?'

Lilac noticed Art glancing a little uneasily at his mother, but she was too tired, frightened and unhappy to worry about it overmuch. Indeed, that night she refused Mrs O'Brien's offer of hospitality and went straight back to her own home. Not that it was hers, of course, but she would worry about that, she decided as she got into bed, in the morning.

'If you're goin' to insist on stayin' at number eleven, then you'd best 'ave a word with the landlord,' Mrs O'Brien said the next day, when Lilac had politely but steadfastly refused her renewed offer of a place under her roof, just until Nellie got home. 'Mr Jackson ain't too bad; you tell 'im 'e'll get 'is money same's before an' likely 'e'll let you stay.'

It had not crossed Lilac's mind that anyone might try to turn her out, but she did not say so to Mrs O'Brien. The more Mrs O'Brien dangled the bait of her own home before Lilac's eyes, the more Lilac realised she must avoid such a fate at all costs. She would share a room not only with mucky Etty but with five other assorted O'Briens, since the two tiny bedrooms meant everyone had to share. And though Mrs O'Brien had bidden her bring her own bed, she had seen at a glance that there was no room for it. No, she would have to sleep on the floor, like Etty and the others did, wrapped in whatever rags Mrs O'Brien had been unable to sell or pawn.

What was more, Lilac enjoyed her food and Mrs O'Brien's idea of cooking was to bung whatever food she had into an encrusted old cauldron, add water and boil for as long as the fire remained lit. She ate well enough herself – shop-bought cakes and puddings, meat pies, chips – but her children rarely fared as well. And anyway, whenever she saw Mrs O'Brien's piggy eyes on her, a most peculiar sensation of fear and dismay sizzled along Lilac's spine. The older woman meant her harm, she was sure of it, though by no means certain how Mrs O'Brien intended to bring it about. And she saw no reason, either, why she should say anything at all to the landlord. In fact unless it was brought to his attention, he was unlikely to know that Aunt Ada had died. Mr Jackson had a rent-man who collected money owed weekly, but provided the money was there, he was unlikely to be at all interested in who paid it over.

'So long as I pay the rent,' she said now, rather coolly, 'there's no reason for Mr Jackson to evict me or indeed, to take any interest in me. So if you don't mind, Mrs O'Brien, I'd rather you said nothing to him whatsoever.'

Mrs O'Brien sniffed and gave Lilac a malevolent look out of the corner of her piggy eyes, but she said nothing more and Lilac quickly changed the subject.

On the day following the funeral, Lilac got herself ready for school and went out wrapped up well in her brown overcoat with a long scarf over her head and shoulders. She took a sandwich for dinner since there was no point in her coming home like most children did. She had not lit the fire, which would only go out before she was back, but it was laid and ready. She would light it when afternoon school was finished and until then, she felt a good deal more comfortable as far away from Mrs O'Brien as she could get.

On the way to school she voiced some of her unease to Art.

'Art, what does your mam mean when she says Mr Jackson might kick me out? And why does she want me to come and live at your place?'

Art shrugged. His eyes slid about, clearly trying to avoid Lilac's frank gaze.

"Ow the 'ell do I know?' he said almost irritably. 'I suppose she thinks we'd all 'ave more to eat with Nellie's money comin' in. You wouldn't 'ave to pay us rent, see? But you're best off keepin' your own place, our Lilac. What 'ud Nellie say if she come 'ome and she didn't 'ave no 'ouse? No, gal, you stick to your guns.'

'I will. I'm awful glad you don't mind, Art, but it worries me when your mam keeps on the way she does,' Lilac said a little timidly. Art grinned at her.

'Oh aye, I know the feelin',' he said. 'Wait for me after school, chuck, an' we'll take a look round Paddy's market. You can get a lovely dish of pea soup for three ha'pence and a big chunk of soda bread for a ha'penny. That'll do you for your tea, save you cookin'.'

And it's an excuse for not going round to Mrs O'Brien's, Lilac thought; Art was a good friend. But they were nearly at their respective schools so she slowed, smiling up at him.

'Thanks, Art, that'll be really good. Will you come round, later? I'll have homework, we could do it together.'

He nodded, then raised a hand.

'Sure I will. Thanks, Lilac.'

A week later, Lilac was spread out across the kitchen table, writing a letter to Nellie, when someone knocked at the door.

With a sigh, Lilac sat up. Art sometimes came and did his homework with her, the two of them sharing the table, but tonight Mrs O'Brien had demanded her son's presence. She was taking the younger children to buy coats at Paddy's market later in the week and since her mother-in-law had said she would pay for the garments, a visit was important. The older Mrs O'Brien lived some way away, on Fairclough Lane, so Art had agreed to go along – and to sag off school, an activity of which Lilac disapproved. Art, seeing and rightly interpreting her look, had called her a tight-mouthed little proddy and Lilac, taking exception to this, had called him a thick cogger with more hair than brains. Art had rushed off in a temper, Lilac had stalked into her house and slammed the door. So who was it, knocking to come in at nine in the evening on a cold and wet November day?

But it was no use sitting here and wondering; she would never find out that way. Reluctantly, because she was still only halfway through her sums and because she would have to discard Aunt Ada's old black shawl, which she wrapped round herself in the evening to combat the multitude of draughts, Lilac got up and made her way across to the door.

'Who's there?' she asked, and that was an odd sort of thing to do, but on the other hand most people announced their presence along with the first knock … Art would just have pushed the door open.

She swung the door back a bit and peeped out through the crack. A thin, sharp-faced man dressed in a bowler hat and long black overcoat stood there. When he saw her he took off his hat and bent slightly at the waist.

'Mrs Threadwell?'

'Oh ... no, I'm sorry ... but I'm her niece. Can I help you?'

'Ah, then you'll be Miss Threadwell; may I come in?'

Lilac swung the door wider and the man came in and stood for a moment, looking appreciatively round the room.

'Very nice, very cosy,' he said with almost official approval. Lilac stared at him as he put his bowler hat down on the table and turned towards her. She saw, now that he was inside in the lamplight, that he had pale red hair and a thin, pale red moustache. His eyes, rimmed with white lashes, looked colourless and his mouth was wide and narrow-lipped, his ears so flat to his head that for one awful moment Lilac thought that he had none.

'Now, Miss Threadwell, perhaps you would like to explain to me just where your aunt has gone and why you've remained here without her?'

'My aunt died some weeks ago,' Lilac said, annoyed that he should ask what he so obviously knew. Otherwise, she reasoned, he would have assumed Auntie to be either already abed or out visiting. 'As for remaining here without her, what choice have I? And who are you, anyway?'

The man smiled and bowed again; mockingly, Lilac thought crossly.

'I'm Rudolph Jackson. My Pa owns all the houses in Coronation Court, or did, rather. He passed them over to me six month ago. So I'm your landlord, Miss Threadwell. So now we're introduced.'

He held out a thin, pinky-red hand. It reminded Lilac of a loin of uncooked pork, but since he was her landlord she supposed she had better be polite. She shook his hand gingerly; it was as cold and damp and thoroughly nasty as it had looked.

'How d'you do,' she said gloomily. 'Nice to meet you. Well, if that's all ...'

Rudolph Jackson smiled. He had pointed teeth which all seemed to angle inwards. Lilac saw that he looked weaselly and sly when he smiled and sinister when he did not; on the whole, she preferred the sinister look, she decided, though neither was exactly pleasant. Besides, she did not see why he was here. Her rent was paid weekly, she gave the money to kind Mrs Lennox who lived at number six and was old and infirm, so was always there when the rentman called.

'No, my dear, it is not all. Your name isn't Threadwell, for a start.'

Lilac frowned.

'No, it's Lilac Larkin, but people often call me either McDowell or Threadwell. It doesn't seem important,' she said. 'Anyway, Larkin's only a made-up name, because they didn't know my real one at the Culler.'

His pale eyebrows rose and his eyes rounded. So no matter what he might think, he did not know everything, Lilac saw with satisfaction. But the eyebrows came down again, to scowl over his pale eyes.

'So it's an orphan brat,' he said softly, almost to himself. 'Now I wonder why I wasn't told that?'

'Probably because it isn't true and it's no one's business but mine anyway,' Lilac snapped. 'Look, Mr Jackson, I know this is your house, but I pay rent for it, and ...'

He was shaking his head, smiling. His eyes glowed in a peculiar way and he kept licking those wide, thin lips.

'No, Missie. Mrs Threadwell's my tenant and she should pay the rent. If she's dead then you've no right here, and I'd be obliged if you would pack your bags tomorrow and get out.' He smiled again when she fell back involuntarily, her mouth dropping open. 'That's to say, Missie, it's my *right* to tell you to go, and I *could* tell you to go. But I ain't going to do so ... not if you'll do right by me.'

Lilac was so relieved that she actually smiled at the man and moved forward again.

'Phew, you gave me a scare,' she said, just for a moment very much a child again. 'I couldn't make out what you meant, Mr Jackson ... but it's all right, I'll do right by you. I'll pay the rent same's Auntie did, the money will be with Mrs Lennox every Friday. And I'll keep the place tidy and that.'

'Oh, you will, will you? Well, that's very nice ... but I shall be puttin' the rent up in a week or two – what will you do then?'

'Pay it, so long as I can,' Lilac said stoutly. 'So will everyone else, I guess.'

'We'll see,' Mr Jackson said. 'Now how about showin' me you're grateful? How about a nice cuppa?'

'Of course,' Lilac said readily, though her heart sank a little at the prospect of having him in the house for any longer than she had to. 'Sit down, Mr Jackson. The sofa's quite comfortable.'

He sat. She saw him shrugging out of his coat, unwinding his muffler, then she went into the back for the teapot. The kettle was already singing by the hob, now she pulled it over the flame and heard it begin to purr. She had poured the hot water in and picked up the pot, ready to carry it back to the table, when she felt him just behind her.

Startled, she tried to turn and the pot tipped. Hot tea splashed her wrist. She said a bad word beneath her breath and went to set the pot down ... and felt hands take her by both small breasts.

The shock was so great that she almost forgot the teapot, but she set it down quickly on the table, and

then shot an elbow backwards, into the yielding softness of flesh.

'Stop that!' she said loudly. 'Let go or I'll scream!'

'What? And I thought you was going to show me
some gratitude? Look, all I'm asking for is a bit of
friendliness, a kiss, a cuddle ...'

He was thin but wiry and strong. Lilac kicked out
and struggled and he lifted her off her feet, panting,
breathless. Then he sat down on the sofa, with Lilac
still uncomfortably imprisoned in his arms.

'Now come on, my dear,' he said in a nasty,
wheedling sort of voice. 'Why can't I take a look at your
pretty ...'

He was wrenching at the neck of her blouse, buttons
were popping off. Lilac, who hated sewing, felt, above
the fear and disgust, a surge of pure rage. How dare he
make more work for her!

She bit. Blessing her excellent teeth she sank them
into his hateful, freckly wrist. She felt the bone, tasted
blood ... and he gave a high shriek, like a woman's, and
let go; indeed, he almost threw her from him. He began
to moan, holding his wrist, and Lilac saw that he had
somehow undone the front part of his trousers so that
something nasty bulged beneath the dangling shirt-
front.

Lilac had landed on the floor. She was struggling to
her feet when he came at her again, this time looking
the very epitome of evil, his lips drawn back from his
teeth in a horrible grimace, those odd, light-coloured
eyes glowing with an emotion which terrified her.

'A child of spirit! I like a child of spirit,' he said
breathlessly. He leapt at her, treading brutally and
deliberately on her bare foot, then his hand swept
round, hitting her so hard across the head that she fell
to the floor, seeing stars. He dragged her to her knees

and put both hands beneath her armpits, propping her against the table as though she were a rag doll, and hit her again, across the face this time. A double blow, first on the right cheek, then the left. Lilac felt her teeth rattle in her head and screamed, trying to fight back. She felt another punishing blow, this time in the stomach, and she folded up, groaning. He seized her and threw her down and she was flat on her face on the flagstones, one arm bent up behind her. She knew he was kneeling over her, breathing heavily, she felt the air cool on her as he fumbled with her clothing...

She whimpered, but he grabbed her by the hair, lifted her face clear of the floor, and then slammed her viciously on the back of the head. There was no avoiding the impact. Lilac felt a fierce pain in brow and cheekbone, then she knew no more.

She could not have been out for long, yet when she came round everything was different. She was on the sofa, for one thing, and someone was trying to cover her up, not undress her. A voice she knew murmured her name, someone was talking to her, gently, persuasively.

'C'mon, flower, I've sent 'im packin', open your eyes, Lilac, I made you some tea ... '

It was Art. Lilac opened her eyes and looked fearfully round her.

The door gaped, open to the darkness of the court. There was something lying just beyond the doorway, a pile of clothing, perhaps?

Lilac raised her head and looked. The pile of clothing moved, moaned. Art followed her gaze.

'Well, he'll be gone in a moment,' he said. 'What an animal though, Li – I 'ad to belt 'im with all me strength to get 'im to let you alone.'

'He'll come back,' Lilac said weakly. 'Suppose he comes back, Art? He's a man grown ... he'll come back and ... '

Art stood up. For the first time, Lilac saw he was taller than she had realised. Taller than Charlie, taller even than Stuart! And though he was skinny, she could see he was also strong, and not a bit afraid of Rudolph Jackson, either. He went over to the door and grabbed the bundle of clothes, heaving it to its feet. Mr Jackson's venomous face was sickly pale now, almost green in fact. He shied away from Art as though Art was a big beefy coal-heaver instead of a fourteen-year-old lad.

'I'm going, I'm going,' he whined. 'Where's me hat? Don't you try to steal me hat!'

'Here; shove it on your bleedin' 'ead,' Art said roughly. He picked the hat off the cobbles and jammed it down on Mr Jackson's red hair. It went right down to his eyebrows, crookedly, and Lilac, remembering the extreme flatness of his ears, thought he was lucky it had not continued on until the jut of his nose stopped it, so hard had Art pushed it on. 'Now git goin'.'

'I'll 'ave the pleece on you,' Mr Jackson shouted from the safety of the court entrance. 'I'll go straight round to Dale Street and lodge a complaint.'

Lilac got off the sofa and tottered palely to the door. She hugged her torn blouse round her, and the shawl Art had swathed her in.

'Oh, yeah?' she shrieked. 'I'll go down Dale Street, that I will, and I'll tell 'em all about you ... child-beater! Filthy little toe-rag! And don't you ever come back, do you hear me? Else I'll rip out your guts and use 'em for garters.'

Art, sniggering, pulled her back indoors and shut the door firmly. Then he went into the scullery and came back with two chipped white mugs.

'I'll pour us both a cuppa,' he said. 'Well, our Lilac, you tek the biscuit! Most gals would be weepin' and wailin' for their mams, not talking about the pleece and makin' threats. I say, you're a mass of bruises.'

Lilac looked down at herself. Her arms were already turning purpley-blue and her feet were almost black with dirt and abrasions. She knew one eye was half-closed and her lip felt like a great, throbbing cushion and a cautious hand to her face informed her that there was a big cut on her forehead and blood had trickled from it down one cheek and into the hollow of her throat. What was more her blouse had two buttons intact instead of its original eight, her skirt was crumpled and rucked and she ached as though she had been through a mangle - which was not far from the truth.

'Yes. He hit as hard as he knew how,' she said wearily. 'I hope you've broken lots of his bones, Art, for I'm sure he's bust most of mine. Oh … tea … I was so thirsty!'

She sank onto the sofa but Art drew a chair up to the table, picked up her pencil and a sheet of paper, and began, laboriously, to write.

'What are you doing?' Lilac asked presently, when the worst of her thirst had been satisfied. 'Is that to the police, Art?'

'No. To Nellie,' Art said briefly. He folded the page, put it in one of Lilac's envelopes and sealed it down. Then he began to address it. 'She'll have to come 'ome, chuck. You can't stay here alone.'

'You think he'll come back,' Lilac said. 'Oh … I'll move in with you and your Mam then, Art. No need to worry Nellie.'

Art, still writing, shook his head.

'No use, queen. Who d'you think tipped ole Jackson off that your Auntie was dead?'

'Oh, Art ... not your mam?' Lilac gasped after a moment's stunned silence.

He looked up then. His eyes were very bright; if Lilac had not known that tough lads never cry she would honestly have thought Art was crying.

'Fraid so, queen. So you'll have to get right away. Or get Nellie back, of course, which is what I 'opes I've done.' He jerked his head at the small brown envelope on the table covered in his square, practical writing.

Lilac had done her best to be brave and sensible ever since her aunt had died. She had run her small home, paid her rent from the contents of the envelopes which Nellie and the boys had sent, kept herself clean and her clothes neat and mended. She had gone to school, done her shopping economically, continued with her Saturday job. She had longed for Nellie's return, but she had soldiered on without her because she knew it was her duty. And now, suddenly, she was betrayed. Mrs O'Brien had pretended to be her friend, had taken offered food and clothing, had given advice and said she admired Lilac's housekeeping.

And now Lilac knew she was a traitor and a wicked woman.

It was all too much.

'Wh-why?' she croaked, through the tears that wanted so badly to be shed. 'Wh-why, Art?'

Art looked up at her for a moment, then down at his work once more.

'For money, chuck,' he said quietly. 'For money.'

Chapter Twelve

When the latest bunch of letters reached her, Nellie left the hospital and walked along the quiet, flat road which led to the beach. She sat down on a sand dune above the cold North Sea with a pale and wintry sun trying to struggle, now and then, through the thick, lowering snow clouds and spread the letters out in her lap.

She had come away from the hospital because she felt she simply must get some fresh air and escape, for a moment, from illness and death. No one, she supposed now, with the half-dozen letters still in their envelopes and her long grey cloak wrapped round her against the cold, had really thought about the end of the war. What would happen to all the nurses, and to their patients. She was still here, though the eleventh hour of the eleventh day in the eleventh month of 1918 was long gone and Christmas was fast approaching, nursing seriously injured men who could not be moved. There were gas victims who coughed half the night and vomited if you couldn't get the oxygen cylinders to them quickly enough, who stank of the mustard gas they had inhaled. And men with shell-shock who thought they were still in the trenches – one tried to strangle a nurse holding a hypodermic syringe who appeared, to him, to be a Hun with a fixed bayonet, come to kill. And still they were nursing hundreds of men with Spanish 'flu, though the staff thought it was easing, now.

Nellie stayed because she was needed, and because

she had not come to France until early in 1917 so she did not feel she could just go home when others, who had been here longer, stayed. And she stayed because Lilac's letters told her that her girl was happy, working with Aunt Ada to keep their home nice, studying hard at school, settling down nicely. And because Stuart was still in Egypt and not expecting to get home for a while. So what was the point in leaving people in the lurch when they needed her?

Lucy was with her, and Sarah, Emma, but others had gone when their leave-time arrived. Those who remained had been promised that in another six weeks, four, two, they would be sent home but somehow, when you saw the sick and wounded and the strained faces of the doctors you had come to admire, you hung on, said you'd stay another week ... two ... four.

Conditions were a bit better. They no longer slept in tents but were billeted in a country house not far from the hospital. Food improved slightly; they even had fruit sometimes, and the tea was strong enough to taste. Shifts were still long, but at least when a man left, to be shipped home to Blighty, he was not immediately replaced by another. You felt, Nellie concluded, gazing out towards the horizon which hid England, home and Lilac, that you were slowly but surely winning.

One of the letters was from Stuart, one from Aunt Ada, one had handwriting she did not recognise and the rest were from Lilac. It was tempting to save Stuart's until last – or to read it first – but Nellie was always strict with herself. She read them as nearly as she could in date order, that way it was a bit like one long, continuous chat with a friend.

The first letter had been written not long before Armistice Day. It was from Aunt Ada and her uneven, ill-spelt message seemed to be that she and Lilac were enjoying life. Lilac had kept her job with the Coppners and they treated her well. Aunt Ada had given Nellie's old blue coat to Mrs O'Brien, who was turning out to be a good neighbour for all her sluttish appearance.

The next letter was from Lilac. Brief. To the point. Aunt Ada had died during the street party to celebrate the Armistice. Lilac's employers, the Coppners, had done all the funeral arrangements, she was sad and rather lonely, but managing.

Nellie put the letter down whilst the news sank in. Poor Aunt Ada, who had taken the boys in when they needed a friend, and she had taken Nellie herself in, too, when the Culler had done its work. And now she was dead. It was terribly sad, but so many people died ... only they weren't all her relatives, they weren't all the nearest thing to a mother Nellie had ever known.

She sat and stared at the horizon until it blurred, then she blew her nose, wiped her eyes and tore open the next letter.

Lilac again. Managing. Doing well. Art being a good friend, Mrs O'Brien being neighbourly. It all sounded satisfactory.

Next. Nellie slit open the small brown envelope with cold fingers, for the pale sun had given up its fight and the clouds were supreme, now. She read how well Lilac was doing at school, how clever she had grown at housekeeping, how she knew that Nellie would come when she could and in the meantime she was seeing to everything. 'Perhaps you might come for Christmas?' the letter ended hopefully. And was signed, 'Ever yours, dearest Nellie, Lilac.'

The wind was getting up. Only two letters left, one from Stuart and one from the stranger. The postmarks were indecipherable in the faint, greyish light. Nellie succumbed to temptation and opened Stuart's.

He was fine, hoping to be home for Christmas, trusting that she would be back then, too. He intended to go round to Coronation Court anyway, but would be bitterly disappointed if she was not there. Had he ever mentioned how he felt about her? That she was the one thing on which he pinned his faith for the future, the only person who truly mattered to him? He believed he had, once or twice – he could not wait to tell her again, in person, to hold her in his arms.

With a sigh of contentment, Nellie lay down Stuart's missive on the thin, crackly blue paper and picked up the one addressed in a strange hand. She opened it, her eyes flicking briefly from the salute – *Dear Nellie* – to the signature – *Art O'Brien*. Good lord, whatever was Art doing, writing to her?

It was quite a short letter, but it shocked her more even than the news of Aunt Ada's death had done.

'*You better come home, Nell,*' Art had written. '*Your Lilac's been in a bit of bother … the landlord come and tried it on. I reckon she do need you, whatever she may think. First time it happened I come in and knocked him cold, but I reckon he'll come back.*'

She was reading it for the second time when the storm struck. A cold and steady wind started it, then the snow began. Nellie got to her feet, bundled her letters into her apron pocket, for she was in uniform under the cloak, and began to scramble down the sand dune. It let her get halfway, then collapsed on her so she slid, fell, was covered in wet and soggy sand.

Scrambling to her feet, Nellie made for the road. Despite the force of the blizzard all she could think about was poor little Lilac. Ada dead, and that awful landlord, Jackson wasn't it, actually daring to try to molest the kid! She was in a fever to get back to the hospital, to tell Sister, see Matron, and try to get herself back home ... what on earth should she do? She was too far away for immediate action ... she closed her eyes against the snow and began to pray; God take care of her for me, God help me to get home!

But presently she began to realise she had walked a long way and still there was no sign of the hospital. She could scarcely see more than a foot or two through the thickly whirling flakes, and the cloak was no barrier against such weather, but if she had been going in the right direction, surely she would have seen something by now? Soon her front was iced up, her hair soaking, her hands and feet so cold she scarcely knew how to bear them. She stumbled on, longing desperately for the warmth of her billets, wishing she had waited for Lucy or Sarah to accompany her, remembering – too late – that the nurses were not supposed to leave the hospital grounds unless they were accompanied.

She finally acknowledged she really was lost, must have taken a wrong turning, when she blundered into something concrete and hard which smelled of sacking and petroleum. It was an old gun emplacement overlooking the Channel and right now it was at least a shelter from the blizzard raging outside. She crouched in it, low to avoid the wind howling through the embrazures which had once held guns and huddled her cloak round her and tried to work out just where she was.

Finally, she decided that she had not noticed the spot where, usually, she would have turned off to the left, but must have clung so close to the straggly verge that she had actually turned right without noticing. With the snow so thick and the wind howling like a banshee and buffeting great clouds of snow across the path, it would have been an easy mistake to make.

Encouraged by the feeling that she now knew where she had gone wrong, Nellie unfolded herself from her crouching position and left the gun emplacement. The snow was still just as thick, the wind as vicious, but this time she took care. She watched through the whirling flakes and saw the road bend to the left, knew that she should now go straight ahead. And presently she fell in with a soldier, wrapped in his British warm and with a great, striped scarf round his neck. He hailed her gleefully, told her she looked like a pillar of salt and no doubt felt like one too, and advised her to 'hang on to me, Sister'.

Nellie was glad to obey and presently found herself safe in the hospital again, though very wet indeed, as well as shuddering with cold.

She went up to the ward and explained that she had been caught by the snowstorm and soaked on her way back from her billet. Sister raised a brow and Nellie admitted she had just walked down to the coast for a moment's quiet.

'I'll get Nurse Mayberry to take you back to your billet and see you into a warm bed,' Sister said. 'Don't do such a silly thing again, Nurse.'

'Oh, but I want to tell you … to show you one of my letters … ' Nellie began, but was kindly but firmly shushed.

'Not now; you're perished with cold. Go to bed, get someone to make you a hot drink and a hot bottle, and come and see me in the morning. No matter what your letter may say, I know you need your bed after a drenching like that. You don't want to make yourself ill, do you?'

From bitter experience both Lilac and Art knew that

letters sent do not always arrive and if they do, it is generally a lot later than either the sender or the receiver wish. So the day after Mr Jackson's unexpected and unwanted visit, Lilac took herself off to the clinic. She had a splitting headache and although she had been half-teasing when she told Art that the landlord had bust her bones she was in a good deal of discomfort and wanted to make sure that she really was all in one piece.

She went and saw Sukey and arranged for her friend to explain to the teacher that she had gone to the doctor, then she set off. She was sadly remembering her last trip on this particular tram route, with Aunt Ada sitting on the wooden bench and chatting to her, when the vehicle clattered up the steepest part of William Brown Street, between the back of the St George's Hall on one side and the beautiful stone buildings which were the museum and the free library on her left. Lilac remembered her vow to come up here and see if she might borrow some books; she had never done it, of course. Perhaps she might do so today, when she had seen the doctor.

She got off the tram at the same stop and walked to the clinic. She would have liked to see the doctor who had been so kind to Aunt Ada, but his name was not above any of the doors, so she simply chose the shortest queue. A smiling, grey-haired man examined her and gave a disbelieving grunt when she said she'd fallen.

'Who did it, m'dear?' he said, looking at her over the top of his little gold-rimmed spectacles. 'This is a matter for the police.'

'Well, it was the landlord, because I didn't like him squeezing me,' Lilac mumbled, looking fixedly at the bruises on her thin white legs. 'My friend Art came in and knocked him down though ... but my aunt died and I'm scared he – Mr Jackson – might come back.'

'Have you no parents? No brothers or sisters? A young girl of your age can scarcely live alone!'

'Well, I do, since me auntie died,' Lilac admitted. 'She died on Armistice Day. She'd been ill for a while though, so I'm used to looking after meself.'

'And the *landlord* did this to you? My dear child, it's only by a miracle – and the fact that you've green young bones – that you aren't using crutches right now. The man's a brute, he should be handed over to the police. They'd put him inside where he could harm no one.'

Lilac liked the two large policemen who walked up and down the Scottie and came into the courts as though they knew each inhabitant personally, but she knew that with money, most things could be bought. Mr Jackson had money and she and Art had none. If Mr Jackson chose to lie, it might be Art who ended up inside.

'I'll think about it,' she said gruffly, however. 'I've got a sister, Nellie McDowell, who's nursing in France. We've writ her to come home.'

'And until then, you think this fellow might come back?' The doctor looked worriedly across at his nurse, who pursed her lips but still managed to look kindly at the bruised and battered patient. 'You won't go to the police, will you? And upon reflection, I don't blame you. Such things can complicate life almost unbearably, especially for those ... ah, I do have an idea. Will you go outside and wait, Lilac? It may be a longish wait, but I think it might be worth your while. The nurse will come out and fetch you in again when I'm ready for you.'

Lilac went and sat outside, on one of the empty

benches, for time had passed and the queues of patients were shrinking. She looked round her, at the scuffed and peeling brown paint, at the dusty floor and the rough wooden benches. The windows were dirty, even the rooms where the doctors worked were pretty grim, for all they put clean sheets on the examination couch and kept the instruments sparkling clean. The doctors had an ordinary kitchen chair to sit on and wrote their notes sitting at a plain deal table – not exactly the sort of furniture to which they were accustomed.

And yet these doctors gave their time here free, so that people who could not afford a doctor could still see someone. That was a good thing to do, it meant these doctors were good men. So it followed that whatever her new friend was going to suggest, she should try to go along with it.

She had been sitting outside for a couple of minutes when the doctor's door opened and the nurse came out. Lilac got ready to jump to her feet but the woman gave her a quick smile and walked right past her and out of the building. After much longer – possibly an hour, though Lilac could not see a clock – the nurse came back again. She carried a white envelope in one hand and this time she winked at Lilac as she passed. Lilac waited again and after perhaps half a minute the nurse came to the door again, smiled and beckoned her in. Lilac got slowly to her feet – she was stiffening up after all the punishment she had received – and went back into the consulting room. The doctor smiled at her. The white envelope lay opened on the desk and the doctor held a thick, expensive-looking piece of notepaper in one hand.

'Lilac, I have thought of a solution, of sorts. I'll tell you and you can see what you think. You've been looking after your aunt, right?'

'That's right,' Lilac said, nodding.

'And keeping house for her?'

'Yes, I done that, too.'

'So it follows that you're no stranger to domestic work?'

Lilac nodded. What was he getting at?

'Well, my dear, although the war is over there is still a great shortage of people to do various jobs of work. Many have been killed and wounded, and even more are sick with this new type of influenza which is sweeping the country. And last evening my friend and colleague, Dr Matteson, told me that his maid had left him to go and nurse her mother, who has the 'flu. They have other staff, but I know they are elderly and could do with a younger person to run up and down stairs and so on. Now Dr Matteson has a surgery not far from here, so my nurse very kindly took a note round, and brought back a reply. If you would like it, Dr Matteson is willing for you to take his maid's place just for a few weeks. You'd be well away from your landlord, but you could leave your rent money with a neighbour and just say you'd gone to stay with friends.'

'Oh, that would be wonderful,' Lilac gasped. 'But I'm still at school … what'ud I do about that, sir?'

The doctor smiled. His eyes behind his glasses twinkled down at her.

'What a good girl you are, Lilac. Provided you do your work, which is mainly straightforward house cleaning, Dr Matteson quite understands that you must continue to attend school. I said you were not yet fourteen.'

'And school holidays start in a couple of days,' the nurse said affably. 'Dr Matteson's ever so nice, dear, and his wife's nice, too. You'll like them and they'll like you, just you see.'

'So if you would like to give it a try I'll write you a note which you can take round, a sort of introduction,' the doctor said. 'The Mattesons live in Rodney Street – do you know that area of the city at all?'

'Quite well,' Lilac murmured. 'We lived there, once. Oh thank you so much, sir, you're ever so kind.'

The doctor scribbled on a piece of paper, then looked up at her.

'Want to hear what I've said?'

'Yes please,' Lilac nodded vigorously. She had not wanted to open the letter, it seemed sly, but she knew she would have done so had he not told her what the note contained.

'Right. I've said, this is to introduce Lilac Larkin, who would like to try the job of housemaid for a few weeks, until her circumstances improve. All my best to you both. Alex.' He smiled at Lilac. 'I'm Alex Jacobs ... Dr Jacobs to you, of course.'

'I hope I can do the work all right,' Lilac said, gingerly taking the note and putting it into her coat pocket. 'Let me see, Rodney Street ... had I best go home first, sir, and make my arrangements? Then I can catch the tram back to Leece Street and walk through.'

'Excellent,' the doctor said heartily. He held out a large, clean hand. 'Goodbye, Lilac, and take good care of yourself. No more fist fights with men twice your weight!'

'I'll be careful,' Lilac said. 'And thank you very, *very* much!'

Lilac came out of the clinic and the sun was shining. It seemed like an omen. She caught the tram home, changed into her best things, packed a small bag and locked the door behind her. She would have to come back each week of course, to pick up her letters and pay the rent, but other than that she could forget the Corry for a bit.

But not Art. He might not be her one love, that was Stuart, but he was still her good friend. She went along the Scotland Road with her bag weighing heavier and heavier as the bruises and abrasions stiffened and ached, and hung about in Newsham Street by his school until he came out, hair on end, a bag of books slung carelessly over one shoulder. He saw her and his eyes lit up, then he grinned.

'Puddin' face,' he said. 'Poor ole Lilac, I bet you're sore. What's 'appened?'

He knew her well enough to guess from her expression that something was up, Lilac realised.

'A bit of good luck,' she said jubilantly. Until the doctor proposed his solution she had not realised just how much she was dreading the evening to come. 'I'm to go for a maid in Rodney Street, just till Nell gets back. I'll give me rent to old Ma Lennox, as usual, but can you keep an eye on the house, Art? I could leave you the key, then you could see me letters was safe, 'cos there's money in some of 'em.'

'I'll see to it,' Art said grandly. 'But I'll miss you, our Lil!'

'No you won't, because I'll still be in school, and I reckon I'll be in and out,' Lilac said. 'Come to that, I'll miss you.'

'But you'll be a deal safer, till Nell gets 'ome,' Art said wistfully. 'I 'opes as how it all goes smooth for you, chuck.'

'Well, I've not met them yet, but Dr Jacobs, who found me the place, is the nicest man in the world, I should think. Want to walk me to Rodney Street? Only we'd best take a tram most of the way, or they'll wonder what's keepin' me.'

'I better,' Art said, falling into step beside her. 'How'll I know where you are, else? I say, ain't Rodney Street where the Culler is?'

'That's right. It'll be strange to be living there again, but as a proper person and not an orphan.'

Art walked along the pavement with her, then, when they reached the house, he took a long look at it, grinned and waved. Lilac stood watching until he had disappeared onto Leece Street once more, then, with a small inward sigh, she climbed the clean whitened steps and lifted the bright brass knocker. She knocked rather hesitantly and was admitted to the tall, imposing house by a girl not a lot older than herself in the standard uniform of a dark dress with white collar and cuffs, an all-enveloping white apron and lace-up shoes. She had a small, round face, screwed up and puggy, a fringe of shiny black hair and a pair of bright, slanting black eyes. She was also wearing clothing which had clearly been made for someone at least a foot taller and quite a lot fatter than she. She grinned cheerfully at Lilac, however, held the front door wide, and after a quick glance over her shoulder to make sure they were alone, sank into a deep curtsy.

'Welcome, me lady,' she giggled. 'You'll be the gairl what's come to take Joan's place, and a good thing too, if you asks me. Joan was that idle, no one but the mistress would 'ave stuck her for two minutes. Oh, I'm Polly ... Polly Clark. What's your name?'

'Lilac Larkin. I've got a letter for Mr and Mrs Matteson.'

'Oh aye? Give it 'ere, I'll tek it through when I tell

'em you've arrived. Ah, 'ere's Mrs Jenkins, the 'ousekeeper. She's the boss, fierce ain't the word.' She giggled again, turning to the gaunt elderly woman approaching them across the sweep of the polished parquet flooring. 'She's come, Mrs J! She's called Lilac.'

'That's good,' the older woman said. 'I hope you'll be happy here with us, Lilac. We work hard, but we're valued and that makes hard work a pleasure.'

She smiled brightly at Lilac, revealing a set of improbably white false teeth framed by vivid pink gums. The smile made her look very like one of the big shire horses Lilac had watched being shod by the smith in the Scottie. Lilac, smiling back, felt an instinctive liking for 'the boss'.

'I'm not afraid of hard work, Mrs Jenkins,' she said. 'And I hope I've been taught to do a job properly if I'm to do it at all.'

That was Culler-talk, but it had risen to her tongue unconsciously, without a thought. She had heard it so often, she supposed, on the lips of various teachers, and it sounded like the sort of thing an employer would like to hear. But it had an unexpected affect on at least one of her hearers. Polly's mouth and eyes both rounded though she said nothing.

'Here, Polly, your legs are younger than mine; just take Lilac up to her room and show her the uniform and then bring her back down to the kitchen. I'll take her up to madam when she's dressed and ready.'

Polly nodded but grabbed Lilac's arm when the younger girl turned towards the gracious sweep of the stairs.

'No, not that way, silly! You're a servant now, you don't trip up the front way ... leastways not unless you've a reason to do so, and we're 'eadin' for the attics.' She led Lilac through a green baize door which shushed richly on the stone flagged corridor along which they made their way, but stopped short at a flight of narrow, uncarpeted stairs which led sharply upwards.

'Ere, where did you say you come from? Only ... I'm a Culler girl, an' the times I've 'eard them very words ... *If you do a job at all, do it properly.*' She stared hard at Lilac for a moment, then said triumphantly, 'It's true, ain't it? You've spent some time at the Culler. Now why don't I 'member you, eh?'

'I don't remember you, either,' Lilac rejoined. 'Yes, I was at the Culler until three years ago. I thought I knew everyone there, particularly people around my own age.'

'Oh aye, that accounts for it,' Polly said. 'It's ten year since I been there. I'm only little, but I'm older than you'd think. What did you guess, eh?'

'Fifteen?' Lilac suggested. 'Sixteen?'

'Twenty-six,' Polly said triumphantly. 'How about that, eh?'

'Gosh, you don't look that old,' Lilac admitted. 'Do you remember someone called Nellie McDowell, though? She would have been about your age.'

'Nellie? Oh aye, course I do! Hey-up, don't say ... you ain't that babby she used to cart around everywhere, are you?'

'Yes, that's me. Well I never did!'

'It's a small world,' Polly agreed. She set off ahead of Lilac up the narrow stairs. 'I didn't go far from the Culler either, you see – come 'ere when I were fifteen as kitchen maid, been 'ere ever since. I fell on me feet and I knew it, so I stayed around. Where's Nellie, then, or 'ave you lost touch?'

'I'll never lose touch with Nellie,' Lilac said. 'She's like a mother to me, or a big sister. She's nursing in

France right now, but I hope it won't be long before she's home.'

Nellie allowed Maude Mayberry to accompany her to her room, to make her a hotwater bottle and bring her a hot drink. She drank it, feeling hotter and hotter as she did so. But it was not a lovely, glowing warmth but the strange, unnatural heat of someone who has been chilled to the bone too long.

She got into bed; despite the bottle the sheets felt like ice. She gasped at the touch of them, but cuddled down and closed her eyes. She supposed she must have fallen asleep, for when she woke the room was in darkness. She felt absolutely dreadful, boiling hot, with a terrible, dry heat, as though someone had installed a small personal furnace somewhere in her chest.

She tried to struggle into a sitting position, but to her amazement she could not do so. Someone seemed to have tied her in a bundle ... she was suddenly convinced she was in the middle of a roll of carpet, being smuggled out of England by a white trader.

She struggled, but she was so weak she could not so much as move an arm or a leg. She began to weep helplessly – she was so hot, so dreadfully hot ... and she felt sick!

She was sick. She scarcely made any noise, just a few gulps and then there was a wetness by her face and a sour and dreadful taste in her hot, swollen mouth. A light came on ... it was agony, it hurt so badly, that light. It seemed to be directed at her like a searchlight ... she moaned a protest and someone touched her face. The touch hurt, she wailed like an injured kitten and a voice, huge and echoing, boomed: 'Maggie, she's on fire! Oh goodness, fetch a doctor!'

It was Lucy's voice, distorted somehow by the roll of carpet. Nellie tried to turn her head and opened her sticky and disgusting mouth to speak, but no words would come, only little moans.

'I don't think she likes the candle,' boomed Lucy. 'Stand it outside the door, Maggie ... I'll clean her up whilst you fetch someone.'

With the candlelight dimmed by distance, Nellie could just about bear to open her eyes. She saw Lucy waveringly, as though they were both under water. It was a strange enough phenomenon for her to simply watch for a few moments as Lucy poured water into a basin and pattered over to the bed with it. Her shadow was enormous, long and black ... as Nellie watched it became solid, it reared over the bed, it was a monster, it was going to devour her!

She thought she screamed as the hot, wet mouth dabbed at her face; the creature was licking her prior, presumably, to swallowing her alive. She cried out for Lucy to help her, but Lucy boomed, 'Just let me wash your face and neck, sweetheart, then I'll swap your horrid pillow for my nice clean one and you'll feel much better, you'll see.'

The cruel roughness of that mouth was only Lucy, was it? Cleaning her face with a flannel? And now someone wedged an iron bar beneath her sore and delicate shoulder blades and heaved her as upright as they were able; the pain was appalling, she shrieked again, except that what she had believed to be a full-throated roar emerged as a tiny kitten's mew.

'There; is that nice?' The horrible pillow had gone and a cool one was nestled beneath her cheek. They lay her down again, and there was a lovely breeze blowing over her ... suddenly she was standing on the pierhead, with Lilac holding her hand, and they were waiting for the ferry to dock so they could go aboard. There was sunshine, and that lovely cool breeze coming across the Mersey, and seagulls swooping and soaring in the blue sky overhead.

Someone caught hold of her, fingers of steel dug into her raw and painful flesh. She was back in the roll of carpet, only they were unrolling her with cruel thoughtlessness. Someone caught her leg, someone else grabbed an arm. They were mauling her about ... a lion raked her with metallic claws, she felt the blood run and wept, imploring someone to help her.

'Going to take you to hospital ... flu's infectious ... you'll be better where we can keep an eye ... '

Muddled sentences, mad voices, all booming and echoing in her aching head, talked across her. Sometimes someone addressed her but since she could not answer she scarcely bothered to listen. Sit up, lie down, drink, let me bathe your forehead, lie down, sit up, drink ... the words and sentences interspersed the periods when she dropped into an exhausted, nightmare-haunted sleep. They dug daggers deep into her poor right arm, they sucked her blood, they tore her hair out by the roots ... when she was baking hot they made her hotter, then she would suddenly shiver with the intensity of the cold and they would drag the covers off her – she knew now that she was not wrapped in a roll of carpet but was in bed and could not move for the weakness that their treatment engendered – and subject her to torrents of icy water which fell from so great a height that they seemed to bruise her flesh.

And then, waking in what seemed the middle of the night, she opened her eyes and saw, not a monster, not a lion, not a tormentor, but Maggie. Walking quietly past, skirts rustling, with a jug of something in her hand.

'Maggie?'

Maggie came over to her. She stared incredulously into Nellie's face, then smiled delightedly.

'Nell, you recognised me! Are you better?'

'I don't know. I've been ill, haven't I?'

Maggie chuckled and rolled her eyes.

'Ill! We've thought you were going to snuff it several times, you poor little thing. Matron says we're all underweight and overtired … worn out in fact … which is why some of us have got so dreadfully ill. But you are better, because you know it's me. You've been delirious for more than a week.'

'More than a week?' Nellie said wonderingly. 'It feels like years since I was on the ward. Can I have a drink?'

'Oh, my love … willingly! What would you like?'

'Tea, please,' Nellie said, without even having to think about it. The thought of a cup of tea actually made her mouth water. 'Oh, but it's the middle of the night, where will you get tea?'

'Sister has a kettle and a gas ring,' Maggie said. 'I won't be long, you'll have that cup of tea before you know it.'

She was as good as her word. Nellie had barely taken in the ward, which was quite a small room only containing three beds, when Maggie was back, carrying a small tray. She had brought Sister's own tiny teapot, a big jug of hot water, a small jug of milk and a feeding cup with a short, fat spout.

'Do I need that cup?' Nellie asked as Maggie began to pour. 'Can't I drink from an ordinary one yet?'

Maggie finished pouring the tea and looked up, smiling.

'Don't underrate what you've gone through,' she advised. 'You'll be weak as a kitten for a while yet.' She handed the feeding cup over. 'See whether you can manage that.'

Nellie took the cup and had difficulty just raising it to her lips. Her hands shook and when she began to drink, her throat ached with every swallow. Yet the tea was so good, like nectar!

'Go steady,' Maggie advised as Nellie began to tilt the spout towards her mouth. 'Little and often is best, you know. Everyone's felt like a limp rag for at least a week once the fever abates. Lucy's in the bed nearest the door, I don't suppose you realised that, did you? And little Emma's opposite. You three are the only ones in this side ward, because the others are all soldiers. Emma's much better, but Lu's had a dreadful time.'

'When did she get it? Long after me? Does it take everyone a week to get over the worst stage?' Nellie said huskily. She sipped the tea once more, then handed the cup back. After drinking less than half the tea the ache in her throat defeated her thirst.

'Lucy got it within a couple of hours of you coming onto the ward,' Maggie said sombrely. 'But she's sleeping quietly enough now, so we'll hope for the best. Emma was two days behind the pair of you, but she's younger and not so tired, so she recovered first.'

'Could I have some more tea?' Nellie said. 'Just a sip. It's so delicious, so refreshing.'

'Just a drop, then.' Maggie handed the feeding cup back. 'When you've finished your drink, would you like a wash? I could use the rest of the hot water in the kettle to sponge you down.'

Nellie took another sip of tea and put the cup down. She allowed herself to think about her body, to check it over as it were. She was stiff and aching, she felt as though she had been thoroughly mangled, and there was that ugly, dried-sweat smell whenever she moved. Her head ached and her throat hurt, but no longer with the angry violence which had filled her nightmare-ridden sleep.

'I'd love a wash,' she admitted. 'I just hope I don't fall asleep on you!'

'Who cares?' Maggie said, smiling as she picked up the empty feeding cup. 'Nurse McDowell, I think you're on the road to recovery!'

It was another week before Nellie was able to eat an ordinary meal and stay awake for more than an hour, but by then she was so much better that Sister decided to move her out of the small side-ward.

'You can't go back to your billet, but you can go into Ward Five, where the other nurses have been put,' she said. 'You'll recover quicker with people around you.'

Emma had been moved out two days before, but Lucy was still very ill. She had periods when she was conscious and knew where and who she was, but then she would plunge back into feverish dreams once more, her temperature would soar and nothing the nurses did seemed to give her any relief.

'What about Lucy, Sister?' Nellie asked anxiously. 'Isn't it better that I'm here? If she needs help I can either call out or fetch someone.'

Sister shook her head.

'Lucy is fighting a battle which only she can win,' she said soberly. 'We will do our best, but ... '

'Then I really should stay,' Nellie argued. 'Surely I can be of some help?'

But Sister's word was final. Nellie was moved to Ward Five and within twenty-four hours she was told that Sister had been struck down.

'She's forty, and she's been nursing all her life. She's tough,' some of the nurses said, but others feared for the woman who had kept them – and many wounded men – going for so long.

Maggie, who seemed immune to the infection, came to and from the small ward with news of her patients. She was sanguine about Lucy's chances, but clearly deeply worried over Sister. Nellie, feeling better with every day that passed, was talking about going onto the wards again and hoping to be able to help Maggie out, but Matron still insisted that she have her full convalescence first.

'I don't mind, in a way,' Nellie said to Emma as they sat together, sewing. They had been given heaps of sheets and told to sew shrouds, for the men were still dying of the Spanish 'flu, though not in such great numbers as at first. 'Did you know I was hurrying back to the hospital when I was first taken ill because I'd had a worrying letter about my sister? Our aunt had died and the landlord was making trouble for Lilac. Well, I've had another letter since. She's gone into service with some wonderful people, they're letting her continue her education but she's safer with them than she could possibly be at home. So I'm not too anxious about her. But since I am here, I feel I ought to be nursing, not just sitting around getting better.'

'And sewing shrouds,' Emma said gloomily. 'Honestly, what a thing to ask us to do! You can't help thinking … well, you know what I mean.'

'I do. I'm just jolly thankful I'm sewing them and not wearing one,' Nellie said frankly. Because it was a cold day they were sitting round the wood fire, toes held out to the flames, whilst outside the snow tapped on the panes. Christmas had passed whilst Nellie was delirious; she had not missed it, had not given it a

314

thought and now January was more than half over. She put down her work and picked up another log from the basket, then lay it on the glowing embers. 'Just think, Em, in another five days Sister Francis says we may wrap up warmly and go as far as the canteen and have a proper meal, sitting at a proper table.'

'It'll be nice,' Emma said. She put down her sewing and rubbed her eyes. 'You think you're so much better, you want to do more and more, and then you sew one seam and you start to ache again.'

'I know. I wrote a letter to Stuart and then kept crying,' Nellie said, genuinely puzzled. 'But he's on his way home, I expect, at least he's much safer than before, so why on earth should I cry?' She finished her seam, oversewed it and laid the work aside. 'Look, I'm going up to Ward Five to have a word with Maggie, see how Lucy is. She must have turned the corner by now.'

'Didn't you know?' Another girl leaned forward, laying down her own work for a moment. 'Maggie's ill. She's probably got the 'flu too.'

'Oh no, not Maggie! Why, she was marvellous with us ... she's nursed so much 'flu I'd have thought she was immune.'

'Well, it may not be 'flu, it may just be exhaustion, but she's in bed and she's in the side ward where Lucy is. Melissa Brown was moved out of there early this morning; she said it was to make room for Maggie Netherwood.'

Nellie got to her feet.

'I'm going up there,' she said firmly. 'Poor Maggie ... she worked like a slave over us.'

'I'll come too,' Emma said. 'Wait for me!'

The two of them hurried up the room. Most of the other patients were up for at least part of each day here, but they were all lethargic still, slow-moving, easily

315

tired. Several girls spoke to the two as they hurried along and everyone wanted to be remembered to Maggie, who had nursed most of them at some stage or other.

They reached the long ward; soldiers sat up on their elbows and called out to them.

'Sister, you look much better!' 'You comin' back soon, Sister?' 'Oh, Nurse, we 'aven't 'alf missed ya!'

The two girls replied in kind, then went to have a word with Sister Francis, taking temperatures down the end of the ward. She was happy for them to visit the side ward, particularly as she was temporarily without a nurse.

'Nurse Abbott has gone to fetch today's milk,' she said. 'They forgot to deliver my usual supply. I miss Nurse Netherwood very much, she really has a way with fever patients.'

'That's very true,' Nellie said feelingly. 'She did wonders for all of us. We'll come back for a word when we've seen them, then, Sister.'

The two girls walked back along the ward and into the corridor, then slipped into the smaller side ward.

Lucy lay on her back, propped up by pillows. She was sleeping, breathing heavily, the breath almost rattling in her throat. Nellie noticed the dark circles under her eyes and the yellowy skin, but she only patted the bed lightly as she passed it. She was anxious about Maggie.

The other girl lay as Lucy had, her head sideways so that her cheek rested on the pillow. A tube led from a blood-bottle on the stand down into her wrist. They were giving her a transfusion, evidently. Nellie knew that in cases of extreme weakness a blood transfusion sometimes helped.

'Maggie? You poor dear, that you should get it when

you worked so hard to get us well again! Is there anything you want?' Maggie's eyes flickered open. Her cheeks were waxy but Nellie could feel the heat of her from a foot away.

'What ... oh, Nellie!'

'Would you like a little drink?' Nellie said, immensely heartened by the other girl's response. 'Sister's on the main ward, but she said we could give her a hand just for a minute.'

'Drink?' Maggie said vaguely. 'Well, there's always lemonade.'

'I'll get some,' Nellie said eagerly. She turned to Emma, smiling broadly. 'She must be better ... I'll just run up the ward and ask Sister if she's got any lemonade made up. If not I'll squeeze the lemons myself. I remember how I enjoyed the lemonade when I began to improve.'

'No, I'll go,' Emma said. 'Nellie, love, I don't think Lucy's so good. Stay and have a talk to her – see if you can get her to agree to some lemonade too. She's been sick a long time.'

Nellie swung round at once and went and knelt by Lucy's bed.

'Lucy? Lu, my dear, it's Nellie. Would you like a drink of lemonade? Emma's just gone to get some.'

Lucy's heavy lids lifted slowly. Her dark eyes were lustreless, still dry from the fever. She licked pale lips.

'Nell? Is that you?'

'Yes, it's me, love. Don't you recognise me?'

'I ... I can't see you; it's so dark and ... and thick,' Lucy said in a tiny, painfully hoarse whisper. 'Where's Maggie? She's been so good.'

'She's not here right now – she's off duty. But I'm come to look after you instead,' Nellie said. She tried to keep her voice steady but Lucy's words had shaken her. She stroked the heavy hair off Lucy's thin, yellowy forehead with a hand that trembled suddenly. 'Don't worry, you'll soon be well again.'

'Nellie, when you go home, will you see Mother and Father for me?'

'You'll be coming with me, when I go,' Nellie said robustly. 'You're going to get better, our Lu!'

'And you'll write to Sid? I liked him ever so much, Nell, but it was hard, because of Johnnie.'

'Of course I'll write to him, but you'll be writing yourself in a few ... '

Her voice trailed off. Lucy's lids had slowly drooped over her eyes and her mouth had slackened. She's asleep, Nellie thought gladly; poor soul, she needed her sleep, she had fought this dreadful fever longer than any of them, she needed all the rest she could get.

She patted the thin hand, then stopped. She looked closer. Oh God, she could see no movement of Lucy's breast, that hoarse, uneven breathing ... it had stopped!

She flew across the little room and out into the corridor. The door crashed noisily shut behind her. Sister, emerging from the main ward, looked at her in surprise, her eyebrows rising sharply.

'What's happened, nurse? As you know, we like to keep our patients as quiet and serene as possible ... '

'Oh Sister, come quick! I think Lucy ... Nurse Bignold ... oh please come!'

Emma, returning with a jug of lemonade, followed them into the small side ward. Sister leapt at Lucy, trying to sit her up further, snapping orders at the others. Fetch the oxygen cylinder over, call for Doctor Simmonds, get me a saline drip!

The flurry lasted seconds, then Sister lay Lucy down on the bed again, adroitly removing all the extra pillows.

'She's gone,' she said. 'I didn't think she could recover, she'd fought so long and hard. But it's always a dreadful shock when a girl you've worked with and nursed with all your skill passes on.'

Nellie stood at the foot of the bed whilst Emma dragged the screens around and Sister pulled the sheet up over Lucy's head. Her last glimpse of her friend was of a face like a colourless mask, with no hint of the lively, brave young woman she had known and grown to love.

'Peace at last,' Sister said quietly. She took the chart off the end of the bed and there was a finality about it which underlined what had just happened in Nellie's mind. 'She fought so hard, like a little tiger, but she was tired, as we all are, and couldn't win. She's gone to her reward.'

Nellie, who had been staring blindly at the bed, turned to face the older woman. She found she was trembling with useless anger, her cheeks hot with it, her hands shaking.

'Her reward? My God, how can you talk like that? She was the brightest, most hardworking girl I've ever known, and the reward for her courage and self-sacrifice is to be *death*? Talk like that makes me sick to my stomach!'

Emma stood the jug of lemonade and the two feeding cups down. She looked frightened but she looked angry, too.

'She's right! Poor Lu lost so much – her husband, her hopes for their life together, but she'd met someone else, she was happy … now he'll be heartbroken and Lu – Lu won't be anything!'

Sister took Emma's hand, then reached out and took Nellie's, too.

'I'm sorry, it just seemed better to say it the

conventional way, but I was wrong, you know too much, have seen too much. I've said it so often lately, to grieving widows, weeping mothers … it's a comfort to them, you see, to think of their loved ones going on, being happy. You are like me, like all of us. There's no comfort in death.'

She spoke drearily, leading them out of the side ward and back into the corridor.

'I'm sorry I yelled at you, Sister, it weren't your fault,' Nellie said, painful tears beginning to run down her cheeks. Her own illness was too recent to allow her to hide her feelings. 'You feel like we do, I know that. And it isn't as if you let anyone go without a fight; you fought harder than anyone to bring 'em back, Sister dear.'

Sister pressed Nellie's hand, pausing at the doorway of her tiny office.

'Bless you, Nellie. I'll ring for the porters to come … could you be the wonderful nurses I know you are, and go back and talk to Maggie for ten minutes, just in case … ? The death of another patient always affects those on the same ward, but when the other patient is a dear friend, someone you've laughed with and teased and, at the end, nursed … it can do great harm. Try to keep it from her, but if she knows, make it easier for her to accept.'

The two girls returned to the side ward, keeping their eyes resolutely away from the closed screens. Maggie seemed to be drowsing, but she opened her eyes and looked at Nellie very straight.

'She's gone, then? Poor little Lucy. Nell, I did try, but it wasn't any good, I could see her sliding away no matter how hard I worked! She had drips and a blood transfusion, oxygen … But it was too late, she'd struggled for too long, she was too weak. Earlier in the day I thought she'd gone, but she dragged herself back. I reckon she was waiting for something. Or someone. I reckon she couldn't go until she'd spoken to you, Nell.'

'That can't be so,' Nellie said uneasily. 'All she did was to ask me to visit her mother and father and write to ... '

Her voice faded. Of course, that was why Lucy had hung on! She had always been thoughtful of others, eager to help. She knew how they would grieve, her parents and the man she loved. She had wanted to ease their grief as much as possible.

'And you'll do it, she knew that,' Maggie said quietly. 'I'll have a drink now please, Emma.'

She sipped at the lemonade and presently the porters came and took the body away on a stretcher and Nurse Abbott returned from her errand.

'We'd better go; Maggie will be all right,' Emma whispered at last. 'Sister Francis is putting Anna Barlow in here to keep Maggie company. We'll only be in the way soon.'

The two girls returned to their own convalescent ward and presently Nellie and Emma began to work on the shrouds once more; their work would be needed soon.

Lucy was buried in the big war cemetery not far from the hospital. It had been suggested that her body should be taken home, but the nurses knew better.

'She nursed here; many of her friends and patients lie here. Lucy wouldn't want to leave,' Nellie said. 'Her parents are old; this grave will probably be tended long after a grave in an English churchyard had been forgotten. She's amongst friends here.'

321

So now Nellie and the other nurses stood in the cemetery on a clear February day and watched as the coffin was lowered into the ground. In Nellie's head the words which had started this mad adventure replayed themselves. *Sometimes I want to get away so badly ... from John's parents, from my own, even from Liverpool, because that's where we were happy*. Poor Lucy, she had got away from everything, even life. Was it possible that, without even knowing it, she had found what she sought? Was she with her lover at last?

Chapter Thirteen

Rather to her own surprise, Lilac was happy in Rodney Street, with Polly as her favoured companion and Mrs Jenkins as a mother-substitute to them both. Her day began early, at five o'clock when it was still dark. The Mattesons were too posh to employ a knocker-upper, so it was not to the sound of a stick rattling on the windowpane that Lilac awoke, but to the buzzing whirr of Polly's little alarm clock. It stood on the table between them and sometimes Polly would reach out in a daze and try to turn it off and push it onto the floor, where it would lie, ringing steadily, until one or other of them got up and silenced it.

Then Lilac's day started. Not Polly's, because she did not have to finish her work before school, she could lie in for another hour, almost. Lilac had to jump out of bed and have a cold water wash, always undertaken in a hurry, and then scurry quietly down to the kitchen. There, she riddled the stove, which was an all-night burner and kept the kitchen beautifully warm, and put fresh fuel on, shooting in coke from the long black hod onto the greying embers. After that she cleaned the stove with a damp cloth, which hissed and stuck as the metal heated up. Then she put the big, blackened kettle over the heat and scurried through to the family's living rooms.

Here she lay and lit fires, cold despite the fact that she always put on her overcoat. She had a basket with paper, kindling and matches in it and in each room there was a hearth-brush, a small shovel and bellows so that when the first coal caught she could encourage it to flame.

She raked out last night's ashes, cleaned the grate and surround, lay the new fire, lit it, tended it through its first infantile splutterings until it was bravely flickering, then moved on to the next.

In this way an hour passed like lightning, and it was time to make a pot of tea for the rest of the staff. Mrs Jenkins, Polly, Martha who did the cooking, Emily who helped and Mr Jones, the butler, made up the staff. Mr Jones had been a fine figure of a man, famous for his kindliness to the staff and snootiness to visitors, but now he was old and wizened and had difficulty in crossing the hall at anything but a snail's pace. Lilac, only there some of the time, scarcely counted, any more than Maudie did. Maudie came in three times a week to do the hard scrubbing, and there was a boy who polished shoes and lugged coal and kept the garden tidy.

'I did the fires before you came, and I'll do them again when you leave,' Polly said resignedly, when Lilac asked who had done her work before. 'That Joan could never seem to get the knack, some'ow.'

It was true that firelighting was a knack and one Lilac was glad she possessed. Not that she had been born with it, it had been taught her by Ruth, at the Coppners', on a Saturday. How to place the paper, to make a wigwam of sticks, to balance small coals here and there. She had passed on her lovely job, with secret fears, to mucky Etty, but Art said Etty was that grateful, and the Coppners seemed pleased with her. Lilac thought rather unkindly that at least doing the fires was not likely to make Etty any dirtier, then felt bad when Art thanked her for thinking of his sister.

'She's cleaned 'erself up suffin wonderful,' he said. 'She 'as a little bit of soap what Ruth give 'er, an' that blue dress of yourn; she looks a tidy sight better, I tell you.'

Other things were nice, too. Since she was used to leaving the court each morning with a piece of bread to eat as she hurried to school, and getting a drink of water from the tap in the yard when she arrived, Lilac had no expectations of the Matteson household feeding her before she left, and was astounded as well as delighted to find that Martha made her a big dish of porridge each morning and a mug of tea, too.

'She even packs me carry-out,' she told Art when they met during their dinner-hour. 'Lovely bacon sarnies, or a bread roll with fish and mayonnaise, or hardboiled eggs and bread'n butter. And cake. And an orange, often.'

'That's good,' Art said. He was growing taller every time Lilac saw him; he needed feeding, she thought anxiously, and told Martha about the friend who had saved her from Mr Jackson. After that Martha packed a bit extra for Art, and he was always glad of it.

When Lilac got home from school there was always time for a piece of cake and a drink before she was scurrying round once more. Cleaning, with Polly to show her how to polish brasses, get the soot off gas mantles, bring a shine to the long mirrors in the bedrooms. Dusting, she doing the bannisters and table-tops, Polly doing the bannister rails and table legs, being as she was smaller, she explained.

Martha cooked the dinner and Mrs Jenkins and Polly served it, with Lilac serving them – seeing that the dishes were ready for them, that plates were hot, water iced, vegetables served with a little pat of butter melting amongst the peas, or carrots, or new potatoes.

Emily washed up and cleared away, with help from anyone who could be spared.

Then it was staff supper, always something good, then Lilac did her homework until it was time to rush upstairs, light a fire in the master bedroom, turn down the bed, bring up hot water ... by the time they had finished for the day she was always glad to reach her attic and she had no trouble sleeping.

'I could sleep on a clothes line, like they did in Waytes's lodging house before the war,' she used to declare, and she told Polly the story of the lodgers who could not afford a tanner for a bed being accommodated on a clothes line for a ha'penny, or so the story went.

'But Nellie says they never slept on the clothes line, they slept on the floor, the line just marked out where their bit of floor was,' she told Polly. 'I've been past Waytes's on the tram and you can see the dozens and dozens of old mattresses through the window. But no clothes lines.'

She did not see much of the Mattesons, not at first. They were childless and seemed old to Lilac, she in her forties, he perhaps fifty. Polly told Lilac that Mrs Matteson had been the daughter of an important man, a lord, and was thought to have married beneath her, but since she and the master had been deep in love and were still very fond, perhaps that did not matter much after all.

Once Mrs Matteson had had a lady's maid though, and sometimes, when she saw Lilac cleaning upstairs, she called her into her room to tie ribbons, do up buttons down the back of a dress, or simply to fetch some small item of clothing which had been recently washed and ironed and was still downstairs in the scullery.

She was a handsome woman. Her thickly curling, mid-brown hair was streaked with white and her skin was soft and paper-pale but she had large, dark eyes which were alight with interest in the human race and her sweet expression soon drew people to her. Although at first Lilac was very shy, she gradually thawed under the warmth of the older woman's personality and was soon looking forward to their encounters. And one day, amused by a small happening at school, she told Mrs Matteson the story and was rewarded by her mistress's interest.

After that, their relationship became very much warmer and closer. Lilac saved up little anecdotes to relate and Mrs Matteson, more practically, saved small articles of clothing and bits of trimming which she thought Lilac might be able to wear or use. Mrs Matteson formed the habit of ringing for Lilac when she went to her room to get ready for dinner, and though often there was little that Lilac could do to be of practical help, the two of them, so different on the face of it, chattered happily of their lives like two old friends. Or, as Polly remarked, like mother and daughter.

'She had a little daughter once,' Mrs Jenkins told them as they wiped up the dinner dishes. 'A dear little soul. Died of scarlet fever when she was ten ... she was fair-haired. It wouldn't surprise me if the mistress didn't fancy she saw a likeness.'

Time began to pass very quickly now, with Lilac enjoying both her work and her leisure. Polly and Lilac, sharing a room and their work, were good friends. Lilac could always make Polly laugh with tales about the Culler when she was small, or by relating stories which Nellie told in her letters.

And in return, Polly told her stories about the houses in Rodney Street and the people who lived there.

She chose quiet times, when the two of them were cleaning silver, polishing brass, or hemming dishcloths, and usually she told her stories when the older members of staff were out of the way, for they would have called such innocent talk gossip, a pastime of which they strongly disapproved.

'Up the road, quite near the Culler, there used to be a family called Harrison,' Polly said one day, when the two of them were energetically cleaning all the brass hearth instruments, sitting in the kitchen by the fire whilst the older servants had what they described as forty winks. 'Awful snooty they was ... their noses was so 'igh in the air they tripped over their own feet! But there was a son of the 'ouse, Albert 'is name was, and 'e seemed different as different from 'is Ma and Pa. He 'ad lovely golden 'air an' blue eyes, and 'e always gave you a smile and a lift of the 'at, no matter that you were only a Culler kid, and 'e'd stop to chat with the older girls an' all. We thought that was so kind, see, we used to call 'im Bertie the beauty, or Harry the gent, until we found out 'e weren't no gent at all, but a right villain.'

'Why? What did he do?' Lilac asked idly. She held up the brass shovel she had just polished and pulled a villainous face at her reflection, then grinned at Polly's expression. 'Sorry! Go on, so Harry was a right villain. What did he do?'

'It ain't funny, young Lilac. He'd always had an eye to the gels, we knew that, but the family took on a maid from the Culler and rumours flew; they said 'e'd persuaded 'is ole man to employ the gel because 'e was already sweet on 'er. Then one day young Bertie did a moonlight. Yes, for all 'e came from a good family an' that, 'e flitted. The Harrisons advertised an' all, not just in the *Echo* but in the big dailies. It were ... let me see, 1904 or 1905 it musta been, but they never saw 'im again, or they 'aven't so far, an' it must be fifteen year since 'e went.'

'What happened to the girl who went to be a maid there? Did he take her with him?' Lilac asked hopefully. A runaway love-match between a Culler girl and a young toff would be just the sort of story she liked.

'Nah! She were a nice gal, not more'n fifteen or so, called Maeve Malone. That golden-'aired boy took advantage of 'er something shameful; they threw 'er out after six month. She went into the work'ouse, 'cos no one else would 'ave her, see? Then when the babby were born they took it away and poor Maeve went funny in the 'ead. She's still in the work'ouse, poor bugger.'

'They took the baby away? Why, Polly, it might have been me,' Lilac said, much struck by the story. 'No one knows who my mother and father are ... oh, but I wouldn't like to think I was a workhouse brat!'

'No, chuck, it couldn't be you! Mind, the timing would be about right, but they don't put work'ouse brats on doorsteps, they 'and 'em over to the orphan asylums, names an' all. Official, it is. I reckon the asylum gets a grant from the work'ouse or something like that.'

'Yes, of course,' Lilac said, much relieved. 'Do you know who your mam and dad were, Poll?'

'Yes, course I does! They died when I was a nipper, that's 'ow I come to be in the Culler. They was Bert and Mary Clark an' I 'ad a dozen brothers an' sisters. Some of 'em were old enough to fend for theirselves when Mam and Dad died, but the rest of us went into orphan asylums. We don't keep in touch, though,' she added regretfully. 'Too difficult, once you've been years apart.'

'Well, I could be *anyone's* child,' Lilac said, polishing

vigorously. 'But I have a strong feeling that my mother was very rich and beautiful and definitely wasn't in a workhouse. Besides, I wouldn't want a father who ran away when he knew I was coming ... was that the way of it, Poll?'

Polly admitted that it had probably been the case and after that they talked of other things, but it was this conversation more than anything else which set Lilac to wondering about her parentage. She was writing regularly to Nellie, who had now recovered from her 'flu and talked rather desperately of having to stay until most of the wounded had been shipped out. As she said, it was first in, last out, and she and her friends had not travelled to France until early 1917 so of course they must do their bit and take care of the wounded whilst they were needed. But Lilac could tell that Nellie was longing to get back to Blighty herself, now that the fighting was over.

So now when she wrote, Lilac told Nellie that she would like to find out who her mother was. Nellie wrote back, saying it was very unlikely that anyone would own up to dumping a child, but Lilac was sure there must be a way of finding out. Only she decided that if her mother turned out to be some backstreet slut she would keep such knowledge to herself.

'You might not be able to, chuck,' Polly said feelingly when Lilac confided how she would act. 'Backstreet sluts 'ave a way of pushin' their noses in where they ain't wanted. Why don't you leave it, eh?'

But Lilac was curious and determined. She began to examine the smart ladies who came to the house, wondering, wondering. There was one very beautiful woman, Mrs Thomas Manders, who could have been her mother if fair hair and blue eyes had anything to do with it and another, Mrs James Prescott, who Lilac fancied as a parent because she was so kind and pretty, known to speak to the girl who opened the door or took her coat just as if they were members of the family. Of course in the old days it would have been Mr Jones who opened the door, but because he was so slow the girls were usually ahead of him, though Mr Jones took over as soon as he panted up to them, and led the ladies or gentlemen up to the drawing room with great dignity, if slowly.

Lilac spent a lot of time dreaming and even more time cross-questioning people. She went off Mrs Manders after she heard that lady telling Mrs Matteson that if her Lucinda had come into the drawing room with jam round her mouth she would have her whipped. Mrs Matteson, who frequently entertained her two small nephews and who loved them dearly, frowned a little but said nothing. Toby, the jammy one, was the apple of her eye, at five a handsome, noisy, normal little boy. Mrs Matteson often got down on the hearthrug the better to play tigers, or to join in a game with Toby's wooden tramcars. Lucinda Manders, on the other hand, had a stammer and bit her nails.

Lilac heard Mrs Matteson relating the whole affair to her husband that night at dinner whilst she waited at table, Polly having succumbed to a heavy cold.

'Sally Manders can't keep a maid more than a month,' Dr Matteson remarked as Mrs Jenkins put down the dishes of vegetables and Lilac reverently brought in the gravy boat. 'Her main aim in life is to enjoy herself, so I doubt she's ever seen either of her children in less than pristine condition. But she shouts at them and keeps dismissing their nursemaids – no wonder Lucinda stammers and Felicity keeps wetting the bed.'

'You are their doctor, Gerald. Can't you say

anything to her?' Mrs Matteson asked hopefully. 'Whenever I see those poor little souls I wonder what they've done to deserve such a fate. I'm just so grateful that my sister is as fond of Toby and Benjy as I am.'

'I see the nurserymaid and the patient, not the mother,' Dr Matteson said. 'Sally Manders leaves the children very much to her staff. Socially, we measure up because of your parentage, my dear. But I'm just a general practitioner, someone she probably wishes she could ask to use the tradesmen's entrance.'

'Just let her dare … ' Mrs Matteson began, a frown beginning to form on her white brow, whilst her fine, dark eyes flashed, but then Lilac and Mrs Jenkins left the room, having no further excuse to linger.

Back in the kitchen, Lilac glanced curiously up at Mrs Jenkins.

'What about that then, Mrs J? Fancy that beautiful Mrs Manders being such a wicked woman!'

'It don't do to listen when you wait at table, dear,' Mrs Jenkins said repressively. 'We only hear half a tale most of the time. Just you shut your ears to it and concentrate on your work.'

Able now to concentrate on Mrs Prescott, Lilac took to lurking. She shamelessly listened at doors when her victim came calling, but apart from learning that Mrs Prescott was called Charlotte and greatly admired Italian opera she discovered nothing whatsoever about her.

March came, a windy, boisterous March with high blue skies and scudding white clouds, with brief rain showers and long periods of sunshine. The evenings lengthened and when they had done their work Polly and Lilac became delivery girls, for Dr Matteson had a great many patients needing medicine, which the two girls carried importantly from Dr Matteson's tiny dispensary in an upstairs room to addresses all over the city. As a result, Lilac learned to know Liverpool pretty well – she and Polly even visited the Culler, where they were kindly greeted, to say nothing of a foray into Dunn's devils' territory, where they were boisterously welcomed and sat down in the kitchen with a cup of hot cocoa and a biscuit, the evening being late and chilly.

'Them boys are lucky,' Polly said after that particular visit. 'The Dunns treat 'em like their own kids ... we was treated like bloody nuisances from the first.'

'Not in the nursery,' Lilac said quickly. She still had fond memories of her early days at the Culler, before Miss Hicks took a hand in her upbringing. 'Miss Maria was nice.'

'It weren't Miss Maria when I were small,' Polly reminded her. 'Come on, let's step out, we don't want to miss staff supper!'

One of the reasons they were allowed to deliver medicines was undoubtedly due to the fact that there were still not as many men about as there had been before the war; demobilisation took time, and some of the troops were coming from distant theatres of war and could not leave until there were ships to carry them. Even so they were warned to be careful out on the streets.

'Keep to the main thoroughfares and come home before Mr Elphick gets this far if you possibly can,' Mrs Jenkins had advised. 'Stay together and don't talk to strangers. Then you'll be all right.'

Mr Elphick was the lamplighter. Before the war there had been a bright young man on a creaking, elderly bicycle but now it was Mr Elphick, who was seventy and as creaking as the previous lamplighter's cycle. But he was goodnatured and chatty and quite often the girls would meet him as the dusk deepened and walk home with him, exchanging gossip all the way.

In this fashion Lilac and Polly became familiar with the crowded slum-courts of Hampton Street and also with the marvellous houses built around Abercromby Square, with its trees, grass and beautiful walks. They delivered to the huge Deaf & Dumb Institute on Selbourne Street and visited a wounded soldier who lived with his bedridden mother in Roscoe Lane. On their way to and from Maghull Street they explored the intricacies of Wapping Dock and prowled around the goods station whilst Lilac told Polly how she had stolen coal when their money ran out and Polly remembered pinching ollies from some kids in St James's cemetery, whence she had gone to put a holly wreath on her parents' grave.

'It's ages since I played ollies,' Lilac said wistfully, for indeed sometimes her childhood seemed to have vanished into the mists of time. 'I won a big blue glass one, a real whopper, once. But someone took it off me.'

'Did you ever play skipping?' Polly asked. 'They didn't let you at the Culler, but I saw other kids doin' it. It looked great.'

'Oh aye, we always skipped; used to get the yeller ropes off the orange boxes, and use them,' Lilac remembered. 'We didn't get oranges during the war, but the ropes were still about. I were good at it, better than Art. Tell you what, Poll, when the evenings draw out a bit we might have a go at skippin'. In the back somewhere, away from carts and that.'

'Right, it's a date,' Polly said. The two of them shook hands solemnly, then set off again, the big basket almost empty, now, of medicines, pills and potions, slung between them. 'Come on, only a couple more deliveries and we can go home!'

And Lilac, casting an eye at the cathedral which was still only half-built and God alone knew how long the rest of it would take, thought that she had only been with the Mattesons three months and already their house seemed more like home to her than anywhere else on earth.

The Corry was nice, and Aunt Ada's house was cosy when we had the fire lit, she thought to herself. But I truly was born to better things, that's why I've settled down so well and feel so at home at the Mattesons'.

It did not cross her mind that Polly, who had no claim to be high-born, felt equally at home in Rodney Street.

At the end of April, a big change came about in Lilac's life. As it happened she was passing through the wide upper landing, carrying a jug of hot water up to her attic so that she might scrub the floors, when Mrs Matteson appeared in the doorway of her room.

'Ah, Lilac. Come in here a moment, my dear.'

Lilac stood the jug down on the floor, rubbed her damp hands on her apron, and followed her mistress into the bedroom. Mrs Matteson was studying a letter which she held in one hand whilst the other held the cup of coffee which Lilac had carried up to her room earlier.

'Sit down, dear.'

Lilac sat on the little velvet footstool whilst Mrs Matteson continued to frown over her letter and to sip her coffee. Whilst she waited, Lilac looked round the room; how nice it was, with a big vase of sweetly scented white narcissus on the windowsill, a posy of dark purple violets on the dressing table and the big glass bowl of *poudre naturel* smelling faintly of roses.

'Lilac, I've a letter here from a cousin of mine, Blanche, Lady Elcott.'

She waited, and Lilac murmured politely, though she had no idea what response was expected from her.

'She wants me to spend a week or ten days at her home in Southport; she says her little dog, Spider, has had a litter of three puppies, she thought I might like one of them. She also thinks the sea air will do me good, or that is what she says, but in fact I believe she's lonely. Her only son was killed in France and her husband, Lord Elcott, is busy with estate matters and is being sent abroad quite soon to represent Britain at a conference on agriculture. Of course I can't stay long, Dr Matteson would not like that, but just for a week or so ... '

She paused again. Lilac said politely that it sounded very interesting. She did not mean it; to go abroad must be wonderful, but to a conference on agriculture? And a home with two old people in it would not be much fun for her, though she supposed that there must be servants – after all, this fellow was a lord. And then there was the sea. She had been to New Brighton once ... it had been wonderful, she longed to go again.

'Yes. I would like to go, but ... well, the fact is, Lilac, I don't have a child of my own, and I wondered if you would care to come with me and ... '

She's going to adopt me as her own little daughter, just like in a novel, Lilac thought. She was about to clasp her hands rapturously before her in the manner of one of the heroines of her favourite *Peg's Paper* when her mistress completed the sentence.

'... and take care of the puppy, if I decide I would like one? I know very little about dogs, though we always had them at home when I was growing up. But here in Liverpool, Dr Matteson thought it unfair to keep a puppy always within doors.'

A puppy! Lilac had seen puppies wrestling and playing in the markets and occasionally on the end of long leads in the street, but she had never expected to be able to lay hands on one. Now, at the mere prospect, her fingers itched to stroke, to play, to cuddle.

'Oh yes please, ma'am,' she said at once. 'It would be really lovely to have a dog here … Polly and I could take it round with us when we deliver medicine.'

'That's what Dr Matteson thought,' Mrs Matteson said, colouring a little. Lilac could see she was delighted to find a fellow dog-lover as eager as she for the puppy to come to the house in Rodney Street. 'He thinks that owning a dog would be good for me since he has long recommended that I take gentle walks two or three times a day, so if you would not object to being out of the city for a week or so, we might set off at the weekend. I'll write a note to school for you, of course.'

'Thank you, ma'am,' Lilac said. 'Oh, but … '

Mrs Matteson was engaged in putting a smear of *poudre* onto a swansdown puff before transferring it to her nose. Now, she looked enquiringly at Lilac through the mirror.

'Yes, dear, what is it?'

'Won't anyone mind if I go with you? I mean I'm the newest and Polly's my friend, I wouldn't want … '

'Polly is a good girl, but she has never aspired to help me with my clothes or my toilette. One of these days, Lilac, it is possible that you might wish for a position as lady's maid, so to travel with me and to help me when I need you is a necessary part of your training. Besides, I don't believe Polly cares for puppies and someone must remain here and take care of the doctor for me. Now if that is all, you had better come here to my room first thing in the morning and we will go over your clothes together to see that you are suitably dressed for your stay at the seaside.'

In the kitchen, Polly congratulated Lilac on her luck and Mrs Jenkins told her to remember to speak nicely, like a little lady, and to mind what Lady Elcott's servants said.

Art, when she told him of the treat in store, was less sanguine.

'Cor, you'll be swimmin' in deep waters, our Lilac,' he said gloomily. 'Don't you go gettin' ideas above your station. What'll you do with yourself all day, though? She won't let you play on the sand an' that, not likely she won't!'

So Lilac told him about the dog and saw the light of true envy shine out of his round brown eyes.

'Oh, Li ... a dog!' Art gasped. 'Oh, I've always wanted a dog of me own ... can I 'elp you tek it for walks?'

'It won't be mine, Art, and I don't know whether she'll let me take it out yet either,' Lilac pointed out. 'But I'll do me best to let you have a look at it, whilst it's still small.'

'Lilac, you're a reg'lar brick!' Art said fervently. 'I'd 'a had a dog years since, only me Mam says as it's just another mouth to feed. We might teach 'im to beg, an' die for 'is country!'

'We'll see,' Lilac said, delighted with his reaction to her news. 'Give us a kiss goodbye, Art O'Brien, 'cos you won't see me no more for a whole week!'

The prospect of a week in the home of a real Lord, even if he didn't live in Liverpool, fuelled Lilac's interest in her parentage as nothing else could have done. Now her dreams centred round a lordly father and a titled mother. She examined herself in the spotted mirror which hung between her bed and Polly's and decided that her glorious red-gold hair and smooth, creamy skin could only have been passed down to her by a member of the aristocracy. She confided this information to Polly, and was rather cast down to be told that Elaine Gunny, one of the prettiest of the fruit-selling mary ellens, was reputed to have the most beautiful skin in the whole of Liverpool, yet everyone knew she was the daughter of a whore.

If Polly had hoped to cut Lilac down to size, however, she failed. Lilac was far too excited, and set off in the hired car which the Elcotts had sent with high hopes, which were not cast down by her reception at Elcott Hall.

For a start, the staff in the big, Georgian house on the outskirts of the town did not treat Lilac as a servant at all, because that was not how she appeared. Mrs Matteson told everyone that Lilac was staying with her whilst her relatives were abroad, and insisted that Lilac should sleep in the small dressing room off her own room, and when she dressed in the morning, changed for dinner, made ready for bed, Lilac was on hand to help. Lord and Lady Elcott knew the truth of course, but the servants assumed Lilac to be a favoured poor relation, a sort of companion, and treated her accordingly.

Lady Elcott had a proper lady's maid, a stiff, sniffy woman known as Belter, which seemed wildly inappropriate to Lilac. She was not friendly and thought herself a cut above the rest of the staff, so when the Elcott servants discovered that Lilac, despite being their mistress's cousin's companion, was delighted to give a hand in the kitchen, chat to the other girls and do anything she could for her mistress, they were pleased to welcome her to the kitchens and to show her the well-appointed house and extensive grounds. She was even conducted round the walled kitchen garden with its netted frames for soft fruit, its raised violet beds, the fan-shaped peach and apricot trees espaliered against the south wall and the glasshouses where vines and orange trees grew and fruited in their season.

Everything delighted her. The dairy with its gleaming marble tables, the laundry with its enormous copper and its range of mangles from the small, neat one for collars and handkerchieves to the huge monster which devoured household linen. The rose garden was nothing more than what looked like dead bushes, but Lilac could imagine how beautiful it would look in June, and right now the beds were ablaze with early tulips and camellias and daphnes delighted the eye and scented the spring air.

Within two days of moving in, however, Lilac had a problem, and the problem was George.

George was Lord Elcott's eldest grandson, and was in direct line for the title. His father had been killed in October 1914 at the battle of Ypres, at a point where the German attack had been fiercest and most successful. He had died bravely, leading his men into a position where they might 'putty up' the gaps left in the dismounted cavalry division which had been deployed between Haig's force and the III Corps. So young George was therefore being drilled in the craft of a country landowner by his grandfather in order that, when he came into the title, he might honourably take his father's place in the scheme of things.

George was tall and handsome, with curly, light

brown hair, pale blue eyes and a charming, deprecatory smile. But his good looks hid a nervous disposition and a tendency to expect others to do things for him and at first Lilac found his sudden devotion a blessed nuisance. He hung about the kitchens waiting for her to be free and he frightened the life out of her by lurking in dark passageways upstairs, pouncing on her as she passed with hot water for her mistress, or a newly ironed morning dress.

He had served in the Rifles himself at the tail-end of the war but had been brought home by Lord Elcott, who knew him to be under-age, when a shell-splinter had pierced his lung and almost ended his life. The fact that he had hated every minute of his army career and had in fact written to his grandfather for help was something he did not boast about, but not unnaturally, he was proud of being wounded in defence of his country when not quite sixteen.

Being an only child he had never known the rough and tumble of family life and when he returned from France his mother might have ruined him by over-indulgence, so his grandparents took over, treating him as an ordinary young man and insisting that he take instructions from them and from their staff so that he would understand the workings of the estate from the grass roots.

When Lord Elcott had brought him back from France there had been fears for his future health, and indeed he suffered from breathlessness if he over-exerted himself and from occasional bouts of palpitations, when his heart seemed to go at double its normal rate and he had to sit quiet until it slowed. But being young and strong he had quickly regained his strength and had then spent the next six months avoiding his doting mother, eating a great deal to make up for his enforced diet in France, and learning the craft of estate management.

He had been making excellent progress, until, like a bolt from the blue, Lilac – and love– had entered his orbit for the first time and reduced him from a hard-working young man who was fast being licked into shape to what his grandfather scathingly described as a gibbering idiot.

'But it was bound to happen, I'm just glad he didn't make a secret of his infatuation, because we can undo the damage now,' he said, when he and his cousin were discussing the matter. 'However, it won't do, you know that, m'dear. Can't have the lad getting ideas just because he's young and she's pretty. I've had a word with him, told him to remember he's got responsibilities as my heir and they don't include playing fast and loose with the servants, so if you tell young whatsername to keep him at arm's length I'd be much obliged.'

It was a sensible approach and one which Mrs Matteson heartily endorsed. The trouble was that George, with all the instincts of a young and eager male animal, simply could not be shaken off. Lilac, though she was secretly very flattered by George's attention, could still remember all too well the clammy hands and objectionable behaviour of Mr Rudolph Jackson. She thought George very handsome but also weak and easily led, and she had not forgotten Polly's story of poor Maeve Malone. George only had to lay a finger on her sleeve and horrid thoughts of being slammed up in the workhouse went through her head, whilst she imagined the shame of it, and the pain of it ... and was able to skip out of young George's way and scarcely regret at all that she had to do so. Besides, he was not half the man Stuart was – nor Art, for that matter.

'Don't you like me, Lilac?' George asked plaintively after one such rebuff. They were crouched over the basket of puppies in his grandmother's small sitting room and he had put out a gentle finger and stroked her cheek. 'You behaved as if I'd meant to throttle you, dammit!'

'I like you very much, but you shouldn't pat me, you know,' Lilac said. 'You're going to be Lord Elcott one day, and I'm just plain Lilac Larkin, although ... '

She stopped, eyeing him uncertainly over the head of the puppy she had snatched up into her arms. It was a fat spotted spaniel with a drooping, humorous eye and long, silky ears. It wriggled in her grasp, then reached up and licked her chin with its soft pink tongue, nudging her at the same time with its wet button nose. Lilac sneezed and laughed at the same time, then put the puppy back in its basket.

'What do you mean, you're plain Lilac Larkin? You aren't plain, you're by far the prettiest girl I know.'

'It's nice of you to say so,' Lilac said, not bothering to deny the undoubted truth of the remark. 'But you know what Lord Elcott said.' She looked thoughtfully across at George. It had suddenly occurred to her that George might have the key to her own particular mystery ... it was clear that he really did like her, so why did she not put his liking to some real use? Why not see if she could involve George in her Quest, as she had come to think of it. Her Quest to find her rich relatives?

'No it's not *nice*, it's the truth,' George said rather crossly. 'As for my Grandfather, he shan't rule me over this. I mean to be your friend. Come to the woods for a walk, Lilac! There are heaps of rabbits and sometimes you see a weasel or a stoat. And of course there are lots of squirrels and birds by the score.'

Lilac guessed he had seen her fascination with the puppies and had noted the way she hung round the stables and brought sugar lumps and bits of bread for the horses. Naturally, he thought she would like to see rabbits and he was right, furthermore. She was entranced by the prospect, though it would not do to let him see how easily pleased she was, not if she really meant to make use of him.

'Well, all right, I'll come,' she said. 'But George, there is something you could do for me, if you would.'

'Anything!' George said, ardently. 'You have only to ask.' He then rather spoiled it by adding apprehensively, 'Only if you're going to tell me to go away and let you walk by yourself, that ain't fair!'

Lilac looked across at him. His chest was heaving rather; she must not forget that the shrapnel had collapsed his lung, for though he was now quite well excitement or too much exercise could make him wheeze and gasp for air. If he was to help her – and she was more sure with every moment that passed that he could – he must remain in good health!

'No, it's all right, it was just something you might know. Look, we can't talk here, I'll tell you all about it as we walk.'

And once they were away from the house she did. What sort of sense George made of her garbled tale – truth, fiction, dreams and downright wishful thinking jostled for first place once Lilac really got going – she could not tell, but he was certainly excited by it.

'It's a real romance,' he breathed. 'And you are the heroine of it, Lilac.' He took her hand and she did not snatch it away. How sensible he was, he had taken the point at once. When he squeezed her fingers she smiled at him and fluttered her lashes.

'Yes, it is rather romantic, isn't it? So you see, I feel

it's very important to find my mother and father, or at least to discover who they were. If, as I suspect, they were well-to-do, perhaps even famous, or at least people of substance, then there could be no reason ... I mean it would be very much easier ... '

'You mean Grandfather would allow me to ask you to be my wife,' George said, jumping to a conclusion Lilac had not even considered. But now that George had said it, she began to see that a rich parent would indeed be advantageous if it meant she could marry George. She loved Elcott Hall already and might well grow fond of its heir, in time. But George was smiling at her, speaking. 'Not that anything or anyone would stop me asking you to marry me, dear Lilac, when we're old enough. I'm only seventeen and you're three years younger, but one day ... '

'So if you could ask around, Georgie, we might discover who I really am,' Lilac said when his voice faded into silence. George slid an arm round her shoulders and she tried not to stiffen and pull away. And once she got used to it, it was rather nice, a warm and friendly feeling. 'Will you do what you can to help me with my Quest?'

'A Quest, by golly! Yes, of course, I'll do anything! And Lilac, you go home in a few days.'

'Yes, I know. But although I'm in Liverpool and you aren't, I still think you're more likely to discover the truth than I, because you are on easy terms with the sort of people I'd like to question,' Lilac pointed out. 'I'll do my best, of course, but it's harder for me. And we can exchange letters, you know.'

'Don't forget that my mother lives in South John Street, so we needn't just write, we can meet quite easily when I'm at home,' George said at once. 'We'll keep our friendship dark, of course, but Uncle

Matteson is my doctor, so I can always make some excuse to pop in.'

'Yes of course, I quite forgot,' Lilac said rather apprehensively. She had not bargained on George actually pursuing her to Liverpool, though she supposed that it was unfair to say 'pursue', since the young man could scarcely help living in the city. 'It might not be too sensible to come to Rodney Street though, George, since I've never told Mrs Matteson anything about my Quest or the mystery of my birth.' She liked that; *my Quest* was good, but *the mystery of my birth* was better. It sounded a whole lot more romantic than saying *I don't know who my mother was,* which smacked of carelessness on someone's part, if not on hers. 'We'll make an assignation.'

She liked the sound of that, too, and so did George, she could tell. He brightened; he had looked momentarily sulky when she had suggested it was foolish of him to visit her in Rodney Street.

'Oh, right ... an assignation! Still, that's for later. Now we'll walk very quietly into the woods and see what we can see.'

They stayed in Southport for a fortnight in the end, and both Mrs Matteson and her protege enjoyed every minute of it. The food shortages, which had affected everyone in Liverpool except the really rich, did not seem to make much difference here. Besides, with the war well and truly over, goods from abroad were coming back into the shops. Lilac was given oranges which she peeled and ate with great enjoyment and she watched cook making a syllabub with real lemons, a great deal of sugar, thick cream and Napoleon brandy.

When they first reached the hall, April had been

more than half over. By the time they left, May had arrived. The trees were in early leaf, the rhododendrons were blossoming. The drive was a tunnel of blooms of every shade from deep purple to palest pink and the rockeries were brilliant with blue aubretia and pink rock roses. Lilac tried rather half-heartedly not to consider the place as good as hers, but it was tempting to stroll around the gardens and plan what changes she would make, or to examine the dreadful, faded wallpaper in the state bedroom and consider how nice a bright, floral pattern would look.

Whilst she was with the Elcotts, in fact, the mystery of her birth was usually on her mind, particularly when Mrs Matteson took her shopping in Southport and she saw the slim, beautifully dressed women who walked down Lord Street. She watched enviously as they visited the wonderful shops and sauntered into the cafes and restaurants to while away the time with coffee or a meal. And try though she might she could not help eyeing these fortunate people a little wistfully. How nice it must be to stroll around the shops, buying whatever took your fancy, to go into the biggest cafe of them all and order coffee and fresh cream cakes, to fritter a morning away chatting to your friends! When my mother claims me ... Lilac's thoughts usually began, despite her intention not to let her dreams run away with her.

And at Elcott Hall itself there was still George. Despite Lord Elcott's strictures he was very attentive, particularly over their mutual aim – to discover her parentage. He, who had never taken any interest in the many beautiful women who came within his social sphere, began to look at them with real attention. Anyone who resembled Lilac in the slightest – and it was surprising how many golden-haired ladies there were, he told his young friend – was immediately the object of his interest. He got a list of names and, when possible, their addresses, as well as whether they had at some stage resided in Liverpool.

'You were born just before Christmas, 1905,' George said, as the two of them sat on a mossy bank in the wood, watching from their hiding place as tea was laid out on the terrace. 'So we want to know what all our suspects were doing at that time – right?'

'Not the fathers,' Lilac said. 'I'm not quite sure if I've got it right, but wouldn't it be … earlier … '

She felt her cheeks flame, but George, absorbed in calculation, merely grunted. He frowned down at his hands, then said: 'The thing is, Lilac, it's going to be impossible to find your father until we've got your mother. It's difficult for a woman to hide a baby, but a man doesn't look any different. So for now, let's concentrate on the ladies. Right?'

'Yes, of course,' Lilac said, her cheeks still hot. 'Did I tell you we're going home the day after tomorrow? For definite this time.'

'You didn't tell me, but Grandfather told Grandmother that he'd be happy when Friday arrived, so I guessed what he meant. Well, he shan't stop me from seeing you, I swear it! Another thing, I can always call in Rodney Street to find out how the pup is doing; it's the spotted pup you're taking, isn't it?'

'Yes; Petal. Mrs Matteson says we may call her Petal. I like it because it's a flowery name, like Lilac.'

Petal was already the apple of her eye. Small and fat, white with liver spots, she was the prettiest of all the cocker spaniels in Lilac's opinion. Although she did not want to go home, for she had never been happier than she was at Elcott Hall, she was reconciled to the move because it would mean being with Petal a great deal and having the schooling of her. Mrs Matteson had made it clear that she would expect Lilac to undertake to housetrain Petal as well as teaching her good manners.

'George, dear, where are you? Do come and have your tea.'

From the small group of people on the terrace, Mrs Matteson's clear voice floated across the long green lawn.

Lilac stayed where she was and George, though he got sulkily to his feet, did not actually move but looked down at her imploringly.

'Go on, George,' Lilac said briskly. 'There are crumpets. And an orange and ginger cake. I watched cooky making it and she let me add the candied peel. We'll meet again later.'

Chapter Fourteen

1920

Nellie stood at the rail of the ship and watched the heaving grey ocean and hoped she would not disgrace herself. Truth to tell she had so looked forward to this moment and now that it had come it just seemed a huge anti-climax.

She could have gone back earlier, of course, had she been set on it. But once Lilac had moved out, it seemed only sensible to sub-let the house. It had taken a bit of time, Aunt Ada's daughters as well as Nellie's brothers had had to be consulted, but they all felt that the house would only deteriorate left to stand empty – unless a family desperate for accommodation simply moved in and took over.

So for a year a family of four had lived there, a woman and her wounded husband and their two small children. But then the husband had died and the wife, a native of Manchester, had gone home to her own people, leaving number eleven empty.

And the hospital in the chateau was only half full now, the patients were being moved whenever possible, either home or to other hospitals. The girls who remained were restless, prepared to face the possibility of unemployment at home rather than continue to live in a foreign land.

Lately, Nellie had dreamed of standing by the ship's rail and seeing France get smaller, until it was just a smudge on the horizon. She had not expected to feel a traitor, as though by leaving France she was also leaving Lucy.

Lucy! It was a full year, now, since her friend had died, yet it sometimes seemed to Nellie as though Lucy influenced everything she did. Every dream of home had contained her friend, every wistfully imagined sailing had been with Lucy by her side. And when she had finally been told that she was to leave in so many days' time, that Emma and Sarah and Maggie would be going home too, all she could think of was Lucy, left here alone.

She knew it was stupid, because Lucy wasn't here any longer, hadn't been here since that awful moment in Ward Five when her hoarse, painful breathing had stopped. There had been nothing of Lucy in her face two minutes later, so why should she imagine, now, that Lucy wailed, ghostlike, across the flat French countryside because her friends had left?

She was gripping the rail so tight that her knuckles had whitened and her hands felt as though they were frozen to the metal. She carefully unclenched her fingers and turned her head. Maggie stood by her. She, too, was straining back towards France. She saw Nellie looking at her and turned, sighing.

'Nell, have you thought what we're going to go back to? Nothing will be the same again, not now we've known freedom, responsibility, the thrill of being not just useful but important, a person who could help a man to live, or ease his dying. We've done our duty and more – it's over a year since the war ended, we stayed whilst we were needed – but that won't matter to the folk at home. How will I go back to living over a greengrocer's shop, doing as my mother wishes, dusting the furniture in the mornings, embroidering pillowslips in the evenings? And why should I do it? Why the hell should I? What are my chances of marriage, now? In case you hadn't realised, Nell, the pillowslips were to be my trousseau.'

'And Ned was killed at the battle of the Somme,' Nellie said. 'But you must have met a hundred other young men, Maggie, and you'll meet a hundred more. You'll marry, I'm sure of it.'

'Are you? Take a good look at me, Nell. A good look. When the war started I was twenty-one. I knew nothing, and you could see it on my face. Now I'm twenty-seven and look ten years older. I've worked until my nails were down to the quicks, I've scrubbed floors and shovelled coal into the boiler, I've changed dressings and cleaned suppurating wounds. I've laid out the dead and tried to ease the agony of the living. What have I got to offer some young man who's longing to forget what he saw and suffered in the course of the war? Nightmares? Shared horrors? Believe me, Nell, the men who survive won't want reminding of it by the woman in their bed, they'll want to forget with ... with a dewy-eyed twenty-year-old who faints at the sight of blood and is proud of her filbert nails.'

Nellie looked at her companion, at the sensible, short-cropped hair, the lined face, the work-weary hands. Maggie was tired and looked it, but surely that would not make her unmarriageable? Surely someone would see, not the tiredness nor the cruel lines that sorrow had bitten into her face, but the courage, the gaiety in adversity, the indomitable spirit which had brought Maggie through?

She said as much. Maggie smiled wearily.

'I wish you were right, but I don't believe you are. Men who want to forget will look elsewhere for a bride and men who never suffered won't want me as a continual reminder that they were the lucky ones. Still, I can't face the flat over the greengrocer's for the rest of my life, so I shall either continue to nurse if they'll have me, or I'll try to start up a little business of my own – God knows what.'

'You need money to start a business,' Nellie said slowly. 'And in one way we're the same – I've got to go back to whatever awaits me, and pick up an ordinary life again. I don't know how Stuart will feel when we meet again. But you and I will settle down, find our place in the world.'

Maggie smiled and turned to go down below and Nellie thought of her own circumstances. She had jumped at the chance to stay on for a further year once she knew from Lilac's letters that she was happily settled. Nellie was grateful to the Mattesons, of course she was, but also, perhaps, the tiniest bit jealous. And ever since Lilac's visit to Elcott Hall, Nellie had been worried by her changing attitude. She seemed to have got it into her head that she was descended from royalty, or at least from titled people, and all she ever wrote about was her Quest, as she called it. She had been fond of Art O'Brien, but that had fallen by the wayside when Lilac realised that he was powerless to help her find her parents whereas George Elcott could be very useful. And Nellie was sure, from the tone of Lilac's missives, that she was hoping George would ask her to marry him.

Foolish child, Nellie thought fondly now, smiling to herself. As if he would be allowed to do so, even if he wanted marriage in four or five years' time. But Lilac would grow up, as she, Nellie, had grown up, and see the error of wanting the impossible. If she stuck to her schooling and worked hard, then the world was her oyster, and with looks like hers ...

Thinking of Lilac's future calmed Nellie's agitation for a while, but then she thought of Stuart, who was with the Army of Occupation in Germany, reporting on the war trials. He was learning the German language and getting on well with it and was now settled in Berlin as the correspondent for a national daily. Their close correspondence still went on, sometimes he talked longingly of meeting when they both went home ... but would it mean anything when they did see each other again? Would the magical warmth have withstood the long separation? And, naturally, she wondered sometimes whether she should have given herself to him, but then practical commonsense took over. He was a good man, he would not despise her for the pleasure they had given each other. She had read in his letters his longing for her and had told him frankly that she felt the same. No; that night in the big bed, clutching, holding, touching, learning, had been a gift from the gods and she had no intention of wishing it undone.

Nevertheless, doubts hovered, for she knew she had changed, as Maggie said. Lucy's death had changed her, the suffering she had seen had made its imprint on her soul. But so would Stuart have changed; if she went home and Stuart followed, then she would soon know where she stood.

Alone? If Stuart had grown away from her with all his new responsibilities, then she might indeed be alone, for Lilac would probably want to move away from her in a couple of years. Dear God, was loneliness to be her reward for doing her duty?

Sighing, she turned back to the rail and gazed, this time, towards England.

They docked in London, and the girls who were Liverpool-bound got on a train which took them through a country they remembered vaguely from that other journey, the one they had taken as innocent girls eager for a part in the war.

England looked green and pleasant in the spring sunshine, with flowers blooming, trees in bud, people beginning to wear lighter clothing as the warmth of the days increased. Nellie remembered France; they had been taken on a tour of the battlefields and the black-ened emptiness of the landscape, without even a tree or a village, would haunt her until her dying day. She had walked over the lines with Maggie, Emma and the others, deeply depressed to think that she, as a member of the human race, must bear some responsibility for this sea of mud, this ruin of what had once been fair fields, pleasant places.

But now was the time for forgetting. She sat back in her seat, with Maggie's side warm against hers. Maggie lived in Chester, they would part soon, but surely they would meet again? They had been so close this past year, since Lucy's death. It seemed impossible that, tomorrow, there would be no Maggie to joke with, no Maggie from whom to ask advice.

The train jerked, slowed. A station loomed, grey and black, shut off from the green and gold of the country-side. It was a practical place, smelling of concrete, coal burning, the sulphurous reek of the steam. On the platform a man with a cart was selling hot bread rolls with sausages in. Maggie and Nellie bought one each. They ate with enjoyment, then sat back in their seats and gazed out of the window at the peaceful country-side as the train chugged on.

The train slowed again, clattering over points, and drew up alongside another grey platform. A porter, hat at an angle, a spotted scarf round his throat, announced that this was Chester. Nellie had been dreading this moment and now that it had arrived she saw that

Maggie dreaded it too. But they were practical women, no longer foolish girls. Nellie helped Maggie with her luggage and stopped on the platform long enough to give her friend a parting hug, to promise to write or to visit. But even as the train began to move and she waved from the window to the diminishing figure in the drooping grey cloak, Nellie was sure it would never happen; they would be swallowed up by their own lives once more the moment they stepped from the train.

It was too much to bear. She had not wept since Lucy's funeral; now she wept all the way to Liverpool Lime Street.

She had not expected to be met because she had not been able to tell Lilac what train she was on. Nevertheless, it was awful arriving at Lime Street station to find nobody who knew her on the platform. And it was busy, too, crowded with people, a good few of them still in uniform, as she was. Demobilization had taken longer than anyone had anticipated; here it was, mid-March 1920, and there were still troops in Europe and probably further afield, too.

But Nellie picked up her heavy box and the lighter bag which she slung across her shoulders, and set off, suddenly eager to get away from the limbo world of the station, the bustle of arrivals and departures, and to emerge into the real, civilian world at last. Out there the sunny March day awaited her – and Liverpool, her home.

Nellie stumped out of the station, passing directly under the grimy windows of the North Western Hotel. Lime Street was very wide here and horses, carts, cars and lorries streamed by whilst Nellie waited for a chance to cross. A tram approached, the driver clanking the bell warningly, then leaning out to shout at a lad who had skipped across the road in front of him. Nellie found the bustle confusing after so long in a land where military convoys were almost the only traffic on the road and paused by the kerb, blinking. Directly opposite her rose St. George's Hall on its wide plain with the statues of the famous black against the pearl-grey stone building. Just to the left of that she could see the trees in St John's Garden. Their branches were bare still, but big with buds. Pigeons, dusky black, fudge-brown, dove-grey, squabbled for crumbs which a nursemaid and her charge scattered round the equestrian statue's plinth. Occasionally a passerby would cause the flock to rise into the air for a moment and then the wings flashed white and gold in the sunshine and the child would crow with delight, throwing back his head in its red tam o'shanter and clapping at the sudden flurry.

This is my place, my home, Nellie told herself, dragging the box across the road and suddenly loving every cobble, every stone, every feather on every pigeon, though she knew that, near-to, they would probably prove to be a scruffy, scurvy bunch. She sniffed the air and smelt the clean buffeting breeze from the Mersey, the smells of food and vegetables from St John's, a whiff of cod and haddock from the fish stalls and the odd dry, tinny smell of the trams lined up on Old Haymarket, waiting to leave.

She walked down William Brown Street, still full to bursting with love for her city; how had she borne to be away? She had left here once before, to go to Moelfre, but she had been scarcely more than a child, then. Now she was a woman and could feel the deep, abiding love for this place which had been growing in her all her life and had finally come to its full flowering. She glanced across to the Free Library. There were daffodils in the beds, nodding their golden heads, and a few frail primroses. Ahead of her the Wellington monument loomed black against the blue sky.

Her tram was second from the front when she reached the line-up, which was good, since it meant she would have a shorter wait for departure. She climbed aboard, gave her money to the conductor in exchange for a ticket, and let him stand her box in the doorway, where it would not impede other passengers. She sat on the shiny wooden seat and stared eagerly out through the glass. She felt as if she could never have enough of the place which she knew like the back of her hand. Presently, with a jolt, the tram started, and she could see for herself that it was the same, it had not changed. Straight up Byrom Street, like an arrow from a bow, the tram charged, the bell ringing warningly at every intersection, the conductor calling out the stops. At Gerard Street, where they stopped to let people off, she heard and felt the rumble of an underground train as it sped on its way to Waterloo station. Home! A stranger would not have known what that rumble implied!

The conductor sang out 'Arden Street, anyone for Arden Street?' and Nellie's smile broadened even as she felt an unaccountable urge to weep. She was home! They were on the Scottie! Any minute now it would be her stop and she would be lugging the heavy case into the Court and through her own front door!

'Raysho Street, Raysho Street,' shouted the conductor. They never got it right but everyone knew what they meant. Nellie made her way to the entrance and the conductor winked at her and heaved her suitcase down onto the flags.

'There y'are, queen,' he said. 'Home at last, eh?'

Nellie nodded, too full to speak. He knew she was a nurse of course, because she was still in her grey cloak and uniform dress. No one had civilian clothes in France and she had no money to buy them with, not yet. Anyway, if she continued to nurse …

But right now she simply could not think about the practicalities of her future. She did not know what the options were to be, let alone what she wanted. She heaved the heavy box under the archway and into the court. It was just the same! Doors were left wide open, women called from house to house, small children played ollies, scrambling after the roughly rounded clay balls. A girl of fourteen or so skipped rope, keeping an eye on a couple of scrawny babies who slept, tangled together like puppies, on a filthy piece of blanket laid out on the flagstones.

The girl looked round. It was Hannah Batterby from number eighteen.

'Wotcher, Nellie,' she said. 'They're tekin' on at the tobaccer manufactory so me mam tole me to keep an eye on the kids. 'Ow's life, then? What d'ya think of the ole city now you've been away from it a whiles?'

'It's the best place in the world to be,' Nellie said seriously. She glanced across at number eleven, the only door which was closed. 'I'm real glad to be home, Hannah … who's got the key, d'you know?'

'Dunno, unless it's Mrs O'Brien. Nah, it won't be 'er, come to think on, it's Art what goes in most days since the Thompsons left, I seen 'im, but 'e's at school now, acourse. He don't come 'ome dinnertimes no more either. Tell you what, Nellie, if you leave your luggage in our front room, you can walk up to school an' get the key off of Art. Don't worry, I'll keep an eye on your stuff.'

'Oh Hannah, that is good of you,' Nellie said gratefully. She put the case down just inside the open front door of number eighteen and turned away, digging in the pocket of her cloak. She found two pennies and gave them to Hannah. 'I'm real grateful. Here, nip down to Taverners and get yourself some sweets.'

'Ooh, I could just do wi' some taffy,' Hannah said, eagerly taking the pennies. 'Thanks ever so, Nellie!'

Relieved of her burden, Nellie strolled out of the court again and turned right along the pavement. She would have liked to wait outside Lilac's school, but suppose she did so and missed Art? Then she remembered that Art and Lilac usually walked home together; she went on past the end of the street and turned left after St Anthony's Church, then walked quickly along the pavement until she reached the school.

It was a grim-looking building, the bricks long blackened, the tall, narrow sash windows each divided into many small panes scarcely adding to the building's good looks. The school yard was deserted now, but presently it would resound to the remonstrances of teachers and the clatter of boots as the boys rushed out into what remained of the afternoon's sunshine.

Nellie cast a couple of wistful glances over her shoulder, in the direction of Lilac's school. She knew the child would have to hurry back to Rodney Street, but surely she would wait until Art came out, so that they could walk some of the way together? And she really could not risk meeting Lilac but missing Art, because if Art went off with her key she would be unable to get into number eleven!

The prospect of not being able to get inside her home was daunting, so Nellie stayed where she was. And presently, five minutes at least before the bell rang, she was rewarded. A small, green-painted door to one side of the building opened and a figure slipped out. It could not be Art, who was small and stocky ... yet it was. She recognised the way his hair stood up in a quiff in front, the sturdiness of him, a certain something in his walk. He came down to the gate, walking with long strides, and Nellie waved to him.

'Art! It's me, I'm home!'

Art stared. Nellie stared too. He was tall, broadshouldered, quite a young man now, no longer a boy. Yet in her letters Lilac always referred to him as though they were both children still. Or perhaps she did not, perhaps it was Nellie, assuming.

'Wotcher, queen,' Art said as soon as he got near enough. 'I come out early so's I can see our Lilac afore she 'as to rush off. She'll be out in a few minutes, so we better 'urry.'

And hurry they did, arriving outside Lilac's school just as, with a noise like a flock of starlings, the pupils emerged.

If Nellie thought Art had changed, she was astonished, even shocked, by the change in Lilac. Not a child, not even in the unbecoming school uniform, but a young woman, emerged from the throng of scholars. In fact she would not have recognised her but for that startling hair and the fact that Art, standing by her elbow, nudged her and pointed.

'There's she is! Good gairl, early for once. Look who's 'ere, our Lilac!'

Lilac started to run towards them and Nellie stared and stared at the child she had loved ever since she had first held her. She had always thought Lilac pretty, but this was a beautiful young creature with great, dark blue eyes, a milk and roses complexion, and the slim yet rounded body which Nellie had previously associated only with stars of stage and screen. And it was not just beauty, she discovered as Lilac drew near. There was a sort of chuckling charm in her smile, a delightful impishness, the confidence of someone who expects admiration and takes it for granted that she will be loved. How different from me, Nellie thought, sadly but without self-pity. I'm always delighted when someone's nice to me, takes a bit of notice. I'm bowled over when someone shows me affection!

But right now, Lilac clearly had eyes for no one but Nellie.

'Nellie, Nellie, Nellie!' she gasped as she shot through the school gates and onto the pavement. 'Oh Nell, I've missed you ever so ... don't you look so sweet in your grey cloak – I declare, you're no taller than me, but of course I've grown, and you'd done all your growing before you went to France. Oh Nell, it's so good to have you home! Will you be back in number eleven tomorrow? Oh, how I wish I could come back with you now, but it wouldn't be fair. Mrs Jenkins expects me home in about half an hour, she'll want things done, and now I'm a sort of companion to Mrs Matteson, I have to speak nicely and always look neat – do I sound different, Nell? Oh lor', and the Mattesons have their dinner at night, d'you know? We have supper – ever such lovely food we have, Nell. Well, ask Art – my carry-out is heaps nicer than most people's – Art and me often share, don't we? Oh look ... my tram ... I'd better run!'

She set off at a lope, looking over her shoulder at them, smiling, charming. Dismissing, too. But Art kept pace with her, looking into her face, a detaining hand on her arm.

'Mrs Jenkins won't mind if you tell 'er as your Nellie's come 'ome,' he said persuasively. 'She's awful good, your Mrs Jenkins. And Mrs Matteson is even better, you've said so often.'

'Oh yes, they're both ever so nice, Mrs Matteson particularly. She takes such good care of me, but I can't let her down ... perhaps tomorrow ... '

'It's all right, Li,' Nellie said. 'I'll have a word with Mrs Jenkins and the Mattesons tomorrow, thank them for taking you in and keeping you safe and happy. And you sound as pretty as you look! So if you pack your traps this evening, or first thing tomorrow, I can collect 'em for you, then you can come straight home after school.' She had to raise her voice above the rattle of the tram which was drawing up almost beside them. 'Tell you what, I'll come down with you now, it's early still, perhaps they might let you come home tonight!'

Lilac hopped aboard the tram and darted up the stairs and onto the top deck. Nellie followed rather more sedately, first paying their fares, and sat down on one side of the younger girl whilst Art took the other. The three settled themselves, then Nellie turned to Lilac once more.

'So I'll talk to Mrs Matteson tonight, eh, queen? She's awful nice, you said.'

'Oh yes, very nice,' Lilac agreed faintly. 'But ... not tonight, Nellie! They depend on me, honest to God! I'll have to give 'em a chance to get fixed up somehow, though I don't know... but not tonight, Nellie.'

'Not?' Nellie said rather blankly. 'Well, perhaps you're right, luv. It's a bit sudden. I'll come round tomorrow and ...'

'Look, let me speak to them first, then call round for me after school tomorrow and I'll tell you when to come,' Lilac said. 'They've been so good, Nell, I don't want anyone upset.'

'All right, if you say so,' Nellie agreed after a short pause. 'Where do you get off, queen?'

'Depends which tram this is,' Lilac said rather sulkily. 'Either Leece Street and walk through, or by the pub on the corner of Knight Street. You were talking and I was in a hurry, so I didn't look at the destination board.'

'It don't matter, though,' Art pointed out. 'You'll know soon enough, queen! If the tram turns left by St Luke's then it's the Leece, if it goes straight it's t'other one.'

Lilac said nothing for a moment, then she asked Nellie, in a rather strained voice, whether she had had a good journey.

'Not so bad,' Nellie said. 'It took a long time ... do you know I've not even seen number eleven yet? Well, apart from the outside. I left my luggage with young Hannah from opposite. But you've been popping in from time to time and seeing it's tidy, I suppose?'

'Since the Thompsons left, do you mean? Art does,' Lilac said quickly, with a rather defensive note creeping into her voice. 'After all, what with school and work in the house, I'm pretty busy. I barely have time to pick up my post ... why didn't you write, Nell, and tell me you were on your way?'

'I did,' Nellie said flatly. 'But since you said it was better to keep writing to the court, you'll likely not have received it yet. I wrote two weeks ago that it would be soon, though I couldn't give an exact date.'

'I don't take the post out,' Art said, since Lilac did not reply but continued to stare out of the window. 'I don't always get outer school in time an' there's no point in me havin' the letters.'

'Very true,' Nellie said. She was beginning to feel uneasy. Lilac had grown so pretty and self-confident, but surely the old, clinging, loving Lilac was still there, somewhere, beneath the exterior of this calm and self-assured young woman? She turned to say something to this effect just as Lilac said brightly, 'Oh, I know which tram this is, it's the one that goes down Berry Street and past the cemetery. I was looking down at the tram stop whilst the people got on and there's an old woman with a wooden leg who catches this tram every night. She's never on the tram which turns off down Leece so I suppose she lives by the docks, somewhere, and couldn't walk that far.'

'Well, now that we've solved which tram we're on … ' Nellie began, to be interrupted once more.

'Nellie, honestly, it's awful good of you to come home with me, but you can't come in, not tonight, so why don't you and Art stay on the tram? If you stay on until the terminus you can come back on it, all the way to the Scottie. It 'ud save you hanging about.'

'Very sensible,' Nellie said dryly, after another awkward pause. 'That's thoughtful of you, Lilac. Well, I'll see you after school tomorrow, then.'

'Yes, of course,' Lilac said eagerly. The conductor shouted 'St Mark's,' and she jumped to her feet. 'Here's my stop. Thanks ever so much for coming with me, Nell, and it's lovely to have you home! See you tomorrow, then.'

After she had gone the tram continued to rattle along whilst Art and Nellie did their best to keep their balance and talk at the same time.

'Don't get upset 'cos of Lilac not wantin' you to see them Mattesons,' Art said presently. 'She don't want me up there, either. She lets me meet 'er outa school, but that's about me lot, these days. She talked about some feller – George, 'is name was – who's helpin' her in some way. But I reckons those Mattesons tek good care of 'er, like you said, so it's good that she likes 'em. Per'aps it's better not to interfere, eh?'

'Yes. But Art, what about coming home? To the Scottie?'

Art stared at his boots. Nellie registered that they were very large boots for very large feet and that they were quite new, as well. But all she could think of, really, was Lilac.

'Would you ... would you mind if she stayed with them Mattesons ... just till she's old enough to leave school?' Art enquired at length. 'They feed 'er well, she 'as the best of everything ... you've only gorra look at 'er to see that.'

'I did my best and so did Aunt Ada ...' Nell began, but Art put a very large young hand over hers and squeezed gently.

'So you did, but we don't live like them, queen! They treat our Lilac more like a daughter than a servant, honest to God. An' that can't be bad, eh? She looks so growed up, but she's only a kid at 'eart and she's enjoyin' the good things, the good times. She's got a dog called Petal ... leastways it's Mrs M's dog, but they let Lilac do all the trainin' and walkin' and she do love Petal. An' I don't know if she said anythin' to you, but she's desperate keen to find 'er mother an' she seems to think she's close, now. Per'aps it would be cruel to make 'er come away.'

'But what does it matter who her mother was? And anyway, she *is* a servant, Art, even if they treat her like family, and that isn't what I wanted for her! She's so bright and clever, she could be a teacher, she could work in a bank, she could do anything, if only she keeps on her with education!'

'Oh aye?' Art looked down at her from his superior height with compassion in his round, brown eyes.

'Well, last year it were quite a struggle to stop 'er leavin' school, but I managed it and she's still there. Whether she'll stick it much longer I wouldn't like to say. And she's rare 'appy in Rodney Street, Nellie. Don't that count for anything?'

'Yes, of course it does! But she could be happy with me, couldn't she? In Coronation Court?'

Art raised his brows and then fell to contemplating his boots again.

'Aye, perhaps. She's growin' up fast though, Nell.'

Nellie laughed suddenly, with genuine amusement.

'So are you, Arthur O'Brien! I hardly knew you. And just why are you still at school? You must be fifteen, going on sixteen.'

'That's right. But it's different for me; I've got me way to make. Mr Wainright says if I keep on workin', there's no reason as I shouldn't get into a bank! That's steady work, right? I could mek a good 'ome for someone with a job like that.'

And Nellie, looking hard at Art's averted face, knew who he meant and, in her turn, squeezed his hand. It was not only she who would be left alone if Lilac turned finally to the Mattesons. But Art did not grudge Lilac her happiness. Art was prepared to let the little bird fly, hoping that she would, in the end, fly home.

I could learn a lesson from this lad, Nellie told herself. And I must go careful, or I'll alienate my girl for ever.

It was good to be back in the court again, though the house seemed tiny, dark and cold despite the sunny day that had just passed. Looking round it, Nellie wondered how she could have imagined it was a cosy little home, a home a girl would enjoy coming back to – after years in a great, clean hospital and billets where the ceilings were high and the beds soft, this place seemed dank and unwelcoming, the entire way of life of the court dwellers narrow and deprived.

But the same was not true of the inhabitants of Coronation Court. Old and young alike, they went out of their way to welcome Nellie and tell her how they had missed her. Nellie had never really liked or trusted Mrs O'Brien but even she seemed well-disposed towards the girl they had last seen over three years before.

'The Thompsons were awright, but we 'ated the 'ouse empty,' she announced. 'Not nat'ral. I brung you some scouse; just warm it up an' it'll feed a little thing like you for a coupla days.'

It was greasy and sour-tasting, but Nellie appreciated the thought behind the gift. She accepted it and mixed it with a bag of mouldering oatmeal she found in the cupboard, then sneaked it round to Mrs Lennox, who kept four chickens penned into a corner of her living room since she said, rather mysteriously, that the house was too big for one.

Mrs Lennox, delighted to feed her hens free for once, said she was powerful glad Nell was home.

'Bring the tiddler back too,' she said earnestly. 'That's a good gairl, that Lilac a yourn.'

And Nellie was busy, too. That evening and all the next day she hardly had time to think. She scrubbed and brushed, cleaned and polished, lit fires and bought kindling, coal and logs. She stocked the cupboards fiercely full, then scolded herself for trying to bribe Lilac back. But with every hour that passed the house grew pleasanter and cosier, and gradually Nellie managed to convince herself that Lilac would come home willingly, gladly, once she had had a chance to square things with her benefactress.

'She's a good kid,' she told herself that second after-noon, as she arranged the table for tea, laying two places, and banked up the fire. 'She's a good kid, if her head's been turned by these people, who can blame her? Everyone wants a comfortable life; well, she can have one here with me just as much as skivvying for the Mattesons.'

It was another blowy March day so she had taken the opportunity to wash her print dress and the grey cloak. They dried quickly, blowing on the line, and she heated the flats on the stove top and ironed everything, then polished her shoes, made sure the seams of her stockings were straight, brushed her hair until it shone and set out at last for school, convinced that everything would be all right.

Lilac would soon be home, where she belonged.

Lilac had gone home after leaving Art and Nellie on the tram, with her mind afire with conflicting desires. What on earth should she do – what did she really want to do? She did love Nellie, and Nellie had always made a home for her, but she was really happy at the Mattesons, she saw George Elcott once or twice a month, they discussed the search for her mother, and Lilac just knew that Nellie, if she discovered what was going on, would put a stop to it.

Besides, the most important thing in her life, right now, was to find her mother. Not only because it would enable her to marry George when they were both old enough for matrimony, but because she did not intend to go through her life rootless, a foundling. So if it came to the crunch, Nellie would jolly well have to lump it – Lilac needed to know that her mother was a high-born lady, and find out she would! And if Nellie didn't approve of her marrying George, why she would have to lump that, too.

In the deepest recesses of her mind, Lilac knew that if Mrs Matteson knew what was going on she would be none too pleased. And as for Lord and Lady Elcott ... well, she shuddered to think what they would say if they knew George was intent on marrying to disoblige them, as the saying went. For George was now most definitely courting Lilac, and Lilac was, if not encouraging him, not dismissing him out of hand, either.

But of course they both pretended it was the search for Lilac's mother which drew them together. George pretended it, Lilac knew, because it was the only way he could be sure of getting Lilac to himself and Lilac pretended because she was being very careful. She loved life at the Mattesons, the food, the warmth, the easy acceptance of the good things of life. And she had begun to see that her best hope of getting such a life for herself was to marry well.

Nellie had wanted her to be a teacher, but the teachers at Lilac's school wore grey skirts smudged with chalk and had chilblains in the winter time. They lived in neat little houses compared with the courts and terraces of the city, but they lived carefully and almost never seemed to marry. Lilac liked the Mattesons' comfortable house, but even more she liked Elcott Hall. All those servants, the marvellous grounds, the dinners and dances ... and it would all be George's one day. His father was dead, his mother a complaining lady who took little interest in her only son ... and the grandparents were, in Lilac's eyes, incredibly old. They disapproved of her, but if she could just produce a high-born parent then marriage to George would be not just a dream but perfectly possible. She still yearned after Stuart, but he had not written or visited and almost without noticing it, she had begun to see her future as being shared with George, her life as being lived out at the Hall and in the town house in South John Street.

Yet she loved Nellie, she really did. She knew that without Nellie she would not have amounted to much ... well, probably not, anyway. But the meetings with George would soon stop if she had Art and Nellie watching her, and she had no faith in her ability to hold George's interest for long without these meetings, for George was eighteen and almost a man. Although she was getting on for fifteen, she was very much afraid that she lacked the arts of older women. Now that she was virtually Mrs Matteson's personal maid she had a small room of her own adjoining that of her mistress. So it became possible for George to sneak up to her room sometimes, when the weather was too inclement for the long walks which they shared.

They had done nothing to be ashamed of, though, Lilac thought defensively now, tossing and turning in her comfortable bed as she tried to make sense of her own very mixed feelings. They kissed and cuddled and lately she had allowed George to put a trembling hand down the front of her blouse and caress her breasts, but that was the extent of it. So far. She wanted to do right, to save herself for marriage, but if George showed signs of straying ... well, it would be tempting to let him have what he wanted, and then to persuade him to marry her.

Not that she knew what he wanted, far less whether he wanted it! He was so diffident, so easily shoved off, but she supposed that his urge to fondle her breasts could have been turned to her advantage – if only she could work out just what that advantage was.

Lilac sighed and pushed the blankets down so that the breeze coming through the window could cool her hot flesh. What was more, they were getting close to her mother, she was sure of it. George had a lead! It was all terribly complicated, but he really did think it was a possibility. Apparently his mother, of all the unlikely people, had begun to talk about a cousin of hers, a very high-born lady, who had had a wild, tempestuous *affaire* with a young man which had ended mysteriously.

'I might not have asked about it, except that I met her, d'you see, and was much struck by her, she's the most glorious creature ... with hair the very colour and texture of yours, Lilac. So of course I asked Mother about her when she had gone – she was paying a morning call – and she told me what she could. Apparently this cousin lived with Mother's family after her own parents died. Well, when they were quite grown up her cousin went away to stay with friends and when she came back she kept to her room for several weeks; her maid said she had scarlet fever, the doctor came and went ... and then one day she was fit as a flea once more,' George said impressively. 'I couldn't help but think it was possible that she'd had a baby and managed somehow to get it to the Culler, for Mother said that though her cousin was beautiful she was sly and difficult to live with, only I expect there was some jealousy there, don't you? My mother is no beauty – though very nice, of course.'

The two of them were walking in St James's cemetery at the time, since it was quiet and seldom frequented by members of the Matteson household. Having imparted his information, George put his arm round Lilac's shoulders and gave her a squeeze. Lilac, conscious of obligation, snuggled against him.

'What was this cousin's name, do you know?'

'Well, she's Mrs Herbert Allan now,' George said. 'She's been married twice, though. Why? Does it matter?'

'No-oo, only I'd like to know my mother's first name ... if she is my mother.'

'We'll find out for sure,' George said confidently. 'I'll think about it and you must do the same. Apparently the Allans have just moved back to the city after being in London for twelve years or so. They're living in Abercromby Square, in a positive mansion – Mother said trust her cousin to fall on her feet!'

Everyone wants to know who their mother is, Lilac thought defiantly now, turning over yet again and laying her hot cheek against the cool pillow. She would stay with the Mattesons until she had got her parentage sorted out and then – perhaps – she would consider making some changes in her life. She must remember, however, that Nellie, though nice, was nothing to her really, no relation, nothing. So she need never go back to nasty, common Coronation Court.

So when Nellie met Lilac out of school that day, the die, so far as Lilac was concerned, was already cast.

'Do come and see Mrs Matteson,' she said cordially. 'Only my mind is quite made up, Nellie dear. I'll visit you often at number eleven, I promise, and I'll come back for my holidays, but I'm going to go on living in Rodney Street. Look, I get pocket-money, and they feed and clothe me, and when I leave school in the summer Mrs Matteson is going to take me on full-time, properly, as her personal maid. Then I'll *have* to live in ... and Nell, dearest, jobs are so difficult to find in Liverpool, you must know they are! I can't risk losing one where I'm so very happy!'

'L-leave school?' Nellie stammered. 'Oh, but queen, your career ... your education! I thought you'd try for a teacher ... I want more for you than I'll ever get ... I don't mind for meself ... '

'Oh Nell, you're so good – I don't deserve you,' Lilac said, hugging the older girl's arm. 'We can go back to the court now, Mrs Matteson said of course I must spend some time with you, just so long as I'm home before ten o'clock ... she's given me money for a tram! Can you forgive me? Dear Nell, try not to hate me for what I'm doing.'

But Nellie, hugging Lilac back, scarcely heard anything past the word 'home'. So Rodney Street was home to Lilac now – and it served her, Nellie, right. She had gone off twice, once to give birth to the little son she had never set eyes on since, once to escape from that little son's father. She had not meant to go for long the first time, but the second time she had known she would be away for months, perhaps years. Who was she to blame Lilac if the kid had made a satisfactory life for herself whilst she was away?

'Nell? Are you cross?'

'Oh queen, how can I be cross when I can see that you're doing the right thing? I did want you to keep at school, but if you've got a good life and a happy one, then you stick to it! I'll miss you, I won't pretend otherwise, but I'll settle down, pick up the threads.'

The two girls had been walking whilst they talked, and turned into Coronation Court on the words. Lilac hesitated, then walked steadily forward, but Nellie had noticed the hesitation and suddenly, for an instant, saw the court as Lilac must be seeing it, and not just seeing, but remembering.

The place smelt, even though it was not yet high summer; when summer came, it would stink. There were only two dustbins for all the houses in the court – sixteen of them – and they weren't emptied as often as they should have been, either. And the privy, shared by all, hummed now, but would be worse when the weather warmed up. Come summer, flies and bluebottles would be thick around the bins and the privy, and inside the houses the women would wage a constant war against fleas, bed-bugs, lice and worse.

The doors were all open today, and once more children played on the dirty flagstones. Dirty children, Nellie realised anew, with runny noses, cold sores round their mouths, greasy, tick-ridden hair. Oh, not all of them, some of them were kept as nicely as one could expect, but some were always neglected, dirty, hungry. She had thought that if she closed her door and polished away, spread the table with good things, kept the fire lit, then she was somehow apart from all this. In fact she could not hold herself aloof, any more than Lilac would be able to, if she returned.

They went across to number eleven and opened the door. Nellie put a log on the fire, then pulled the kettle over the heat.

'Tea won't be long,' she said cheerfully. 'Wash your hands, queen.'

Whilst she bustled about she realised that there was a draught cutting in under the door enough to take your feet off at the ankles. The houses were always draught-ridden, icy cold in winter yet hot and stuffy in summer. Who could blame Lilac for preferring the comforts of the house in Rodney Street?

'Kettle's boiling,' Lilac said. 'Can I mash the tea, Nell?'

'If you wouldn't mind,' Nellie said. 'The tea's in the Bruno tin on the mantel. Aunt Ada's nice red caddy seems to have disappeared.'

'Walked with the Thompsons, I expect,' Lilac said cheerfully. 'It's nice to be together again, isn't it, Nell? I'll come often, shall I? When Mrs Matteson will let me.'

Nellie opened her mouth to say come as often as you like and quite different words emerged, words which she had not known she meant, let alone meant to say.

'You're always welcome, queen, but I shan't be here long, meself. I've been told I can go before a hospital board to start training as a properly qualified nursing sister. I might get a place in a Liverpool hospital but then again I might have to go away. Still, until I go you're always welcome, as I said.'

'Oh!' Lilac said rather blankly. 'Oh, I see. And what'll happen to the house?'

'Well, I don't want it and you don't want it, and from what I've heard the boys don't want it, so the landlord can find another tenant,' Nellie said cheerfully. 'I couldn't afford to live here by meself, chuck, not on the sort of money I'm likely to earn nursing. Besides, nurses live in, usually. I wrote to Matt and Charlie when we first decided to sub-let and they said I might do as I pleased. They're all settled. Matt's with Charlie in the Lake District and Bertie and Unity live across the water in Woodchurch; none of them are likely to want a home in the 'pool.'

'I see,' Lilac said again. 'Will you come and visit in Rodney Street then, Nell?'

'Yes, of course I will,' Nellie said, giving Lilac a quick kiss on the cheek as she passed. 'But we're both big girls now. We'll do very well.'

All evening they talked over old times, told each other stories, laughed and joked. At nine forty-five Nellie put on her cloak and walked Lilac to the tram, got on with her, saw her to her door, then walked home. Alone.

Next day she went round to the Northern Hospital and spoke to one of the Administrators there, explaining that she wanted to take up full-time nursing training.

She had excellent references from her previous nursing posts and after a short interview, was accepted as a probationer. By the end of the week she had packed up all her things – they were not very numerous – and moved into the nurses' home attached to the training hospital to which she had been assigned. A couple of days after that she sold all the furniture and bits and bobs which no one wanted from the house in the court and sent the money to Ada's daughters, half each as arranged.

She wrote to Maggie and her other nursing friends, explaining what she had done and giving them her new address. She wrote to Stuart, too, of course, telling him what she had done and where she was to be found. She was desperate for news of him because he had not written lately and though the war was over, accidents did happen. But she managed to make her letter cheerful and informative, hiding, to the best of her ability, the pain that Lilac's defection had caused. She loved Stuart so much, she thought painfully, that marrying anyone else was simply out of the question, she would rather never marry than settle for second best.

Then she settled down to gain her qualifications as quickly as possible, because when she had returned to number eleven that night, after seeing Lilac home, she had also seen the sort of future which might lie in wait for her if Stuart changed his mind, and it had frightened her.

So even the life of a grim, tight-mouthed Nursing Sister, living in cramped accommodation in various nurses' homes, was better than degenerating into a lonely, underfed spinster ekeing out a miserable existence in a tiny house in Coronation Court. Perpetually hungry and increasingly lonely, that spinster would work at some menial job until she could toil no more, then she would let rooms until her tenants realised she could not force them to pay the rent. Then she would starve to death and be found in her filthy, rat-ridden kitchen, just a little heap of bones and grey, greasy hair.

The depressing picture scared Nellie. If she was nursing, at least she would be amongst people, earning her living in a job she enjoyed and at which she could excel.

She went twice to the Matteson house, but found it difficult to talk easily to Lilac under someone else's roof.

Stuart did not reply to her letter.

Chapter Fifteen

Lilac was sorry that Nellie had felt she must move out of Coronation Court, and sorry, too, that Nellie was not able to visit her often, but as spring turned into summer and summer into autumn, her Quest began to assume gigantic proportions in her mind.

There was no doubt about it, she was close ... getting warmer, getting warmer, as kids shouted when they played hide- and-seek and the seeker drew nearer and nearer to the apprehensive hider. And now with the coming of autumn, the opportunity to see for herself was suddenly within her grasp.

Lilac was in the kitchen, ironing Mrs Matteson's blue dress with the lace collar. It was a difficult task but one she enjoyed. Using the iron with great care, she steered it round and over the intricacies of the lace and saw the material become beautiful under her hand. On the hearth-rug Petal lay, toying with a bone. Perched on a kitchen stool drawn up to the table, fingers stained, eyes dreamy, Polly dipped the cutlery into the pink polishing powder and rubbed until the stains were gone, then handed each piece to Madge, who polished the powder off again. Then the cutlery was passed to Emily, who washed it in hot soapy water, dried it on one of the best glass cloths and returned it to its baize-lined drawer.

It was a peaceful domestic scene into which Polly, all unknowing, dropped a bombshell.

'Hey up, gels,' she said suddenly, wiping her brow

with the back of her hand. 'Anyone want some extra spondulicks? 'Oo could do with some spare cash, eh? Cos there's a big party being give on Abercromby Square an' they want extra maids to serve the grub around.'

'Oo said?'

That was Madge, who had come to replace Lilac after she had been moved upstairs. She was fat and giggly, with a round, childish face, small, bright blue eyes, dark curls and rather a lot of spots. She and Polly got on well, but the friendship between Polly and Lilac had survived even Lilac's swift rise to the status of personal maid. The two girls had so much in common, Lilac sometimes thought, that no one could come between them. Polly knew all Lilac's secrets; she knew about George, and even about Lilac's Quest, to say nothing of the Mystery of her Birth, and Lilac knew she would never breathe a word.

'Oh, 'oo said,' mimicked Polly now. 'I said, tatty-'ead! Me young man told me, if you must know.'

Polly had a young man at last. He was a very young man but that scarcely mattered when you considered that Polly only looked about twelve. And he was nice – chauffeur to a family who lived halfway down Black-burne Place. His name was Tom Hedges and because he drove the family everywhere they wanted to go he was a fount of knowledge and gossip. Polly adored him and had great hopes of becoming Mrs Hedges some time in the next two or three years.

'Which house, Poll?' Lilac said idly, finishing the lace collar and starting on the cuffs. 'What's the name of the people, did he say?'

'Course 'e did, 'ow else could I apply? It's Mr and Mrs Allan and I'm applying since we're savin' up, Tom an' me.'

'I wouldn't mind myself,' Lilac said, doing her best to appear nonchalant. What a bit of luck! As soon as Polly mentioned Abercromby Square she had thought of the Allans, but had not dared hope they were actually the party-givers. She often walked up to Abercromby Square and looked at the big houses, but George could not go with her. Too risky, he said, since he had actually met Mrs Allan – was related to her. But by herself she had had no luck. The big houses had remained infuriatingly closed, their windows blandly, blindly shining. 'What are they paying, Poll?'

'Three bob for five hours,' Polly said. 'It ain't bad, cos the work won't be hard, an' it'll be interestin'. Goin' to come?'

'Might as well,' Lilac said. 'When is it?'

'Oh … Sat'day night. It's a masked ball, Tom says. It'll be ever so posh with lots of food an' champagne, and the women will dress in their best and everyone will 'ave these little black masks on. There's a Dixieland band, very modern, an' they've done the ballroom floor with chalky stuff so's their feet slide nice, Tom says. Anyway, it's seven till midnight, only Tom says it'll be more like two a.m. before all that washin' up an' clearin's over, so we might make five bob if we're lucky.'

'I'm on,' Lilac said. 'What about you, Emily? You, Madge?'

'I'm game,' Emily said. She had been the kitchen maid but was now the cook, a quiet girl with nice manners who might, the girls thought, step into the job of housekeeper when Mrs Jenkins retired. 'Do we have to apply in person?'

'Yeah, go to the kitchen door an' give in your name. It's black and white acourse, wear your own, an' Tom says to put your name down quick, afore word gets round.'

'Tom says, Tom says,' mimicked Madge, getting he
own back. 'I'll go along an' all, Polly. Cor, five bob f
'avin' a lark – can't be bad!'

Lilac finished the dress and stood the cooling fla
iron down on the stove top. She reached into the bi
wicker linen basket and pulled out Mrs Matteson'
long, full, white cotton nightdress with the embroider
round the neck and wrists. She laid it down, sprinkle
water from a jug by her elbow, and picked up the fla
nearest the heat, then tested it by spitting onto i
shining surface. The spitball disappeared; Lilac waite
a moment, to let the flat cool a bit, then commence
work. When the embroidery round the neck had bee
dealt with she started on the sleeves, glancing casuall
across to where Polly sat as she did so.

'Are we all on, then? What's the woman's nam
again, Poll?'

'She's a Mrs Herbert Allan,' Polly said. She finishe
the last knife and threw her filthy piece of rag into th
pink-stained saucer of knife powder. 'Cor, what I'
give for a cuppa!'

'So I've put my name down to work there on Saturda
night, for at least five hours,' Lilac finished trium
phantly. 'Mrs Matteson laughed when we told her an
said we should go, it was about time we saw some life
She and the doctor don't have parties, just an At Hom
a couple of times a month. Well? What do you think c
that, Georgie?'

'You're splendid, Lilac,' George said admiringly
'You might not be able to find out much whilst you'r
working, but at least you'll see Mrs Allan. I wish she'
ask me to her party,' he added wistfully. 'I could do th
real Sherlock Holmes stuff – go through her desk

question people and so on. But even if she asked us, Mother would say no. She doesn't like her cousin very much ... she's jealous, I'm sure.'

'Why don't you just turn up?' Lilac suggested. 'Polly's Tom says everyone will be wearing little black masks so you might not even be recognised. Go on, why don't you?'

'I might,' George said. His pale blue eyes sparkled and for a moment Lilac thought not only that she would like to marry him but that she might almost fall for him when he looked like that. Unfortunately, however, he then started to cough and she felt the old familiar impatience rise up in her chest. If only he were more like Stuart – decisive, capable, full of humour and good sense! Even knowing that George's cough was because of a weakness left over from his war-wound did not soften her attitude. She thought that, had he been a proper man, he would not have let her keep him at arm's length for so long ... then she remembered how she hated babies and pain and decided she would rather have him as he was.

'Oh well, see what you can do.'

They were walking down by the Salthouse dock, with the strong wind from the Mersey snatching strands of Lilac's hair and turning her carefully coiled bun into a parody of its former self. That was the trouble with Liverpool, Lilac thought resentfully. The bloody wind never stopped!

'Lilac ... would you like me to come to the party?'

'Of course I would,' Lilac said at once. She wished George was not so easily cast down. 'It would make it much more fun ... but I do understand that it's difficult for you, being a relative and all. And George ...'

'Yes?'

'Well, if you were discovered by someone, taking a

close look at something which the family didn't want seen, it would be far worse for you than for me. I mean a maid can always get lost, no one would imagine I was snooping, but a cousin ... '

'I see what you mean,' George said, looking relieved. 'Well, if I'm invited I'll go, but if not I leave it to you, Lilac.'

The maids had been told to arrive at the house in Abercromby Square no later than seven o'clock, which meant leaving Rodney Street at a quarter to the hour. The girls were excited, giggly. They wore their best blacks, starched white blouses with high collars, and did their hair either piled on top or tied back and fastened with narrow black ribbon.

Lilac, because a party was a bit of excitement when you didn't get out much, chose to pile her hair up on top, with a black velvet band round it. She had not previously arranged her hair so and received several compliments.

'You look charming,' Dr Matteson said, meeting her crossing the hall. 'It's much prettier than the modern hairstyles, I like a girl to look like a girl, not like a boy.'

'Cor, get you,' said the garden-boy. 'Can I 'ave your autygraph, Lady Muck?'

'I say, quite the little belle of the ball,' next door's handyman said. 'Goin' dancin' wiv the toffs at the Pally?'

Lilac sniffed and checked that her hair was still neat. Despite the doctor's strictures she longed to have a fashionable bob but Mrs Matteson said that one's hair was one's crowning glory and anyway, unless you could also wear the new skirts with their dropped waistline, the fringes, the flowerpot hats, then bobbed hair would probably just look silly.

'We're going to a party,' she said grandly. 'At Abercromby Square.'

The handyman guffawed. The October gales which
had only just begun to ease had brought the leaves
tumbling down and a sudden gust whirled a pile of them
into the air. The girls shrieked and clutched their skirts
and Polly advised the handyman to button his lip and
mind his manners just as Tom Hedges, in his employer's
new Wolseley, drew up alongside them. Whilst they were
still clutching their coats around them he leaned across and
cranked down the window on the passenger side.

'Here we are, gels, you're goin' to the party in style!
Polly love, come and sit by the driver so's I can give
you a squeeze.' He grinned at them, then got out of the
driving seat and came round to open the back door,
bowing as though they were all ladies 'with five
'undred a year,' as Madge put it.

Polly got into the front passenger seat and Madge,
Lilac and Emily got into the back. There was plenty of
room on the wide leather seat and they appreciated
every moment of the short journey, luxuriating in the
comfort of it.

'Wish we had a motor,' Lilac said with a sigh. 'But
Mrs Matteson says it's not worth it, not with the
doctor's practice being mainly in the city. Now if he
was a country doctor ... '

'If he was a country doctor he wouldn't be able to
afford a motor,' Emily pointed out sensibly. 'But he's a
fashionable city doctor with patients who won't go to
anyone else because they know he's the best, and they
get charged according. In fact, if he didn't do so much
work at the free clinic, he'd probably be able to afford
two motors.'

'One for each foot,' Madge said, giggling. 'Ooh, ain't
it comfortable, though? Better than the tram!'

'Too quick,' Lilac sighed as the car drew up, not in Abercromby Square, but in Bedford Street North. 'We're here already ... oh, what a shame, I could have sat here for hours.'

'Here we are, your Highness,' Tom said, turning round to grin at his passengers. 'You're bound for the corner house, so you'll go in the back way, through that little brown gate, down the steps and into the kitchen. You can't miss it.'

The house was even larger seen from here than it had appeared from Abercromby Square. The windows were a blaze of light, the curtains looped back, though from where they stood, in a small group on the pavement, they could only see the upper windows over the high wall.

'Well, gels, off we go!' Polly said. She led the way across the pavement and in through the gate. 'No loiterin', ladies, no stoppin' or starin', we're 'ere to work our bloody fingers to the bone!'

The gate led them into a tiny back yard from which a flight of steps descended to the door of the basement kitchen. It stood wide open, sounds of great busyness and smells of good food greeting them as they descended cautiously into the warmth and noise from the fresh autumn evening.

Polly was first down the steps and into the kitchen. She rattled on the door as she passed but did not pause to see if she had been heard.

'We've arrived, Mr Lumsden,' she said cheerfully, above the clatter of preparation as the live-in staff loaded trays and trolleys with food, crockery and cutlery. 'Where'll we put our coats?'

It was an unforgettable evening. Used to the quiet

dinner parties and the At Homes given by a childless, elderly couple, the girls had come to believe that the jazz age had passed Liverpool by. Now they saw that it had not.

Taking coats was their first task. They stood in the wide hall as the butler greeted guests and passed them into the main reception room. Those who had coats took them off and the Rodney Street girls carried them into a small cloakroom, put them on coat-hangers, and slid the hangers onto long wooden stands provided specially for the purpose.

And when the coats were removed, what a dazzling display was revealed! High-heeled shoes in silver, gold, scarlet and blue. Dresses with dropped waists, fringes, low necks, no sleeves. Pretty, bouncy girls with boys' figures, bobbed hair, bangles and beads.

'They're wearing *make up*,' Lilac hissed to Madge at one stage. 'And the pretty one in the scarlet and white dress who keeps shrieking and grabbing the men because her heels are so high – she's not wearing a petticoat. And did you see those earrings?'

Madge could only nod, wide-eyed. Even Polly, thought to be sophisticated, with her young man a chauffeur – chauffeurs were known for a tendency to use the back seats of their cars as places to despoil their ladyfriends – was stunned by this sudden introduction to the younger set.

'I'd like to know where they buy their knickers,' she muttered darkly as one bright young thing came down the stairs so rapidly that her short skirt flared out, revealing chubby knees in shiny silk stockings, garters and what looked remarkably like bare skin. 'I've heard as 'ow flesh-coloured knickers is all the rage, but they looked like invisible knickers to me, an' them I 'ave *not* seen in Blacklers! Tell you what, gels, they're *fast*!'

'Where's the lady of the house?' Lilac asked presently, when the steady stream of guests had dwindled to a trickle. 'They all seem to be very young.'

'Mrs Allan's in the main reception room, greeting her guests,' the butler said, overhearing. He was a tall man with a roman nose which looked like the prow of a ship. 'Run along, girls, you'll be wanted to set out the supper presently, and take round the trays.'

Back to the kitchen the girls went, to be handed big, heavy silver salvers laden with glasses.

'Go to the ballroom,' someone told them. 'A tall man with a blond moustache will fill the glasses for you in the ante-room, then you carry the trays round and guests will help themselves.'

I'll see her now, Lilac thought triumphantly. I'll see the woman who might be my mother!

Two minutes later, she knew it was not to be that simple. There were probably a couple of hundred people in the ballroom, and a great many of them had donned small, black masks and were talking very loudly, laughing, flirting and moving about constantly. You had to be very careful or you would get trodden on, knocked down – and your tray of drinks would bite the dust.

But Lilac was slim, strong and quick. She glided around the floor, with half an eye on the dancers and the rest on the guests. At first, she thought that no one noticed her at all, which suited her well in one way though not in another. She was accustomed to being whistled after, smiled at, spoken to, but these people did no such thing. She was a servant and as such, more a part of the furniture than a person.

Soon however, she began to enjoy herself. It was fun to inch one's way through the crush towards a young man with an empty glass, offer him a full one, slip away towards a girl with a sulky mouth and unnaturally pink cheeks, watch her take the fresh glass, raise it to her lips ... and go on your way once more, heading for the pretty girl in scarlet who was twiddling her long string of beads round one slim, red-tipped index finger and eyeing the young men with an overt hunger which Lilac found more shocking than the weary suggestions made to passing sailors by the whores on the docks.

When her tray was empty she was able to stand for a moment and watch the dancers. She thought their gyrations very ugly and probably wicked, too – the women's bodies in their brief, silky dresses which left knees, upper breasts and shoulders bare, were clasped far too close to the men's black evening suits.

'Hey ... you, with the yaller hair! Fetch us a drink!' A thick-lipped, oily-haired young man shouted at her, then leaned over and tapped her tray. 'This is supposed to be kept full, or are you so stupid you hadn't noticed it was empty?'

Lilac, hating him, muttered an excuse and returned her empty glasses to the kitchen, then loitered as slowly as she dared to the ante-room for the refills. She thought what fun it would be to tip the tray of drinks all over that unpleasant person, but by the time she returned to the ballroom he was dancing again, hanging all over a short, square girl with a sequinned pink dress and bulging, myopic eyes. He had either forgotten his champagne or got a glass from someone else.

'Look lively, girl ... they'll be going in for supper in a moment, get back to the kitchen, someone will tell you what to do next.'

That was one of the real servants, a tight-lipped elderly woman who had nevertheless astonished the girls from Rodney Street with the speed and efficiency with which she dispensed drinks.

'All right, I'm coming,' Lilac muttered to her disappearing back. Honest to God, some people wanted slaves, not servants, and the servants themselves were worst of all!

And then, for what seemed like hours, she was truly on the go. Carrying silver salvers laden with every imaginable sort of food from the kitchen to the supper room, serving the salads and the dozens and dozens of different delicacies, fetching and carrying for the chef, an enormous man in a tall white hat who was very gracious to the guests but who shouted and hit out at the maids if they did not at once do his bidding.

But the speed slowed as the guests' plates and glasses were filled at last and they took their places round the tiny tables set out in the supper-room. The tight-lipped one gestured to the maids to leave the room and took them back to the kitchen.

'There's sangwidges,' she said grudgingly. 'And there's tea in the big urn. Best get some down you ... we'll be serving the desserts in twenty minutes or so.'

The sandwiches were very good when you were young and hungry, even if they did not measure up to lobster patties and smoked salmon on brown bread, two of the delicacies Lilac had eyed with interest. They contained nice things – cheese and lettuce, ham and pickle, egg and tomato. And the tea was served in large white pottery mugs and went down a treat, Polly said, when you'd been run off your feet all evening and were thirsty enough to drain a ditch dry.

'It's a dry night, though windy,' someone remarked as they ate. 'That means some of 'em will go onto the terrace and even into the back garden.' The woman who spoke was smart in her blacks, but she had a coarse way with her, Lilac considered. 'Ha, Ned'll be moanin' tomorrer about his flattened chrysanthemums and ruined dahlias.'

'The men like to smoke,' the housekeeper said. 'Some of the ladies, too. The mistress likes a cigarette – she's very modern, Mrs Allan.'

'I don't like the smell of it,' Polly remarked, helping herself to another sandwich and speaking rather thickly through her first bite. 'When they smoke in the motor, it's awful, really horrid.'

'Oh, well.' One of the menservants stretched out and took a packet of cigarettes off the sideboard behind him. 'I'm off into the yard for a puff. Anyone coming?'

'I'd like to … to tidy myself up a bit,' Lilac said shyly. She knew everyone would assume that this was a euphemism for using the lavatory and so it proved.

'Oh, right. Straight out of here, down the corridor, turn left, first door on your right,' the tight-lipped one said. 'Don't be long!'

Lilac hurried out of the kitchen, her heart bumping beneath her starched white blouse. What should she do, now that she was, for a moment, free to take a look around? Mrs Allan must be with her guests down in the supper room, her husband too. Other staff were in the kitchens … but what could she discover in the bedrooms? What tiny clue to her past?

She glanced into the first door she reached; a pantry, stone-floored, with shelves from floor to ceiling. The next door hid a cloakroom with staff coats, hats and boots. She ignored the rest but went through into the house itself. And here she had a piece of luck. A girl, tall, fair-haired, stood in the hall looking the picture of misery. When she saw Lilac, however, she brightened.

'Oh, hello … do you work here? Some clumsy idiot trod on me whilst we were dancing and tore one of my floating panels and it's a brand-new dress … could you put a stitch in it for me? It wouldn't take you a minute.'

She smiled beguilingly. Lilac, smiling back, thought that here was a real young lady, not one of the brash creatures who had ignored her all evening. The girl's skirt was a reasonable length, her shoulders covered, albeit only with light gauze, and she had a breezy, bright sort of beauty which needed no help from powder and paint.

'I'll do my best,' Lilac said now. 'Umm ...'

'The things are upstairs, in Godmother's dressing room,' the girl said. 'I'm Sarah Kingsley, Mrs Allan's goddaughter. I'm twenty-one, old enough for Godmother's parties now, my father believes. Though I don't think he realises quite how modern Mrs Allan is,' she added thoughtfully.

'Yes, she's very modern,' Lilac said brightly. 'Once we reach the dressing-room I can mend that tear without any trouble, Miss Kingsley – I just hope I can find the right colour thread,' she added.

She hung back a little and Sarah Kingsley mounted the stairs in front, chattering all the while.

'It's great fun of course, and I am enjoying myself, but normally I only see Godmother at our house, or on At Home days, so ... but Father and I are very old-fashioned, we live quietly in the country ... that was why he wanted me to come, and to come without him, what's more.'

'Don't you have a mother, Miss?' Lilac said rather timidly as the two of them entered what seemed to be a small sitting-room with pastel roses on the walls and a carpet so pale that it would, Lilac was sure, show every footprint. 'You haven't mentioned her.'

'No. My mother died when I was two, so I don't remember her at all. But my father is a wonderful man, truly. And there's Auntie Lena, who keeps house for him and taught me to ride and swim ... oh, we're very happy at home, even if we *are* old-fashioned.'

She said the last a little defiantly, as though her old-fashioned attitude had been held against her, and recently. Lilac thought of the people downstairs, the blonde in scarlet and white with her long red nails, the girl in black and silver with the provocative glances, the young men with their sweaty hands and gleaming, oily hair. She could well imagine that they would despise the fresh, open-air beauty of the girl beside her. But that was something a servant could scarcely say! So she scrabbled through an elaborate work-box until she found what she wanted and turned to Miss Kingsley once more.

'Here we are, Miss, blue thread, just the right blue, as well,' she said chattily. 'If you'll just sit down for a moment ...'

She settled the older girl in a comfortable chair and began to stitch the pale blue gauze with tiny, delicate stitches. Miss Kingsley waited until the job was nearly finished and then turned her head.

'Don't you sew nicely? I'm dreadful at it, Father says he thanks God fasting that he no longer has to pretend to use the handkerchieves I used to make him, or wear the gloves I knitted. When I was small I used to struggle away to make him presents at birthday and Christmas and he was always so good, maintaining that the handkerchieves were the finest he had ever owned, trying to get the gloves on even when I knitted a pair with one finger missing, which I did when I was ten.' She paused, then said, 'But how I do rattle on! What's your name and what do you do for my Godmother? I don't remember seeing you before.'

'My name's Lilac Larkin, Miss, and I'm only hired

for the evening,' Lilac said carefully. She would have lied shamelessly to anyone else who asked, but not to this glorious girl. 'I work for the Mattesons, on Rodney Street.'

'Not Doctor Matteson? Why, he's looked after me since I was a tiny thing, because Father knew him years ago, when they were both at Oxford together! Isn't that an odd coincidence? So I don't suppose you're any more used to such events as this than I? Dr Matteson and his wife are very quiet and busy.'

'Finished, Miss,' Lilac said, cutting the thread off short and putting her needle carefully back in its small case. 'Yes, the Mattesons are quiet and don't entertain much, so this is ... a real change for me.'

'Well, be careful not to get caught in any dark corners by that disgusting young Willoughby,' Miss Kingsley said frankly. 'You're not very big compared with me, and I had a struggle to stop him mauling me as if I were a kitchen maid ... oh, how offensive of me, I *am* sorry, it was just a figure of speech.'

'It doesn't matter; but I'm very strong,' Lilac assured her new friend. 'Hadn't you better go back to the party now, Miss?'

'Yes, I suppose ... ' Miss Kingsley was beginning reluctantly, when the door swung open.

A slender woman stood there. She still wore a little black mask outlined in sparkling glass diamonds but her fingers were fiddling with the ribbons, and she tugged at it, obviously trying to take it off. She had quantities of rather brassy, red-gold hair, pale, puckered skin and a scarlet mouth. Her dress was off the shoulder, the upper part transparent, and it clung to her shape as though it had been wetted. The colour was a clear blue, reflecting the shade of the eyes which Lilac could see through the slits in the mask.

'Sarah, what on earth ... and who the devil are you?'

It was Mrs Allan, it could be no other. Lilac began to stammer that she was one of the maids, that she had been helping the young lady, when the woman made an impatient gesture and took a step nearer.

'Quiet! Just who are you? A young friend of mine said ...' the mask was half off and must have made it difficult for her to see before, for suddenly, almost as though she could not believe her eyes, she ripped it right off and stared, her eyes widening horribly for a moment and then narrowing dangerously.

'A servant! My God, what in heaven's name ...'

And then, before Lilac could speak, she drew back her hand and slapped the younger girl across the face, so hard that Lilac fell against the door panels.

'Get out!' Mrs Allan hissed. 'Get out of my house!'

'Godmother!' Sarah Kingsley shouted, bounding across the room, putting a protective arm around Lilac's shoulders. 'Oh, Godmother, she was only here because I asked her to come and mend my dress, what on earth did you think she was doing? It's all right, she's only doing as I asked ... are you unwell, God-mother?'

The woman in the doorway swayed, then threw her discarded mask to the floor. Lilac, straightening from the blow, saw the blaze of big blue eyes and the wreck of a once-beautiful face. Powder and paint could do so much, but they could not cover up the ravages either of time or of reckless living, which Lilac could see on the face so near her own.

'Get out – the pair of you!' Mrs Allan hissed again. She sounded frighteningly insane to Lilac. 'Get out, get out, get out!'

The two young things exchanged scared glances,

then obeyed without further demur, running from the room, only pausing halfway down the stairs to glance back, make sure they were not pursued.

'Gosh, what a temper!' Miss Kingsley said. 'Lilac, I'm most awfully sorry, I can only suppose my god-mother has been drinking. She does, I know, though my father has no idea that ... Oh, please don't go, you've worked so hard, I'll speak to Cobbett ... '

'I'd better go,' Lilac said feelingly. 'I don't think your godmother likes me ... I'll just run and fetch my coat, then I'll make an excuse and go home if you don't mind.'

'I don't mind – I don't blame you, but look ... I'll speak to Godmother as soon as she's herself again, make sure you get paid, at least,' Miss Kingsley said, obviously much concerned. 'No, I'll have a word with Dr Matteson ... I was never more shocked in my life!'

'Don't worry; I startled her,' Lilac said. 'I'm ever so glad I met you, Miss, and thanks.'

She hurried along to the cloakroom and claimed her coat. Then she found Polly, up to the elbows in suds as she washed up what looked like a million plates.

'I'm not feeling so good and we've mostly finished,' she whispered. 'I'm going now. We'll talk later.'

She left by the back way and as she hurried past the jigger which served the big houses she was hailed by a young man who had apparently left the party to get some fresh air. He made a rude suggestion which caused Lilac to tilt her nose loftily but she ignored him, making her way gladly back towards Rodney Street. What a shame that the party had finished so horribly, yet despite the fracas, she was suddenly aware that she was smiling.

I must be mad, she thought. Her cheek stung from the woman's double slap, her knees felt a bit weak and wobbly, but there was a great enormous happiness within her and she could have sung and danced along the pavement despite her tiredness and the lateness of the hour.

When Mrs Allan had taken off the mask she had seen at once that this person could not possibly be her mother. Oh, the colouring was the same, but there all resemblance ended. Mrs Allan had a mean little face, lined, raddled skin, and a cruel, thin-lipped mouth. She was thin and brittle, harsh voiced and spiteful, and her hair was dyed and lifeless, without gleam or gentle waves. And she had hit Lilac with all her strength, just out of sheer nastiness, since Miss Kingsley had made it plain as plain that Lilac was with her.

So why am I so happy, Lilac asked herself. But she knew the answer. Her Quest had just bitten the dust and she was glad from the bottom of her heart.

What do I want with a high-born mother? Lilac asked herself happily as she plodded homeward. Why, what a fool I've been and what a lot of time and energy I've wasted! My own dear mother's been right by me all the time – Nellie's my mother, and a better one never lived or breathed. She's my dear little mother, and it's high time I told her so!

Mrs Allan had been told, downstairs, that her god-daughter had gone off to have a seam stitched or some such thing, and she had followed her because she had drunk too deeply of the champagne – as she so often did – and wanted to ask Sarah what she thought of young Willoughby. She had noticed with some annoy-ance that Rex Willoughby had seemed more than a little taken with Sarah's buxom charms ... Mrs Allan looked down at her own sticklike contours and felt only satisfaction ... so it would be interesting to find out how Sarah felt about him.

Mrs Allan had been pursuing Rex Willoughby for a month and had not invited him to her party just to see her goddaughter waltz off with him, but Sarah did not know that – yet. So clearly she must be told that the young man, though eligible enough, was not a suitable *parti* for Gerald Kingsley's adored only daughter.

Unfortunately by the time she was halfway up the stairs the champagne, and her own salacious imagination, had managed to convince her that she would find Sarah not alone or with a maid, but in the hot embrace of young Willoughby. The more she thought the more convinced she became that she was about to be thwarted. And the more convinced she became, the angrier she grew. Sarah owed her something, young Willoughby owed her more, she would not be forced to lose the man she urgently desired just because she was not quite as young as she had been and Sarah, damn her eyes, was as fresh and green as a snowdrop in spring.

She burst into the room, remembering the mask at the last minute, struggling to snatch it off, determined that they should know who had found them out, know who they had betrayed. Anger, painful jealousy, bitterness, fought for supremacy as she glared at the young person who stood before her.

But it was not Sarah! Who on earth was it?

And as the first red mist of her rage cleared from her eyes, Lucille Allan saw – youth. Aghast, she stared at the pale face, the big blue eyes shining with innocence, the mass of red-gold hair gleaming like a crown on the small, shapely head. It was like looking in a mirror, but a mirror into the past. She was seeing the girl she had once been, when she had been young and innocent,

before she had married an old man and become disen-
chanted with the life of a rich, spoilt society darling.
Before she had begun to find consolation in fast living,
champagne and young men.

And suddenly she had been devoured by a jealousy
and a rage greater than she had ever felt before. She
hated that innocence, she hated that youth, she hated
everything about this fresh, childlike servant girl – she
would have killed her if she could. But all she could do
was to hit her, hard, across the face and rejoice as the
wide-eyed innocence crumpled into bewilderment,
then turned from her, ran from her ... leaving her the
victor, breathing hard, clenching her hands into fists
and driving the nails into her palms, then forcing herself to pace carefully down the stairs, to call for more
champagne, to clutch young Willoughby and giggle
against his ear ... and taste only bitterness, only defeat,
because she could never know youth – or innocence –
again.

Chapter Sixteen

'Sadie, are you doing anything this evening? I thought I'd go along to the Pivvy; they're showing *One Arabian Night*, with Pola Negri. It's supposed to be good, but I hate going to the flicks alone.'

'Pola Negri? She's all right, but I'd rather have a good laugh any day. There's a Mack Sennett comedy at the Electric with Louise Fazenda; wouldn't you rather see that?'

Nellie and her room-mate, Sadie Pickerfield, were in the nurses' sitting room, huddling round a rather inadequate fire. They were both what Nellie cheerfully described as 'long in the tooth', compared with some of the probationers, since they had learned a good deal of their nursing during the war, but experience tells and they were finding the work very much easier and pleasanter compared with their wartime experiences. It helped, of course, that several of the senior staff had nursed with the two girls at one time or another and knew their worth. And right now, they were on a surgical ward with Sister Francis, back from France, in charge – and Nellie had always got on well with Sister Francis. The Sister remembered most of Nellie's friends and a good many of her soldier patients and they often fell to reminiscing as Nellie made beds or set up blood transfusions.

Now, however, Nellie leaned forward and gave the fire a vicious prod with the small brass poker which stood in the hearth.

'A comedy? That's not a bad idea. I could do with something to make me laugh – other than Mr Williams, of course.'

Mr Williams was a confirmed grumbler. He moaned about everything. His operation, which was only to remove a gigantic bunion, was the most painful anyone had ever experienced, the surgeon had done it wrong anyway, the houseman had prescribed the wrong painkillers, the nurses were rough, the dressings impossible to bear. Mr Williams crouched in a chair in a hairy brown dressing gown and scraped his plate clean at mealtimes whilst saying the food was inedible and someone would be in trouble when he put in his report.

What this report was he never said, but the nurses, fed up with his continual carping, had taken to leaving his dressings until last, avoiding him as they came down the ward, and becoming mysteriously deaf when he shouted for attention or rang his bell.

'Mr Williams is a pain,' Sadie agreed now. 'But what about Teddy Matthews, then? He's comic, if you like!'

Nellie dealt the fire a last ferocious blow with the poker and sat back in her chair.

'Teddy isn't funny, he's probably my last hope of getting out of this place and leading a normal life,' she said, whilst Sadie giggled. 'He can't help his spots, or his funny voice, and he's the first person to tell me he loves me for … oh, for a lifetime.'

Teddy Matthews was nineteen, a tall and skinny insurance clerk with acne, frizzy blond hair which stood up as though he'd just seen a ghost, and a voice which emerged as though through a mouthful of ollies. He was a keen amateur rugby player and had fractured his shin playing for his team, Sun Assurance, against Royal Life. The fact that he was deeply enamoured of

Nellie McDowell amused everyone, even, at times, Nellie. In vain she had explained that she was nearly ten years older than he; Teddy Matthews thought that Nellie and Nellie alone had been responsible for his badly broken tibia beginning to heal after weeks of traction. He said her smile made the day worth living and a touch of her hand brought his blood pressure up. When he was on his feet again he planned to escort her all over, to theatres, cinemas, smart restaurants. Even when Nellie brought him a bed-bottle or helped him to sit on the bed-pan his ardour remained undimmed.

'You oughter give 'im a blanket bath,' one of the other probationers giggled. 'That 'ud do the trick.'

But Nellie said primly that unfortunately a blanket bath merely increased his overpowering urge to make Nellie his mate – or she assumed it did, due to certain physical manifestations ...

The girls shrieked, but everyone knew it was what you might call an occupational hazard. Men fell in love with nurses, it was as simple as that.

And if she were honest, Nellie reminded herself now, only half listening as Sadie read out the film reviews in the Echo, having Teddy's wholehearted admiration did make her life seem less empty. She had always believed, in her heart, that Stuart would come back for her but she had heard nothing since arriving at the hospital and Art said the new people in number eleven had received no letters for her, or not so far as he knew. So it looked as though Stuart's affection had not survived their long separation ... she refused to believe that he had dropped her because she had allowed him to make love to her, that was absurd. But she could not help the little ache in the back of her mind which hinted that had she been a nicer girl ...

So Teddy was a comfort, though she had no

intention of going out with him when he left hospital, because she knew very well that once he was released his ordinary life would catch up with him again and she would be, very rightly, forgotten. But it made her realise that she was still capable of arousing affection, even if it wasn't the affection for which she longed.

Because now that Lilac had declared her allegiance, decided to search for her real mother and live with the Mattesons, Nellie began to realise what real loneliness was. She had lost Lilac and had given up any hope of hearing from Stuart; she supposed drearily that at least he had realised it was over, had not bothered to try to rescuscitate a dead affection. Yet, acknowledging that, she still missed him fiercely, imagined she saw him in the street, followed similar back-views until a turn of the head or a gesture revealed her mistake.

Then there was Davy. She didn't miss Davy, but now she envied Bethan the love which she had once thought hers by right. And Richie, the baby boy she had put so firmly out of her mind five years ago, chose this moment, in her thoughts, to reproach her for her neglect. So he believed himself to be Bethan's child; well, that was no excuse for Nellie to try so very hard to forget him, to read the letters Bethan sent and then destroy them immediately, before the images which rose in her mind when she read could hurt her. You should be hurt, Nellie McDowell, because you deliberately lived a lie, she told herself. You don't deserve peace of mind and perhaps you'll never get it.

'Last one. Clarine Seymour in *The Idol Dancer*,' announced Sadie, slamming the paper down on the small table beside her. 'Well, McDowell? If it's to be the flicks, which one do you prefer? Clarine's on at the Rotunda, just a tram-ride away.'

'Since you ask so nicely, Pickerfield, I'll plump for

The Idol Dancer; then we can have some supper at one of the cannys on Scottie Road afterwards. You coming? I'll have to change.'

Sadie sighed and said she wanted to go down to the office to see if her parcel had arrived. Mrs Pickerfield, convinced that her daughter could not possibly be eating properly in a hospital, sent parcels of country food weekly. They were a great comfort not only to Sadie, but to her room-mate, too.

Nellie was hard up, but at least what money she had was not sent away to support someone else any longer. She saved up and bought herself clothing, she went to the cinema, she had meals out sometimes. It was about the only thing, she reflected, climbing the stairs to her room, that she never felt guilty about, for the improvement in Lilac's looks and figure had shown her that proper food and exercise created a beautiful woman, whereas insufficient food and too much hard work simply made one skinny and gave one spots.

She reached her room and looked doubtfully at the clothes hanging on the rail. It was cold today with that grey, miserable chill which is typical of November. Would a gabardine skirt, a woolly jumper and her light macintosh be warm enough? She was hard up for winter clothing still, though she did have one nice dress, a golden-brown wool mixture with brass buttons which she was buying at so much a week from Sturlas's. In about two weeks it would be paid for, then she intended to get herself a pair of stout shoes and a proper coat for the cold months ahead.

Deciding that the skirt and jumper would have to do, she slipped them on, then brushed her hair and washed her face. She looked pale, so she rubbed her cheeks vigorously with the palms of both hands. She was tempted to slip on her grey cloak, but heaven knew she had spent enough time in various uniforms in the course of her twenty-eight years. She would be warm enough in the cinema, anyway.

A rattle on the door and a muffled shout announced that Sadie was outside. Nellie opened the door and what looked like a walking parcel entered, but it was only Sadie, bearing her mother's latest offering.

'I think she's baked a fruit cake and some pies,' Sadie said breathlessly, dumping the parcel on her bed. 'And there's a ham, I can smell it. Are you sure you want to go out for supper, Nell? We can eat here, if you'd rather.'

But Nellie, tying the belt of her macintosh firmly round her small waist, shook her head.

'Thanks very much Sadie, but I'd rather eat out. It'll take my mind off … things.'

Sadie was relaxing company because she knew nothing about Lilac, or Stuart, or anything to do with Nellie's past. She knew Nellie had been a Culler girl but that was about all, and since she did not come from Liverpool but from a small village called Tarboke Green she knew almost nothing about Scotland Road, the courts, and the lives of the people who lived there.

'Oh all right, spurn my mother's goodies,' Sadie said good-naturedly now. She began to untie the string which wrapped the parcel about, then changed her mind. 'No, I'll leave it till later. We want to catch the last house.'

The two girls came out of the cinema with their heads in the clouds; Clarine Seymour's performance had carried them with her into a land of dreams but now, marching arm-in-arm up the pavement, they wanted supper and then their beds.

'We're on too early tomorrow to risk getting to bed late,' Nellie said briskly as they walked. 'Besides, we don't want to miss the last tram. Do you want to go to Paddy's for a bite, or Dolly Pop's canny?'

'Dolly Pop's do those lovely pies with mashed potato on the top,' Sadie said wistfully. 'Loads of meat inside, too. But the apple pudding at Paddy's takes some beating. Oh, I'll never decide – you choose, Nell.'

'Dolly Pop's, then,' Nellie said. She had spent too many pennies in Paddy's with Lilac beside her, she wanted no more reminders of the good times, not today. 'I like their spotted dick and custard.'

They walked up the Scotland Road with the lamps hissing and flickering overhead and a crowd of people good-naturedly jostling along the pavement. Dolly Pop's was crowded but they found a seat and ordered their meal, then sat back to look about them until it arrived.

'Hello, Mrs Preswick, evening Mr Halford,' Nellie murmured, as people she had once known well came and took the few remaining places. To Sadie she said 'These people were my neighbours until I moved into the nurses' home. I miss them.'

The food came. It was delicious and nourishing. Nellie, tucking in, thought of the many times she'd had to walk past this door because she didn't have the pennies for a meal. Ah well, she was older now, she had left such times behind. Soon she would have a career, in time she would be a Sister with a ward of her own to rule. At the end, a pension, two rooms and a few friends of her own age, all slowly heading for senility together.

She pulled herself up on the thought, shocked. What on earth was the matter with her, today? She was just so depressed – perhaps it was the grim November weather, or the fact that she had come off a busy shift tired out and instead of collapsing into her bed had gone with Sadie to the pictures.

But whatever the reason she must stop going over and over it in her mind, otherwise she'd go insane. Think about your holidays next year, when you're due for a week or so off, she commanded herself urgently. Remember what you'd planned? To go back to the Isle of Anglesey and to stay somewhere near Moelfre, so that she could see the child but, hopefully, not be seen herself. That would be fun, and you never knew, she might get in touch with Bethan without Davy finding out and arrange to meet. Through all the years in between she had never ceased to love Bethan, how good it would be to see her again, and why should she not? After all, Davy and Bethan had a good life, she had no claim on either of them save the claim of friendship. Why should she not try to meet her friend?

But she knew she would not do it, not really. So, with a sigh, she dug her spoon into the treacle pudding she had ordered to follow the delicious, crispy-topped cottage pie, and smiled across at Sadie.

'Yours all right? This must be my treat, Sadie, because you'll never let me pay you anything for sharing your parcels.'

Sadie's parents farmed successfully, but Sadie had not settled when she returned home after the war. It said a lot for the relationship between parents and child, Nellie thought, that they had sent her, with their blessing, to train for a nurse.

'Ooh, lovely,' Sadie said now. 'I wish you'd said before, it would have made the food taste even better! Lucky you, to be able to come here when you were a kid … I didn't even have fish and chips until I came into the city to do my training. Small country villages don't go in for cooked food, much. Oh, goodness, that reminds me!'

'What?' Nellie said, scraping her spoon round her bowl. 'My, that was good! What my brothers would have called a sinker.'

'I meant to tell you, but we were in such a rush to get off to the cinema that I forgot. Someone was asking for you earlier, only you were on duty.'

'Oh?' Wild thoughts of Stuart chased through Nellie's head. 'Who was it? Man or woman?'

'Oh, woman. Well, more like a young lady, really. An awfully pretty kid, got this amazing red-gold hair ... she asked what time you'd be free tomorrow, so I told her and she said how about meeting in the Crinoline Tearooms in London Road tomorrow, at around four. She'll wait for you there. I'm awful sorry, Nell, it just went clean out of my head.'

'It doesn't matter; if tomorrow's early enough then it can't be exactly urgent,' Nellie said. 'I'll be free from about three ... wonder what she wants?'

'She didn't say. Who is she, Nell? A relative?'

'Yes. An adopted sister,' Nellie said. She put down her spoon and reached for the cup of tea by her plate. 'Actually, we've not seen each other for a while, we had a bit of a disagreement, so it'll be nice to be back on good terms.'

'I'm sorry I forgot,' Sadie said remorsefully. 'But still, you can go down there tomorrow, can't you? You'll enjoy that.'

'Yes,' Nellie said absently. 'Have you finished, Sadie? Because if so we really ought to get a move on. We're usually in bed and asleep by now!'

'We'll catch a tram,' Sadie promised. 'We'll be in bed and asleep in thirty minutes anyway, if we get a move on.'

'Right,' Nellie said, jumping to her feet. She had

aken her mac off when they sat down, now she tugged
t on again. 'Only I hope we don't have to run for the
ram, I've eaten far too much.'

But they did have to run, and only just leaped
aboard as it was moving off.

The tram was already crowded so they headed for
he stairs and settled themselves happily on the top
deck.

'Where have all the crowds come from?' Sadie asked
presently, as the tram swayed along the road. 'Oh, look!'

'It's Homer Street market,' Nellie said. 'The stall-
holders reduce their prices as time goes on rather than
have their goods go bad on them over Sunday, so of
course frugal housewives shop later and later. I've had
some good bargains myself when we lived here,' she
added. 'Especially meat; you could get meat at less
than half the proper price if you were prepared to hang
on until eleven or so.'

'Sounds good,' Sadie observed. 'I say, this tram must
be full, we're going to go right by the next stop.'

'They sometimes do that if there's another close
behind and no one wants to get down,' Nellie said,
leaning forward to peer at the group of people waiting
t the stop. 'Oh ... oh ... oh!'

She had jumped to her feet but Sadie clutched her,
preventing her from trying to go down the stairs whilst
he tram was bucketing along.

'What's the matter, Nell? What did you see?'

'Stuart! It was Stuart standing waiting at that tram
top. I've got to get off, I really must ... it was Stuart, I
know it was!'

'All right, chuck, but wait for the next stop,' Sadie
said, hanging onto Nellie's arm. 'The driver won't stop
for you between stages, you know how they are, so get
at down. Who's Stuart, anyway?'

'A friend. The best,' Nellie said breathlessly. 'I' have to get off at the next stage, Sadie, honest to God will.'

'Then I'll come with you,' Sadie said resignedly. 'Bu if there's a tram close behind ... oh well, I can se there's no reasoning with you.'

She was right. At the next stop both girls alighte and, with Nellie leading, ran back to the previous stop

The small crowd waiting looked at them curiousl as they panted up.

'One's just gone, gairls, so you got plenty of time,' th young man at the end of the queue informed ther lugubriously. 'It'll be ten minutes afore the next 'un come along.'

Nellie turned to Sadie.

'I'm sorry, chuck. You were right. He's not here. I it was him, of course.'

'Oh, Nell, I'm sorry.'

'It doesn't matter,' Nellie said dully. 'I don't know why I made such a fuss. If he'd wanted to see me, h knows where I live but he never even replied to my las letter. And anyway, he's got no call to come up this en of the city.'

'Unless he thought you still lived off the Scotlan Road,' Sadie suggested. 'Suppose he'd just forgotte you weren't here any more?'

Nellie stood very still for a moment. Then she turne to Sadie. Her whole face was alight with hope.

'D'you think that's possible?' she said breathless ly. 'D'you think my letter might never have reached him Do you think he's been trying to find me?'

'It seems likely,' Sadie said. 'If I lost touch with you Nellie McDowell, I'd try to find you – and I'm not a feller

Nellie gave a little squeak and flung her arms roun her friend, then gave her a smacking kiss on the cheek

'Oh Sadie, I love you!' she cried. 'I could fly to the moon tonight!'

Nellie arrived at the Crinoline Tearooms at a quarter to four and found Lilac there ahead of her. The younger girl was sitting at a window table, gazing out at the people passing, and had not noticed Nellie, so she was able to stop and have a good look at her young friend.

Lilac was wearing a suit in a deep burnt orange colour, with a dark brown fur collar and cuffs. The skirt was flared and met the tops of a pair of dark brown Russian boots and to top her outfit off nicely, a tiny brown fur hat was perched on her gleaming hair. She did not look like a skivvy out on the spree, nor even a servant taking the air. She looks a real little lady, Nellie thought, pride mingling with sadness that it had not been possible for Lilac to wear such charming clothes when she, Nellie, had been her sole provider.

A waitress cleared her throat and Nellie realised she had been standing in the doorway for several moments. She apologised and set off across the room towards Lilac.

'Here I am, early too, but you're earlier,' she began gaily, to be interrupted. Lilac jumped to her feet and gave Nellie a big kiss and then hugged her fiercely. Nellie could feel her shaking. Tenderly, she put Lilac away from her and sat down, eyeing her protégé keenly.

'What's the matter, love? Oh, it's so nice to see you ... I've missed you more than you could ever guess.'

'I can guess, because I've missed you much worse. Nellie, can you ever forgive me for thinking that it was more important to look for my mother and to live with

the Mattesons than anything else? Can you? Because
was a fool, and greedy, too. When I really though
about it, really, with my heart, why on earth should
care who my real mother was? After all, she care
about me so much that she dumped me on the doorste
and never even tried to make sure I was alive. But you
Nell, you had no cause to love me, or look after me
And how did I repay you? By dumping you, just lik
she dumped me! Nell, you're all the mother I've eve
known, and you're all the mother I ever want, and
had to tell you!'

Nellie leaned across the table and clasped Lilac'
hands in hers. She could feel tears shining in her eye
yet she was laughing, too.

'What are you on about, our Lilac? You don't wan
to get yourself in a state, queen, because I never though
you'd cast me off, not really, not after all these years
And if you had, it would have been a part of you
growing up and my own fault for going off to France th
way I did. I never told you why I did it, because you wer
too young, but you aren't too young any more.'

It was a drizzly afternoon and the Crinoline tea
rooms had few customers. The waitress came an
brought them tea and cakes and put another lump o
coal on the fire and Lilac listened attentively whils
Nellie told her everything ... about trying to find Davy
and finding him married to Bethan, about giving birt
to the child. And then of her shock at discovering Davy
was not dead, that he was actually in the hospita
where she nursed and would be a patient for man
weeks ... and had sent for his wife and child.

'So I went to France to get away from them, and no
just to do my duty,' she admitted ruefully, watchin
for some sign of condemnation in the small, fair fac
opposite her own. There was none, only deep attention

'I let you down, Li, but all I could think of was getting away, before Bethan arrived.'

'And Richart,' Lilac said softly. 'Didn't you want to see him, Nell?'

Nellie shook her head.

'No. I've never set eyes on him since he was a few weeks old and I knew that was the way it must be. Davy knew nothing, you see, and that's the way it must be, too. I was so afraid ... so I ran away.'

'You left your own baby for me,' Lilac said softly. 'Nellie, dearest Nell, I always knew you were special.'

There were tears in the big eyes, brimming, tipping, tumbling down the smooth, damask cheeks. Nellie got out her hanky and tenderly dabbed them away.

'Don't cry love, and don't forget that you were pretty special too, or I daresay I'd never have done it. And since then we've both done things we regret, I daresay, but we love each other very much, and it's love that matters. Is that why you wanted us to meet? To tell me what I always knew, in my heart? That we loved each other no matter what?'

'Since you've told me, I'll tell you,' Lilac said bravely. 'It's rather a long story ...'

It was. She began right at the beginning when Polly had first aroused in her an interest in her mother, and continued up to the moment at the party when Mrs Herbert Allan had slapped her face.

'And walking home, I was so *happy*,' she said, a little smile tilting her mouth as she thought back to that moment of revelation under the gas lamps around Abercromby Square. 'It was such a release, not to have to pretend it mattered who my mother was, not to try to love George Elcott, not to deny the court, and the Culler and all the other bits of my childhood. And running through my head, like a little, sprightly dancetune, were the words, 'Nellie's my mother, she's the one I care about, I can't wait to tell her she's all the mother I want.'

'Oh queen, they're the best words in the world,' Nellie sighed, cradling her cup of tea in both hands and leaning forward earnestly. 'But I've given up the house now, and you're settled. Do you want me to leave the hospital and make a place for you again?'

Lilac shook her head until her curls danced, her eyes alight with amusement.

'Nellie, as if I'd ask such a thing of you! One of these days you're going to marry, and so shall I. We'll both have our own homes. But I want you to know that ... you're the person who matters most to me in the whole world, and always will be. I doubt if anything will change that.'

'It will,' Nellie said, smiling right back at her. 'It's only right and proper that it should. One of these days, Lilac Larkin, you'll meet a feller who'll put all thoughts of me – and of everyone else – right out of your head. But we'll still love each other dearly, I hope.'

'And see lots and lots of each other, even after you're married to Stuart,' Lilac said gaily. 'Because he'll come back for you, dear Nell. Only a fool would let you go. And as for me, all I want right now is my good friends, lovers can wait. I'm going straight round to the Corry tomorrow after work though, to tell Art ...'

'To tell Art what? What he already knows? That you and I love each other?'

Lilac smiled and shook her head.

'No, not that. Something he'd much rather hear. I don't know what he'll say, Nell, but if you come round to Rodney Street at about eight tomorrow evening, you could find out! I explained to Mrs Matteson that it was difficult for us to talk in the nurses' home, with you sharing a room, so she's going to let us use the small parlour. There will be a fire, a tea-tray ... and we can have an evening together every week.'

Nellie did not ask what she meant by her enigmatic reference to Art; she hoped she knew. And presently they parted, Lilac to hurry back to the Mattesons to help her mistress dress for dinner, Nellie to return to her room in the nurses' home and ponder happily on the past couple of hours.

And it was not only her reconciliation with Lilac that filled her with warmth and optimism, either. She had imagined Stuart a hundred times, seeing him in the street and accosting total strangers, but from the top of that tram, she had been *sure* . And he had been on Scotland Road, just as though he had been searching for her at Coronation Court, and if he really was searching for her, they were bound to meet!

Just the thought of it kept her happy until it was time for bed.

I wonder how I am to meet up with a young man who doesn't have a clue where I am, but wants to find out? Nellie asked herself next evening after work, as she set off dutifully for Rodney Street. If it had not been for Lilac she would have gone off to Coronation Court with all possible speed, since the people there could scarcely have missed Stuart, had he been searching for her. Not that they knew where she was, she remembered, save that she was nursing. But it would only take Stuart so long to comb every hospital in the area, he should catch up with her eventually.

It was dark, of course, and by the time she left the hospital the street lamps were lit. She walked to the tram stop through an increasingly soaking downpour with the wind rising and above her head, grey clouds scudding across the sky. Fortunately she did not have to wait too long for a tram, but when she got aboard her cloak was drenched and she shivered as the night wind gusted through the door every time it opened to admit a new passenger.

There were not a great many people about. It was Sunday and though some people were probably making their way to church it was not by tram. Nellie sat on the vehicle almost alone and got out at St Mark's, to face the bitter wind and clutch her cloak round her tightly

Walking down Upper Duke Street with only the railings between her and St Mark's churchyard, Nellie felt suddenly alone and very vulnerable. She had been looking forward to an evening with Lilac, but she wondered how she should greet Mrs Matteson if she appeared once they were both indoors. But it did no matter, it was kind of the woman to suggest that they met at the house and once the weather was better and the evenings lighter they could do all sorts, tram-rides trips on the ferry, tea down by the pierhead. She remembered taking Lilac there once, as a birthday treat ... they had eaten cream ices and drunk lemonade .. but it would have to wait for the better weather.

She reached the corner of Rodney Street and the wind, howling along St James's Road, hurled the fallen leaves from the trees round the cemetery up into the air, so that they flapped round her head like tiny, wet birds. It was a relief to dive down Rodney Street though the wind followed her, tugging at her cloak disarranging her soaked and draggly hair.

Walking quickly, Nellie suddenly thought of that other person who had come along Rodney Street on just such an inclement night almost fifteen year before. How odd that she should remember that girl and her shawl-wrapped baby so clearly, and yet she had never actually seen the girl, only the child and the fine wool shawl. Poor girl, she thought now with real pity and understanding, how hard it must have been to leave your baby, how cruelly hard! It had been different for her, Richart had been left in the best possible hands, not with strangers. She also wondered how the girl had made out the Culler on such a wild night, for she herself was having to peer up at the doors to find the numbers and it was more by luck than judgement that she reached the right one at last.

She mounted the three steps and pulled at the bell. She listened and heard, faintly, the distant clang.

Stuart came down Rodney Street at a quick pace, his boots splashing indifferently through puddles and mud. He had got back to the city two days ago, coming via India, where his paper had sent him on an assignment, and he had gone straight to Coronation Court to find Nellie. He did not understand why she had not written, unless of course he had been en route for India when her letter arrived. His landlady in Berlin had probably thrown any letters which came after his departure on the fire – she was not fond of the English, she had lost two sons in the war.

But he had drawn a blank at the court. Friendly neighbours said she was nursing, they advised him to try all the hospitals, so he had started with the Alder Hey and intended to move gradually into the city centre itself.

He had visited a couple of hospitals earlier in the day without any luck, and had given up for today because despite his furious impatience, there were things he had to do. So deciding that he must buy a few small presents before he paid his duty call this afternoon he donned his dark suit, tie and shiny shoes, and set off for Lewis's.

The streets were busy and the big store crowded. Stuart wended his way from department to department. Despite his preoccupation with finding Nellie, he put a lot of time and thought into choosing his gifts. A few toys here, a pretty hanky there, a pouch of pipe tobacco, a bag of bright beads for threading. He enjoyed choosing but after an hour he had bought something for everyone so he set off, down the stairs.

Halfway down, glancing idly over the heads of the people below him, his eyes were drawn irresistibly to one particular head. Richly red-gold, it seemed to attract more light, more brilliance, than ...

Lilac! It had to be she, and if he could find Lilac then Nellie was only seconds away from him!

He plunged down the stairs, pushing between couples, dodging round the elderly, hurrying through the crowd. The red-gold head was a yard away, a foot ... he put his hand on her shoulder, half-swung her round towards him.

'Lilac, I've searched all over for you ...'

The red-gold head turned. It was not Lilac but a much older woman. She stared, narrowing large, dark-blue eyes, then smiled invitingly.

'Hello, young man; can I help you?'

Stammering, disclaiming, Stuart apologised, moved away, almost ran through the crowd. What a fool he had made of himself, he really must be more careful ... tomorrow he would go to the other hospitals, he would try the schools, he might even pop in to the Culler since he would be only a street away this very afternoon.

He caught a tram and got off on Leece Street. He was

visiting friends on Pilgrim Street so he thought he would pay his call there first, and get rid of the heavy bag of gifts, then he would just pop in to the Culler.

He was greeted rapturously on Pilgrim Street and spent some time there, talking about old times, telling his war stories, asking for old friends. They wanted him to stay but he pleaded a prior engagement and left, hurrying along beneath the hissing gas lamps, glad of their light to show him the way now that he was on less familiar territory.

He knocked at the door of the Culler and asked to see the matron. Her name was Mrs Simpson and she was plump and smiling with a gentle expression and softly waving dark hair. Stuart thought her a friendly person even after she had said that she knew neither Nellie McDowell or Lilac Larkin.

'But I've only been here two years,' she explained. 'I'm so sorry I can't help you, Mr Gallagher.'

Stuart thanked her politely, touched his hat and left, thinking how much pleasanter she seemed than the awful old witch who had ruled here for so long ... what was her name? Hansom? Transom? He ran lightly down the steps of the orphan asylum and set off into the windy darkness. He was thinking of Nellie, remembering her. He had loved her, he believed, from the very first moment he saw her, a thin, rather pathetic little figure, draggle-haired, nervous, dressed in that awful brown uniform ...

Someone was standing on the doorstep of a house not a dozen doors from the Culler. She was small and thin and she wore a drooping, rain-darkened cloak just like the one the Culler girls wore, but he could see that she was grown up and anyway it was unlikely that a Culler girl would be attempting to gain entrance to one of the smarter houses on Rodney Street.

He drew level with her ... and gave a shout.

'Nellie! My God, by all that's wonderful, it's Nellie! Oh my dearest girl ...'

She was down the steps and in his arms in a second; they were rocking together, clutching, kissing, and she was as familiar to his arms, as dear, as though they had known one another always and had never known the agony of separation.

'Nellie, what on earth ... ? Oh come out of it, my darling, let's get away from here before they open that door!'

They ran like kids, like naughty schoolchildren, down the road, around the corner and out of sight.

'Was that the bell?'

'Oh Lilac, you lazy cat, you know very well it was. Isn't that sister of yourn coming for you this evening? Well, old Polly isn't gettin' off of 'er perch to let your visitors in, Lady Muck. Go on, do, afore she rings again.'

The girls were in the kitchen, roasting chestnuts over the fire. Mrs Jenkins had gone to her own room, cook was asleep in a chair, but Lilac, Polly and Madge squatted on the hearthrug and fished the hot nuts out of the fire with the tongs and knocked the burnt shells off them, squeaking and laughing.

'Oh all right, in a minute,' Lilac said, getting to her feet and sucking her burnt fingertips. 'Save me some nuts ... I'm going to take Nell up to the small sitting room for a bit, but she'll want to meet everyone so we'll come down and have a cup of tea, later. Shan't be long.'

She left them. Madge blew on a nut, then gingerly popped it into her mouth. She hissed in her breath, then began to chew.

'What 'appened to our Lilac at the Allans' party the

other day?' she said, eyeing Polly. 'She went 'ome early, but she was ever so pleased with 'erself next day, you'd ha' thought she'd found a sovereign!'

'Dunno,' Polly said. 'She was pleased with 'erself awright, but she wouldn't say nothin'. Just kept gigglin' and huggin' herself an' sayin' she'd got a nice secret. But I reckon it 'ad to do with this Nellie, 'cos they fell out a while back an' Lilac weren't 'appy about it.'

'But now she is?'

'Now she is,' Polly confirmed just as the door opened. 'Hey up, Lilac, weren't it your Nellie, then?'

'No, there was no one there,' Lilac said, looking very cast down. 'Oh, and I was that sure it was her! Never mind though, I suppose she was on a late shift. Perhaps she'll come tomorrow.'

'No one at all? Or just no one for you?' Madge said suspiciously. She knew how singleminded Lilac could be. 'Bells don't ring of theirselves, chuck.'

'There was no one at all, just the wind and the dark, and the rain blowing almost horizontal,' Lilac assured them, round-eyed. 'The street was empty. Whoever rang was long gone.'

It was ridiculous, stupid, but they could not bear to let go of one another. All down the street they clung, right to the tram stop on the corner. They climbed on the first tram which came along and Stuart propelled Nellie carefully up to the top deck. They neither knew nor cared where it was, all they wanted was the chance to talk – and to be alone.

'Why didn't you write?' Stuart said as soon as they were seated. They were the only passengers on the top deck and the tram swayed as the wind caught it. 'Why didn't you tell me you'd moved out?'

'I did write. Truly. I thought it was you who hadn't written.'

'Your letter must have gone astray, or arrived after I'd left Berlin for New Delhi. But I've written at least a dozen times and probably more from India, telling you all about it. Oh, Nellie, how sweet you are, how soft and cuddly ... how dreadfully I've missed you.'

'I've missed you as well, only I kept telling myself we were almost strangers ... do you realise, Stuart, that you knew Lilac as well as you knew me?' Her hand flew to her mouth. 'Oh lor', I was supposed to visit Lilac this evening, we'd agreed that I'd go round to the Mattesons, meet her employer and her friends ...'

'Really? Then just what were you doing in Rodney Street?'

Nellie smiled and touched his mouth with soft fingers.

'Lilac lives there now. She's in service with a family there. She's personal maid to Mrs Matteson, a doctor's wife. Oh Stuart, I don't feel that you're a stranger at all, I feel as if I've known you always.'

'Well, you've known me for quite a while,' Stuart said. He put his arm round her and drew her head down to rest in the hollow of his shoulder. 'It must be fifteen years.'

'Never! I met you for the first time out in France, when you were convalescing near the hospital where I was nursing,' Nellie reminded him. 'What do you mean, fifteen years? You aren't saying it feels that long, I hope!'

'Well, it does, because it is. I guessed you'd not recognised me that time and somehow I was always too busy to say. We met on Christmas Day as I recall and you were in church, with a baby, I suppose it was Lilac, in your arms. I gave you my chocolate bar; *now* do you remember me?'

Nellie was frowning up at him, then the frown cleared and she gave a little crow of delight.

'Oh Stuart, don't tell me you were the boy with the olly! The Dunn's devil who was playing ollies in church!'

'Didn't you recognise me, in France? Thought not, but I knew you at once,' Stuart said in a hurt voice. 'You'd got a lot prettier and curvier, but you were still my little love, because when I looked at you snatching up my olly that Christmas Day and keeping it safe for me, I thought, *She's the girl for me*, I thought. And wasn't I right?'

'I can't *believe* it,' Nellie said in a stunned voice. 'I can't believe you were that boy! You never said you were a Dunn's devil, Stuart!'

'You never said you were a Culler girl, only I knew, of course,' Stuart said. 'We never needed many words then, Nell, and we shan't need many now. Are you going to give me a kiss or am I going to take one?'

There was a short silence whilst their faces gradually drew closer. Nellie began to smile, then his lips touched hers and she moaned softly against his mouth. She had been so alone, she had felt cast off by everyone, and now ... now ...

'Tickets, please. Where d'you wanna get down, chucks?'

They flew apart, Nellie at least with burning cheeks. But Stuart fished nonchalantly into his pocket and handed the conductor a sovereign.

'As far as you like and back again,' he said grandly. 'Only don't let any other passengers up here, there's a pal. Keep the change, wack!'

'Now I know you're truly a Dunn's devil,' Nellie murmured as the conductor, chuckling, descended the stairs once more. 'Oh Stuart, I thought you were so nice

423

when you were just a scruffy kid, but I like you even more now.'

'Likewise,' Stuart said, tightening his grip round her and turning her so that their faces were close. 'Likewise, my dearest Nell.'